Sideshow

SHERI S. TEPPER
SIDESHOW

SPECTRA ™

BANTAM BOOKS

NEW YORK   TORONTO   LONDON
SYDNEY   AUCKLAND

SIDESHOW

A BANTAM SPECTRA BOOK / MAY 1992

SPECTRA and the portrayal of a boxed "s" are
trademarks of Bantam Books, a division of
Bantam Doubleday Dell Publishing Group, Inc.

BOOK DESIGN BY JAYA DAYAL

Library of Congress Cataloging-in-Publication Data

Tepper, Sheri S.
Sideshow : a science fiction novel / by Sheri S. Tepper.
p. cm.
ISBN 0-553-08130-6
I. Title.
PS3570.E673S54 1992
813'.54—dc20   91-40420
CIP

Published simultaneously in the United States and Canada

Bantam Books are published by Bantam Books, a division of Bantam Doubleday Dell Publishing Group, Inc. Its trademark, consisting of the words "Bantam Books" and the portrayal of a rooster, is Registered in U.S. Patent and
Trademark Office and in other countries. Marca Registrada. Bantam Books, 666
Fifth Avenue, New York, New York 10103.

PRINTED IN THE UNITED STATES OF AMERICA

BVG   0 9 8 7 6 5 4 3 2 1

To all those
who ride the great dragon
Wonder

heaven longing ape
angel who stumbles
blind light bearer
who falls and fumbles
worshiper of error
seeker after truth
hurting and aging
lover of lovely youth
wild beast raging
craven and brave
freak of fashion
and custom's slave
puppet of passion
lowest and loftiest
a sideshow gape
god's fool, nature's jest
heaven longing ape

"M A N"
Koi Bashi

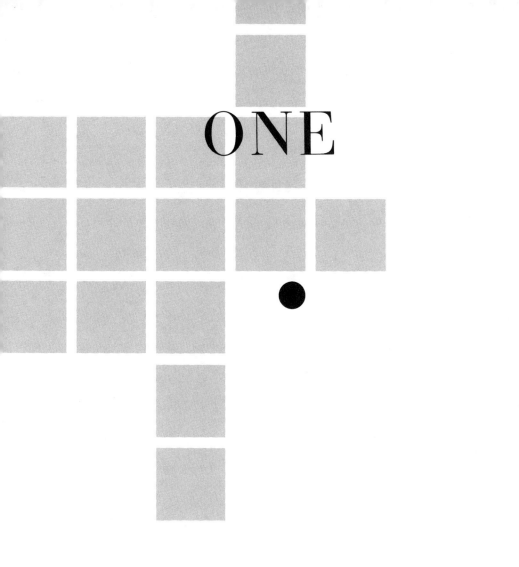

ONE

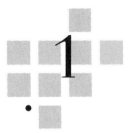

1

Humanity was saved from certain destruction when, on their wedding night, Lek Korsyzczy informed his wife that their first child was to be a son. Certain intelligences (the Celerians, actually) established later that this was the event setting causation in motion. It happened at around one o'clock on an October Sunday morning during the 1990s, common era. Lek made the remark as Marla was about to get into bed with him, his voice slightly slurred from the wedding champagne, but with nothing tentative or doubtful in it to indicate that Marla had any choice in the matter.

Marla thought he sounded like a builder, like one of the customers at the lumberyard where she worked, matter-of-factly ordering framing timbers. She gave her new husband a thoughtful, rather troubled look. "Leksy, I think that just sort of happens how it happens, you know? Like my sister Judith, the one married to the plumber, she had four girls before she had Buddy."

Leksy shrugged. His heavy shoulders were covered with large orange freckles and a pelt of fine, red-blond hair. Marla had already decided he would have to wear something with sleeves when they made love, because his fur tickled. She was sure, ticklish as she was, they would start doing it and she'd start laughing, and laughter, so her sister Judith had informed her, was never a good idea then.

"They don't tell you how ridiculous it is," Judith had confided in the rest room, after five glasses of champagne at the wedding supper. "The nuns sure don't tell you. The priests don't tell you. They go on and on about sin, but nobody says how ridiculous it is. And then there you are, doing this silly thing—oh, don't get me wrong, it can be fun—and you start thinking what it must look like and you want to laugh, and let me tell you, don't! That's one time you do not want to laugh. You wouldn't believe how bent out of shape some men can get!"

So, now, looking at the tickly pelt of hairs on Leksy's shoulders and arms, almost to the wrists, Marla knew she'd have to take steps to avoid laughter. "I mean," she told him, "I wouldn't want you to get your heart set on a boy right away, or anything."

"You don' unnerstan'," he told her, hiccuping slightly as he slid completely under the influence of the multiple toasts he had drunk. "I got it all work' out with the Blessed Virgin."

"You what?"

"I got it all work' out." And with these words Leksy's eyes fell shut as his mouth opened to emit a tiny snore. It was only a raspy breath, a mere puppy gargle so far as snores went, but it was definitely a snore, not something else. Not lust, for example. Not passion.

Marla sat looking at him, not sure whether she wanted to laugh or cry. It was kind of like a dirty joke, him falling asleep that way. "There was this guy, see, and he drank too much at his wedding and that night his new wife stayed in the bathroom a long time, so he fell asleep before anything happened, see. . . ." Not that she'd been in the bathroom that long! On the other hand, his being asleep gave her a little time to think about what he'd said, that he'd worked it out with the Blessed Virgin. It didn't exactly surprise her. Well, it did, but then it didn't. Lots of things Leksy did seemed kind of surprising at first, but not after you thought about them. The whole Korsyzczy family was religious. No, pious. That was the word. Maybe a little more pious than was good for them. Who else did she know besides Leksy who had five sisters who were nuns and three older brothers in holy orders. Holiday dinner at their house was like a convocation! And they were all the time dragging religion into everything, like God was watching every breath you took! Like your whole life was bugged for holy!

Marla was tired and just a little bit drunk herself, which meant queasy in the stomach, because she couldn't drink, not really. Whenever she tried, she either threw up or passed out. She decided to have a nice long hot bath and not worry about it. It wasn't romantic of Leksy to fall asleep that way, but their marriage would probably get off to a better start if he slept off the champagne. And she'd enjoy things more if her stomach was settled down. They'd both be better off for a little sleep.

Leksy would probably wake up in an hour or two, and then they could do what he'd been self-righteously keeping them both from doing for the past six months since they'd gotten engaged.

The bath helped. Afterward she lay down beside him, expecting he'd wake up pretty soon. Several times during the night, she came out of a doze, thinking he was about to, but he only snored that same puppy snore and snuggled more deeply into the pillows. Along about four o'clock, she fell soundly asleep, and when he finally reached for her, around seven, she couldn't rouse herself and wasn't really aware how annoyed she was with him until she heard her own response.

"Don't," she said sharply. "I'm too sore." Judith had warned her about *that*.

"Sore?" he asked stupidly, looking at her bleary-eyed. "Sore?"

"I think you ought to have more consideration, Leksy," she said. "I'm not used to this, and four times is just too much all at once." And she turned over with a little secret smile and went on sleeping, leaving her husband to puzzle, then grin, then chortle as he got up and went in to take a shower. That small happening continued the chain of consequences that had begun with Lek's announcement and would culminate with the arrival of the Alien and the saving of the planet Earth, for, as Marla's eldest sister Sizzy had been fond of saying, you just never know.

That small happening also became a marital sandbag for Leksy, part of the accumulated grit any two people rub off each other that ends up reinforcing the family levees against the outside world. Marla didn't realize that's what it was. She had meant it as a joke, not a shibboleth, and she didn't think twice before sharing the story with her sister Judith. Sometime later, Judith told her husband about it, and a year or so after that, during a drunken party, her husband told a guy he worked with, and a couple of years after that, the man remembered it during a fishing trip and told someone else. The town was a small one on the U.S.– Canadian border, the kind of town where everyone knows everyone, and though the story wasn't one of those knee-slappers that move like wild-fire, it was a sort of amusing anecdote that hung around in people's minds and got retold from time to time. It took almost seventeen years before it got back to Leksy.

Meantime, it was business as arranged for and sanctified, which, by the end of the honeymoon, had pretty much settled into the pattern it would occupy in their lives for the foreseeable future. Nothing fancy. Leksy had a horror of anything fancy. Fancy was stuff whores did. Fancy was stuff you could go to hell for or get AIDS doing. Mouths were for kissing only, and hands could be used discreetly at the beginning only, and the rest of it was up to the parts designed for the purpose, provided the one was securely inserted in the other before anything went bang. So said Father Jabowsky, and so Leksy believed because that's the way he had done it every time he'd done it, and he hadn't had any complaints. Of course, his mostly willing though often drunken partners hadn't been asked for critiques.

It never occurred to Leksy to inquire whether Father Jabowsky was giving him good advice. Father was father, so it was the right advice, necessarily. The priest was almost seventy-five; he firmly believed that Vatican II had been a hallucination; he still said Mass in Latin whenever he thought nobody was listening; and he had never, even as a boy, felt in himself the slightest sexual urge, a fact he mentioned from time to time during premarital counseling sessions with a kind of quiet pride. Father Jabowsky took marital sex on faith, the same way he took transubstantiation. The church said the sacrament was there, so it was there, even though Father couldn't see it, smell it, or taste it. You could tell it was there from the effects. Grace on the one hand. Babies on the other.

Marla rather wished Leksy had another confessor. She thought she knew a lot about sex, mostly from watching Oprah and Donahue, and though she found her relations with Leksy generally satisfying, she would have liked a little more variety. Maybe, she told herself, when Father Jabowsky died or retired, she could ask the new priest to talk to Leksy. Judith said some of the younger priests had actually studied about sex and were able to counsel about it intelligently. In the meantime, however, Marla amused herself by teasing Lek about "the way he did it on their wedding night." Whenever they made love, and he asked if she'd liked it, she said yes, but she wished he'd do it the way he'd done it on their wedding night.

Leksy couldn't admit he didn't remember. A few times he went so far as to say he couldn't remember he'd done it any *different*. To which Marla merely smiled an enigmatic smile that drove him crazy because he got to wondering what he'd *done*, and whether it had been something maybe, you know, *perverted*, only it couldn't have been because whatever it was, she'd liked it!

Aside from the teasing, Marla didn't worry about it much. The main thing was to get pregnant, and people got pregnant in the missionary position as well as any other.

Except that she didn't. After six months, she went to the doctor for a checkup. The doctor ran tests and filled out a long questionnaire and asked her to have her husband come in for a sperm test. Marla tried to explain about Leksy, who wouldn't submit to a sperm test in a million years, while the doctor muttered something about ritual and superstition and being back in the Dark Ages.

"Well, since I can't find anything obviously wrong with you," he said at last, "next time you have intercourse in the morning, come on in as soon afterward as you can. We'll take a smear and try to determine from that."

Which meant waiting until the next time Leksy had a weekday off, so they could stay in bed almost until the doctor's office hours, and then pretending she had an appointment with the dentist to explain her rushing off, even before breakfast. And it turned out useless, after all. "Enough sperm to populate the planet," grumbled the doctor into his microscope. "All flapping around like trout."

So another six months went by, and still no pregnancy. Leksy's relatives were beginning to look at her funny. Father Jabowsky came right out and asked her during her confession if she was using birth control, which made Marla very upset with him, and she called him something—well, not him exactly, she just said people who suspected things like that had dirty minds—so he ended up loading her penance. That certainly wasn't fair. He was the one with the nasty uncharitable thoughts.

After that, she stopped going to St. Seraph's and started going across the parish line to Holy Redeemer. A lot of the younger people did, so that was all right. Even Leksy knew that, and he didn't say a word about it.

She had the doctor repeat the tests when they'd been married a year and a half, even going so far as to have him look at Leksy's sperm again, just to be sure. By this time she was so upset she spent almost an hour crying in the doctor's office.

"You're trying too hard," he told her. "Relax."

Relaxing wasn't exactly what she was able to do. Leksy kept at her and kept at her. She told him he was wearing her out, but he said marriage was for babies, so until she got pregnant, it was his moral duty to keep at it and there was no sin involved. Besides, since she'd quit working at the lumberyard—Leksy had thought maybe it was her job that kept her from getting pregnant—she could always take a nap in the afternoon. Leksy wasn't worried. He had it all worked out with the Virgin, and nobody was accusing *him* of using birth control.

At the end of two years, Marla was on the verge of a nervous breakdown.

"Three and four times a day," she said. "I can't even turn around if he's in the house or he drags me into the bedroom. I like sex, Doctor, or I used to, but this is getting ridiculous."

"There's this new drug," he told her. "Ovitalibon. Made by one of the big European drug companies, just recently released for use in this country. I've used it with some success in situations like yours, cases of unattributable subfertility."

"I've read about those drugs," she said. "Women pregnant with nine babies, like a mama dog with a litter. All of the babies die. Or they have to abort some to let the others live. Leksy wouldn't do that in a million years. He'd leave me first."

"No, no," the doctor huffed, making pursey little lines around his mouth. "By this time I'm well aware of your husband's religious hang-ups, Marla. No. That's a different drug you're talking about. Ovitalibon doesn't do that. It does slightly increase the incidence of twins, but it doesn't cause multiple births. In fact, we're not entirely sure how it works."

By which Marla understood that the drug had probably been invented for some other condition entirely, then had been found to have fertility effects, but nobody knew why. Just like the birth control pill had originally been invented for infertility. Watching Donahue kept her well informed, though it had also made her slightly cynical.

"You're sure it won't give me like five or six babies all at once."

"I'm sure," he said. And he was. About that.

The drug was miraculous. Within two months she was pregnant. As soon as she was sure, she told everyone and peace descended like a dove. She told herself peace came exactly like a white-winged dove. Fluttering down. All soft and cooing. Leksy let her alone. Her relatives let her alone. For the first time since their wedding, she got a full night's sleep. For the first time since their wedding, she found herself ecstatically, totally content.

Everything, so says Jordel of Hemerlane (whom you will meet in due time), is connected to everything else. Time imposes no limitation on this rule. Everywhen is connected to every-other-when. Tit floweth from tat, tut floweth from tit. Past, present, future, are not disparate things but a continuum, a recoiled helix of interconnections in which time no more serves to sever than does distance. Here and there are not separable. Now and then are not divisible. Everything burrows through the myriad wormholes of reality to become part of everything else. Time and space are coiled like some unimaginable DNA, pregnant with both possibility and certainty. In this multidimensional womb, separation is a fiction, all things are adjacent, and twentieth-century Earth snuggles close against the warm cheeks of the planet Elsewhere. . . .

. . . Elsewhere, at the far end of an attenuated galactic arm, surrounded by a clutter of cosmic debris. Elsewhere, lit by one middle-sized yellow sun and accompanied by a scattered handful of heavy little planets and moons. Elsewhere, which had been set up—so said Council Supervisory—as the last refuge of humanity from enslavement by the Hobbs Land Gods, that botanical plague that had swept across the galaxy over a millennia before, bringing, so it was said, slavish conformity in its wake.

Some of the urgency had seeped out of that claim over the centuries, during which time Elsewhere had remained so inviolate that one might question whether the Hobbs Land Gods knew or cared it was there. Considering that Elsewhere had been set up and populated in secret, this was not astonishing. Still, Elsewhere had indisputably been designed as a refuge, and from the moment the first fleeing groups arrived to settle provinces of their own, each one was guaranteed the uninterrupted continuance of its own language and religion and customs and dress and anything else it considered important. Elsewhere, managed by Council Supervisory, was designed to insure the immemorial diversity of man.

Council Supervisory had made the rules to start with, and they had not changed since.

No province would be allowed to cross its own borders to infringe upon another or to make common cause with another to infringe upon a third; evangelism across borders was forbidden along with treaties and alliances; travel and trade were allowed, within limits; and any and all groups would be welcome so long as they *let one another alone!*

If provinces did not leave one another alone, if a Situation arose,

Council Enforcers would be sent to Attend the Situation. Enforcers might go winging or striding or riding some ancient, patient animal; they might go singly or in groups of hundreds; they might carry simple weapons or a complex armamentarium. However they went, the Situation was always Attended to. Provinces on Elsewhere really did Let One Another Alone. If they would not do it on their own, the Council Enforcers made sure they did it anyhow.

One such Council Enforcer was Zasper Ertigon, who at a certain point in his career found himself in the city of Molock. The city was the capital of a province also called Molock, on the continent of Panubi, which was well settled around the edges but otherwise largely unexplored. Zasper had been in the city for a few days on routine Council business that was almost concluded. After checking out his vehicle and while waiting for his colleagues, he'd given in to thirst if not to the pleasure of the company, and now occupied a tottery stool in a ramshackle shelter near the vehicle park, drinking what passed locally for ale in company with a local guard officer.

"Goin' home now?" the sweating guard asked him, belching voluminously.

Zasper nodded, holding his breath against the noxious emanation and fingering the thick braid of slightly graying hair that signified his rank and status. "Back to Tolerance," he acknowledged, meaning the quasicity on the polar plateau that was headquarters to Council Supervisory and all its works. "We'll leave as soon as my colleagues arrive." Actually, the persons he had conveyed to Molock were not colleagues, that is, not Council Enforcers. They were Council technicians charged with maintaining the ubiquitous monitors that speckled every province like seeds on a bun, but it was Council policy that all technicians be escorted by and treated as Enforcers when on duty out in the field. Zasper wasn't Elsewhere's greatest pilot and he found escort duty dull; but when ordered to do it, he did it.

"Tol'rance your home?" the guard persisted.

Zasper shook his head. "No," he admitted. "I'm from Enarae originally."

"What category's that?" the officer wanted to know.

"Category seven," Zasper replied. Category one was untouched wilderness and category ten was quintessential tech, so a rating of seven meant only a little better than halfway civilized, which was a comedown for people who originated in sea-girt Phansure, once home for the galaxy's preeminent engineers. Or so Zasper had been taught as a boy in school. Molock was only category four. Molock was primitive and, in Zasper's privately held opinion, barbaric. Enforcers weren't supposed to have private opinions about provinces, but many of them did.

"What's it like in Tol'rance?" the guard officer asked.

Zasper drank deeply and stared toward the fireglow of Molock city, ruddy against the overhanging cloud, trying to come up with something that would be both permissible and inoffensive. When he thought of Tolerance, he thought of the Great Rotunda, where Council Supervisory policed and protected the varied remnants of humanity, where the monitors clicked and chuffed and whirred and now and then beeped, as they had been designed to do, bringing scurrying minions to see what each and every beep portended. When Zasper thought of Tolerance, he thought of obsessive attention given to cleanliness, no escape from boredom, and an excess of piddly little customs that didn't mean anything. He also thought of comfort, marvelous food, and quite outstanding drinkables.

But he couldn't talk about that. So, he fell back on geographical details, told in dull generalities, while he swallowed more of the tasteless ale and wished he were either drinking back in Tolerance or out Attending to something urgent.

Though Zasper didn't know it, the something urgent was present, just across the landing field where two persons and a child huddled in the darkness outside the circling fence. The child's name was Danivon Luze. The two adults were his parents, Cafferty and Latibor. They had given Danivon something to make him quiet and a little sleepy.

"It's there," Danivon's mother said, staring through the fence at the bulky Council vehicle, parked not far from the gate. "But so are the guards."

"Wait," whispered Danivon's father. "They just finished a circuit. In a minute they'll go in the hut. They always do. They spend most of the night in there gambling and drinking with their officer. Every night I've watched them it's been the same. . . . ."

"Yes, but the Enforcer's in there!"

He raised his head and sniffed the air, like an animal testing for predators. "It won't matter. They won't let that bother them."

"It has to be tonight," Danivon's mother murmured, the softness of her voice barely holding the hysteria that bubbled just below the surface. "It has to be tonight."

"Cafferty, I know," he said, shaking her gently by one shoulder. They both knew. When they glanced over their shoulders toward the town they could see the looming bulk of the temple pyramid silhouetted against the glow of a thousand cookfires. The shadowy bulk of the temple had a watchfulness about it, a living presence, like some great crouching beast that might rise up on its legs and come hunting them. On that temple height within the next few days certain rites were expected to take place, rites in which the child, Danivon Luze, had been chosen to feature prominently and painfully. His parents weren't supposed to know about it, but they had sniffed it out. The danger was real and imminent.

"I keep wondering if anyone here in Molock has any idea who we are," Latibor mused.

"No," she reassured him, more out of habit than conviction. "You know they don't. We'd smell suspicion in a moment. This business has nothing to do with who we are. Danny's being chosen for this new rite of theirs was pure chance. When he got to be three, his name went in the pot with all the other three- to five-year-olds. We had no business being here, that's all. We had no right to risk a child in a place like this."

"It wasn't that bad until recently. And you wanted a child," he murmured, nostrils flaring as he watched the guard move slowly away. "You wanted a child."

"We wanted a child," she corrected him gently. He liked to think he was more reasonable about it than she. "Oh, Latibor, we talked about it, remember, when we came here. We thought we'd find out everything there was to find out and get out. We thought we'd be out of here by a year ago. Statistically, we thought we could risk it."

He made an apologetic grimace. She was right. He'd wanted a child as much as she had. They hadn't thought about having children when they'd offered to come to Molock. The old woman, Jory, had said she needed information, and as without Jory there'd have been no Cafferty, no Latibor, they owed her. But once they were here, settled into the joyless life of the place—they had wanted a child.

"Funny," he said in an unamused voice. "Other people's risks are statistical. When it's your risk, your own child, it isn't statistical anymore."

"We should have been out of here by now," she said hopelessly, telling him what he knew. "If we'd been able to reach Jory . . . If we'd . . ."

"Unfortunately, Jory isn't answering our messages just now." This worried him too. When he couldn't reach the old ones, he always felt less secure.

"Quick," she whispered. "The guards are going into the hut. Help me over the gate."

Her face swaddled in a dark scarf to keep it from showing in the faint light from the guardpost, Cafferty climbed over the gate and reached up to accept the sleepy child, sliding him into the sling on her back before she half scuttled, half crawled across the expanse of bare gravel, taking advantage of the shadows thrown by parked vehicles. Latibor stayed at the gate, checking his belt for the knife, for the short, heavy club. The guards wouldn't come this way, but if they did . . .

With their customary arrogance, the people from Tolerance had left the vehicle unguarded, never dreaming anyone might take advantage of that. Cafferty hoped they'd been careless enough to leave the cargo door unlocked, as well, and that it would make no noise when opened.

Hope was fulfilled. The cargo door slid noiselessly. She crept in, found a small crevice behind a pile of boxes, and pointed it out to the drowsy child, who crawled in with his little mattress pad while she piled the packaged food and drink behind him. In anticipation of this moment, they'd been playing this hidey-hole game for days. So far as Danivon knew, he was merely playing the game again. He knew how to curl up in his blanket and go to sleep, how much of the food to eat each day (drugged food, so he would be placid and quiet), how much to drink, how to find a hidden place to go potty. He knew not to cry out loud, and that he mustn't be found for some time. That was the purpose of the game, not to be found. If he played well, he would win something extra special.

Danivon knew numbers and colors and his name and the names of many ordinary things, but no words or names to connect him to Molock, not the name of the place or the names his parents used. He'd been kept away from other children. He'd been told the name of the place was Duffy danty boddle bock, for if he knew the real name of this place, he'd be brought back.

Cafferty kissed him, her face wet with tears. She took the medallion from around her neck and placed it around his, whispering that he must keep it always. She slipped out of the cargo hold and shut the door, then crawled away, unable to stop sobbing. When she came to the dark gate, Latibor helped her over, and they stumbled off down the road toward the place they'd most recently called home. From there they would head for the river, leaving a clear trail the first part of the way. If they were followed, they'd be followed there. No one would think of looking here until it was too late.

They were halfway down the road toward the city when they heard raised voices and the slam and heave of metal. The inspection vehicle rose with a whoosh of air and moved away into the night. They didn't stop to watch it go. They'd done all they could.

Inside the ship, Zasper set the controls to return the ship to Tolerance. The technicians muttered and yawned and retired to a sleeping compartment, gabbling incomprehensibly to one another in a jargon Zasper neither understood nor cared about. Left alone, he did some yawning and muttering of his own. The powers that be had chosen to rearrange his customary travel schedule. Molock, normally a midway point on the maintenance loop, had been the last stop on this occasion. Normally after a last stop, he would sleep on the way back and do all the inventory checks after arriving in Tolerance. But since he never slept well after visiting Molock because of feelings about Molock being or having recently become an abomination—feelings an Enforcer had no business having—he thought he might as well do the checks first, thus reducing the time spent in arrival formalities on the morrow.

Cafferty's stratagem had depended upon the cargo hold being empty for some little time. Zasper, all unaware that his decision was not merely a distraction but a matter of life and death, took the inventory cube, inserted it into a File reader, and got on with the duty. He was standing in the cargo compartment beside a pile of monomol-packed replacement parts when he heard the sigh. A tiny sigh. The merest breath, meaning nothing except that it occurred in a place where nothing was supposed to be breathing but himself.

It took no time to find the child, asleep behind the pile of cartons, small packages of food and drink stacked near him, a little pad beneath him to speak of concern for his comfort, concern for his life. None of the food had been eaten, none of the water drunk. All the evidence indicated he'd been put aboard in Molock.

Duty required that Zasper Ertigon return the vehicle to Molock and turn the child over to the guards. Nonetheless, he stood for a time, looking at the rise and fall of the little chest, hearing the soft breaths, again, again. The child was a good-looking little rascal, dark-haired, with skin the color of sand. His eyelashes were unbelievably long, the way some children's were, giving his eyes that fringy, vulnerable look. Zasper made an impatient gesture, went back to the control compartment, and turned the ship.

Shortly the glow of the city came up beneath him, the light of cook-fires reflected from a suspended layer of smoke and cloud that formed a level ceiling slightly above the flier. Directly in his path, looming out of the glare, the temple pyramid thrust a wide ceremonial platform toward him, like a rudely outthrust tongue. This time of night the temple complex was empty. Zasper lowered the ship upon the platform, a little awkwardly (flying had never been one of his talents), and got out to stare over the smoky city.

Enforcer duty brought him to Molock from time to time. He'd seen the Molockian temple, though never before close up, and what he hadn't seen, he'd heard about. After a moment of indecision, he climbed the short flight of stairs leading to the top, where the level rock-paved summit seemed to hang only a few feet below a layer of flame-colored smoke and cloud, the space between suffused with a bloody glow.

He wanted to see if what he'd heard described was really there, and it was, not ten paces from the top of the stairs. Centered upon the paved square was an iron rack made up of wavy spikes, ten wide, ten deep, ten high. On each spike rested a skull, a thousand skulls, all little ones, all from children possibly four or five years old.

The ten skulls from the back row of the top layer had been removed to the stained altar and lay there lined up beside two stone mauls. Twice each year the ten oldest skulls were beaten into powder and distributed to the worshipers as a guarantee of fertility for the fields, the flocks, the men and women of Molock. To the dreadful pounding of drums and the shriek of flutes, all the other skulls were moved up a notch, and twelve little boys were hung upon the sides of the rack to die slowly of thirst and hunger before the eyes of their parents who, during all that long dying, were carefully restrained and fed and given water to drink before the eyes of their sons. The first ten who died were used on the rack. The last two left alive were given back to their parents and sometimes they survived. Seasonally, ten skulls were removed and replaced with ten new ones.

Zasper counted the skulls, as though the act of enumeration might change the total number. He had heard about the rite when it first began, marking it down as another delightful thing about Molock to make him avoid the place. He had refused to consider details then, but now they confronted him in a way he couldn't simply pretend not to see. In order to have accumulated a thousand skulls in the short time since the rite began, the number of children sacrificed at first must have been many times the current number, which was quite bad enough. Obviously there was only one likely reason for someone having put the child in the cargo compartment: to save that child from ending up here.

He peered into the eyes of the skulls, which seemed to stare back at him. Some of them near the bottom bore shreds of skin and hair. Among them something squirmed and dropped with a sickening plop to the stones.

Molock. Category four. Barbarian. And its temple. Which Zasper was sworn to protect, or at least sworn not to allow any interference with whatsoever. He was a Council Enforcer. His oath and the oaths of those like him were all that stood between the diversity that defines humanity and the loss of humanity itself. Cultural relativism. The necessity of maintaining a nonjudgmental attitude. Diverse but not therefore perverse. Those were a few of the phrases he was accustomed to. Still, he looked at the skulls and didn't move, feeling sickness clench deep in his bowels.

Abruptly, without thinking about it, he went back to the ship, raised it, and returned to his former course. With a little judicious stage setting, he could make it look as though the child had been in there for days. He could scatter some wrappings about. He could empty some food and water containers. After all that beer with the watchman, he could even manage a few convincing puddles.

As he went about planting evidence, he thought about the new rite instituted at Molock and all the implications of it: the new cruelty, the new fury, the new pain. Had it anything to do with the increasing persecutions at Derbeck? The higher death rate in Enarae? He called to mind other changes observed here and there and more or less everywhere, none of them for the better and all of them to do with the worship of this god or that god, the persecution of this or that heresy, the requirement of this or that conformity.

As though the provinces had all of a sudden gotten hungry for blood and suffering, he told himself. Not that some of them hadn't been like that before, but lately they had been more so. Getting still worse all the time. As though something . . . something were changing, yet what could be changing? The status quo was a sacred trust! He and some thousands like him enforced it, preserved it, protected it. What could be changing?

When the flier arrived at Tolerance, Zasper let the technicians disembark and go about their business while he fiddled and fidgeted, unnecessarily computing fuel consumption for the third time. At last he took his inventory sheets and with ostentatious clamor opened the cargo hold.

Everyone in the vehicle bay heard the shout of surprise when he found the child. Members of the maintenance crew heard him cursing and found him holding a little boy against his shoulder as he pointed with an outraged finger into the hold.

The crew chief demanded to know when he got in there.

No way of telling, said Zasper. The trip had included over twenty stops. They hadn't had to get anything out of the cargo bay since the third or fourth stop. The boy could have been in there for days. Look at all the food wrappers, Zasper urged. Smell the urine where the kid had piddled behind boxes, against the sides of the compartment. And look there. Shit!

Both piddle and shit were added artistry, his own, but he didn't think anyone would bother with an analysis. To keep them off balance, he fulminated, counterfeiting outrage.

"Cute kid," said a female crew member, reaching for him.

The boy put his arms around her and laid a weary little head on her shoulder. She smelled rather like his mother.

"Who are you, little boy?" she asked.

"My name is Danivon Luze," he said clearly, gazing at her from under his incredible lashes, like a fringe of reeds around little sky-colored lakes. "I'm four years old."

"Danivon. That's a nice name. Do you know where you live?"

"Duffy danty boddle bock," he said clearly and very seriously. "That's where I live."

The crew laughed at that, some of them, making the child look first doubtful, then tearful, while Zasper gave thanks that someone had been reasonably clever.

"That's all right," said the woman, wiping the child's tears. "They weren't laughing at you, Danny."

"I suppose we ought to report this," said the crew chief doubtfully.

"Oh, no," cried the female crew member. "No, Jerrod. Hey, don't. You do that, no telling where they'd send him. Let's keep him. He's a cute little kid."

Zasper, fading purposefully into the background, looked back to find the boy's eyes fixed upon him. The little boy's nose twitched as he settled into the curve of the woman's shoulder, never for an instant taking his eyes from Zasper's face.

And what're you going to grow up to be, Danivon Luze, Zasper asked himself, without an instant's suspicion of how very important the answer to that question could be.

In the other time and place, on Earth, the first small cloud on the sky of Marla Korsyzczy's contentment appeared during the fifth month of her pregnancy when ultrasound revealed two babies. A bit of a surprise, yes, though twins could not be considered a disaster. If one wanted lots of children anyway, which Marla and Leksy did because they couldn't hold their heads up in the family otherwise, twins were an efficient way of getting there after what Leksy's family insisted on calling a slow start. The doctor said he had a little trouble distinguishing between the two heartbeats, but everything appeared normal.

"I'd like to do an amniocentesis," he told Marla.

"Why?" she asked. "What are you looking for?"

"Don't you want to know what they are?" he asked. "Boys, girls, boy-girl?"

Marla thought about it. If there was a boy in there, no problem. If there was no boy in there, she might very well have a problem, but it would be the same problem later as now. Maybe it would be better simply not to know just yet. Leksy had already picked out a boy's name and painted the nursery blue. He had already thanked the Virgin with numerous candles and by referring to her several friends of his who had only girl children.

Marla said she thought she'd just go along with uncertainty, which, after all, had been the usual way of things until recently. The doctor went along with that. Still, when he ran the scanner over her bulging belly and looked at the ultrasound screen, he looked a little puzzled.

"What's the matter?" Marla asked, alert to any nuance.

He shrugged. "They're just in a rather odd position," he said. "Relative to each other. We'll take another look in a month or so."

Another look disclosed no change. The babies were lined up as though on parade. The doctor bit the bullet and told Lek and Marla that the babies might be joined.

"Siamese twins!" blurted Leksy, horrified.

"Joined babies," corrected the physician in his calmest and most professional tone. "Almost all joined babies can be successfully surgically separated. Let's not borrow trouble. Let's just wait and see." He did not remind Marla that he had told her the medicine caused a slightly higher incidence of twins. He didn't want to remember that himself.

Marla leaned forward and fastened the doctor with a scalpel eye. "What about natural childbirth," she asked. Marla had been attending classes since the third month.

"If the babies are joined, you'll have to deliver by cesarean," the physician said, glad to change the subject, if only slightly. The word "cesarean" got them off on a discussion of scars, how big and where they would be. Leksy wasn't great shakes on innovative lovemaking, but he did like to look at her nude, which Father Jabowsky had told him was all right if it served to get him in the mood to do what the books on Moral Theology said was all right to do.

The doctor discussed scars at some length because he did not want her to think about this Siamese-twin business. Ovitalibon had never, never been known to produce *Siamese* twins, but still. It could be argued. In court. That he should have known. Or shouldn't have recommended. Or should have let God's will be done in not letting Marla get pregnant at all, because when she didn't maybe that was God saying no. The doctor could imagine what the woman's husband would say on the stand. In this church-ridden town they would probably call in the priest as a witness! Either that or subpoena God Himself.

So he sweated and prayed that God, assuming there was one, could still be merciful to poor doctors who were trying their best. First, let the babies be born healthy. Second, let the separation be easy and let both babies live!

He got only part of what he prayed for. Marla went into labor, the obstetrician did a cesarean and delivered her of two bouncing, screaming somethings, nobody was quite sure what.

"Boys," said the delivery-room charge nurse in a gloomy voice. "Without a doubt. Listen to them complain!"

"They don't have penises," whispered a younger nurse.

"One sort of does. Besides, they have scrotums," the charge nurse answered.

"One of them does. Sort of."

"Well, they don't have vaginas," muttered the charge nurse.

"I think one of them does. Sort of."

After a quick analysis of the twins' chromosomes, the doctor attempted to explain to Leksy what the problem was. They were both XXY, and though the doctor did his best, Leksy either wasn't able or willing to understand the implications.

"The one born first is a boy," said Leksy, who was still visualizing the babies being born as kittens and puppies are born, one at a time in a slimy sack, not being lifted from the open abdomen in one very much connected and already yelling bloody chunk. "First born is a boy. I know that. If you have to do some surgery, I understand that. God gives us these things to try our faith, but it's a boy because the Virgin said it was going to be a boy."

"I've always wanted a daughter," sobbed Marla from the depths of an extreme postpartum depression. She wasn't thinking at all. She had resolved to give up thinking. Look where thinking and worrying had got her! Now she only cried and said exactly what she felt, no matter how silly it was. "Look at her, so sweet." She was looking at the left-hand twin, who was, in fact, slightly smaller and sweeter-looking than the right-hand twin. Not that there was anything wrong with the looks of either of them. They were pretty babies. All there, except for the sexual anomalies. Five fingers on each hand, five toes on each foot. Two little umbilici. Lots of dark hair and cute little curly ears and squinched-up eyes. Just like any two normal children, except for the broad pink tube of flesh that joined them from between right-hand baby's left armpit to slightly behind left-hand baby's right shoulder and extended downward almost to their hipbones. The flesh was full of throbbing, heaving movement. It wasn't just skin and muscle. It was obviously full of innards. Somebody's.

Preliminary reports revealed that separation was a vain hope. The babies shared one heart that was hooked up in a very unusual and complicated way. They seemed to share a liver and part of one lung. Besides, they were born in a Catholic hospital that had a medical ethicist on staff. At one time there had been a priest who had said yes or no, but now there was a medical ethicist who said the same things. The surgeons emerged from their conference with the ethicist with no joy whatsoever. One child could not be sacrificed for the other. Both lived, or neither, and there was no question that there were two separate children. They had, for example, two quite separate brains. The priest who, just to be safe, baptized them immediately after birth did it twice. There was no question in anyone's mind that there were two babies there.

By this time there were several physicians involved, all of them aware that a great many people who, believing they were men or women and living acceptable lives as men and women, were actually, genetically speaking, something else again. The deciding factor in cases like these had to be how the parents intended to rear them. The surgeons consulted again. The baby on the right did have sort of a penis, though the urethra opened at the bottom of it, next to his body. Well, that could be fixed. Also, right-hand baby had either testicles that were undescended or ovaries where they belonged, but whichever they were could be moved down and out, as it were, into a scrotum constructed from this and that. This would give right-hand baby a set of masculine-appearing sex organs. With the baby on the left, they could leave the gonads where they were, in the abdomen, and then modify the external complications into an acceptable vulva. There was already a sort of vagina, though it didn't go anywhere, and an isolated scrap that, from the quantity of nerve tissue, would serve as a clitoris.

"Look," said Surgeon A to Surgeon B, running his trembling hands across his bald head, "granted, we can come out with some reasonable-looking sex organs, male and female. But, we do this, these persons are going to have a hell of a life. Where're they going to go to the bathroom, for God's sake. Whose locker room do they use at school?"

The surgeons attempted to reason with the parents, in the presence of their priest.

"He's a boy," said Lek stubbornly. "His name is Bertran."

"A daughter," insisted Marla, who was angry with Leksy for getting her into this. Also, she knew in her heart she would never have another child and it was this time or never. "My little Nela."

"We pray God will bless your knowledge and skill," said Father Jabowsky, who was convinced that whatever the doctors did was irrelevant, that sexual organs could be dispensed with entirely for they would make no conceivable difference in the next world, which was the only one that mattered.

The surgeons, who thought they would probably be sued if they did and would undoubtedly be sued if they didn't, bowed to the inevitable, called their attorneys, and had five pounds of waivers generated to be signed by both parents, their parents, and all the relatives they could find. The surgeons who had been recruited to do the work itself were professors emeritus at the medical school, reconstructive surgeons called out of retirement on the theory that by the time the babies themselves got old enough to sue, the doctors would be dead. So far, no one had mentioned malpractice out loud, but no one was taking any chances.

The operations, several of them, were performed. Tissue healed, several times. Time went by. On a fine spring day at St. Seraph's, the twins were christened Bertran and Nela Korsyzczy, children of Mother Church, inheritors of the faith. Bertran wore a little blue velvet suit with a white lace collar. Nela wore a pink satin dress with an embroidered ruffle at the bottom. Marla held them, beaming with determined cheerfulness. Lek stood at one side, little Bertran's right hand curled around one of his big red fingers. Marla kept her mind on all the pretty little dresses she would get to make when Nela started school. Lek was wondering how old his son would have to be before he could start teaching him baseball. He was also resolutely not looking at the image of the Virgin standing in the little chapel, just behind the baptistry. Recently Lek had the feeling the Virgin had somehow let him down.

Neither Lek nor Marla were being realistic about the situation, but then, it was a peculiar situation to be realistic about. Both fully expected the day would come when the children would be separated—"As techniques improve," the doctor had said repeatedly in his most emollient voice—and until then (surely not long! Not more than a year or so!) it was merely a matter of prayer and patience.

But no more sex. Lek couldn't bring himself to do it anymore, at least, not with Marla. Not seeing where it had led before. He blamed himself, keeping after her that way. He'd told her it was his moral duty, but hell, he'd liked it. Every time. He'd lusted after her, and lust was one of the seven deadly sins, and maybe he was responsible for this having happened.

Lek didn't know about the medication, of course. Marla had never told him. Somehow, she felt it was better not to. Maybe she was responsible for what had happened. She considered telling Lek she couldn't have any more children, which both she and the doctor thought to be true, because during the cesarean he had spotted certain anomalies that hadn't shown up on tests, but what if something miraculous happened and she got pregnant again? She couldn't make sure she wouldn't, by using birth control, because Lek would find out somehow. Even though the doctor offered to put up pills in a bottle with a different label, like for anemia or something, she'd have to confess it to the priest. And somehow Lek would find out. So, she didn't, he didn't, they didn't.

Which meant, since both of them were normal, with normal appetites, that they became more than a little snappish with each other. Whenever things were difficult, however, throughout all their trials, Lek reminded himself of Marla's words on their wedding morning, when she had said to him four times was too much. Like a keepsake gem, that remembered moment gained importance as time went by, losing its own content and context to become an abstraction freighted with other, deeper meanings. As other enjoyments failed, it was the memory of how he had felt at that moment, the great gush of pride and wonder and fulfilled manhood, uncorrupted by actual memories, that enabled him to be unfailingly loving to the twins. Marla did not share that memory, but she had other myths that served a similar purpose.

Marla made clothes for both the twins until Bertran got to the age where little boys stopped being babies, and then she bought him jeans and checked shirts and tiny boots. Nela always wore dresses, wee pinafores with blouses and skirts with suspenders, and shorty white socks and black Mary Janes. The flesh between them was always kept decently covered by a dark length of stockinette that wrapped around the join in a kind of sleeve and had Velcro tabs to fasten it securely to itself and to the matching holes in the twins' clothing.

Lek built a double-width swing in the backyard, and a teeter-totter with a forked end, and a double-width slide. When they got to the right age, Marla tried to enroll them in nursery school, but there weren't any willing to take the twins except one for exceptional children, all the way over in Peaks Hill. They tried it for a week, but the twins were miserable among all the retardeds and autistics. One thing, something Marla didn't know if she was grateful for or not, the twins had excellent minds. By the time they were four and a half, they were learning to read and asking questions she sometimes had a very hard time answering.

Lek tried a few times to teach Bertran to play catch, but the child couldn't really manage it, connected to Nela the way he was, even though he wore lifts in his shoes to get his shoulder above hers. Lek also tried taking them fishing (Nela got seasick), and to a football game (Nela was afraid of crowds). Lek told Marla it was all her fault, she was the one who filled Nela's ears with how sick she, Marla, got in boats and how she, Marla, hated mobs.

"She's like her mommy, is all," said Marla. "You couldn't expect her not to be like her mommy."

"She should be exactly like her brother," Lek said. He had been discussing his problems with a counselor at work, one hired by the management to keep the production line functioning, despite the employees' personal problems. The counselor, up to his ear holes with drugs and sex and alcoholism, had welcomed Lek's situation as a taster might relish a rare vintage found among a clutter of vins ordinaires.

Lek went on, "The psychologist says they have to be geneic . . . genetic . . . the same. He says it's a law of nature. They started out as one egg and one sperm, and they're exactly alike!"

Lek had come to this understanding too late. It was no longer true. Biology had been bypassed. Reality had left genetics gasping. Gender had been imposed. Nela looked up at her daddy through her eyelashes and smiled at him flirtatiously, her delicate hands picking at the smocking on her muslin dress.

"Have you got me a present, Daddy," begged Nela, winsomely.

Bertran scowled manfully, his hands thrust deep into the pockets of his jeans.

"Hi, Dad," said Bertran. "Whudja bring me?"

"How can you say they're alike?" Marla demanded in a shrill, angry voice. "How can you say such a thing, Leksy. Why, they're nothing alike. Nothing at all."

Tolerance on Elsewhere: the Great Rotunda. There, on what is still called the Arrival Floor, brightly uniformed guards stand in imperturbable immobility around the Doors. The big Door, the one all the refugees arrived through long ago, is thought to require guards. Persons could still come or go through it, theoretically at least, and the guards are needed to make sure no one does. The other Door, the twisted, corroded loop of metal, is an Arbai Door, not unlike many other such Doors that the enigmatic Arbai left scattered around the galaxy. Despite the seeming dormancy of this one, there is always the possibility it might be functional, so it too is surrounded by a complement of Frickian armsmen. Besides, in the opinion of Council Supervisory, it makes a pleasant symmetry to have uniformed men around both Doors during the ceremonial changing of the guard.

An excellent view of these recurrent rituals can be had from the mezzanine, a high-ceilinged, softly upholstered dining balcony reached from the Arrival Floor by a dramatically curved flight of stairs. By convention, certain sumptuously furnished tables on the mezzanine are set aside for senior members of the Council Supervisory. Other tables, more sumptuous still, are located upon a small upper balcony used only by members of the Provost's Inner Circle. The upper balcony is quite private. Conversations held there cannot be overheard. Not least for this reason, it is a place much favored by Boarmus, the current Provost.

Today Boarmus has an appointment with Zasper Ertigon, sometime Council Enforcer, who has petitioned the Council for retirement so he may return to his native province of Enarae. Boarmus knows a good deal about Zasper, as he does about most Council Enforcers. He is inclined to grant Zasper's request, but before he does so, he wants something in return.

Zasper has given as his reason for retirement that the burden of constant travel is wearing him down, which is not precisely true. He hasn't really minded the travel; his real reason for retiring is this other thing he's been noticing and feeling and worrying over without being able to pin it down. This nastiness that seems to be getting worse. The extent to which twisted people are doing nastily kinky things, even in places where twisted people and kinky things have been more or less usual.

More child sacrifice, more female and child slavery, more wife killing, more ritual rape.

More pain and flagellation and maiming of celebrants.

More complicated torture. More mobs, more mayhem, more murder, more meanness.

Zasper has been around long enough to notice the increase, and he wants out. If it takes some kind of pro forma meeting with the Provost to get out, he'll attend the meeting.

So they come together on the upper balcony, the jowly Provost and the stocky Enforcer, the latter now dressed in undistinguished civilian garb, the former—so far as anyone knows—extending this exceptional courtesy to a good Enforcer now growing old, who is—so far as anyone can tell—enjoying the honor of a personal farewell. That neither of them has ever much liked the other isn't considered important, even by themselves.

"More tea?" offers Boarmus, ignoring Zasper's untouched cup.

"Thank you, no," says Zasper, who drinks ale when he can get it and believes herbal infusions to be at best old womanish and at worst disruptive of the bowels.

"I asked you here to take advantage of your experience," says Boarmus smoothly, making no further offer of refreshment. "In the field, as it were."

"Sir," says Zasper. It is an all-purpose word, essentially meaningless. "Confidentially."

An interesting interpolation, but the same word serves. "Sir."

Boarmus sits back and looks at his guest, almost smiling. Stiff-necked bastard. A good Enforcer. One of the best, but no give to him. Which is what's wanted. *"Confidentially,"* he says again, with an unmistakable emphasis.

Zasper blinks. "Yes, sir. Of course, sir."

Boarmus takes a package from his lap and places it on the table. Only Zasper sees his quick sidewise glance, both directions, to see if anyone's watching. No one is. The hour is early for the evening meal, late for midday. The upper balcony is deserted except for themselves.

"I received this recently," Boarmus says, removing the wrappings, though only enough for Zasper to see what's inside.

On the table between them lies a plaque of metal (Zasper thinks gold, it looks like gold) with fancy work around the edges (Zasper thinks gems, they look like gems). The words graven on the plaque are in a language commonly spoken on Elsewhere.

> THE PEOPLE OF ELSEWHERE
> ARE RESPECTFULLY REQUESTED
> TO RETHINK THEIR POSITION
> WITH RESPECT TO THE REST
> OF THE UNIVERSE
> •
> *R.S.V.P. NOPLACE: Central Panubi*

"Ugh," says Zasper, completely taken by surprise.

"These are not predispersion times," says Boarmus. "When precious metals and jewels had great intrinsic value. But even here and now a trifle like this is somewhat . . . extravagant."

"Ah."

"As much for the workmanship as for the materials," says Boarmus. "My consultants tell me that though the gems are extremely rare, it is even rarer to have something like this handmade. The lettering is hand done, for example. By an actual person who spent a good part of a lifetime learning how."

"What does it mean?" asks Zasper, cutting through the chatter.

"I don't know. It's the fourth such . . . petition we've received," says Boarmus. "All of them different. According to my predecessor, Chadra Hume, the first one popped up in the Files about a century ago. For a full day, nothing but a message similar to this would appear in response to any request for information. Various languages, but the same message. The second message appeared during an orbiter surveillance of the highlands of Denial fifty years later, and that one was spelled out in

letters a mile high, bright purple crass-brush against the tundra. My predecessor told me about that one too. Twenty-five years later, a third
one. I saw it, also on orbiter: herds of grazing animals on the Bi-flom
plains forming letters and words, a square mile or so, all with an ornamental border of migratory bat-swans. That was twelve years ago. Now
this one."

"How did you get it?"

"Found it on my Files access one morning."

"Ah," says Zasper again.

"How much did they teach you about the origins of Elsewhere?"
Boarmus asks in a low voice, casting another quick glance around him-
self. "I don't mean in Enforcer Academy, but when you were in school.
As a boy."

Zasper shrugs, furrows his brow, and tries to remember. "I learned
what most kids learn, I suppose."

Boarmus stares at him while trying to recall what children are taught
about Brannigan Galaxity, the greatest institution of learning in the galaxy, and how it had established Elsewhere as a refuge from the Hobbs
Land Gods. How much are children taught about the refugees being
promised complete freedom to live as they liked? About Elsewhere being
settled by a thousand different peoples, all of them with ancient gods to
propitiate, ancient wrongs to settle, or ancient duties still to perform?
Surely Zasper knows this much; surely everyone does!

Still, one has to be sure. "You learned about the Hobbs Land Gods?"
Boarmus asks.

Zasper nods. "Of course. A kind of fungal plague."

"Not one that killed, unfortunately. You learned about Brannigan
Galaxity?"

Zasper leans back with an amused look on his face and nods again.
"I learned that Brannigan had this committee to study the Great Question, and when the Hobbs Land Gods began enslaving humanity, the
committee felt that threatened their work, so they set up Elsewhere as
a refuge"—Zasper sniggers very slightly—"for humanity, including
themselves."

Boarmus adopts an offended expression. "I've never heard it alleged
that Elsewhere was set up as a refuge for the members of the Great
Question Committee particularly."

Zasper's mouth curls in amusement. "There's a thing we kids used
to sing when we chose up teams. 'Breaze and Bland and Thob and Clore /

ran till they could run no more / then Jordel of Hemerlane / chased them all right back again. One two three four / you're it.' " He starts to laugh, then stops as he notices the color drain from the Provost's face.

Boarmus reaches across the table and lays a slightly trembling hand across Zasper's mouth, saying in a shaky voice, "Don't! Remember where you are!"

"Sorry, Provost," murmurs the Enforcer in confusion. "I wasn't aware . . ."

"I don't ask you to be aware," growls the Provost. "I ask you to use courtesy and good sense. It is not . . . appropriate to mock the . . . founders of Elsewhere, certainly not here in Tolerance. It's true there were Brannigan professors named . . . the names you mention. And it's true that Jordel of Hemerlane was an engineer much involved in the Elsewhere project, but this makes neither them nor their many colleagues suitable subjects for ridicule."

"Well, the way I was taught the story," says Zasper irrepressibly, "is that they set Elsewhere up in secret, kept it a secret, and were the first ones here!"

"That's also true," agrees Boarmus in a whisper. "They were almost the first ones on Elsewhere. It was a long time ago, however, a thousand years, give or take a few, and their names are . . . historic. To be used with gravity!"

"You asked me, Provost!"

"What I was trying to establish was whether you understand the historic connection between Elsewhere and the Great Question."

Zasper snorts. "Every kid knows that connection. Grown-ups won't give you candy on Great Question Day unless you can go through the question-and-answer routine. There was a verse about that too: 'There once was a girl from K'van / who was asked the Great Question of Man. . . .' " He catches Boarmus's expression and goes on hastily, "Though, quite frankly, Provost, I don't see what this all has to do with this thing you've received."

"Then you're not using your imagination, Ertigon!" Boarmus flushes angrily, suspecting the man opposite him of willful ignorance or dumb insolence or both. Most likely both! "This petition, if that's what it is, suggests we 'Rethink our position regarding the rest of the universe.' The rest of the universe, this galaxy of it, at least, was long ago taken over by the Hobbs Land Gods. Only Elsewhere is free of enslavement.

Thus, only on Elsewhere may the Great Question be answered. So, to a suspicious mind like mine . . ."

"You think maybe someone . . . something doesn't want the question answered?"

"The thought had crossed my mind. Which is one reason I'm talking to you. The petition says R.S.V.P. Noplace: Central Panubi. You've been on Panubi."

Zasper, remembering a few times he'd been there, keeps his face expressionless. "Many Enforcers have been on Panubi."

"That's true. Unfortunately, few of you have been over the wall to Central Panubi, which should have been explored generations ago!"

The excuse originally given for not having explored Central Panubi before settlement was that there hadn't been time. The advance of the Gods had been swifter than anticipated. There had been ecological adaptation delays on Elsewhere. There had been the construction of the Great Rotunda to get finished off and a Frickian army to transport and house. There had been staff to hire and settlement protocols to be developed. There had been on-planet Doors to set up for transporting refugees to their provinces. Exploration of Central Panubi, it had then been felt, could wait until all these matters were taken care of. The reasons given now were different ones, but exploration still waited.

Boarmus's musing over this fact is interrupted by Zasper's impatient question.

"Provost, what do you want from me?"

"Well, I don't want the matter talked of here, for one thing. Since you're going home, you won't be here to talk about it. We Council members are not people of action. We don't think that way. We like precedents. We like rules. You, however, you're a man of action, so you can tell me what a man of action would do under the circumstances. That's what I want from you."

"I'd send someone to Central Panubi to find out what's going on," says Zasper firmly.

"Well, I have considered that," Boarmus replies, offended once more. "That seems self-evident, rather. The former Provost and I both considered doing that. But it's very difficult to send anyone to do anything and keep it secret! One man, maybe. But one man couldn't be expected to . . ."

Zasper thinks about it. "You don't want to mount a major expedition?"

"I don't. I don't want the talk. All it takes is the least bit of tittle-tattle and all Tolerance buzzes like a hive, all the charge monitors get themselves in a muddle, and nothing gets done for ages. Work backs up. The status quo is threatened. No, we couldn't have a major expedition without talk."

"Well, if I couldn't send someone to find anything out, then I'd simply wait. You've probably noticed that the intervals between messages are getting shorter. Whoever or whatever it is may be growing . . . less patient. If you wait, the petitioner may come to you."

"If you had to guess, what would you think this thing means."

Zasper, well schooled in tactics at the Enforcer Academy, ticks off the possibilities on his fingers: "Agitation, misdirection, misinformation."

"Meaning?"

"Meaning these messages may be mere harassment, attempts to throw you off balance. Or something or someone might be trying to make you look at Central Panubi so hard you don't see something happening somewhere else. Or perhaps there are beings in Central Panubi who believe they can get us to leave Elsewhere, some of us at any rate, going out where we'd be vulnerable—*or* who simply believe we ought to; no accounting for some people's idiocies." Zasper nodded. Idiocy was one thing Enforcers knew could be counted on.

He went on musingly, "Inasmuch as this thing suggests we turn our attention outside our own system, I could suspect the Hobbs Land Gods have something to do with it. Of course, there is another possibility, which is that the messages are meaningless. They may be created by some entity who's just fooling around. Maybe even a series of entities. It could have started generations ago with some kid recently brought to Tolerance from Heaven, and then he passed the joke on to succeeding generations."

Zasper feels this latter alternative is not unlikely. Kids do silly stuff. Even he, as a kid . . . Well, no matter. Of course (he has to admit this, proud as he is of being what he calls a realist) his feeling that this is foolishness could be just him getting old, losing his resiliency and perceptivity. He doesn't mention this, however, any more than he mentioned it to the Supervisors when he asked to go back to Enarae and become a mere provincial Enforcer again.

Boarmus frowns thoughtfully. "None of the reasons you mention would require that any of us actually go to Panubi."

"No," agrees Zasper. "None of them require that you go there. At least, not right now. Later, maybe. I can't help thinking that whoever sent that didn't really expect a response. The message is too enigmatic. Were the others equally so?"

Boarmus nods gloomily.

"Well then, he, she, or it may not expect an answer. The fact it's so nonspecific really lends weight to the idea that someone's playing games."

"Then we should wait, you think?"

"I don't think what you should do, Provost. That would be presumptuous of me. But it's what I'd do."

"Thank you for your opinion, Enforcer."

"Sir!"

In the other place, on twentieth-century Earth, Bertran and Nela Korsyzczy became bookish, both by necessity and inclination, their fondness for stories stimulated by Marla's habit of reading to them at bedtime. The comfortable hour she spent each evening sitting beside the twins' bed holding the pages of a favorite book in the glow of the little lamp with the ruffled pink shade was Marla's favorite time.

One night, while she was reading *Alice in Wonderland,* a new edition, with many colored pictures, Bertran broke into the story to ask, "Do you have to read girls' stories all the time."

"It isn't a girl's story," Marla said in surprise. "It's a classic. Alice could just as well be a little boy."

"She could not. She's all the time crying and talking to herself and doing stupid stuff."

"Well, she has to talk to herself," Nela objected. "There's nobody else there for her to talk to."

"A boy wouldn't," said Bertran stoutly. "A boy wouldn't talk to himself like that. He'd do something!"

"Oh, pooh," said Nela. "What would you do?"

"I'd smash that caterpillar for one thing."

"Boys are always smashing something," sneered Nela.

Bertran subsided with a glower.

"I'll read something for you tomorrow night," his mother promised. "You pick it out."

"Read the turtle," he demanded when the time came. "Not the Ninja one, the other one!"

Marla wondered why the turtle was more a boy's story than Alice had been, but Nela was making no objection so she burrowed for the raggedy old book. It was behind the fairy-tale tapes, on the bottom shelf, much creased and worn and stained with jam or something worse. It was called *The Turtle Who Wanted to Fly*.

" 'Once there was a turtle,' " she read, telling of the turtle who swam in the pond and dwelt in the mud, who ate green things and wormy things and listened to the splash of water and the humming wings of the dragonflies, who saw the swallows dipping the silver surface of the water.

" 'Came autumn, a time of gray thorn and gray leaf and gray mist rising,' " she read. " 'Turtle saw the glimmer of the swallows in the evening mist and wondered at them, for he could not see them clearly, darting as they did, their silver bellies and sapphire backs making bright arcs and darting dances along the ripples. "Oh, I want to see them," cried the turtle. "See them close and feel their feathers and the whisper of their wings, for I believe if I could see them closely, I could learn to fly. . . ."

" ' "To see them closely, you must go to the secret sanctuary of the birds," said the bullfrog, whose eyes were so constructed that he could see only the movement of the birds, not the birds themselves. "My grandfather told me of the place high on the windy mountains."

" 'So turtle went, by long ways and sad ways and hard ways always, gray tree and gray stone and gray wind blowing, until he came to the secret sanctuary of the birds.' "

And there he saw the birds, as he had longed to do. And there he was made a certain offer that he could not accept.

"I don't like that story," cried Nela, tears on her cheeks, anger in her eyes.

"I do," said Bertran, wiping his eyes on his forearm. "It's real, that story. Things are like that, they are."

"Only a fairy tale," said his mother, shocked at the depth of his feeling. "Berty, it's only a story!"

"Real," he insisted. "The way he feels."

"You know," said Marla in a slightly confused and worried voice, "if you practice, very soon you'll read well enough to read to yourselves. Then you can each read what you like."

She wiped Nela's tears and found herself longing for the person who had once wiped her own tears, her older sister Sizzy. It had always been Sizzy who had read to Marla when she was a child, always Sizzy who comforted her when things went wrong. Sizzy had left home long ago. Sizzy would be in her forties by now. Marla hadn't heard from her in over two years and didn't even know for certain she was still alive, but at that moment, wiping Nela's tears away, powerless to help whatever was really wrong, Marla wanted Sizzy very badly.

When the twins were six, they went to first grade at Holy Redeemer parochial school. The nun in charge—the school actually had a nun in charge, and some teaching nuns as well, despite the diminishing number of religious nationwide—made a halfhearted attempt to refuse them admittance on the grounds they didn't live in the parish. There were other nonparish children in the school, however, and Marla had a few choice words to say about the Pope's stand on birth control and the sanctity of life, ending with the question: Would Sister have preferred that the twins had been aborted?

Sister, shamefaced, said no, and forgive me, and we'll work it out somehow. The perennial rest-room question came up yet again, and was solved simply by letting the twins use the private toilet off the teachers' lounge, which was, presumably, unisex anyhow. Marla bought a duplicate of the small stool the children used at home, one they could move from one side of the toilet to the other, as necessity demanded, so both could sit while one was eliminating.

There was some teasing from the other kids to begin with, though old Sister Jean Luc soon put a stop to that. The twins sat at the back of the room, so the other students couldn't stare, occupying two chairs set side by side behind a small table brought in from the library where it had formerly held the big dictionary. Everyone tried very hard to be understanding and civilized, and the twins did not feel at all handicapped at any intellectual level.

Sports were something else again. The only exercise they were able to engage in was walking, which they managed in the manner of a three-legged race; Bertran, wearing his elevator shoes, his inside arm about Nela's shoulders, Nela's inside arm thrust into the front of her jacket, their outside arms swinging freely. The only problem with walking any distance was that neither of them enjoyed it very much. Their single heart had to work quite hard just to keep them both going; putting extra strain upon it fatigued them both to exhaustion.

Anything that required hitting a moving ball was out. Anything involving hitting a stationary ball was out, since neither of them could get their arms into a good position for whacking anything. Sister Jean Luc found them crying in the teachers' lounge one afternoon after a particularly trying attempt at kickball.

"Why?" demanded Bertran, more angry than sad. "Why are we like this, Sister? We can't do anything! Why?"

Marla would have told them to be patient, it was only for a time. Sister Jean Luc was less comforting though more truthful. She had a strong feeling that if the children could be separated, someone would have done it by now, that encouraging them to think they could be separated was much akin to lying to them.

"God always has a purpose for everything," she said firmly. "The fact that you were born in this strange way and must live differently means that God needs something from you he cannot get from ordinary people. Of course it is hard. Being a tool in God's hands is always hard." Sister Jean Luc considered herself a tool in God's hands, knew how hard it was, and believed what she was saying. Her words were implacably convincing.

Thereafter, most often at night when they were in bed together, they would remind one another of what Sister Jean Luc had said. When the day had been difficult, they would remind each other that being a screwdriver wasn't easy, being a hammer wasn't easy, being a pipe wrench wasn't easy. The idea wasn't exactly comforting, but it gave them something to hold on to, something to bolster one another with.

"Being a left-handed jackplane isn't easy," Bertran would say, trying for a laugh.

"Being a plumber's helper isn't easy," Nela would respond with a giggle.

Though they shared many of their thoughts and fears, they tended to keep their dreams and longings to themselves. Bertran dreamed waterskiing dreams in which he skimmed across white-topped waves. Nela fantasized being a ballet dancer and not merely a ballet dancer but a premiere danseuse, leaping weightless through waves of applause. They feared to share these visions with one another and had no way to share them with anyone else. They had learned to be wary of one another's feelings, since the unhappiness of one inevitably became the unhappiness of both. They shared misery through the bloodstream, like oxygen. This did not stop their bickering, which those closest to them eventually came to understand was more a recreation than an expression of real annoyance.

They encountered puberty, as their pediatrician had feared they would.

At age fourteen, various indeterminate organs began pumping hormones into their bodies and an endocrinologist was added to the working group of physicians who met from time to time to confer on the matter of the twins.

"There's no way we're going to be able to keep her on estrogens without him being on them too," the hormone expert snorted. "No way we're going to get him on testosterone without her growing a beard."

"What are they producing naturally?" one of the surgeons asked.

"A most god-awful mix," gloomed the endocrinologist. "Like a ragout."

"They're both growing pubic hair and breasts, if you can believe that."

"Feminizing hormones, then."

"Well, yes. Except they're both growing hair on their chests and faces too."

"Don't forget the libido," said the pediatrician. "Their mother says they're definitely sexual." That hadn't been what Marla had meant, exactly, though she had mentioned the fact.

"With each other?" asked the geneticist, inexplicably horrified.

"Who else?" sniggered someone, unforgivably.

The twins were, in fact, *sensual* with one another and had been for some time. Though their carefully constructed organs were not reproductive in nature, they were well equipped with nerve endings. Bertran and Nela, deprived of many other joys, had discovered certain mutual comforts when they were about six. Prohibitions against such activity, which they encountered in religion class and which all seemed to involve sins against reproductive nature, simply did not apply in their case. So Bertran had assured Nela, when they were about twelve. Nela told him she was sure Father or the nuns could think up a reason since they could think up reasons most everything nice was sinful.

"Even though we can't ever make a baby," she said. "The doctor told us that."

"We could pretend to have one," Bertran suggested tentatively, hearing sorrow in her voice but uncertain whether her grief was related to the matter of babies.

"I suppose we could," she said doubtfully, wondering why Bertran would suggest such a thing, but thinking perhaps he was sad over not being able to be a father. "What shall we name him."

"Turtle," said Bertran, the word coming out with no thought at all. "Call him Turtle. Turtle Korsyzczy."

"Not Korsyzczy," she objected. "What happens is, when he grows up a little, he changes his name. He says, 'Korsyzczy is too much of a mouthful. I want a name that says who I am, not who I'm related to.' "

"Well, who is he then?"

"Well, he's our turtle, Berty. Gray-wind-rising turtle. Only, let's pretend he can fly. Call him Turtle Bird."

Bertran thought about this. "I don't like Bird," he said. "It sounds too much like that long ago president's wife, the one our history teacher said got the billboards down along the highways. Something else with wings, maybe."

"Butterfly? Angel? Moth?" Nela suggested. "Eagle? Owl? Duck?"

"Dove," he said suddenly, liking the sound of it. "Turtledove. Like in the Bible, the voice of the turtle, you know."

Turtledove he became, their child, Turtledove. He, a boy, and never any discussion about that. Nela hadn't demurred. Their child was a boy by virtue of being a "he," but he never did anything that could not have been done equally well by a she or an it. The twins made up marvelous stories about him, though they never mentioned Turtledove to anyone else, any more than they mentioned what went on between the two of them. And aside from Marla's plaint to the pediatrician and the pediatrician's sneer to his colleagues, no one mentioned their intimate activity to anyone, least of all to the twins' father.

Lek was, therefore, totally unprepared when he entered the twins' room without knocking one morning and found them intimately engaged. He had entered silently; they didn't know he was there. In wordless shock, blank-faced and blind-eyed, he departed as soundlessly, left the house, and went to work. During a coffee break, a new coworker, one who was unfamiliar with Lek's family but who had recently heard something about him, made sniggering allusions to the foolishness of a man who believed he'd made love to his wife four times on their wedding night when he'd actually been asleep the whole time.

Though he did not seem to hear, the words went through Leksy like a knife. Without a word to anyone, Leksy put down his cup, left the plant, and went to a bar. All through the (mostly) sexless years, it had been the memory of that morning that had kept him relatively constant. Not what Marla had said or the idea of it, or even the confirmation of his own maleness, but the *feeling* of the moment. The surge of contentment and joy and fulfillment. His whole body and mind had seemed to glow from within, as though lit by a joyous flame. He remembered it as the happiest moment of his life, shining like a star, and he had held that light before him, guiding himself with it, determined from the depths of his despair that it would someday be like that between them again, if not on this earth, then in heaven.

Now, he saw the star flicker out, a coal, a cinder, a black hard nothing. It had been a lie. His joy had been a lie. Marriage was a lie. Fatherhood, children, all that was a lie. Things coming out right if you just had faith and worked hard, that was a lie. He drank for a time, without becoming at all drunk. The alcohol went through him into some dry other place where all the liquor in the world could not have made a splash. There was no change in his feelings, his arid hopelessness. Finally, he got off the bar stool, went to a car lot, sold his car, took the money, and got on a bus. By suppertime he was two hundred miles away, headed toward the Atlantic seaboard, nothing in his mind but flight and emptiness. When he got to New York, he called one of his brothers, a priest, to say that his and Marla's life together had been a sin and a delusion, that he was going, he didn't know where, and would not be back.

The brother called Marla. She screamed, then wept, then blamed herself and threatened suicide. They talked her out of that, repeatedly. There wasn't much anybody could do. No one knew where Leksy had gone. No one knew exactly *why* he had gone, though everyone guessed at part of the truth. Everybody on both sides of the family pitched in to keep Marla and the twins fed and clothed and the rent paid. Leksy had had some savings too, and there was a welfare fund at the plant. After a couple of months, Marla went back to work at the lumberyard.

Leksy's folks made a modest effort to trace his whereabouts, without luck. Months later, one of his brothers heard through the clerical grapevine that Lek had joined a contemplative order of monks in the Atlas Mountains of North Africa, an eremitic order living in a high rock city where everyone ascended by ropes and no female person or animal of any kind was allowed to enter.

Marla lasted less than eighteen months by herself. She grew accustomed to going out for long lonely walks after the children were abed, trying to wear herself out so she could sleep. She couldn't marry again because Leksy was still alive, somewhere. She couldn't seek the company of men for anything less than marriage. She couldn't do what Leksy had done and run off, leaving the twins alone. He had been able to do that only because he'd known she was there to care for them. Men, she thought, had always been able to seek holiness when they wanted to because some woman was back at home taking care of their obligations. That's why most of the saints were men and why most of the women saints were virgins. Sometimes she spent the hours wondering if suicide was actually a mortal sin.

During one of her long, introspective hikes, she was accosted by a mugger who demanded her money or her life. She laughed hysterically at this. Judith had been right. Some men get awfully bent out of shape when they are laughed at. Marla's funeral Mass was well attended.

Neither set of grandparents felt quite able to take the twins. It's true that all of them were far advanced in years.

Aunt Judith, who by now had ten of her own, shook her head in dismay. Sorry, she said, but . . .

Most of the other aunts and uncles were in holy orders one place or another, and children were not allowed.

And then, out of the blue, the twins' Aunt Sizzy showed up. Marla's oldest sister Sizzy, who hadn't been seen by any of the family for years; Aunt Sizzy with her apricot-dyed hair and sapphire-blue eyelids, her bright-glossed lips, bangles halfway to her elbows, a cigarette habitually dangling at the corner of her mouth even now, even after everyone knew it could kill you. Fifty-some-odd-years-old Aunt Sizzy who, everyone said, hadn't changed a bit.

"I've come to get my niece and nephew," she announced. "I've kept in touch through old friends here in town." She didn't remind anyone it had been her choice in friends that had contributed to her departure in the first place. No one needed to be reminded. "I know what a problem the twins would be for you people who have families of your own, but I'm alone, and I can take the twins with me."

None of the agencies that might have moved in to investigate Aunt Sizzy, which *would* have moved in to investigate Aunt Sizzy had she been going to take anyone but the twins, none of them did zip. All of the agencies in town had been involved in the twins' life since Lek had gone, and all of them had thrown up their hands, some in pity, some in exasperation. Not one social service employee checked out Sizzy's lifestyle. Not one intrusive do-gooder nun or priest stuck his nose into her past. Not one relative asked Sizzy where she planned to live, how she planned to support them all. As a matter of fact, the relatives kept the conversation very, very general and genial, never admitting to themselves for a moment that they didn't really want to know.

So, when Sizzy departed in her little red car with the bemused children in the backseat and the modest proceeds from Marla's life insurance in her purse, no one had an inkling as to where they were going.

Sizzy, who knew the town intimately, who knew all the relatives well, who had had years apart from them in which to make calm judgments about them, had chosen not to mention her destination. She chose not, even though she had known since she first heard about the twins that she would someday invite her niece and nephew to live with her, in her milieu, in the place where Sizzy herself had found both refuge and work for many years: in Matthew Mulhollan's Marvelous Circus.

Zasper's petition for retirement was granted routinely. The personnel Files found no reason not to do so. There were always more provincial Enforcers wanting Council status than there were open slots for them.

"But I don't want you to go!" cried Danivon Luze, now seventeen. When Zasper had rescued the toddler Danivon from Molock, he had not foreseen that Danivon would grow up to attribute to Zasper many virtues and qualities Zasper himself was not at all sure of. Danivon had just enrolled in the Enforcer Academy at Tolerance, a prestigious institution that would prepare Danivon to be, so Danivon said, just like Zasper himself.

Zasper thought Danivon would be better trying to be like someone else. He had even considered dissuading Danivon from an Enforcer's career, giving up the notion only after several days' worrying about it. He had no right to influence the boy. Letting People Alone was more than mere slogan, or so Zasper had always believed, though he'd become less certain of it latterly. Just because Zasper himself had this sick feeling about Enforcement didn't mean Danivon was going to. Besides—and this was the critical point—there weren't all that many avenues open to a foundling in Tolerance. All the servants, guards, and technicians were Frickian and had always been Frickian. All the Supervisors were whatever they were, some hereditary class or race or group or tribe; Zasper didn't know what and had sense enough not to ask. Information that wasn't freely offered was better not asked for, at least in Zasper's experience. It did a man no good to get a reputation as a prynose.

Whatever Danivon was, he wasn't Frickian, and he wasn't Supervisor blood, either, being a great deal taller than the former and a good deal handsomer than the latter. Though his mouth was a bit wider and his hair a bit curlier than Zasper's idea of perfection, he was a handsome, articulate, well-built lad who should get on with life. Full of the juices of youth as he was, Danivon no doubt had a good deal of life to get on with!

Danivon didn't see it that way, complaining that Zasper had no right to go off and leave him. "I like the Academy," he explained. "I really do. I like the other students too, almost all of them. It's just, I get lonesome sometimes. When some of them talk about home it makes me wonder why I don't have one." He confessed this to Zasper in a whisper, as though it were shameful.

When this subject came up, Zasper always swallowed deeply and reminded himself there were excellent reasons not to tell Danivon what he knew about Danivon's origins. Not least that telling the boy might get both of them killed.

"Nothing wrong with wondering where you come from," Zasper said. "Anybody would." Thank heavens the boy didn't look Molockian. If he had looked Molockian, Zasper's bit of playacting all that time ago might not have worked, and Danivon Luze could have ended up as one of the skulls on the top of that blasted temple. Zasper shook his head, driving away the thought, and repeated something he had said so often it had become rote: "We saw about twenty provinces on that journey; you don't really resemble the people in any of them; I can't be any help to you." Though wholly false, taken phrase by phrase the statement was quite true.

Danivon merely stared, his nose twitching. When he did that, it made Zasper feel uncomfortable, as though the boy knew something he shouldn't. Knew something he wasn't saying. "Besides," Zasper said hastily, attempting to divert that gaze, "from what I hear, you're not that lonesome that often. Not so far as feminine companionship goes, at any rate."

"Oh, that," said Danivon Luze with a self-deprecating grin that admitted everything but specified nothing. "I didn't mean *that*, Zas. But never mind. Even if you go back to Enarae, I'll come visit you. They make real good guns in Enarae, so I've got a reason. I'm not going to let you just disappear. I just won't."

It was true, they did make real good guns in Enarae. Zasper's home province was not remarkable in most regards—not to anyone who had seen Beanfields with its Mother-dears, or Derbeck with its Old Man

Daddy, or City Fifteen, full to its walls with dinka-jins. However, En-arae did have an unusual preoccupation with personal weaponry, due to having been founded by weapons engineers descended from sea-girt Phansure, the legendary homeworld. Shrines to the Guntoter stood on every other street corner; citizens were accustomed to the chatter and blast of weapons, the hushed slump of falling bodies, the ritual (some-times sincere) wailing of the bereaved. Five classes were recognized in Enarae: Executive, Professional, Wage-earner, Trasher. And, of course, Outcaste. The lower one's caste, the more one's self-esteem could de-pend upon prowess with weapons. In acceptance of this fact, Zasper did not disarm himself before returning home.

Immediately after he arrived, he went to Old Town, the entertain-ment district, where he strolled Tyme Street from end to end, examin-ing the displays outside every joy shop, relishing the menus recited outside every café, savoring every familiar sight and smell. At the bottom of the street, where a rusted iron railing leaned above the sluggish river, he turned the steepish corner and looked down a slanted flight of stone steps into the Swale. Whenever he thought of himself as a youth, or-phaned and lonely, he remembered himself doing exactly this: walking down Tyme Street, slowing his steps as the street narrowed above the river, almost stopping as he heard the clucking water at that final corner, wondering each time what marvel would be around the bend. Now, as he came around it once more, he knew no matter what else might have changed, the Swale had remained the same.

Now as always it seemed strangely empty for such a populous place. On one side the river crawled under ancient piers and around the hulls of silent boats. On the other, vast timbered structures pocked with blind niches leaned toward one another over narrow alleys. Every wall was pitted with doors, massive doors, iron-hinged doors, tightly shut or barely ajar. There were peepholes too, and windows where heavy curtains quivered continually, as at the touch of a restless hand. Behind the doors one could catch glimpses of tortuous corridors leading off into dimly lit interiors, and twisting stairs bending upward to tiny tilted landings that seemed built more for spiders than for people. Dank walls dripped with river sweat and stank of damp rot. Everything in the Swale suggested the disreputable and decadent, the presence of debauched and covert pleasures. The sound of the Swale was a muted growling, the murmur of a swarm in a hollow tree, not immediately visible or threatening, but ominously present, nonetheless.

A short way down the Swale was a gambling establishment run by Zasper's oldest friend, Ahl Dibai Bloom. Zasper was no sooner in the door than he heard the greeting:

"So you've come home, eh, Ertigon?"

"Better late than never, Bloom."

"Thought it'd be never, so I did." Bloom scuttled across the room and zoomed his elevator legs, looking down on Zasper from on high. "Thought I'd see you never again, Ertigon."

That had been what Zasper had thought too, once.

Bloom tugged him to a table more or less secluded from the ruckus going on.

"So, what brings you back again, Old Man?"

Because Bloom had more sense than most people, Zasper tried to explain.

"Lately . . . lately, do you get the feeling something isn't right?"

"You mean in addition to the normal everyday constant things that aren't right. Like these phlupping taxes, and the number of babies getting knocked off in the street, and . . ."

"I mean," said Zasper with a good deal of dignity, "something else, Bloom. A kind of feeling I've had lately."

Pressed for details, he could offer only generalities. He said it was only a feeling, as though some hideous danger lurked just out of sight. Danger was an Enforcer's constant companion, of course, and Zasper said he didn't mean any ordinary danger, like maybe getting killed, but something worse than that, far worse than that.

Bloom listened without being impressed, but then it took a lot to impress Bloom. Still, he was a friend and Zasper hadn't that many friends left alive. Whether Bloom understood or not, Zasper was still most comfortable in Bloom's place or around the Swale.

He came there often in the evenings when the river mist rose thickly and the lamps made balloons of light in the soggy air. Sometimes he stood at a corner for an hour or more, listening, watching, soaking up the quality of anticipation he had always felt there, the expectancy that hovered, as though something remarkable were about to occur, some wonder were to creep down the nearest alley, emerging at any moment. If he turned his back, he would miss it. The opportunity of witness would be gone unless he waited, patiently, for whatever it might be.

One evening while engaged in this solitary occupation, his scanning eyes detected movement where no movement should have been. Turning his head slowly, focusing on the shape of a crouched shadow, he translated the image into a scarcely credible reality—a girl child. A girl child, moreover, full of nervous twitches, half-suppressed fits and starts and trembling shivers that betrayed her presence beside the bulky hinge post of a tightly closed door. The door was carved in high relief with assorted pornographic scenes to advertise the establishment behind it, a brothel of a particularly unhealthful sort.

A girl this age had no business anywhere near there. Who was she? What child would dare these threatening alleys to hide herself in such a place? An older and more experienced person would be ill advised to do so. A girl child had no business in the Swale at all!

He moved silently, as Enforcers are taught to do, around and behind, coming up from a direction she would not expect. He did not speak until he had one iron-hard hand fastened firmly on her shoulder.

"What in hell are you doing here, girl?"

It wasn't so much a question as an exclamation, and though his voice was purposefully harsh, his prey did not seem frightened by it as she hung almost limp in his grip. He thought she drooped there like some little animal, too shocked to struggle, maybe playing dead the way they do, waiting for him to drop her so she could scurry off.

Instead, he drew her into a half-lighted doorway to get a good look at her, a pale-skinned child, thin as a scabbard, topped by a tangled mop of flaming hair. He noticed her gnawed and bleeding fingers when she pushed the hair away from a tear-runneled face, away from stone-green eyes not so much scared as watchful, the skin around them dark as a bruise. He'd seen eyes like that before, also in a child's face, but it took him a minute to remember where. A dozen years before. In Tolerance. A little boy, peering over a shoulder. Those eyes, Danivon's eyes, had been watchful in this same way.

"Child," he said, shaking her gently, made mild by memory, "what are you doing? It's damned dangerous here."

"I come here all the time," she said, staring into his face. She saw a stocky man with a gray braid over one shoulder and an Enforcer's badge on the other. Enforcers were mysterious, almost legendary creatures. She had no answer for the question he had asked. She didn't know what she was doing in the Swale. She came there, that was all. She sometimes thought she came here to get away from . . . whatever she wanted to get away from. Other times she thought she came here because of what was here. Though she lacked sufficient vocabulary to define the place, she could feel its essential nature. It suited her because it was like herself.

"Not a good place to come ever, much less all the time," he said.

She was moved to attempt explanation. "It's . . . it's like sort of secret," she said. "Or like the shrines. Sort of like me too." Struggling to understand the nature of the Swale, she had come up with amorphous concepts of taboo and sacred things.

"What'd you mean, like you?"

She shrugged. What she meant was, special. What she meant was, holy, but she didn't even have that word. What had occurred to her was that perhaps the reason she was here alone and not with other people was that she was different. Destined for something extraordinary. The idea had come from nowhere, sneaking into her mind bit by bit, like a little warm breeze, thawing her chilly heart. Being different would explain a lot of things, like why nothing worked out for her like it did for other people. She wasn't sure she really believed the idea, even though it was comforting. Comforting ideas didn't always—or even very often—work out, either, so she hadn't dwelt on it much. Still, she didn't *disbelieve* it, not yet. She could be destined for some particular purpose, maybe, and if so, she wouldn't be harmed by haunting the Swale as ordinary people might be. Coming here—it was almost a test!

"My name is Zasper Ertigon," he said. "What's your name?"

"Fringe," she said. "Fringe Dorwalk."

"There are better places than this, Fringe," he told her.

"Where?" she asked him, intrigued. She had been looking for better places as long as she could remember.

Their friendship began with that question. Remembering his own youth, he did not waste time in admonitory lectures. Instead, he showed her some better places, safer at least, like the way to get into Ahl Dibai Bloom's gambling house from Tyme Street, without going through the Swale. Ahl Dibai Bloom, bobbing up and down on his elevator legs as he did when he was amused, said he could use a young person to sweep the gambling rooms and stack the bottles, winking at Zasper over her head as he hired her for this duty.

After that, Fringe spent a lot of time at Bloom's, often when Zasper was there, mostly listening as they talked. Zasper told her a censored version of his life as an Enforcer, and she talked artlessly about herself, as though about a stranger. Little by little, he came to know who and what she was, though there was little enough he could do about that. Enforcers who had left off being Council Enforcers to become provincial Enforcers were just that. They had no great status, except among old colleagues. Still, they had a certain reputation and were not often interfered with. Habitués of the Swale, at least, soon learned that Fringe was Zasper's bit of harmless amusement and better left alone.

Freak shows were still current on Earth toward the end of the twentieth century, though less fascinating than in some former times. Television had made freakishness a commonplace; the *National Enquirer* and its ilk had made aberration a matter of mere momentary titillation, of no more duration than a headline. The world's fattest woman was only a person with a glandular disorder. Human skeletons were merely anorexic. The seal woman was a thalidomide baby. Bearded ladies and giants were no longer fantasy but matters of endocrine malfunction. A child born with an extra leg, the result of an incomplete twinning, would have had his supernumerary appendage amputated at birth. Elephant men had been reenacted on Broadway and in the movies. Dwarfs and midgets were merely little people who could take the roles of Munchkins or Time Bandits or small furry spear-carrying Ewoks in *Star Wars* epics. In cosmopolitan places, in urban areas, where the abnormal was ordinary, wonder at the bizarre had been lost.

In rural areas, however, eyes still widened and mouths still gaped. There the birth of a two-headed calf was still cause for a visit from the neighbors, hexing was a day-to-day possibility, the evil eye a fact. There credulity reigned and one of *them* was born every minute, fair target for the one-ring sawdust circuses, the dog-and-pony shows, still playing beneath canvas, their often dilapidated but brightly blazoned trucks moseying from smallish town to smallish town, their performances long on smaller animals and acrobats and totally deficient as to elephants or tigers. There, the snake charmer was still good for a three-dollar admission, and the cooch dancers brought out the boys who had no local topless bar for their after-work delectation. There, though the glitter was tarnished, the glamour faded, and the repair budget was always in arrears, the authentic aura of circus enchantment could still be found.

Mulhollan's had all the essentials, albeit on a small scale: taped calliope music tootling over the P.A. system, the whir of a cotton-candy machine, the shout of the straw-hatted ticket seller from his high booth, the barker's spiel outside the sideshow tent, the hum and mutter of the crowd; the smells of wet canvas, hot grease and caramel corn, horseshit and sawdust and hay; a dangle of trapeze ropes, a strut of plumed horses, an awkwardness of ruff-necked dogs dancing on their hind legs. Mulhollan's had Clown Alley, oleaginous with greasepaint, spider hung with fright wigs and balloony pantaloons. It had Sizzy's souvenir stand, its roof striped red and soiled white, its tattered sides emblazoned with peeling silver stars. The shelves inside were crowded with gimcrack junk: whistly whirly-birds on a stick, clown-faced coffee mugs, silver caps with horns and ears, plastic boomerangs and Frisbees, tiny wooden acrobats that swung around a bar when one squeezed the uprights together, ashtrays with pictures of dogs and snake charmers on them and the words MULHOLLAN'S MARVELOUS CIRCUS in curly P. T. Barnum letters.

Mulhollan's circus was Sizzy's circus, where long ago she had found refuge from small-town memories, ultra-pious kinfolk, priests, nuns, and people who had to be lived up to. Mulhollan's circus was Sizzy's circus, where neither she nor the twins had any history requiring explanation.

"What are we going to do here?" asked Bertran, looking around himself in a mix of awe and amazement, prey to an unfamiliar bubbling feeling he did not recognize as elation.

"You're going to be in the sideshow," said his aunt. "You're going to earn a living, the only way you can, until you grow up and they maybe cut you apart, and then you can do what you want."

"I don't think child labor's legal," said Nela, without conviction, feeling what Bertran felt and recognizing it no more than he.

"You're not going to labor," said Sizzy. "You're going to stand on a stage, all dressed up. After everybody's had a look at you, we'll put a curtain between the two of you, and the women in the audience can take a peek at Nela and the men can take a peek at Bertran. For five dollars extra."

"Look at me naked?" screamed Nela, shivering pleasurably.

"Naked," said Sizzy. "Just a peek."

"She's got hair on her chest," said Bertran.

"That's what Nair is for," his aunt announced loftily. "And hot wax treatment, and maybe even electrolysis."

"She doesn't have much boobs."

"So she'll get implants," Aunt Sizzy said, undismayed. "Look, kids, be practical. Nobody wants the responsibility. Nobody's ever known what to do with you, including my poor fool of a sister. At least here, there's some purpose to your life, right? And some enjoyments too, I'll bet. Marla was my favorite little sister. She wasn't long on sense—none of Mom's babies born after she was forty had good sense—but she had a good heart. I owe it to her to see you get some enjoyments. Fun, you know?"

They didn't know, but they learned. After the initial shock, it turned out to be not bad. Good, in fact. The best thing was that the circus was completely matter-of-fact. After all those years of strain and prayer, circus life was sensible and acceptable. No giggles. No pointed fingers. No labored three-party consultations in the confessional. No arguments about what bathroom they were going to use. Just, "Hi, Berty. Hi, Nela," from a clown. Just, "You kids going to eat or what! Get over here before I throw it out," from the cook. Just, "Try on your new costumes before noon so I can get them done before the show tonight," from Mrs. Mangini. The Manginis were mostly trapeze or horse people, but Mrs. Mangini was too fat to ride or fly, so she did a lot of the circus sewing instead.

The twins had a new double fold-out bed in Aunt Sizzy's trailer. They had a wire-haired fox terrier named Flip who belonged to them but also did acrobatics in the clown act. With them in the sideshow was a hairy-nosed geek named Ralph, who ate live chickens and was billed as the Alaskan Wolf Boy. They had Sappho and Archimedes Lapin, billed as the smallest man and woman in the world, even though they weren't nearly the smallest. They had the cooch girls (any female below the age of thirty who wasn't otherwise occupied) as the opening act, including the girl who doubled as Madame Evanie, the World Famous Snake Charmer. They had the marvelous Timber Head, who could drive nails into his face. They had Countess Vampira, with her long, long fangs that not even the dentists in the audience could tell from real because she'd had them done in Los Angeles where dentistry had attained the status of an art form. They had Tiberias, the mind reader, who usually didn't but sometimes could. And they had Bertran and Nela Zy-Czorsky (which Nela had made up out of the letters of their own name and pronounced Zee-CHORsky), the Eighth Wonder of the World, the only male-female Siamese twins in the universe.

Bertran's costume was midnight-blue, bow tie and tails, with a gleam-

ing white shirt. Nela wore a shimmery pink dress, all sequins and ruf-
fles. They stood side by side on the platform, long enough for people to
get restless and start to question the whole thing, then they turned away
from each other, just a little, showing the broad pink band of flesh that
joined them. Aunt Sizzy would shout, "Is there a doctor or nurse in the
audience?"

Sometimes there was. Aunt Sizzy always insisted on seeing identifi-
cation if anybody claimed to be a doctor or nurse. If there wasn't one,
somebody from the circus would claim to be, come up on the stage, feel
the flesh, look where it joined, act astonished. "My God. They really
are!"

"Yeah, but maybe they're both men or both women," some smartass
would inevitably call. If someone didn't, a shill would. "Yeah, but."

"For five dollars," Aunt Sizzy would say, starting into her spiel. She
had a chart and a pointer. She explained about chromosomes and how
all other Siamese twins were either boys or girls, and how Nela and
Bertran were a miracle, a one of a kind. Then she'd pull the curtain,
the one with the slit in it to go over where they were joined, and all the
women who wanted to pay five dollars would go to one side and all the
men would go to the other and look.

It wasn't bad. Even the peeping wasn't bad. Aunt Sizzy wouldn't
allow any touching, and it was only women on Nela's side and men on
Bertran's. Bertran would unzip and unbutton, showing the hair on his
chest, the genitals, small, but masculine-looking. Nela would untie,
showing her androgynous chest (depilated the night before by Aunt Sizzy)
and her own organs, unmistakably nonmale. Then the audience would
leave, men asking their wives and girlfriends, "Was she?" Women asking the men, "Was he?" Each assuring the other that he was, she was.

The school authorities caught up with them, of course. Aunt Sizzy,
who had been meaning to phony up a birth certificate to make them two
years older than they were, had to lay out a bribe plus enough to buy an
acceptable curriculum, and they had to study it enough to pass the semiannual tests, but it was nothing. Nothing! They could pass the tests
without half trying. Whoever laid out that curriculum had never been to
parochial school under Sister Jean Luc!

That first year, when they went into winter quarters, Sizzy arranged
for Nela to have breast implants. Not very big. Too big, said Aunt Siz,
and nobody would believe it. Kind of small ones. Just right for a teenage
girl. Nela had electrolysis too, to get rid of the beard and the hair on her

chest and to straighten out the line of reddish-blond pubic hair across the bottom of her belly, so it would look more feminine. Aunt Sizzy put them both on a diet, so they wouldn't have a lot of what she called "unattractive podge." Bertran dyed his hair dark, all over, to emphasize the difference between him and Nela, who stayed blond. After Nela healed up, she and Berty visited back and forth with the other circuses, the big ones, where there weren't any freaks who were called freaks, and the little ones like theirs, where there were. They made a lot of friends.

Also, starting in Florida and continuing everywhere they went, they frequented the bargain counters in bookstores, always leaving with an armload of books. In their trailer at night they lay side by side in the double bed, each with a night-light and an eyeshade and a book. Nela read romances and natural history, reveling in love and zoology. Bertran read history and math texts and biographies. Both of them read about religion, fascinated by it, not as a belief but as a subject. Though the matter had never been discussed with them by their parents or the priest or any of the nuns, they both realized that religion had paid no small part in letting them be born as they were. Sometimes they even talked about that, wondering whether, if they'd had the choice, they'd have been born this way at all. Sometimes, when it had been a good day, they thought they would. Other times, despairing, they were sure they wouldn't. Aunt Sizzy, who overheard one of these conversations, told them everybody felt that way. Some days, she said, everybody wished he or she hadn't been born or wished he or she could just die and be finished with everything. The smart thing to do was wait and see if a few days didn't change things. If it didn't, well, then it was up to people to do what they had to do, and she didn't believe anybody went to hell for suicide, not as overpopulated as the world was, but, she emphasized, usually a few days was enough to change a point of view.

Sometimes they thought she might be right. Other times, the few days stretched to weeks and they despaired. It was possible, they told one another, to be so depressed by what they were that they were incapable of doing anything about it even though they wanted to. That's why they went on, they said, sometimes capable of laughing about it. They went on because they were too depressed to kill themselves.

Sometimes they mitigated depression by holding long involved conversations about Turtledove, how he was doing at school, how he was doing at Little League, whether it was sensible for him to keep up his lessons on the violin.

"So expensive!" said Nela.

"But his teacher says he has genius," said Bertran. "What would we think of ourselves, years from now, if we denied him his chance at genius."

Meantime, no matter how they felt, they took dancing lessons from one of the Mangini girls, and learned elocution and comebacks from Matt Mulhollan, owner and ringmaster, and picked up a few sleight-of-hand tricks from one of the clowns. Their act was fine as it was, but as Sizzy said, mere titillation was limited by both prurience and credulity, while entertainment had no boundaries. "If you entertain people well enough, they don't care you're a fake," said Aunt Sizzy. "Most people don't give a damn about the truth, anyhow." She mentioned some politicians, including a recent president, as examples. "The world's biggest phonies, not very bright, but they entertained people, so nobody cared." The others in the show agreed, helping the twins practice their routines over and over, until the two of them oozed charm at every pore.

It helped that they were bright. No one, not even themselves, had ever doubted that. They turned their minds to the task, realizing their own welfare depended upon it. They worked on their voices, Nela raising hers, Bertran deepening his. They developed a sharp line of patter and a clever way with hecklers. They made the magic tricks sparkle.

"It's not easy being a power sander," said Bertran. "Not easy being a polisher."

"Don't tell Turtledove," said Nela. "He'd be so embarrassed if the other children knew his mother was an edger and finisher."

It was not long before their act began to draw, began to bring people in, began actually to increase attendance. A marked increase, commented Matt Mulhollan to Sizzy, during one of their regular late-evening conferences over a few beers and a little habitual sex. A steady, marked increase.

Sizzy passed this along to the twins. When they began to preen a little, she said, "Now, don't go feeling important. Sure, you're a draw. Anything new is a draw. But you're not the main event. You're in the sideshow, not under the big top. It doesn't do to puff yourselves up too much, because you'd just be setting up for a fall. Remember, no matter how classy you think your act is, there's always something bigger and classier coming along!"

Matt Mulhollan, who was no fool despite having been a little down on his luck recently, plowed most of the increased income back into the business. He bought new costumes. He repaired equipment. He added some acts he'd been unable to afford previously. Almost as an afterthought, he raised Bertran's and Nela's salary, and Aunt Sizzy went on doing with it what she'd done from the first: investing it in their names in blue chip stocks with a conservative brokerage firm.

Good fortune continued. The circus began to attract notice. During the twins' third year, it was featured as one of three notable small circuses in a nationally televised special on educational TV. The twins avoided the TV interviews. They still weren't of age, and they didn't want to risk someone from their hometown coming after them, not that they considered it likely. Not long after, Matt Mulhollan called everyone together to make an exciting announcement. Mulhollan's Marvelous Circus was to tour the European continent during the following year, a kind of exchange program in return for a Czech circus coming to the U.S. and Canada. Also, there was a possibility they might go to China the year after that. If the circus was granted permission to do so, certainly one reason, said Matt, being kind, was the attractive presence, among the more standard fare, of the Eighth Wonder of the World, Bertran and Nela Zy-Czorsky.

In Enarae, Zasper came to know all about Fringe Dorwalk. From a word dropped here and an implication there, from this tale and that recollection, Zasper managed to put her story together so that he felt he understood it. Perhaps, he told himself, it was part of his Enforcer's habit, always to seek reasons for things. An Enforcer charged with Attending a Situation had to be able to judge what had caused the Situation, after all. Though perhaps, he admitted to himself, he was merely a snoopish old man who, having no family of his own, let himself dig into the interstices of other people's. Or, he admitted somewhat wryly, it could be that he simply cared about Fringe.

Whether it was fondness or mere curiosity, he did learn about her, and about her family, most notably her father, Char Dorwalk, scion of the Professional class. Professional wasn't top class, not Executive, but it was far from trash, as Fringe told him, quoting her grandma Gregoria Dorwalk. Professional class was the good life, plenty of perks and not many risks, so Char had been born lucky. All he had had to do to have a good life, said Fringe, still quoting Grandma, was be sensible: set up in a profession, find a Professional-class spouse, and settle down.

"The way you say that, I guess he didn't do it," said Zasper.

No, she told him in Grandma Gregoria's words, Char hadn't been sensible. Char didn't set himself up in a profession and pick a Professional wife. Instead, he picked a pretty little chirp of a Wage-earner woman who kept the books at the debt-slave market. Her name was Souile Troms, and as if Wage-earner class wasn't bad enough, she was clerk caste to boot.

"Clerk caste isn't *exactly* trash," Fringe quoted Grandma Gregoria once more. "But when you get that low, you're getting close."

"Does your grandma always tell you anything that comes into her head?" Zasper asked, dumbfounded. "Including stuff about your ma?"

"Grandma says my ma is a perfectly nice woman," Fringe explained with some surprise. "She just isn't suitable for my pa."

Zasper shook his head. "Didn't your pa think she was suitable when he married her?"

"Oh, my pa! He was all in a fine fever of dedication, saying he'd draw her up to his level," Fringe replied, quoting Grandma Gregoria once again. "Grandma told him he could draw Ma up all he liked, but what was he going to do about her family?"

"Her family?" asked Zasper.

"The Tromses," said Fringe. "Ma's ma and pa. They live with us. Their names are Nada and Ari."

Further questioning by Zasper elicited that the Tromses were from the very bottom of the class structure, Trashers—sometimes nicknamed Troughers, because they had their noses in the public trough. Souile Troms, born a Trasher, had done well to rise to Wage-earner class by her own efforts, but raising up her folks had been beyond her.

"If your ma wanted to marry Char, she should have left her folks behind," Grandma Gregoria had said. "Her brother and sister went off and left them behind. Souile might have had a chance if she'd done that. I tried to tell my son, before he took them all in, but he wore me down. I finally told him to do whatever it was he was going to do. I couldn't stop him, and after arguing and arguing, you get so tired you quit trying."

Char had done what he wanted. Souile would not leave her parents behind, so Char had taken the setup money left by his father—every respectable Professional family provided funds to set up each child in a profession—had "invested" part of it, and with the rest bought a house large enough to hold them all plus the children he and Souile planned to have.

No house could be large enough for both Tromses, however. Their continual battles ranged from room to room and the smell of old Ari permeated any space he occupied. An hour after Nada and Ari moved into the room allocated to them, Nada moved out and into the space intended for children, which she had to herself until Fringe came along. Fringe had few memories of herself as a young child, but many impressions of that room, full of sniffles and groans and cries heard through the darkness.

"Don't you dare talk to me like that! I'm your mother! Ah, my heart, my heart. When I'm lying dead, you'll realize what you've done to me. Oh, help me to my bed. Let me lie down."

"Ma's dying, oh, Char, she's dying, she says . . ."

Char's voice, his dark-time voice, the one Fringe never heard in the light. *"She's always dying. Never a day goes by she isn't dying. So, let her die, if she'll just let us alone. Will you all let me alone! Never any peace, no peace at all!"*

"Hush, Char! Pa'll hear you. All he wants is . . ."

"Let the filthy old fart have whatever he wants. I'm too tired to argue."

"I guess Pa thought they'd all get along all right," Fringe said to Zasper in the careless voice she always used when she talked about her family. "I guess it just didn't work out."

"Things like that often don't work out," said Zasper. "Despite good intentions."

"Yeah," mused Fringe.

"It takes a strong man to turn back from a bad choice." This was Enforcer wisdom, hard-learned.

"Yeah," said Fringe again, this time with a quick sidelong glance to say she'd noted that one down for future reference.

Certainly Char hadn't turned back. Instead, he'd taken to spending most of his time away from the house. Nobody knew where he went or what he did. He wasn't practicing a profession, that was certain. Rumors came that he was gambling. He did that a lot. Ma was gone most of the time too, but Fringe wasn't supposed to ask where, and Nada wasn't supposed to tell, even though she did tell in a shamed whisper: Souile was out earning money.

"We need it to buy food," Nada whispered. "We need it to pay the school fees. But don't tell your pa."

"Grandma Gregoria says working for wages is disgraceful for a Professional-class person," Fringe explained to Zasper. "Ma should go to the E&P Wives Club instead. She should go there and do acceptable activities."

"E&P Wives Club? Acceptable activities?" asked Zasper. Though he'd been reared in Enarae, he didn't recall hearing about acceptable activities.

"Acceptable activities, you know," said Fringe. "Things your class says are acceptable. Like, if you're a Trasher, you can gang-fight, but not if you're a Professional. Professional women are supposed to go to the Executive and Professional Club and do women things. Wardrobe development. Conversation salon. Social dancing. History of Customs and Courtesy. E&P games. Acceptable activities. You know."

Zasper's Outcaste youth had been spent in activities that weren't remotely acceptable, so he didn't know, but he took her word for it.

Little girls, according to Fringe, learned about acceptable activities by playing with the E&P dolls their mothers gave them. E&P dolls had large wardrobes and extensive talk programs built right in.

"Tomorrow is the fifth of Springflower, Great Question Day," a doll would say. "Everywhere on Elsewhere, people will consider the Great Question of man's destiny. Here in Enarae red and gold are the traditional colors for Great Question Day. What will you wear?"

". . ."

"We must all look our best for the festivities. I've done my eyes a new way. They make me look lovely, don't you think? Do you like the new way I've done my hair?"

". . ."

"Do you suppose I'll be picked for the promenade?"

". . ."

Girls were supposed to fill in the blanks with conversation about grooming and style. That way, when they went to school and had conversation salon or grooming-and-style classes, they'd have a head start.

"At school they say we're supposed to consider the Great Question," said Fringe to Zasper, screwing up her mouth. "But nobody talks about the question at all. I mean, that could be kind of interesting, that question, about what mankind is for, but what we really do is play dolls. And all the dolls look alike. Exactly alike. They all have precisely the same face."

Zasper noted her expression, which was of someone about to spit out something nasty. "Don't you like them?" he asked innocently.

"I hate them," said Fringe, who had always managed to break her dolls almost as soon as she got them, though she never exactly planned to. "Maybe if I had someone to play with. But Ma and Pa are always gone. And Grandma Nada is always dying."

"Always?" asked Zasper.

"Well, every few days. Grandma Gregoria said she does it to keep in practice."

"Who takes care of you and your brother."

"Grandma Nada. When she isn't dying."

Certainly it was Nada who kept Fringe and Bubba fed and clothed. Sometimes Ari would come out of his reeking room and amuse them with wild tales of his ganger youth. By the time she was old enough for school, Fringe had picked up the Tromses' attitudes and accents, their habits of speech, their habitual actions and responses to the actions of others; Nada's defensiveness, Ari's belligerence, the Tromses' low-class vocabulary.

"Fringe talks like trash," Grandma Gregoria said to Char, making a moue of distaste, either not knowing or not caring that nine-year-old Fringe was behind the door, listening and watching through a crack. "Your daughter talks like trash, Char. She's low! And your son will be!"

The words shocked Fringe. She knew the two sides of the family hated each other, but though the knowledge was painful, she hadn't thought it had anything to do with her. Now, she realized she was mixed into it. She, Fringe, was right in the middle of it!

Shortly after the conversation between Grandma Gregoria and Pa, Bubba was sent away to a Professional-class boarding academy. Pa couldn't have paid for the school, so Grandma Gregoria must have done it. Though Grandma Gregoria had a daughter and several granddaughters, Bubba was her only grandson.

Fringe wasn't sent away, which meant she was all right as she was. Either that or it meant she wasn't all right, but Pa just didn't care.

"Do you suppose that could be it," she whispered to Zasper. "He just doesn't care?"

"Do you think about that a lot?" Zasper wanted to know.

She really didn't. She tried not to think about it at all, or about the other stuff that went on. She found she could shut out the real world by pretending things inside her head. Sometimes she went for days not even noticing the real world. Except for some things.

Like the old woman who'd taken to following her around. Fringe thought between Grandma Gregoria and Nada, she had enough old women already, but this old woman kept showing up, here and there, not doing anything much, but sort of always there, a white-haired old thing with keen black eyes that seemed a lot younger than her face.

"Why do you always show up where I am?" Fringe asked her angrily, confronting her in the alley outside Bloom's place.

"Do I?" asked the old thing. Today she was with a man almost as old as she was, and she looked at him with her head cocked to one side. "Do I show up where this child is?"

"I thought it was the other way 'round," said the old man. "I thought this child was always appearing where we were."

"There you have it," said the old woman. "Contiguity does not prove causation."

"What does that mean?"

"It means we're not necessarily following each other around."

"I think she is, though," said Fringe to Zasper. "Her name is Jory and I think she's a spy."

"For whom?" Zasper wanted to know. "Or what?"

Fringe couldn't tell him. The only reason someone would spy on her was if she was special for some reason. But she didn't want to talk about being special. If you talked about things you wanted, or things you hoped for, somehow that fixed things so you never got them.

So, she changed the subject.

"Ma's sick all the time now," Fringe said.

"What kind of sick?" he asked, thinking he already knew.

"Just sick," said Fringe.

These days Souile often lay abed with the horrors, glaring at the ceiling with wide, frantic eyes. The sickness came from near-lethal doses of mood-spray, but Souile never admitted that, not even to herself.

"Before I married Char, I saw my children in my mind," Souile said to Fringe when Nada sent her with a bowl of hot broth. "You were never babies. You were always grown-up, poised and perfect. You moved like dancers. You were successful. You didn't need anything from me. I knew you would be beautiful, and healthy and clever. I knew you would be talented and everyone would admire you, and me, because I was your mother. I thought if you were born Professional class, that's all you'd ever need. . . ."

"She said that, then she cried," Fringe told Zasper, her eyes wide and ringed with shadows. "She threw the soup on the floor and cried, and she couldn't get her breath, and I was afraid she was going to die."

"What did you think about that?"

"I knew it was my fault."

Zasper gave her a horrified stare. "Why would you think that?"

Fringe threw up her hands in a gesture learned at Grandma Gregoria's knee. Why would she think that? Because she hadn't done any of the things a good daughter should have done. She broke her dolls. She hadn't learned to be classly. She hadn't cared enough about style. She hadn't learned to do conversation. She didn't even know how to play the E&P games she was supposed to know.

"I've decided to take all the classes I'm supposed to," she told Zasper desperately. "I'm going to do better."

He didn't say anything. He had never been a Professional-class child. He didn't know what to say.

Fringe signed up for classes in conversation and personal style. She studied her fellow students, desperately intent on doing and saying the acceptable things, exhausting herself in an effort to make sense of the seemingly pointless rituals. No matter how she tried, she couldn't believe in them, she could not fit herself into the pattern. She tried to act the part, but she didn't feel it. Some rebellious part of herself kept rearing itself up and sticking its tongue out, going nyah, nyah, nyah just when she had to concentrate!

Despite all her resolutions, she didn't fit. She knew it and the Exec-class, Prof-class girls she was with knew it.

"Today one of the girls said I was crude," she told Zasper in an expressionless voice. "She said I talk like a Trasher. She said I have no polish and my clothes don't go together. She said I smell."

"What did you do?"

What she had done had been without thought, without decision. It had just happened. "I hit her. Then I bit her."

Sharp language, and sharper teeth (a Trasher trait, anger and fighting, learned from Ari). She'd known what the girl said was true though she had had no idea what to do about it or whether, if she had known, it would have been worth doing. She didn't smell nearly as bad as Ari did.

"What classes are you good at?" Zasper asked gently.

"General classes, like mathematics and systems technology and weapons."

"Those are important."

"Nah. Nobody cares about those. Not for Professional-class girls. Professional-class girls don't use weapons or math much."

"What happened today when you fought with the other girl?"

"They put me out of the E&P classes. They told me not to come back." Her eyes were dry when she told him this. She'd finished crying over it, but the guilt was still with her, some guilt at having failed the classes but more—much more—at having felt glad when they'd thrown her out. How could she be a good E&P daughter for Souile if she was glad when they threw her out!

After that, it was pointless to try very hard at school and too painful to try very hard at home. What was easiest was to be where nobody expected anything from her at all. She spent even more time at Bloom's, with Zasper, or ricocheting around the Swale.

"I like it better here," she said. "I'm not always messing up when I'm here."

"None of the messing up was your fault," said Zasper, turning away to hide his face. "I like you just as you are. Remember that."

Oddly enough, the old woman said the same thing. There Fringe was, just going down the alley to the Swale, and there the old woman was, sitting on the low wall that ran along Tyme Street, eating a meat pie.

"You look a bit worn and raggedy today," said the old woman.

"Everybody hates me," said Fringe in a nasty voice, thinking it was none of this old person's business what she looked like.

"I like you just as you are, child," said the old woman, with a strangely penetrating glance. "Raggedy or not. Sit by me and I'll buy you a meat pie."

"Rather have a sweet one," said Fringe, glaring angrily from beneath gathered brows.

"A sweet one then," said the old woman, patting the wall beside her, so nothing would do but for Fringe to sit down there and have a hot fruit pie all to herself, fresh from the vendor's kettle.

"Your name's Jory, isn't it?" demanded Fringe. "I know your old man's name too, he's Asner."

"That's right. What's yours?"

"Fringe. Are you Professional class?" Fringe asked, wondering who else would have time to sit about all day, eating pies.

"Only in a manner of speaking," said the old woman. "Actually, I'm not from Enarae at all."

"You're here all the time."

"Vacationing. Seeing the sights."

"Not much to see," snorted Fringe, who, as an habitué of the Swale, thought she had seen it all. "People from Denial and Sandylwaith. Globs once in a while. Dinks from City Fifteen."

"Dinks. You mean dinka-jins."

"People parts in boxes," sneered Fringe. "Obs."

"They eschew the flesh," said Jory thoughtfully.

"Hah," barked Fringe. "Like I said, Obs and Uglies."

"But they're still people," said the old woman. "Interesting people. Some of them are very, very smart."

"Maybe in City Fifteen they are, but not the ones who come here," Fringe snorted.

"Possibly not. But still, I like people. Picking them out, you know."

Fringe didn't know.

"I picked you out," said the old woman with a smile. "I really did, Fringe. Did you know that?"

Fringe held her breath. "Why?" she asked.

"Why?" The old woman cocked her head and considered this. "Because you obviously aren't satisfied with yourself the way you are, that's why. You keep popping out in all directions, playing at being other people. But then, don't you get dreadfully tired of people who like themselves a lot? Just the way they are?"

Fringe's eyes stared wide in wonder. "How did you know that?"

"Well, because we're alike, I guess. Both special in our own way. And then, too, I've spent years and years picking out people, all over Elsewhere."

This came so close to her dream that Fringe didn't dare listen, didn't dare believe! "How can they be special if there's a lot of them?" she sneered, sure it was all deception.

"Not lots! I never said lots. I said all over Elsewhere. Someday you'll come visit me, perhaps, and I'll tell you all about them. Introduce you to them."

Though it was possible the old woman might actually be telling the truth, Fringe took the promise with a grain of salt. It would hurt to believe it and find out it wasn't true. Grown-ups were always making promises they didn't keep.

Great Question Day on Elsewhere. Carnivals and street dancing and solemnities. Processions with bands and clowns and red and gold banners. Music from the rooftops, and children going from door to door begging candy for the traditional give and take:

"Where is the Great Question asked now, child?"

"On Elsewhere, only on Elsewhere!"

"Why only here, child?"

"Because only on Elsewhere are there any humans left!"

"Long ago, where did they ask the Great Question, child?"

"At Brannigan Galaxity! They asked it there!"

A rattle of candies into the proffered container. A whoop and a scamper, off to the next house.

Brannigan Galaxity.

Oh, say the name reverently. Say it with awe. Say it as you might utter the secret name of God.

The center of the academic universe. The repository of all knowledge. The hub around which all reputable research had revolved. The quintessential fount of academe that was.

"Brannigan," the human teacher had said, in the remote village on the tiny world, laying her human hands upon the heads of her rose-lipped charges. "Study hard and maybe you'll get to go to Brannigan."

"Apply effort diligently," the docentdroids had cried on the eduscreens, to urb-pale students they would never touch, never see. "You may be selected for Brannigan."

Fat chance. One in ten million had been accepted at Brannigan. Un-

questioned and prodigious genius might have gained an interview, if one
had known the right people, if one's parents and grandparents had gone
there, if one had been on the AA list. Otherwise, dream on!

Vast auditoria reverberating to words deathless as Scripture. Labora-
tories where ideas fell thick as pollen, packed with potentiality. Hall-
ways vibrant with scuttering youth, with striding maturity, with ponderous
age. Ramified structures, lofty towers, cloud-touched, star-noticed, sky-
surrounded.

Voices raised in song:

Brannigan we sing to thee!

A thousand colleges, each with its own history, its own traditions, its
own glories to recount. A thousand colleges, each with its own feudally
owned worlds to provide goods and services, each with its own recruiters
at large in the star-whirl, moving among the lesser schools like sharks
among the shoals, picking the little scholar fish who would grow into the
intellectual leviathans of the future!

Fountain of diversity!

Libraries sprawling in wandering tunnels of stone across continents of
lawn. Mile-long stacks, loaded with volumes numerous as stars, copies
of copies of copies from originals long ago turned to dust. Automatic
retrieval ladders disappearing into the retreating distance of painted ceilings where figures out of forgotten legend disported themselves. Was
that Wisdom teaching the multitude? Or the Queen of Denacia, issuing
writs of attainder to her bailiffs? Was that Agriculture with the garden
springing up at his feet? Or was it the Winter God Hembadom, readying
himself to trample the fertile worlds of Borx? One time the docents had
known, had pointed upward while lecturing to legions of tourists and
hopeful candidates.

Here twisting stairs clattering beneath niagaras of pounding feet. There
dim corridors, endless as roads, running into vaulted passages that grew
silent as they left the tenanted areas. And there, at the end, corroded
doors opened upon cavernous spaces shrouded in cobwebs, home to the
beetle and the fly, where bindings were only templates of green mold
and pages had turned to inscrutable powder. No matter. All that was
here was also in Files, incorruptible.

May thy golden towers rise . . .

Brannigan: glorious with the names of former scholars who had risen to untold heights: the Chairman of the Council of worlds; the Emperor of Eltein; the Goddess-elect of Vamie; the Virgin Inheritor of Rham. . . .

As a beacon for the wise. . . .

Brannigan: whose emeriti had stood in glittering rows along the Halls of Tomorrow, preserved in impenetrable vitreon, awaiting the day the Great Question would be answered. They were to have been raised then, from senescence into eternal youth.

Immortal may thy children be. . . .

Lost. All lost except the Great Question itself. Gone, Brannigan. Gone the towers, the libraries, the teachers, the students. Gone the hope, the pride. Gone as all the galaxy is gone, down the gullets of the Hobbs Land Gods, leaving only . . .

The Great Question, the Only Question, still to be answered by this remnant at the end of the star-wheel, this tiny spark against the long-dark:

WHAT IS THE ULTIMATE DESTINY OF MAN?

On Earth, success followed success for Mulhollan's Marvelous Circus. Despite Sizzy's adjurations of modesty and humility, Nela and Bertran sometimes felt they were indeed the main event. Sometimes they were sure the whole circus focused on the freaks in the sideshow tent where the attraction was the people themselves. Other attractions were only tricks, as when a monkey pedaled a bicycle or a bear juggled a barrel or someone did three somersaults between the trapezes. But in the sideshow, no matter how professional their act, it wasn't the tricks or the sparkle that mattered. It was they, the sideshow artists, who were the show, what they were and suffered. It was their oddity that brought people in.

"Turtledove writes that he is terribly proud of us," said Nela. "We have been reviewed in *The New York Times*."

"It isn't easy, being a jackplane," Bertran admitted with a wry grin. "But we're getting good at it!"

Even so, oddity alone would not satisfy the audience once it had seen. Once the spectators had sated their curiosity about whatever peculiarity had piqued them, many of them lingered, looking for something more. Nela learned to recognize that searching stare fixed on her, on Bertran, that perusing eye that caught her own and asked recognition of it. And when she nodded or smiled, acknowledging the unspoken question, the viewer nodded too, as though saying to himself, herself, *Why, she's like me, he's like me, no matter what they look like, they're like me after all.* It was the oddity that brought them in, but it was the humanity that let them go again.

"If they wanted only difference," Nela explained her thought to Bertran, "they'd go to an aquarium. Or to a museum, to see a collection of fossils. They'd seek out spiny creatures, things with many legs, aliens, weirdnesses, but they don't go there, they come here, where the strangeness is people, because it isn't the strangeness they're really looking for, but the fact we're people, no matter how we look. It's the identity under our skins they want to assure themselves of. Now, I wonder why that is?"

It seemed to Nela there had to be a reason. Something beyond mere curiosity. Something, as she sometimes thought, intended.

Bertran agreed it was the humanity behind the freakiness the audience wanted to see. However, he said, though most of them went away afterward chattering and relieved, some of them were strangely silent, as though the humanity behind the barker's chatter had not been enough. "They're looking for something they don't find," he said, wondering what they were looking for. Something more meaningful or knowing. Some definition, perhaps, of what humanity was, a definition that *had* to be sought in sideshows because the answer could not, never would be found among ordinary, everyday mankind.

"Turtledove believes that people are seeking an oracle," Nela said. She often quoted Turtledove as saying things she herself felt or thought but, for some reason, did not want to have to defend as her own opinion. "People want a seer." Though she wasn't sure, she thought this might be true. People wanted someone to drop key words in their ears, the revelation they needed right then; help, surcease, pity, forgiveness, hope— the secret of existence. They were looking for all those things in a sideshow because they hadn't found them anywhere else.

The audience didn't get any of that. Not help nor hope. All it got was a moment's wonder, a wink of complicity, plus magical rings, disappearing scarves, and patter. "Which is all we've got to give, Nelly," said Bertran. When he said it, he believed he spoke the truth.

It was during the third European tour, ten years after the twins had joined the show (Turtledove, they told one another, had just won an international violin competition and had fallen in love with a girl named Sylvia Syllabub who played the bassoon), that Bertran and Nela met the Alien. The circus was performing in Rakovnik in Czechoslovakia, in a building constructed for year-round performances of circuses. Bertran and Nela had just left the sideshow after the last performance. The rest of the artists had joined the performers and support personnel to discuss a minor wage problem they were having, something to do with the rate of exchange. Bertran said he and Nela had talked about it enough, that they were going back to their trailer. Nela, as was unavoidable when Bertran made pronouncements, went along. They were still dressed for display: Nela, fluffy and pretty in her sequined and beruffled dress; Bertran, saturnine and handsome in his tails and stiff shirt.

Both were in good spirits, their mood currently rising after a few days of that episodic and paralyzing depression they had long ago learned to recognize, a depression that physicians over the years had blamed upon the weather, the work, or perhaps on Nela's ovaries or whatever they were attempting to be cyclical. Nela herself called the episodes NMS, or nonmenstrual syndrome, and both she and Bertran had learned to suffer through them stoically (eschewing any thoughts of suicide until later) in anticipation of the euphoria that very frequently ensued. Bertran was reading a note that had been passed to Nela during the performance, and his current upswing kept him cheerful about it, though he didn't find the contents honestly amusing.

"This man wants to marry you," he said with a wry grin.

"I know. That's my fifteenth proposal, Berty. I've kept count."

"They never want to marry me." He pulled a long face. "Here I am. Always a bridesmaid. . . ."

"Well, they want to do what they *do* want to do, with you."

It was true that Bertran had been propositioned from time to time. "Only because you'd be there," he said. "Your inescapable presence makes the prospect excitingly wicked." Bertran contorted his mouth as though to spit. He claimed not to be intrigued by those who propositioned him, though he sometimes found Nela's suitors truly amusing.

She shook her head, pouting. "I think the ones who want to marry me want it for the same reason. Let's tell this one yes and see what happens. What's his name? Ladislav Something?"

"Poor fish. When you tell him I'm coming along on the honeymoon, he'll gasp and his little gills will quiver. He probably thinks we're a fake."

She nodded in agreement as they swerved to the right, into the stables, where they moved between two lines of glossy horses, all munching, stamping, looking up with glowing dark eyes to greet whoever was coming through. The twins enjoyed this short detour after every show, and they paused to stroke sleek flanks and soft muzzles, receiving whickers and nuzzles in return.

"Why do these crazies want to marry me, Berty?"

"Because you're exotic," he said. "Beautiful, but very, very strange. It's the same thing we've talked about before. Some people hunger for the strange because they have not found answers in their ordinary lives. They want to be different."

"None of them would trade places with us. We're different."

He thought about it. "Well, perhaps they desire singularity more than difference. They feel their humanity is not all, not everything, not enough. They feel strangeness immanent inside them, and they want to understand it as singularity without displaying it as oddity. They want to be pointed out for their distinction, not because they're weird." He looked down at her. "Or, perhaps, they lust after variety, diversity, newness. Who knows?"

Bertran's gaiety flattened somewhat as he considered the matter. From time to time, unpredictably, he quivered with indefinable longings and nostalgic melancholy quite distinct from the depressive episodes, times during which he thought he must be yearning for some place he had forgotten or had not yet seen. He called these moods *ubalgia*, where-pain, but only privately, to himself, never speaking of them, not even to this, his probably dearest and certainly nearest kin. From time to time he dreamed, dark reflections of dreams he had had in childhood, now more erotic and more perilous. He tried not to dwell on these, either, realizing without asking that he was probably not alone.

During one late, restless night fairly recently, in fact, Nela had spoken into the empty darkness, almost a whisper, as though to herself.

"I want to sleep. Except I dream about Turtledove, at least he starts out as Turtledove, but then he turns into the heavy little turtle who

spied on the birds. 'Gray thorn and gray leaf and gray wind rising.' "
Her voice had seemed to inhabit the darkness like a lost spirit. "And
then suddenly he has feathers, and he is Turtledove, really, with wings
and he's reaching for me, calling me, Mommy, Mommy, and I'm trying
to find him. . . ."

Her words summoned a picture of a moon peering through mist while
voices from childhood called in the dark, "Berty! Where are you, Berty?"
Fog and autumn smoke, and a nostalgia bittersweet. Where had it been?
Who had been calling him? Not Mother. She had called "Nai-lah . . .
Ber-tee," both names, always. Who was it who had called him alone,
just him, as though he could answer as the turtle had answered, alone,
"Here I am!" That's what the little turtle had cried when he heard his
friends calling, his plodding, heavy little friends, searching for their long-
lost comrade, high on the windy mountain.

Caught in his where-pain, Bertran hadn't responded to Nela's whisper
in the shared dark. Instead, he had lain quiet, pretending he hadn't
heard, and after a time he had fallen asleep. The memory hadn't left
him, though, and it was of that calling voice he was thinking as they
emerged from the stables with the last of the sunset in their eyes, a
rose-violet glow, bright enough that the figure stepping from behind the
nearest wagon was silhouetted against the light and showed, for that
moment only, as a stalky and featureless blackness.

"Please do not be alarmed," it said. "I am not from your world. May
I have a moment of your time?"

The accent was patrician, if anything, delivered in a mellow though
slightly raspy baritone. It was Alistair Cooke's voice. Bertran immediately guessed it was intended to be reassuring, since anyone with senses
would know at once the creature was not human. Not human, not animal, not earthly at all. Bertran had been with the circus for over a decade. He and Nela had traveled over most of the world, the more thickly
populated parts of it anyhow, and nowhere had they seen or heard of a
striated, very skinny, seven-foot-tall, L-shaped creature with four legs at
the bottom and two arms at the top, centaur style, rather pale in color
and looking much like a huge stalky vegetable. There were even frilly
protrusions at the top and at the joints of the extremities that appeared
leaflike.

Nela thought, from the midst of an icy calm, that if one scattered
some facial features at the top of an immense stalk of bent celery, it
would resemble what confronted them. Without panic (even while re-

minding herself she would undoubtedly have hysterics later) she studied the creature as she waited for Bertran to respond. In cases of surprise or emergency, it was easier to let Bertran do the talking because even if she spoke, he would invariably interrupt her.

"What did you want to talk about?" asked Bertran, his voice betraying no apprehension, though he felt it. It had been a long time since he'd been startled over anything—working circus tended to make one almost startle-proof—but this thing had appeared when he was already feeling somewhat off balance, and there was a definite yaw in his perceptions.

The Alien took a moment before answering, "We have come from a far place. We would like to talk with you about—our presenting a Boon."

The creature's face wasn't much. A small vertical orifice that emitted speech, another two or three triangular depressions of ambiguous purpose, several roundish ones that glinted rather like eyes, or at least more like eyes than anything else. It had a strong vegetal smell, also. A summery smell. Heavy, but not unpleasant. Like mown hay and gardenias over a faint breath of rain-wet soil.

"We've got some time," said Bertran. "If you'd like to come to our trailer." He rather wanted to get out of sight, preferring that this encounter continue without witnesses. The instinct to hide was a holdover from childhood, when any new or possibly embarrassing thing needed to be considered in private before the twins were forced to deal with it in the public gaze. Even if the Alien proved dangerous, it would be better to meet that danger in private. So his blood said, hammering in his ears, no matter what cautions his brain urged upon him.

The Alien nodded. Since it had no neck, the whole body bobbed, almost a curtsy, the four bottom legs folding and unfolding like springs. They were set at right angles to the body, like insect legs, and looked tacked on. Assembled. Like a plastic toy. Fit pegs A, one through four, into holes B, likewise.

The twins moved toward their trailer, at first tentatively, then picking up speed as the thing trundled closely behind. Nela hoped the other sideshow people were still involved with their meeting. If this parade was observed, she and Bertran would never hear the end of it. My God, that time the baby goat from the animal act had become enamored of Bertran and had followed them home, they had been baa-ed at by their colleagues for days! What would they say about this?

The creature had some trouble getting into the trailer. Human-type steps were obviously not spaced well for its legs. Once inside, however, it managed to curve itself into a chair and tuck its bottom appendages beneath and around it, out of the way, showing that it knew what chairs were for, though it obviously needed one of a different shape.

"My name is m'dk'v*dak'dm#," [Muh-*click*-duhk-*click*-vuh-*rasp*-dak-*click*-duhm-*gurgle*] the thing said, making a chain of mechanical and consonantal sounds.

"I'm afraid I'd find that a little hard to say," said Bertran with his most studiedly charming smile. He patted at the sweat along his hairline with an immaculate handkerchief. His breath was slowing. Both he and Nela were growing calmer. The thing did not seem threatening at all. "Would you mind if we called you Celery." He put the handkerchief before his mouth to hide the fact he was nervously chewing his lower lip.

"Celery," the Alien said in a musing voice. "Vegetable. Comestible. Considered worthy. Valued. Often associated with ritual or holiday occasions shared with kin and close friends. In some cuisines, a customary ingredient. No inimical implications. Why not Celery."

Bertran nodded and smiled in automatic response as he and Nela moved to their usual places on the small couch across from the single chair. There were some folding chairs in the closet, for occasions when they had more company, but usually the couch, the chair, and the dining table with its two benches were all they needed for seating during tour. They had a larger trailer back home, one they had bought when they stopped sharing with Aunt Sizzy. This small one seemed suddenly very crowded, overwhelmed with aroma and presence.

"To what do we owe the honor of meeting you?" asked Nela, deciding simultaneously on participation and formality.

Celery considered this for a moment. "You are the most . . . the most similar-to-us being with language we have found on this planet. Since we are constrained by the death of our late, illustrious, much valued comrade to provide your planet a Boon, we sought a similar-to-us to hear our offer. Our sensitivity is so great, we cannot deal with those who are not similar to us."

Nela and Bertran didn't need to look at one another to share the questions both of them felt. Bertran's left arm was across Nela's shoulders, where it usually was. Nela's hands were folded in her lap. Their thighs were pressed together, not too tightly. Their heart beat as one.

Their breathing was slow, controlled. They understood one another's feelings completely.

"Explain, please," asked Bertran. "We don't quite understand."

"We share certain attributes," said Celery, its gesture including them and itself. "The persons on this planet are, almost without exception and regrettably, singular, isolated, unable to fully empathize. You are not singular, not isolated. Neither are we, though in appearance we may seem so. While you are side-by-side, we are some-in-one, eventually many-in-one. Our own experience assures us it is the correct way to be!"

Bertran struggled with this concept and decided to let it pass for the moment. "What is this Boon?" he asked.

"I will utter in greater detail." Celery scrunched slightly, achieving a more recurved configuration. "We are a people who have only recently been granted the great concession by the powers."

"Great concession?" asked Nela.

"Permission to leave our galaxy. Permission to . . . expand."

"You need permission?" she said disbelievingly. "From whom?"

Celery gestured vaguely. "You . . . you lack the concept. I search your language in vain. I find words: 'quarantine,' 'border guards,' 'Ellis Island,' 'immigration,' 'quota' . . . None of them are right. You must simply accept what I say. We have only recently received permission to travel. Now we are on our way. You would call us, perhaps, pilgrims. Pilgrims to the holy land."

"I see," said Nela, who did not see.

"When in the course of our journey a comrade dies—as is inevitable, for all life hath an end—when our comrade dies, it is our custom to memorialize by providing a Boon to the nearest inhabited place. One Boon. One thing that, in our judgment, will be of greatest value to the inhabitants."

"You can do this? Provide this . . . this Boon? Something of value?"

"We have done so from time to time."

"World peace? Immortality?"

"We have done peace, yes. World peace is simple. We identify all inhabitants whose racial or tribal loyalties take precedence over their planetary ones and eliminate them. Peace inevitably results. Immortality, however, is one of the exceptions."

Bertran and Nela shared a glance. "Exceptions?" Bertran asked.

"We do not regard immortality as a Boon. Theoretically, it is possible. Philosophically, we consider it an abomination. Also, in multiracial worlds we do not regard extermination of any intelligent race as a Boon, though other races might consider it so. We would not eradicate all your aboriginal humans or all your cetaceans, for example, not that you do not seem to be doing that very well on your own. And we do not regard sharing our knowledge as a Boon, except in limited fashion. If we were, for example, to decide upon the cure of some disease as the Boon for your planet, we would share enough of our methods to provide the cure, but only that. We ourselves have no disease. Unlike your race, which would perish utterly without disease to control its prolificacy, we no longer have use for it."

Nela said, "Nobody is going to believe this."

Bertran nodded. "She's right. Nobody is. I can see it now. 'Freaks Claim Contact by UFO!' 'Aliens Invade Big Top.' "

"Oh, we know you'd be disbelieved," said Celery. "We have relied upon that and upon your pragmatic realization of that fact. We do not want to be known. Searched for. Noticed. We are pilgrims, not visitors. Our destination is far from here. Only the necessity of memorializing our dead comrades brings us into contact with other races at all."

Bertran shook his head. "Then why come to us? Why involve any of the inhabitants?"

Celery looked embarrassed. Afterward, Nela tried to decide what about the creature had made her think of embarrassment. Perhaps the slight flush of green about the features. Perhaps the slight jerkiness of motion in the limbs.

"We have already decided upon the Boon for your planet. However, we are going . . . a long way. We hope to be on time for a particular event that, our great prognosticators tell us, will occur in foreseeable time. If we stay to accomplish the Boon, we may get sadly out of phase. It has been suggested that you might accomplish the thing for us, without compromising our journey, for a suitable reward."

"Accomplish what?" Nela's mouth fell open. She found herself unable to imagine anything she might do that would benefit the world.

Celery scrunched itself once again. "Shortly, within the year, on your planet will manifest a thing originating from a great distance. Let me see. How shall I make it clear to you? Another race of creatures—a race your people will know, in the future, as the Arbai—have adjacently established a transportation and communication network that is spreading automatically throughout the galaxy even though the Arbai, so we believe, either already are or are about to be extinct. The Arbai envisioned a universe unified by their network. One of the, ah, way stations? Nodes? Gateways? Doors? One of whatever you choose to call them will manifest itself on this planet shortly.''

Nela caught her breath. "How marvelous!"

Celery nodded, then shook itself, saying yes, no. "Indeed. The Arbai, though a people of inflexible philosophy, have subtle and wonderful intelligences regarding the natural universe. They are capable of marvelous things. But, no, this gateway will not be marvelous for you Earthians, for if it is left here, it will first contribute to great unrest among all the people of Earth, after which it will allow a plague to enter that will exterminate the human race."

They stared for some moments, trying to absorb this. "How do you know?"

"Prognostication is our science. We are very good at it. Not perfect. Nothing is ever perfect. But we know of the Arbai and of their network. And we have seen with our science certain consequences that have happened or will happen. We speak a close approximation of truth when we say the way station, the gate, the door, must be closed if your race is to continue. A close approximation to truth is the best that can be achieved. To anticipate the opening of the door, to close it before mankind ever becomes aware of it, this is the Boon we provide."

"And you want *us* to close it?"

"We will give you the means. A simple matter. The door will open near where you will be at the time. It will not inconvenience you. And we will reward you for your help."

"How?" Bertran asked bluntly. "How? What will you offer us?"

"What would you like? Riches? Your people enjoy riches. A long life? We can offer that."

"Could you separate us?"

The creature before them shivered all over, as though stricken by cold. It made a gagging noise and bent awkwardly in the middle, shaking again, then composing itself with seeming difficulty. "No," it gasped. "We would regard that as an obscenity. We came to you because you are, as we are, multiple. Would one of us willingly separate? Would we commit such an atrocity of isolation upon one of our kind? We cannot even discuss matters with separated persons!"

Nela started to say something, but Bertran laid his hand over hers.

"If you were attempting to discomfit me, you have succeeded," the being muttered. "I should not be offended. Undoubtedly I discomfited you. Let us proceed gently."

Bertran asked, "Do we have to decide about the reward now? You've given us very little notice."

"No," Celery said, pulling itself into rigidity once more. "No. We can grant your wish later on, even from a great distance. Be as quick about it as you comfortably can, but leave it for now."

This time it was Nela who spoke. "What do you want us to do?"

The matter was simple enough. Celery repeated it several times, being sure they understood it completely. The thing would manifest itself at a time and place foreseen. The twins would be there when it happened. They would fasten upon it a device, and the door would demanifest. The world would be saved. No one would know. Later, when they decided, the twins could request their reward.

"Discuss your reward," suggested Celery. "State it in words, clearly, saying what you mean. Then speak it into the transmitter I will leave with you and smash the transmitter against some durable surface. We will get the message."

"One reward for both of us?" asked Bertran, wondering if, perhaps, he might achieve a personal desire that Nela did not share. Once. Just once.

It was not to be.

"One for both of you, when you agree," the thing confirmed, with obvious distaste, as though asking the question had again transgressed a taboo. It fell silent, as though thinking. When it spoke again it was in a tone conveying both grief and pride. "This Boon will be the m#dk'clm*tbl [Muh-*gurgle*-duhk-*click*-cullum-*rasp*-tubble] memorial. m#dk'clm*tbl was not only a great friendship but a related aggregation. We have warm memories of them/it. This Boon will be suitable, in memory of very great camaraderie."

It gave them the device, a thing about the size of a lipstick. It told them how, when, and where to use it. It gave them another, slightly smaller device, the transmitter. It got up, bowed or nodded, went out the door, stumbled down the steps, strolled across the hard-packed earth of the parking area and around behind the Mangini trailer. It did not emerge from the other side. Bertran and Nela went out to look. There was no one behind the Mangini trailer. There was nothing there at all but the trampoline frame and the practice trapeze rig where the youngest Mangini daughter, Serafina, spent her mornings training to do multiple somersaults.

"Do we believe this?" asked Nela wonderingly.

"Does it matter?" asked Bertran in return. "Even if we don't, should we take the chance on not doing it? Celery said he was sure the world would die. . . ."

"Remember Sister Jean Luc?" asked Nela suddenly.

"Yes. Of course."

"Remember what she told us, about God needing us for something. The creature talked to us because we are as we are, Berty. If we'd been ordinary, he wouldn't have talked to us at all. Perhaps . . ."

"You think this is what God's purpose is?" asked Bertran. He didn't mean his question to sound ironic or cynical, and yet it did, a little.

"Why not?" she demanded. "Good Lord, Berty, saving the world and all its people is a fairly big thing, wouldn't you say. Reason enough. . . ."

He hugged her. "Reason enough," he agreed, tears in his throat. Why didn't he believe it?

They went back into their wagon, shutting the door behind them, leaving the parking area untenanted except for a strolling cat who stared at the sign on the side of the wagon without interest or comprehension. "Bertran and Nela Zy-Czorsky, the Eighth Wonder of the World!"

"You were here in the Swale all day yesterday," Zasper said to Fringe, offering her half the fried berry pie he'd just bought from a passing cart. "Don't you ever go home?"

"I told you before about how Ari's sister came to visit. She's a real old lady."

"Ah?"

"I mean, she's really old, Zasper. Everybody said it was just for a visit, but she's not going anywhere else because she doesn't have anywhere to go."

"Where did she come from?"

"One of the Seldom Isles, I think. Something dreadful happened there, and most everybody died."

Zasper nodded, his lips tight. Yes, indeed. Something horrible and inexplicable had happened there, quite recently, and no one had been able to find out how, or why. Enforcers had been sent and come back paler than usual. No one had figured it out.

Not noticing his distraction, Fringe went on, "Yesterday, Ari got this old room module for her to live in and put it out behind the house." She pursed her lips. "I mean, he stole it."

Zasper drew his mind back to the conversation and elicited the story. Everyone in the family knew the module was stolen. There had been a yelling match between Char and the Tromses, at the end of which Fringe, with a fine show of indifference, insisted on moving into the module herself, "So Aunty and Nada could be together."

The two old women had always hated one another (Ari had confided this to Fringe, laughing heartily over it), but angry as Char was, everyone was keeping quiet, so by the time Char and Souile had calmed down enough to pay attention, Fringe was already moved.

"Nobody's going to find the module there, behind our house," Fringe said. "The local Enforcers aren't going to find it. It's so banged up, I'll bet they aren't even looking. I said I liked it, I told them all really, I like it."

"Do you like it?" asked Zasper when she finished her tale.

She sighed. "Well, it's real little. And it's pretty drafty. And the saniton doesn't always work."

"But?"

"But what?"

"But something, Fringe. Your voice had a but in it."

"But, it's better to have a space of my own." Far better than trying to hold on to her sense of herself in a room with one or both of the old women. Nada filled whatever space she was in, leaving no air for anyone else to breathe. Adding Aunty made a suffocation. Fringe felt herself smothering. The two old ones hawked and sniffed and got up and down all night long. Their bits and pieces littered every surface. They bickered with each other, and when they tired of picking at each other, they pecked at Fringe. *Aren't you finished with that schoolwork? Turn off the Files. Turn off the light. What's that funny noise you're making. Quit coughing. Quit chewing your fingers. Quit picking your nose. What are you doing under the covers? Your clothes are on the floor! You'd think you were a boy, the way you leave your stuff around for other people to pick up!*

Either that, or they talked about her as though she weren't there. *Look at that outfit. She looks like the pig's dinner. Miss Professional, tryin' to be like the Dorwalks; thinks she's something, don't she? Chaffer can't change its shell; pig can't change its smell; she's in for a surprise.*

"It's bad I don't like them better, my own kinfolk," Fringe confessed. "But they make me feel so . . . so gone."

"Don't you like them at all?"

Truth was, she did rather like them, in a large open space, one at a time. They had interesting things to say sometimes, when they forgot she was there and didn't pick on her. It was just when one got closed in with them, with doors shut, with walls around, that they seemed to turn into other creatures, some kind of birds with pecky beaks and claws, looking speculatively at her with those beady dark eyes as they tore little pieces of her away. Among them, she felt herself dwindling, felt herself becoming tattered, pecked into raggedy lace, infinitely fragile and angry and lost.

"They eat me," she said to Zasper. "If I didn't fight them, they'd quit, but I have to fight them because they get me so I don't know who I am. Sometimes I think my whole life is just going to be eaten up by old women. Sometimes I think that's all I'm for, for them to eat up. They don't seem to have any other use for me!"

There was something else. Something she hadn't mentioned to Zasper. When she was alone, she had these visions, kind of. A light, beckoning. A voice saying words she could almost understand. She could lie there, half asleep, and almost see it, almost hear it! But when the old women were around, she couldn't remember what it had been.

She sighed, continuing, "When Aunty came, I saw her, and at first I thought she was that other one, the one who follows me around all the time."

Zasper nodded. "Is she still doing that? Following you around? What's her name?"

"Jory. I still see her, if that's what you mean. Sort of here and there. Sometimes she buys me a pie. Sometimes she talks to me about things."

"What things?"

"You know. Just things. How I feel about things. About how I'm to go visit her one day. But she doesn't really look like Aunty. Aunty just looks old and sort of ragged out and gone. That other woman, she looks really old too, but like she had a fire in her."

Zasper shrugged. He had not yet succeeded in catching sight of Fringe's follower. Sometimes he thought Fringe imagined her. Fringe imagined a good many things.

"So now you're living in a module," he said, returning to the former topic. "But you're never there. You're always here."

"I like it better here." This was said pleadingly, as though she feared he might force her back to a place that wasn't where she wanted to be. She dwindled there. She vanished, even to herself. Except when she was with Zasper or sweeping the floor at Bloom's she couldn't keep in mind that perhaps she was meant to be odd, as she was, for some reason. It was important to have some reason. Otherwise . . . otherwise why exist at all? There had to be some reason for it, sometime, somewhere. Like her very own Great Question. What was she meant for?

Nela and Bertran had been told the manifestation was to occur on the seventeenth of May, some ten months after the Celerian—which is what Bertran and Nela called him—had visited them. The visit itself had come almost to occupy the realm of myth or shared dream. They would no longer have been sure it had happened, except that Celery had left them two small things. One was golden and featureless except for an oval lens set into one side. Since it had a ring at the top, Bertran put a chain through it and wore it around his neck. The other thing was wasp-waisted, about three inches long and as thick as a finger. This device was to go on the door when it manifested itself. They kept it in a kitchen drawer in the trailer. A few times, when they opened the drawer, they found it glowing. A few times they heard it make a sound, a remote clicking, like death-watch beetles in some other room.

The gate was to manifest itself late in the evening in the middle of an orange grove that lay only a few miles from the circus's winter quarters. The twins went there under the guise of taking a little drive and eating out. Nela had learned to drive and did it quite well, though Bertran could not keep himself from telling her what to do next. She continually told him to buy a right-hand drive and do it himself, otherwise to keep quiet. He never did the one or the other. In truth, it was hard for him to put both arms in front of him. His left arm was almost always around Nela's shoulders.

During the previous month they had scouted the grove several times, enough to know it well. Celery had been able to identify the exact place for them, within a few feet. Between the eleventh and twelfth rows of trees from a certain fence, between the fifteenth and eighteenth trees in the row. When the thing showed up, they were to place the device at the edge of it, at the bottom, fitting its concave sides between two protrusions.

By a quarter to eleven, they were in place. They had brought a couple of folding stools to sit on, and Bertran had the device in his shirt pocket. They wore their favorite leisure clothing: sneakers—Bertran's made especially for him, with lifts, to raise his shoulder over Nela's—and dark-colored sweat suits, the ample material Velcroed together to hide their mutual flesh.

At precisely eleven o'clock the fragrant air among the trees wavered with a coruscating oval. Irresolute, it glimmered for some time before solidifying into a lopsided plane of fire, a slightly warped screen of light. The twins got up from their stools and walked around the thing. It was the same on both sides. Close up, they could see the twisted loop of dark metal that framed the fire, the whole upon a solid base of the same material. The protrusions they had been told to look for were duplicated on both sides. Simultaneously, they shrugged. Presumably, either side would do. They knelt at the base. Bertran handed Nela the device, Nela leaned forward and positioned it as they had been directed to do, hearing it click into place. She shut her eyes, murmured a few words of prayer remembered from childhood. If this was the reason for their existence, she wanted to accomplish it with some sense of divine purpose.

Bertran, however, was struggling to his feet, and she, perforce, came up with him, still leaning slightly forward. Nela put one foot out, off balance. . . .

She felt something move under her foot and looked down to catch a glimpse of a dark ovoid. Bertran, also looking down, saw the same shape. It might have been Bertran's arm that pushed Nela, for he had put out his right hand to catch himself and it had gone through the plane of fire into nothing. He fell forward with Nela inevitably beside him. They went on falling. A moment later the screen of fire disappeared, together with its frame and base, just as the Celerian had said it would. The Celerian had not said, of course, that the Zy-Czorsky twins would disappear with it, though the strong probability of that event had been foreseen.

Their car was found at the edge of the grove. Two parallel sets of footprints led partway into the grove and then vanished. Two canvas stools sat side by side. The only living animal creature found in the grove was a small tortoise, staggering laboriously along beneath the trees. The disappearance became, like the twins themselves, a purely temporary wonder.

The world had, in fact, been saved, though no Earthian knew it at the time. Afar, in other places, the Celerians conducted a chaste and tasteful celebration. The likelihood that the twins would fall through the gate had been accepted as an appropriate risk: the twins had, after all, been honored in the saving of their world. A shortened time upon that world was a small price to pay for such honor. In terms of total life loss, the Earthian Boon was at the extreme low end on the scale of Celerian Boons. Other Boons had resulted in enormous, though always justifiable, death tolls.

Celery and his age and aggregation mates were proud of their prognostication. Even they admitted, however, that foretelling had its uncertainties. This seldom kept them from changing the immediate future, even though the Great Aggregations among them, who reviewed those changes, were occasionally moved to comment on what had been done.

So, following the departure of the twins, a Great Aggregation came before the assembled crew of the ship(?) and announced with comfortable asperity that the Earth Boon had shaken the very fabric of time! "Look here," it/they said to the younger, smaller, and more facile aggregations, "look here! If the Boon had been provided in a different manner, none of this would have happened. Look here at the place called Grass. Look at this place called Hobbs Land. Look at this place called Elsewhere. Look at these humans, Danivon Luze and Zasper Ertigon. Look at this human girl called Fringe. Look at this old, old woman who calls herself Jory now, and this old, old man who calls himself Asner! See what they portend! See here, how our journey will be altered, our future interrupted as we are called away from our proper pursuits, all for naught? All to no point, for we will be able to do nothing!

"See how the great concession we have so lately earned, with what enormous effort, is threatened by the way in which you have granted this Boon!"

TWO

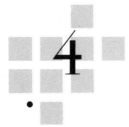

4

Tolerance on Elsewhere: the Great Rotunda, where, on the upper balcony, Boarmus the Provost sits thoughtful. His companion, Syrilla, is unaware of his thoughts. In Boarmus's opinion, Syrilla may be unaware of any thoughts at all. Though a longtime member of the Inner Circle, she seems incapable of connecting cause and effect. Her forte is hysteria; her singularity to freight even the most irrelevant remarks with enormous import.

As now, when she dilates beaky nostrils and cries dramatically, "I cannot understand why Danivon Luze would have done such a thing."

"You know why," Boarmus says lazily, without stirring. His wide-bottomed form is well settled into its velvety chair like an old monument into turf, slightly tipped, but massively immovable. "If you're speaking of Danivon Luze the Council Enforcer."

Syrilla gestures with an apparently boneless hand and raises her eyebrows to her hairline, miming astonishment. "Of course, Danivon Luze the Council Enforcer." Danivon Luze, once a foundling child, the pet of Tolerance; then Zasper Ertigon's youthful protégé; now a strikingly handsome though controversial officer. Who else?

Boarmus snorts, a muffled plopping, like boiling mud. How long has he come here in the afternoons to occupy this same table, this same chair? How long has he drunk one thing or another while looking down upon the uniformed guards, the two Doors, the ceremonial changing of the one about the other? Whatever time it has been, nothing has happened in it. Well, very little. A few minor rebellions, relentlessly put down. A few new ideas, squelched. A few innovations, which always turned out to be reinventions of things forgotten centuries ago. And now, at last, something. Something happening, and though in the past he had thought he longed for something to happen, he now wonders if such longings had been at all wise.

"My dear Syrilla, Danivon did it because he's been trained to do it. Enforcers are trained to report wickedness." He brackets his speech with sips from a porcelain cup heavily crusted with gold. Members of Council Supervisory have recently reinvented (for the umpteenth time and under another name) both teatime and the Baroque.

"Did he have to be so public about it?" she asks in a high, affected voice, a little-girl voice belied by the ageless cynicism of her eyes.

Boarmus grunts impatiently, weary of the woman. She's a stick: thin to the point of emaciation, a well-groomed, talkative, much ornamented stick. He is bored with her and others like her. He is tired of himself, of being who he is, where he is. He is a much put-upon man. He had never wanted to be Provost, so he now recollects, conveniently forgetting many of the evasions and contortions he had gone through to end up with the job. Besides, that was long ago, when he was young and inept—and ignorant!

He says: "The rule is that one must assert guilt in the Rotunda, loudly, so a great many people hear the charge and it can't be hushed up. Danivon Luze was taught what we're all taught, that we can be forgiven for being naughty, but never for being covert about it. We all learned that as children, back in Heaven." He longs briefly for that island home of the Supervisory people, that sea-washed paradise of tropical foliage, breeze-cooled days and velvety, star-washed nights. Small enough payment, Heaven, for what they go through!

"Of course," Boarmus continues in an ironic tone, "we of Council Supervisory *unlearn* it during our first tour of duty here at Tolerance. Not being one of us, Danivon never unlearned it, that's all."

"Poor old Paff."

Boarmus slits his pouchy eyes and runs a pudgy hand over his bare and sloping skull, murmuring, "Poor old Paff has been raping and murdering children since he reached puberty. We preferred not to notice, that's all."

"But he was one of us, Boarmus! And they were only ordinary children. Molockians and that."

"Quite frankly, I don't think—"

"No. It's no excuse. Of course not. The Diversity Law admits of no exceptions. He had no right to take any children, not even Molockians. He had to Let Them Alone. I know that, Boarmus, I was merely feeling sorry for him."

"Damn his nose, nonetheless."

"Paff's nose?"

"Danivon Luze's nose."

"I haven't heard anything about his nose. I know who he is, of course."

Boarmus contradicts her. "No one knows who he is. We only know who he became after he got here."

"What is it about his nose?"

Boarmus's laughter bursts in a soggy spray, like a mud bubble. "He sniffs things out. Corruption. Or trouble. Or whatever."

"How very odd."

"Odd, perhaps. But useful," he replies, nodding ponderously. "I have found Danivon to be quite irreplaceable."

"Just by virtue of this smelling out? I mean, really. . . ." She subsides into silent thought. Poor old Paff. A pedo-necrophile, without question, but such a courtly man. Always so elegantly dressed. Paff would take advantage of the finalizer booth, of course—the only honorable thing to do. If he couldn't bring that off, something would happen to him. The Frickians would manage it quietly and neatly. They always did in such cases.

Boarmus muses, stroking his massive chin, regretting he has mentioned Danivon's usefulness. He hadn't intended to discuss Danivon with Syrilla, whose discretion he trusts no farther than he can fart against a high wind. Danivon has recently committed a tactless act. One might almost say an indiscretion. Boarmus knows about it, but no one else does, yet, and Boarmus hopes to remedy the matter before anyone does. Danivon Luze must get out of Tolerance before he has opportunity to repeat his lapse. Not that Danivon has done anything purposefully wrong. He has erred out of mere curiosity, Boarmus is sure—though there are those who will assume worse motives for the act, if they find out.

"I'm not sure I've ever actually seen him. Danivon, I mean," says Syrilla, still following her own thoughts.

"As a matter of fact, he should be here momentarily," Boarmus announces. "I've decided to send him to Panubi."

"You're sending him to find out about the dragons!" squeals Syrilla in pretended surprise.

Boarmus glooms at her from beneath his heavy brows. Why does the fool woman insist upon this girlish posturing! All the fashion just now, posturing. Every social occasion given over to giggles and squeals and standing about with one's hands flapping like some wide-winged wader bird about to take off! Well, no amount of squealing and chattering can make a surprise out of the matter. When people on Panubi report seeing dragons where there have never been dragons heretofore, certainly someone has to be sent to look into it.

"And that must be him coming now," cries Syrilla, clapping her hands and gesturing awkwardly toward the stairs up which an erect, brightly costumed figure is approaching. "All done up in ceremonials too."

"As is proper," Boarmus mutters. "Though damned conspicuous." No one on the lower balcony can miss those nodding purple plumes, that swirling, wide-sleeved purple coat, those scarlet trousers and shirt, the tap-tap of those lustrously polished gaver-hide boots.

Danivon Luze, striding up the stairs as though on parade, knows he is showy. Considering how rumor runs floodtide in Tolerance, he'd planned it that way, wanting no appearance of connivance or conspiracy when summoned to a meeting with Boarmus. Danivon doesn't really trust Boarmus, doesn't think he likes Boarmus, though he's not really sure. Sometimes Boarmus smells like old sin itself, and other times like Uncle offering cookies. No telling in advance whether today's summons is for naughty Luze or neffy-with-a-sweet-tooth Luze. So, Danivon comes as though on parade, which makes him conspicuous, yes, but also anonymous, his individuality subsumed into the regalia, so to speak, into a uniform formality of manner and stance: not Danivon Luze at all, but merely a Council Enforcer, Tolerance Post.

Danivon stops the requisite number of paces from the tea drinkers, executes a stylish salute that ends in a bow, the appropriate depth of which has been calculated to the last finger's width. Straightening, he assays an appropriately deferential manner. "Sir," he says, sweeping bonnet into hand. "Ma'am," standing easy, relaxed.

Boarmus doesn't ask him to sit down, but then Danivon hadn't expected he would.

"You've heard about the messages from Panubi," Boarmus says. "This business about the dragons."

"Only in passing, sir. Nothing definite." Actually, Danivon probably knows more about the so-called dragons than Boarmus does. Dragons, certainly, but also sightings of other, indescribable things, plus screams in the night and people gone (or mostly gone) in the morning, an unusual roster of horrid happenings, even for Elsewhere. All this has been served up for Danivon's delectation in the Frickian servants' quarters, far below this exalted level. Boarmus doesn't spend time as Danivon does, down with the flunkies, hobnobbing with messengers from the provinces or with recently returned maintenance techs and supply vehicle drivers.

Boarmus purses his full lips and pontificates, mostly for Syrilla's benefit: "So far as we know, no animals resembling dragons exist on Elsewhere, though there's nothing to prevent persons from low-category places from costuming themselves as dragons, or persons from high-category places from manufacturing bi-oids to resemble dragons." He sips his tea, noting with satisfaction that his voice has betrayed no urgency, no overtones of panic.

Settling the cup into its saucer, he goes on: "There is an additional matter. Some years ago, while you were still a youth, I received a message from Panubi. Not from one of the provinces, but from some other entity, centrally located on the continent. It was one of a series of such messages that seemed unimportant and equivocal at the time, not to say enigmatic. Now, however, inasmuch as this dragon business has come up . . ." He sips, watching Danivon's eyes. Was Danivon, possibly, smelling something useful?

"Might one ask what the message said, sir?"

"Um," says Boarmus, "a petition is how I took it. To the people of Elsewhere. To . . . ah . . . leave Elsewhere, perhaps."

"Ah," says Danivon, unenlightened.

"Ah?" says Syrilla eagerly. "You never told me that, Boarmie."

"There was nothing to tell. Someone or something located in Central Panubi sent a message. It could have been a joke. It could have been the work of a madman." Boarmus shrugs, elaborately casual, and turns to Danivon once more. "The message concluded with these words: 'R.S.V.P. Noplace, Central Panubi.' I talked to your friend Zasper about it at the time, as a matter of fact. Twelve or thirteen years ago, it was."

"Ah," says Danivon again, considerably confused.

"Zasper felt it didn't warrant an answer. Now, however . . ." His voice trails off, as he considers. He doesn't intend to mention that a fifth petition has arrived. Syrilla doesn't need to know that. Neither does Danivon. Particularly not the undignified details. He does not often take a woman to bed these days, and when he does, he does not expect her to go into hysterics at the sight of words suddenly printing themselves in large purple letters across the skin of his buttocks and belly! "Rethink their position," indeed! Luckily she had the good sense to keep quiet about it.

Boarmus sets the humiliating memory aside and perseveres. "Your talents are unique, Luze. You're well equipped for the task. I suggest you begin by consulting with Zasper Ertigon. He may have had some further thoughts in recent years."

It isn't quite what Danivon had expected. He had sniffed something in the air, but not this. Even now, here, with Boarmus not two paces away, he sniffs something other than this. Old, cold Boarmus, lizard-eyed Boarmus, greedy Boarmus, is lying to him. No, that doesn't smell right either. Maybe not exactly lying. Just not telling the whole truth. Just not telling something . . . something very important.

"Sir." Danivon nods, concentrating. His nose twitches sharply, and he suddenly knows some of what is in Boarmus's mind. "You have wondered whether these so-called dragons might actually be enslaved persons?"

Even knowing Danivon's ability as he does, it is hard for Boarmus not to show surprise. In light of the strange invitation, the idea of enslaved persons had indeed crossed his mind, but it isn't a thought he intended to mention in Syrilla's hearing. Well, too late. He shrugs, yawns. "I suppose anything is possible, my boy."

"How would enslaved of the Hobbs Land Gods get here?" demands Syrilla in an apprehensive tone. "Our defenses are proof against the Hobbs Land Gods. Our Door is guarded; our force-net would report any incursion from space!"

"You're perfectly right, Syrilla," Boarmus murmurs.

She substitutes melodrama for apprehension, laying a twiggy hand on her chest to cry breathily, "Just think! Enslaved ones!"

"Well, all these matters can be examined simultaneously," Boarmus says smoothly. "Dragons and enslavement and invitations and 'noplace,' wherever that is, plus whatever routine Enforcer duties may pop up on the way."

"Sir," says Danivon mildly, trying to digest this all at once. "Am I to go alone."

Boarmus doesn't care whether he goes alone or in a company of hundreds, not so long as he *goes*, but saying so would trivialize the matter. For Boarmus's purposes, this mission must look quite important indeed! Not an *emergency*, which might frighten Council Supervisory into fatal spasms, but important, nonetheless.

Boarmus frowns to show he is considering the matter. "Not if you think it best to take others with you. I'll leave the details to you, Luze. I have every confidence in your abilities."

"Sir," says Danivon again.

Boarmus nods weightily. "Offer what inducements you think appropriate. Requisition whatever equipment you consider necessary. Before you leave, check with the Complaint and Disposition schedule: there will undoubtedly be some routine business to take care of on your way." He waves a negligent hand, illustrating the trust he places in Danivon Luze. "Besides, it's time Central Panubi was explored."

He said this to Zasper years ago. He has said it to others since. After twenty or so generations of human occupation on Elsewhere, the center of the continent is still labeled "Panubi Incognita," one of those places on maps where the lines trail off into emptiness and cartographers traditionally print "Here be dragons." Considering that some pixieish conceit led the original cartographers on Elsewhere to do just that, perhaps no one should be surprised now that the dragons have actually shown up.

Allegedly shown up, Boarmus reminds himself. Allegedly. Though whether allegedly or actually, Panubi Incognita serves as a good excuse to get Danivon gone before . . . someone finds out what he's done.

Danivon receives a dismissive nod, bows, about-faces, hooks his right thumb in his belt to give his coat a swagger, and stalks off toward the stairs, gaver-hide boots gleaming, purple plumes nodding, purple coat swirling at the hem, golden badge on his shoulder shining, soft red shirt and trousers rippling beneath in silken perfection. Behind him the two supervisors sip at their cooling tea and watch him go, Boarmus with slight perturbation, Syrilla with appreciation for the fine picture he makes. Exemplary, she thinks. Truly exemplary.

A Frickian servant brings hot tea and pours. A long, silent moment passes. Syrilla leans forward to set her cup upon the table when a sudden motion catches her eyes. On the Rotunda floor a guard has moved! She leans farther forward, disbelieving. Even though Door guards aren't supposed to quiver so much as a muscle, one of them has moved! No . . . two . . . two have moved!

Boarmus has seen it too. "The Door!" he breathes.

Her eyes flick across the big Door as she follows Boarmus's pointing finger. Not the big Door. The Arbai Door? But the Arbai Door doesn't do anything! It has never done anything!

It is doing something now! Scintillating, sparkling, flinging coruscations of bright light around the Rotunda and through the high-arched opening into the balcony, sequined schools of spark-fish, swirling and reversing. Most of the guards are moving, shifting uncertainly toward and away from the glittering gate, casting doubtful glances over their shoulders, waiting for someone to tell them what to do, their weapons twitching in their hands.

Syrilla is half out of her chair when the clap of thunder sounds. She has time to see the guards cowering, and then the Arbai Door flashes like lightning, blinding her, blinding everyone. When she can see again the light has gone, leaving a dark spidery blotch struggling on the Rotunda floor.

Guardsmen raise their weapons. Someone—Danivon, it is—shouts a command as he descends the last few curving steps at a dead run. The weapons are lowered, reluctantly. Danivon arrives at the struggling thing on the floor at the same time as the officer in charge. In a moment they tug at the blotch, the thing, raising it up.

Syrilla and Boarmus stare in disbelief as they move toward the stairs, actually breaking into a trot as a confused babble rises from below.

Later, after Danivon assures everyone that his nose tells him the creature(s) is essentially harmless, after an Alsense machine is obtained and set before the arrival so that its (their) language can be understood, after the creature(s) explains that it (they) had, only moments before, existed in Predispersion times, a time so remote that only Files has any detailed knowledge of it at all—only then do the people of Tolerance learn that their accidental and extremely agitated guest(s) are Bertran and Nela Zy-Czorsky.

Elsewhere on Elsewhere, in Enarae.

Fringe's pa died all of a sudden. His name appeared in the daily bulletin published by Enarae Executive Systems for the benefit of the next of kin. When Fringe, now in her early thirties, followed custom and went to review Char's Blood Book in the Hall of Final Equity, however, she found she wasn't Char's daughter anymore.

Blood Books of all deceased were posted in the Hall for the convenience of family and claimants. The first page always listed family members, since they would be liable for the debts of the deceased. Char's Book had only one name in it: Yilland so-called Dorwalk, adopted daughter of Char Dorwalk. There was no mention of Fringe herself or of her brother Bubba.

Fringe kept herself still, even when the surroundings blurred a little. She felt something rather like pain, though it wasn't really—maybe more a final awareness, like stepping off a cliff and only then noticing it really was a long way down.

"I didn't know," Fringe blurted, almost in a whisper, not meaning anyone to hear.

A huge, shiny-headed bystander, who'd been glancing curiously at Fringe, jerked his head toward someone across the hall and mumbled, "That's her. That's Yilland."

The only woman in that direction was talking in a high, distressed voice to one of the Final Equity arbitrators. She was wispy, skinny, perhaps a little younger than Fringe, and though her words didn't carry, her voice did—an abrasive sound, like a knife being whetted.

"Don't want to intrude," the bald-headed giant offered. "My name's Curvis. Last time I saw you, you were just a little thing with a great mop of red hair. Now here you are, all growed up, but you've still got it!" He stroked his glistening pate and made a wry mouth. "Still got those funny eyes of yours too."

Fringe nodded, acknowledging that she still had her natal accoutrements. Did the nosy ogre think she might have sold her hair? Her stone-green eyes? Or given them away? Well, why not. People did sell their features sometimes. Features, organs, appendages. Sometimes they were forced to.

He made what was meant to be an apologetic grin and shrugged one enormous shoulder. "Somebody told me your pa adopted her. You honestly didn't know?"

"I didn't know," she repeated, so surprised she forgot it was none of his business. "But then, I haven't talked to Pa for . . . well, for quite a while."

"Old barstid," commented Curvis, shaking his massive head as though this confirmed an earlier opinion. "Doing a thing like that to his own blood." He stroked a capacious pocket on his chest where something moved beneath the fabric. Some device. Or a live thing, maybe.

Fringe swallowed the lump behind her breastbone and said with an expressionless face, "Since it eliminates my debt risk, I ought to be grateful." Despite her words, she was still thinking it might be some kind of mistake.

She took up Char's Book to look again, but it wasn't a mistake. The new daughter really was the only family member named, as well as the sole heir. Fringe felt a cold wash of sadness, like a flash flood down a long dry gully, not for the inheritance (she'd never thought there'd be anything to inherit) but because there was no word there for her. And because the Book said Char had adopted the new daughter and written off his natural one at a time he had made a promise of quite a different kind to Fringe.

She took a deep breath and put the Book down, the little chain that linked it to the claim desk rattling noisily. One of the uniformed assemblers frowned up from his workstation, then went back to the figures rolling by on his tabletop display. Someone's lifetime transactions being put together there. Everything came here, in the end. Whatever you hoped or dreamed or actually managed to accomplish; whatever you failed at or fell short of, it all came to Final Equity, where creditors, friends, and kinfolk, who could be creditors of a different sort, looked over the result amid confused murmurs and muffled sobs and angry mutters. The vaulted hall soaked up the sounds, softened them. There were always deaths and killings, so there were always books set out for people to examine. They came and went, their feet making shuffly whispers in the quiet. It was all very ordinary, Fringe told herself sternly. No cause for tears or guilt or sentimentalism. He's dead, that's all. He left you no word, but then, if he didn't talk to you while you were alive, why should you expect a word after he died?

When Fringe looked up again, she caught the woman, Yilland, staring at her with an avid, restless expression, like some hungry animal in too small a cage. Fringe let her glance slide across the woman's face, and then back to the book, wondering whether the balance in it would be enough to satisfy the claimants against Char's Book, or whether the woman across the room would be asked to make satisfaction. Heirs were sometimes sold, entire or in parts, to cover the debts of a deceased. Creditors had been known to get nasty carving up an heir. Fringe had paid out a good bit on debt insurance over the last fifteen years. She'd been more than a little anxious, knowing Pa as she did. Well, wasted credit. She needn't have worried. She was out of it.

And Yilland so-called Dorwalk was in.

Fringe nodded a farewell to the bald ogre, then turned and walked away, eyes straight ahead, striding from the Hall like a woman with somewhere to go, only to be accosted by a uniformed flunky at the portal. The Final Equity Exec begged the courtesy of an interview, said he. She glared in disbelief, but he nodded and beckoned and pressed his lips together impatiently until she followed him. Curvis, the giant, was watching this encounter from across the room, head cocked to one side. She cocked her own in reply, and shrugged. Who knew what Execs wanted?

She was led down the echoing corridor into the office wing behind the Hall, where the flunky paused at a tall door, rapped on it, opened it, and bowed her through. The Exec sat behind a desk that looked carved from a single block of chalcedony, though Fringe, mentally computing weight and noting the relatively fragile structure on which it rested, believed it a fake, symbolic, an accoutrement of Executive class. No other class handled money matters so well, no other class displayed such elegant contempt. People born Executives didn't need money, so they could disdain it. No other class could pretend to justice so convincingly, for Executives didn't need that, either. This man was classly dignified and alert too, she could see that; but then, Executives were the only class that could and did declassify members for being stupid.

He turned a serene gaze upon her and took his time assessing what he saw. "Char Dorwalk's Book came up on the Files to be approved by this office," he said. "The scanner advised me you were present in the Hall. Examining the record, it occurs to me you may wish to make a death claim against the estate of your natural father. Disinheritance is always subject to review by this office, and so far as I can see from your father's Book, you were cut off for no valid reason. I find no record you were ever notified or given a chance to object. You're entitled to file a death claim."

"By this office," indeed. Why couldn't the damned Execs just say *me*, like anyone else? They were always "this office," or "this council," or "this governing body."

"Shit," she said, allowing herself to sound more like a Trasher than usual, "why should I?"

The Exec raised one high-bred nostril. Such language was not often directed at top castes, certainly not by shapely, red-haired, light-eyed women of middling-young years and uncertain classification. What was she? He could usually tell, but not with this one. Despite her language, she wasn't Trasher class, that was sure. Trashers tended to be either obsequious or defiant, but he detected neither in Fringe. She showed neither Wage-earner servility nor Professional-class hauteur. The quality of her clothing was almost Executive, but if she had been Executive he'd have known her. Besides, the weapon on her hip was not the usual Executive toy. Maybe she was Outcaste, one of those interesting oddities who didn't fit the system. An artist or entrepreneur, perhaps.

Fringe laughed openly at his puzzled expression and almost winked as she said, "Offended, sir? I do beg your pardon. Hell, I don't want anything from him. Let his classly adopted daughter have what she can salvage."

The Manager had enough sensitivity to realize she might be distressed. His expression softened. "His wives both died some time ago. And you're entitled—"

"To nothing," she said firmly, surprised by the pain she was feeling. She had forgotten that pain, mostly. Now she ignored it as she explained: "He did not approve of me, good sir. I disappointed him. If I take nothing from him, I am free of that. Owed nothing, I owe nothing. I may go my own way."

"I have the feeling"—smiled the Manager, suddenly taken with her—"that you've always done that."

"And well, perhaps I have," Fringe said, her eyes fixed on some distant scene that only she could see. "There were times it seemed there was no other way to go." She was thinking that there had been Dorwalk on her father's side and Troms on her mother's side; she couldn't be both, so she had ended up neither.

The Equity Exec had been watching her musing face with complete attention. "I know it's a personal question, but what's your classification?"

"Born to, earned, or claimed?" she asked.

"They're usually the same thing." He gestured sameness.

"Born Professional, earned and claimed Outcaste," she said with a matching gesture.

"You're an artist then?" he asked, charmingly, to show how sympathetic he could be, how open-minded. Even Executives associated with certain Outcastes, like artists and singers. "Or an actor, perhaps?"

"Not exactly," she said, the weapon she wore on her hip seeming to leap of itself into her hand. "What I do is, I Attend to Situations." The eye of the weapon stared at him as her thumb twitched above the power stud.

The Exec swallowed, stood up quietly, opened the door for her, and stood aside, bowing very slightly as she left. When he sat back down at his desk, he noted with some astonishment that he was trembling. The weapon had been aimed between his eyes. If she had wanted him dead, she could have pushed the button and he'd have been scattered atoms or fried meat, depending on how tidy she was. He touched the ornamental weapon at his own belt, almost with revulsion. It was good for little. High-class persons carried weapons mostly as costume accessories. It was the custom to carry them, but no one ever used them. Well, hardly ever.

He licked his lips. It was a matter of pride with Executives not to be caught off guard. Someone should have warned him. He should have been more careful in checking before he invited her in. The Files had said merely Fringe . . . Fringe Dorwalk. He keyed through the records before him. AKA, blinked the small codiforms squeezed in between two other things he hadn't bothered to look at. AKA: Professional Name. . . . She had rearranged the letters in her name to spell something she liked better.

And she was a licensed Enforcer.

In Tolerance, Supervisor Syrilla had invited her young protégé, Jacent, to lunch. Jacent was a mere boy, only recently arrived from Heaven for his first tour of duty at Tolerance, but he was part of her "family" and therefore her responsibility.

"What do you make of this Arbai Door arrival?" asked the Supervisor of her young kinsman. "Do you believe it?"

"One believes one's eyes," he said firmly, tossing up one hand in an ebullient gesture. "You believe yours, Aunt Syrilla. You saw them come through."

Syrilla frowned. Among themselves Council members cultivated a languid and unruffled demeanor, one which sought to convey they had seen it all and were not surprised at anything. Seeing her expression, Jacent flushed and put his hands in his lap. He had been warned not to wave his arms about except in public. When on display, yes, be shrill and mannered as a cageful of birds, but not when closeted, as now.

They were on the terrace outside Syrilla's living quarters: she standing at the railing, he seated at the table where he lingered over the delicacies Syrilla's Frickian cook had provided. Frickians made excellent servants as well as soldiers; there were several thousand of them employed at Tolerance, and a great many more employed back at Heaven. Jacent was fond of Frickian food, though he was not fond of much else he'd found at Tolerance.

Syrilla persevered. "I mean, do you believe they are primitives? Really? From before first dispersion?" She sounded not only puzzled but apprehensive, and Jacent looked at her covertly from beneath his abundant lashes, wondering at her tone. Why apprehensive? The creatures, however spidery and archaic, could do no harm.

"Well, of course, we've all asked Files what Files thinks," he admitted, meaning we, the youngsters, the lower orders, the dilettantes and chatterers who had not yet learned discretion, those who did the routine work of maintenance and monitoring until they were old enough to do something essential and even more boring. "Files does not *disbelieve* it. Files went searching through the old, old records and found several widely separated accounts of contacts with this Celerian race. A very old, old race, or so Files extrapolates, who were leaving our little spiral on their way somewhere else, who said, according to the strange twins, they had been granted the concession to do so!" He laughed. The idea was amusing. Who and what had granted this supposed concession? They had talked about that a great deal, down in the warren below the Great Rotunda.

He sobered at her expression and went on, "Also, joined human beings *are* occasionally born in primitive societies, even here on Elsewhere. Files has found references to that, as well."

"I know all that," said the Supervisor fretfully. "But I have never heard it theorized that the Arbai Doors could be used for time travel. In fact, I've always been assured that time travel is impossible!" She whined, perhaps a little hysterically.

Why should the subject of time travel be so upsetting? Particularly when there was quite enough here in Tolerance to be upset about without borrowing trouble?

"Well, of course, the technicians have talked that to shreds. The current theory seems to be that when these persons demanifested the Arbai Door on Earth all those millennia ago, they caused some kind of malfunction that prohibited their going anywhere at all. They were simply sidetracked into nothingness for some thousands of years . . . on their way here."

She turned and stared at him. "There was no time travel?"

"No. No time travel. Merely an extremely lengthy hiatus in their awareness." He smiled, noting the tension going out of her shoulders, her neck. Interesting. "Files tells us there have been other strange incidents with Arbai Doors. For example: A woman went into one on a planet called Grass millennia ago and turned up a thousand years or so later (absolute time) on a planet called Thyker. She had aged a great deal but was not, you know, mummified or anything. The only way she could have lived all that time was through some such lapse or series of lapses. The Door engineers and technicians are greatly agitated and interested. I am told they have not been so wrought up since the machines in City Fifteen came up with a cure for our newest plague before we'd even used it."

Syrilla stiffened. It was considered not nice to mention such matters except during official sessions. Plagues and assassinations and small, limited wars were necessary in maintaining diversity, but casual talk about them could make one seem coarse and unfeeling. She made a moue at the boy, shaking her head very slightly.

"Sorry, Aunt Syrilla," he murmured, flushing, aware he'd breached convention again. There were so damned many things one didn't *say*! Or *do*! At least, not in social contexts. Sometimes he doubted he would ever learn to behave properly. Sometimes, when he was feeling particularly resentful about this place, he doubted he wanted to! There was something very wrong here at Tolerance, something that none of the old folks would identify or admit to, but something that made them jumpy and peevish nonetheless. Jacent kept his facial expression pleasant, giving Aunt Syrilla no hint of what he was thinking.

She waved away his apology and turned to the forest once more.

"Something about this troubles you?" he said in his prettiest voice, hoping the tone would excuse the presumption and make her forget he had been gauche. He very much wanted to know why she cared.

"Yes," she cried. "Yes, Jacent. No one seems to have thought what time travel would mean. It would mean that the Hobbs Land Gods could go back in time and get here before our people came, and then . . . It could mean they are here now. On Panubi. That possibility has been mentioned, but I didn't take it, well, you know, seriously. But now, well . . . we *don't* know what's on Panubi, so they *could* be there. Boarmus is concerned about Panubi. He has sent Danivon Luze to find out about . . . all this business of dragons. It could be enslaved ones, you know. Not dragons at all. We don't really know what enslaved ones might look like." She shuddered, her face becoming momentarily skull-like and horrid with fear.

He gasped silently, terrified by her terror, then waited, holding his breath.

At last she spoke again. "It's disturbing, Jacent. The idea that the Hobbs Land Gods might actually be here, now. Just waiting to leap out at us, take us over, enslave us as well. . . ." She sighed, patted her forehead, and then whispered, "I have dreams about it sometimes. Like smothering. Like not being able to breathe. Like being stuffed into some impossibly small space until I'm all . . . smashed." She swallowed, painfully, tried to smile.

"Of course, if there is no time travel, my concerns are . . . without foundation. The people from the past are merely . . . as you say . . . harmless." She laughed, lightly, while fear danced madly behind her eyes.

Jacent was more than merely interested. He was intrigued! He did not think he had ever been as afraid as she obviously was. And though he'd learned in school to dread the Hobbs Land Gods, he'd never really thought about them. Oh, he'd seen the docudramas, all about how Elsewhere was set up as a refuge from the Gods, about Lady Professor Mintier Thob and Madame Therabas Bland, about Subble Clore and Orimar Breaze and the rest of the committee members, how they'd come here all that long time ago. None of it had ever frightened him.

It obviously frightened Aunt Syrilla. He felt it best not to pursue the matter. So, he said nothing, and the silence extended.

"What is to be done with the strange twins?" she asked at last. "I haven't heard what has been decided. Are they to be sent to Heaven?" Though the subtropical island of Heaven was reserved as a homeland for Supervisors and their Frickian servants, a few members of other races were allowed to live there also, if they were harmless or interesting or had talents the machines couldn't duplicate.

"Rumor is that Danivon Luze has a use for them," Jacent replied. In the lower regions, that rumor was causing endless speculation. In the lower regions, Danivon Luze himself caused endless speculation. The mystery of his origins made him quite the romantic figure, somewhat to Jacent's annoyance. "Only a rumor, of course."

"Oh, my," whispered Syrilla, remembering what Boarmus had said about Danivon Luze. Such a complicated knot that would make: Danivon, and Panubi, and dragons that were maybe really enslaved by the Hobbs Land Gods, and the strange twins from the past.

"Oh, my," she said again.

Fringe had intended to startle the Executive at the Hall of Final Equity. Meant to scare the piss out of him, if truth be told. Executives and Professionals, by and large, gave her the gripes. She understood why this was so, but understanding did nothing to change her feelings. She resented the Executive and Professional classes in their entirety, and had done so as long as she could remember—at least since she'd been given those damned E&P dolls as a child.

She had privately acknowledged the resentment when she turned sixteen and realized, suddenly and undeniably, that though she'd always been told she was a Professional, there was no chance she could retain that class. For most of a year she had heard her schoolmates talk of the Professional training they would be starting, the businesses they had been bought into, the apprenticeships their families had paid for. Though Grandma Gregoria had always talked of the Professional class as being governed by a kind of natural law that guaranteed that its children became Professionals in their turn, no training, no business, no apprenticeship had been arranged for Fringe. No start-up money had been set aside. Some essential part of the natural law had been left out in her case.

It was ironic, Fringe reflected, that Souile had been born Trasher and had rebelled against that class early to raise herself up, while Fringe had been born Professional class and had not realized she had to rebel against anything until it was too late! Now she had only a short time of free schooling left and no resources beyond her own energy and determination. Being honest with herself, as continuing association with Zasper was teaching her to be, she knew the best she could do for herself at this late date was retain the level Souile had achieved. If she was unwilling to be a Trasher, which she was, she would have to be a Wage-earner. Though it wasn't admirable, it was respectable.

She had learned a degree of pragmatism from Zasper and from Ahl Dibai Bloom, both of whom advocated action rather than what Zasper called "wiffling around." "If you're going to wiffle around once you know the facts," Zasper often said, "might as well have no brain at all."

So, she would not wiffle. The first step was to switch from Professional education level to Wage-earner training level at school. The one had been theoretical, the other would be entirely practical. She already knew she was better with things than people and very good at working with her hands. Once enrolled in training, she asked her instructors to help her find a job, and one of them referred her to a nearby weapons shop where she was hired to make adjustments and repairs during the late afternoons and evenings. All of these rearrangements of her life, job included, were accomplished in less than ten days from the time she made the decision. Zasper, when she told him of it, said she showed gumption and good sense, that he was proud of her.

No one else seemed to care. Though Fringe made no attempt to hide what was going on, neither Souile nor Char seemed interested. Of course, they were both preoccupied with other things. Char was not often at home anymore. When there, he shut himself up in his study and was outraged at interruption. Souile had grown even more withdrawn in recent years; she emerged less and less often from her room, and when she did, she seemed not to see what went on around her.

So matters went on, with Fringe's life largely unregarded, until one evening she arrived home to be met at the door by old Nada, who had obviously been waiting for her. This in itself was a rarity. Nada and Aunty spent most of their time in their room, quibbling with each other.

"Fringe girl."

"Yes, Nada."

The old woman twisted her hands against her abdomen and blinked her watery eyes. "Your ma, she died today."

Fringe could think of nothing to say. What went through her mind, unforgivably, was that it should have been Nada because Nada had had so much more practice at dying, but Nada was standing there, peering nearsightedly at her, and Fringe saw herself, as though from a distance, with her mouth gaped open and the only words she could think of unsuitable to the occasion.

"Where's Pa?" she choked out, evading what was happening.

"Char's in his study. The door's locked. Ari's locked himself in too. Fond of her, he was. Liked her best of his children."

"Aunty?"

"Upstairs. Crying. She's been crying all day."

"Bubba?"

"At his school, you know."

"Where's Ma? You know. Her . . ."

"Gone," whispered old Nada, tears running down her cheeks. "Char had her taken already. She's gone."

Fringe hugged Nada because she knew of nothing else to do, because she needed to hang on to something, and they cried together though they were unable to offer any words of comfort. Fringe kept trying to remember when the last time was she'd seen Ma, or when the last time was she'd seen Ma acting like a real human person who laughed and said sensible things and seemed interested. Fringe couldn't remember when that had been. If that had been ever, it had been a very long time ago. Years. Maybe when Fringe was a child, long, long ago.

And what could she say to Souile's mother? That Souile had died of stress, of trying too hard, of walking a tightrope with Char and his folks pulling from one side and Ari, Nada, and Aunty pulling and tugging from the other, even her daughter a disappointment to her? That she'd died of mood-spray and of being eaten alive? Fringe didn't say that. She didn't say anything. She felt guilty that she did not grieve, then grieved because she felt guilty.

Two days later she came home to find the Tromses gone as well. Char had sent them to the so-called Pighouse, the provincial home for elderly indigents.

"But, Pa, you can't just . . . They lived here!"

"No more."

"But this was their home."

"No more," he said. "I can't take any more. I couldn't do anything while your ma was alive, but they're not my folks. They've got another daughter; they've got a son. Let them do it! I can't do it anymore."

It was the first time Fringe had thought about the Tromses having other children. There'd never been any evidence of them. She hid herself away in the module to consider the matter. Was she glad Nada and Ari and Aunty were gone? Would she go visit them? Would it be better to do that or not to do that?

"By the way," said Pa over supper. "I want you to move out of that damned module. You can move back in the room where you used to be." His voice was harsh and demanding, and he did not look at her when he spoke. She understood it not as a suggestion but as a command, though she could not fathom the motivation behind it. Was she now to be a daughter again, she who had not been a daughter for years?

She hadn't been in the room in years, either. She stood in the door, peering at dusty surfaces, unlit panels, at a clutter of keepsakes, at the circulation units the old women wore on their feet and hands to warm their always-cold extremities, at the so-called Auto-nurse, actually little more than a timed medications dispenser and monitor. The room smelled of old women, sour-sweet, vinegar, and dried flowers. It hissed with old voices, old coughs, and sniffles and whines.

That night Fringe trailed into the room, half-swathed in a blanket she had fetched from her module, a cocoon to wrap herself in, a second skin to keep the room from touching her. She lay down atop the bed she'd used as a child, the one Aunty had slept in. She kept telling herself the room was empty, but she felt the usual occupants going about their customary business. No matter that Nada and Aunty were gone away, their ghosts still moved about the room. Not only their spirits, but Souile's as well. From a veiled distance, they whispered together, about her, about Fringe, saying the things they had always said. She could hear the whispers and guess at the content. She did not fall asleep until almost dawn.

She went to the Pighouse the next day, to visit them. They sat in chairs, vacant-eyed; the air was thick with the scent of the stuff sprayed about to keep them quiet. When Fringe spoke to them, they nodded slowly, scarcely hearing.

"Is the food all right?" she whispered. "Nada, is the food all right? Are you getting enough to eat?"

"To eat," murmured Nada. "To eat, Fringe girl."

And, "Did you know Souile died?" Aunty asked.

That night, Fringe tried the room again, only to feel their eyes on her, the weight of presences, the force of personalities, the accusatory whispers, the weight of habitude. Their spirits were here, in this house, not there in the Pighouse where their bodies had been taken. Though she could have done nothing to save Souile, nothing to keep Nada and Aunty from the Pighouse, she felt guilty that she had not tried. Maybe she could have found Nada's other daughter, Nada's son. Why hadn't she at least tried? Was she glad? Could she actually be glad?

She made a faltering attempt to talk about it with Pa. She might as well have talked to a rock. As usual, Pa didn't talk about things. He merely became angry and told her to get her things out of the module.

"I've sold it," he muttered, not meeting her eyes. "I've sold it. The man's coming to take it apart and move it today. Besides, you'll do better in your old room. Look at you, for heaven's sake." His voice oozed contempt. "Look at you." He gestured at her, her chewed fingertips, her rat-tailed hair, her blotchy skin, her tear-stained face. "Look at you," he repeated in disgust.

She opened her mouth to try once more, then shut it. There was no point in trying to explain how she felt. She wasn't sure how she felt, except that with Souile and the old folks gone, she couldn't stay in this place. Pa had something in mind, some role he wanted her to play, and she didn't know what it was. No matter what it was, she couldn't do it. The time was past for that. She couldn't be a daughter for Souile, so she sure as hell wasn't going to be a daughter for Char! She could hardly be herself for herself. She could not be someone else for Pa.

Back in the shabby module, she totted up the credit chits she'd earned at the weapons shop, the old tattered ones she'd earned working for Ahl Dibai Bloom. They were all there, virtually untouched, enough to keep her for a time if she could find a cheap room near her job and the school. Other Wage-earner youths lived in such places. She spent the afternoon looking, settling for a place no smaller or shabbier than the module had been, with a bed no narrower or harder, a saniton no less functional. The next day she packed up her personal things and moved out, without telling Pa she was going.

That night she went home at suppertime, sat in her usual place, and waited for Pa or Bubba to ask her where she'd been. Bubba talked about the training program Grandma Gregoria was setting him up in. He was to be Professional class, architect caste. He was full of the thrill of it, the challenge, the newness. Neither of them mentioned her absence. She wondered if they even knew she had moved out. Perhaps where she was, was less important than the module being gone.

If they found it easier to pretend, she would pretend. She lived in her rented room but went home for dinner whenever she could bear to or was too hungry not to go. Occasionally she went to Grandma Gregoria's. No one ever said anything about what she was doing, though both Pa and Grandma carped about things in general and Fringe's many failings in particular.

When she couldn't face going home and wasn't too hungry, she spent her time using junk and discards from the weapons shop to make complicated little machines that spun and glittered and were company of a kind. She rather longed for a pet but could not afford to feed one. Though she knew herself to be unattractive (Zasper said that wasn't true), male companionship was offered from time to time. Each encounter left her feeling more alone than before, and she told herself she was safer without. She was less likely to make idle comments that others took as commitments or insults, less likely to let her insecurity bubble up in teasing gibes that only made others angry. Alone, she didn't make mistakes that came back to haunt her. Except for her friendships with Zasper and Bloom, she hadn't the hang of relationships. People always wanted her to be something else.

"Men don't work out for me," she told Zasper when he asked her about her love life. "I don't have the right . . . oh, I don't know, Zasper. It doesn't feel right, that's all."

He shook his head, but he did not argue with her. Perhaps love didn't work for her. There were people like that. Zasper thought he himself was probably one of them.

Besides, she told him, she got plenty of company at work, where they did approve of her.

Her job included the provision of target accuracy certificates for repaired arms. Most of the technicians used a firing stand, but Fringe preferred to shoot from the hand, becoming so skillful that her customers came to rely upon her work and her opinion. Even Zasper said, half in jest, that a girl with her target scores was wasted in a repair shop. To hide her pleasure at this, she remarked offhandedly she'd probably inherited the skill from some Guntoter forebear on Earth, thousands of years ago.

Then one afternoon she went to Grandma Gregoria's and tried to be mannerly over a plate of grilled fish while Grandma snarled with more than usual vituperation about Fringe's Trashish and unforgivable behavior and how beneath himself Char had married.

"If it hadn't been for your ma," said Grandma. "If it hadn't been for those Tromses, you might have turned out to be something. . . ."

Fringe had been much alone recently. The plate before her was the first food she had had in several days. She was still very young and often frightened. Day by day, she tried to keep bewilderment at bay, tried not to think about anything except the next minute, the next task, hold-

ing herself together with endlessly frayed and continually patched resolve. At the sound of the carping voice, something inside her tore. She
felt it rip, felt the fabric of her life tear asunder, letting something molten and horrid show through.

"If I'm a Trasher," she blurted, "it's because Pa is so fucking arro-
gant he took on more than he could manage. Then even though he
looked down his nose on the Tromses just like you did, he let them
raise me! Then he despised me because I turned out to be just like
them. Who else would I have been like? Take your tongue off me and
my ma, Grandma, because we both turned out just the way you and Pa
made us!"

It had been then that Gregoria, eyes bulging and mouth spraying
fragments of fish in all directions, told Fringe to get out of her sight and
never come into it again.

Fringe went in a mood of cold desperation, not so much angry as
chilled and shocked, as though she were bleeding inside. She couldn't
stop trembling. She couldn't get warm. The only warm place she could
think of was Bloom's, so she went there, or near there, stopping in an
alleyway nearby because her stomach cramped, bending her double, and
she couldn't move.

"Are you sick, Fringe?" asked a voice.

For a moment she thought it was Nada. The voice had some of that
quality, though without any whine to it. The speaker was half-hidden
in a doorway, wearing the kind of cloak and hood that tourists sometimes wore in the Swale, tourists who wanted to see without being seen.

"I'll be all right," gasped Fringe, waving the nosy intruder away.

"Something happened," said the hooded woman. "Something bad."

"Something," agreed Fringe, taking deep breaths, suddenly remembering that voice. It was Jory—the old woman who'd followed her around
back . . . back when she was only a kid. "What are you doing here?"

The old woman put back her hood and came closer, ignoring the
question. "You've been hurt," she said. "By somebody who shouldn't
have hurt you, but did."

Fringe's mouth dropped open and for a moment she forgot to breathe.

"What's your second name?" the old woman asked. "I don't remember your second name."

"Dorwalk. Fringe Dorwalk."

The cramp surprised out of her, Fringe moved around, trying to get
a good look at whatever it was behind the woman, something large and

shadowy moving there, just out of sight. A mystery. That's all she needed right now, another mystery intruding on her life.

The old woman reached out, lifted Fringe's chin, dried her face with the backs of her old hands. "I'm going to give you a new name," she said. "In my opinion, that's what you need. New names often help. New names create new people; new people can leave old habits behind and handle things better."

Fringe merely stared stupidly. Who did this . . . this thing think she was?

"Owldark," said Jory. "Your new name. The letters of your old name spell your new name: Fringe Owldark—a totally different person from Fringe Dorwalk, don't you think? Say it."

Fringe, too stupefied to argue, said it obediently, watching the shadowy something shift and move. "Fringe Owldark."

The old woman nodded to herself. "Fringe Dorwalk had an uncertain future. Ways were closed to her. She was anxious. She chewed her fingers and cried herself to sleep. But Fringe Owldark is one of *my* people. I told you that long ago, didn't I? One of my people, chosen by me to . . . to do wonderful things. To become something special. Yes, Owldark has a totally different future before her! All she needs to do is go find it." The old woman patted her cheek, turned, and was dissolved into the shadow. Fringe took a step forward, but the doorway was empty.

Perhaps she had dreamed it. Likely she had dreamed it. Hunger dreams. Visions. Sometimes she had those.

"Fringe Owldark," she said aloud, no longer crying, suddenly wanting to tell Zasper all about it.

She went to him full of the story, but when she got there he greeted her by thrusting a plate full of food at her and quoting a remark some friend of his had made, touting Fringe's skills at weapons repair. He said yet again that she was wasted in the repair shop, a remark at which Fringe Dorwalk had always flushed and bridled, not sure how to react.

Fringe Owldark, however, her mouth full of succulent roast meat and the juices running down her throat, knew with absolute certainty she had indeed been wasted up until now. She was not going to be hungry again!

"I want you to sponsor me to the Enforcer Academy," she said firmly, surprising herself as much as Zasper.

"Ah, Fringe," he said with a pang, the expression in her eyes reminding him suddenly of Danivon Luze, "nah, nah, you don't want to do that."

Fringe Dorwalk might have equivocated, but Fringe Owldark did not. The request had come from a spewing well of desperation that could not now be capped and ignored. "I have to do something, Zasper. I can't go back home and I'm barely making it on my own. I'm tired of being hungry."

"You can always come here to me! Never a day I'd let you go from this place hungry!"

"I don't want to have to go to anybody, don't you understand! I don't want to go to anybody for anything. I don't want to have to depend on anyone. I want to be on my own. I want a place, food, clothes I don't have to ask for. I'm tired of people feeding me and clothing me and all the time resenting me because I'm not what they had in mind."

"I'd never—"

"I know that! But it would still be you, Zasper, not me! What I want is your sponsorship. Help me. Sometime I'll pay you back."

He sat her down, gave her a glass of black ale, and begged her to listen to him. "Fringe girl, I'll help you any way I can, but listen. There's something . . . something changing on Elsewhere. Was a time when everything was clear and plain, even for Enforcers. These days, things are cloudy. It's like, like something . . ."

"You're not saying anything, Zasper," she cried. "I need help and you're not saying anything!"

"All right, all right, listen! Pretend I'm a flea living on a dog, all right?"

"You're a flea, Zasper. I can believe that." She choked with hysterical laughter, tears running down her cheeks.

He pounded her, forcing her to listen. "Right. And I begin to think something's wrong. And all the other fleas laugh at me, because there's nothing different. The sun comes up, the sun goes down. The dog eats his breakfast and shits on the grass. Then, one day, the dog falls down dead, and I suddenly realize: That was it! The dog was sick!"

"So?"

"So there's something sick happening to Elsewhere, Fringe. Something sick and dangerous."

She stared at him, shaking her head. "*Life* is sick and dangerous, Zasper. You try and tell me different!"

That wasn't what he meant, but he couldn't make it any clearer. "Being an Enforcer, it's hard, Fringe."

"I don't care how hard it is."

Sometimes Enforcers failed of their duty, he said. He himself had sometimes not come up to the mark. He had never learned to operate a flier well. And there was a little boy he had once saved from certain torture and death, against the rules. And he had opinions all the time. "You will either break your oath or you will hate yourself sometimes," he said.

"I hate myself all the time now," she replied. "Hating me just some of the time would be an improvement."

She insisted, overriding his warnings, his confessions of what he said were his failings, wondering at his telling her, telling anyone, for if someone reported him, he'd be in trouble. Not that she would. Never. Not Zasper. She came close to him, put her hand on his arm (something she seldom did or allowed), told him she knew it wouldn't be easy, she knew some of the work was hard and unpleasant, but no matter how hard or unpleasant, it was better than where she was now.

Zasper shook his head at her, opened his mouth, then shut it. He had no more arguments and nothing to offer her instead, any more than he had had anything else to offer Danivon Luze. Zasper had been an Enforcer for decades. He knew what being an Enforcer had done to him. After years of doing it by the book, he'd asked himself what he was, what was this Zasper Ertigon? A man with ugly feelings hidden away, emotions he couldn't express, judgments he couldn't make. He'd been raised with certain ideas of right or wrong, but over the decades he'd felt a certain moral atrophy, an inability to decide what was right. Now he laughed at the thought. As a child here in Enarae, yes, there had been right things and wrong things, but what did an Enforcer want with such puzzles? That isn't what Enforcers were for! They were for doing the will of the Council, which meant enforcing right *and* wrong and any other damned thing. They were for protecting diversity through the status quo. They were for not thinking or feeling any more than they could help.

Turning the question around, however, he had to admit there were Enforcers who seemed to like the work. Many of them enjoyed the pay and the respect; some of them relished the power.

"Zasper," she begged, tears spilling. "Please!"

It actually hurt him to say he'd help her. It would have hurt only a little more to have refused her.

Later, she remembered she'd been going to tell Zasper about getting a new name, but somehow she'd forgotten. Though she didn't get around to telling him the story for a long time, she didn't forget the name. Owldark. It was hers. Secret, for the time being, but hers.

One qualified sponsor was all she needed to get into the Academy. Candidates paid nothing in advance of their study. Graduate Enforcers were expected to compensate the Academy for their training by paying high dues to the Enforcer Posts later on, during their more profitable years. So, without telling anyone else, she dropped out of the Wage-earner school, left her shabby room, and moved into one much like it, though rather cleaner, at the Enarae Academy. It was, said Zasper, the second-most prestigious Enforcer Academy on Elsewhere, surpassed in reputation only by the Academy at Tolerance itself.

Each day she rose before dawn to stand at parade with her fellows, to be told the ancient history of an indomitable people who would not be taken over by the Gods; to hear of the glories of Phansure of old and of Enarae the First, and of Enarae in Exile here, on Elsewhere; to feel her chilled blood warm and stir at the thudding drums and the flickering lash of the long-tailed banners. She recited the oath, every word burning itself into her heart. She heard the Masters cry: *"Enforcers! A Situation!"*

She rose with a hundred others to shout the response: *"We Attend the Situation!"*

She swallowed it whole. Enforcers were honored and honorable. History flowed through them, like power through a fiber, illuminating and warming all it touched. Without Enforcers, there would be no diversity, and therefore, no humanity. She and her fellows were the gallant few who kept the unthinking majority safe. Her passing doubts she put down hard, buried them, wouldn't consider them. Any flicker of her old rebelliousness she dealt with the same way. She had chosen this! She would not allow anything to sully her choice.

She learned weapons, weapons she hadn't known existed until now. She learned drill and signals, overt and covert, to be used among Enforcers. She learned command, how to make people obey her, even when they didn't want to. She joined in case studies of provinces that had strayed from the status quo in the past and how Enforcers had put them back on track.

She became almost proud. Her rat-tailed hair turned glossy. Her chewed nails grew out. Her skin cleared up. She stood up straight with her head high! She was someone, someone special at last!

Even Zasper had to admit she bloomed.

Had she thought about it, she would have known she was too happy for it to last. Something had to come along and destroy her contentment. The blow came in the form of a message from her pa, demanding that she come see him. Full of trepidation, she went, not knowing what to expect.

He regarded her morosely when she came in.

"I've found out," he said.

Her jaw dropped. Found out what? She'd hidden nothing.

"You're to leave that place," he said.

"Leave?" She gaped, then laughed almost hysterically. "Leave! You mean the Academy?"

"Do you have any idea what it will do to my reputation as a Professional to have a daughter at the Enforcer Academy!" It wasn't a question. He didn't expect an answer.

By this time, Fringe had quite an accurate reading on her pa's reputation as a Professional. She shook her head stubbornly and said, "I have to do something, Pa."

"There are a hundred professions!" he trumpeted, sounding so much like Gregoria that Fringe was astonished. "A hundred professions!"

Though in the past she had been inarticulate when confronted by Pa or Grandma or even the teachers at school, she was voiceless no longer. Not since that day at Grandma Gregoria's had she been silent or tongue-tied. Now she was hot, fiery, and she matched Char's vehemence with gritty resolution.

"There's a hundred professions, that's right, but they all take schooling or apprenticing or buying in. And all of that's expensive and has to be paid up front! Where is the setup money, Pa? Professional-class girls all have setup money. You wanted Ma enough to risk everything for her. I understand that. Well, you got her, you got her people, now she's dead, they're gone, I'm gone, it's done and over. You risked what you had, used it up on them, and there was nothing left over to keep me a Professional. I'm not mad at you. I'm done crying about it. But don't try to stop me making my way, Pa!" Despite her words, she had been unable not to cry, feeling the wetness dripping from her jaw.

Pa turned red, then white, then he surprised and disarmed her by weeping in his turn. She had never confronted him before. Except for his own mother, no one had ever confronted him. He did not know how to deal with it. He had not been prepared for it. Tears flowed in streams as he promised her he would move in with Gregoria and sell the house to provide setup money for her. She was right! It was owed her. He would do it at last. She must not blame him! He would make it up to her!

And although she knew it would mean pain and rejection and loneliness all over again, Fringe clung to him in a great flood of warm sentiment, pledging herself to becoming a Professional. They hugged each other and smiled tremulously into each other's faces, and Fringe went away aching with a longing she had almost forgotten. Come morning, she told herself, she would resign from the Academy. She would apologize to Zasper and beg his forgiveness, but she would resign. That night she chewed her fingers to the quick and broke out in spots, but remained resolute.

When morning came, however, she made herself sit quietly and think the matter over. There had been times . . . times when Ma and Pa had cried all over each other, promising this, promising that, things that never came to pass. She'd seen Char promise Grandma Gregoria too, and those promises hadn't usually meant anything much. Besides, she had nowhere but the Academy to live, and if Pa was going to sell the house, where would she stay? Would she be welcome at Grandma's? Perhaps it would be better to wait until things were a little more definite. . . .

She told herself this, refusing to admit real doubt. She thought of going to Char and getting the details straight, but told herself that might be pressing him too much, even as she suspected it might be pressing herself too much. Days went by. She heard nothing more about setup money. Her emotions wavered from anger to relief, back and forth, like a children's balance board, up and down, up and down. She hadn't really wanted to leave the Academy. And yet, if he truly would provide . . .

At last, telling herself she needed to make an end of the uncertainty, she went to ask him face-to-face. The house was empty. A neighbor saw her standing there and told her Char was away on a long trip, a marriage trip. He had married again. A Professional-class woman, a widow. The house was being expensively refurbished against his return.

The cold that washed through her was no worse than it had often been before. Pa had obviously decided it was better to get himself a new wife and start over than saddle himself with the old wife's daugh-

ter—particularly since she wasn't really a credit to him. Too spoiled by
the Tromses, no doubt.

She went back to the Academy and put the memory in that place she
had put other memories, that locked, secret place. Why become a Professional Dorwalk when she wasn't Dorwalk at all? She was Owldark.
She had been gifted with that name and had been carrying it about with
her for some time now. She liked the sound of it. Sneaky, and quiet,
and unseen, that was her. She would become an Enforcer, she would
become Owldark, she would have a place of her own.

Though she sometimes dreamed of him thereafter, she never saw
Char Dorwalk again.

Jacent, Syrilla's protégé, found Tolerance increasingly intolerable. He
hovered between tedium and terror most of the time, being bored by
mind-numbing routine in the days and panicked by nightmares at night.
The med-tech from whom he shamefacedly sought help recommended
a sleep inducer and spoke of the difficulties of adaptation to a new environment. Give it time, the med-tech urged. Jacent gave it time, waking night after night with his heart thundering in his chest, fighting to
catch his breath, frightened out of his wits for no reason he could name.
He knew he spent far too much time worrying about it, but there were
no distractions to keep him from worrying. No workshift was distinguishable from any other. Persons and events seemed to flow together,
fungible as water. Nothing had any edges. All was pose and habit, all
eccentricities smoothed away. He was not allowed to appear concerned
or show surprise at anything real. Though some of the provinces he
monitored had unbelievably nasty customs, it was custom to accept them
without comment. In public he was expected to twitter engagingly about
trifles, but never to mention anything important or significant. The whole
structured artifice was too much to bear.

Jacent told himself he wasn't old enough for all this habit! He needed
some exciting reality! Perhaps if he had something interesting to think
about, he would be able to sleep! His chance came when he was invited
to join a group of giggling youngsters in their exploration of the abandoned installations north of the Great Rotunda.

"There will be tunnel rats as long as your arm," whispered Metty, a
girl almost as recently arrived as Jacent himself, a friend, someone who

shared his brooding boredom, his disenchantment and discontent. They talked about their plans late at night, under the covers, between more or less successful attempts at erotic distraction.

"Rats and maybe serpents," said her brother Jum, he of the curly hair and extravagant clothing, when invited to join the group. "We'll take net-guns and capture some for the zoo!"

There was a stasis zoo at Tolerance, where odd flora and fauna brought by settlers were preserved, at least those species that hadn't fit into the terraformed ecology originally adopted on Elsewhere. Capture of interesting creatures would provide a reasonable-sounding excuse for the unauthorized expedition, though one of doubtful legitimacy. Capturing animals was Frickian business. In fact, in Jacent's opinion, anything adventurous and fun seemed to be Frickian business, while everything routine and dull was the business of Supervisors.

"How do we get into the place?" Jacent asked. "I thought all the old army quarters were sealed off."

"Oh, they were," said laughing Kermac, known for his incautious adventures among the Frickian servant boys. "But we've broken one set of seals and pried open a door. There's oodles of corridors down there, and lots of the lights are still working."

So it was with these and another half-dozen temerarious adolescents that Jacent sneaked into the lower corridors and through the narrow crack that was the best Kermac had been able to achieve with the stout and obdurate door. Anyone less lithe than the youngsters could not have wriggled through that narrow slot at all.

They emerged into a variable dimness that was, so Jacent soon decided, rather worse than darkness, for in darkness he would not constantly think he saw things that, on second glance, did not seem to be there. The place also provoked a breathlessness that reminded him unpleasantly of his nighttime terrors. He thought apprehensively of the noxious gases said to gather in ancient vaults. The others, however, were having no trouble breathing, as their chatter indicated. He took himself firmly in hand, assuring himself the seeming lack of air was all imagination.

The place was a labyrinth. Corridors connected and divided. Rooms had multiple doors, which often opened at unexpected places; stairs plunged up and down with little regard for system or direction. It was impossible to get any sense of *where* one was in relation to where one had been shortly before. Had it not been for the hansl, the trip recorder Kermac had borrowed (unauthorizedly) from Supplies, they would have been hopelessly and helplessly lost within moments.

With the lifeline of the hansl to depend upon, however, they progressed ever more deeply into the tangle, finding nothing interesting but continually hoping to do so. Walls and floors had been uniformly gray to begin with and were now uniformly laden with velvet dust. All the surfaces were featureless. Glow beads along the floors let them move about without stumbling. Here and there work lights came on at their approach, letting them actually see where they were, though there was nothing to see. No interesting sights, no sound at all, not even the subliminal hum and hiss of moving air. When the work lights came on, they created a gray and swampy glow, bordered by shadow. When the lights turned off behind them, they left a darkness deeper than before.

At the bottom of an uncertain number of stair flights they found a short corridor debouching into echoing space, into what might once have been an assembly hall. Their chatter had long since been stilled by the dusty silence. Now, in this huge space, the quiet weighed upon them so heavily that their spirits demanded interruption of it.

"We're hunters," Metty shouted suddenly. "Haii, we're hunters!" She waved her net-gun, as though to some invisible watcher.

Her voice went out into a silence so utter that each of them stopped, poised to flee, hearing the shocking sound escape into nothing, awaiting the echoes that had to come back from the hard-surfaced labyrinth. Their ears pricked in anticipation of the sound they knew was coming, and their minds supplied the expected reverberation: ". . . ters . . . ters . . . ters."

The reply, when it arrived at last, was a mere insinuation, a flabby softness on the ears, as though the velvety dust were capable of devouring the bones of sound and leaving only its fat and skin.

"We're . . . hungers. . . ." The words, though soft, came clearly, then the repetition, falling away into silence once more. ". . . gers . . . gers . . . gers," the sound gulped hungrily.

The young people looked at one another uncomfortably, each wondering if the other had heard what he or she had heard.

"Hungers?" whispered Jacent. "Is that what you yelled? I thought you said hunters?"

Metty shook her head at him, suddenly haunted by the vision of some soft and repulsive creature crouched just out of sight around the nearest corner, cunningly capturing words and twisting them as it sent them back, making the explorers doubt not the echo but the original utterance.

"Hunters is what I said," she whispered from a dry throat.

Her brother Jum, white-faced but restive, raised his voice, challenging the darkness.

And again the echoes came, meeping and maundering, twisting the words into different, quite dreadful meanings.

Jacent, feeling the hairs on his neck stand up, knew it could not be an accidental effect. It had to be deliberate. Such intelligible warpings would not happen by chance! He started to say so, then caught himself. He shouldn't say so, not here. His ears had heard vile obscenities Jum's tongue had never uttered, but it would be wiser, far, far wiser to pretend not to have noticed. He glanced at Metty, to see her flush and look away. Well, then. So she had heard the same.

The two of them were standing beside a huge pillar at the center of the hall, the ceiling invisible above them, the walls showing only as a distant limit to the darkness. Unlike other walls they had passed, these were covered with murals: Frickians in arms, Frickians involved in great battles, the landscapes of military engagement. Jacent took Metty's hand and drew her to the pillar, as though to refuge, like some small forest creature to a tree, putting the bulk of it between them and the sounds.

Leaning against it Jacent could hear the footsteps of the others, amplified through the great support post into the sound of an ominous army marching, around, around. What if he cried out "Beware!" or "Danger"? He imagined himself shouting out the words, imagined them coming back like an avalanche, sending his friends fleeing wildly. He knew what would happen then. They would become separated. They would be lost. All of them. That would be something real, an actual happening, something Council Supervisory could not merely wave away, something they'd have to deal with! Search parties would have to come from the Great Rotunda! The Inner Circle would have to do something!

He swallowed the hysterical impulse to scream such a warning and breathed deeply, as he did on waking from his nighttime terrors. Kermac had the hansl, and Kermac was across the vast room, near the opening of a corridor. If Kermac was startled, he would flee down that corridor, leaving Jacent and Metty where they were, abandoned to the voices of this place. Jacent did not want to be abandoned here. Not even for the sake of excitement. Tugging Metty after him once more, he went to the place where Kermac and Jum stood.

Jacent no longer believed the reverberations they had heard were really echoes. Had he ever believed they were echoes? Well, if he had, now he didn't. They were voices, real voices, growling ominous threats and accusations from some not far distant room. Not far distant enough, at any rate.

"What was this place?" he asked, almost in a whisper.

"The army barracks," Kermac said very softly. "From settlement times."

"Why should an old barracks be . . . be like this?" Jacent wondered, still whispering. "I mean, it was just Frickians, wasn't it? You'd expect a place like this in . . . oh, Derbeck, maybe. Or Molock. Or what's that place in Enarae, the Swale?"

"I've monitored the Swale," said Metty. "It's a little, you know, depraved, but this is really spooky!"

"But why?" Jacent persisted.

"It's worse the farther down you go," murmured one of the girls from over their shoulders. "You notice that? The more stairs we go down, the worse it gets."

"Oh, you and your farther down," said Jum defiantly. His face was white and drawn. There was fear in his eyes, but his determination to fight the fear made him reckless. Jacent saw that. Jum was doing the same thing he, Jacent, did, when he wakened from those damned nightmares! Moved by both sympathy and fear at what Jum might do, Jacent put out his hands—too late. Jum darted away from them to face the empty distance, the vacant corridors, the lurking dark.

"You don't scare me!" he cried. "I can laugh at you!" And he did, screaming laughter into the brooding quiet. "Ha ha, ha ha ha," forced hammer blows of mocking laughter.

On the tail of his laughter the sound came back, without an instant's delay, and they went down before it like grain before a scythe. The laughter was a drum roll of thunder, an earthquake of sound. Somewhere a chorus of monsters was enjoying a terrible joke. The adventurers rolled on the floor, their hands over their ears, trembling in a frenzy of horror while the demonic sounds abated.

An expectant silence drew in about them as though awaiting the next jest.

From afar off came a liquid swallowing.

One of the youths whispered, "This was a rotten idea. This is a nightmare."

"I have nightmares," Jacent murmured into his hands. "All the time." He looked up to find a circle of eyes fixed on him. "Don't you?"

There were flushes and nods of assent as they rose, brushing the dust from their knees.

"Why?" he whispered.

"I don't think this is the place," Metty murmured from her position beside Jum, still crouched, still covering his ears. "Not the place to talk about it, Jacent."

It was not the place. They agreed wordlessly to that. Jum struggled to his feet, and the group turned as one toward the door through which they had come. Kermac led them back, all of them on tiptoe in a straggling line, everyone trying to be quiet, wanting no noise at all. Jum shook his head at Metty when she tried to help him, waving her away. She came to walk beside Jacent once more.

"He's frightened. It makes him angry," she whispered.

Jacent nodded. Being scared half to death always made him angry too. Later on. When he thought about it.

They caught themselves glancing toward the walls, all of them now seeing what Jacent had seen on the way in, the movement of things that weren't there. Right-angled corners shifted into unaccustomed configurations. The line where walls and ceilings met wriggled like serpents, along with the tops of the doors, the edges of stairs.

Shadows, Jacent told himself firmly, ignoring the fact that the light was shadowless, and if there had been shadows, what would have made them move?

At last they came to the door they had left ajar, the door they had unsealed and wished now they had left alone. They wriggled through it one by one. When they had pushed it shut, Kermac set about renewing the seals while the others stood together, saying very little, not sure what to say.

"Where's Jum?" asked Metty suddenly. "Where's my brother?"

"He was right behind me," said someone. "He was bringing up the rear."

"We have to go back and get him," cried Metty.

No one moved.

"I'll go alone!" she cried. "I have to find him! Kermac, give me the hansl."

Kermac swallowed. "I already wiped the trip record. As soon as we got to the door. I didn't want it in there. . . ."

"You didn't!" she screamed. "You couldn't have."

He shouted at her. "I borrowed it from the supplies room. I didn't want anybody to know. . . ."

She ran down the empty corridor toward the Great Rotunda, her feet clattering, the sharp, clean echoes coming back at them like slaps. "I'll get help," she cried. "Help."

The others stared at one another guilt-faced, then went after her, slowly, shamefully slowly, far too slowly to catch up with her. At the first intersection, one of them turned off, and another at the next. Soon Jacent found himself alone in the main corridor near the monitor section. The rest of them had gone away, here and there. They were not going to get involved if they could help it, so much was clear.

So what should Jacent do? He couldn't simply abandon Metty. She was his friend! After a moment's thought, he went into the monitor section and sought out a Files access, one which was not only vacant at the moment but also set in a corner that hid it from any human or mechanical observer. When he asked for the plans of the Frickian barracks, he used the general work code for the current shift, not his personal code. The plans materialized before him, and he flicked back and forth through them, locating the door by which they had entered, retracing the way they had gone. The area was ramified and labyrinthine indeed, but not particularly mysterious. Several levels down he found the vast hall where they had heard the filthy echoes. It was the only space of its kind and size they could have reached in the time they had spent getting there. So, even without the trip recorder, it should be possible to trace the way they had gone. If Jum had stayed put, he could be found. Jacent would find Metty and tell her.

As he was about to erase the plans and go in search of her, however, his eye was caught by a red-lined access route leading from the vast assembly hall, through a narrow sideway, and thence downward into blankness.

"Query," he asked. "What's here?" indicating the vacant space.

Files was silent. A red light flickered at the bottom of the Files access, one which told him he was about to receive assistance whether he wanted it or not. Abruptly, Jacent flicked off the access and left the room. He was barely in time. Behind him the unit came back on, and a querulous voice asked, "Who just used this access? Enter your personal code at once!"

Damned officious, interfering . . . Even in the library back on Heaven, he had sometimes had a librarian materialize out of nothing to ask why he wanted to know this, why he wanted to know that. It hardly ever used to happen, not when he was much younger, but in the last few years it had begun happening all the time! Files seemed to be getting very touchy about questions to do with certain things. Early times, mostly.

He stood hidden at one side of the doorway, peering up and down the corridor. In both directions monitor lights came on, waiting for him to pass, waiting to identify who was here, who might have used that access. There were just too damned many things one couldn't do in Tolerance, and asking the question he had just asked was obviously another of them. So, if it was forbidden to ask what lay below the old barracks, what was going to happen to Metty when she got back to the Great Rotunda or wherever and started screaming for help? Hah? When she told someone, anyone where they'd all been? When she mentioned names? What was going to happen to all of them then?

Nearby was one of the almost invisible doors giving access to the servants hall. Jacent slipped through and up a twisting ramp. "I wasn't involved," he rehearsed as he wound his way back to his personal quarters via ways reserved for Frickian flunkeys, corridors which were not, so far as he knew, monitored at all because no one cared where servants were, where servants went. At least, not Frickian servants, because Frickians, as everyone knew, were incapable of conspiracy or rebellion. If he didn't let Files see him leaving the area, Files wouldn't know who had asked that particular question.

Of course, this meant he couldn't offer to help Metty. If he told her, then Files would know who'd been looking up the plans. Perhaps . . . perhaps in a day or two, when things settled down. Jum wouldn't starve in a day or two.

Where the servants hall intersected the corridor to his own rooms, he waited until a talkative crowd came by, then joined it as though he had been part of it all along, laughing, chatting, finding out where they'd all been for the last watch, what they'd been doing. If necessary, he'd say he had been with them. If asked. Only if asked.

.   .   .

When Metty had left the others, she had run toward the monitoring center, or rather toward the storage area that lay beneath it. The center itself was two levels above, and there were shift mates on duty today, people she knew, people who could raise the alarm and get a search party together. Asking for help would mean being found out, of course, which would mean some form of discipline, and she didn't look forward to that! Nonetheless. . . .

Jum was such a fool. He didn't have sense enough to just be scared. He always had to put a brave face on everything, even when it was just stupid to do it. He'd been the same as a little boy, always facing up to bullies bigger than he was, always determined to fight or die. He'd probably gone back, by himself, needing to prove he could! Poor little muggins. That's what their mother had always called him. Her little muggins. "Take care of him, Metty," she said when Jum first came to Tolerance. "Take care of him."

And what had she done but gone and lost him! Ahead of her she could see the paired red doors that led into one of the Files storage levels. Beyond them were the lifts, people, help.

Around her, the air shifted horribly, as it had done in the old barracks. She staggered, feeling an abrupt, agonizing pain in her hip. She put her hand on it and drew it away wet. Bloody.

Damn, she'd run into something.

The pain came again. Worse.

She looked down. Blood was flowing, soaking through her clothing, pouring out of her.

She opened her mouth to scream. Nothing came out but froth, pink froth.

She gasped. No air. No air at all. The pain was everywhere, in both hips, in her shoulders. Everything was going black.

She fell, sprawling, gurgling, flopping on the floor, unable to get up. Her right leg twitched, jerked, tore away at the hip, and moved away. She could see it moving away, like something tugged at the end of an invisible string. She tried to scream and couldn't get it out. Then the left leg. She saw it go, tugging away. Then the arms, one at a time. Blood poured out. Her chest still heaved. Her mouth still moved. She kept trying to call someone, beg someone. . . .

Then darkness came down and it was all gone.

Her body parts lay quietly on the dusty floor, like the parts of a puppet, disassembled. A leg moved farther away from the torso. An arm twitched. No one came this way except an occasional Frickian patrol. It would be some time before this was found. At the edges of the carmine pool, blood began to clot. The parts continued to move, here and there, making different patterns, smearing the blood into different patterns, letters, words.

Fool. That was one word. With the blood still dribbling from the left shoulder, something wrote that word on the floor several times, then another word, over and over.

Shadows moved at the edges of the walls, along the corners of the walls, accompanied by an interested sound, a satisfied gulping sound. Almost, but not quite, a chuckle.

Fringe Owldark's home was a loft above a river-trade warehouse, four tiny rooms and two large ones that looked through tall windows at the passing barges; four tiny rooms and two large ones made up mostly of bare and shining space. The bedroom held only a simple float bed and the most complete information-entertainment console available in Enarae. Through the narrow windows, Fringe could watch the boats moving slowly by, night or day. Three doors along the inside wall opened into the saniton, into her wardrobe, and into her workroom.

The other large room was hardly ever used, not it, not the food synthesizers in the tiny kitchen. It was a room for guests and she never had guests. Four skeleton chairs, like dark fish bones, poised on the polished floor along with one sculptural table and a few blocks of polished precious stone with *things* on them, *things* that spoke to Fringe, whether or not others would have found them meaningful.

It had taken her years of moving about before she found this space. It had taken a lengthy time of living in it before she'd felt fully at home. She could count on her fingers the times she had brought anyone into this home space with her. She preferred that it be hers alone. She preferred to find it empty, untenanted, its air unbreathed.

Evenings when she was not on duty, she most often spent alone, perhaps lying quietly on her float bed, thinking of not much, watching the turgid flow of the river. This is what she was doing a day or two after her interview with the Final Equity Manager, when the evening reverie was interrupted by a call from Yilland so-called Dorwalk. If Fringe didn't mind, Yilland said after introducing herself in a too-bright voice, she would like to come for a brief visit.

Fringe did mind, with a flush of anger so bright and shining it seemed it would set the place afire. The heat dwindled however, giving way to a mild curiosity. What did Yilland so-called Dorwalk have in mind?

The question was answered as soon as she showed up, for Yilland could barely conceal her frantic embarrassment as she chirped her plaint in an aggrieved voice.

"These last few claims that just came in, they're claims from your mother's brother and sister, and there's no way Father's Book can meet them!"

Yilland's hair was slightly disheveled. Her face was blotchy from recent tears. Her comfort and poise were further compromised by the latest Professional fashion in clothing, a ridiculous profusion of bobbles, dangles, and drapes.

"My ma's kin?" Fringe asked, gesturing to one of her skeleton chairs and seating herself across from the woman. "I heard it mentioned that Ma had a sister and a brother, but I never knew them. What claim might they have?"

"They're claiming damages against Char for letting their father die before his time. In the Pighouse."

Fringe snorted. "Ari was as old as sin. He spent the last year or so in a life box, being pumped in and out, with no more brain than a chicken. If his children wanted the old man, why didn't they claim him earlier?"

"They say they didn't know their sister died, didn't know their father's habitation was threatened, changed, oh, you know. They claim they should have been informed."

"Who knew where they were? I certainly didn't. They'd taken some pains to disappear, the way I remember the story." Fringe shrugged, feeling angry. "You can probably buy them off for almost nothing."

"But there's nothing left, and they're demanding I sell myself. . . ."

Fringe said patiently, "The claim is unrighteous and unenforceable, and chances are they know it! They're owed no such debt."

"I know that!" Yilland shrieked, putting a hand over her mouth as though in shock at the sound she had made. "I know I probably wouldn't have to do it. But they won't let me alone and I don't know what to do! They won't let me alone!" Her face twitched, in spasms.

Fringe read the signs and got up, her lips quirking with a barely suppressed snort, half amusement, half anger. Wasn't this ironic! Pa had repudiated her because of her chosen career, at least that had been his excuse, and here came his chosen classly daughter, wanting an Enforcer!

"You want me to Attend the Situation?"

"Would you. Oh, please. They frighten me!"

Fringe got out her pocket file and clicked it open. "Names?" she asked.

"The man says he's your uncle, Zerka Troms. The woman's name is Zenubi."

"Where are they staying?"

"At Bridge House number three." Yilland put her hand to her lips once more, as though to stop their trembling. "I have no right to ask you to do this, except they're your kinfolk. . . ."

"I suppose they could be, in a manner of speaking. But they're not making any claim against me."

"I know, I know, it's just they're so . . ."

"Crude," suggested Fringe. "Brutal, vulgar, common, gross. . . ."

Yilland couldn't find a response.

"Like me," finished Fringe.

"That's not . . ." She gulped. "That's not—"

"Oh, Yilland. Of course it is! That's what Grandma Gregoria always thought. What she said the day she told me to get out of her sight and never come back. How is Gregoria, by the way? Did she die? Finally?"

Yilland nodded, her face flaming. "Before Char . . . before he married Mother. That's why Mother married him, because he had inherited. . . ."

Another thing Fringe hadn't known. But of course, if he'd inherited from Grandma it would have opened up whole new worlds for him! She sighed.

"Both Pa and Grandma Gregoria were very clear about my being crude. And Trashy. Which is no doubt why I was deposed in your favor. I didn't find that out until he died, did you know that?"

Tears ran down Yilland's face. "I never asked him to. I never even knew you didn't know. He didn't tell us you were still around, anywhere. I thought you were gone away, that you didn't need anything. . . ."

"And if I had needed anything?" Fringe asked curiously. "Would you or your mama have helped me out?"

Yilland flushed again, face quivering, and Fringe felt guilty, as though she'd slapped a child.

"If he inherited from Grandma, what happened to it all?"

Yilland gestured helplessly. Gone, her waving fingers seemed to say. Evaporated. Vanished. Well, that was typical.

"Oh, go on home, Yilland," Fringe said impatiently. "Don't worry about the claim. I'll take care of it, because I'm curious, and because you ask me, and for the fee. No, no, you needn't pay me now. Later will do. When you get yourself married to some classly Professional."

Yilland turned a floral red from her neck to her forehead. "I have no right to ask. Mother and I . . . we thought you had betrayed Char," she whispered, unable not to confess her true feelings. "Well, he said you had. Betrayed his Professional status by becoming what you are. . . ."

Fringe felt first a blinding fury, then a surge of laughter coupled with something almost like pity.

"You have no idea what I am," she whispered.

Yilland paled and stepped back.

"You have no idea," said Fringe again. "You and your classly mother, and all the self-satisfied people of Enarae. All the folk of Elsewhere! They live because of me and people like me! Char Dorwalk lived on the blood of people like me. It is we who keep you all situated in your familiar worlds, we who keep you comfortable. If it were not for me and those like me keeping things together, those you despise so readily would rise up and eat you! Or the Hobbs Land Gods would swallow you up and perhaps that would be best for you all!"

It was what Enforcers said about themselves. Even Fringe didn't believe it all. But at the moment, it felt exactly the right and final thing to say.

Night in Tolerance, with nine tenths of the population asleep, the corridors still, and only the night shift on monitor duty. These are the vacant hours, the time for inexplicable happenings. Corridor doors deep below ground swing open of themselves. Distant sounds filter through from ancient armories. People waken from dreams sweating, their hearts pounding. Night workers think they see things at the corners of their eyes. There has been more of this lately, a great deal more. The med-techs are concerned, wondering if there is some kind of epidemic brewing.

If so, Boarmus is a sufferer, wakening at midnight, lungs heaving, as from a dream of torture and despair. The room flickers around him, as though thronged with transparent creatures. He believes he sees faces, hands, arms writhing like tentacles. He knows he hears voices. Dead men. That's what Boarmus calls them. Dead men. They never used to come here like this, but lately—lately they seem to wander around to suit themselves.

Boarmus heaves himself out of bed and goes out just as he is, in his rumpled nightshirt, uncorseted and bleary-eyed. The corridors are vacant except for the flickering, wavering shapes he sees along the walls, except for the pairs of dim white orbs following him down the narrow back hall to the secret tubeway, which opens at the sound of his voice and drops him a thousand feet down and horizontally, clanking through voice-code activated security locks before opening into a small metal-walled cube with blank walls.

Before the former Provost, Chadra Hume, had retired to Heaven, he had brought Boarmus here once. There had been no marks on the walls to guide Chadra Hume then; there are none to guide Boarmus now. He simply has to remember where the touch plates are. Three paces left of the lift door at shoulder height (where he thinks he sees two spectral faces howling into his own). *One.* Six paces the other side, waist high (where he puts his hands through the guts of a wraith). *Two.* Straight across from the lift door, eye level (under that clutter of ghostly hands). *Three.* If he's done it right, there'll be a click. If he hasn't done it right, he must go up, come back down, and try again.

The click is slow in coming, muffled and reluctant. One of the metal walls moves to the right, leaving a floor-to-ceiling slit at the corner. Boarmus shambles into the opening before the wall stops moving, and it closes behind him as he shuffles down soft-floored twisting corridors flushed with effulgent light. Like being sucked down a glow worm's guts, he had thought more than once. The corridors are lined with rows of cabinets, all of them stuffed with sensory recordings and official transcripts—a millennium's worth of records of God knows what by God knows whom!

The door at the bottom opens into darkness. Only when the door has locked itself behind him do the lights come on, showing the console, the speaker, the transparent plate set into the lower wall and floor through which he can observe the crystalline structures below. This is the Core, the first thing built upon Elsewhere. Before the armory, before the Great

Rotunda, before all the ramifications of Tolerance, this was built, an enormous, complicated device extending in repeated spirals down to the limit of vision, deep as a mine, wide as a chasm. Spirits cluster thickly upon the spirals, like rotted grapes upon a dangling vine. Boarmus can't see them. Not really. But he believes they're there.

"Boarmus," says a dead man in a toneless voice.

"Here," he answers. It is cold in this place. It is hard to keep from shivering, but he tells himself it has nothing to do with the ghosts, only with the temperature. He has forgotten to put on a coat. Next time he must remember.

"You have not come timely, Boarmus." Gulp.

Boarmus shrugs elaborately. He calls this voice, one he dislikes, the gulper. Boarmus has studied the biography book, over and over again. He thinks he knows who this voice is, but he dares not address it by name. Perhaps, by now, it has become . . . someone else. Boarmus shudders inwardly at the thought.

He has made it a matter of pride not to show fear, not before any of them. Chadra Hume had confessed that he sometimes came back from these nightmare forays shaking in his shoes, pale and sweat-beaded. He had puked, he said, puked like a sick dog, heaving dryly as spit ran down his chin. Boarmus has sworn he will not react so.

"There's still a day or two before the deadline," he says expressionlessly.

It has not been quite a year yet since his last visit. The rules say annually, when the residents of the Core wake up. A fleeting thought related to this disturbs him, but before he can consider it, the voice goes on.

"We've been waiting. We should not have to wait." The words accuse him, but the tone doesn't. The machine has only one tone to serve for everything. One tone for anger, joy, hope, pain. Why should there be more? What do dead men know about such things?

As for their having waited . . . why would a dead man wait for anything? Tomorrow or the next day, that's when they were supposed to waken. Chadra had spoken of his own lengthy waits as he fidgeted about in this icy room forever until some one of the dead men warmed up enough to receive his annual report.

The voice goes on, still in the same tone. "Files tells us there are people from the past. Files says there are dragons. Explain these things!"

So they'd been awake long enough to go burrowing through Files! Damn!

Boarmus breathes deeply, invoking the deity of deadly boredom. He explains the twins in the dullest possible words, managing to convey a yawn in every sentence. The last thing he wants is for the dead men to become interested. They have rarely been interested up to now. Most often they have merely accepted the annual report that he as Provost has been required to give, and then they have gone away. Less often they have become agitated, like this: demanding and intransigent and threatening. So Boarmus talks of people from the past who had showed up, yes, but dull, dull, nothing to concern yourself with at all. They came through the Arbai Door. Everyone knows about Arbai Doors. Even the dead men know about Arbai Doors, and about this particular Arbai Door, which was found on Panubi when Elsewhere was first settled.

The matter of dragons, however, he is unable to explain to the dead men's satisfaction, and the voice of the machine sizzles and pops its irritation, like fat bones in a fire. "You aren't explaining!"

"I've sent someone to find out about them," Boarmus says, keeping his throat quiet to avoid tasting the bile at the back of his tongue. "He's putting together a team right now. If I could explain it, I wouldn't need anyone to find out about it! I'm sure it's nothing very important, but when I get a report about it, I'll let you know."

A long, reverberating silence. During such silences, Boarmus imagines the colloquy going on. This dead man talking to that dead man. He hasn't seen what lies below in the great coiled mass. He doesn't want to see it. He imagines the insides of those ramified crystalline structures, something far worse than the dinka-jins in City Fifteen, which are quite bad enough. He doesn't need to see it to know about it. He has read the original specifications several times, specifications informing him that they are down there below, all their fleshy parts severed and cold, white-rimmed and asleep; all their mind patterns being awakened once a year to run through the matrix like scurrying pets on an exercise wheel, whirring, whirring as they update themselves and take exercise, prior to going back into unconscious stasis once more. So the specifications say.

And then his former fleeting thought returns, suddenly, all at once to leave him gasping at his own obtuseness! How could they be here now if the specifications were being adhered to? How could they have been disturbing him, making those ghostlike appearances, if things were as they should be? If things were being done in accordance with the specifications, the dead men could not have wakened until tomorrow!

With sick realization he knows the dead men have not been sleeping

their year-long sleeps, they have not been waking only annually to update their information as the specifications *very clearly spell out.* Oh, no.
Breaze and Bland and the rest of them have been awake! What had
Zasper's silly song said? "Breaze and Bland and Thob and Clore ran till
they could run no more." And what did the song mean? What had they
run from or to? From the specifications, maybe? Could that silly children's rhyme actually date back to the first days of settlement? Well,
what else could their being awake mean? That they've recently been
awakened *by* something? Or maybe recently *chosen* to stay awake? All the
time? Or only some of the time? Are they doing it now just to harass
him?

The cabinet containing the specifications and the Provosts' logs and
the biography book is outside in the corridor. The biography book has
pictures and histories of every person who went into the Core, all one
thousand of them. Boarmus knows those faces as he knows his own. In
the log each Provost in turn has recorded the substance of his reports to
and conversations with the dead men. In addition to these documents
there are stacks of private sensory recordings left behind by those in the
Core, sweet reminders of youth, probably, so they can relive old times
after they wake up and come out.

Boarmus has only glanced at the logs from time to time. He has never
bothered the private sensory records. Of course not! Though, perhaps. . . .

"Dragons," says the voice, sounding like another person. Though it
is always the same mechanism, sometimes it gives an impression of difference, which means, so Boarmus believes, that it is moved by a different consciousness, a different pattern. He thinks of this voice as female,
even motherly. "Have you asked Files about dragons?"

Boarmus decides to risk it. He is too curious not to risk it. "To whom
am I speaking?" he asks courteously.

"To . . . Lady Professor Mintier Thob," says the voice after a moment's hesitation.

"Lady Professor, I have asked Files about dragons, of course." She
(it) no doubt knows as well as he that Files holds thousands of years'
worth of dragons. Lizards that are called dragons, extinct and living.
Artworks depicting dragons, ancient and modern. Dragons in legends,
human and nonhuman. Intelligent races that resemble dragons, both fossils and flesh. Boarmus had perused them all and now says so.

That humming silence again. "The Arbai resembled dragons," says the machine. "Files has pictures of them. Files has data. Where is the Arbai Door that was here on Elsewhere when we came?" The words seem tentative, if a machine can be tentative.

"It was brought to the Great Rotunda during the early days of settlement, and it's been there ever since," says Boarmus. "Nothing has come through it before, if that's what you're wondering. Besides, there were Arbai Doors everywhere. All across the galaxy. As for the Arbai themselves, they are extinct."

"So are we," says the first voice once more, and for a moment Boarmus believes he can hear hideous laughter. "In a sense. But it doesn't matter. We can do more . . . extinct."

"If that's all," Boarmus says, only with great effort keeping it from sounding like a whimper. He wants out of this place, away from them. He needs to consider the implications of this. He needs to think!

"No. It isn't all." Though the voice is toneless, Boarmus interprets the words as threatening. "Someone has asked questions about us, Provost. Someone has asked questions of Files."

His mind shudders in panic, like a child caught in a bit of naughtiness. It was such a little thing! He hadn't expected them to notice. Possibly he should have expected it, but he had hoped. . . . Damn. Damn Danivon Luze. Well, Danivon is well away from Tolerance, so what?

"Tell what happened," the voice demands.

"About what?" He feigns ignorance.

"Someone asking . . . about us?"

Boarmus shakes his head, making a tsking sound. "I don't believe that anyone has knowingly asked about you. From time to time people who are reading history come upon some reference to the early days of settlement, that's all. Every Great Question Day people consider the early days of settlement, and the committee, and the fact that the members of the committee came here to Elsewhere. That doesn't mean people know about the Core, or know that you . . . are still here."

"They think we're dead!" says the voice flatly.

"They think you lived out your lives here and died, yes. That would have been the normal course of events," muttered Boarmus. "No one knows about the Core but me."

No one had ever known except the current Provost, and his living predecessor(s), if any. Though what difference it would make, Boarmus can't imagine. Before the first refugees arrived on Elsewhere, the Core had been set deep into immemorial stone, cased in impenetrable vitreon, double housed in a power-shielded hull along with its own storehouses, its own factory, its own power sources. The Core has never depended on Elsewhere for anything! Even if every person on Elsewhere knew about it, what difference would it make? It isn't as though any fool with a hammer could break in!

"The person you speak of was not the only person. There were other persons asking about this place, where we are. Asking about this place is also forbidden."

Another person? Boarmus swallows. He had no idea someone else had been asking. . . . "Well, I'd have to review the recent Files to determine what they actually wanted to know. Questions about . . . places aren't forbidden, exactly. Some answers just aren't available, that's all." Boarmus manages to yawn convincingly, though he is in a perfect fever to find out who the voices are speaking of.

"You're sending one of the questioners away," says the dead man.

Boarmus raises his brows. "If you mean Danivon Luze, he's the one I'm sending to investigate this business of dragons on Panubi. He's the best person I have for the job." Boarmus does not mention the petitions. He hopes the dead men do not know about the petitions. If they are set off by a few harmless questions about history, what will they think of being asked to rethink their position about anything!

Silence. The silence is somehow worse than the voice, for it has a hungry howling at the back of it, barely detectable. In the vault he believes he sees the dead men twisting like snakes, coiling upward toward the glass. Chadra Hume had confessed to having dreams in which snakelike arms actually came through and seized him. Boarmus shuts his eyes and recites bawdy verses to himself. *"Here's to the girl from Denial / who thought dinka-jins worth a trial. . . ."* The dead men are harmless. They may be able to counterfeit appearance and sound (though perhaps it is only suggestion that makes him think he can see and hear them), but they cannot touch him.

The silence thins into a knife edge of unsound. Then the gulper's voice once more:

"We do not want anyone asking questions, Provost. It is not fitting that mere . . . mortals should question us. Not who we were. Not who we are. We will . . . rid ourselves of those who ask questions. Likely we will rid ourselves of Danivon Luze. Also the others when we find out who. . . ."

They will rid themselves? *They?* How will they manage that? And *mere mortals?* Where did that come from?

"Danivon Luze is invaluable to me," Boarmus blusters.

"No matter about you," the voice says, chuckling. "We have the power, Boarmus. All the power. We are becoming . . . more than mere mortals, Boarmus!" The voice chuckles gulpingly.

Boarmus fights to keep his face calm and unresponsive, not to react to this outrageous statement. What do the dead men mean? And how will they kill anyone?

He has to think about this. He has to get away from here and think about this. He licks his lips. "If that's all," he says again.

No response. Then, a whisper. "I already killed two of them, Provost. Young ones. Sacrifices. To us." A long pause. "To me."

Boarmus swallows, feeling the acid burning in his throat. What have the dead men done?

He looks away for a moment, breathing deeply, gaining control of himself. When he looks back, he sees only the machine with most of its lights out, only a few flickering madly to show the Files are being accessed, the dead men are thinking. He rises from the chair and goes out into the twisting hallway, to the nearest cabinet where he searches frantically among the Files, removing several containers of material he has not bothered with before. No record, no sensory recording, is supposed to leave this place, but Boarmus cannot stay here long enough to look through them. Remaining here has become a physical impossibility.

Thus burdened, he goes back the way he came, distracted only briefly as he approaches his suite by the sight of someone hiding behind a half-opened panel. There is not time to stop and challenge. Once in his own place he vomits and defecates all at once, just as Chadra Hume had said he did, like a sick dog. It has never happened to Boarmus before, and he is sickened at the indecency of it, at the frailty of his own response.

He cleans up after himself, washes himself, rinses out his mouth, and flings himself on his bed to lie there taking deep breaths. "Two young ones," the dead man said. Sacrifices to themselves, itself. Who would that be? And who had been hiding outside?

He summons Files with an outthrust hand. "Personnel check," he says. "First item: identity of young person hiding outside my quarters when I returned here moments ago. Second item: Are all Tolerance staff members or guests present or accounted for?"

Files clicks and hums. Monitors throughout the enormous complex are alerted. Recent past-this-point traffic records are recalled and tabulated.

"First item," says Files. "Named Jacent Sturv. Male kin of Syrilla. Recent arrival from Heaven. Second item: two unaccounted for. Metty and Jum Duschiv, siblings, recent arrivals from Heaven."

"Find the two missing ones," says Boarmus from a burning throat.

Files blinks and chatters. Outlying monitors come awake, Frickian guards are roused and directed to patrol unused areas. Boarmus sits on the side of his bed, his jowly face sweating into his hands, waiting.

The news comes at last. Metty Duschiv, found messily dead in the corridors several levels below the Rotunda. On the walls, words written in her blood. "Fool" is written there. And a word that looks like "adore." Boarmus thinks it isn't "adore." Boarmus thinks he knows what it is.

The girl's brother Jum is nowhere to be found, though a door into the old barracks appears to have been forced.

Have the dead men done this? And if so, how? And for the love of all humanity, why?

Outside Boarmus's suite, behind a half-closed panel in a corridor alcove, Jacent stirred uncomfortably and decided that nothing else was likely to happen tonight. He had seen Boarmus go, accompanied by a certain weirdness, not unlike the weirdness in the old barracks. He had seen Boarmus return all alone. He had been close enough to see Boarmus's face on the return trip, not a face that would encourage Jacent to follow in Boarmus's footsteps. A terrified, sweaty, sick-looking face. There for a minute, he'd thought Boarmus had seen him too, but evidently not.

And right after that, every monitor had awakened, Frickian patrols had gone bustling past, one of whom had eventually told Jacent about Metty when Jacent asked what was happening.

After hearing that he went to his own place and crawled into bed, his mouth dry, watching his walls for that telltale shift, that shadowy sinuosity, listening for that glottal sound. There was something here in Tolerance he wanted to know about, but he preferred not to get dead finding out, particularly not the way Metty had gotten dead. Something very strange was happening, something interesting. Something Boarmus no doubt knew all about.

Jacent, mouth still dry and limbs jumping nervously, lay on his bed, sickly fascinated by the thought of something—anything!—happening at Tolerance!

On Elsewhere's technology scale of one to ten, in which category-one places were unsettled wilderness roamed by a few eremites or savages, and category ten were state-of-the-art technological habitat, a category-seven province like Enarae had sufficient technology for comfort while retaining enough nature to provide pleasantly parklike spaces for the inhabitants.

Particularly parklike were the Seldom Isles, reached by swamp-river boat or by the farflung tentacles of Number Three Bridge, lofting upward from the western outskirts of the city and continuing in that direction all the way to the neighboring province of Denial. Fringe Owldark had spent holidays in the Isles and knew they were about as far as possible from the farm town of Fineen, which lay in the flat, sparsely settled agricultural lands across the city to the east. If putative Uncle and maybe-so Aunty came from Fineen, Fringe thought it very strange they'd be staying at Number Three Bridge House. If, on the other hand, they came from the Seldom Isles, as a good many gangers and vagrants did, their place of lodging made perfect sense.

"Probably bogus," Fringe advised herself as she asked for Zerka and Zenubi Troms and was given the location of their quarters, cheap ones, at the back of the complex, almost under the bridge itself. Fringe settled her Enforcer's garb, brushed lint from her coat, and keyed the annunciator. The elderly woman who answered the summons resembled no one Fringe had ever known. She looked like neither Ari nor Nada, not like Aunty, not like Souile.

"Yes?" she asked in an Islish drawl that made two syllables of the word.

"Zenubi Troms? I've come on behalf of Yilland Dorwalk," Fringe said. "To settle the matter of your death claim against her father."

"Our claim's against *her,*" said the woman. "He left nothing."

Fringe smiled her bloodletting smile. "Does enslaving one member of the family make up to you for the loss of another?"

The woman snorted. "Not my family, she. His first wife, she was family."

"Let's see, that would be Souile?"

"My baby sister," the woman sighed. "Sweet Souile."

Fringe pretended to refer to her pocket caster. "Whom you abandoned, leaving her to provide total support for your aged parents."

The woman looked startled. "She married well," she snapped. "We knew she would."

"And now that she is dead, and he is dead, you want money to soothe your grief at having abandoned your parents," said Fringe, snapping the caster closed.

A man came from another room and stood in the doorway, glowering at her. "Who's she?" he demanded of his kinswoman.

"I am here on behalf of Yilland," Fringe repeated.

The man scowled and took a threatening step forward, only to find himself staring at the business end of a rather large aitchem weapon, so-called from the initials HM, for *hurt and maim.*

Fringe smiled at the woman once more, and intoned, as though it were formula: "I am here to inform you that Fringe and Bubba Dorwalk, Souile's natural children, are filing blood claim against you for two thirds the total cost of providing housing and sustenance to Ari, Nada, and Aunty Troms for varying periods of years, plus accrued interest, which expenditures increased their father's indebtedness and led him to unwarranted and arbitrary actions deleterious to their interests, depriving them of status and comfort. Since this falls within the category of a long-standing and outrageous indebtedness, as defined by the Executive Council of Enarae City, it is being filed in life court for immediate dispensation."

She was surprised to find that she actually felt angry, not against these pretenders but against Souile's real siblings, wherever they were. Even if they'd been only Trashers themselves, they could have helped!

"We are not residents of Enarae City!" the woman cried, both outraged and frightened.

Fringe yawned ostentatiously. "Notices of the suit have been sent to all wards, including Fineen, which you have given as your place of residence. I am an Enforcer retained to pursue the indebtedness should you attempt to leave Enarae before it is adjudicated. As an Enforcer, I must inform you that Fringe Dorwalk is outraged by your claim and has agreed to accept vengeance in lieu of settlement." She held up her caster. "I have recorded the fact that you were both warned. Is it necessary to inform any other member of your family?"

It was all bluff and fluff, but her two victims obviously didn't know that. The man had gone pale and seemed to be having trouble breathing.

"Yes. No! No. I'll tell them," the woman screamed at her.

Fringe left quietly, pausing just long enough to stick an ear on the door before finding her way to a quiet table in a corner tavern where she sipped at a mug of ale while eavesdropping through the receiver behind her ear. Even over the chatter of the tavern, she heard the flurry of hysteria and imminent departure. So much for the imposter kin, who were making a hasty return to the Seldom Isles. Fringe detached the receiver from its bone socket, dropped it into her belt kit, and turned her full attention to the remaining ale. It was good. Better than she had tasted lately. She noted the name of the tavern: somewhat out of the way, but worth the visit.

"Nicely done," said a voice at her shoulder.

She sat very still, without moving anything except one finger that moved slowly toward her weapons belt.

"No threat," said the voice casually.

She stopped moving the finger and turned. He was a sand-colored, black-haired man with curly lips, a fine beak of a nose, and a wide, firm jaw. When she looked at him, something inside her lurched, and she swallowed her errant innards down, holding them still by not breathing for a time. A man to move one's blood around, her own blood told her, while her mind did a careful assessment, weighing and measuring. His clothes were ordinary enough in style, though fine in quality, and he wore them superbly, a trait Fringe always noticed. Now who was he? Or what? She breathed gently, testing to see if her stomach would stay where it belonged.

He gestured at the seat across from her, and she nodded, a mere jerk of the head. She couldn't stop him joining her. Or maybe didn't want to.

"Nicely done," he said again, seating himself and raising dramatically curved eyebrows at her. "That business with the kinfolk who weren't kinfolk."

"You were spying on me?" she asked, more surprised than offended.

"Been observing you," he said comfortably. "Enough to overhear your little show. They aren't even related to you, are they?" He gave her a steamy look, saying, *They couldn't be related to you, woman, not that kind.*

She couldn't quite ignore the look, but she breathed deeply and let her quickened pulse slow of itself. One thing she had learned. Usually the body followed where the mind went. One had only to take firm control of where that was!

"I think not, though I did quit listening," she said, concentrating on the tile pattern of the tabletop.

"My bet is they're part of a gully tribe." He fingered the medallion at his throat, his long fingers tugging at it, turning it.

Fringe grunted. She'd already decided that. Such scavengers were common enough in mid-category places.

"Somebody dies in some province or other," the man mused, as though talking to himself. "The nearest tribe sends a couple gullies along to act the part of wronged kinfolk or people owed a debt. Seldom it's anything that will hold up to examination by the powers that be, but most people don't risk that. Instead, they settle, just to be rid of the chaffers." He mimed stripping one such bloodsucker from his exposed arm, making a face.

"Char Dorwalk's adopted daughter had nothing to settle with," she said crisply.

"Well, no," admitted the man. "My name's Danivon Luze, by the way."

"Fringe Owldark," she said, giving him her hand somewhat reluctantly, noticing that her fingers didn't go up in flames, though she'd felt they might. She swallowed before saying in a carefully neutral voice, "What's your classification, Danivon?"

"Outcaste," he said. "Like you. When I'm here."

Which meant he moved around and could be almost anything. "Where?" she asked.

He gestured expansively, ending with a snapped finger at the youth serving drinkables. When he'd been provided with a tankard and had thirstily dipped his nose, he sat back with a sigh, singing the first line of a well-known vagabond song in a pleasant baritone: " 'On this world of Elsewhere, elsewhere's where I go.' "

"Do not try to hold me, dear. Tomorrow I'll be far from here," her mind continued the verse as he fished a border pass out of his pocket and opened it on the table between them. From the pass, his face stared up at her beside the patterns coding his essential being, physical and mental. She wished she had decoder eyes and could read them, give herself that advantage, at least. At the bottom were the words "Danivon Luze. Universal Pass."

"Aren't you something," she said, half enviously. There were reputed to be fewer than one thousand Universal Passes on all of Elsewhere, and most of them were held by Council Enforcers. He hadn't said he was an Enforcer, but he hadn't said he wasn't. He wasn't wearing a badge, but then he wasn't required to unless he was Attending a Situation. "Now that makes me mightily curious," she said.

"As it would anybody," he said, still comfortably.

"You've been observing me, you say?"

"We have."

"We?"

"A friend and I."

He was being too smug for her. "Am I to winkle words out of you one at a time?" she demanded, working at being annoyed. "If that's so, I've no time for the exercise. No time and no appetite. You approached me, *colleague.* If you have something to say, say it!" Or get out of here and let her temperature settle to normal, which she devoutly wished for.

He seemed not one whit upset at her impatience. "I'm what you might call recruiting. I've been asked to mount an expedition. I came here to consult an old friend, and he mentioned your name. When he did, my nose twinked. So, I took the trouble to see what you're like, how you work." He tugged at his medallion again, a nervous habit. The thing was shiny from the touch of his fingers, the design on it blurred by long touching.

"Indeed," she remarked, laconic in her turn. "Your nose twinked." Damned if she'd ask him who had mentioned her name. She looked at the tabletop once more in order not to look at his nose. Not to look at him at all. Here she'd been working at making herself man-proof, and this creature had to come along to test her resolve. Well, test away, damn him!

"Well, my nose does that," he muttered. "From time to time."

"Have you found what I'm like?"

"We give you high marks for self-control, and for thinking on your feet. We're not looking for any ganger-caste mavericks, out for slaughter."

Fringe lifted a nostril at him. In truth, she felt a grudging empathy with gangers. Old Ari had often spoken of gangers knowingly and with nostalgia, though Fringe had been in her twenties before she'd admitted to herself that he knew so much about them because he'd been one.

"They do have a tendency to kill first and identify later," she remarked. "I've met a few."

Danivon smiled at her. "I know you have," he said.

"You know too much. How much?"

"Everything. I've been through your Book." He looked up and smiled at someone approaching the table. The newcomer sat down beside them without invitation.

Fringe found herself glaring at the huge, bald-headed man who had called himself Curvis. This time she was truly angry, and she snarled at both of them: "Spies, the two of you. Blood Books are private. Until I'm dead, you've no right!"

Curvis merely grinned. Danivon tapped the Universal Pass. "He has one of these too. They're good for more than just getting across closed borders."

She subsided, growling, curiosity getting the better of her. "So, what's my balance?"

He tipped his hand to and fro, like a scale, wavering. No big debts. No big credits. In balance. Almost.

"What's the job?" she asked.

Curvis grunted. On his chest, his pocket moved, and he unfastened it to let something tiny and furry peep out with shiny purple eyes. Danivon scratched his head and made a comical face. "Fringe Owldark, answer me a question first, will you?"

"If I can," she said indifferently, watching the sleek little animal move out of Curvis's pocket onto his shoulder.

"How is Elsewhere different from Everywhere?"

"You're playing at riddles, man. I've no thirst for nonsense."

"No nonsense. I'm serious. How?"

She stared at him, one finger tapping the tabletop. "Luze, everywhere else there are Hobbs Land Gods, but not here."

"And if I said there's a possibility the Hobbs Land Gods have come to Elsewhere? Then what, Fringe Owldark?"

She felt her pulse slow, then race, her face pale, then flush. He might as well have stuck a knife in her side, or told her she'd just been poisoned. She knew nothing about the Gods except what she'd been taught to know, taught to think, taught to feel, which was simple terror.

Those taken over by the Hobbs Land Gods were no longer men, no longer children of God (by whatever title), no longer the concern of heaven (of whatever type). Though the people who had fled to Elsewhere disagreed about virtually everything, about this one thing they agreed: To be taken over by the Hobbs Land Gods was to lose one's soul, one's chance at salvation, one's hope of eternal blessedness—or the equivalent. So said those who ought to know! The Gods were the bogeyman, the thing with teeth, the monster in the dark.

If the Gods came, she would not be herself in any form, but a slave shape, a used being, a kind of puppet on invisible strings, without even the wits to resent it,

He laid a hand on hers. "Ah, now, don't faint."

She breathed deeply, noticing it was his hand that trembled. "How melodramatic!" she managed to say. "A good scare tale, hoicked up for the occasion. Did you dangle it there to see whether I'd scream and fall on the floor?"

He smiled again, a smile that went no farther than his lips. "You didn't, so you passed. It is remotely possible the Gods could have come here. When something happens nobody can explain, we always suspect the Gods." Boarmus hadn't said that, of course, but it was true, nonetheless. True enough that Danivon occasionally woke up shaking from nightmares about it. He too had been taught to fear the Gods, and something long ago in his childhood reinforced that fear. Something he could not even remember, though abandonment might have been part of it.

"Something inexplicable has happened, has it?" she asked.

"Dragons," he said laconically. "Very strange mysterious dragons. Council Supervisory has been appealed to concerning these dragons. So, Council Supervisory in the person of the Provost says, 'Danivon, my lad, get up a team and go find out. No hurry. Take your time, but find out if there's really dragons there, or maybe some other thing that looks like dragons.' One wonders what the 'some other thing' might be, of course."

Fringe took a deep breath and kept herself still. She had been an Enforcer for a dozen years now. She was of middling-young age, attractive still, but no longer girlish. Still, Danivon's words were causing an inappropriately girlish reaction—that shivery, half-hysterical negation that comes when one is barely pubescent, that tantrum tumult of the mind, which screams denial at an unhearing world, before one has learned resignation in the face of unavoidable realities. She breathed quietly and reminded herself of who she was, an Enforcer in good standing. A person worthy of respect. She would not panic at the thought of the Gods, or dragons, or Danivon Luze, or any other damned thing.

Consider dragons. What did honor require an Enforcer to do about dragons? What did her own self-image insist upon? What did her oath demand? And, come to that, what was she more frightened of? The Gods in the guise of dragons coming to Elsewhere, or herself going off with Danivon Luze? She felt the heat of him from where she sat, and she badly wanted advice.

"What are you thinking?" Danivon asked her curiously.

"Of a man called Zasper," she replied soberly.

Curvis and Danivon exchanged glances.

Well, so, she thought. It had been Zasper who'd mentioned her name!

The little animal put his nose in Curvis's ear and whispered to him. Curvis gave it a square cracker that it took in tiny paws and began to nibble at, turning it around and around, making a perfect circle of it, holding the circle off and admiring it before taking another series of tiny bites around the circumference.

"What is that?" she asked, wanting the subject changed. The little creature had pale violet fur and a long tail with a fluffy tassel at the end. Its habit seemed to be to drape the tassel over its eyes, half hiding them.

"A pocket munk," said Curvis.

"Not from here?"

"From the forests along the Roga coast." He prodded his pocket, and another of the little animals peered sleepily forth. "Amusements," Curvis said. "And friends. They hear people talking, then they come and repeat what they hear. Or one hears in one place, the other repeats it somewhere else. Most useful at times."

Fringe took a deep breath and settled herself. "Tell me whatever it is you came to say," she demanded.

"Do you know where Panubi is?"

"Near the equator, somewhere south of the Curward Islands."

"What do you know about it?"

"It's a continent, a place."

"I mean, do you know what kind of place?"

"Hell, Danivon! A partially settled place with a lot of provinces around the edge and empty territory in the middle. Full of weirds and odds, it's said, though it's never really been explored. So I was told at Academy. One of Elsewhere's little mysteries. Is that where your dragons are?"

"Indeed. So it's said."

"Send a mechanical, an automatic. Why risk people?"

"Devices have been tried. They don't come back with anything useful. Of course, neither have people. . . ."

Fringe took a deep breath. "No need to impress me, man. Or frighten me, if that's what you're attempting."

"Listen to her," said Danivon to Curvis, miming wide-eyed admiration. "Very well, Enforcer. You're being offered a chance to join an exploration company."

"How much?"

"Would you consider fame? Honor? How about glory?"

She grinned her bloodletting grin and fingered the fatal-hands dangles below her Enforcer badge. "Piss on that, Danivon. Only dead Enforcers get paid in glory."

The two men exchanged a significant glance. "Here's the deal. Appointment as Council Enforcer, twice standard rate, weapons allowance, all expenses, and a lifetime annuity."

She took another deep breath. Of course, employers didn't offer a lifetime annuity unless the odds were long against there being any substantial lifetime in which to collect. But appointment as Council Enforcer was likely bait! Then she could have a Universal Pass of her own!

"Who else is going?" she asked.

He looked uncomfortable as he replied, "A couple people."

"Who?"

"Some strange people. What difference does it make?"

She shrugged. He shrugged a mocking reply and got up to get another drink.

"He won't know for sure who all's going until he smells 'em," said Curvis conversationally, one massive forefinger tickling the little animals who lay close to his chest on the table before him, noses on paws, watching her.

She stared at him, uncomprehending.

The bald man shook his head admiringly. "He's got this . . . this talent. Like . . . suppose there's a situation that won't give. A bad situation. And other Enforcers try this and they try that, and it won't give. Danivon comes along, and he picks this one and that one and some other one, and he takes them into the situation, and all of a sudden, *powee*, things change."

"How does he do that?"

"He says he smells 'em." Curvis grinned at her and winked, as Danivon came back to the table. "Catalysts."

Fringe told herself she couldn't handle any more of this at the moment, not Danivon, not his friend, not the little animals lying there on the table, each with its tail over its eyes, each with a little stack of now-circular crackers, each one staring at her through its tassel, as though waiting for her to do something amusing. She stood up, laying coins on the table for her own drink. "I'll let you know. Where will I find you?"

"We'll find you," said Danivon, returning to the table.

She left it at that. As she walked away, she heard her own voice saying, "I'll let you know. Where will I find you?" and turned to see one of the little animals looking after her. It opened its mouth and said it again, making a comical face. She shook her head and stalked away. Pocket munks, for the love of heaven. Why did they chew things into circles like that?

When she had gone, Curvis asked, "What'd you think?" He pocketed his pets and stared at Danivon, waiting for an answer.

Danivon Luze gestured vaguely and stared at the wall for a long time before he said, "Oh, she's right. I'm sure of that. But something about her's not quite . . ."

"Not quite what?"

"I don't know. Not quite solid, somehow."

"Looked solid enough to me."

"I don't mean her body, Curvis. Not her health. Not her abilities, which Zasper says are good enough, though I'd like to see her use a weapon."

"Well, stick close for a few days and we probably will. Lot of stuff going bang here in Enarae."

"True."

"Those strange people from who knows when, those twins. Do they smell solid."

"For what they are." He smiled a lazy smile. "I guess."

"Why are you taking them along?"

Danivon slapped the table with his hand, almost angrily. "Damn, Curvis, I've told you a thousand times I don't know! Ask an artist why he's putting blue in the shadows. Ask a dancer why she bends sideways. . . ."

Curvis interrupted, "All right. You don't know why. Do you know if we need more?"

"All I know is, the team isn't complete yet."

Curvis started to ask how he knew and who next, but caught himself in time. "You want another drink?" he asked instead, receiving no answer at all. Danivon was sitting there, head down, nose twitching, smelling something, his eyes half-closed.

Sometimes when he got into these moods, he didn't move for hours. "Shit," said Curvis softly as he went off into the crowded room to find himself some amusement.

Danivon, left behind, was wondering the very things Curvis had been wondering, why and why. What might have happened had he been a different child, a different youth? If he hadn't so early gained a reputation for helpfulness, for example. He'd done that since he was just a kid, shown up when someone needed a hand. Sometimes even before the helpee even knew it, here'd be Danivon, grinning all over his face, explaining, "I smelled you needed somebody."

It was true, though no one had believed it at first, not even Zasper. At first everyone thought it was some kind of joke, that someone had put him up to it. Later they learned he really did smell such things. At least, he received information in a way that seemed to him like a smell, whatever it may actually have been, not reliably always, but often enough to be useful. He smelled people needing help; he smelled difficulties that wouldn't come unraveled; he smelled women lusting after him—or after other people; he smelled solutions to problems; he smelled people who could do things together they could not, or at least did not, do separately.

He smelled hatred and lust. He could sniff a crowd and tell whether it would become a mob or merely a purposeless pack that would get bored and break up. And though he could never explain what his talent really was or how it worked, Danivon's nose had become very valuable to Council Supervisory. He had done lots of things for Council Supervisory, though doing their work had sometimes bothered him a lot—though he never let it show. Bothered him, but it had never frightened him until now.

Why now? Why this smell of trouble? Why this stench of darkness? Why these smoky twinings and luminous blotches, always seeming about to resolve into faces, never quite doing so? Why? Not a dream. He couldn't remember any such light, any such darkness. A threat, yes, but more than merely a threat. Fear, heart-stopping fear, the nightmare kind he sometimes woke from almost screaming, heart hammering! He heard cries, pleading, as though through some linkage with some other place, an echo of a sound. The stink of sweat, somebody's sweat, somebody scared and running.

Not precisely the most hopeful signs and portents with which to start a journey. And why the strange twins from the past? Why Fringe? He might have added her, anyhow, just for the way she looked, the sidelong glance she gave him, the light flickering deep in her eyes, the way she walked and spoke, as though carelessly, but with that tension in the tilt of her head, as though she were waiting for something to happen. Yes, he might have wanted Fringe just for herself, but adding her, adding each of them satisfied that sense within him he called smelling, a kind of rightness, an unquestionability. It didn't change the overall aroma any. That was still there. Fear stink. Fear all the way down into wherever fear takes root.

Which was really beside the point. There had been no good way to duck the assignment. Boarmus had said go, and he was going. No threat, Danivon had said to Fringe. No threat. That had been pretty much a lie. He didn't even believe that himself!

Tourists from categories eight, nine, and ten often came to the Swale. *Tour down, trade up* was the policy established by the Supervisors, which meant one usually traveled to and imported from places more primitive than one's own. While some argued that "primitive" wasn't the right word at all, the fact was that most tourists in the Swale came for the thrill of danger, came hoping to see someone killed, or maybe to kill somebody. In Enarae, tourists were of no more importance than any scruffy Trasher or Outcaste, so inevitably some of them ended up getting killed instead.

Though Fringe had long considered the Swale her natural environment, she could not deny its essential quality. Shrines to the Guntoter were ubiquitous. Every recess could and often did hide a thrill seeker. Aware of this, knowing she was on a stage with no cover, she always took a moment at the corner to adjust her boots, check her weapons belt, and see to the fastenings of her clothes. Behind the peepholes could be a thousand eyes, a thousand stares, each fixing her in place like a bug on a pin, booby-trapping the short flight of steps and the few yards of slimy street between her and Bloom's place. It might be real. It might be a game. How was she to get from *here* to *there* while surviving that lethal barrage of eyes!

Confronted by such obstacles, fancied or real, one didn't wiffle around! She polished her Enforcer's badge with the ball of her left thumb, took a deep breath, and went where she chose to go, all in a rush, down the steps and across the dangerous street to take shelter in the entryway of Bloom's place. Keeping in practice, she told herself, relishing the surge of fear that had accompanied the self-induced panic, knowing it would have been easier but far less exciting to have come in the back way. Safety was for children. So said all Enforcers worth their pay.

Inside, Bloom bustled up to greet her, extending his legs and kissing her on the cheek, which she resignedly permitted. Bloom would do it when he liked, with fine disregard for sex or age or present affectional situations. Though Zasper had never presumed to kiss her at all, much less in public, Bloom had been kissing her since she was twelve; he wasn't likely to stop now.

"Owldark," he murmured. "Too long, lady love. What've you been up to, Fringy?"

"This and that," she said in the offhanded Enforcer's manner that made no admissions of involvement in anything specific. "Here and there." The hall swarmed with life and noise and was thick with smells: food and drink; sweat and drugs; boxes, bales, and baskets of exotic stuff from a dozen other provinces, brought here as barter. Her nose wrinkled and she sneezed.

The Bloom made a face at her and shortened his legs, yelling at her on the way down. "There's a man here from Gaunt's showing the new gimmicks. They've modified the Finalizer seven-aught-nine, would you believe? Twice the kill power with half the weight. Want to see him?"

She shook her head, making a face at him.

"No? Looking for work?"

Fringe preferred to get her contracts at the Enforcement Post, where things were more predictable than at Bloom's. Not that he was unethical, just that he was casual about contract terms—little things like dates of completion, and acceptable solutions, and getting paid. She grinned and shook her head again.

"Not that either? How about a game? Want a table?"

"No weapon, no job, no game, Bloom. I'm looking for Zasper. He been around?"

"Here now," admitted the Bloom with a shrug. "Doing badly and welcoming interruption, I'd say."

"Where?"

He jerked his head back, indicating the balcony stairs halfway across the room behind him, then shot high on his legs to watch her snake off through the heaving crowd.

She wove her way among the revelers: Enaraenians, Sandylwaithians, a few Supervisors pretending to be something else, Denialites, pretending to disapprove of what they were doing, scattered parts of some City Fifteen dinka-jins visiting the Swale to experience reality. Dink eyes darted about, peering; dink noses slunk, smelling. The modulator boxes had to be across the room somewhere, along with the arms and legs and other parts. She didn't bother looking for them. Assembled or disassembled, dinks were not her favorite thing.

Upstairs, she found Zasper in the gambling room nearest the street. Wet river light fell on one side of his face as he glared across the table at a player with his back to her, glared until he saw her, then growlingly excused himself and came out, his face split into a welcoming grin. A strong old hand crushed her shoulder, and she accepted the familiar pain impassively. He led her to a small table near the balcony railing, overlooking the organized chaos below.

Fringe, who disliked crowds, kept her eyes on Zasper. Though he'd retired from provincial Enforcement a few years back, he still wore his gray hair in the long braid, still looked meaner than a scorched chaffer, still wore his badge with the fatal-hands dangles—on his left shoulder to show he wasn't active. Retired or not, he hadn't stopped being her friend. He knew her better than anyone.

"Heard your pa died," he grunted now.

She gave him a look. If he'd heard that, he'd heard the rest of it, as well.

"Too bad." He knew how she felt, how she'd always felt. There'd been times he'd known that better than she did.

She shrugged. "Not why I'm here, Zasper."

He raised an eyebrow. She leaned forward and told him about Danivon's offer. "Yesterday this happened," she said. "I've been thinking about it overnight. You give him my name, Zasper?"

"Well, I knew him when I was at Tolerance," he admitted, choosing to admit no more than that. "Some call him a wonder boy with fireworks for blood."

"But not burned out yet," she murmured. Oh, no, Enforcer Luze was far from burnt out!

"No, not so far's I know. 'Course, he was only a kid when I left there, but friends from Tolerance tell me he's fatal hands with bells on. He gets results."

"Flaming ego?"

"No. Not that I've heard. Not one to walk over bodies in spiked boots. No more than any of us."

Sometimes walking over bodies was part of the job. Not all Enforcers worked for the Council, but no Enforcer could work against it, such was the rule of the Craft. Adam-the-man could hire any Enforcer he liked to protect him against all threats except those posed by Council Enforcers. If CEs came looking for him, other Enforcers stood aside. When a CE lifted his hand in salute and recited a complaint and disposition number to confirm he was Attending the Situation, other Enforcers were expected to remember pressing business elsewhere. Sometimes afterward there were bodies to walk over.

"I've heard whispers about that Panubi dragon business," said Zasper. "Interesting. What do they offer?"

Fringe told him and he whistled between his teeth. "Couldn't do much better than Council Enforcer and twice standard! Plus an annuity."

She snorted. "If I survive."

"There's always that."

Down on the floor below, Bloom was shrieking at a croupier, his truncated form erupting out of the swarm like a jumping fish from roiling water. Strictly speaking, Bloom's legs were not category seven. He'd imported them from some nine or ten province in defiance of the ban against higher category imports, but nobody in authority seemed to care.

Fringe touched the service button and a voice said, "Yah?"

"Black ale," Fringe muttered. "Two."

Black ale had been what Zasper offered her when she had come begging his sponsorship at the Academy. It had been what she offered him the day she graduated, after he pinned the Enforcer's badge on her shoulder. It was part of their relationship. She turned half away from the hubbub below and said musingly, "There's this giant goes around with Danivon Luze, you seen him?"

Zasper nodded. "Curvis. I know him. Sometimes a little . . . rigid. Mostly reliable."

"He said Luze smells out who he's going to work with."

"That's what I've heard." Zasper grinned to himself. "Smells out all sorts of things, like who's bluffing and who's not."

She waited, but he offered nothing more.

"You're not saying much, Zas! I come to you for help, and you don't say pollywhop. Just sit there smirking."

Two sealed pods slid onto the table from the service hatch, popping lids and extruding handles as they arrived.

He shrugged and went on smiling. "What's to say, girl? Tell you to send him packing and stay safe here? Tell you to go for the prize? Tell you you're Fringe Owldark, all grown-up, got to make up your own mind? What?"

"Well, hell, something, Zasper!" She put her nose to her mug and drank. "Did I ever tell you how I got the name Owldark?"

He cocked his head. "Thought you made it up."

Grinning, she told him about the time Jory had named her. "Did you ever catch sight of her, Zasper? I used to tell you about her. She told me I was one of *her* people. I keep expecting her to show up again, but she never has."

He frowned, finding the story ominous without being able to say why. "Sure she was a woman?"

"Looked like a woman. She had something with her, though, something that could have been a glob. Something shadowy. Maybe that's what reminded me of her. What Danivon said. Monsters in the shadows, nobody knows what they are. He says the Gods may be here on Elsewhere."

"That scares you?"

"You know it does!" She swallowed painfully, shuddering a little. "Having those things eating your soul, doesn't it scare you?"

Zasper waved that away with one hand. "Every few years, somebody says the Gods are here on Elsewhere. Whether they are or not makes no difference to what you're going to do, does it? Want me to tell you again what your trouble is, you don't trust who you are. Hell, you know that already! How many times we talked about that? All the time second-guessing yourself. Remember the story I used to tell you? The one about the warrior maid and the gylphs?"

"I remember," she said, making a face. Zasper had dwelt on that story overlong and overoften. Poor weighted-down heavy-armored warrior, envying the magical gylphs their power of flight, not satisfied to be herself but not willing to take off her protective armor, either.

"You've always told me you thought you were born for something special," he said, raising his voice to be heard over the whoops of laughter from below. "And either that's true or it isn't. If it's true, likely you'll find out when something like this comes along. If you duck it when it comes, what does that mean?"

Fringe diddled, drawing pictures on the tabletop with one wet forefinger. "I'm not ducking, Zasper. I don't mind the thought of dragons, not if that's what they are. The idea of Gods scares me spitless. When I hear there's a possibility of that, I sort of shrivel. Like there's no hope, no reason to go on."

She looked at Zasper to see if he understood what she was saying. "But even if I'm scared, I swore to protect diversity and humanity, and the only diversity and humanity that's left is right here on Elsewhere. I believe in it. It makes more sense than anything else I was ever taught, so I can't just let them come on and take us over if maybe we could stop it. And besides, it may not be the Gods at all. I have to go, I guess. It's just Danivon . . . he's . . ."

"I know what he is. He cuts a swath through the girlies. Pulls like a magnet. Gets at you, huh!"

She gave Zasper a look. None of his business, dirty old man. Except he was the pa hers hadn't been, the brother hers hadn't been, somebody who listened. "Yeah," she admitted. "Sort of."

"So, tell him. You'll go, but keep it business because sex disrupts your efficiency. Drops your weapon scores. Makes you miss easy targets."

Damn him, he was laughing at her. "It does not!" she blurted. "You know that's not it!"

Now he really was laughing. "Fringe! What the hell you want me to say?"

She shook her head, half amused, half tearful. "I don't know, Zasper. Maybe I'm afraid I'll be homesick." Her clean bare rooms. Her things. Comfort. Safety. A place where she could lock the door against the clamoring world.

"You going?" he asked her.

"Prob'ly," she admitted.

"Well then. Something I want to tell you about." He leaned forward, his lips within inches of her ear, and told the story of his last interview with Boarmus, concluding, "Danivon say anything about those petition things?"

"Not to me, he didn't."

"Well, my bet is Boarmus told him. Just figured you ought to know. Dragons probably aren't all he's after."

She thought about it, but it made no sense. "Who's petitioning who?"

Zasper shrugged. "You know what I know. R.S.V.P. Noplace. That's all I know."

She decided to change the subject. "The Bloom says they've improved the Finalizer seven-aught-nine."

He grunted. "That's his opinion. It's lighter, faster, and you can hit what you aim it at maybe one time in ten if you're real careful. I borrowed one from Gaunt's man, just to test-fire it. Fool thing's all over the place. Real good weapon for nipping, Fringe."

Nipping, the more-or-less accidental slaughter of Non-Involved Persons, wasn't considered professional when done by Enforcers, though Trashers did it all the time. Fringe said disapprovingly, "Then the Bloom shouldn't have said it was improved!"

The Bloom, as though invoked by the mention of his name, appeared at tableside, still bouncing up and down. "Hey, lady love, this old fart bothering you?"

She shook her head, trying to grin. "No more'n usual, Bloom."

"If he is, I'll call him out. Two shots, fifty paces. Make him pay, worthless old chaffer."

"Yeah, I've heard about you and fifty paces," rumbled Zasper. "You get up-sun of the guy, and before he gets a shot, you zoom your legs and let him have it out of the glare. You shoot dirty."

"Dirty takes the pot! Which is better'n you've been doing," Bloom said severely.

While Zasper had never admitted to it, Fringe assumed that since his retirement, Zasper played for Bloom's. Zasper's response seemed to confirm that.

"Chaffer spit, yes. Got to recoup," he said, struggling to his feet. "Listen, girl. I'll finish this game sooner or later. Prob'ly sooner, since I've already shot my credit." He cast a sidelong glance at the Bloom. "I'll buy you dinner. We'll talk about it."

"That's all right, Zasper," she said. "I knew what I was going to do before I came down here, that is, if you didn't say I was crazy. When Enforcers swear to protect diversity and humanity, they can't turn down the protecting when it comes along, I guess. And only a fool would turn down a chance at twice Council standard!"

"Twice Council standard!" said Bloom reverently. "Now there's a dream."

"Maybe more than a dream," she said. "Maybe more than, Bloom."
She left them, going back down the stairs and through the crowd where
the dinks still swarmed. At least they'd left their genitals home, or were
carrying them in closed boxes. Fringe had never gotten used to penises
zipping around on their own hovers, rubbing up against anything that
felt good. Female parts were even worse, cozying up to the nearest hands.
She looked around for dink modulator units and found three of them
over by a gambling table with three sets of hands and one pair of eyes,
playing Four Ladies.

A dink nose sniffed intimately at her as she went by, and she slapped
it without thinking. From across the room, a dink voice box screeched,
"Violence! Violence!"

"Kill the damn thing," a bystander urged her with barely controlled
belligerence. "Kill it, Enforcer."

"Open borders," screamed the voice box in a hysterical soprano. "Open
borders."

Fringe shrugged an apology. The voice was right. Enarae had open
borders. It welcomed tourism. Even dinks, who, thank the 'Toter, seldom showed up anywhere but in the Swale.

A voice spoke in her ear, "What's the matter, killer? You don't like
dinks?" Another dink voice box, this one a sneery baritone, with an eye
on top and an ear at one side. A conversation module, no less.

"No," she said. "I don't like dink noses sniffing my crotch. I don't
like dink eyes looking down my neck, or at my cards when I've got a
bet down. I don't like dink hands grabbing anything they can grab or
dink pricks shoving up against me. Open borders means open both ways,
box! You don't like my not liking, then the border's open to get out."

"Now, now," said Bloom, appearing at eye level. "Now, now, bad
Fringe! Bad box! Naughty. Play nice or Bloom will insist upon assembly." He waved at the sign over the bar, which read, "Bloom reserves
the right to refuse service to globs and disassembled entities."

Fringe muttered an apology, while the voice growled something
threatening. Ignoring the sulky mutter, she went out into the street.
Empty, as always, except for a meat-tart vendor who'd parked his smoky
cart fifty paces away at the bottom of the stairs and was stirring his kettle
of hot fat with a long slotted spoon. The smells of woodsmoke and frying
meat filled the street. Fringe swallowed, suddenly ravenous.

She had juice dripping from her chin and her hands full of hot food when Bloom's door crashed open and one of the dinks came out, evidently hastily assembled, though all its interlocking parts were arranged more or less in anatomical order.

"Hey, girly!" it yelled in its sneery baritone. "Hey, Enforcer!"

Still chewing a mouthful of succulent meat and pastry, Fringe turned slowly to confront the aggregation. Its left arm had been disassembled, probably for parts, leaving only a forearm and hand unit, but the muscular right arm was complete, including a shoulder cantilevered from the modulator core. The assembly had a weapons belt strapped around it, hanging low on one side. Fringe choked on a bit of crust. It looked like a caricature of the Guntoter icon. Like an animated costume rack in some ancient predispersion gunfighter myth. Fringe had seen them all as re-created by the Files. When she was about ten she'd watched nothing but gunfighter re-creations for days at a time. She swallowed the laugh that came bubbling up, reminding herself survivors didn't laugh at challenges, no matter who they came from.

A long time back, you might have laughed at some idiot carrying a weapon because you knew he had no skill. Then technology superseded skill, and the weapon itself did the killing. The one the dink was carrying was a case in point, a broad-beam aitchem that could do her serious damage if merely discharged in her general direction. Fringe had only a pain needler on her belt. In skilled hands that would ordinarily have been quite enough. Unfortunately, most dinks had been disconnected from pain. The worst she could do was make it itch, which the dink damned well knew.

Bloom's doorway was full of dink eyes, watching, dink ears, quivering.

"Are you provoking a fight, dink?" Fringe called curiously. "That what you want?"

"Damn right," yelled the dink, its hand jerking up and down near the weapon.

Fringe dropped the remains of the tart and herself to the street, rolled sideways with her legs curled under her, came up with her right hand full of the weapon she had been carrying in her right boot, and shot the dink assembly through the modulator, upper left corner, where the brain can usually was. Her boot weapon was always loaded with explosive slugs. Shreds of the dink flew in all directions while what remained sizzled, smoked, and fell apart into disparate boxes, some of which trembled for a time while the voice went "Gaaaaaahhhhhh," in a terrified and dying wail.

The dinks who'd been watching disappeared inside Bloom's place like snakes down a hole.

"For a dink to provoke a fight with an Enforcer is not a smart thing," she remarked to nobody in particular, the monitor, maybe, if the stupid thing was listening. "Which information should be disseminated to every cocky box as it arrives." She walked forward and blew the dink's weapon apart with another ear-shattering jolt. No point leaving it around for some crazy to maim thirty noninvolved pedestrians with.

Bloom's door had closed abruptly, but something moved at the upstairs window. She brought up the weapon, but it was only Zasper, waving. He'd been watching the whole thing. She waved in return. Bloom's door opened, and a salvage machine with a Guntoter icon on its snout came out to suck up the shreds of the dink. Fringe walked back to the food cart and told the recumbent vendor to get up off the street and give her another tart to replace the one she'd rolled on. She took it from his trembling hand and climbed the stairs to the corner, leaving the Swale.

Behind her, in the window of Bloom's place, Zasper turned to the man beside him, the player who'd been winning steadily.

"She killed it," Zasper said.

"Thought she would," said Danivon Luze, his fingers stroking the medallion at his neck. "No hesitation at all."

"Were you expecting hesitation?"

"I was expecting something," said Danivon Luze in an unsatisfied voice. "Something I smell about her. Something sort of . . . uncertain."

"There's nothing uncertain about Fringe's skills," said Zasper stiffly. "I told you she was good and I meant it. Any uncertainty has to do with other things. Wouldn't want you to mistake that, Danny! You sure she's the right one to go along?"

"Oh, yeah, she's the right one. One of the right ones."

"You didn't tell her about the petitions, but I bet Boarmus told you!"

"Haven't told anybody. Not even Curvis. I will, when it seems appropriate."

"I told her."

"Well, damn, Zasper."

"She's a friend of mine, Dan."

"So?"

"You know. Treat her like a friend."

"Do my best," said Danivon, flushing, not sure what his best might be in this context.

"What is it you're smelling, Danivon Luze?"

"Oh, I don't know. Everybody talking about dragons and petitions and possesseds, scared of all of 'em, scared of anything new because it might mean changes. Of course, expecting Council Supervisory to welcome change is like expecting a chaffer to fly. 'Change' is a naughty word on Elsewhere. We all know that."

Zasper stared in the direction Fringe had gone and nodded, well aware that everyone did, indeed, know that.

In Tolerance, Jacent was attending his first committee meeting.

Business before Council Supervisory, Complaint and Disposition Review Committee A., Day 26, Period 10, Year 1353 P.S. (Post Settlement)

AUTHORITY: Articles of Organization, Council Supervisory of Elsewhere, Rule Number 53, Paragraph M, Section xiii. *"All dispositions entered by C&D machines shall be reviewed by Council members (human) before implementation."*

AGENDA
COMPLAINT AND DISPOSITION
Items one through one hundred fifty-nine
of this date.

ITEM 1: Complaint by the brotherhood of dinka-jins, City Fifteen (category ten); one of their members wantonly killed while traveling in Enarae.

DISPOSITION: Official warning to brotherhood of dinka-jins that members travel at their own risk. Enarae is category seven, confrontational, weapons-using society, and killing is not untypical of that province.

No penalty.

"Aye," said the members of the committee.

> *ITEM 2: Complaint by the brotherhood of dinka-jins, City Fifteen; citizen of Enarae found using category-nine bionic prostheses in category-seven province.*
>
> *DISPOSITION:* Complaint denied as not meeting criteria for legal standing. Only Enaraen citizens may complain about internal matters.

No penalty.

"Aye," said the committee again, as with one voice.

> *ITEM 3: Complaint by the brotherhood of dinka-jins, City Fifteen; citizen of Enarae guilty of importing category-nine prostheses across borders into category-seven place in defiance of ban against higher category imports.*
>
> *DISPOSITION:* Standing affirmed. Any citizen may complain of categorical border violations.
>
> > Probability illegal importation across open border: .967.
> > Penalty assessed, Enarae. Fine of cr. 1,000.
> > Probability illegal importation perpetrated by category-ten dinka-jin tourist in return for gambling credit: .978.
> > Penalty assessed, City Fifteen. Fine of cr. 1,000.

"Aye," said the committee, a few of them smiling slightly. C&D machines sometimes seemed capable of a sly humor.

> *ITEM 4: Complaint by High Priest, closed-border province of Molock on Panubi. Inhabitants avoiding child sacrifice by escaping via riverboats trading in foodstuffs with neighboring provinces.*
>
> *DISPOSITION:* Enforcer will investigate and will if necessary assess penalty against riverboat owners or workers or provinces involved. Enforcer will reaffirm to persons in

Molock that inhabitants of closed-border provinces have no rights of escape.

"Aye," the committee muttered.

Jacent looked out the window, his mouth moving but making no sound, full of an obscure discomfort. A quick look at the faces around the table showed them unchanged. Obviously, the other members felt the matter of Molock was merely routine.

"Diversity," Aunt Syrilla had preached at him. "We neither approve nor disapprove of individual provinces, Jacent. Some of them are, no doubt, quite distasteful, but our interest is higher than approval or disapproval. Even provinces that murder their own children are accorded favorable recognition by us, and in so doing, we continue a chain of diplomacy that has come unbroken from remotest times on Earth itself. We assure the diversity of humanity. No one system has within it all answers to all human needs. So much we know from history. The task set before us is to answer the Great Question of man's destiny, and from diversity the answer will emerge. So we are taught. So I believe. Only here, on Elsewhere, does diversity exist, and our lives, yours and mine, are given to assuring its continuance."

Her tone had been one of aunty concern and lofty assurance. The Great Question and the value of diversity had been drummed into him since childhood, so he'd agreed with her. Of course he'd agreed with her; what member of Council Supervisory could disagree? But still, when one heard the words "child sacrifice," it did make one pause. He looked around the table again. No one else had even blinked. Well, he would undoubtedly get used to it.

ITEM 5: Complaint by hemi-province Salt Maresh that hemi-province Choire is overbreeding in order to obtain a few very fine voices, thereby burdening Salt Maresh with supernumerary children, including many who can carry a tune.

DISPOSITION: Council will suggest to Salt Maresh that it (1) refuse acceptance of children; or (2) that it petition Council for full provincial status, thereby abrogating its agreements with Choire and insuring the integrity of its borders; or (3) that it request Enforcer review of Salt Maresh/

Choire mutuality agreements together with whatever solution Enforcer thinks most suitable.

"Like what?" Jacent whispered to his neighbor, a much older, plumper
individual who assented to each disposition in a subdued monotone. Jacent, who had spent the previous year monitoring the C&D machines,
had only recently been appointed to this, his first assignment by Council, and was still unfamiliar with it. "What would an Enforcer think suitable?" he asked.

"Oh, he might decide on a small plague in Choire that would reduce
their population to the point they'd need all their children, or maybe a
small plague in Salt Maresh to do likewise, or he might decide on a fine
against Choire for every child sent to Salt Maresh who isn't tone-deaf.
There's lots of possibilities." Jacent's neighbor scratched his nose. "I'd
say the likelihood in this case is a fine, since there's no real abrogation
of contract to get nasty about. You've watched the machines for a while,
haven't you? You've learned then that before the machines make a disposition, they consider every precedent we've accumulated for hundreds
of years. We very, very seldom overrule the machines."

Jacent put his hand over his mouth to keep from yawning.

His neighbor looked at him sympathetically. "I know. By the time
we get to item number fifty, it'll really get boring."

> *ITEM 6: Complaint by citizens of New Athens that a tyrant has
> gained power and is depriving citizens of basic human rights and
> freedoms.*
>
> *DISPOSITION:* Constitution of New Athens (q.v., ap-
> pended) assures all citizens basic human rights and free-
> doms. Enforcers dispatched to Attend to tyrant and
> supporters.

"Aye," murmured the committee with some satisfaction. Later they
would see the recorded consequence of this vote. Some such assassinations made rather exciting viewing.

> *ITEM 7: Complaint by citizens of Derbeck that torture and exe-
> cutions by chimi-hounds of suspected malcontents has reached
> unconscionable numbers.*

DISPOSITION: Derbeck is a theocracy based on religious and political orthodoxy. Arbitrary executions and torture are integral to such systems.

No penalty.

"Aye," said Jacent, yawning once again behind his hand.

ITEM 8: Complaint by a citizen of Denial . . .

"So, what've you decided?" asked Danivon Luze. He was sitting on one of Fringe's fishbone chairs, staring at the object on the nearest stone pedestal.

She shrugged, as though she hadn't made up her mind.

He sighed, shaking his head at her lack of decisiveness. "Don't wiffle around," he said, surprising her. "What's that thing?" He was pointing at the pedestal.

"A shell," she replied.

"It isn't pretty," Danivon commented.

"No," Fringe admitted. The thing wasn't pretty. It was the shell of a turtle, one of the Earthian animals man had carried with him throughout all his generations. Fringe had found the shell at the top of a very tall tree on one of the Seldom Isles. Turtles did not climb trees, and yet the shell had been there, sun-faded and empty.

"Why do you keep it?" Danivon asked.

Fringe shrugged. He might have read her Book, but that gave him no right to her thoughts. The shell meant mystery. Wonder. How had it come where she had found it? It was like herself, a strangeness, and none of his damned business.

"And this thing?" Danivon said, stroking a curved element at the top of another pedestal. It was one of the machines she made as a hobby, now in sunlight and therefore in motion. It shivered and glittered as it carried tiny beads of light from its base to its tip, dropping them into nothingness, over and over again.

"Just something I made," she said.

"Why?" he asked. "What's it good for?"

She shrugged again. It was good for just being what it was, and if he couldn't see that, to hell with him.

He'd been staring at the stuff in her room ever since he arrived. As though it held some kind of message. Some kind of code, maybe. She was becoming fairly annoyed with him.

"So, when are you going to decide?" he asked.

"I've decided," said Fringe, thankful he'd stopped looking and started talking. "I'm still a little ambivalent. Partly because you didn't tell me everything. I'm a good Enforcer and I like being trusted. You should have told me about the petition things."

"Zasper told you!"

"He did, but you should have. Despite that, I've decided to go, provided the terms of the contract are recorded and approved."

"They are." He smiled at her, an invitational smile.

"When, then?" She ignored the invitation.

"I guess in a couple days." He sighed. "I'm like you. Ambivalent. I've been fooling around, thinking there should be somebody else going with us, thinking someone might show up. Well, maybe there's someone else, but not here. Not anywhere near. Not that I can get a sniff of."

"Maybe on the way," she suggested.

"Likely," he assented with a gloomy face, glancing at her from the corners of his eyes. The woman was like a good bow, all shiny curves and elegant tensions, making his hands itch to stroke her, bend her. There weren't all that many women Danivon lusted after, not that many he enjoyed, but those he enjoyed seemed to enjoy him too, so it wasn't as though he expected some one-sided thing she'd come to regret. But this Fringe Owldark gave him not so much as a twinkly look, not she! She was all quiet-faced business and no joy. Still, he couldn't misread that tilt to the head, that glance, that tension. . . . Could he?

She, meantime, was thinking that even gloomy the man set off drums inside her. *Tumty-tumty-tum*. Rotten little drums, making her feet twitch as though they wanted to dance, so she'd let them and find herself danced right over some precipice. Enough of that, Fringe Owldark.

"So, who do we start with?" she asked in her calmest voice.

"Five of us. You, me, Curvis, and two people from the past. Their names are Nela and Bertran Zy-Czorsky, and they're joined people."

"What the hell is that? And what do you mean, the past?"

He described Bertran and Nela, their oddity, their odyssey, making it dramatic for her amusement. Though who knew what would amuse this one!

Fringe succeeded in visualizing this unlikely concatenation only with some revulsion. "They're going to get parts cloned and be unjoined before we start out, I hope!" she said with fervor.

He shook his head. "Takes too long. Later. When we get back. Disconnecting them's the price I offered them, like I offered you twice standard. None of you get paid up front."

"Then I sincerely hope there's no danger where we're going, Danivon Luze, for these folk sound like a real handicap to me."

"There's that," he admitted. "Nonetheless. . . ." He stroked the medallion at his neck.

"Your nose says not."

He smiled, surprised. "My nose says not."

The motion of his fingers drew her eyes to the medallion around his neck.

"What are the plans so far?" she asked in a practical voice, staring at the thing he was stroking. Talk of dragons! He was wearing one around his neck, a toothy monster ridden by a robed figure. Man or woman, she couldn't tell.

"We fly to Tolerance. Bring your ceremonials along because you'll need them for your initiation as a CE."

"Oh, shit," she groaned, half under her breath.

"Can't serve as a Council Enforcer without being initiated," he said firmly. "It isn't done."

She grimaced, throwing up her hands. She hadn't thought about the initiation as Council Enforcer. Damn. She hated that. Attending solemnities was the worst thing about being an Enforcer, even though it was only a semiannual obligation. She liked parade, that was fun, but ritual made her teeth itch, her legs twitch.

Danivon went on, "From Tolerance, we go to the Curward Isles, and from there to Panubi by boat. We could fly, but the twins need to learn the local language, and that'll give them time to pick up a smattering. Then once we get to Panubi, we'll go upstream by riverboat, taking care of routine items as we go."

"What do we travel as? Enforcers? Traders? Explorers? What?"

"Now it's interesting you should ask that question," he said thoughtfully. "Boarmus says we're not the first to go looking around Panubi. Enforcer types have gone there before. I thought it might be better if we didn't make a big thing out of being Council Enforcers, at least not when we got near the unexplored parts, and when I mentioned it to the Zy-Czorsky twins, they suggested we travel as a sideshow."

"As a what?"

Danivon attempted to explain a sideshow, fumbling for a concept that he only partially understood. Eventually she got the idea. telling herself that the rest of the party were freakish enough, though how she herself would fit into such a pattern eluded her. When Danivon eventually took himself off, saying he'd return on the morrow, she still hadn't figured out how she'd fit into a troupe of oddities.

Her best talent was with weapons, but knife throwing or target shooting would call attention to her Enforcer training. Unarmed combat was likewise out. It had to be something else, something that would appeal to the ignorance and superstition rife in low-category places, but not anything overtly violent.

A late-afternoon sunbeam fell through the tall windows to bring one of her machines to life. Bright bits rose to the top, plunged down, disappeared, only to appear again, rising. The movement was relaxingly repetitive, yet irregular enough to be enjoyably unpredictable. The sporadic rise and fall had been inspired by Bloom's legs, except that Bloom's legs carried Bloom, while Fringe's machine carried nothing but random sparkles.

Of course, she could make it carry something, if she wanted it to. Something like . . . omens, maybe. She sat staring and planning for some time as the sun dropped lower, her eyes fixed on the silent gyrations of her devices. When the light went at last, she nodded to herself and went into her secured room to get her tools.

When Danivon returned the following morning, he found her working on a skeletal array, a bony assemblage of rods and tracks and bright bits of moving mirror reflecting shards of lasered light.

"What in the devil?"

"Tell your destiny, Danivon?"

"My what?"

"Tell your destiny?"

He gave her a questioning look. "I suppose."

She beckoned him to sit where she was sitting. Before him sprouted a forest of little levers, some gemmed, some plain, some colored, some black, variously shaped.

"Pick some at random," she told him. "Any of them."

He pressed some half dozen, mostly blue ones. The machine made questioning sounds, hummed, glittered at him as though it were looking him over. Light flickered into his eyes and away, quick mirrored glances.

Bells rang, singly and in harmonic series. Small bright capsules plunged down, while others spun off into remote parts of the maze. A capsule was retrieved from some distant siding, edged nearer in repeated orbits, then dropped into a bin before him where it was joined eventually by another and yet another. The machine tinkled and became quiet.

"Now what," he asked.

"See what they say," she suggested, turning a capsule so he could see the word written on it.

"Journey," said one. "Ancient," said another. "Danger," said a third.

"We journey into ancient danger," she intoned portentously. "But then, we knew that."

His mouth dropped open. He closed it with a snap. "You had it set for that message! How random is it?"

"It won't repeat itself, if that's what you mean. Not if I put each word in the pot only once. The capsules aren't all shaped alike. Actions fit on one track, descriptives on another, entities on a third. It'll deliver from three to five words, assorted." She pressed a key, dumping the capsules back into the machine's innards. "This one is only a sample. It isn't nearly complicated enough. To be properly impressive, it will have to be more complex, with more noises and movement to it."

"What do the levers have to do with it?"

"Not much," she admitted. "They all press the same start bar. I'll change that on the final model. Make different levers start it at different places."

He laughed, his eyes squinting shut in amusement. "What do we call it?" he asked. "What's our hype?"

"Hype?"

"That's what the twins say we need. Hype. They tell me hype is the message that evokes wonder or desire in the observer. Excited words. Loaded language. Hype. Evidently many activities in their time depended upon hype."

Fringe considered what would make the device seem more marvelous. "We can say it's ancient," she offered. "People are always fascinated by ancient things. We say it was discovered in some uninhabited place. Desolations are intriguing too. Maybe we'll say something about the mysterious creators of the machine and how they vanished. We'll call it the Destiny Machine. . . ." She paused, thinking. "Oh, I know! We can pretend the Arbai invented it."

"Make it look corroded like the Arbai Door, then."

"I've never seen the Arbai Door."

He described the convolutions and corrosions of the Door while she nodded thoughtfully. When he had finished, he took in her intent expression and laughed. "Fringe Owldark. I didn't expect it of you. I marked you as lacking imagination."

She flushed, angry at him. "I have as much as I need, Danivon Luze. Isn't it the kind of thing you wanted?"

"Oh, yes. It's quite marvelous. Finish it. Tell me what you need, if anything. You'll have to have some kind of traveling crate for it. We're leaving in two days' time." He stood smiling at her, obviously enjoying what he was looking at.

She flushed again, at first in embarrassment, then in annoyance at his smile. It knew too much. It belonged to one who had read her Book. Who had transgressed upon her privacy. "Well then," she said in an angry voice, "let me get on with it."

"It's almost mealtime," he wheedled. "You must have a favorite eating place. Let's go there."

She shook her head, still peevish. "No. I should get this thing mostly finished before we go, though I can add the final bits and pieces on the way. Besides, I'm not hungry." Her palms were wet, and she wiped them on her trousers, a gesture of rejection. "We'll have plenty of time for lunches in Tolerance."

He flushed. "No. Sorry. I've received orders. . . ."

"Orders?"

"I'm not to return to Tolerance. For some reason old Boarmus wants me to stay clear of the place. He's invented a job for me in Denial. Curvis will go with you to Tolerance, and I'll meet you two and the twins in the Curward Isles."

She stared at him in bewilderment. Why should Danivon be warned away from Tolerance? Him, a Council Enforcer? She didn't ask that question, but instead, "Why do I have to go to Tolerance at all then?"

"Don't you want to be initiated as a Council Enforcer?" he asked.

"Is it required?" she demanded.

"Well . . . not strictly, no."

"Then I don't."

"It's a nice ceremony, very impressive ritual."

"I don't like ceremony. I don't like ritual." She avoided either, whenever she could. They reminded her unpleasantly of other things, other times.

He shrugged. "Well, take your ceremonials anyhow. Boarmus will probably want to see you. He does that with all the Council people." He rummaged in a pocket and drew out a travel disc that he dropped on the table by the machine. "Here's your authorization. There'll be a CE flier at the northeast flight center, first watch, day after tomorrow."

She nodded, silently.

"You'll need help with your machine."

"I'm competent," she muttered. "I can manage."

"I was only offering. . . ."

"Not needed," she said, dismissing him, standing where she was until he had gone, until the door was shut behind him, until she could catch her breath.

"No," she said to no one in particular. "Absolutely not needed."

She did need help with the machine, but she got it from Ahl Dibai Bloom, who brought two craftsmen over and stayed most of the day. They came to help her finish the construction and build a traveling case, but they got so involved in playing with the gadget it was hours before they accomplished what they'd come for. When they were finished, the device was larger and vastly more complicated than the one Danivon had seen. Also Fringe had done what she could to make the machine look old and mysterious, with capsules that seemed truly oracular by virtue of their odd spellings and dim archaic lettering.

"I want one, Fringe!" Bloom demanded, chortling over his fortune—his eleventh or twelfth, all different. "I want a machine like this, a bigger one, for my place in the Swale."

"So, we'll build another one, Bloom," she said, dropping some newly lettered capsules into the supply box.

"When?"

"When I get back."

"And when will that be?"

"Your guess is as good as mine."

"I was afraid of that. Will you take care, lady love?"

"Always, Bloom. If you'll say good-bye to Zasper for me."

"I think he plans to do that for himself."

Zasper did plan to do that for himself, arriving at the flight center as the Destiny Machine was being loaded. He didn't come directly to the place Fringe was standing, but went off across the field to where Danivon was packing himself into another flier. Fringe noticed, to her amazement, that Zasper hugged him like kin. When he came back across the field, he greeted Curvis like an old friend before taking Fringe's hand and presenting a tiny box.

"What's this?" she asked suspiciously.

"A present," he said. "A nothing, Fringe. A keepsake."

She choked, felt herself getting red.

"No," he said firmly. "You're not to get angry and flustered at me. I want you to take it and wear it to remember me by. When you see it, you say, 'Zasper thought I was all right whatever I wanted to be. I didn't need to be anyone else for Zasper.' "

She felt tears.

"Promise you will?"

"Promise," she said softly.

"Fringe," he said as softly. "You know, a long time ago I told you about that boy I saved. It might be wise not to mention that on your way to . . . to wherever." His eyes flicked sideways, to the place Danivon's flier had been.

"Hell, Zasper. What do you take me for. Of course not." She said it, but her mind was elsewhere, putting together the hug, the glance, his obvious discomfort. So Danivon had been the little boy Zasper'd rescued. Well!

"Well then. Good luck, girl. Attend the Situation!" He saluted, turned himself about, and stalked away, back rigid, shoulders straight.

When she was in her cubicle aboard the flier, she opened the box. A circlet of gold and a chain. The circlet made up of the words "Just as she is."

It hurt. It hurt like that time Char had offered to sell the house. What she felt was something grabbing at her, something holding on to her. She knew it as pain, a pain she'd learned to avoid. She hung the circlet around her neck, buttoned her shirt over it, felt it burning against her skin, and tried to forget it was there.

Why couldn't he just have said good-bye?

The people of Tolerance were charming and hospitable and so mannered that Fringe felt they stuck to her like swamp slime. The place itched her. It dripped into her boots. Being here made her want to bathe, over and over, and she could not tell why. There was something severely amiss in Tolerance, though no one seemed to notice but her.

"Relax! We're only here for a day or so," said Curvis, giving her a curious look. "Are you always this jumpy?" They were returning from the Rotunda balcony where Fringe had moved the components of an excellent dinner around on her plate without eating any of them.

She twitched, flushing. "No. I'm not. I don't know what's the matter with me. If I were Danivon, I'd say I was smelling something very wrong."

Tolerance seemed no different to Curvis than it had always been. There was always a good deal of tension in the place. And then recently there'd been that case of dismemberment and disappearance, but that mystery would no doubt soon be solved. Some visitor gone mad, no doubt. It happened sometimes. Curvis had never been alert to nuance, so he had no inkling of what was bothering Fringe.

Nonetheless, he attempted reassurance. "Tolerance always has a kind of agitation about it, too many people in too small a space, monitoring, fussing, like that."

"Agitation alone wouldn't make me feel like this."

"Do the twins make you uncomfortable?"

She shook her head. It wasn't the twins. She had at first been in an agony of embarrassment over the twins, but it wasn't them. "They speak Lingua very well," she said lamely. Though learning to talk with such strange beings, even in Lingua, was a problem she had struggled with. "Though it's a little hard for me to figure them out."

Bertran and Nela had noted her discomfort. She had been obviously anxious to say the right thing or, at the least, to avoid saying the wrong one, and their first interchange had been marked by long silences and inconsequential mutters. After a time, however, she had devised a solution that suited her, for she began to act toward them as she might have done toward two totally independent persons. She stopped trying to make sense of their condition, stopped saying "you" to include them both, and began to address them as Nela and Bertran, speaking to them separately, as distinct people.

"As I was saying to Nela just a while ago," she would say to Bertran, ignoring that he must have heard. Or to Nela, "As I remarked to Bertran . . ." She had decided to pretend that only one of them was present at a time, though the time might be only momentary. After an hour or so of being amused at her, they adapted to her pretense, finding it novel if not entirely convincing.

Fringe, to her own amazement, became quite comfortable with them, more than she was with most people. When in company, she usually felt herself to be the anomaly. Compared to Bertran and Nela, she was ordinary. By the second day, she was becoming confidential with them, almost voluble.

"She belongs in a sideshow," Nela remarked to her twin. "Just as we did. You see how easy she is getting to be with us? Yet, see how she behaves with others, all flushes and starts, or silent as a rock. Gauche, Aunt Sizzy would have said. No poise, except when she is being professional."

"I don't understand," said Bertran, who had been thinking of something else.

"She thinks she's a freak," explained Nela softly. "Don't you see? No matter what person she is being, she feels others will judge it to be inadequate. So, she's constantly on the defensive. And so are we, in a way, all of which makes us colleagues, friends. Now that she is used to me, when she sees something amusing, she gives me a girlish glance, making me her coconspirator. She's never had any friends, but she's becoming our . . . my friend."

"Why would she not have friends?" he asked, amazed. "She's a beautiful woman!"

Nela nodded thoughtfully. "The beauty has come upon her recently, I think, and she doesn't acknowledge it. And who knows exactly why? Something to do with the way she was reared, perhaps. Rejected by this one or that one, perhaps. For whatever reason, she thinks she's a freak." She shook her head. Something about Fringe troubled her, some mystery hiding behind those stone-green eyes.

"Well, so does Danivon think he's a freak," her twin said. "That's obvious."

"Oh, no, not Danivon," said Nela. "Though he really is an oddity, he takes himself for the paradigm of Adam-the-man with bells on. Danivon was reared in an atmosphere of general approbation. Like a pet puppy. He is very pleased with himself. You can tell. Danivon is the very opposite of Fringe Owldark."

"If he really is odd, Fringe ought to get along with him at least as well as she does with us," Bertran persevered.

"No. I think she will not," Nela said soberly. "But it won't be for lack of collegiality, love. I'd wager that'll be sex."

Fringe took the oath as Council Enforcer in the Grand Master's private office, without ceremony, accepting with reasonable grace the purple coat they gave her to replace her Enarae Post blue one. They also attached a jeweled fatal-hands dangle on the bottom of her Enforcer's badge, the one Zasper had had made for her with the warrior and the gylph on it. Enforcers could have any device they liked on their badges, but the dangles were all alike and so were the words around the edge: I Attend the Situation.

She was headed back to her room after the ceremony when a Frickian flunky came to say the Provost wanted to see her.

The Provost! That would be Boarmus. Well, she thought, as she followed the Frickian up endless stairs and down lengthy corridors, this was the last bit of business in Tolerance she had to get through. She cast a sidelong look at herself in a long series of mirrors and was satisfied to find herself quite correct. Leather belt and boots polished. Purple coat swinging absolutely straight from shoulder to ankle. Purple bonnet tilted to one side, hiding the helm beneath, plumes bushed up like a cock's tail on the other side. Red silk shirt and trousers flowing and snapping, full everywhere except neck and wrists, and there tight as her skin. She faced dead ahead and clamped her teeth together, being resolute.

Boarmus was a jowly man with furzy eyebrows and an unhealthy pouchiness around his eyes, like a man who has not slept well in some time. The corners of his mouth lost themselves in pinch wrinkles, as though he clamped his lips tight often, to shut in words, perhaps.

"I'm Boarmus," he told her, giving her a long, measuring look. She was impeccable, leather gleaming, coat falling in immaculate folds. Her Enforcer's badge shone on her shoulder, the two gold fatal-hands dangles attesting to her years of experience, the gemmed one to her new status. He continued, "I am Provost, thus head of the Council."

"Sir!" she said, standing easy. Bridling at his look would only gratify him. Besides, it would do no good. The best defense against that look,˗ so Zasper had always said, was not to notice it. She stared straight ahead.

"You took an oath tonight," he reminded her.

She had scarcely had time to forget. She lowered her eyes to meet his and found them veiled, unreadable.

"It was an oath of loyalty to the Council," he said.

"Sir!" Did he think she hadn't noticed what she was swearing to?

"And, therefore, to me, as head of the Council," he went on.

She wasn't at all certain of that. She had an idea that loyalty to the Council meant to the whole body of it, not just to one person, even if that one was Provost. She waited to hear what he would say next.

"You are going into an unknown territory. We need to learn everything we can about it." He put out his hand, and she took the small cube he gave her. "You will carry this transmitter with you, and you will let me know if anything unusual happens."

"Sir! I was told Danivon Luze was head of this expedition." Without expression.

Boarmus smiled a lizard smile. "All Council Enforcers are under my command. You will be loyal, as you swore to be, or you will be forsworn." His tone threatened she would not survive long in that event. "You will not even mention this matter to Danivon Luze."

She did not reply, merely uttered the all-purpose word again. "Sir!" She much wanted to ask, why me, but it was better to ask nothing, say nothing. Best not to object. Not to inquire. Not to argue. So Zasper had said, on more than one occasion. "Try never to ask a question of a superior unless you already know the answer and are doing it for form's sake. Always be sure where you are standing before you draw a line and dare another to cross it."

Boarmus nodded dismissively. She bowed, only the requisite bow, and left the Council Provost staring balefully after her. She could feel his eyes and believed she had given him no satisfaction, but neither any justification for anger. Zasper had been clear about that too. "Don't let commanders play games with your head," he had said. "If you are absolutely correct in your manner, they can't fool with you. That means no expression at all. No insolence. No dismay. No annoyance. Nothing. Your face should be blank as a chaffer shell. You should show no feelings. Better yet, you should have no feelings." It helped to be wearing ceremonials. The silks and leathers and flapping coattails always made her feel depersonalized anyhow.

Fringe was wrong about Boarmus. In his opinion she could not have been more perfect. Totally poised. The true and perfect Enforcer, down to her bright little boots, and very nice they were too. A provincial Enforcer just up from the provinces might have been excused for being a bit awed and stuttery at being brought before the Provost, but this one had given no sign of it. Boarmus had counted on that, on the fact she was from Enarae and that Zasper Ertigon had been her sponsor. Enarae being the kind of province it was, Enforcers from there received experience early and often. Zasper being what he was, she was as advertised. Owldark would serve his need.

"Dead men, sleep," he muttered to himself. Perhaps he would be lucky. Perhaps they would do nothing more, nothing worse than they had done, and he, Boarmus, would need to do nothing. But if they did something, at least he would have let Danivon know.

Back in her quarters, the subject of Boarmus's consideration stripped off her ceremonials and put them in their case. The purple coat was too fine a fabric for daily wear. She would have a heavier one made when she returned. If she returned. Since they were not going on this expedition as Enforcers, she might not need Enforcer dress—except for her badge, to identify herself if need be. She pinned it to her undertunic. "I Attend the Situation." And so she would, whatever it might turn out to be.

Whatever old Boarmus decided it would be. She didn't much like this business with Boarmus. It smacked of sneakiness, ordering her not to tell Danivon. A team could have only one leader; how many times had she been told that? And what did Boarmus want to hear from her he would not hear from Danivon Luze?

The transmitter cube lay on her bed, beside the bonnet, featureless, seemingly inert. She picked it up and turned it in her fingers, eyes suddenly riveted as words appeared on all faces of it at once, words brought into view, presumably, by the warmth of her hands.

"Give this secretly to Danivon Luze. Silence!"

Even as she read them, they faded, and the cube was blank once more. Her fist closed around the cube as she pushed it deep into the pack she would be carrying. Well! Boarmus, saying one thing, had done another, had engaged in misdirection, as though someone was watching him! He didn't want anyone knowing he was sending a message to Danivon Luze. Clever fat old man. No one could have seen the words on the little cube. It had gone from his hand to hers. No one could see it where it lay now.

And, come to think of it, it had been Boarmus who had ordered Danivon not to return to Tolerance. Was Danivon in some danger? Or was it the Provost himself who was in danger?

Who? she asked herself quietly, moving slowly and deliberately, showing no outward evidence of the sudden anxiety that she felt. Who could be watching Boarmus? There was no one above the Provost, no one superior to him! Provost was as high an office as one could achieve on Elsewhere.

Inescapably, however, one had to consider that if Boarmus was being watched, perhaps those he met and talked with were also being watched, including Fringe herself.

Zasper's tutelage had covered such possibilities. Enforcers routinely went into category-nine and -ten places where they might be watched, overheard, spied upon. She pretended unconcern. It wasn't necessary for her to feign weariness. She got into bed fully intending to sleep at once. "Sleep when you can, pee when you can, eat when you can" was the common wisdom among Enforcers. She didn't sleep. Instead she lay long-time wakeful in the dark, going over the stories she had heard about the girl who had been found dead, the boy who had disappeared, considering the tension in the place, wondering until the mid-hours of the morning what in the name of holy diversity was going on.

Curvis, Fringe, and the twins flew to the Curward Isles on the following morning. Danivon awaited them there, and Fringe put the transmitter cube into her pocket, ready to pass on to him. Though she approached him at various times during the day, Fringe had no opportunity to speak to him alone. Curvis always hovered at his shoulder, or one of the sailors was there, or some official concerned with loading their baggage. By midafternoon, when the five of them embarked on the *Curward Industrious*—a cargo ship of the Curward fleet—no appropriate occasion had presented itself.

To her dismay, no proper occasion arose at any time on the ship, a crowded vessel upon which privacy was nonexistent. The message to her had said "Secretly" not "Urgently," therefore (she assured herself) Boarmus had considered confidentiality more important than immediacy. During each of the ensuing days, she looked for a time or place to pass the cube along without anyone noticing, but there were no opportunities. Who knew what eyes and ears might exist on the ship? Who knew which of the sailors might be a spy? If the message was to be passed in complete secrecy, she would have to await an appropriate and natural occasion.

There was no such occasion. She was never out of hearing of the sailors or other members of their group. After a few days of frustration,

Fringe put the matter out of mind. She would deliver the message as soon as possible after reaching Panubi.

Meantime, the members of the sideshow spent each day on the forward hatch cover, returning to the tiny shared cabins only after the night winds had cooled them. Danivon and Curvis exchanged Enforcer stories and Fringe taught the twins the local trade language. Fringe was a reliable teacher, though more conscientious than talented. Luckily, Nela and Bertran acquired languages easily. The Curward sailors offered considerable help with the more vulgar words, since they called out bawdy suggestions whenever Curvis and the twins practiced their sleight of hand, making things vanish from Curvis's hands to reappear in Bertran's, or vice versa. The twins knew they were improving when the sailors quit jeering at their patter and started whistling and telling them jokes in local patois.

Each morning Danivon stripped to his smalls and poured buckets of seawater over himself, watching Fringe from the corners of his eyes to see if she was appreciating him. He had an appreciable body, or so he'd been told, not that she seemed to notice. Danivon found himself getting peevish about it, spending time contemplating assault, or rape, or both successively. The damned woman would not be anything but impersonal. She would not meet his eyes. Would not . . . anything.

"What's wrong with me?" he asked Curvis in their cabin aboard the ship, peering at himself in the mirror, meantime, to see if he'd grown two heads, though she, Fringe, seemed fonder of two heads than one! She got along well enough with the twins!

"Nothing," grunted Curvis. "Nothing the matter with you."

"Then why does the fool woman act this way!"

"Shit, Danivon! We're on a mission. Attend the Situation. Leave her alone." Curvis had no objection to women, particularly as cooks or bedmates, but Danivon's preoccupation with Fringe was becoming an annoyance.

"I don't want to," Danivon said softly. "I just don't want to. She's . . . different."

Curvis laughed shortly. "The only difference with that woman is she wants nothing to do with you. It's the novelty of that fact has you fascinated." Fringe was not a type that appealed to Curvis, and he did not take Danivon's infatuation with her at all seriously.

"Why doesn't she want to?"

Curvis glared at him, then grinned. "If you want to understand Fringe, ask Nela. Close as the two halves of a chaffer shell, Fringe and Nela. Bertran will be a good fellow and pretend not to overhear."

So Danivon waited until Fringe was below and asked Nela.

She thought for a moment, recalling things Fringe had said about her childhood. "On the surface, there's little mystery about Fringe, Danivon. When she was a child, she thought the world began and ended in her daddy. She talks about him, you know, but always about him when she was a toddler, a little child. She was no doubt adorable, as many little beings are. Wide-eyed. Bright-haired. With baby skin and baby talk. So he petted her like a kitten. Then when she grew older and became prickly and difficult, as many young folk do when confronting the reality of the world, he shoved her aside as troublesome. I doubt he meant her harm. He was preoccupied with other problems and had no idea how to deal with a girl-woman." She shook her head, reflecting that things had not changed much in thousands of years—not so far as families and children were concerned.

Bertran had the same thought. "It amazes me, Danivon Luze, that human nature, which had changed little in the several thousand years before our time, is still unchanged all these millennia later! Man has swept himself along on wings of technology, but he remains psychologically much the same. As I read it, Char Dorwalk's life was unconventional enough that it let him in for a good deal of criticism from his class and family. Perfection in his children would have justified his break with convention."

"Bertran may be right," Nela said in a doubtful tone. "Since his daughter was not perfect, she justified nothing. He may have resented her falling short of his expectations."

"Which has what to do with me?" growled Danivon.

"Only this," said Nela. "Little girls learn about men from their fathers. They learn to trust, or not; to respect, or not. And Fringe may remember her daddy being handsome and charming and herself being of little value to him when push came to shove. And aren't you handsome and charming also, Danivon Luze?"

"I wouldn't treat her like that!"

"Of course not," Nela said, turning her attention to the costume she was sewing for Fringe. "Oh, of course you wouldn't, Danivon Luze."

When Danivon left, Bertran asked, "You said, 'On the surface,' Nela. What did you mean?"

She gazed at the sparkling waves, her hands for the moment still.

"Only that it's all too easy an explanation for how Fringe is, Bertran. You know, some people are the way life has made them be . . ."

"A truism, dear sister," he interjected.

". . . and some are the way they are, despite what life hands out. I'm not sure which applies in her case. There is something about Fringe that feels . . . immutable."

Bertran hadn't noticed it, but he took her word for it.

Nela was curious enough to mention the matter to Fringe. "He's a good-looking man," she said to Fringe. "You're sure you want nothing to do with him?"

"Certain sure," muttered Fringe. "Listen to the man talk. Never a woman mentioned except as someone met on the way who gives him directions to the nearest alehouse. I think that unlikely."

"True," mused Nela. "When a man like that expresses no grief over a lost love, no sorrow over a failed one, it would give one pause."

"Perhaps he is simply chivalrous and chooses not to speak of women," Bertran offered.

"If he chooses not, it's because they were so few they are sacred to him or so many he's forgotten most of them," Fringe flared up.

Bertran laughed. "You choose neither to blaspheme his relics nor be added to his trivialities, is that it?"

Yes. That was it. She thought that was it. "An Enforcer can't afford that kind of distraction," she said soberly, believing it quite sincerely.

The twins had no idea what an Enforcer could afford. Since members of the Craft were habitually either reticent or euphemistic about most aspects of their work, the twins had come to picture Enforcers as made up of equal parts public health inspectors and accountants. Though they asked endless questions about other things, somehow they never thought to find out about Enforcers.

"I want to know about these Arbai creatures," demanded Bertran late one afternoon, when they had all wearied of other diversions and were lying about, half insensible from the sun. "And also about these Hobbs Land Gods. The religion in which I was reared would say they cannot exist, but you all seem to accept their existence."

Danivon exchanged looks with Curvis. Fringe continued her exploration of her toes, which had lately acquired a pesty itch.

"Well?" demanded Bertran.

"What can we tell you," droned Fringe.

"Just tell me all about them, or it."

Fringe took a deep breath. "Well, as to the Arbai, I can't tell you much. They made the Doors and scattered them around, and they went extinct from a plague. That's all anyone knows about them."

"Not quite," said Curvis.

"That's all I know," she said.

Curvis shook his head. "They wrote books, which have been translated and can be found in the Files, though they don't make much sense to humans. And they built cities. Actually, there's quite a bit about them in the Files, if you're interested. It's true, though, that they're extinct."

"Well, tell about the Hobbs Land Gods, then," asked Nela.

Fringe said, "Some time ago, quite a number of generations, the human settlers on a farm world called Hobbs Land discovered . . ."

"Were discovered by," amended Curvis.

". . . a kind of parasitic growth that propagates through soil and rock and into trees and buildings and flesh. . . ."

"A kind of net," said Curvis.

"A root system," corrected Danivon. "That grew in people."

"And animals," said Fringe. "That is, intelligent animals. And other races."

"How dreadful!" cried Nela. "Couldn't they kill it?"

"They didn't try," said Danivon.

"They liked it," said Fringe with disgust. "And I would appreciate being allowed to tell this story without interruption. After all, it was my ancestors who fled from the Hobbs Land system, not yours!" She glared at Curvis and Danivon.

"I didn't know that," said Danivon. "Enarae was settled by people from the Hobbs Land system?"

"I'll tell it my way, all right?"

The others subsided.

"From your tone, I assume this thing, this fungus or whatever, did not kill the people or animals involved," said Bertran, with such distaste as to imply it had been far better had the stuff killed them instantly.

"It did not kill them, no," said Fringe. "It mushed them up with animals and other races until they could all sort of read one another's minds and it made them into something they called Fauna Sapiens."

She shuddered dramatically. "The point is, of course, that they were all enslaved by this thing, humans and other races both. Once enslaved, some of them sneaked into the galaxy spreading the stuff around!"

"Saint Sam," said Curvis, interrupting once more. "Wasn't it Saint Sam?"

"Saint Sam was the one who went through the Arbai Door in search of the Thyker prophetess. However, before all that, people went from Hobbs Land to the other planets in the system, to Thyker and Phansure and Ahabar. My forefathers were weapons engineers who lived in one of the northern provinces of Phansure. Our people would not be enslaved! Before the Gods got to their province, they fled all the way across the galaxy to Enarae the First. Even that turned out not to be safe, because the Gods kept spreading."

"And no one could kill them, it?"

"Once it had hold of you . . ."

"It must be like a drug," said Nela firmly. "Something addictive. We had that, in our time. Drugs that could be absolutely lethal, you could know they were going to kill you, but you used them anyhow."

"But this wasn't a drug and it didn't kill you," corrected Fringe. "That was it, you see. It didn't. But it did make people not people anymore. Not human. That's why my ancestors ran away!"

"How, not human!" demanded Bertran.

The three Enforcers looked at one another and shrugged. "Not human," muttered Fringe. "That's all. Enslaved, like I said!"

"Why did people like it so much if it wasn't like a drug?" asked Nela in an obstinate voice. "I mean. . . ."

"Because," said Fringe, "it sort of . . . got rid of a lot of their problems, I guess."

"Well, drugs do that. Or seem to."

"No, this really did. That's what made it so insidious."

"What kind of problems?" asked Bertran.

Fringe shrugged. "Problems between people. Environmental problems. You know, problems. The kinds people have."

"That would be insidious," he murmured. "You're saying it was benign, then. Beneficial."

"If something makes you a slave, how can it be beneficial," cried Danivon, shivering angrily. He found the discussion intensely disturbing. "Even if you're . . . superficially more . . . peaceable, if you don't do it yourself, if it's imposed on you . . ."

Bertran felt argumentative. "Well, in our time, in our religion, for example, we might say a man incapable of solving his problems by himself could do so by God's grace. Would that have made him a slave to grace?"

"It's not the same thing," Danivon said furiously. "You might have had enough of this grace to solve your problems, but it would still have been just you, individually, not everybody all mushed up together. . . ."

Bertran said, "You're talking about some kind of hive mind? People lost their own personalities? Their own minds?"

Fringe nodded slowly. She hadn't thought about it in those terms before, but that sounded right. "No diversity," she added. "They were all alike. Not like here." All of Enarae—all of Elsewhere—believed this was true. It was the ultimate horror. "They all thought, believed, acted the same."

The twins regarded each other with a measure of skepticism. "In our world," said Nela at last, "there were certain authoritarian regimes that regulated what beliefs people could have. At least, the beliefs that could be publicly spoken of."

"We have those too," said Danivon. "Molock, for example. Also Derbeck. And there's a whole bunch of totalitarian provinces over by the Throckian Gulf."

"People could be imprisoned, or tortured and executed, for saying or writing things indicative of the wrong attitude?" asked Nela.

Danivon nodded. "Yes, that's true in Molock and Derbeck too."

"Or for trying to escape?"

"Yes. That's also true in Thrasis."

"We had some societies that were divided along racial lines, with one race being enslaved by another," Bertran went on.

"Derbeck again," said Curvis. "Where the High Houm lord it over the Murrey, and the chimi-hounds over them all."

"Or where the military ruled the civilians. . . ."

"Frick," said Danivon. "In Frick if you're not from a military family, you're nothing."

Nela took up the inventory. "Though there were also some supposedly freedom-loving countries, though they had rather burdensome bureaucracies. . . ."

"New Athens," said Danivon. "They make a big thing out of freedom in New Athens, but even they know they're slaves to their bureaucracy. They make jokes about it, but they don't really think it's funny."

"We had so-called benevolent despotism in some places. Where a strong man ran the country but most of the people approved of the way he did it."

"Sandylwaith," said Curvis. "High Lord Say-so in Sandylwaith. You obey the law—and the law's sensible mostly, for it's a peaceful, lovely place, Sandylwaith—and you get along fine. But if you break the law, there's no second chance. High Lord Say-so will have your ears off first, then your feet and your eyes next, with what's left of you sitting in the square as a warning to the populace."

"Dreadful," shuddered Nela.

"Well," Danivon offered judiciously, "there's no crime or violence to speak of in Sandylwaith. No thievery. No rape. The people there like the system, even though you might say they're all slaves of the Lord. Of course, what happens when the current High Lord Say-so dies, who knows? Some of them haven't been so sensible."

"We had religious dictatorships, run by old men, hereditary cultists, where women had no rights at all," Bertran said.

"Thrasis," said Cruvis. "We don't even send female Enforcers to Thrasis. Women go veiled in Thrasis; they are property, first of their begetters and then of whoever they're sold to. If their owners die, they go into the towers of the prophet, for the prophet owns all otherwise unattached females in the country."

"They are all his property," said Fringe, making a face.

"Enforcers do not have opinions on the internal matters of provinces," said Danivon in a mocking tone. "Don't make faces, Enforcer!"

He was right! She hadn't even realized she was doing it. She flushed.

"Of course," Danivon went on, "in Beanfields, men have about the same status as women do in Thrasis. Mother-dear rules in Beanfields, and every man is owned by his mother. Not his real mother, but his surro-mother. Whoever his real mother gives him to. When male Enforcers go there, a female Enforcer always goes along as their mother. Otherwise they're up for grabs."

"And this is the diversity you are sworn to preserve?" asked Nela.

"There are one thousand and three provinces," said Fringe. "We have mentioned only a tiny few of them. On Elsewhere, mankind is free to be whatever he can, or will."

The twins thought about this for a time before Bertran asked, "Let us suppose one of the women of Thrasis wishes to escape. Or one of the—what did you call them? The Murrey?—one of the Murrey from Derbeck? Let us suppose a civilian from Frick grows weary of being ruled by soldiers. What recourse have they?"

"I don't understand," said Danivon. "Recourse?"

"Are they free to leave?"

"Of course not," said Fringe. "Persons must stay in their own place, in the diversity to which they were born."

"But . . ." Nela offered, "if they try to escape, aren't they *being* diverse? I mean, even *more* diverse, when they choose to be something else?"

"Where would they go?" asked Fringe gently. "There's no place for them. Except for the middle of Panubi, all the places are taken up."

"Whether there is any place for them or not, if they cannot leave, then Elsewhere is not devoted to what *I* would call diversity," said Bertran. "All of its people are imprisoned in their own systems, though each system may be different."

"What would you call it then?" asked Danivon curiously.

The twins thought about this for a time. It was Nela who spoke at last.

"I'd call it a people zoo," she said. "Just like zoos on Earth of long ago, with all the people in habitats."

Fringe and Danivon shared a pitying glance. Poor things. They had no idea what they were talking about at all.

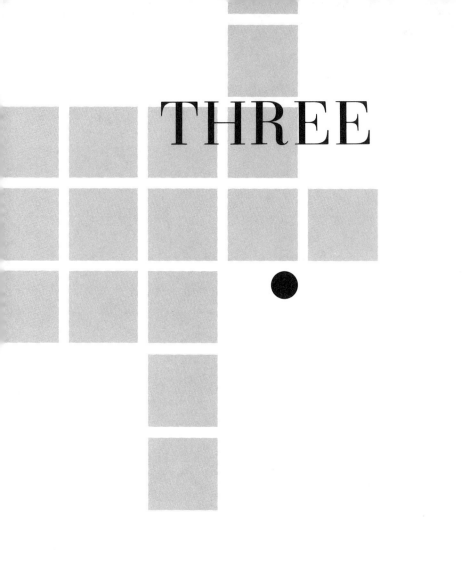

THREE

7

The sideshow arrived in Shallow late one afternoon when the ship dropped anchor near a lagoon of blue lilies, a scene of such tranquillity that it was only the muttering among the sailors that told the travelers something was amiss.

"What are they going on about?" Curvis asked of the captain.

"They're wonderin' where the people are," he said in a puzzled voice. "And so am I."

"People?"

"The folk of Shallow. Every time we come in here they're swarmin' about in those little round gossle boats, but today's like there was a sign on us sayin' 'plague.' Where are they?"

The question was partially answered after some little time when a bargelike vessel moved toward them from far across the lagoon.

"What is that?" asked Danivon, pointing toward the building from which the vessel came, a sizable structure with several wings set on pilings above the water. The piazzas running the length of each floor spilled with flowering vines, like gardens piled in terraces above the water.

"Heron House," the sailor said. "An' that'll be the Heron House gainder-yat comin' to get you. Best get your bundles up."

"Heron House?"

"You folk are goin' upriver, so you'll need someplace to bide until your river-yat comes. That's it: Heron House, built and managed by the Heron family of Shallow, them that run the yats. You'll stay there unless you fancy growing webs on your fingers and paddling upriver in gossle boats, the way most folk in Shallow do." He looked about them at the empty water and amended his discourse. "Usually do, that is. I'd like to know what's happened to 'em all, I would."

So would we, thought Danivon. *So would we!*

They brought their bundles up, though their preparedness did nothing to hurry the approach of the gainder-yat, which took its own good time, making several lengthy stops on the way. Waiting was not unusual in Shallow, so said the Curward sailors. "Slow folk in Shallow," they said. "Deep folk in Deep, and wearisome folk in Salt Maresh." Even when the boat finally arrived, it stood a distance from the Curward vessel while those manning it looked them over and whispered to one another in fearful voices.

Danivon's nose twitched painfully. Something badly awry here. The people from the hostelry were extremely apprehensive, no question. Fearful they were, but of what?

Eventually the Shallow folk decided the Curward vessel held no risk, and the gainder-yat came close enough to gather them into its capacious wide-bottomed self before wallowing away across the lagoon, its sculling oar plied by half a dozen web-fingered folk who started at every sound or movement their passengers made.

Except for a few cleared waterways leading toward the hostelry's entry float and stairs, the lagoon was carpeted with the blue-flowered lilies. Long-toed birds ran across the pads, snatching at jewel-winged flies and being snatched at in turn by toothy gaver snouts that emerged explosively from among the leaves. From the edge of the lagoon something made a melodic thumping among the reeds, as though on a set of tuned drums.

"A new place," cried Nela. "Bertran, a new place." She clapped her hands, determined to be joyful.

Her twin stared morosely at the water, thinking of diving, of swimming, of disporting himself like a penguin, like a seal. Or even like one of those toothy gavers with their sleek hides and webbed feet. Alone, of course. Unencumbered. If this expedition turned out well, he might return here, alone, unencumbered. He did not speak of this to Nela. It seemed a bitter thought when she was trying so hard to seem happy.

"A new place," he agreed, imagining the water flowing along his naked skin, imagining that skin sleek from hip to shoulder, not bulged and emerged as it was, not shared, but his own. As always, these thoughts brought a mingled feeling, part guilty pleasure, part hopeless pain. It would never happen. Though he dreamed and dreamed, it would come to nothing.

They docked at the Heron House float. Web-handed folk dressed in wraparound skirts came to take their bundles and precede them up the wide stairs to three adjacent rooms at the end of a corridor. They were told food would be served shortly on their shared piazza, at the end of which woven panels had been pulled across to give them privacy.

"Someone or something important to us is going on here, in this place," remarked Danivon to nobody in particular as he leaned over the railing. "I can smell it. But there are no public rooms! How are we to find out what's going on?"

"We'll do what we planned to do all along," said Fringe as she went to stand beside Nela and Bertran, who were already leaning across the railing. "We'll do our sideshow business down there on the float and see who gathers."

"What a beautiful place," said Nela, taking Fringe's hand and squeezing it affectionately. "Lucky people of Shallow, to have settled here."

"Lucky indeed," said Danivon moodily. "For I doubt they were given any choice in the matter."

"Didn't the people who fled here settle where they liked?" asked Bertran, puzzled.

Danivon shook his head. "They were met by a Frickian army and assigned where to go by Supervisors. Since the people of Shallow already had webbed hands and feet, the Supervisors did at least give them a wet province, for which I suppose they were duly grateful."

Fringe turned toward him, her eyebrows drawn together in a thoughtful frown. "I'd always assumed Council Supervisory was selected to run the planet after all the original Brannigan people died. Who were they then?"

Danivon snorted. "I've already made the mistake of asking that question. Files said it had no information. My rule has been that when Files is silent, it is better not to pursue the matter." He laughed ruefully, almost silently. "I broke my rule and asked the question a second time. Since then I've been smelling trouble." He'd been smelling something a good deal worse than that, but no point in frightening the others.

Still, he could not completely disguise his apprehension, and Fringe was stabbed by sudden anxiety. Since their first meeting she had thought of him in bold bright colors without shadows, one of the hero-type Enforcers much touted at Academy, one of those Zasper called the fireworks boys, who skated always on the edge of risk, laughing at death, fearless and puissant. What she had heard in his voice was simple fear, however, which she well recognized. With a pang of conscience, she remembered the transmitter cube in her pack. Perhaps he had good reason to be fearful. Perhaps that was why Boarmus had told her to deliver the thing privately.

Certainly a puzzle! She glanced at Danivon from under her lashes, seeing his brooding face fixed upon something distant and invisible. Despite all the rules she had set herself to live by, all her rejection of involvement, a part of her yearned to comfort him or, at the very least, share his concerns. A colleague could do that. She could offer him friendship at least.

No. It would only end in pain, she told herself sternly. Friendship wasn't what he had in mind. Friendship wasn't what *she* had in mind, either. Leave well enough alone!

You've survived pain before, so use that, a leering voice inside her whispered. *Use it to get the job done!*

She flushed guiltily as she felt Nela's hand on her own, squeezing it.

"Your heart's in your face, lady."

Fringe flushed. "Not my heart, Nela. Quite a different part of my anatomy, I'm afraid. And I didn't know it showed." She flushed and cast a sidelong glance at Bertran.

"Berty doesn't listen to girl talk."

Nela and Fringe had engaged in a lot of girl talk on the voyage. Chitchat about themselves and their feelings. Bertran, who had been an unfailing listener (even with his eyes fixed on a book to pretend noninvolvement), wondered at complexities in Nela he had never known of. Complexities and affections, for Fringe was Nela's first real woman friend, and Fringe was genuinely fond of Nela, a situation he found both ironic and amusing. Fringe should, he told himself, have been equally fond of them both, though she obviously was not. Of Bertran she was almost as wary as she was of Danivon.

"There's nothing to talk about," Fringe replied now, compressing her lips, making a face. "I'm not going to get involved, Nela. It wouldn't be sensible."

Nela heard the self-doubt in the words and shook her head in sympathy. "I guess I can understand. Though I sometimes think I'd give . . . well, a lot, just to have the chance to get involved."

Beside her, Bertran took a sudden breath, and she came to herself with a start, aware he might well have misunderstood—or understood too well.

"Sorry," Nela muttered, looking around desperately for something to change the subject. She pointed toward the long-toed birds stalking across the lily pads. "Remember the story we told on the voyage, the one about the turtle who wanted to fly?" she said brightly. "It's a pity our turtle didn't choose those birds to emulate instead of swallows. Waders, not fliers. Turtle might have done quite well as a wader."

Now it was Bertran who flushed guiltily, aware his thoughts would have been as wounding to Nela as her words had been to him. Perhaps he should make up his mind to stay a wader himself. It might be more profitable than this endless wanting!

All this private agonizing was interrupted by a flap-footed woman of Shallow who bustled onto the piazza to hang lamps above the long table and set it with plates and goblets preliminary to the arrival of two servitors bearing covered platters of food. They looked, so Fringe thought, like frog angels: webbed hands, wide mouths, and bright halos of frizzed hair glowing in the lamplight.

"Can you tell me who's staying here?" Danivon asked them.

"Persons," the woman answered, gesturing with a webbed hand. "Women from Beanfields, people from Choire and from Salt Maresh. Some prophet's men from Thrasis. Come to buy fish or baled fye fiber, mostly."

Danivon persisted. "Have you heard any rumors of strange things happening lately? Here or up the River Fohm?"

One of the servitors shivered, almost dropping the platter he was carrying. He was, Fringe thought, a very frightened frog angel, his face drawn and pallid.

His fellow came to take the platter from him, and they murmured together.

"Tell me!" Danivon insisted. "I know something's wrong. What's happened?"

"Noises," said the second man, almost belligerently, his arm about his friend. "Noises coming from the reeds. And people go out in the gossle boat, then there is only the empty boat. His son went in a gossle boat to fish. That's all we found, the empty boat, but there was . . . flesh in it."

The other man gasped, gulped, and fled.

"Have you seen anything at all?" asked Danivon, more gently.

The woman answered soberly, "Some people have seen shining places in the reeds. Sometimes . . . sometimes dead people, or parts of what might be dead people. Maybe that could be gavers, but gavers don't leave flesh neatly cut."

The man nodded abruptly. "We hear also of dragons."

The sideshow exchanged glances among themselves.

"Dragons?" Danivon prompted.

"We have not seen them here. The men of Thrasis bring word of dragons. They see them from their borders, off in the distance." The servitor shivered again. "Is it the dragons, taking our people?"

"We don't know." Danivon shook his head. "We'd like to find out. Can you tell us anything else."

They shrugged. Abruptly the woman said, "You asked who was staying here. I forgot the old people."

"Old people?" breathed Fringe.

"The old woman. The old man. Very old." She mimed a tottering ancient, stumping along with a cane. "We have never seen people so old. They ask the same questions you do. What have we seen? What do we think? They are away, just now. Soon they will return."

"Where are they from?" asked Curvis. "What province?"

"Noplace," said the servitor firmly. "We asked them, and they said noplace."

He shivered again, making an apologetic gesture, then he and the woman slipped away, like frogs into a pool.

"I take it you expected that information?" asked Bertran with a curious glance at Danivon, as he pulled two chairs close together for himself and Nela.

Danivon, who had started at the word "noplace," came to himself. "Dragons, yes. Disappearances here in Shallow, no."

"There was that in Tolerance too," said Fringe.

"What do you mean?" asked Danivon.

"There was a disappearance in Tolerance just before Fringe and I arrived there," said Curvis. "And a mysterious death. Two youngsters. I'd forgotten to tell you."

Danivon's face paled.

"Talk about that later," said Nela firmly. "I don't want to hear about such things over dinner. Did you expect to hear about old people, Danivon?"

Danivon took a deep breath. "I didn't expect to hear anything about old people, no." He sat beside them distractedly, paying no attention to the plates they were passing about. "How do we find out more about these dragons?"

"We'll set up the sideshow on the landing float," repeated Fringe, watching Danivon from beneath her lashes. "People will see us from these porches and come down to see what we're doing, and we can ask about dragons. That was the idea, after all, wasn't it?"

Danivon looked up distractedly. "I suppose that was the idea, yes," he grunted.

"Evening? Morning?" Curvis demanded, annoyed by Danivon's distractions.

"Not enough light this evening, it's already getting dim. We'll wait for daylight. Tomorrow morning."

"Tomorrow," agreed Fringe thankfully. She longed for an evening spent alone, now that the crowded voyage was over. She would bathe, lengthily. She would luxuriate in quiet. She would wash her hair!

Will you now? her conscience demanded. *And what about the transmitter cube Boarmus gave you for Danivon?*

This fretted her, making her sorry she had remembered it. Danivon was sharing a room with Curvis, however, so she couldn't simply take it to him. But soon they would go upriver in a boat no less crowded than the Curward vessel had been. No privacy there!

She dithered, wondering how to get him alone without being obvious about it. Well, shit, he was an Enforcer and so was she! There were all those covert Enforcer signals she had learned and almost never used. All she had to do was wait until Curvis was out of the room.

Though Curvis seemed determined not to leave the room. He stuck to Danivon like glue. When he did leave at last, Danivon was right behind him.

"Danivon," Fringe said, getting him to turn in the doorway. "Sleep well." She made the surreptitious gesture that requested a private meeting.

"Good night," he answered absently, eyes on her hands, his surprise betrayed by one soaring eyebrow.

Well, so much for secret signals, she reflected sourly. Probably he hadn't used the damned signals any oftener than she had. Anyone watching his face would have wondered what was going on. She turned, then blushed to find Nela's speculative eyes upon her.

The tap at her door came late.

"You wanted to see me?" he said softly when she let him in, casting a quick look around the room to see if they were alone.

She had looked over the room as best she could, without obviously searching it, but there was no way to tell for sure that there weren't spy eyes watching. So, if she were to pass the cube along secretly, as Boarmus had ordered, it would have to be done in the guise of something else. She'd planned the most misleading thing she could think of: an embrace, a hug, maybe even with some kissing and fondling.

"I thought it was time we got to know one another better," she said throatily, purposefully seductive.

His mouth fell open. "Well." He stared for a moment, then grinned. "What took you so long, Fringe Owldark?"

She moved toward the chair by the window, barely able to keep herself from snarling at him. The monstrous ego of the man! She took a deep breath and turned, ready to utter the next flirtatious phrase she'd rehearsed, only to find herself against him, her chin pressed into his chest. She tried to step back, but his arms were around her. She started to say something, but his lips were on hers. She had planned on this happening, but not so quickly. . . .

Everything inside her loosened in an unfamiliar way and she couldn't remember what she'd been going to say. He half dragged, half carried her toward the bed and they fell onto it together, arms and legs already entwined, tangled in their clothing, she dizzy, trying to think of words that would get her out of this, he busy finding flesh to touch. When she thought of something at last, his mouth was still on hers; she couldn't breathe, then didn't want to breathe.

After which she forgot about breathing or speaking or doing anything. Anything that needed doing was doing itself. The room was washed by dim ripples of torchlight reflected from the water outside. The only sounds she could hear were the cry of a night bird, the sob of her own breath, the murmur of Danivon's voice saying not-quite words. Then everything went to pieces in mirrorlike shards, inside, outside, the sky breaking apart, her thought shattering into splinters that didn't connect to anything. He said something urgently, but she couldn't tell what it was. The room rocked on the wavelets, gently, as though it floated.

After a long, quiet time, she opened her eyes and stared through the window at the stars, half in wonder, half in anger. She'd planned this! She'd planned to do this, well, not exactly this, but something like this. But she hadn't planned . . . hadn't planned for the sky to come apart.

Damn it. Why had that had to happen! Why had she done it? Why had she thought she could pretend . . . then pretend she hadn't?

Angry tears filled her eyes, and she wiped the wetness away with one hand as she reached for her pack with the other, feeling automatically for the comb she'd made sure was there on top, next to the cube Boarmus had given her. Her hand came out, the cube hidden in her palm, the comb in her fingers.

"Danivon," she said huskily, her voice seeming to come from some unfamiliar place inside her.

"Fringe," he whispered, inviting her, drawing the word out, making a caress of it.

She refused to understand him as she put her lips against his ear. "Boarmus gave me a message for you."

He started, but she held him down with her full weight, keeping him from moving, afraid that if he moved . . .

"Secret, Danivon. He believes he's being watched. Maybe we are. The message is here in my hand. Take it. Don't examine it until you're sure you're alone, where no one can see. Not even Curvis."

"Fringe," he murmured, as in a dream.

"Shhh." She lay beside him, closing his hand around the cube, holding it in her own. In a moment, he breathed deeply, half asleep once more, and she sat up to comb her hair, hearing the snap and spark as the comb slid down the long tresses. No one was watching, but just in case . . . just in case. All she was doing was combing her hair. Not braiding it, because she wasn't an Enforcer, not here in Shallow. She was just a woman kissing her lover and combing her hair. That's all. Let spy-eyes make what they would of that! She sought her fastener among their tumbled clothing, knotted her hair on the top of her head, and pushed the teeth of the fastener through it, feeling the fangs as though they went into her flesh.

Then she extricated herself bit by slow bit, her clothes, her limbs, her feelings, all of her, back together in one place. So. Now what was she going to do? She'd sworn she wouldn't get involved with Danivon Luze, and she'd done it anyhow. She'd let it happen. Lying to herself. Calling it duty when it had probably been lust all the time. She didn't call it love, didn't think of that, didn't let herself think of that, even though she wanted to lie down beside him once more, lay her lips at his throat, lose herself. She wanted to feed on him, sate all her hungers with him, soak him into herself, root herself in him. Be whole with him, whole as she had never been. That's what love must be for, to feel like that.

At least, so Souile had said once. Love was to make yourself whole. Well, it hadn't worked for Souile, had it? Or for Char. It hadn't worked for anyone Fringe knew.

And when it didn't work, it was worse than nothing. It was regret, sorrow, love sucking you in until you couldn't move, holding you down, making you stop struggling and taking you over, just as Danivon had done. Like the Hobbs Land Gods. Taking you over. Eating you up and leaving you too stupid even to know you didn't exist anymore!

She took a deep, trembling breath and told herself she would not, that's all. If it had really happened, it would be a mistake, so it had never happened. She had given Danivon the message, that's all. A little playacting. Unthink it. Nothing happened.

She took a blanket and sneaked away silently, out onto the shared piazza where she found a comfortable chair and cocooned herself into it to watch little lights moving among the lilies where the people of Shallow were night-fishing with torches and spears, the gossle boats moving around the lagoon like black bugs with shining eyes. After a time, hypnotized by the moving lights, she slept.

Danivon slept as well, a smile curving his lips. Sometime later he was wakened by a fisherman's shout and reached out for her, only to find her gone. Half-dressed, dragging his discarded clothing, he looked onto the piazza but didn't see her buried in the depths of the chair. Puzzled, he made his way to the room he shared with Curvis, finding it dark and silent except for an occasional explosive snore.

The thing she had given him while he lay half dreaming was clutched in his hand. This thing she had said . . . said what about? Said to be private before he looked at it. He went to one of the sanitary cubicles cantilevered out over the lagoon, a primitive arrangement, but a reasonably private one, lit by a fish-oil lamp suspended from the ceiling. The light was dim but adequate to show him a standard transmitter cube. Well. So? He went back to the room, inserted the device into his reader, and let it whisper into his ear.

"Danivon, you are in danger," it said in a whimper that sounded not at all like Boarmus. "There's a kind of force here on Elsewhere, and it's after you, after the people with you. It says it intends to kill you. I don't know if it *can* kill you, but it wants to. When I see it, it looks like a ghost. Maybe it will look like a ghost to you. It's taking people over, enslaving people, killing people, Danivon. Not the Hobbs Land Gods, Danivon. Another thing. Be careful."

Which didn't sound like cold old Boarmus at all. Which sounded so unlike him it sent a chill through Danivon, along with a smell of old, corrupted ice. Boarmus was talking in generalities, in hints and clues. As though to be specific would be even more dangerous—for whom? Boarmus or himself?

"Try to stay alive," the cube sobbed in his ear. *"Be very careful! I may need you."*

How long had Fringe been carrying this thing? Since Tolerance? Why hadn't she given it to him before! Considerably shaken, Danivon wiped out the message and dropped the cube among others in his kit. So the danger he'd been smelling was not merely for the usual kind of risk. It was something bigger than that. Worse. And whatever it was had evidently come to Shallow. Sparkling and noises and people disappearing. Had the danger followed them? Or was it lying in wait?

He lay back on his bed and considered matters. Nothing had changed, except that he knew Boarmus knew. He shouldn't be furious at Fringe for taking so long, except that he was angry. Last night had seemingly not been what he had hoped it was!

By morning, his feelings were thoroughly confused, sleepiness mixed with erotic longing for Fringe mixed with fury at her for . . . for being Fringe! He went to her room, went in without knocking, and found her sitting at the window.

"Rude of you," she remarked in a toneless voice.

"Fringe. Come on, we need to talk about—"

"What about, Danivon?"

"About?" he exploded in a whisper, conscious of Curvis on the piazza, of the twins standing outside at the railing. He came close, reached for her. "About us. About . . ."

She leaned against him, put her lips close to his ear. "Us," she said, still tonelessly. "Colleagues. On an assignment together."

"No." He shook her. "About us together. . . ."

"On an assignment," she insisted, staring coldly into his eyes. "That's all, Danivon. On an assignment!" She made a gesture, a warning flicker of fingers, another Enforcer sign, this one conveying caution.

He snarled, pulling her close. "You mean you . . ."

"I mean I was told to deliver it secretly," she hissed into his ear, barely audibly. "And I tried to do just that, and you're about to foul everything up."

"You weren't pretending," he said softly. "Damn it, Fringe. You weren't pretending. And I wasn't pretending."

And she hadn't been pretending. He was right. For a moment her body sagged against him and his arms tightened. Then she pulled away in desperation. "We've work to do, Danivon." Fear dictated the words. She needed him to get away from her, now, leave her alone, before she was lost! "Damn it, Danivon, I can't afford this!"

He stepped away, seeing the expression on her face, offended by it, not understanding it in the least. He had never forced himself on an unwilling woman! No woman who wasn't a target for Enforcement had ever, ever needed to be afraid of him, and no woman ever had needed to be afraid of him sexually! But there was no mistaking her expression: she was afraid of him or of herself, and did it matter which?

She turned away, her back rigid, and after a long silent moment he left her there to go trembling away, not sure what he was feeling. Sympathy, maybe? Or grief? What? Maybe anger, that was easiest! Except that anger might be self-defeating, for this mood of hers might depart in time.

Very well. He swallowed anger and decided to give her time.

When she sat near him at the table and served herself breakfast, however, her closed face looked through him, or past him, as she had been looking at him more or less since he met her in the tavern in Enarae. She sat beside Nela, but she didn't even look at Nela.

"We didn't sleep well last night. When we did, I dreamed I was that little turtle, in the story," said Nela, half to Fringe, half to the air.

Fringe said expressionlessly, "It must have been a sad dream."

"No sadder than the story you told us about the warrior maid and the gylphs," murmured Nela.

"It's the same damned story," said Bertran, sounding irritable. "We are many of us raised on the same stories. In fact, many of us *are* the same stories. At least, so I've decided lately."

Danivon tried unsuccessfully to catch Fringe's eyes. She turned away from him. He said urgently, "Speaking of turtles, Fringe has a turtle shell in her house. She keeps it upon a pedestal but will not tell me why."

"A turtle shell?" asked Nela, much interested.

Fringe looked at Danivon and shook her head slowly. "I found it on one of the Seldom Isles, at the top of a tall tree. So far as I know, turtles do not climb trees." Fringe thought it likely a predatory bird had taken it there, though it could have been Nela's turtle, seeking the secret sanctuary of the birds. Perhaps it climbed up there and couldn't get down, and so it died, high up, staring at the sky. Actually, she preferred that explanation. *If you were going to rise to such heights, better do it on your own than be grabbed up and eaten!*

"And you will not tell Danivon why you keep it?" Nela teased.

"If Danivon knew me at all, he would know why," she said wearily, fixing him with her eyes. "I keep it to remind me that even small creatures may have longings for something higher and more wonderful than they have ever known. Even small creatures can try to climb, can refuse to be sidetracked by temptations of comfort and . . . kindness."

She had intended to sound cold, but the words came out as a plea.

Danivon flushed. Nela saw and understood, but her twin, his eyes on his plate, missed the exchange.

Bertran laughed ruefully. "You surprise me, Fringe. I might once have thought someone reared in Enarae couldn't possibly understand ancient Earthians like Nela and me, yet the very fact that we both have similar feelings about our turtle stories tells me we share many of the same feelings."

"There is not so much real diversity among folk as we are led to believe," Nela said, trying to lead the conversation to a less emotional level.

This was heresy! Curvis immediately rose to the bait with an impassioned defense of diversity as found upon Elsewhere, while Fringe, with a feeling of relief that they were talking of something impersonal, made herself concentrate on their performance planned for this morning.

During their voyage from the Curward Isles, Nela had insisted upon stitching a fancy robe and headdress to go with the Destiny Machine, a flowing garment glittering with beads and a tall cap with painted panels falling stiffly on either side of the face. More hype, said Nela. Fringe must look like an oracle, not like an Enforcer! Immediately after breakfast, Fringe got into this outlandish garb and helped Curvis maneuver the Destiny Machine down to the float, stopping long enough to invite a few of the servitors to come have their futures foretold. In the bright light of morning it seemed apprehensions had been laid aside for they chattered about the machine, giggled over their individual fortunes, and raced back into Heron House to tell others. It was not long before there was a crowd gathered around them, all laughing and talking and pointing fingers as Curvis made the munks disappear only to reappear twenty paces away in Danivon's pocket; while Nela and Bertran did sleight-of-hand tricks to amaze the audience; and finally while Fringe busied herself with all the hypish nonsense Nela and Bertran had suggested, including gong-whacking and the sonorous invocation of recently invented and strangely named powers of past, present, and future while volunteers from the audience had their destinies loudly foretold to great awe and amusement.

As a second act, Curvis juggled burning torches, catching them behind his back, Nela and Bertran told funny stories—at least, stories the Curward sailors had assured them were funny, though many of them seemed pointless to the twins—and Danivon went about sniffing at people, either whispering or trumpeting his smellings as he went. "You are in love," he whispered. Or "Your lost flail is lying under a pile of chaff on the threshing floor," he said loudly. The crowd cheered, becoming larger the longer they performed.

"All we need is cooch dancers," Nela said, giggling, almost happily. "And a bearded lady and a contortionist and a lightning calculator."

"I don't think these people would care about lightning calculators or cooch dancers," said Bertran, who was finding the joyous naiveté of the audience irresistible. "We seem to be doing well enough as we are. They certainly accept us as an amusement!"

"Have we attracted any people from Thrasis or Beanfields yet?" Nela asked.

"There, crowded around Fringe's machine," said Curvis, indicating various outlanders with Danivon already sniffing among them like a hound on the trail. After a time he beckoned to his colleagues, and they concluded their performance with many bows and congratulations to their audience.

When they had put their heads together, Danivon reported:

"None of the Thrasian or Beanfields people have had any disappearances or funny air or any of that. The men from Thrasis have seen dragons, creatures taller than men but not huge, of various colors, who have been seen to carry things, perhaps tools. Sometimes they wear clothing, and they are always seen at a distance, never up close." He was speaking to Fringe, as though she were the only one present, a fact that Curvis noted with distaste. "The women of Beanfields have seen them only rarely, though they assert that Mother-dear has decided the dragons are friendly."

"Friendly?" asked Curvis in a sneering tone. "How would she know?"

"How do Mother-dears know anything?" Danivon shrugged, annoyed, though whether at Curvis's question or his manner the others couldn't tell. "Maybe she merely means inoffensive."

"The fact they have been inoffensive where the local people are concerned doesn't mean they will be with us," drawled Curvis. "They may find us offensive. Or rather, you, Danivon. You have some history of being offensive, do you not?"

Danivon said stiffly, "If you're referring to the reaction of the Inner Circle when I denounced old Paff. . . ."

"Old Paff?" asked Fringe.

Curvis drawled, "A member of the Inner Circle. He had a nasty habit of picking up children from places like Molock or Derbeck and using them to satisfy certain personal desires."

"What did you do?" Nela asked Danivon.

"I stood on the stairs in the Great Rotunda and denounced him, as I was taught to do in cases of abuse of power."

"What happened?" Fringe was suddenly interested despite herself.

"Paff killed himself, shortly before I left Tolerance."

"I don't understand how you could have offended anyone," cried Nela. "They should have been glad you uncovered such wickedness."

Curvis gave Nela a long look that changed from annoyance to amusement. He turned to Danivon to say jeeringly, "It seems you have not explained our ways to our guests, Danivon." He turned back to Nela. "The Inner Circle already knew about old Paff. Had known about him forever."

"Please," cried Nela. "I don't understand this. You are saying your ruling circle knew this man was a child killer. It did nothing. What kind of a place is this? Where is your law?"

"Here," said Fringe, tapping her chest.

"You are the law?"

"Enforcers are the arms and hands of the law," she said. "I am, and Danivon and Curvis. And the Council is the voice of the law. If there is a situation that needs attending, we Attend the Situation!"

Another silence, interrupted when Nela said in a tiny voice, "So, the three of you are what? Executioners?"

"I rather imagine," said Bertran in a distant voice. "Hit men. Hit women."

"Enforcers," said Fringe stiffly, detecting the brittle dismay in their voices, hurt by it, but not in the least understanding it. "It is an honorable thing to be. And we have honor to maintain." She badly wanted the understanding no Enforcer would ever beg for.

Nela ignored her tone. "Where does honor enter in?"

Fringe stiffened. "Honor enters in in that we are not skulkers. We do not kill unless we must. Even then, we do not maim, we do not torture. If we kill covertly, we do it only to save apprehension or disorder. When the circumstances require it, we go face-to-face. Honorably."

"Oh, goody," said Nela angrily. "*High Noon*."

"I don't understand."

"You shoot it out, you and whoever? To see who's the fastest gunslinger. Is that it?"

Fringe felt herself growing angry at this slighting reference to the sanctity of Guntoter. In Enarae, one did not say "gunslinger" in that scornful tone! "If Council Supervisory has ordered it, yes."

"So you're only following orders," said Bertran.

Fringe wiped all expression from her face and regarded them both coldly. "You seem to have become unfriendly toward me, but I don't understand why."

Nela shook her head. "What Bertran means is, in our time there were evil men who did some extremely nasty things, and when they were brought to trial, their defense was that they were only obeying orders, or if not orders, then the wishes of their superiors. It was a cliché in our time, to excuse all crimes."

"But if they obeyed orders, they did not commit crimes and the men were not evil," Fringe objected hotly. "If proper authority says we are to do something, and if, as sensible men, we have acquiesced to proper authority, why then—"

"I gather it was not so in your time," interrupted Danivon curiously.

"No," Bertran asserted, patting Nela's shoulder to calm her. "At least not entirely. We did have a good deal of disagreement about what constituted proper authority. It was asserted by many that natural human rights took precedence over the authority of the state."

"Human rights?"

"The right to peaceful existence in one's home, to be free of unreasonable harassment, of false imprisonment or torture, to speak freely one's feelings and opinions, to assemble with like-minded friends, to worship or not, as one liked. If I hear what you are telling me, there are no human rights on Elsewhere."

Nela shook her head, confused. "But that can't be, not if Danivon denounced this man because he murdered children. . . ."

"No," said Danivon, offended. "That's not why I denounced him. That would have been improper."

They stared at him, and he at them, neither understanding the other.

"Our job is to protect diversity," he said through gritted teeth, "the very diversity from which the answer to the Great Question will emerge, the very diversity that is the essence of humanity! In that diversity children are always being killed for any number of reasons. If the killing is proper to that place, then it is proper. But this old man took children across *borders*. He *interfered* in the affairs of a province! Here on Elsewhere, we let one another alone."

Nela quivered in outrage. Bertran squeezed her shoulder and said softly, "There is much we have to learn about Elsewhere. I don't think we have the right to comment. Not yet."

Fringe looked pleadingly at Nela, who turned her head and stared angrily away over the lagoon. She started to speak, but felt Bertran's fingers pinching. It was an old signal between them, and they excused themselves. As by mutual consent, they headed toward the sanitary facilities at the top of the stairs.

"What have we come to?" Nela whispered as they climbed.

"Nothing we have any control over," he replied sensibly. "I think we should take breathing space and withhold judgment."

"But, I liked her! I really liked her, Berty. I liked Danivon too. And they have no more moral sense than a pig, or a tiger," she cried.

Bertran shrugged, sending a like tremor through his sibling, as he whispered, "Look, Nela, we grew up in a religious family in a small town. We were educated in parochial school, which you have to admit is hardly a microcosm of things as they are. Then we went to the circus, and except for some raging egos, that was fairly well insulated from the world too. I can't say for certain that our time was all that different! We'd be wiser not to judge too quickly."

She shook her head stubbornly.

"Besides," he went on, "we're stuck with them, Nela. We haven't any choice. Even if we decide we detest this world and all its works—including Danivon and Fringe, who, you have to admit, have been damned nice to us—we're here, with no chance of going anywhere else."

"I don't care," she said stubbornly.

He shook her. "Unless you're suddenly avid for martyrdom, we can't toss away friends because they're not . . . maybe not the friends we would have chosen at home."

She bit her lip and was silent.

While Fringe stared after the twins with troubled eyes, the others gathered their equipment into a pile, ready to carry it back to their rooms. They had just finished when a shout from across the water drew their attention from their paraphernalia to an approaching gainder-yat.

Fringe heard the cry and turned, still so preoccupied with what she had been thinking that she thought the old woman on the deck of the yat was Aunty or Nada come alive again. The old thing was staring at her with that alert, fowl-eyed look that had typified Fringe's kin, a look that seemed to search her soul for something edible. However, as the yat drew closer, she saw this wasn't Nada or Aunty, but someone even older, a wisp of a thing, a clutter of bones in a tight-drawn skin. The man leaning on a stick beside her was also very old, though not so old as she, and Fringe recognized them!

Curvis put down an armload of juggling gear and moved to catch the ropes the oarsmen tossed him. The others straightened from their tasks and watched. When the plank shuddered down, the old woman tottered toward it without taking her eyes from Fringe. Something shadowy moved behind her, moved and shifted as she cried out in a shrill bird voice:

"There, Fringe Owldark! Carry an old woman down."

Fringe, astonished, found herself carrying. She had a confused impression that she was not the only one carrying, but on the landing stage she was the one setting the old thing on her feet once more and keeping an arm around her so that she didn't blow away.

"Why, girl, you've grown beautiful," the old woman cried, releasing a hand to pat at her cloud of white hair. "Remember me? Jory. Jory the Traveler."

Fringe repeated the name, "Jory, Jory the Traveler," as though the title might do something to solve the mystery of this old one's appearance here, at this far corner of the world.

"Fringe?" said the old woman. "I am disappointed! Don't you know me?"

Fringe stared at her helplessly. Recognize her, yes, but know her? "When I was a girl," she said at last. "Long ago."

"Not *that* long ago! Why, it was I who gave you your name. Did I tell you, Asner? It was I who gave her her name."

"You've told me," said the old man, pushing between the two of them. He'd needed no help getting down the plank, plunking slowly along with his stick. "Don't let her fuss you, girl. She does that all the time. Travels around. Meets people. Then pops in on 'em half a lifetime later, all innocence." He mimed a teacup, lifted eyebrows, " 'Well, of course we met, thirty years ago at the carnival in New Athens.' 'Don't you remember, we shared a dish of thusle custard fifty years ago in Denial.' Half of it's sheer fiction, made up for the occasion."

"This isn't fiction," the old woman said with a laugh. "We've been down along the shores of Deep, fishing."

"Did you catch anything?" Fringe asked stupidly.

"Not what we needed," replied Jory, looking over Fringe's shoulder to catch Danivon's glance. He was standing a little distance away, staring as though his eyes would fall out, his nose twitching. Then he came forward in a rush.

"Who?" he murmured, thrusting in among them. "Now who're these people, ah?"

"Jory," muttered Fringe unwillingly, indicating the old woman with her free hand. "And Asner."

"The people from *noplace*?" crowed Danivon. "Is that who you are? Ah?"

"Asner," complained the old woman with a hint of laughter. "Did you tell the Shallow people that? That we were from noplace?"

The old man shrugged. "I might've," he said. "When you've been as many places as we have, it's hard to remember where you're from."

Danivon grinned and sniffed. "People from noplace. Now isn't that strange. Someone I know received a rather peculiar . . . suggestion from noplace. Would you know anything about that?"

They turned on him looks of bland incomprehension, which he met with studied calm.

"What's on your mind, boy?" demanded the old man in a grouchy tone. "Don't fuss us, now. Don't play about making conversation. I can tell there's something on your mind."

"How can you tell that?"

"How can you tell when it's raining, boy! By the water on your head! Don't waste time. You get as old as we, there's no time to waste."

Danivon sniffed deeply, smiled slowly, like a sunrise. "We're planning an expedition upriver and you seem to be headed that way. Am I right?"

"Think of that," Jory interrupted. "An expedition. So exciting, expeditions. Moving about, place to place, seeing new things, unraveling mysteries. Even when you think you've seen everything there is to see, there's something else . . . beckoning."

Asner regarded Danivon with a skeptical eye. "What're you wanting, boy? Directions?" He looked up, his eyes widened, he nudged Jory and murmured, "Would you look at that?"

Nela and Bertran were descending the stairs in their synchronized fashion, Bertran's arm around Nela's shoulders.

"I do think that's ziahmeeztwinz," murmured Jory.

"Joined people," said Fringe.

"What I said," the old woman remarked. "Now isn't that interesting. Wonderful how travel broadens one, isn't it?"

"I don't know," said he. "What's ziahmeeztwinz?"

"Two babies born joined together," she said. "Except they're always two boys or two girls."

"Not in this case," said Fringe. "And how do you know about such things?"

"Oh, my dear, a person as widely traveled as I knows bits and pieces about a lot of things."

"I've been in most places on Elsewhere," said Danivon. "And I don't know about ziahmeeztwinz."

"But you haven't been where I've been, boy. I don't mean *here*," said the old woman. "I don't mean *now*." She smiled sweetly at Nela and Bertran who had, by this time, joined the group. "I've never met a pair of ziahmeeztwinz before."

"Siamese twins," cried Nela. "How do you know that word."

The old woman said something in a language Fringe could not understand. The twins replied in the same language. The old woman fumbled a bit with it, as though it might be a language she had not used for a long time. Still, the twins seemed to understand her well enough, and soon the three of them were babbling away like birds on a branch while the old man gloomed at them and the three Enforcers listened with their mouths open.

"Think of that!" Jory cried at last, turning to Fringe. "We're almost countrymen. Virtually time-mates."

"They got caught in an Arbai Door," said Danivon, gesturing at the twins. "Caught and left in limbo forever. And you?"

The old woman cocked her head, regarding him with complete attention. "An Arbai Door! Isn't the galaxy full of wonders! Now, what's this about going upriver?"

Danivon's nose twitched. She hadn't answered him. She wasn't going to answer him. His nose told him that. "Perhaps we need you to go along."

"So lovely to be wanted," she cried, clapping her hands. "We'll go, of course. Won't we, Asner?"

"If you say so, Jory. Whatever you say." He sighed dramatically. "She'll get her way no matter what I say, so I just give in right away to save trouble."

"Now, Asner, that's not fair."

"Fair or not, that's the way things are." He winked at Danivon. "Women!"

Danivon, casting a glance at Fringe from beneath half-closed eyes, did not respond. She, however, grasped him firmly by one arm and drew him to one side.

"You have to be joking," she said.

He shook his head at her. "Not."

"Danivon! She's . . . she's old! Look at her! She doesn't weigh as much as your left leg from the knee down. Bird bones held together by skin. First sniff of danger, she'll be dead!"

He tapped his nose and said again, "Not."

"Isn't that thing ever wrong?"

"Hasn't been yet. And what's it to you? She wants to go. She isn't your granny."

Fringe flushed. The old woman wasn't her grandma, or old aunty. And yet. Yet. "She's something to me, Danivon. I may not have known it till this minute, but she is something to me!"

"They're talking about you," Nela was saying to Jory. "Fringe feels it would be unwise for you to go along."

"What does she care?" asked Jory with a secretive smile.

Nela persisted. "She's concerned about the danger to you." Fringe's concern for the old woman was welcome to Nela, who did not want to believe Fringe was the amoral monster her earlier words had made her out to be. "Quite frankly, I think she's sensible to be concerned."

"Child, you worry too much," said Jory, patting Nela's cheek. "I've lived a long time. Isn't that right, Asner? You get to be our age, you don't worry so much."

"Doesn't do any good when you do," said Asner. "So after a thousand years or so you give it up."

Fringe, meeting Danivon's obstinacy, threw her hands into the air and turned her back on him to face the group once more. "Everybody's crazy!" she cried. "Old woman, you mustn't do this."

"What's this device?" asked Jory, paying no attention to Fringe's remonstration as she ran her fingers up and down a shiny track on Fringe's machine.

"It's a Destiny Machine," said Bertran heavily.

"A fortune-telling device," explained Nela.

"Oh, goody," cried Jory. "Well, then, why don't we leave it to the machine. Your machine, Fringe Owldark, to answer your own objections. Show me what to do."

Fringe sulkily pointed at the levers, and Jory picked three of them to touch, gently. One red. One green. One blue.

The machine trembled. Small bells rang tunefully. Fringe stiffened. She hadn't arranged for melody. The bells were random; they rang when hit by one of the traveling capsules, sometimes in harmony, sometimes in dissonance, but there was no way to make them play a tune. "In this world of Elsewhere," they rang. "Elsewhere's where I go. . . ."

The tune played on. Glittering gems moved out from the center of the device and spun at the far edges, spiraling like a tiny galaxy. One far light gleamed brighter than the rest. It shone, like a little sun. It spun, moving onto a nearer track, circled, coming closer, still closer, then fell into the bin. Abruptly the music stopped, the machine quivered and was still.

Fringe glared at her invention. It wasn't supposed to stop until it had delivered at least three capsules.

"Now what?" asked Jory, peering into Fringe's face.

Fringe picked the capsule out of the bin and turned it in her hand, seeking the word she had lettered upon it. It was there, but not in her handwriting. Not in her letters. Not a word she had painted at all.

"Go!" it said.

"Go!" read Asner, taking it from her.

"Go!" whispered Jory to Fringe, her eyes glinting like cut gems in the sidelong light. "Well now, isn't that nice."

Houmfon: capital city of the province of Derbeck, a river port half a day's sail up the Ti'il from its confluence with the Fohm. Cobbled streets, arcades, shaded gardens, and a town square beside the Palace wall where the great iron gates are shut tight and draped with purple. In the Palace, Old Man Daddy is dying.

He has lived a long full life. He has killed all his enemies face-to-face and most of his friends from behind. He has eaten from golden plates and drunk from goblets of pearl (after his taster has tried everything first). He has had seven wives and a hundred concubines (though only one son), and now he is dying. He lies on his canopied bed in the lowest tower room, a rock-walled round beneath the treasure vaults, his breath wheezing in and out, his eyes rolling blindly beneath their shuttered lids, his hands twitching on the covers as though they needed to grab one more thing, one more time. On the curved benches around the walls sit the dozen chiefs of the chimi-hounds and the dozen high priests of the dabbo-dam. The dabbo-dam holds the manifestation of Chimi-ahm; the chimi-hounds hold the fount of power. Old Man Daddy has held both, but now they are slipping away. His breath rasps and his fingers grab at nothing.

Around the walls the chiefs and the high priests exchange significant glances. Old Man Daddy has been a much loved son of Chimi-ahm, a faithful practitioner of dabbo-dam, a generous patron of the chimi-hounds, no less in his latter days than in earlier ones. Recently Old Man has known he hadn't much longer, recently Old Man has arranged everything. The chimi-hounds have been paid and new, powerful weapons smuggled in from a category-six province have been put in their hands. The priests have been paid and gifts made at the altars. After the funeral and the proper period of mourning, an election is to be announced. The result of that election, already paid for by Old Man Daddy, is to be foretold by dabbo-dam and assured by the hounds.

It has been arranged. If people do not agree, the hounds will put an end to dissent. Mutterers will go flying, leaking from many holes. Old people. Women. Brats. Blood everywhere. That's what makes elections.

When all the blood is washed away, Old Man Daddy's only son, Fat Slick, will have been elected Holy-head of Derbeck. In Houmfon, the great image of Chimi-ahm will smile, confirming the work of man. Then there'll be fireworks and barbecue and everybody singing and no doubt Chimi-ahm himself will come down to walk with the people, for Chimi-ahm (unfortunately) has been doing that frequently of late.

Chimi-ahm, in fact, has become almost as worrisome to his priests as he always has been to the populace at large. Before now, Chimi-ahm usually did what the priests thought best. Now, strangely, it seems to be the other way around.

Still, the knowing glances dart from chieftain to high priest to chieftain again, sliding across the ladder against the wall, the ladder leading up to the treasure vaults. Though Old Man Daddy named him as successor, Fat Slick is a witless wonder, a slob-lipped nothing much. His mama was a luscious though brainless High Houm often possessed by Zhulia the Whore, the female personage of Chimi-ahm. Old Man Daddy has always claimed Fat Slick was his own get (and who'd have said different), but with Old Man no longer able to say . . . well, maybe Fat Slick isn't Old Man's son at all. Maybe he's nothing much. Who's to say who's been bought and what's been paid for? Chimi-ahm whispers maybe it's some other man's son? Maybe the high priest's son? Or the son of the boss chimi-hound chief? Or the boss chimi-hound chief *him*self, old Houdum-Bah?

Outside, in the hall, where the long tables are kept stocked with drinks and eatables and sniffables, outside are whisperers, scurriers, fetchers, and mutterers, dressed all in white with white cloths twisted around their heads, naked feet painted blue, backs of their hands painted blue, blue stripes on forehead and cheek, little people, servant people, the zur-Murrey, which means "blue boys" in the old language, the tongue most of the people still speak. The Murrey are as human as the highest of the Houm, but they are beige and small, with stiff black hair that stands up like a brush. Only the paint on hands and feet and face says which color-tribe each one belongs to.

"They won't go for Fat Slick," says one of the blue boys to one with yellow feet and ankles, yellow dots beside his eyes and down his jawline. "Fat's for the chop, the flop, the drop, the long hang down. Fat's for the pit, the spit." And giggles then, hysterical giggles, for there's scarcely a Murrey in the palace, male or female, who hasn't been handled by Fat Slick in one way or another, none of them nice.

"Ten on sunset," breathes a green boy to a blue, the keeper of the last breath pools. Ten derbecki that Old Man Daddy will draw his last breath as the sun falls. "Ten more on sunrise!" Ten derbecki that Fat Slick will draw his last at dawn, on the gibbet. Those in power don't like Fat Slick. Though Fat Slick is stupid—and ordinarily the priests and hounds would prefer somebody not quite bright—for some reason they've taken against him. Whisper says Chimi-ahm himself has taken against him! So, money flows like water, up and down in the Palace, everybody betting. Betting makes it more real, more actual, more sure. Oh, to see either one of them dead! Oh, to see both of them dead in the space of one day!

Others of the Murrey, even some of the High Houm, the aristocracy, consider ways of getting out of Houmfon for a time until things settle down. It isn't only Old Man Daddy dying, it isn't only the election, it's other things too. It's Chimi-ahm manifesting himself all the time lately, it's people going to a dabbo-dam and never coming back. So, the Houm think of going off to take care of a sick relative in the country, maybe. Or they think of going down sick themselves, maybe, in some well-fortified back room, and staying in there until well after election: out of sight, out of mind. No point just going to another town. The other towns are no better than Houmfon. If one goes anywhere, one has to get clean away, out into the forests. The only thing sure about Old Man Daddy's dying is that someone will be set up in his place. So, there'll be one man going and maybe more than one coming, *and* the dabbo-dam eating people like chug-nuts, forces coming together like the stones of a mill, and who but the zur-Murrey and the jan-Murrey and ver-Murrey caught between those stones? Blue boys, yellow boys, green boys, no matter, the streets and the altars will run bloody when tenancy changes in the Palace. That's how the old saying goes. *All rou-Murrey when the topman goes. All red-boys when Old Man dies.*

Not that the little people don't run red other times too, whenever the chimi-hounds get aggravated at something!

So, even now, before Old Man Daddy is properly dead, there are people headed upstream or down. It is mostly flatland along the Ti'il, until one gets to the roots of the river where the country rises up into mountains, into forests, into a thousand little knobs and swales and chasms where one can find a scatter of huts set in garden patches, and maybe even a milk animal or two, or a flock of gimmers for meat and hides. Not that the chimi-hounds couldn't come there; they could and sometimes do; but usually, they don't bother. Why go so far to kill a few when you can stay in town and knock off dozens?

Downriver is Du-you, the port at the confluence of the Ti'il and the Fohm. Du-you is no good. Chimi-hounds run Du-you, from the docks to the farms along the delta. But along the low banks of the Fohm, east and west, lie miles of reed beds where anyone can disappear. Reappearing is sometimes a problem, what with the blood-birds and the monster chaffers and the gavers that sit on their piled nests of rotting reeds, but those you can look out for. There are islands among the reeds, and people living on the islands. Some of the people have been careful for so long that the chimi-hounds don't even know they exist.

It is one of these islands the refugee couple almost happens upon, he and she, well into middle age, found lying in sodden exhaustion, surrounded by a circle of patient blood-birds, some little distance from a nameless village. Such places have sentries well out, and the sentries find them.

"Out along the reed canal," the sentry tells the headman, Ghatoun. "Lying up in the reeds, half-dead."

They are not half-dead. A quarter, maybe, from being sucked by chaffers and scratched by swamp briar and covered with bites from stingers, cuffer-noses, and swutches, none of which is usually lethal.

"Who are you?" Ghatoun wants to know. He knows already they aren't chimi-hounds. A chimi-hound wouldn't have a woman along.

"Latibor Luze," says he.

"Cafferty Luze," says she.

Both are gray at the temples and wrinkled a bit around the eyes. Both have open faces and shining, open eyes, like those of children too young to know about Chimi-ahm, though there is something watchful there, as well. And something sad, but then, in Derbeck, that's the usual thing.

"And where from?"

"Houmfon, most recently," the man sighs.

Most recently? And where before that? The headman looks Latibor Luze in the eyes and wonders if he really wants to ask.

"From Beanfields before that," says Latibor softly, giving Ghatoun a straight look. "Some years. And before that, all over. For a long time." It's a risk to tell this to Ghatoun, but not a large risk. Ghatoun's people wouldn't be out here, living among the reeds, if they were in sympathy with what goes on in Derbeck.

"Chaffer spit," Ghatoun mutters to himself. He doesn't want to hear it. Border crossers! Maybe even agitators, maybe with Council Enforcers after them, and if not Council Enforcers, then surely chimi-hounds, eager to kill off nonbelievers. The very kind of thing that was most dangerous!

"Who knows you're here?" he demands harshly. "Who might be looking for you."

"Nobody," whispers Latibor in an exhausted voice. "We'd only been in Houmfon a short time. When we heard Old Man Daddy was dying, we decided we'd better get out, but before we left, we told our neighbors we were going upriver, to the Viel Gorge."

"Somebody looking for you in Houmfon?"

"Probably not at all," says Cafferty. "Certainly not yet. They'd have no reason to. We're just folk."

They aren't just Derbeck folk! Though human enough, they're too big to be Murrey; too wide-mouthed and high-nosed to be Houm; too sandy-skinned to be High Houm. They are, in fact, distinctive, and Ghatoun doesn't believe for a minute there won't be somebody looking for them. Still. . . .

"You believers in Chimi-ahm?" asks the headman very softly, so softly not even his own folks hear him. "You dabbo-dam?"

"No," whisper the strangers. "We aren't believers. We've never been *taken*."

Could be, as many places as they've been, they're immune to being taken by the hungry ones, Zhulia the Whore, and Chibbi the Dancer and Lord Balal and all the minor manifestations.

"Well then, stay awhile," the headman says. "Rest."

They both smile gratefully, tremulously, and do rest while the headman speaks to the sentries, doubling their number, putting them twice as far out as usual. So the strangers say nobody's looking for them. So they say nobody's missed them. So. Maybe they believe it. That doesn't mean Ghatoun has to. He'd be within good sense simply to kill them off and send their bodies down the river. Still, wasn't it that kind of thing what he'd left Houmfon to escape, long ago, not wanting it for him, or for his wife-mate, or his children, or his people. Wasn't it that kind of thing what he hated most?

Jory and Asner had arrived on the *Bright Winged Dove*, a two-masted river-yat with a crew of eighteen including the captain, and this ship now took the others aboard. Danivon's troupe now totaled seven, if one included the old folks as part of the show. Danivon, though temporarily elated at Jory's arrival, was beginning to think of his expedition as notably ridiculous: seven people, two of them so old they could barely stagger, two of them mated like the halves of a scissors, only three able-bodied persons, and one of those a fool woman who attracted him as no other woman ever had, yet acted like some female Thrasian in purdah. All of them off on a mission to find out what these putative dragons might be, and if that wasn't a sideshow right enough, and well within the meaning of the term!

"Where do we go first?" asked Nela, excited despite having decided to disapprove of the entire undertaking and everyone in it. If withholding her approval was the only thing she could do, it was at least something. She would not, she had told Bertran stubbornly and at some length, condone.

"We stop at Salt Maresh," said Curvis, referring to his pocket file. "Too many children have been sent down from Choire, and we're to Attend the Situation there on our way upstream."

"Won't that tell everyone on Panubi we're Enforcers and not show-men?" asked Fringe.

"According to the captain, the *Dove* is the only ship plying the Fohm at this season," Danivon replied. "So there's no one to carry word upstream ahead of us. Besides, stopping at Choire will give us a chance to hear the music. I haven't been to Choire in years, but I remember the music."

Fringe asked no more questions. Since the revelations in Shallow, she had been much aware of a recurrent disapproval in Nela's manner. Fringe was trying to set aside their burgeoning friendship as she had set aside other relationships over the years. Nela, however, refused to be set aside. Despite her occasional coolness, she broke out every now and then with a giggle or a sidelong glance or a whisper to Fringe, as though she'd forgotten to be angry, and when she forgot, Fringe forgot too.

So, they sat near one another beside the rail, watching the delta pass by: the reeds, the gardens, men setting their nets for birds, fishermen checking their lines, gaver hunters sharpening their spears as they dried gaver hides over their smoky fires, women on the stamped-clay threshing floors forking shiny showers of dried grain into the air to let the wind blow away the chaff. Everywhere the color and smell of lilies, everywhere spicy blossoms hanging from the rich muddy banks. Everywhere the little round gossle boats, skimming the waters, like water bugs, darting. Everywhere the plash and murmur of folk. Fringe had seen much apprehension in this place, but not a single weapon. She had heard voices shaking with fear but not raised in anger. To one reared in Enarae, this equanimity was unbelievable.

"Don't they ever fight?" she asked Jory and Asner, who had just come up on deck.

"Not the folk of Shallow, no," replied Jory, while Asner nodded agreement. "They are of calm temperament and cheerful disposition. They work, not hard, but steadily; they make proper occasions to rejoice."

"With all this peace and tranquillity, I'd think they would have overpopulated their province by now," Fringe opined.

Jory shook her head. "Their custom dictates that each woman is entitled to keep two living children under a certain age. If she has more than that, they are given to the Fohm."

Fringe turned from the peaceful scene with a sense that something had shifted inside her. "To the river? Drowned?"

"They are put into a reed basket and sent downstream."

"Into the ocean? To drown?"

"Except for the few picked up and adopted by Curward sailors, more likely they are eaten by large gavers, many of which throng the delta and middle reaches of the Fohm. A quick death, and sure."

"But . . . but . . ." Fringe wanted to say, "That's dreadful. That's terrible." She said nothing. It was not dreadful, not terrible. It was only diverse, her indoctrination told her. Diversity. Holy diversity. She shut down her momentary disapproval and focused on one of the mind-relaxing exercises she'd learned at the Academy. "Difference is always disturbing," her instructor had said. "Learn to calm yourselves and accept."

Nela, however, voiced the thought before Fringe could suppress it. "That's dreadful!"

"Look about you," said Jory. "Do the people seem dreadful?" She turned toward Nela and fixed her with a bright-eyed stare. "It is no worse than is done in other places. For example, in your time and country, were there not many children killed?"

Nela said, "Many were, I suppose. But not like this!"

"In your time a primary cause of death in children was by violence, no?"

Nela nodded. "Well, yes," she admitted. "But the deaths were accidental! Children weren't specific targets! Or, if they were, it was some crazy person killing them!"

"Oh, I see. If they died by accident, they were not really so dead? It is better to die if your killer is crazy?"

Bertran blurted, "There's a difference!"

Jory shrugged. "Whether eaten in a basket on the Fohm or killed by a madman with a gun, the children became equally dead. Each form of death is acceptable to its own culture."

"Of course they weren't *acceptable*," cried Nela.

"If they had not been acceptable, something would have been done to stop them. Accidental deaths are usually acceptable, even expedient. And it's often the business of government to obscure the connections between cause and effect so that expedient deaths will seem to be . . . accidental."

"Expedient deaths?" questioned Nela.

"I know what she means." Bertran turned aside, and they saw sourness cross his face, a fleeting shadow, as on the face of someone who has unwittingly bitten into unripe fruit. "If you are overpopulated, or have an underclass, as in our time, it's to the advantage of everyone if they kill each other off."

"One advantage of the Hobbs Land Gods," murmured Asner. "That there is no overpopulation, no underclass."

"If you don't mind being enslaved," cried Fringe.

"Actually, I've wondered about that," said Asner thoughtfully. "I've been places where the Hobbs Land Gods were active, and it didn't seem that bad to me!"

Fringe backed away from him as though he were contaminated, her face drawn into an expression of disbelieving horror.

"He's not going to infect you," said Jory impatiently. "He was just trying to tell you something."

"I don't want to hear it!"

"I do," cried Nela. "I want to hear it!"

"I merely wanted to point out," said Asner, "that those who were influenced by the Hobbs Land Gods—"

"Enslaved," spat Fringe.

"Influenced," repeated Asner. "Those who were influenced were happier and less violent but no less curious or intellectually free than any of us here and now."

"I don't care," cried Fringe. "A slave is a slave." She turned away, angry and embarrassed. "No matter how the slavery feels to him."

"I merely remarked—"

"Who are you to remark anything!" demanded Fringe. "You, Asner, who are you, to talk so of the Hobbs Land Gods? What gives either of you the right to meddle in my . . . all our lives?"

Jory fixed her with an amused eye. "As to who I am, Fringe Owldark, I have been a number of people: wife and mother to persons long departed, lover and friend of unhuman marvels, savior of humanity (so I have been told), far-traveler, prophetess and guide, bender of time, explorer of the far reaches, and now—"

"And now retired," interrupted Asner, jabbing her with his elbow.

Jory turned an amused stare on him, concluding, "As for the rest, I meddle when I can. To the extent I am allowed."

Fringe flushed. "Well, if you're going to meddle with me, I have a right to know why!" Hot with annoyance she looked down at her writhing hands and worked them, finger by finger, as though readying herself to take up weapons and do battle.

"She's right, you've hectored her and them enough, Jory," said Asner, turning to gesture across the railings at the surrounding watery landscape. "You've philosophized and theorized sufficiently! If Fringe prefers to be miserable in her own way rather than be happy in some other way, it's her choice. The preference isn't unique or original with her, so let us discuss something else. Geography, for example. We're getting near the border of Shallow, at the top of the delta. The water meadows of Salt Maresh will begin to show up soon, with their long-legged fishers. There's a small river port not far upstream where we'll be stopping to—"

"Oh, Holy Mother," cried Nela, staring across the moving waters.

"What?" Fringe looked up.

"Is that your diversity!? Oh, oh, Holy Mother." Nela leaned and pointed. Following the extended finger, Fringe saw. A basket floating out in midstream, bobbing on the wavelets, carrying a child some three or four years old who held tight to the closely woven rim and cried silently, mouth open, eyes and nose streaming.

"You said babies . . ." said Fringe to Jory, surprised and offended at this event following so soon upon her catechism.

Jory corrected her, "I said children."

Nela cried, "Why would anybody . . . why would they send a toddler instead of an infant. I don't understand!"

"Perhaps the toddler is a boy and the family prefers a newborn daughter," suggested Asner calmly. "Or vice versa."

"Perhaps the toddler is defective in some way," suggested Jory quietly. "Or, perhaps, the child and its mother simply did not get along."

The basket bobbed on the river waves. The child looked up, saw them, stretched out its arms, and cried across the water. "P'ease . . . p'ease. . . ." The river flow swept the basket on past, the child's voice still rising in a wail of fright. "Oh, oh, pick Onny up, p'ease. Pick Onny up. . . ."

Bertran heaved himself away from the rail, Nela thrashing in his wake, sweat beading both their foreheads. "I can't believe this," Bertran snarled. "I can't. . . ."

Where the basket bobbed, something large and many toothed raised itself from the water and gulped hugely.

Fringe turned blind eyes away from the water, shutting out the sight, driving out the memory of it. Such things were. Diversity implied both pleasure and pain, both justice and injustice, both life and death. That's the way things were. She excused herself and stalked off, brushing by Danivon as she went.

"What's the matter with her?" demanded Danivon, who had just come from below.

Asner pointed where the basket had been and explained in a low voice, "A big gaver came up from below and gulped down the child. I think Fringe was upset by it."

Danivon snarled. Well, he had told her, back in Enarae, that some places on Elsewhere would have disturbing habits. She should have prepared herself then! What did she think he'd been talking about? Table manners? One couldn't go getting outraged over every child floating down the Fohm, over every skull on the rack at Molock, over every bloody pile of street-corner corpses in Derbeck. And what would she say when she saw the women in Thrasis! Well, she wouldn't, luckily, since women Enforcers didn't go into Thrasis, which thought reminded him to fume once more that there was no good use for Enforcers who were unsuited to the work.

So far as Danivon was concerned, that included most women Enforcers. He started to say so, angrily.

Then, noticing the tears running down Nela's face, the expression on

Bertran's, he decided to say nothing for the time being. Their faces reminded him that Fringe was not the only one being exposed to true diversity for the first time. There were things several of them had to learn about accepting diversity without getting upset. There were things about being a Council Enforcer—or being in an Enforcer's company— which undoubtedly took a little getting used to.

Night comes on the river, and dark. The people go to their rest, all but one. Jory stands at the railing of the *Dove* listening to the chuckling water. The voice that speaks inside her head is familiar as her own, dear as a lover, treasured as a friend she has known forever.

"Evil here, woman. Growing day by day. You feel it." A sigh comes, vast as hurricane winds, and Jory's hair stirs in the breath.

She can feel the evil. She nods and says tiredly, "The question is the same one I've been asking all along, where's it coming from? Evil comes from unchecked power; only Council Supervisory has power; but this evil is not theirs. Where is the power from which it comes?"

A feeling, as of a frustrated shrug. *"Not from outside."*

"Not from outside, no. It's from here, on the planet. But where? It's everywhere. There seems to be no focus, no place of origin. . . ."

"Not Tolerance?"

"Well, I thought so at first, but where in Tolerance? Not Boarmus, poor fellow, doing his muddled best. Not Council Supervisory. They parade their cruelty openly, calling it diplomacy, calling it expediency, as governments always have. But still, they have a certain gentle-folkian standard that prevents their being brutes, rather reminding me of the democracies, back in the centuries of my era. Wanting to be good, you know. Wanting to be on the side of the angels. Able, once in a while, to muster the support needed for a brief crusade, but never able to continue in righteousness for long against the demands of opposing constituencies."

"A good argument for a benevolent despotism."

"Oh, give me that every time, so long as I can be the despot." She laughs, then sobers, reflecting. "No, this new horror has no limits on its brutality. When empowered ones sink into the barbarism of torture and indiscriminate death, then not only they themselves but also the society that empowers them are evil, root and branch, twig and leaf. This alone would tell me the horror doesn't come from Tolerance, for Tolerance still sets itself certain standards of behavior. Besides, the source can't be anything Danivon has been close to, or he'd have smelled it out."

"A strange one, this Danivon Luze. Also this Fringe Owldark. Odd ones for you to have picked!"

"I didn't pick Danivon. I picked his parents, and Danivon sort of happened along. I did pick Fringe, and I hold by my choice, old friend. I look at her and I see myself all over again. Oh, she was differently reared and has different ways of reacting. I was reared on words and she on silences, I on a system of philosophy and she on none at all, but inside. . . . Well." She is silent for a long moment, before saying, "She will be the right one, I think. When—"

"We will not speak of that."

"Not out loud, no. But *we* must. Eventually."

"We will not speak of that."

She sighs. "Danivon's in love with her, of course. She could be with him, but she refuses to be. She prefers not to be in love with anyone." Jory laughs with wry amusement. "She prefers not."

"You felt so once. A familiar response."

"Oh, hush!"

"And the twins?"

"Also very strange. They have decided opinions, though they aren't quite sure what they are from moment to moment! I confess that I'm enjoying them, quite selfishly. Hearing them talk of Earth is almost like having my girlhood back again."

"Do you want it back again?"

She considers this, staring into the black where the rim of the wheel of stars made a vast snowy road across the sky, as though to see some other world, some distant sun. "Not really. I was such a prig. So driven to do good, to fix things, that I didn't allow myself many enjoyments."

"You haven't changed."

She laughs. "I guess not. Here I am, come to this world totally by chance, trying to save it. I have a perfectly nice rocking chair at home. I could be sitting there with my cat, watching the horses in the meadow, instead of trying to cure all ills, making a swan song of pushing my nose in. . . ."

The voice in her mind sounds offended. *"Not just your nose. There are several of us."*

"Well, three. You, me, and Asner." She sighs. "I'm guilty of hubris. Having come at last to the peace of Panubi—quite by accident, of course—

having met *them*, upriver, I should have let it go at that. For any normal person, meeting *them* would have made a good finish, wouldn't it? Despite their turning out to be quite different from what I might have expected. Better and worse, one might say. Still, a nice dramatic conclusion for anyone's existence. Any sensible autobiographer would have stopped right there. But no. I wanted one more good thing, one more achievement to my credit. I never thought it would be simple. But I didn't think it was impossible, either."

"Humans are often impossible."

"Look who's talking," she mutters. "Still, I did think this was worth a simple try, a few little nudges that might do some good without much upsetting *them*. I thought we could stimulate discussion, pique curiosity, get a little dissension and rebellion started. . . ."

"Preach the gospel of freedom!"

"One might say that. Given a little time, it might have worked! But now, suddenly, there's this new thing. This malice. This evil. Something dreadful's going to happen, I can feel it!"

"Yes."

"We're both too old for this," she says sadly. "Someone younger should be doing this."

"Asner's younger. By a few thousand years."

"He was already an old man when we found him on my former home planet, staring at that ancient statue of you and me."

"You flirted with him."

"Pah! I simply asked him if he saw any resemblance between me and the statue, and he said he did! You and I looked very brave and beautiful in our prime. Did I tell you it was sculptured by a man I knew?"

"Several hundred times."

"Well, we old people forget what stories we've told. Life changes around us so much we turn to comfortable things. Old events, old memories. Things we've worn smooth with retelling." She fingers the medallion around her neck. "Sometimes I need to remember what I was like, when I was young. Copying my friend's work on a pendant means I can look at it and be reminded. I won't forget him . . . or us, as we were."

"Vanity. All is vanity," he says in an amused voice.

"Your scriptural citations are always correct, old friend. All is vanity. When I stop being vain, I'll be dead. Vanity is its own resurrection. It gives one hope!"

"And you think this one little world is worth . . ."

"You are not the only student of ancient human Scripture. Even long dead religions have had truths written in their names. Think of the ninety and nine in the fold and the shepherd abroad in the windy night, seeking the lost sheep on the lonely hills. . . ."

Together they consider the lost sheep: Elsewhere.

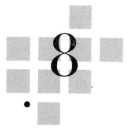

Boarmus was wakened again in the middle of the night. This time he did not bother with the trip down the hall, the tube, the secret doors, and access routes to the Core. This time he didn't have to go anywhere, for they came to him, not as mere wraiths but as actualities, as separate presences.

"Your Enforcers are asking the question again," one cried, waving its hideous arms. "Those with them too, they are breaking our commandments! We can see them. We can hear them!"

Others began to shriek, the sounds making a beast howl in his ears, and Boarmus fought the thrashing sickness in his belly. Only keeping the appearance of calm would save him from them. "What are you talking about?" he demanded. "I can't hear with you all talking at once."

One voice said, "Your Enforcers should not ask questions."

"Ask whom?" Boarmus shouted.

Silence.

"Asking," said the voice. "Talking. We heard them saying things. In Shallow! In Panubi!"

Boarmus thought a moment, cursing silently. "You mean, the people we sent to Panubi have been talking with one another? Telling the people from the past about Elsewhere? That's what you mean, isn't it?"

"Forbidden," the voices gibbered.

How many voices were there? He couldn't tell. Not as many as there should be. A thousand persons had gone into the Core, but there were only a few voices. Since the last time, he had been through the biography book a dozen times. There was that one voice, that one gulping voice, that one name written over and over in blood; there was the female voice that had introduced herself to him; he thought he knew at least two others.

"Why is it forbidden?" demanded Boarmus, forcing the words out against mounting panic.

Silence again.

Boarmus swallowed bile and pressed the point. "Does it really matter if they talk of history or ask questions about Elsewhere? They know about Brannigan. They know the committee members came here. That's public knowledge, discussed on every Great Question Day. But people don't know the Core exists, and they won't find out about the Core because I'm the only one who knows about the Core and I won't tell them. Let them ask all they like. Let them make up stories. It won't matter!"

"Forbidden," cried a horrid voice, joined by echoes, resonances. Perhaps that's all the other nine hundred and some odd were by now, mere echoes, mere resonances. And yet they were dreadful, horrid, turning his insides to churning liquid, making him feel like a bag of loose guts. How? Why this absolute terror, with him powerless to control it?

"Why?" demanded Boarmus again, struggling to keep his voice calm and reasonable, reaching deep into memory for what he'd read in the corridors below, what Chadra Hume had told him. "I can understand your desire for secrecy at first. Your coming here was secret. You believed the people at Brannigan who weren't members of your committee might have resented your coming here. You thought they might regard it as a kind of . . . desertion. You worried that they might be so angry they'd come after you. But that was then!"

He clenched his teeth together and swallowed. "That was then. There's no danger now! There's no threat now. Nobody knows about you anymore. Except for a few rhymes and songs, you've all been forgotten!"

He knew the words were a mistake as soon as they left his lips. Faces faded into the walls. Luminous, flapping forms succeeded them, turned to show faces once more, then faded again and reappeared, each face contorted so greatly it took Boarmus a moment to realize that the emotion they expressed was rage.

"Forgotten," they shrieked at him, deafening him. *"What right have they to forget?"*

Choruses of voices. How many? He couldn't tell. Outside his fear, some cool part of himself listened and noted. There were at least four of them, plus echoes. Were they the ones Zasper had mentioned, so long ago?

"But you *wanted* to be forgotten," Boarmus whispered, barely able to get the words out. "It's in the log, back during the early years. You decided you liked it that way. It was your decision."

"We created this world. If it were not for us . . ."

Boarmus made a placating gesture. Useless. The voices did not pause.

"What I we am are cannot be forgotten! We are . . . we are more than we were, Boarmus. Nobody forgets us anymore, Boarmus. We are . . . we are a new thing, Boarmus. We can do as we will, Boarmus."

He stood slack-jawed, spit flowing up under his tongue as from a well.

"Kneel down, Boarmus. Show reverence," said the gulper, a scream of fury in the voice. "You kneel down!"

"Yes, Boarmus," another voice. This was definitely a female voice, he knew it! "Kneel down. Pray to us, Boarmus. Show us the respect a loving son owes us."

"A loving . . . man owes us," snickered another, also female.

Did he hear laughter? *Do it,* his mind said. *No matter what, just do it. Do it, so they'll be satisfied and get out of here.* He fell to his knees, shivering with a terror so complete he could not have opposed them even if he had thought of it.

His mind still worked, however. Some chilly part of him sat off and asked questions. "Tell me your names so I can be respectful," he murmured. "Please."

"Magna Mater," tittered a voice.

"Most Gracious and Wondrous Lady," said another.

"Almighty and Marvelous," gulped a third.

He didn't ask for further introductions. "Don't kill me, please," he whispered. "Please, almighty ones."

Something like a chuckle, something like a sigh of satisfaction, something like a wailing scream. All at once, from separate beings.

"We don't care what you say," came a fading voice, the male voice. "We will punish . . . if we decide to. Curious people. Blasphemous people. Punish them. . . ."

All right, they were doing it. Now how were they doing it? Not supernatural. He didn't believe in the supernatural. It had to be mechanical or electronic. A combination, perhaps. Sonics to cause apprehension. Combined with holography to create terror. Perhaps focused electromagnetic fields. Could one stop a heart with focused fields? The question was irrelevant. The dead girl they'd found down below the monitoring section hadn't had her heart stopped. She'd been torn apart. Had they done that?

Of course they had. He didn't even need to know why. Why didn't matter. The only question that mattered was how.

He walked to the monitoring station, to the blinking lights and beeping signals and the scurry of persons keeping track of the thousand provinces. *Assume,* he told himself, fighting to appear relaxed and calm, *oh, assume that if they can see what is going on in Panubi, they can also follow you if you leave Tolerance—can and will! Assume they can go anywhere on the surface of Elsewhere. Probably not in the air. Not if they're using sonics and holography and focused fields. Not high in the air, at any rate. Whatever mechanism they use to propagate themselves on the surface, surely it cannot extend through open air. And probably not through or across water. Not yet, at any rate.*

So . . . so, they must be stopped. Of course they must be stopped. The former Provost, Chadra Hume, had known that. He'd told Boarmus that! They had to be stopped before . . . Too late to stop them before. Now they had to be stopped while. Stopped while they were doing these horrible things. And the only minds capable of stopping them were the dinks in City Fifteen. Not just any dink would do. Some of them were ridiculous mechanisms worth no more than a dead chaffer, but some of them were brilliant, geniuses, Chadra Hume had told him once, certainly as bright as those ancient ones who'd gone into the Core, dinkajins who'd chosen to be only brains because that's what they mostly were to start with. Those . . . those were the ones he needed, those were the ones Chadra Hume had told him about.

But how could he get there without the Core knowing? The Core knew everything!

He wandered through the monitoring rooms, nodding, smiling, feeling the skin around his lips crack, trying to ignore the sickness in the back of his throat, the cramps in his belly as he stopped to greet a worker, to peer into a monitor that reflected the abyssal trenches of Deep.

Find an excuse to go somewhere else, he thought, *but don't go there. . . . No. No, for if they expect you to turn up somewhere and you don't, then they'll become suspicious. So, you must go where you say you will go. But then, on the way back, stop off at City Fifteen. And in the meantime, send a message to City Fifteen, telling them what has happened. . . .*

How could he send a message. What mechanism could he use? There was no point in using a code. Down there was an enormous brain full of hundreds of minds, some of them, no doubt, quite competent. A few, perhaps, brilliant. Well, so maybe there were only a few left, they would be the smartest ones, wouldn't they? The fact that they were insane (all? or only some?) didn't necessarily limit their intelligence. Couple that with the fact the thing was located behind an impervious barrier, and it had its own power source and its own workshops and its own warehouse full of everything imaginable (Boarmus had been through the specifications a dozen times) and though it was originally set up to communicate with the outside world only through the Files and the Provost—only symbolically, only verbally—somehow it had found a way to get around those limitations and now it was out!

A code message would be deciphered in the instant.

So, how to send a message to the dinka-jins?

Boarmus peered into a monitor that watched the moon rise over New Athens. He joined an intent group watching a scene in Derbeck, the images flashing up on the array, only to be succeeded by others, then others still.

"Stop it there," said the Charge Monitor for Derbeck, with a bow of deference toward Boarmus. "Right there! Provost, I'm glad you're here to see this. That deity of theirs has actually been showing up on visual recently!"

They watched together as Chimi-ahm, the tripartite deity of Derbeck, strode through the streets of Houmfon.

"Take that eye down," demanded the Charge Monitor, her voice shaking. "I want to see its feet!"

The eye extended its distant lens and focused upon the great crushing feet that broke the cobbles to leave imprints there, feet that crushed the herbage as they crossed a verge, that shattered structures as they smashed through walls.

"It's leaving footprints," cried an observer. "And destruction, real destruction! It can't do that! It's not a material thing!"

"How long has this been going on?" demanded Boarmus, the sickness inside him surging as he watched the striding image. "Am I correct in recalling that the Derbecki god has always been hallucinatory!"

"Has been," said the Charge Monitor tersely. "But *is* something else now, Provost. The damned thing's real."

"Sort of," said another Monitor, bending over a flickering instrument panel. "Not entirely. Almost."

"Make up your mind," the Provost snarled. "Which is it?"

"It varies," the Monitor muttered. "It sometimes is and sometimes isn't. See for yourself."

And they did, watching as the needles flickered and rose and fell. The thing was real, sometimes, for moments. And not real too. Unquestionably, however, real or unreal, the thing *was*. Not quite synchronized, yet, but it was, nonetheless.

Boarmus swallowed. The monitors were looking at him, waiting for him to tell them what to do. They would expect him to investigate this, at once. Perhaps they were expecting him to do it himself, but Derbeck was nowhere near City Fifteen and just now it was absolutely essential for him to get to City Fifteen.

He kept his voice firm and decisive. "We have a team near Derbeck. Danivon Luze's group. Send instructions from me saying they're to make an investigation of this manifestation in Derbeck, as soon as possible." His voice sounded right: concerned but not panicky. Those working as monitors nodded, accepting that he had done the proper thing.

He thought: *New Athens is near City Fifteen. Denial is near City Fifteen. Enarae is near City Fifteen. Zasper Ertigon is in Enarae. I would have legitimate reason to inquire from Zasper Ertigon about Danivon Luze, about Fringe Owldark.*

"I'm going to Enarae," he loudly informed an underling. "I want to talk to former Council Enforcer Zasper Ertigon about two of his Enforcer protégés. Arrange quick transport and be sure Ertigon will be available when I get there." Let the dead men listen, let them hear. What he was doing was appropriate. They could not fault what he was doing.

The underling scurried and returned. "Transport, sir. Down in the garage momentarily. Zasper Ertigon located and holding himself in readiness, sir."

Boarmus made no thanks for this efficiency. Though originality and innovation were rare or totally absent in Tolerance, efficiency was the usual thing.

"Does the Provost wish his travel things packed? Does the Provost wish to take a secretary?" A flunky is what the underling meant. Did Boarmus want somebody along to do the running and fetching. But of course he did.

"Have my travel things packed, yes. And that cousin of Syrilla's. That young man. What's his name?" Boarmus knew what his name was, the one who'd been standing about, spying on him, watching him. The one he'd seen hiding in the corridor last time he'd returned from the Core. Jacent.

"Jacent, sir." Jacent of the lambent eye, the laughing mouth, Jacent the manic, the madcap, the servant-hall comedian. The underling smiled, thinking of Jacent.

"That's him. Get him." Youths of that age had been well educated and well trained and were still fresh enough to have some gumption. Five years from now he would have substituted opinion for fact, pose for reaction, and would be useless—as useless as the rest of Council Supervisory—but just now, Jacent would do. Besides, the boy had been hanging about, obviously curious, and he had a certain daredevil air to him, as though he might be capable of more than mere duty. Boarmus would need more than mere duty.

And in very little time they were aloft, two of them and the pilot.

"We're going to Enarae," Boarmus told Jacent, keeping it to a whisper, his mouth a finger's width from the boy's ear. Even if there was some spying little ear on the flier, likely they couldn't hear him over the whine of the gravitics. "I have reason to think we will be overheard once we are on the ground, so once we are on the ground, you won't say one word about this. You will accompany me to the hotel. You will go with me to the Swale. That's a—"

"I know about the Swale," said Jacent, preening himself in his excitement.

Boarmus seized him with scarcely controlled fury. "Shut up! Don't talk! Listen! In the Swale we'll meet Zasper Ertigon. I'll excuse you, and you'll go off to a gambling house run by Ahl Dibai Bloom. You'll play a little of whatever game you're good at, assuming you're good at anything. You'll watch for a chance to put this packet secretly into the hands of Bloom himself, letting no one see you do it."

The packet was a small one, fitting into the palm of one hand. Boarmus had prepared it after they were aloft, hiding it as he did so. If there was an ear, there could also be an eye. If there were both an ear and an eye, Boarmus was already lost. Best pretend there was neither.

"Yes, Provost," mouthed Jacent, set back by the fury but too curious to let this opportunity pass. "Is this about the ghosts?" he whispered.

Boarmus spun on him, lipping silently, "What do you know about ghosts! Who told you. . . ."

Jacent flushed and stuttered, aware he had erred yet again. "I saw," he whispered. "We were exploring. . . ."

Boarmus drew him close. "You! You were down in the old barracks? You were with that girl who was killed? That boy who disappeared?"

Jacent quivered on the cusp of denial, unable to bring it off.

"Tell me," grated the Provost, gripping the young man's head painfully with both hands. "Quiet as a moth! Whisper me everything!"

Fringe dealt with the children-in-baskets matter as she had often dealt with other confusions, by refusing to think about it. She had learned not-think as a child and she used it now. She would not-think about the children or the baskets, she would not-see them again. She became very busy with other things.

Though Danivon had sought an opportunity to talk to her about the Enforcers' life, as a prelude—he confessed to himself—to another intimate encounter, he took a close look at her shuttered face and gave up the notion. She was in there somewhere, but not immediately available. No point in wasting effort.

In any event, there was no time, for fishponds appeared along the shore, separated from the river and one another by dikes topped with walkways of mud and reeds. Along these walkways the Fisher Folk of Salt Maresh stalked with their burdens of spears and nets. Behind the ponds, in spaces cleared from the reed beds, drying racks stood laden with their strong-smelling burdens among shifting veils of smoke. As the *Dove* came around a curve in the river, the travelers could see the village on a platform set high on pilings. Storklike men with shaven heads came out of their houses as the *Dove* approached, the delicate reed-woven houses making a lacy backdrop to their ominously still figures.

"The Fisher Folk do not bear children," Danivon said to the twins as he cocked his Enforcer's bonnet to the correct angle and gave his coat a twitch. "Their religion requires them to be neutered and eschew sensuality."

"They live spiritual lives," said Curvis in a cynical tone, "constantly inspired by the voices of their kindred upon the heights." He too wore Enforcer dress.

"It's the children from Choire, then, that renew their population," said Fringe.

Danivon nodded. "Choire retains only those with the finest voices, sending the rest down to become Fisher Folk. The complaint is that Choire has recently been sending far too many."

He raised a hand in greeting. The Head Fishers returned the greeting with grim faces. The *Dove* tied up at a piling set in the shallows alongside the stilt-high village.

As soon as the plank had been lowered, Danivon and Curvis went across to the village platform where they were offered ceremonial cups of the local beverage and a catalog of complaint, the latter repeated over and over in more or less the same words for some little time. When the complainants were talked out, the two Enforcers beckoned Fringe from her listening post at the rail, assigned her the role of threatener in the upcoming negotiations, and bade her follow as they rounded up the excess youngsters for return to the heights.

"Where?" Danivon demanded of the Head Fisher who stood beside them on one long leg, the other drawn up, foot in hand.

"There," the Fisher gestured, waving at the reed beds beyond the fishponds. "We told them to build themselves shelters as they would."

"Hospitable of you," grunted Fringe, drawing her polished boot from the mud with some difficulty. "A bit soggy out there, isn't it?"

"We have limited room in the village," snorted the Head Fisher, and indeed, the woven village above them had seemed overcrowded. "They're old enough to take care of themselves. You'll find them through there," and he pointed toward a break in the reed beds, a well-cleared path.

Danivon swore mildly and stalked off along the dike between the ponds, the other two Enforcers following. The path was obviously well used, with many layers of cut reeds laid crisscross into the spongy soil and tramped down to make solid footing. Though clear, the path was by no means straight, and within moments they had lost sight of the village and were surrounded by dark clattering stalks that stood in impenetrable walls.

Danivon found himself walking as softly as possible, stopping every few steps to listen.

His nose said someone . . . No. Some*thing* else was on the path, ahead of them.

"What?" whispered Fringe, watching his face.

He made a face, shrugged, put a finger to his ear to tell them to listen.

The sound came as though he had commanded it, a deep swallowing, as of breath gulped into an enormous maw.

"What in hell?" murmured Curvis.

"Where?" whispered Danivon, palms up.

The other two pointed in slightly different directions.

Fringe grimaced. "What was it?"

"Gaver?" asked Danivon of Curvis.

"Gavers don't make a sound like that. They roar."

They went even more quietly, passing a group of huts that were no more than piled bundles of reeds, unskillfully hollowed to offer shelter. This cluster of squalid dwellings was empty, but another could be seen in a haze of smoke down the trail.

They went toward it, only to stop in their tracks.

"What's that smell?" said Fringe, her nose wrinkling.

"Three guesses," offered Danivon, carefully approaching the nearest hut. He put his head inside only briefly, then came away swiftly to stand beside them, gulping air.

"What?" asked Fringe.

"A body," muttered Danivon. "What's left of one."

Fringe felt a chill upon her skin. "There," she said, catching movement at the corner of her eye.

It was a youngster, scrambling away into the reeds with frantic haste.

Curvis took two long steps and brought him back by the scruff of his muddy shirt.

Off in the reeds, the sound came again.

"How long has this been going on?" Danivon asked the mud-bedaubed youngster, who only shivered and gasped, unable to answer.

"Let him alone," said Fringe, gathering the boy to her. "Come on, boy. Are there more of you?"

The child pointed with a shaking hand.

"Do we dare call?" murmured Danivon, listening with all his attention for the sound to be repeated.

"Do we dare not," she replied, standing tall to shout into the silence:

"We are Enforcers from Council Supervisory, here to take you back to Choire. Come out. You'll be safe with us."

"She says," muttered Curvis, loosening the weapon at his hip and looking alertly around him.

The swallowing sound came again, more remote, but with something in it of . . . amusement? Could that be?

Dirty faces peered from among the reeds. Children emerged, eleven years old, twelve, some a little older.

Danivon wiped the face of one youngster with the hem of his shirt. "How long has this been going on?" he asked.

The boy turned frightened eyes on the three of them. "Every night it gets some of us."

"Have you heard anything? Seen anything?"

The boy shivered. "Nothing, sir Enforcer. We say . . . we say the ghosts are eating us."

"When did it first happen?" Curvis demanded of the youth.

He conferred with some of the others. They thought twenty days perhaps, more or less.

Danivon shook his head angrily. "Is this all of you?"

They counted themselves, taking a tally, one or two going away into the reeds to emerge with others who had been afraid to come out.

"How many were there supposed to be?" asked Fringe.

"About a hundred," said Danivon.

"There aren't more than fifty here."

"I know," he grunted, turning to lead the remnant along the winding trail out of the reed beds.

"The body you saw. How had it been killed?" Curvis whispered to Danivon, not so softly that Fringe didn't overhear.

"It had been dissected," Danivon said flatly. "The organs laid out to one side, this one and that one. From the amount of blood splashed around, I'd say it had been done rather slowly while the kid was alive."

"Boy? Girl?" asked Fringe, wondering why she cared.

Danivon shook his head, saying between his teeth, "An anatomist might be able to tell. I couldn't."

Fringe fought the sickness in her belly, thinking that lately all she'd done was feel sick about this thing, sick about that thing. Maybe Zasper had been right! Maybe she shouldn't have become an Enforcer. Certainly she wasn't doing very well at keeping her stomach or her emotions in line, not as well as the two men. Of course, they'd had more practice. . . .

They came out onto the shore where several of the Head Fishers stood, heads cocked as though listening.

"Why did you bother to make a complaint," snarled Danivon. "A few more days, you'd have had no children to complain of!"

"I told you," said one Fisher to another. "I told you something was killing them!"

The one addressed turned away, making a dismissive gesture. "Not our problem."

"Aaah," snarled Danivon. "Not your problem. What makes you think whatever-it-is is going to stay out there in the reeds? Now we've taken the children, what's it going to do? Hah? What are you going to do when it comes into the village? You'll scream for Enforcers then, sure enough, and maybe they'll just sit tight at the post near Shallow and tell you it isn't their problem." He angrily beckoned to the others, leading them toward the trail that led up the precipitous cliffs to Choire.

So, thought Fringe, with a glow of warmth toward Danivon, *he does have some feelings. He is not totally uncaring.* She soothed herself with this sentiment for a few moments, until it occurred to her Danivon might simply have been expressing annoyance at an unreported predator of unknown type. She fretted over this thought until the climb became so steep she had energy for nothing but putting one foot in front of the other.

Even though they stopped several times to allow the children to rest ("They're half-starved," muttered Fringe, to Danivon's grunted agreement), the journey to the heights did not take long. They were three quarters of the way up the precipice when they rounded a corner in the trail and were met by music.

Fringe forgot her anxieties, her doubts, the sickness in her belly. There was no room inside her for anything but what she heard. Music pulled them along the way. Even the children's heads came up as they ascended the final slope onto the stony ramparts, though most of them fell limply onto the stones at the top. Fringe sagged with them, leaning against a nearby wall with her mouth open, feeling nothing but the wonderful sound. She was caught in a joyous whirlwind! She simply stood, unconscious of anything but the music, lost in harmony.

"They're bred for it," Curvis barked as he passed, slapping her heartily on her bottom to bring her to herself. "Which seems to have caused the trouble. Suppose we earn our pay, Enforcer!"

Recalled to her duty, though still bemused, she followed him to the nearby portico where a group of Choire directors waited, their faces expressing less welcome than annoyance at this interruption of their daily rehearsals. They wore embroidered surplices and carried ritual batons, flourishing these to direct the Enforcers into the vacant hall behind them, all with such an air of tried patience and temperamental disdain that it gave Fringe an appetite for the role she had been assigned should the directors prove intransigent. For the moment she merely sat by, a supernumerary, while Curvis and Danivon began the negotiations.

The complaint and disposition were quoted and explained at length. The directors were not responsive. There was no help for it, they said. The children, and more later, would have to be accommodated in the Maresh.

Fringe took her dagger from her belt and began cleaning her fingernails with it. "The accommodation your children are offered is perhaps not what you planned. They are being sent alone into the reed beds to live as they may. They are not housed, they are not fed. And something is killing them, painfully and bloodily." Her words summoned up the memory of those reed beds, the sounds, the smells, and it was with difficulty she kept herself from gulping.

The directors looked at one another. Fringe tried to read their expressions. Annoyance? Grief? Frustration?

"Surely, that is the responsibility of the Fisher Folk," said one at last.

"Have the children no parents here in Choire to care what happens to them?"

"We have no families in Choire. We have only music."

Fringe threw herself into her role, sighing dramatically and casting her eyes upward. "And lovely music it is. A pity it will be lost to Elsewhere. It will no doubt take many years after the plague for enough voices to be found to sing anything at all."

"We are a healthy folk," said the oldest director in a stubborn tone.

Fringe yawned and juggled the dagger, its spinning blade spitting reflected light into their eyes. "The people in my home province said so too, and they were healthy enough. Then. Those few who are left no longer brag of their health."

"You wouldn't really . . ." said a plump young director apprehensively.

"We would have no choice," said Fringe, slamming the dagger into a carved tabletop with purposeful barbarism and considerable gusto. "You have changed your ways; you are not maintaining the status quo. You were not a numerous people when you arrived on Elsewhere. Thus, your allocated province is not large. Your hemi-province of Salt Maresh can accept about a hundred children a year, not twice that number! Any over that number, you must rear in Choire."

"But, but," the directors babbled.

"We suggest you return to whatever custom you followed when you arrived," said Curvis mildly.

"That would require interference with personal choice," cried the plump director. "Since we have listened to the words and music of Siminone Drad, such interference is anathema to us." He gestured appealingly to the tallest of the directors, a youngish one who stood silently behind the others, chewing upon his knuckle. This was Siminone, who flushed and bowed when his name was mentioned, then went back to worrying his knuckle, like a dog a bone. "Anathema," repeated the director, as though repetition would do what reason would not.

"Having too many children foisted on them is anathema to the Fisher Folk, your kindred," said Danivon firmly. "And it is certainly deadly for the children themselves. You must return to whatever you were doing before."

"But we used to be very strict," cried the young director. "Particularly in expressions of sensuality. It was Siminone who showed us that such strictness also constricts the music, leading to disharmony."

Danivon shook his fist at them threateningly. "You'd best become strict again, or use some other type of limitation."

"To do so would destroy spontaneity," cried Siminone, breaking his silence in exasperation.

Danivon snorted. "There are a number of spontaneous children outside whom you must now make provision for. Though they are fewer than they were, though they are no longer capable of reproduction, every one of them can at least carry a tune. . . ."

"Carry a tune!" exclaimed Siminone. "You think a tune is all that's needed. . . ."

Danivon interrupted him. "We'll leave you to it. When we return, we'll stop here at Choire again to be sure you've understood what we've said. Plague now or plague then, but in any case plague, unless you have accommodated your policies to the status quo."

They returned to the ship, where Jory begged the Enforcers to tell them all about it while the twins, pretending disdain, listened avidly.

"And you would really have spread plague?" Nela demanded angrily.

Danivon smiled at her and reached out to stroke her cheek. "It is almost never necessary actually to do it, Nela. We're not the ogres you think we are. The threat is enough. I've never used plague myself, and from what I was taught at the Academy, it's probably been used only half a dozen times in the last several hundred years, in all cases against badly overpopulated and totally intransigent provinces."

"But how would you keep it from infecting the neighboring lands," Bertran asked. "How do you keep it from wiping people out."

"We use diseases that are spread through close contact, sometimes through sexual contact," said Curvis. "And we use self-limiting strains that never kill the entire population."

"We had a disease like that on old Earth," said Nela. "An immune deficiency disease. It was killing lots of people when we . . . when we came here."

"Such plagues are known to arise spontaneously on overcrowded planets," Jory commented. "When any environment exceeds its carrying capacity, plagues begin to manifest themselves, though humans are always surprised when it happens."

"We have an evil history of destroying the homes in which we live," said Asner. " 'That's all right,' people say to one another. 'Burn down the house. We can always go live with Grandpa God!' " He snorted and threw up his hands. "Enough of this depressing stuff." He winked ostentatiously and patted a pocket. "Let us leave these Enforcers to their business while we go have something to drink."

Bertran tightened his arm about Nela's shoulders as she wiped her eyes, and they both went away after the old ones, somewhat cheered at the prospect of something a bit stronger than tea.

"What Asner said reminded me of Siminone Drad," said Fringe. "Siminone thinks he can burn down his house and still go on making music. Doesn't he see. . . ."

"They don't see," said Danivon. "They never see, or we would not need Enforcers."

"Danivon and I agree that Siminone Drad is the problem," Curvis said firmly. "Now we must do something about him."

Fringe felt very much the junior member, with too little experience to disagree, and after they had settled upon a method and cast lots for the duty, it was Fringe herself who went back to Choire in the late evening to Attend the Situation.

She went up the trail toward the music in a state of controlled unthink. All day she'd been telling herself she need merely do what had been decided was necessary, without thinking about it. Danivon and Curvis were agreed this was necessary, they had more experience than she did, therefore she'd do whatever they thought best. Once at the top, she accosted the first passerby, saying she had returned to ask a question that only Siminone could answer. When she was taken to him, she removed her glove and offered her bare hand. He took his hand from his mouth to put it into hers. She pressed it warmly, running her thumb along the knuckle he habitually chewed. There was no need for violence. The touch of her thumb, previously anointed with material from her Enforcer's kit, was all that was needed. She had scarcely released him when his knuckle went to his mouth again, and he unknowingly licked up the carefully engineered virus she had pressed upon his skin. Fringe put on the other glove she carried in her pocket, its inner surface previously anointed with the suppressant.

"What did you want to know from me?" he asked.

"Who composes the music sung here?" she asked. It was a spontaneous question, one that had occurred to her on the way up.

"I do," he said simply. "Much of it."

She smiled meaninglessly and thanked him. On her way down the twisting trail, she realized that when Siminone died a few days hence of the euphoric disease she had given him, the music he had not yet written would die with him.

She looked at her fingers in distaste, remembering Zasper Ertigon.

"You will hate yourself sometimes," he had warned her.

"I hate myself all the time, now," she had said.

Until the fish ate the child, she had not remembered his words. Until a few moments ago, she had not fully understood what he meant. She had a sudden urge to strip off the glove, suck her infected thumb, and make an end of her involvement in such matters. Better unthink that, as well. She fixed her eyes upon the trail and thought of her turtle shell at home. Gray thorn and gray leaf and gray mist rising. Heights were perilous. Perhaps she should have stayed at home, in her own pond.

When Fringe returned to the *Dove*, she found Danivon on deck alone, staring across the glittering water where the long-legged forms of the Fisher Folk moved along the dikes between the shallow fishponds. Some carried buckets of food for the fish, others carried spears as they searched for the small gavers who fed in shallow waters at night.

He turned and greeted her in a muted voice, thinking her face was more than usually pale in the moving light of the flares. "I waited for you," he said.

"The music we heard today . . ." she said to him, as though she were taking up a conversation they'd been having moments before.

"Wonderful," he said enthusiastically. "No one can sing like the people of Choire."

". . . was composed by Siminone Drad."

"Ah." He shook his head at her. "Gone. Too bad."

"It is worse than that," she insisted. "It's tragic. Why was it necessary to . . ."

"To Attend the Situation?" he asked. "Hadn't Siminone caused the Situation? Curvis and I both thought he had."

"Undoubtedly he had, but we could have talked to him. . . ."

" 'Each Enforcer to his own solutions,' " quoted Danivon sententiously, thinking once more that women were unsuited to this work. Even beautiful women. Even a beautiful, pale woman with hair like a fiery torrent and a body like a cool flame. "You didn't have to go," he said gently. "Curvis or I would have gone."

"Why didn't we consider talking to Drad," she persisted. "I'm not quarreling with you, I'm asking for information."

Danivon settled on the railing. "Talking to him would merely have increased his tendency to think. He is an innovator, and that's what innovators do: They think. They don't reason, mind you. They don't see consequences. And they're never contented with things as they are but must be always fiddling. Siminone might fiddle, for example, with the implications and applications of his former dicta, coming up with other interesting changes he could make. Our conversation might stimulate quite a number of insights. Then, when we came back from upriver, we would find Choire doing something entirely new, different, and reprehensible. A man who makes changes can't stop making changes. You know the rules, Fringe Owldark. 'If one death will do . . .' "

" 'If one death will do, do one death,' " she said. Of course she knew. One death rather than a few. A few rather than many. And many, when one must. Danivon was right. It would probably have been a choice, eventually, of Siminone or plague. One death or many. Reformers were always a problem. But the music. . . .

"One thing that was not discussed with them," she said stubbornly, "was feeding the increased number."

"Feeding?"

"Salt Maresh sends food to Choire. If there are more people in Salt Maresh, then less food goes to Choire. Much less. We could have pointed that out."

"In our experience . . ."

"It wouldn't have worked," she finished for him, remembering Jory's history lesson earlier in the day.

Danivon regarded her with sympathetic eyes. She was being fairly reasonable, for Fringe, so he would give her the benefit of his wider experience. "You heard Jory talking about Earth. It was the same then. Telling people they will go hungry has never worked. When I started out as an Enforcer, I tried preaching good sense. I've said things like, 'Momma, you know you can only get two babies through the dry season, so why did you have three, or five, or seven,' and they tell me, 'They're here now! They've got to eat!' Or, they say, 'Abidoi will provide.' But, after they say their god will provide, it's their neighbors they beg from, the ones who still have food because they've only one or two children. And, often as not, the neighbors give them food and both families watch their children starve, tears all down their faces, never once admitting they're responsible for it themselves. Everybody's possessed by the notion his own children are entitled to life, no matter what happens to other people's."

She turned her face away, hating this talk of death. He spoke so matter-of-factly, so dryly, so unemotionally. She turned abruptly to go to the peace of her cabin.

And found herself standing within the circle of Danivon's arms, her face only a finger's length from his own.

"Fringe Owldark," he murmured. "Fringe, don't fret so. Don't worry so." His hands touched her shoulders, the back of her neck and head. "Don't gnaw over every little thing, Fringe. You can't chew over every decision. You mustn't feel it all so much. Don't be sad. I don't want you to be sad."

"Don't," she thought she said. "Danivon. Let me alone."

"I won't let you alone," he whispered, putting his lips to her throat at the corner of her jaw, just below her ear. "You're alone too much." His tongue made dots of fire down her neck, up onto her cheek. His lips covered hers. "You're alone all the time." And "Shhh," he said when she struggled, only a little.

"Danivon, I don't want this!"

"Little liar," he whispered. "Lovely little liar. Owldark the beautiful. Owldark the perverse. Owldark . . . who makes me shiver, just thinking of her. . . ."

"Danivon. . . ."

There was no one there, no one on the deck. Most of the crew had gone fishing with the Heron Folk. The others of the sideshow were away or asleep. Only if she cried loudly would anyone hear.

She cried softly, so no one would.

Zasper, as requested, met Boarmus in the Swale. At first glance, having no other explanation for Boarmus's eyes glaring between puffy lids, his haggard cheeks, his slightly trembling hands, Zasper assumed the Provost was ill. Zasper, much aware of his retirement from Council Enforcement, felt it was not his role to offer comment upon the Provost's health, so he contented himself with a carefully judged, barely adequate obeisance plus the all-purpose word:

"Sir."

Boarmus beckoned him toward the river. "An excursion boat is just leaving, Ertigon. I have it in mind to see something of the Seldom Isles." His words were a braying whisper, as though he could not decide whether to say or not to say.

This was a puzzle. "Sir?"

"Accompany me aboard. You can offer commentary."

"Sir."

They were the last to board. Boarmus believed the boat would not be spied upon. The dead men hadn't known he was coming here until just before he left. The dead men hadn't known he would be taking a boat. If they were busy doing whatever they were doing in Panubi, probably it was safe to talk on a boat in Enarae. Maybe.

The wallowing vessel thrust off immediately and began making its slow way down into the turgid flow of the swamp river. Boarmus moved to the bow, where no one else was standing, and, drawing Zasper close to him, whispered only inches from his ear, "If you know of any benign local gods who still have any clout, old man, summon them up! We're all in deep, deep trouble, and I need all the help I can get!"

Zasper ostentatiously wiped spittle from the side of his head where Boarmus had sprayed him and regarded the man with distaste. Enough politeness. "What are you up to, Provost?"

Boarmus gripped him harder. "Listen to me, Ertigon. I've something to tell you, and pray heaven we can't be overheard, for if we are, you're dead and so am I, and likely also your protégés, Danivon Luze and Fringe Owldark, both."

Zasper started in surprise, glared threateningly, but kept silent. Boarmus had a twitch above his eye and his skin was gray. He looked like a man frightened half to death, not one to chivvy if one wanted sense. Whatever this was, it wasn't of Boarmus's doing. "Tell me," said Zasper.

"You know about Brannigan Galaxity, Ertigon. You know about Brannigan's Great Question Committee, you know all the members of it came here to Elsewhere."

"So I've been told."

"What you don't know is that they're still here."

"Still . . . ?" Zasper made no sense of this. "You mean, their bodies are still here?"

Boarmus leaned even closer and began whispering rapidly into Zasper's ear, reciting his tale in a frenzy of words that tumbled over one another and had to be sorted out and rearranged by their confused listener. He went on talking for some little time. Zasper didn't interrupt, though his eyes narrowed and his breathing quickened.

Boarmus concluded, "They were supposed to sleep. Wake up once a year and be informed, then go back to sleep. I don't think they've been asleep. . . ."

"Not recently?"

"Not . . . not ever. I try to imagine. What that would do to someone, some normal person. Being awake, in the Core, all that time. . . ."

"But . . . even so. That wouldn't explain—"

"Of course not!" hissed Boarmus. "It doesn't explain anything. Nothing explains anything. I've tried . . . oh, I've tried, I've read, everything they left, all their biographies, everything. Nothing explains anything. But what's happening . . . it's coming from the Core. And they're what was put into the Core. So somehow . . . ."

"You say these people went in there so they could come out once the Great Question had been answered?"

"That's what the documents say. But Chadra Hume, my predecessor, thinks they meant to come out whenever they decided conditions were right. And in the logs down there, one of the Provosts asked when they would come out and they said when they decided to."

Zasper shook his head wonderingly. "And they've been awake in there, all this time."

"They must have changed the specifications."

"Which were designed to keep them . . . sane, I suppose."

"I suppose."

"So now they're not?"

"I don't know! I'm not even sure it is them. Is it just a few of them? Maybe one or two? Or is it all of them? Or . . . is it something else entirely, maybe using their names?"

"Can you shut it down? The Core?"

"No. There's no way. But I think it . . . they know we'd like to shut it down. If it were you, you'd know, wouldn't you? Even if you were crazy . . . especially if you were crazy, you'd know. You'd suspect!"

"You think they're after Fringe and Danivon?"

"How would they get at Fringe and Danivon? Fringe and Danivon are in Panubi. Reason tells me it's impossible for them to reach Panubi, and yet it . . . they spoke of Panubi."

Boarmus fell silent, mopping at his face where sweat ran slickly. "While you and I are talking, my young aide is sending a message to City Fifteen. Secretly, I hope. There's a group there who've been looking at this problem for some time. Chadra Hume informed them a long time ago. Even in his time, he felt something was very wrong. . . ."

"What do you want from me?"

"Anything. Advice. Help." He took in Zasper's blank expression and sighed. "Maybe I only wanted someone to talk to. Oh, I know what you Enforcers think about the Council, Ertigon. We'd have to be complete fools not to know. You take us for pompous idiots, mostly, layabouts who spend our days eating and drinking and engaging in our effete little rituals, none of which mean anything, accomplish anything. You're perfectly right, that's what we are. But then, that's what we were assigned to do. That's what we're here for. It's what all public servants have always been: roadblocks, resistors, interceptors of change, valves designed to shut down the flow of events, inhibitors of revolution, delayers of evolution, servants of the status quo. Here on Elsewhere we call it maintaining diversity, and we send you Enforcers out whenever there's a threat to custom or habit. As we see it, we've been faithful to our charge, Ertigon, just as you've been faithful—more or less—to yours."

"More or less?"

"Well, there was that business of your rescuing Danivon Luze."

"You knew?" Zasper was amazed.

"Most Enforcers do things like that, now and then. You have to let them get away with a few things. Give them a little leeway. Otherwise they crack on you. It's all written down in the Provost's operations manual. How much unauthorized activity to let you all get away with. Better have a guilty Enforcer than a holier-than-thou. Enforcers who feel guilty try to make up for it by being extra conscientious most of the time. Holier-than-thous are a pain. Nobody knows about the real rules, of course, except the Provosts. We keep quiet about it."

"You knew!" Zasper repeated, unbelieving.

"Not only knew but was grateful. Danivon has been very useful. Is, is very useful. I'll confide in you, Ertigon. It's not just that he's useful. I've grown fond of him. I have no children of my own, and he's . . . he's what I would have chosen to be, if we were permitted such choices. He's what I've imagined myself being, from time to time. He's quite a boy. A gallant with the ladies. Ah, well. One can get weary of being Provost."

Zasper stared at him, mouth open. Whatever he had expected to hear from Boarmus, it had not been this.

Boarmus nodded musingly. "And he's not Molockian, of course, even though that's where you found him. I got a cell sample from him. His genetic makeup is closest to the people of Shallow, but it isn't close enough to be proof positive. It may have been modified, of course. So says Files."

"How did you know where I found him?!"

"There are monitors on the inspection ships. For Provost's eyes only. An old saying covers it. Who watches the watchers, eh? Oh, Ertigon. . . . I know a lot."

"But not how to protect us from this thing in the Core," Zasper snorted.

"No. Not that. Sometimes I think whatever it is must be immortal, stewing away down there!"

"And you're scared." It wasn't a question.

"Terrified." Boarmus mopped his face once more. "A Provost shouldn't have to say such a thing, eh? But it's true. I'm terrified. One of the voices, I call the gulper. I think it's part of whatever killed a girl in the tunnels . . . tore her apart . . . wrote words in her blood on the walls. Wrote the word 'fool.' Wrote what we thought was the word 'adore,' but maybe it was the name of one of those . . . Clore. You said that name to me once. The biography book says he's down there, one of the four faction leaders."

"Faction leaders?"

"There were factions on the committee. You know, groups with different ideas. Hell, Zasper, you used the leaders' names yourself, in that damned rhyme you quoted me years ago!"

"Oh, you mean *that* Clore! Bland and . . ."

Boarmus put his hand on Zasper's mouth. "Don't talk about it. If it is them . . . Or if it isn't . . . it thinks anyone asking questions must be plotting against it, them, but at the same time it . . . they're furious at being forgotten!"

"I don't understand that!"

Boarmus sighed. "It's not rational! Don't expect it to be rational!"

"How much of this is fact?" Zasper whispered.

"I don't know," admitted Boarmus in a sick whisper. "Files could probably tell me, or at least give me a probability rating. But I daren't ask Files. *It* would know the minute I did, and it would be furious. Instead, I'm going directly to City Fifteen from here. Chadra Hume told me the dinks there have a shielded system, and I'm hoping it can run probability checks for me. Maybe they can tell me why. Tell me how."

Zasper shook his head slowly from side to side, trying to absorb it all. "Do you think I should go to Panubi?"

"I thought you might want to. If you do, it's not something they'd find suspicious. They'd expect me to want a report on what's happening there. Since Fringe and Danivon are involved, they'll think it's a natural thing for you to do."

"I'm retired."

"Council Enforcers have come out of retirement before now."

"And when I get there, what?"

"I don't know, Enforcer. All I could do up until now was send Danivon a kind of warning, all I could think of at the time. I told you long ago I'm not a man of action, and I haven't the least sticky tail end of an idea what you or they can do. Maybe you can at least offer each other mutual support!"

It was the least Zasper could do, intended to do. In addition to his concern for the young ones, however, he was conscious of a feeling so alien to him, he could hardly believe it. He felt sympathy for Boarmus! Not a bad fellow, he told himself. Considering everything, not a bad old fellow at all.

And Boarmus, relieved at having someone, anyone, to tell his worries to, felt much the same way. A stiff-necked old bastard, Ertigon, but a good man. Yes, a good man.

"I'll go," said Zasper. "Where do I find them?"

"By now they'll be somewhere around Derbeck. The monitors showed a strange manifestation in Derbeck, so I sent a routine message to Danivon, telling him to check on it."

Seeing Zasper's expression, he cried, "I had to! Either that or go there myself. I've got to keep up an appearance of normalcy. That's all that stands between us and chaos!" He heard himself babbling, bit his lip. "Take the Enforcer Post Door to Tolerance. Here's my authority to take the Door from there to the Enforcer Post near Shallow. It's a tiny post, but they have a few fliers there. Take whatever armament you think is most useful. I can't advise you."

Zasper nodded, thinking furiously.

"While I go my way," murmured Boarmus. "To City Fifteen. This lad I've got with me, his name is Jacent. If you receive any message purporting to be from me, ignore it unless he brings it or it has his name. Any message from me alone will be false."

"I'll remember that, Boarmus."

Boarmus grunted, wiping his face once more, trying to keep his stomach from rebelling.

"And, Boarmus. . . ." What could he say to the poor fellow?

"Yes."

"Thank you. Sir."

The *Dove* sailed upriver all day, heading for the main river port of Molock province. For a good part of the day, Fringe kept to her cabin, trying very hard to think of nothing at all, not babies eaten by fangy, armor-plated gavers, not children cut into pieces among the reeds, not an immortal music dead before its time, not even herself and Danivon entwined. She had stayed with him until almost dawn, unable to break away from him. Now she found herself considering him in the same light as she did the Hobbs Land Gods: addicting, enslaving, something to flee from because she could not be with him and remain herself. Not, not, not. She unpacked the Destiny Machine and lay on her bunk twiddling the levers, watching the lights, hearing the bells, ignoring the words on the capsules, hypnotizing herself into thinking nothing at all.

Late that afternoon she emerged to find Jory standing at the taffrail, near where Danivon and Curvis were talking about Molock.

"The thing is," said Curvis, "that this child smuggling isn't being done as a regular thing, or by any certain group. What it is, is individual parents avoiding child sacrifice by stowing their children away on the riverboats."

Danivon said he had never before Attended a Situation in Molock and was unfamiliar with the province.

Curvis described the situation in Molock.

"Ah," said Danivon. "So we're to see that the parents stop trying to save their children."

"You can't make them stop trying to save their children," said Fringe. "You've said so yourself."

Danivon looked up, shaking his head. "But they have no right to avoid the way things are. There's always been human sacrifice in Molock." He reached out a hand, which she evaded.

Fringe's mouth worked as she fought the urge to tell him about at least one human—so-called—who had escaped Molock. "What, exactly, does the complaint and disposition say?" she asked.

Curvis took out his pocket file. "Complaint by High Priest, tum-te-tum . . . Disposition: Enforcer will tum-te-tum assess penalty against riverboat owners or workers or provinces involved and tum-te-tum will reaffirm, and so on."

"So, assess a penalty," said Fringe in a remote, cold voice. "What's the local currency. Derbecki? Fine them five derbecki."

"Five derbecki's nothing," said Curvis.

"I know," she replied, turning away. "But it's enough to comply with the C&D. And post a warning here in Molock. That'll reaffirm."

"What're you carrying on about?" Danivon demanded, newly peeved with her. They had made love twice now, and after each time she had acted like she hated him. She had no right to behave this way! What ailed the woman!

She said, still in that faraway voice, "Remember Shimm-nau, that's all. Didn't they teach you two about Shimm-nau?"

The men fell silent as they considered Shimm-nau, a category-five theocracy, rigidly ruled by a priestly class and constantly subjected to heresy trials, torture, and executions. Because of its proximity to Tolerance, Enforcers had kept the place under unusually tight supervision. Someone in Shimm-nau had discovered a ravenous disease bacteria and had, with the aid of at least a thousand coconspirators, simultaneously infected the water supply in all parts of the province. It was Elsewhere's only case of provincial murder-suicide. There had been no survivors. Shimm-nau was a cautionary example often stressed at Academy.

"You know," Curvis offered in a careless voice, "she's right to say a five-derbecki fine and a posted warning will comply. I mean, that's all that's strictly necessary. If anyone criticizes, we can mention Shimm-nau."

"You have to leave people some way out," said Fringe, turning to glare into Danivon's eyes. "Even if ninety and nine in Molock approve of the way things are done, you must leave the hundredth one a way out! No destiny is right for everyone!"

"But it's the Molockian way," Danivon objected stubbornly, totally missing the point she was trying to make. "I think we ought to do something a bit more forceful than a five-derbecki fine and a posted announcement!"

"What?" she demanded, turning on him wrathfully. "Maybe you'd like to starve a few little kids yourself, just to show they can't get away. Maybe you'd like to beat their bones when they're dead!"

They glared at each other, then Fringe stalked away to stand beside Jory at the rail.

"Women are no damned good at Enforcement," snarled Danivon, now thoroughly angry. "They get too emotional. They can't keep their minds on the philosophical reasons for things."

"You're very angry," Jory murmured to Fringe.

"With myself mostly," she replied sullenly.

"Not with Danivon?"

"Well, him too. There's Enforcement that stays with the letter of the Complaint and Disposition, and there's Enforcement that tramps all over people."

"And Danivon tramps all over people?"

"Sometimes, yes."

"Including you?"

"Well . . ." She thought about this, trying to be fair. "Yes, he does. But I'm afraid when he does, it's because I let him."

"Ah," said Jory. "And that makes you angry."

Fringe flushed and nodded. Of course it made her angry. Acting like that. Acting like any lovesick schoolgirl! Longing for . . . for whatever it was she had longed for all her life, and then forgetting that to lie down for Danivon, like any bitch in heat!

Besides, she kept remembering what Zasper had said to her about the child he had saved. Certainly Danivon had been that child, though Danivon didn't know it. He could have been one of those skulls on the rack, but he didn't know that either. Perhaps it was time he did know it!

She had no intention of betraying Zasper, but she wasn't going to let Danivon get away with murder either.

City Fifteen was three-quarters occupied by dinka-jins, about half of whom were dedicated to the life of the mind. Why, after all, go through disassembly if not to free the mind from fleshly concerns? Why put one's germ plasm on standby, one's innards in cold storage, if not to focus upon the attainments of the intellect?

The other half of City Fifteen's dink population had come up with reasons: reasons erotic, reasons financial, reasons political, reasons of custom. Dinks, so the aphorism said, begot dinks, so they were never in short supply.

The trick to City Fifteen, as Boarmus's predecessor had told him at length, was to be sure you were talking to a brain dink and not one of the other kind. The creature who delivered Boarmus's packet was certainly one of the others, a dilettante tourist dink who had lost heavily at Bloom's—a debt he (she or it) had been unable to pay—and who had been given the choice of running the simple errand or being sold for parts. The dink to whom the packet was directed was Sepel794DZ, a brain dink of the highest order, to whose home/lab/study Boarmus was guided after arriving at a shielded location.

"I brought these things," said Boarmus, dumping the contents of his pockets onto the table before him while carefully avoiding looking directly at Sepel794DZ. He had nothing against dinks. It merely distressed him to look at them.

"Sensory recordings," said Sepel794DZ tonelessly. "Old ones, from the look of them. Where did you get them?"

"Down near the Core. Not in the communications room itself, but in the corridor nearby. There are cabinets full of them. I couldn't bring many, so I picked the ones done by the faction leaders, and by someone called Jordel of Hemerlane. He shows up in the old . . . well, accounts, I guess you'd say." Did one call children's rhymes "accounts"? And why not. Tradition was tradition, no matter who maintained it.

"You haven't accessed them?" asked Sepel794DZ. "You don't know what's in them?"

"I couldn't access them without using Files, and I can't do that without whatever's in the Core knowing. It . . . they know everything I do, every breath I take!" He jittered, feeling the sweat dripping down his neck, under his arms, on his chest.

"Sit down, Boarmus," said the dink in a dry metallic dinka-jin voice that somehow managed to sound kindly. "I had a chair brought in for you."

Dinks didn't need chairs. Dinks didn't need much, Boarmus thought. Except answers. Dinks liked answers.

"I need help," he begged as he sank into the chair, which was too small but no less welcome for that.

The dink tipped one of its boxes. It took a moment for Boarmus to recognize the gesture as a nod. "We've been monitoring the physical effects, just as you have, ever since Chadra Hume brought the matter to our attention. We feel the effects originate in the Core. We've postulated various ways they might be accomplished. Most of us believe there must be some kind of network coming from the Core and extending over wide areas. We've looked for it. Either we've looked in the wrong places or it's shielded in ways we can't even recognize."

"You can't . . . identify it?"

"We haven't yet. And we may be wrong."

Boarmus mused. "You postulate a network?" He tried without success to imagine what kind of network.

"It would have to extend over most of the planet, actually. It would have to include miniature devices, tiny but synchronized. . . ."

"Devices that can make footprints in rock? Devices that can make imaginary things real? Devices that can tear off real arms and legs, kill people really dead? Devices that can hear everything, see everything. . . ."

The dink twitched. "I know it sounds illogical. Of course, we may be wrong."

"You keep saying that!"

The dink didn't reply.

"If it emanates from the Core, what if we isolate the Core. We can't get into it, but what if we dig it up? Suspend it? Cut it off?"

Sepel794DZ made a noise like a snort. "Chadra Hume asked that same question. From what we know, we can't touch the Core; it's too well protected from outside interference."

"Well then, suppose we concentrate on finding this network. When we do, can we destroy it?"

"Yes. Given time. We could destroy it, if we could find it, but while we were destroying part of it, another part could be building. Besides, as I said, we could be—"

"Wrong!" shouted Boarmus. "I know, I know. Stop saying that!" He simmered, thinking.

"The power must come from the Core," he offered.

"Probably."

"Can we shut off the power?"

"Not from outside the Core, no."

"So what do we do?" he cried, feeling tears of frustration gathering.

"Provost, we've been working on that for years! Ever since your predecessor came to us and told us what he suspected."

Boarmus made a hopeless gesture toward the cubes he had brought with him. "Maybe there's something in there that will help."

The dink wagged one of its boxes, a gesture only remotely resembling a doubtfully shaken head. "Perhaps. My colleagues and I will go through them. Even if they don't tell us what's happening now, perhaps they'll give us accurate background."

"What a comfort! We're all going to be dead, but we'll know the background."

"We don't need to bother if you think it's futile."

"How do I know what's futile. Do whatever you think might help." Boarmus made himself look directly at Sepel794DZ. So very plain. So very . . . boxish. Without even any decorations on it, just a few lights and sensors. "How long will it take you to do that?"

"Who knows?" Did the dink actually sound weary? "It may take some little time. I know these are sensory recordings, but I don't know how to access them. It may take a while to find out. We don't feel fatigue, but I know you must be tired. I had a bed brought in for you. It's over there, under the auxiliary files, where it's quiet. There are foodstuffs there as well, and liquids if you need them. Perhaps you'd like to refresh yourself while we get on with it?"

Boarmus sighed again. He couldn't remember when the last time was he had slept soundly, without waking, without lunging up, heart pounding, terrified, thinking the ghosts were about to eat him—or already had. "Thank you."

The box blinked a light beam, showing him the couch against the far wall. It was hard, and too narrow, but Boarmus didn't care. He collapsed upon it, shutting his eyes firmly. He had done everything he could do. Jacent was still back in Enarae, pretending that Boarmus was there with him, entering Boarmus's credit code at one establishment or another, ordering food and drink in Boarmus's name. Perhaps it would be enough. Maybe the thing in the Core was very busy right now. Trying to kill Danivon, maybe. Trying to kill Fringe Owldark. Maybe it was so busy it wouldn't detect the subterfuge. Maybe it wouldn't come looking for him for a while.

When he slept, however, he groaned in his sleep, dreaming of being torn apart by something he couldn't see, couldn't hear, couldn't avoid, couldn't understand.

Upstream from Molock, Nela and Bertran found the captain walking along the deck, repeatedly hanging over the side to stare at the hull, shaking his head the while as he had done now and then since leaving Salt Maresh. He was obviously anxious about something.

"What's the matter?" Bertran asked him.

"We're riding lower than we should," he muttered. "Ever since Shallow. I've had the men down in the hold searching for a leak, but we find no water coming in. I thought some monster gaver might be hanging on the bottom. They'll do that sometimes. . . ."

"Monster gaver? How big?"

"Girl, I've seen them come rearing sail-high out of the river, the length of ten men laid end to end. Once, when I was a mere boy, I saw one take the top watch off the mast with its teeth. Seldom they get that size, true, the young ones being hunted as they are for their hides, but I've seen it happen. Howsoever, we've run ropes under the hull, and there's no gaver there, monster or otherwise. I've taken this old lady up and down the river for half my life, and I know how she rides depending on what we're carrying. It's as though something in the cargo is heavier than it should be, but I supervised the loading myself and nothing seemed out of the usual."

He was more annoyed than anxious, but still he continued his search, leaning over to peer at the waterline. It seemed a small matter to the twins despite his obvious concern, and eventually he seemed to agree for he threw up his hands and made a note in his pocket file.

He pointed to the shore they were approaching, saying: "After this next tack, as we come near the south shore, we'll turn back downstream to Du-you, the main Derbeckian port. It's near impossible either to go straight across the Floh this time of year, or to come into the harbor from downstream. Coming from upstream is far easier on the men at the sweeps."

"Why do we have to stop at Derbeck at all?" asked Nela as they joined the others at the bow.

"Cargo," the captain said, shrugging. "Sorry for the delay, but it's business. I have grain and fiber from Shallow and dried fish from Salt Maresh for my factor in Houmfon, and we'll pick up preserved fruit from the highland orchards."

"We had to stop here anyhow," said Danivon. "Not long ago I got a message from Boarmus. We're to investigate something or other in Derbeck. Unofficially."

"We're not going to show ourselves as Enforcers, are we?" asked Fringe.

"No. Molock was the last official visit. From here on, we're only showmen."

They separated, he silent, she silent, both of them concentrating (though for different reasons) on the snap and billow of the sails, the rattle of chain, the whistle of the wind in the lines, both of them hearing words, what he had said to her, what she had said to him; what he (she) should have said, instead; what she (he) would not say again.

The high Molockian shore receded behind them, its red-clay banks dark as blood above the leaden ripples of the river. Slowly the Derbeckian shore drew nearer, swampy and grown up with waving sedges and taller reeds as far inland as they could see.

When the reed beds were only an arrow's flight away, the ship turned lazily on the current and went downstream, held bow-on by the six men plying the two long sweeps at the stern. "Hauuu," they cried as they pushed hard against the weight of the river. "Lah," as they raised the blade high. Then silence for two beats as the sweep was swung wide for another stroke. It became an endless slow march, full of pauses. "Hauuu-lah." Three, four. "Hauuu-lah." Quiet, quiet.

The top-mast watch first saw the boat, almost a gossle boat so round and clumsy it was, lurching out at them from among the reed beds.

"Boat ho," he cried.

They crowded the rail to see the tiny craft spinning crazily toward them, like a water beetle, rowed by two uncoordinated paddlers sitting either side of a female passenger. One man was squat and dark, the woman and the other man were lean and sandy-skinned, with something familiar seeming about them. It was the dark man who waved at them, shouting words they could scarcely hear over the river sounds.

"Ho . . . stop . . . 'mergency. . . ."

"That's Ghatoun, sir," said the deck officer to the captain. "Head of an encampment along here. We traded fruit and grain for reed mats, last trip."

"I see him, deckman. Tell the men to drop anchor."

"Aye, sir."

Jory and Asner were speaking together urgently, leaning so far over the rail Fringe thought they would fall. She grasped Jory's shirt, holding the old woman down. Came a clangor of chain as the aft anchor went down, a rattle of sweeps brought aboard, the softer rustle of a rope ladder against the side. Then Ghatoun came clambering over the rail near where they stood, murmuring urgently to the captain.

"Scouts say . . . chimi-hounds scouring the reeds. . . . These two . . . not Derbeckian. Border crossers, maybe. . . . Supervisors, maybe. Don't want trouble. . . ."

Fringe cocked her head at Nela and Bertran. The other man and the woman were wearily climbing over the rail, moving like old people or folk tired to the point of exhaustion.

"Cafferty!" cried Jory. "And Latibor!"

"Jory," whispered the man with a ghost of a smile.

"These people belong to you?" asked the captain, turning to the old woman.

"Oh, my, yes," said Jory. "Our dear friends! Come to such a pass. Fled for their lives, I've no doubt."

The two nodded hesitantly, their eyes roaming over the others on deck but returning always to Jory with mingled wonder and satisfaction. They had not expected to find her here, so much was obvious.

"How fortunate we came along!" Jory cried. "You two come below with me. You need to lie down. You need some food."

"They've had food," complained Ghatoun. "And a lie down. Some days of both, they've had, and some days more they no doubt need, but I can't keep them in the village with the chimi-hounds about. Old Man Daddy's dead, and there's some big hoofaraw going on that brings the hounds out, beating the riverbanks."

Jory gave Asner a significant look as she escorted the two strangers below.

"Your good sense and kindness shouldn't go unrewarded," said Asner. "What do you think? A hundred derbecki? A thousand?"

Ghatoun flushed. "A hundred would more than pay for their keep. A thousand would likely get me killed."

"A hundred then." Asner rummaged in his pockets and brought forth a handful of metal, all shapes, all sizes. He plowed the pile with a fingertip, at last finding two silvery coins that suited him. These he handed to Ghatoun.

"Will your people say anything when the chimi-hounds come?"

"And run the risk of getting slaughtered! Don't be a fool, man. We wouldn'ta lasted a year if we had people so silly as that!"

"That's good to hear," Asner said with a smile. "Peace and joy, Ghatoun."

"An unlikely hope with chimi-hounds abroad!" commented the headman. "On your way, now, lest someone see you anchored here and ask why! And keep those folks hid while you're in Du-you, just in case any in Derbeck are interested in them."

Ghatoun was back in his awkward craft and halfway to the reed beds before the anchor was hauled up and the sweeps deployed. The little boat disappeared into the reeds as the *Dove* moved again downriver toward Du-you.

Asner confronted the three Enforcers, all of whom were glaring at him.

"Border crossers?" demanded Danivon. "Were they border crossers, Asner?" Danivon felt himself close to panic. He smelled something, something dreadful and maimed and old. He smelled death and didn't know what to do about it.

Asner shook his head. "Well, now, can't quite say, can I? Last time I saw them, they were headed downriver toward Shallow. Shallow's a freeport, so they could go there. Possibly they were castaways, that's all. Nothing illicit about being a castaway."

"Downriver from where?" asked Fringe. "When you saw them last."

"Downriver from upriver," said Asner. "Obviously. Since that's where we were at the time."

"Thrasis? Beanfields?" demanded Curvis.

"A bit farther up than that."

"In the unexplored region?"

"Well, that's what you say. We don't think of it as unexplored. We know pretty much what's there, don't you know, having been there for some time."

"What place?"

"Noplace. That's what I said before. Noplace. Has no name. Why do people all the time have to go about naming places? Impudent, that's what it is. How do you know what the name of a place is?"

"Whatever it's called, it has no supervision from Tolerance," said Curvis. "No monitors, no systems, no Enforcers assigned duty there. . . ."

"No doubt true," agreed Asner, nodding his head in a not-at-all-sympathetic manner. "Which isn't our fault. Not mine, not Cafferty's. Or Latibor's. Or Jory's. With all you've got to worry about on the rest of Elsewhere, I don't see why you'd be eager to lay your hands on noplace."

Danivon smoldered, but Fringe said, "He's right, Danivon. Your nose told you they were to go along, and this is why. They already know what's up there."

"How'd you get there?" Danivon demanded. "To begin with?"

Asner shrugged. "It's home, Danivon Luze. Cafferty and Latibor came there as children."

"Noplace?"

"Right. Noplace. Some noplace or other." He brushed himself ostentatiously, as though to rid himself of their suspicions, then stumped away to the ladder, calling Jory's name as he went.

When Sepel794DZ said the dinks might find it difficult to access the sensory recordings Boarmus had brought, he had conveyed nothing of the patience and skill the operation required. Boarmus was exhausted. His sleep, though full of fearful dreams, was deep, and while he slept the dinks prodded and poked, burrowed through old files, queried ancient systems, until at last they were able to get into the ancient recordings. As Boarmus said, he had picked sensory data left by five individuals: Thob and Breaze and Bland and Clore. And Jordel of Hemerlane.

As chance would have it, the first recording they got into had been left behind by Breaze, Orimar Breaze.

They saw him as he saw himself. A handsome, white-haired man, strolling among age-gentled walls set in an early spring, trees just budding, their trembling lace spread across time-softened stones, themselves dripping with viny green.

He hears voices raised in song:

"Brannigan we sing to thee."

He hears and feels water splashing. He touches the wetness on his cheeks, feeling the separate droplets, like jewels on his skin.

"Fountain of diversity."

"I am Orimar Breaze, chairman of the Great Question Committee, elder statesman of academe, appointed by the almighty Chancellors to the referendum on curriculum reform, prize-winning author of the greatest erotic work of my century, *Jorub and Andacine*." So he thinks to himself, liking the sound of the words as he murmurs them, contented to be what he is. *"Jorub and Andacine,"* he says again. "A seminal work."

The dinks feel what he felt, hear what he heard. They are proud to be Orimar Breaze who is not like other men. Not like other women. Who is far and away superior to most men, even to many of those here at Brannigan Galaxity, great BG.

Orimar Breaze is on his way to class. Today he will bring the beautiful young into this parklike burgeoning, seat them on the sward, and then stand before them, a first edition of *Jorub and Andacine* open in his hands. He will read aloud, his voice a mellifluous torrent sweeping them along.

Oh, Brannigan:

It is his mistress, his wife. It is his forum, his stage. It is himself, made manifest.

> *Vast auditoria reverberating to words deathless as Scripture. Laboratories where genius falls thick as pollen, packed with potentiality. Hallways vibrant with scuttering youth, with striding maturity, and so on and so on and so on. . . .*

> *"Brannigan we sing to thee. . . ."*

Eyes, bright eyes, the young liquid eyes sparkling between fringed lids, unlined foreheads shining like little marble monuments, sweet mouths curved into succulent questions. Here they are, seated cross-legged on the grass. "Illuminated one," they cry. "Tell . . . tell me . . . tell me everything!"

> *Brannigan Galaxity.*
> *A thousand colleges, each with its own history, its own traditions, its own glories to recount. . . .*

". . . tell me everything," they cry.

He warms at the heat of their voices, feels the excitement of their excitement. Oh, he can teach them things they will never learn from anyone else.

And he loves the names they have for him, the girls particularly.

"Magister." "Sweet teacher." "Lord of my heart and mind." Who was it had called him that? No matter. There would be others . . . others.

Ah, the feel of that young skin against his own.

Ah, the surge of adoration from them to him.

Ah, the surge of . . . of knowledge pouring out of him to them, his body pressed . . . himself pressed. . . . That was in the library, the great library, among the books, she and him.

> *Brannigan Galaxity:*
> *Libraries sprawling in wandering tunnels of stone across conti-*
> *nents of lawn. The infinite distance of painted ceilings where faded*
> *figures out of forgotten legends disport themselves . . .*

They were not the only ones disporting themselves!

[Tourists come here to see the murals. He has never really approved of that. Not in Brannigan, which should be sacrosanct, which should exclude the chattering throngs who stroll along, staring upward, spilling meat sauce upon the mosaics. Oh, they should go away! Depart! This is no place for laity. This is where . . .]

> *. . . legends disport themselves. Is that Widsom teaching the mul-*
> *titude? Or the Queen of who-was-it? issuing thingummies? . . .*

. . . where the body is pressed . . . himself pressed . . . All that working away inside like sparkling wine, bubbling up, pure joy, delight, glory! Glorious these days, these ageless words, these students forever young! Glorious to hear the breathless voice whispering his name. "There he is, Orimar! Teacher! Lover! Oh, Orimar!"

> *Here twisting stairs clattering beneath niagaras of pounding feet.*
> *There dim corridors, endless as roads, running into vaulted pas-*
> *sages that grow silent. . . .*

He does not like silence. Not when he is alone in it.

> *No matter. All that is here is also in Files, incorruptible.*

Incorruptible. He is incorruptible.

Listen to them, the sweet things, gathered before him on the sward, their voices whispering his name, "Oh, Orimar Breaze!" Oh, he relishes it still, in this place, just as he always has.

Though there is one among this group who is not looking at him! One there, to the side, who is not responsive. This has happened before. It is happening again!

When he has dismissed the others, he focuses upon that one. "Come," he says. "What is this? You don't seem to be enjoying the seminar, dearest girl."

She has no reason to reject him. Isn't Orimar one of the illuminati, after all? One of the emeriti, the . . .

> *"May thy Golden Towers rise*
> *as a beacon for the wise. . . ."*

"You need to extend yourself. Be one with the group."

She says something noncommittal. He sees scorn in her eyes. "Old man," her eyes say. "I know you, old man."

What right has she to look at him like that?

He dismisses her, his voice like cutting ice. She will not last, not at Brannigan. He will see to that. One negative report is all it takes, and she may be assured she has earned it from him.

> *"Immortal may thy children be . . ."*

Brannigan, whose emeriti stand in glittering rows along the Halls of Tomorrow, preserved in impenetrable vitreon until the hour they will be raised from senescence into eternal youth . . .

What right had she to think him an old man!

He would summon her to his office. He would give her one more chance.

She is there, before him, her face closed, her eyes shut. He suggests that she do . . . a certain humiliating, undignified thing.

She does not even answer.

Enough then. She has earned her dismissal. Oh, for some other world. Some world in which she could not refuse him in this fashion. A world in which refusal would be sufficient grounds for discipline!

> *"Brannigan, Great Brannigan!*
> *Brannigan Galaxity!"*

Discipline is what that one wants. What she needs. And Orimar could give it to her. He can feel it in himself. Hot. All simmering up, full of lusts. He would strike. He would hurt. He would reduce her to a quivering mass. Eventually he would dispose of her while she still screamed and begged for another chance, just one more chance. He would smile. He would shake his head. Too late.

> . . . on the day the Great Question is answered . . .
> The Great Question, the only question so far as Brannigan is concerned. The Question upon which it was founded, which it has translated and reframed and to which it has devotedly sought the answer. The Great Question, which has plagued humanity since it first came down from the primordial trees . . .
> . . . passion fulfilled . . .
> . . . down from the primordial trees . . .

WHAT IS THE ULTIMATE DESTINY OF MAN?

"Enough," said Sepel794DZ. "We know him well enough. There is nothing there to help us. He was no technician, no engineer. He thought nothing about Elsewhere or the Core."

The other dinks acquiesced. Brain dinks as a class were not deeply into feelings. They had understood only a little of what they had felt in Orimar Breaze. None of them knew why this particular memory had been kept for later reference. They withdrew from Orimar Breaze, all of them eager to find something they understood better.

On his bed, Boarmus shifted.

"Let us try this one," said Sepel794DZ. "This one labeled Clore."

The first sensation they encountered felt roadlike. The road was not, however, a surface of durable substance making up a continuous and more or less cohesive pathway, which is what even residents of City Fifteen usually meant when they thought "road." In the Core, "road" was a less-concrete concept than that. Its parts emitted roadness though they were only remotely and occasionally contiguous. Its nature was of a resilient discreteness, an unwillingness to connect. Sepel and his colleagues were conscious of moving (seeming to move) from rubbery chunk to rubbery chunk, all of which were changing position relative to one another and bouncing apart if they happened actually to touch. There was little indication of distance and "direction" was a matter of arbitrary decision.

"What is this?" a dink asked.

"A dream," said Sepel. "Clore is dreaming, and he has recorded his dream."

"Why would he do this?"

"Perhaps he wishes to review his dreams in all their details, and he chooses this way of doing it. Persevere! Even a dream may tell us something useful."

They persevered. They saw an eruption from the underlying stratum, an exudation of words in several languages, both archaic and current, indicating that they were approaching the lair/kingdom/residence of Great Lord Something. The words could be both seen and heard. They sprouted along the way like mushrooms, then deliquesced, running off in inky utterances among structures that stood here and there, more or less adjacent.

These might have been buildings or chimneys or mountains or trees. As the dream went forward, items became more certainly either thin or flat, finally becoming almost definable. They were proceeding through a dimensionless and arid wilderness that might have been painted by an untalented child of eight or nine on dirty paper with a limited number of colors: ochre, dun, bile-green, dung-brown—those left in the box when all the brighter and more favored colors had been used up.

The farther they went, the more solid things became. More words popped up indicating the approach of the Great God Something. The quality of the surrounding area changed, becoming less sketchy in character and more susceptible to perspective. They came upon definite growths, with perceivable thorns, and at last the dinks felt themselves mounting a ridge of rusty iron where they gazed down upon a fully realized landscape.

The valley echoed with muted howls, the thwack of slack drums and the clash of dissonant cymbals. A vaporous procession wound its way down the ridge beside them toward a vaguely circular chasm of black smoke. Across that chasm and to either side were other ridges, other processions, and through the sullen air came the dirgelike mourning of the mist-veiled marchers.

Within the chasm a stone mesa seemed to float upon the haze, a rock scarcely large enough to hold the hideously ramified bulk of the building upon it. Joining this isolated structure to the deeply creviced lands around

it were bridges of black iron, spiderwebs of cable and strut leaping outward from the central plateau in flat trajectories to bury themselves at
the ends of the squirming ridges. The building lay like a monstrous iron
spider at the center of this web of ways, and like a spider it twitched its
extended legs in great annexial spasms, seeming to shiver in constant
motion, as mirages seem to shiver, an effect possibly caused by the haze
of smoke that rose between the observers and the edifice itself.

Occasionally the chasm belched red fire that oppressively illuminated
the narrow ledge between the building and the chasm, and there strode
a monstrous six-legged being, insectlike, whose three great mouths grazed
bloodily upon the processions attempting to cross the ledge to enter the
great building.

And they were the creature upon the ledge, ravaging the marching
hordes.

"Out," murmured Sepel794DZ. "This isn't helping us."

His colleagues did not argue. They withdrew from the recording.

"This tells us nothing," murmured a dink. "People dream all kinds
of things. Even we do. This was a nightmare. What good can we get
from that?"

"The fact that he saved it," murmured Sepel794DZ. "Only that."

"Shall we try Thob?" asked another wearily.

They tried Thob and came upon a landscape; a shore, rocks, sky in
flat primary colors: shore a line of brown, sea a plane of green, rock
shapes of black, the sky a plane of blue. Was this what the Thob person
saw? Or imagined? Was this her vision of life?

This passed, giving way to:

Clashing spheres, a violence of storm, a hurricane of sound, without
meaning or order.

And this too was gone.

Leaving behind a giant woman with breasts like mountains, crouching
enigmatically beside an endless plain.

The breasts swelled and burst, showering milk onto the plain. It pud-
dled and leaked away in droplets of diamond and pearl, leaving a roiling
net with worlds of its own gathered within it, worlds indecipherable to
the dinks; a mountain of slippery ooze. A slithering womb in violent
contraction. A tentacle that sought to hold, grasp, strangle. . . .

"Get out," said Sepel794DZ. "There's nothing here. Nothing at all!"

•   •   •

Boarmus woke on his narrow couch, sat up, and chewed his fingers for a while, then nibbled at his lips while Sepel794DZ and several of his fellows hummed and clicked. After what seemed a very long time, Sepel made a sound like a groan.

"What?" asked Boarmus.

The dinka-jin shook itself, reminding Boarmus of a dog shaking water from its coat.

"What?" demanded Boarmus again.

Tentacles untangled. Boxes moved apart. Synthesizers made noises like moans, like sighs.

"We read some of them," said Sepel. "One by Breaze; one by Clore; one by Thob. They tell us nothing! Nothing! Nightmares and visions and impressions and pornographic daydreaming. None of them concern Elsewhere or the Core. They were made long ago, on another world."

"And Jordel?"

"We haven't accessed anything by him. Not yet."

"Nothing that tells us what's happening now?"

"Nothing at all. We don't even know for sure that these . . . people are involved."

"Something using the name of one of them is involved," Boarmus insisted. "One of the . . . things introduced herself to me as Lady Mintier Thob."

"That doesn't mean . . ."

"I know. Anyone . . . anything can use any name it likes."

"True."

"I can't stay any longer." Boarmus sighed. "I presume you'll go on looking. Do you have any suggestions as to what I can do now?"

Sepel794DZ shrugged once more, giving a mechanical sigh. "We will go on, yes. We've got a few shielded facilities here in City Fifteen: this lab and one or two others, a flier pad, a few routes to and from. We've shielded our own Files, just in case there is a network. Other than that . . ."

"This is ridiculous," screamed Boarmus. "The Core was made by men! Mortal men! Basically it's just a damned chill box with a few electronic attachments! And you mean to tell me, we're completely at its . . . their . . . whatever-it-is's mercy?"

Sepel didn't answer. The silence was a reproach.

"Sorry," muttered Boarmus. "It just seems so ridiculous."

"We share your feelings. We feel the situation to be basically immoral. Of course, we dinks feel it is difficult to be a man and still be moral. Which is why we've become as we are."

Boarmus thought about this. "Sepel, what's it like, being . . . being a dinka-jin?"

The main box buzzed for a while. "What's it like being the way you are, Boarmus? What's it like being assembled around a stomach you have to keep thinking about and feeding, instead of having your nutritional needs taken care of automatically so you never need to think about it? What's it like only being able to see one thing at a time? What's it like being distracted by pain all the time, or discomfort, or hormones, or heat or cold? What's it like having to eliminate all the time and do other awkward, nasty things with your bodies. . . ."

"All right," sighed Boarmus.

"You asked," said Sepel794DZ.

"I know I did."

"We don't find being men particularly useful, that's all, though some of you are quite . . . decent. We feel our kind of life is saner, some-how."

Boarmus sighed, stretched, too weary to pursue the question further. His mind flailed aimlessly. "What advice can you give me, then. What should I do now?"

The box hummed. "The two usual answers would be fight or flee. There's still a long-distance Door at Tolerance. Of course, once people start for it, they may not be allowed to get to it."

"Fighting's out too, isn't it?"

Sepel794DZ twitched. Boarmus looked away. The dink was making a grinding sound, symptom of concentration, he knew, but it irritated him anyhow.

"I was running simulations," muttered the dink at last. "I found no successful strategy. It . . . they, whatever, has given you indications it thinks it's a god, right?"

"Yes. More than indications."

"Well then, play its own game, Boarmus. Be sneaky."

"What is its game?"

"It says it's a god. Maybe you can make it doubt itself. Challenge it to do something only a god could do."

"Like what?" Boarmus cleared his throat and rubbed his forehead.

The dinka-jin shrugged. "Something godlike, obviously. Like creat-ing a world, or answering some riddle of the universe."

Boarmus grunted, feeling the usual burning in his stomach flare up to make a sudden agony. "I'll think about that. Meantime, I need to send a message to Zasper Ertigon. Privately, needless to say."

"If he has not yet left Enarae for Panubi, that at least we can do."

As the *Dove* went down the Fohm with the current, the three Enforcers, wearing their show clothes, joined the twins at the bow rail to watch for the first appearance of Du-you. Danivon had a dry throat and an ache in his sinuses that would not go away. This was not merely a smell! This was a monstrous stench, a threat made manifest!

Around the next gentle curve of the river, the confluence appeared where the Ti'il met the Fohm, a wide lagoon partly dredged, partly scoured out by the quick spring flow of the Ti'il, separated by over-grown mud flats from the main current of the river. Buoys marked the channels dredged through the flats, and the *Dove* edged toward the near-est set of markers, the men at the sweeps laboring, the captain at the wheel muttering oaths as eddies thrust the *Dove* this way and that. When the ship came into the channel, out of the current, it responded more easily to the helm.

"Hau-la," (silence) the oarsmen cried. "Hau-la. Hau-la." The sweeps beat, raised, and beat again.

Behind them came a clatter, a shout.

A boom had been lowered behind them to block the channel. They could not go out again. At least not by that route.

Curvis and Danivon shared expressive glances.

"What?" asked Fringe.

"Shh," said Danivon.

When they came to the pier, sailors leapt ashore carrying lines to make fast. The riverside was piled high with straw-wrapped bundles, crates and barrels, cargoes coming and going. On the riverfront, white-clad little people scurried madly here and there, wheeling carts and barrows, carrying kegs upon their shoulders, crying their wares in sur-prisingly high and plangent voices, like bells. "The Murrey," said the captain, spitting from the corner of his mouth. Among these little people walked a taller folk, dressed in brightly patterned fabrics and carrying parasols, waving fringed sleeves at one another, chatting in shrill, bird-cheep sounds. "The Houm."

Beyond the scurry at the wharfs were the outskirts of the town, low buildings separated by cobbled streets, then higher structures as the streets rose from the unstable land of the delta and gained the more solid ground away from the river.

Danivon moved uncomfortably, overwhelmed by the stink. It seemed to come at him like a wind from the shore.

"What?" Fringe asked, seeing the pain on his face.

He shook his head gently. Any sudden movement hurt. "I don't know. I've never smelled anything like it before. I wish we hadn't had to stop here." He remembered Boarmus's message. Both messages. The smell of the place was the smell of Boarmus's message. Deadly. Horrible.

Fringe remembered that same message. Though she didn't know what it had contained, its method of delivery meant it could only have been a warning. She cast a quick glance over her shoulder, seeking any sign of the people from noplace. All of them were below and evidently intended to stay there.

She spun back to the rail as a drum spoke warningly from behind the nearer buildings, *TID-dit, TID-dit* again, then a steady tattoo. *TIDdit-'-aTUM-tum TIDdit-'-aTUM-tum*. Those who came shambling behind the drums were neither the little nor the tall, neither the white-clad ones nor the bright folk with their bitsy parasols. These had long and tangled hair, bare arms scarified upon the shoulders and tattooed from there to the fingertips, and they grunted in time with the drums as they slouched forward: *HA-ghn, HA-ghn, HA-ghn*, scattering the Murrey as a great fish scatters a shoal of tiny ones. The fragile Houm dissolved before them.

"Not the Murrey and not the Houm," murmured Curvis, in Fringe's ear. "These are the chimi-hounds Ghatoun spoke of, so watch it."

So much she might have guessed from the weapons they carried. Fringe was suddenly glad of the broad-beam heat gun on her belt and her usual weapon in her boot, either of which was considerably better than anything the chimi-hounds were carrying.

"Captain," the hound leader drawled, making a sneer of it. "Kap-tahng."

"Chief."

"You got pahssen-jhairs?"

"None for Derbeck. Cargo, but no passengers."

"I see your mah-ni-fest, Kap-tahng."

"As you will," said the captain, nervously eyeing the remaining hounds lounging on the pier. He led the way to his cabin, the chimi-hound swaggering after. The remaining hounds slouched insolently at the edge of the pier, staring at the women, making obscene finger talk to one another.

"Nela," Fringe muttered. "If I were you, I'd work my way over to the cabins and go below. Bertran."

The twins were already on their way, walking as casually as they could manage it.

Fringe, Danivon, and Curvis turned their backs on the chimi-hounds and went to the opposite railing.

Danivon muttered, "Boarmus told me to look this place over, but we're not traveling here as Enforcers."

"We don't have to be Enforcers to look it over," said Curvis lazily. "Let's stick with our disguise and see what happens."

The captain stuck his head out of the wheelhouse. "Showman Luze," he called in a tight voice, "could you come in here?"

Danivon went in a hesitating strut, unable to see clearly for the pressure in his head. After a time, Fringe and Curvis were invited to join him. They found Danivon and the captain, both of them white about the lips, confronting a jovial and mad-eyed chimi-hound.

"This man says the boss chief wants us to bring the sideshow ashore," said Danivon. His words were clear, though his eyes were unfocused. "As part of his preelection festivities."

Fringe stared at her lap, where her hands tried relentlessly to control one another. She made them relax.

Danivon turned a vague, unseeing look on her, which she interpreted as a caution. "The boss chief has somehow learned . . . of the performance we gave in Shallow. He is pleased that we have arrived here in Derbeck, where he invites us to perform at the celebration of his election as leader."

"Is small thing to ask," cried the chimi-hound in trade language. "If people say no-can, we wonder why! Such wonder makes us fret. We are silly people when we fret. We do nasty things." He grinned widely, showing sharpened teeth.

"When is the election?" asked Fringe in the same emotionless tone Danivon was using.

"Tomorrow," cried the hound. "So, you see, is only small delay in your journey. You come to banquet. Tonight."

"What banquet is that?"

"Boss chief's banquet, that one, in warehouse at top of Moolie Street. All chimi-hound chiefs will be there. All high priests will be there. Maybeso High Lord Chimi-ahm will be there with Lady Zhulia and Chibbi the Dancer and Lord Balal!"

"Five of us can come," said Danivon. "The two old people are not strong enough."

"Mah-ni-fest say seven in show," said the chimi-hound with hectic gaiety. "All come. Seven. Seven is good number." His eyes glittered and he turned to smile at Fringe, a theropsian smile, full of teeth. The pupils of his eyes were very small. Here and there in his face small muscles jumped, like tiny creatures trapped there, individually attempting to free themselves.

"I'll go speak to Jory," said Fringe in her noncommittal voice.

Below, she blurted out the demand. "There's a threat there." She shook her head, trying to define it. "Danivon looks stunned, or drugged from what he's smelling. I think the hound *is* drugged. His eyes are wild. Somehow, he got word about the show we did in Shallow and he's determined to have us perform here tonight. He's like some crazy animal, tearing at things."

"No matter," said Jory calmly. "We'll come."

Cafferty put her hands on the old woman's shoulders, as though to hold her back.

"But you've got no act," cried Fringe. "No . . . no hype."

"Oh, Jory has an act," said Asner firmly. "Sort of an animal act."

Jory gave him a warning glance and patted Cafferty's shoulder as she said, "Don't worry, Fringe. We'll do well enough. You may tell the hound we'll be ready whenever's time for the banquet."

Fringe returned with this message, no whit comforted. The chief chimi-hound seemed satisfied, however, for he swaggered his way up the hill toward the town, leaving only a few of his men to watch the *Dove* with avid, reddened eyes.

"Serious about it, isn't he?" the captain commented. "What's going on here?"

"I wish I knew," said Danivon, exchanging an undecipherable glance with Curvis. "He's obviously been put up to it by someone. Or something. Perhaps Curvis and I had better do a little preliminary reconnaissance."

"First you'd better do something about your eyes," said Curvis.

Danivon nodded painfully and went off to explore the contents of the med kit. Though he could smell nothing at all, he was able to see fairly clearly by the time the two of them went off down the pier in their show costumes, both pretending not to notice the clot of chimi-hounds who shambled along behind them.

Fringe thought it wise to see to the Destiny Machine. Discretion suggested that new capsules should be lettered in the Derbecki dialect, leaving out all words from which unfavorable inferences might be drawn at the current time. Words like "victory" and "choice" and "leader." Cafferty found her sorting through the capsules and stayed to help her. Between the two of them, they replaced many of the old words, finishing up about the time that Danivon and Curvis returned, both very frown-faced and irritable.

"Damn near riot prevails," muttered Danivon to the assembled group, including the captain. "We stopped in a tavern and listened to the talk. Seems Old Man Daddy arranged for his only son, Fat Slick, to be elected Perpetual Leader. Seems the chimi-hound chiefs weren't all that fond of Fat Slick, so he died of accidental strangulation on the gibbet the morning after his daddy passed on. Then came a pretender from up-country, one calling himself Fees-mew and claiming to be Old Man Daddy's younger offspring. He's gained a considerable following from the lands around the sources of the Ti'il."

"Then," Curvis took up the story, almost with relish, "the boss chimi-hound chief—there's twelve of them together, and this is the meanest of the lot—announced Old Man Daddy had picked him as successor by passing him the key to the treasure vaults just before he died, though this is widely assumed to be a lie because the boss chief has shown no signs of sudden wealth."

"Which wealth," said Danivon, "is still, so far as anyone knows, up in the tower vaults where Old Man Daddy stored it, needing the proper key or combination or whatever, to keep whoever enters the vaults from blowing himself, and it, sky-high in bits."

"So the election is between this up-country pretender and the boss chimi-hound chief, and either of them would give his nose, teeth, and left arm for what's in those vaults," Curvis concluded the story.

"Does the boss chief have a name?" Jory asked.

"Houdum-Bah," Curvis answered with an unamused snort of laughter. "Old Houdum-Bah the Bad."

"And tonight's affair?"

"A preelection victory feast for Houdum-Bah. It's local custom to throw such banquets, to show how confident the candidate is. Meantime, Fees-mew is staying under cover, keeping safe from chimi-hounds who'd kill him gaver quick if they could catch up to him. Each candidate has forces abroad in the countryside, killing off the opposition or anybody who's just standing around."

"And we're entertainment?"

"Too true," Curvis replies. "That we are, in a place that likes its amusements bloody. And Danivon smells trouble."

"I don't smell anything at the moment," corrected Danivon. "Though the drug should wear off shortly."

"How do the common folk feel about it?" Asner asked. "The Murrey, the color-people?"

Danivon shrugged. "They quote at us, is all. They bow and smile and say *'All rou-Murrey when the old man dies.'* And true enough, at that. There's been enough bloodshed already to make the Ti'il flow scarlet."

"They'll do dabbo-dam, tonight," Jory mused. "They'll do dabbo-dam and then some."

"Likely," brooded Curvis.

"What's dabbo-dam?" asked Fringe and Nela, both in one breath.

"Calling down the gods," said Jory with distaste. "Oh, they'll call down the gods right enough, High Lord Chimi-ahm and all."

"I'd like it much, much better out of here," said Danivon. "But Boarmus told us to take a look, so we must."

"Why?" asked Jory, looking puzzled. "Why did Boarmus want you to take a look?"

Danivon shrugged. "That he didn't tell me. Just sent a clear language message telling me to investigate manifestations in Derbeck."

"Manifestations?" she asked, darting a troubled glance at Asner.

Danivon shrugged. "In any case, Jory, there's no way out. The booms are down across all the channels, with chimi-hounds guarding the booms. There's no way for the *Dove* to get back to the river."

He leaned across the rail, staring up at the town, sure that this time and place was the trouble he'd been smelling ever since leaving Tolerance. "I don't know what this Houdum-Bah is playing at, but he seems set on doing it. Safest for us is probably to do what they want and trust in our skills to keep us out of trouble."

"Or possibly get us out," muttered Fringe. "After we're in."

They prepared for their performance in no mood of anticipation. Curvis and Danivon spent some time checking their armamentarium, deciding which highly advanced devices they would carry, deciding on those that could be easily concealed beneath their showman's garb. Fringe carried a heat beamer on her belt, beneath her oracular garb. The twins had sewn themselves counterfeits of their Mulhollan's Marvelous Circus costumes. Jory and Asner came up from below looking frail and vulnerable in their usual loose trousers and shirts, each of them carrying a light cloak.

When Danivon led them off the ship at dusk, the chimi-hounds fell in around them. Fringe, who was nervous as a novice, kept looking behind her, sure some other person had joined their procession but seeing none.

"Relax," said Jory, patting her on the shoulder. "All will be well."

"I keep feeling there's someone coming along," Fringe murmured.

"And why not?" asked Jory soberly. "Why shouldn't anyone come along who might want to."

Fringe shook her head, thinking she'd been misunderstood. She fixed her eyes on the back of Danivon's neck and kept them there. Jory and Asner were behind her, helping her guide the awkward bulk of the Destiny Machine; then came the twins, with Curvis bringing up the rear. The old people set the pace for them all, which wasn't fast enough to suit the chimi-hounds, who chivvied at them as though driving animals, lunging at them with fangs showing and bleats of hysterical laughter.

Danivon paid them no attention as he thrust his way through the crowds of Murrey folk, feeling them part before him like water at the prow of a boat, seeing them flow together behind them seamlessly; jan-Murrey, ver-Murrey, zur-Murrey, all mixed and marbling, the vivid spots on their faces and bodies glittering like bright lizard scales as their eyes flicked across the sideshow in quick glances, fleeing, returning.

"They're curious about us," muttered Jory.

"So would I be," said Fringe. "We're freakish enough." She pulled distractedly at her headdress, bothered by the side flaps that restricted her vision.

"If those bitches' pups don't stop their baying at our heels, I'm inclined to pull their teeth," Danivon growled.

"Caution," she said. "Isn't that what you've advised?"

He made a sound, maybe of agreement, and sniffed, out of habit, smelling little. The drug hadn't fully worn off yet. He focused on his ears instead, alert for every sound. There was much to hear. Frantic ululations from distant rooftops. Drums pounding, a cacophony of rhythms. The roar of a chant howled from many throats, arriving on the wind and then fading with the wind into some other sound. There was no quiet anywhere, and the noises grew more persistent and tormenting the closer to the town they came.

At the top of the slope the road ended at gaping warehouse gates lit on either side by glowing firepits. Spitted carcasses sizzled and spat above the coals, sending up a smoky fume. Stacked kegs at the near corner of the building stood half-hidden beneath a lounging pack of chimi-hounds, their muttering interrupted by occasional shouts of brutal laughter. The place reeked of sweat, smoke, blood, and burning fat. It had a feel to it, Fringe thought, not unlike the feel of the Swale back in Enarae. A muttering threat, barely below the surface.

The leader of their escort sent them between the firepits and through the open gates with a sweep of his arms and a mocking bow before going off to join his fellows. Once inside the cavernous hall, the three Enforcers instinctively turned their backs toward one another with the other four in the middle. Chandeliers hanging from the distant rafters bloomed in the cobwebby dark like distant constellations, lighting the place only well enough to assure them it held no immediate danger. An orchestra of yellow boys diddled and wheeped from one corner, and a troupe of zur-Murrey ran up and down long lines of tables, setting them with mugs and pitchers and plates. Against the far wall, across from the open gates, stood a hastily built platform of planks laid across bales and boxes.

"If that's meant for us, people won't be able to see," said Nela. "The chandeliers are out in the middle of the place. Against that wall is the darkest place in here."

"You'll need to work the Destiny Machine from the floor," suggested Bertran. "Not from the platform. You'll want people to be able to watch it closely."

"It would be wisest to avoid the platform entirely," said Danivon, turning slowly to inspect every corner of the building. "Someone standing alone up there is too good a target and these people are in the mood for targets. Like bowstrings they are, all thrumming with eagerness."

Fringe thought he described it well. The sound of the city shrilled like a cable drawn too taut for its own safety. Here was no law against riot, no control against panic, but instead the deliberate provocation of both: drums, shouts, chants, torches gleaming, ululations, shrieks, cries, a tapestry of sound and movement, of excitement and encitement, a city-wide hysteria being fed and stoked toward some planned-for climax.

"If you're the law here, as you say," whispered Nela, shivering at the sound of the city, "can't you do something about this?"

"Of course," Danivon replied, surprised. "We could do something. We're capable of reducing the place to rubble. But there's been no complaint and disposition nor any violence offered us yet. Nose and experience both tell me it's coming, but Council Supervisory won't accept nose and experience as an excuse for preemptive action."

"So you can't do anything?" She fretted under Bertran's sardonic look.

Danivon himself found her question amusing. "Are you suggesting we commit violence, Nela? Would that be moral?"

She flushed, seeming near tears.

He shook his head at her, patting her shoulder. "I've transmitted a standard trouble message to Tolerance. If, when trouble finally presents itself, we are unable to Attend the Situation, they'll send a retaliation and reduction force."

"Which will be an exemplary lesson for Derbeck," said Fringe in her noncommittal Enforcer's voice, "though not of much use to us personally by then."

Nela gulped and shut her mouth, seeming determined to keep it that way.

"Less talk, more action," said Curvis. "There should be a table on the platform for the high mucky muck Houdum-Bah. Get him up there in everyone's eyes instead of us."

Jory nodded in agreement. "Of course," she said. "Someone should tell the Murrey. Asner, will you take care of that?"

He stumped off to do so, speaking softly to several of the Murrey folk who paused in midscurry, looked fearfully about them, then ran to hoist one of the long tables onto the platform.

"I told them they'd forgotten," whispered Asner when he returned. "Told them I was making a friendly reminder. Poor things, they believe someone forgot to tell them. So, we'll put our things over there to one side, near the platform, but not on it. The light's better there. The boss chief can see us, and so can everyone else."

"What will Houdum-Bah think?" demanded Nela.

"What would you think, if you were the boss chief and arrived at your own banquet to find a table set high upon a platform?" asked Jory. "You'd think it was for you, wouldn't you?"

"How about music?" Asner asked. "Nela, you and Bertran are the experts. What can we do about music for our show?"

The twins went with Asner to talk with the musicians. Coins changed hands. The two drummers nodded as the twins described drum rolls, clashes of cymbals, and when both should occur. After further explanation, the almost trumpeter attempted an almost fanfare, with some success.

Very soon thereafter the Houm and High Houm began to trickle in, each wrapped in gay fabrics and glittering with beads. Blue boys ran back and forth bearing platters of meat from the pits outside the doors and loaves of bread from a store against the wall. Pitchers were filled and emptied and filled again. All was dash and froth and noise. Against the wall, the sideshow set itself in readiness.

"Now's the time to work the crowd," said Bertran. "Curvis, let's work the tables."

"Work the tables?"

"Come on. Let's do some magic." The twins signaled the musicians and moved to the nearest table where they began pulling coins from behind ears, scarves out of women's hair to the accompaniment of drums and bugles and the occasional whang of a timely gong. After watching them for a moment, Curvis followed.

Fringe said, "They're right, Danivon. We'll want the crowd on our side if there's trouble."

He shook his head over her naiveté in thinking Houm or Murrey were capable of taking anyone's side but their own, but he followed her as she tugged the bulky machine to a clear spot near another table.

"Your fortune, ma'am," she chanted. "Your fortune, sir."

Danivon busied himself as her assistant, wafting the incense, summoning the powers of the future.

"Lost . . . Treasure . . . Returns," cried Fringe, reading the shining capsules as they fell into the bin.

"What is it you have lost, ma'am?" begged Danivon, his nose twitching as he held out his hand toward the High Houm woman in her bright green gown. "Was it a pin? No. A ring! Your mother's ring?"

The green-gowned woman responded with cries of delight.

"In the garden outside the window where your washstand is," said Danivon. "That's where it is. You laid it on the sill when you washed your hands, and you forgot it."

"I did!" she wept. "Oh, yes, I remember now."

Her escort dropped coins into Danivon's outstretched palm while others at the table laughed and demanded their own fortunes be told. Fringe worked her way around the table, stopping when she reached the side of a child, a girl of some eleven or twelve years who was looking at her, half in terror, half in delight.

"What's your name," Fringe asked.

"Alouez," the girl whispered. Her eyes were huge and shadowed in the pallor of her face under a misty cloud of hair. She was already beautiful, promising greater beauty to come.

Fringe pivoted, throwing her oracle's dress into a dramatic swirl and taking the opportunity to glance at all the tables. No other children. No other children at all.

"Would you like to hear your fortune, Alouez?" she asked, keeping herself from scowling with some difficulty. Why was this the only child?

The woman sitting next to the girl put her hand to her face, hiding her eyes, not quickly enough to hide the gleam of tears.

"Yes," breathed the girl. "Tell my fortune!"

She picked her own levers, pulled them, listened as bells rang and capsules fell. When they had done, Fringe picked them up, palming one or two to substitute others she had in her pocket. She wanted no message of fear for this child, no matter what the machine said.

"Riches, years, joy," she read, putting the capsules down in front of the child. The tearful woman turned her head away and blotted her face on her sleeve.

"May I keep them?" the girl asked eagerly. The message had erased the anxiety from her face, but Fringe, watching the woman next to the child, knew the reason for that anxiety was still present.

She frowned as she went on to the next table, where Danivon came up to her and asked: "Who's the girl child you were spending such time on?"

"Her name is Alouez," she replied, glancing back at the child over her shoulder. "She's the only child here, have you noticed? She seems very much alone, more than a little frightened. The woman with her is crying, trying to hide it. Something she knows the child doesn't."

"Nasty," said Danivon, catching a whiff of the old familiar stench.

"She seems familiar, somehow."

"The girl?" Danivon grinned fiercely. "Of course. She looks like you. Or as you probably did when you were that age."

It was true, not in the coloring, but in the shape of the face and features. Perhaps in the expression, as well. Fringe had often been fearful at that age. And since, she admitted to herself, trying to think of something that would change the subject. "About that lost ring," she murmured. "That was fortuitous. They were amazed."

"I smelled it, even through all this stink," he said. "Sometimes I do."

"What happens if you smell imminent destruction?"

"I'll scream loudly and we'll all run." He seemed half-serious as he said it, but then he winked at her and caressed her cheek, making her flush. No point in telling her he'd been smelling imminent destruction all day.

Behind them, Curvis and the twins were busy being amusing. Their hands darted and turned, hiding and disclosing, their teeth flashing, they made jokes, people laughed, though warily. By the time the two groups had worked their way around half the tables, many of the High Houm were calling them by name and jesting with them, as were the Murrey folk.

The mood of enjoyment did not last long. From some distance outside came a wavering howl that was taken up by the chimi-hounds at the gates and built into a screaming wail. The assembled diners fell silent in one breath, and into that anxious quiet the clamor of a monstrous drum toppled like an avalanche of stones. Reverberations echoed and died slowly as dust fell from the rafters in spiraling clouds. It was the end of any jollity. The Houm pressed in upon their tables, faces blank, voices stilled, faceless as flowers in a garden. The sideshow members strolled casually back to the corner where Jory and Asner awaited them, managing to get settled into anonymity just as Houdum-Bah's entourage came through the gates.

A dozen drummers first, thundering on balks of hollowed timber, each carried by four men. Armed men second, big men all, laden with weapons, eyes white all the way around, like panicked animals, sleeveless shirts open to the navel, arms and chests tattooed in patterns of red and violet and black, each finger a different color, those fingers weaving an intricate pattern of signs as the hounds spoke to one another in their secret hand language.

The translator in Danivon's bonnet saw the signs and whispered into his ear what the fingers said. "Who put the damned table up there. Houdum-Bah's table? Of course, Houdum-Bah's table! Whaddoyoumean, who?" Then more quick signals. "Are they here? There they are. Well, well, won't they be surprised!"

Danivon, intercepting hostile or amused glances, believed this last interchange referred to the members of the sideshow, and his wariness deepened.

Houdum-Bah himself seemed to find nothing suspicious about the high table. He waved his drummers into a line at the foot of the platform as he heaved his huge bulk upon it and sprawled into the central chair. Murrey ran at once with meat, with drink, with bread. Half a dozen of Houdum-Bah's men mounted the platform and seated themselves on either side of him while Houm got up from the nearest tables on the floor and moved slowly away as the remaining members of the retinue took their places. Within moments, all the entourage was seated and the displaced Houm were edging toward the gates, smiling vacantly as they went, attracting as little notice as possible, leaking through the open gates in twos and threes, vanishing without a word.

Tentatively, the orchestra began to tootle and bang once more, very softly.

"What now?" asked Bertran. "Back to the tables?"

"Not yet," said Jory. "Let them start eating. Then start where you left off. Stay away from the boss chief's men unless they ask you to come over." She sounded very crisp, very young. Danivon peered at her curiously, and she returned the look, winking at him. "I've been in similar situations before," she said. "It's important to look unruffled. Show fear, and they'll be on you in an instant."

"Enforcers know that," said Fringe stiffly. "We're taught that."

"Well, of course you are, dear," Jory murmured. "Of course you are."

More fortunes, more coins from behind ears, more scarves from unlikely places, more transport of pocket munks from one place to another. Now, however, the Houm were not entertained, though they very quietly pretended to be, clearly eager to do nothing or say nothing that might attract the attention of Houdum-Bah or his men. Meaningless smiles. Meaningless nods. Words spoken too quietly to be heard. The orchestra went on tootling, plucking, drumming, but even that sound was subdued, attracting little notice.

"Here, boy," called one of the entourage to Danivon. "Over here."

Danivon bridled.

"Hush," hissed Fringe. "Go, bow, be a sideshow, Danivon."

"I wan' my des-tin-ee," demanded a tattooed giant, a man almost as big as Curvis. "Bring the girlie to tell my for-toon."

"She cannot tell fortunes," Danivon intoned. "But the Destiny Machine may, if it chooses. She does not control it. It does as it will."

Fringe bowed, chanted, lifted her hands, then stood away from the machine, pointing at the levers, saying, "The machine is in your hands. Pick what levers you will."

A bright orange finger flicked at the levers, two, three. The machine began to whir. Fringe went on chanting, standing well away. She wanted no allegations of interference. At last the capsules fell into the bin, and she gestured for the man to pick them up.

"Read it," he cried, his eyes fast upon her face. "You read it."

She picked them up at arm's length and ostentatiously laid them upon the table so they could be seen. Perhaps this animal couldn't read, but someone at the table probably did.

"Great . . . Dragon . . . Comes," she read to her own amazement.

"Wha's that mean?" the man asked between dirty teeth.

She bowed, spreading her arms wide. "I do not know, sir. Only the machine knows, and it will not tell me. Something or someone like a dragon approaches, so I would say."

"Bring her here!" trumpeted a voice. Houdum-Bah himself, beckoning to Fringe. "Here, come give me my destiny, woman! Be sure it is a good one."

Danivon helped her onto the platform and leapt up behind her. Together they moved the machine close to Houdum-Bah. Again Fringe chanted and stood aside.

The man leaned forward, finicky, picking this lever and that. The machine began, lights moving, bells sounding. Silence fell in the great room. There was only the sound of the bells and the tap of the capsules that fell, one, two, three, four.

He read them himself. "Comes . . . Now . . . Great . . . Dragon . . ."

Fringe could not keep the astonishment from her face.

"Wha'?" the boss chief cried, seizing her by the shoulder. "Wha'?"

"It doesn't . . . it doesn't usually give the same fortune twice," Fringe said, biting her lip. "This dragon business must be something important."

"Wha' is dra-gone?" he asked.

She shook her head helplessly.

He bellowed the same question to the assembled diners. "Wha' is dra-gone?"

The orchestra fell silent. Every head was bowed, as for the headsman's axe. No one had an answer for Houdum-Bah. Then, from her place beside the platform, Jory cried in a hag's shriek: "Oh, great Houdum-Bah. There are dragons upriver. I have seen them myself."

"Wha'?" he demanded again.

"Big creatures," she said, coming out into the open space before the platform, curving her skinny arms, extending her bony old fingers, glaring her eyes. "With fangs and spines and plates of hide upon them. And claws, of course. Very fearsome, they are." She shivered all over, making a sound as though her bones clacked.

The man stared at her for a moment, his nostrils twitching, hanging between amusement and annoyance. Then he roared laughter, and his retinue laughed with him, a howled cacophony.

"Houdum-Bah is not feared of beasts, no matter wha' fangs it has," cried one.

"True," said Jory, capering about as she shrieked laughter. "Great Houdum-Bah need fear no beast, no matter when it comes."

"Great Lord Chimi-ahm will deal with beasts," the boss chief declared, rising from his chair. He thrust his arms high and trumpeted into the suddenly silent room, "Great Lord Chimi-ahm will hear of this dragone. Now call the priests, so Chimi-ahm will hear!"

The drummers looked expectantly at the doors and pummeled their instruments, making an earthquake summons. The Houm silently left their tables to press against the walls, turning their faces away as though they wished to become invisible. The Murrey ran, falling over one another in their anxiety to get the tables tugged aside to make a cleared space below the platform. Fringe and Danivon pulled the Destiny Machine off the end of the platform and settled among the others of their party, as intent upon being inconspicuous as were the Houm.

"He's playing at something, is Houdum-Bah," muttered Jory, barely audible under the thunder of the drums. "He's violent and arbitrary toward everyone, but I sense an especial animosity toward us. One he's covering up for the moment."

Danivon sniffed. "True," he admitted. "The man means a particular violence toward us. Of course he means enough violence toward the world at large to get a great many people killed. So, what happens now?"

"You're about to see a dabbo-dam," Jory said. "So, stay alert."

"What does it mean?" whispered Nela.

"The words? Ah. Dabbo-dam means *approach the god*, a ritual during which certain followers get touched or inhabited or, sometimes, eaten by the deity. Keep your wits about you."

"What will happen?" whispered Fringe.

"God knows." Jory chuckled humorlessly. "Whatever it is, it cannot hurt you if you do not let yourself be fooled."

The drums fell silent with the entry of the priests, a dozen of them, bony, dirty, skin-headed, rag-robed, bare-footed. They carried bundles that writhed and stank and torches that smoked, bringing tears to the eyes. They brought an altar with them, a tablelike construction suspended between poles, the gilt-horned altar much stained and scarred. When the poles were taken away, the priests took living creatures from their bundles, killed them upon the altar, doused themselves liberally with the blood, then grasped the horns at the four corners of the altar as they chanted in guttural voices, the smoke of their torches rising in a vaporous chimney toward the distant roof beams. The chant was repetitive, three or four phrases reiterated over and over. The drums took up the rhythm. Several of the Houm added their voices to the chant, then more and more of them until all were swaying and muttering.

"Don't chant with them," murmured Jory from the sideshow's midst. "Move your mouth, but do not say the words. Remember that what you see will not be real. Think about something else if you can. The taste of fruit, perhaps. The pleasures of the bath. I find it useful to think of warm water and soap. I picture it cutting through slime, washing it away."

Fringe moved her lips and thought, as suggested, of bathing. Danivon moved his lips and thought of cutting Houdum-Bah's throat. "Boy," indeed. Curvis moved his lips and concentrated on the coin in his hand that he was making appear and disappear behind Danivon's back. Bertran saw him and did likewise, controlling his own fear even as he felt Nela's fear rising inside him, making him quiver. Nela, trembling, shut her eyes and concentrated upon the turtle. Gray wind, gray leaf, gray fog rising. Poor turtle, coming into such danger.

Houdum-Bah left the platform to join the priests. He grasped one of the horns of the altar and blended his own huge voice into the tumult.

Jory whoofed in surprise, as though she had been hit in the stomach. Fringe glanced up to see an expression of astonishment on the old woman's face and followed her gaze to the smoke where flapping, luminescent flakes had appeared, flakes that gradually joined to one another, coalesced, became a solid thing that shaped itself into a pillar. The pillar gained height and mass, then sprouted roots, branches, became a tree; the tree became a monstrous figure with six arms, six legs, six glaring eyes, six pendulous ears, three sets of great fangs shining from each of its three great mouths that gulped and gulped and gulped again.

"Great Lord Chimi-ahm," shrieked the priests. "Ah-oh, ah-oh, Great Lord Chimi-ahm!"

"Great Lord Chimi-ahm," moaned the Houm. "Ah-oh, ah-oh."

"Great Lord Chimi-ahm," sobbed the Murrey.

The manifestation pointed its multiple arms, a finger at this one, a finger at that. Here a Houm cried out, shaken by spasms. There another began to jerk and sway. Others then, until several score were in motion. Like puppets, they twitched and danced, inward toward the circling priests, flopping and prancing while, in their midst, the god gamboled awkwardly, triple mouths gaping. Among the dancers, two hounds pushed the young Houm girl toward the altar, Alouez.

The child's face bore an expression of baffled terror. Fringe knew that expression. She had seen one much like that one long ago in the blotched mirror of the module behind Char's house. Now the child's mouth opened and she began to scream as she was thrust by an arm, shoved by a hip, knocked and butted forward an inch at a time, unable to resist the violence of the hounds around her.

"Why did they bring that child," Fringe whispered furiously. "She's too young."

"They were told to bring her, I would imagine," said Jory. "I would say that Houdum-Bah ordered her brought."

"Why?" she blurted.

"For himself, of course."

Fringe risked a glance sidewise at the altar and saw the boss chief's eyes fixed on the girl no less hungrily than those of the god looming above. No woman could work as an Enforcer in Enarae without learning to recognize that rapist's look. "She's a child," Fringe cried, horrified and sickened, "only a child!"

"It is said that Zhulia the Whore prefers to pour herself into children," said Asner in an expressionless voice. "So Cafferty has told us. Though perhaps it is the male worshipers of Lady Zhulia who prefer the children."

"Look," whispered Jory.

The tri-une monster in the smoke was splitting. Its three foreheads protruded like the prows of boats, pushing outward, pulling the faces behind them. Eyes followed foreheads, then noses, mouths, jaws as the head came apart into three, each of the three heads striking outward like the head of a serpent, coiled necks following, lashing away from the body, drawing shoulders behind them, then arms, torsos, legs, recoiling then, becoming three beings where there had been only one:

One wide-hipped with a torrent of smoky hair, a wristlet of skulls, breasts like great melons. One mighty thewed, armored, armed, his maleness carried before him like a spear. One slender, flexible, long-legged, narrow-faced, sexless lips bent upward from a sharp-toothed smile. He. She. It.

"Zhulia the Whore, Lord Balal, Chibbi the Dancer," muttered Jory, nodding her head as though confirmed in some private apprehension. "All present and accounted for. Plus some of the minor gods. Look at the hounds."

The hounds twitched and shivered, throwing up their furred arms, opening hands that were now clawed, mouths that were now fanged. Hounds indeed, slavering and staring about themselves with red eyes.

Chibbi the Dancer spun on its toes, arms extended, those arms becoming the spokes of a wheel, the spokes becoming arrows of light that flew out among the twitching Houm, penetrating them. They went on dancing, howling as bones cracked, bodies fell, limbs flailed uselessly. Splintered bones protruded from bloody flesh as the Houm convulsed themselves into wreckage.

The mighty male form of Lord Balal turned toward Houdum-Bah, moved ponderously toward him where he stood below the platform. Houdum-Bah stripped off his garments and awaited the god, arms wide, eyes half-closed.

And before them on the floor the little girl shivered as the female form leaned down, touched her, poured into her like water into a hole. The child seemed to swell. Her clothes ripped away from burgeoning breasts, from wide, luxurious hips, from a vulva thatched with thick, shining hair.

Fringe blinked rapidly, shaking her head, snarling. There was no Lady Zhulia. There was only an eleven-year-old girl standing there. Slight. Breastless. Her little ribs heaving as she panted and tried to cover herself when her clothes were ripped away by one of the priests. A little girl, shivering, her eyes wide and lost.

"No," said Fringe.

"It's their culture," said Danivon firmly, trying to keep his voice from shaking. "This is what they do."

"No," said Fringe again. "Jory, no. He'll hurt her. She's only a child. He'll rape her. He'll kill her."

"This is what they *do*," repeated Danivon desperately. *"Diversity,* Enforcer!"

"No," she said again. "Jory, do something."

Jory stared around herself, her face a mask in which surprise and fury were equally mingled. "What makes you think *I* can do anything, Fringe Owldark?"

"You can. Somebody must."

Jory laughed angrily. "Then *you* do something!"

Without thought, Fringe sprang forward, her weapon leaping into her hand. She seized the girl by the shoulder and drew her away from Houdum-Balal, thrusting the child behind her, threatening Houdum-Balal with her weapon.

He roared with rage, and all the hounds echoed the roar as they came toward her.

She brushed them with heat, enough to stop ordinary men, but they were too hot with rage to feel it. She thumbed the control and tried again, sending them reeling back, all but Houdum-Balal, who came on, arms outstretched, mouth wide in rage, seemingly untouched by the heat.

Fringe backed up, suddenly aware she had no support. Danivon and Curvis were not helping her, were, in fact, reaching out to take the child away from her, to return it. . . .

Jory laughed.

The laugh fled into the smoke and the drums and returned louder. It went out against the walls and returned, louder. It rattled in the corners and returned, louder yet, growing like summer thunder, booming, cracking. The drums fell silent, and the chanting.

"Great Dragon Comes," snarled Jory into the laughter, each word reverberating and growing, each separate, each connected, the whole larger than its constituent words, the phrase bouncing off the walls until it overrode all other sound. "Great Dragon Comes!"

And Great Dragon came, Great Dragon was there, taller than Chimi-ahm, more powerful, one huge paw on the edge of the altar, his fanged maw no more than an arm's length from Houdum-Balal's surprised face.

"No," whispered the dragon in a voice of hushed thunder. "No Chimi-ahm. No Zhulia the Whore. No Chibbi the Dancer. No Lord Balal. None of them. Dabbo-dam is done, boss chief. Dabbo-dam is done!"

Fringe thought she heard the words, believed she heard the words, but they had no sound to them. No timbre she could identify. Almost as though she heard them through some other part than her ears.

Great Dragon was turning, tail flailing, claws reaching, snatching at the priests, tossing them, eating their torches, swallowing their smoke, shredding the images of the gods, sending them screaming out into the night with the dragon in pursuit, leaving Houdum-Bah, suddenly dwindled, with his mouth open and all his chiefdom in disarray.

"Let's go before he decides whose fault that was," said Jory.

The girl child lay behind Fringe where she had fallen, unmoving, her eyes rolled up into her head. Fringe snatched her up, wrapped her in a fold of the oracle's cloak, and carried her along, shrugging aside Danivon's clutching remonstrance.

"Get off me!" she growled at him. "Get off!"

"She belongs here," he whispered, running at her side. "For the love of diversity, Fringe. She's not yours to take!"

"Someone took you!" she snarled in return. "Someone took you. Kept you from ending up on the skull rack in Molock. Kept them from killing you, beating your bones to powder. Zasper Ertigon took you, Danivon! Now I'm taking her. Get out of my way."

And there was no time for argument, for the city came awake like a hive disturbed, with riot and burning and screaming in all directions, for there seemed to be dragons everywhere, pursuing the populace wherever it would run.

In City Fifteen, Sepel and his colleagues set aside the sensory recordings left by Clore and Thob and Breaze and Bland. Those left, only a few, are by Jordel of Hemerlane.

"Join me?" Sepel invites his colleagues.

Tentacles are joined. They are conscious of being Sepel794DZ and colleagues. . . .

Then, in an instant, they are Jordel of Hemerlane.

Jordel of Hemerlane, unconscious of any being save himself, seeing what Jordel saw, knowing what Jordel knew. Being where Jordel had been. . . .

High in the tower room. Such heights usually give him a feeling of exhilaration, an appreciation of the forces supporting such great structures in their skyward reach. Today he feels only depression, frustration, anger. Across from him, outside the windows, clouds scud by on a summer wind. At a distance is a glimmer of banners on pinnacles, a shiver of windblown flags. This is Brannigan Galaxity, heartbeat of humanity.

Before the windows, silhouetted against the racing clouds, stands Orimar Breaze, handsome and silver-haired, his head like that of a prophet. The group is assembled in his place, his important place, this apartment at the top of the highest tower, this apartment that is above even the Pinnacle Study where the meetings of the Great Question Committee are held. And handsome Orimar Breaze is making a scornful shape with his lips as he hears what Jordel has to say.

Jordel feels his tongue flap between dry lips as he pleads with them. ". . . must protest this unwillingness to accept our specifications! We can't risk this!" He swallows, trying to mitigate the panic he feels in the presence of these uncomprehending, unscientific . . . idiots!

No understanding on the face of Orimar Breaze, nor on the faces of Mintier Thob or Therabas Bland, who already have their mouths open in incipient argument.

"Dear boy . . ."

So speaks Mintier Thob as she smiles that patronizingly maternal smile. Though it convinces many people she is sensible and honest, it no longer convinces Jordel of anything:

"When we go into the Core on Elsewhere, you want our patterns to remain in stasis except for fully automated annual updatings. Believe me, dear boy, we understand what you're saying. However, we prefer that our patterns shall *not* remain in stasis and they *shall* be updated and corrected on a discretionary basis rather than automatically."

She smiles, she speaks: calmly, briefly, seeming to cleave to the point while actually grazing it only slightly. So she has enlightened many desperate issues with ignorant complacency. So she does now. Secure in her comfortable, motherly tone, she solicits approval from the others.

And receives it. *Yes,* say Breaze and Bland and Clore. *We prefer our own discretion to your automatics, dear boy. Yes, we do.*

"Then you don't understand the implications," he cries, stung into undiplomatic truth.

"Oh, my boy, indeed!" squawks Therabas Bland, a stringy old hen who eschews body sculpting and syntheskin to sag unappealingly in the dangling beads and flowing draperies of her girlhood. Beauty and grace are nothing to her, she often says, nothing to one to whom the secrets of the universe have been disclosed. She is a mathematician and proud of her mind. She will not believe it might fail her. Her own thoughts must be correct, else she would find them unthinkable. So she waggles a finger at him, cackling, "My boy, indeed, let us say it simply. We prefer to stay awake. We prefer not to emulate some fairy-tale heroine and sleep for a few hundred years. Surely you can understand that!"

What can Jordel say he has not said a thousand times before? He nods, he holds out his hand placatingly. "It is instinctive to respond as you are doing. My gut response is the same as yours. It is not, however, the correct thing to do, and the implications of it are very grave."

"In what way?" Orimar's left nostril lifts only a little; Orimar who never pays attention to the sense of any argument, but only to his own place in it, his own allegiances. His place in this one is beside Thob, beside Bland.

"Error," Jordel hears himself cry, doing his best to make a tocsin of it. "Error will creep in. If the matter of update and correction is left to the discretion of individual minds, we will be wide open to error."

And from across the room sounds a rasping snort as the cadaverous form of Subble Clore rises from a half-hidden chair, wearing an unpleasantly predatory smile that makes Jordel shudder. Clore has made a life-long study of organisms exposed to negative stimulation, of survival or mortality under stress, of the evolutionary response to agony. Clore is a scholar of pain. His place at the Galaxy has been challenged from time to time, but it is whispered he has a hold upon the almighty Chancellors. There are tales of unspeakable agreements made in the pursuit of power, but despite all the tittle-tattle he is here, one of the elect of Brannigan.

"You are saying we are untrustworthy." He lifts his hands, palms up, to the ladies, to Orimar, the gesture a sneer.

Jordel clears his throat. "I'm saying we are all human."

"But some much less fallible than others," remarks Mintier Thob. "Which surely includes the faculty of Brannigan Galaxity. You are one of us, Jordel. Have you no pride! Do you so mistrust yourself?"

Jordel considers pride. Orimar is a narcissist. He will use the Core to go on worshiping himself. Thob is enormous in complacency. She will go into the Core because she cannot conceive of a universe without herself in it. Bland believes herself incapable of error. For her, the Core represents a new universe to set right. Clore . . . Clore's restless mind plays with life and death. He will enter the Core because it will offer new forms of life, new kinds of death. These are not the reasons they would give, but Jordel knows them well. Still, he answers softly, hoping yet. "Of course I mistrust myself, Lady Professor. I've told you that before."

"Enough, Jordel!" explodes Subble Clore. "If you're weighed down by self-doubt, keep it to yourself. Leave it alone, for humanity's sake!"

"It's for humanity's sake I don't," Jordel replies forcefully. "Time in the matrix is not like time outside, it is more like dream time. Episodes that seem to go on for days may actually last only moments. If you are awake in the Core you may achieve many years' worth of memories while a single year passes outside.

"These memories will not be anchored by sensory feedback as they would be in the real world. In the outside world, sensory feedback provides the necessary referents to anchor our emotional and intellectual experiences. Our experiences are separated and made discrete by sensory trivia—by movements, smells, the sound of voices, the sight of a face. In the Core, there will be no sensory data at all, and where there is none, minds tend to create it, just as they do during dreaming.

"So, you will create environments and experiences. And by the time a year has passed, your pattern will have deviated considerably from its original. Returning your pattern to its original configuration would be equivalent to wiping out years, perhaps decades of your life! They will be the most recent, vivid years. To wipe them out will be like dying. You won't . . . we won't be able to bring ourselves to do it!"

Bland smiles, a world-weary smile. "Nonsense, dear boy. I'm an adult, a scholar. I know the need for correction of data from time to time. I can trust myself to take care of it."

"I don't trust myself that much. Truly," Jordel replies.

"Among our peers, I think you'll find yourself virtually alone in that," Mintier Thob responds reprovingly. She strides to the window and gestures outward, across the tower tops to the far horizon, including in the gesture all that is Brannigan. "The academic world is ideal for the development of humane qualities, Jordel. I think we here in this room have proven that. We're more sane than most people. We're more patient. We're kinder."

She smiles her detestable smile, and Jordel, remembering recent bloodletting sessions among these same academicians, tries not to let his reaction show.

"After all," the Lady Professor goes on, "think what trust Brannigan has reposed in our committee: the very destiny of mankind. And we are not about to leave any part of that destiny to an automatic function designed by some mechanic!" She spits the last words, looking directly at him, leaving no doubt just which mechanic she has in mind.

Jordel is silent. So. He has tried. He has done his best. Now let them do as they will do. He will do what he must to protect himself. . . .

And the recording trailed off in feelings of anger, disgust, and firm resolve.

"Twaddle," said Sepel794DZ, angrily returning to himself. "All twaddle. Those people weren't responsible for the destiny of mankind. They were merely discussing mankind's destiny, not creating it!"

"That's manness for you, confusing the manipulation of symbols with reality!" snarled a colleague dink. "And if Jordel was right, it tells us what happened to the inhabitants of the Core."

"But what happened to Jordel himself?" asked another colleague.

Sepel replied: "You felt his intentions as I did. Either he never entered the Core, or he arranged to have himself processed in accordance with specifications. If he found someone—a technician, a fellow engineer—whom he could trust, that person may have begun the little rhyme we learned from Boarmus."

" '. . . then Jordel of Hemerlane/chased them all back home again,' " quoted a dink thoughtfully. "If that's true, then Jordel went into the Core all right. If that's what he meant to do, he's still in there somewhere."

During the return to Tolerance Boarmus steeled himself for the stratagem he had decided upon. He and Jacent discussed it on the trip back, whispering into each other's ears, the boy white-faced but resolute—or perhaps only foolhardy. Boarmus thought that likely. Still, Jacent had been fond of Metty, and Boarmus spared no description of what had happened to Metty and would, no doubt, happen to all of them if the thing or things down in the Core weren't stopped.

"I guess I don't understand how this will stop anything," the boy had whispered, shamefaced.

"We don't know that anything will. This idea may slow it down, that's all. Give us some breathing space. If you can think of something better. . . ."

Jacent couldn't, of course. He wouldn't even have thought of this.

"Remember"—Boarmus put his hand on the boy's shoulder and

squeezed hard to reinforce the point—"you're merely an average citizen. Someone who's concerned about the matter."

"And if it kills us?"

"Then we're dead," said Boarmus flatly. "And maybe better off!"

They did not wait for the ghosts to come to them. As soon as it was late enough for traffic in Tolerance to have fallen into its nighttime mode, Jacent followed the bulky man to the secret tube, down into the featureless room, through it and into the winding way to the Core. It was vacant. No one was there.

"Something will show up," said Boarmus, pressing a lever down. In the ramified structure beneath him, a signal was emitted: Report time. The Provost is present.

"Where will it come from?" whispered Jacent.

"Elsewhere," muttered Boarmus. "Anywhere, boy. Halfway around the world. Hold your water. Look subdued."

It wasn't difficult. He was subdued. He started violently when the voice came from the wall.

"Boarmus," it said softly. Not the gulper voice. One of the female-sounding ones.

"I have been considering what you said to me last," said Boarmus, putting his hand on Jacent's shoulder.

"There is an unauthorized person with you."

"True. He is here as an example."

"An example of what?"

"An example of the awe in which the people of Tolerance hold you," said Boarmus. Under his fingers, Jacent shivered. *Very good,* Boarmus thought. *Let the boy be scared half to death, so long as he doesn't forget his lines.* "An ordinary person of Tolerance. Not a Provost. Not a member of the Inner Circle."

"Does he hold me in awe?"

Boarmus shook him. "Do you hold, ah . . . her . . . in awe, boy."

"Oh, yes." Jacent shivered. "Yes, I do."

"In reverence?"

Jacent nodded, and had to be prodded into speaking aloud. "Oh, yes."

"What does he think I am?" The voice managed to sound curious.

"Now," signaled Boarmus's fingers, almost gladly. He'd worried about working the conversation around to this point; now he wouldn't have to.

"Well," said Jacent from a dry mouth. "Some people think you're god. But others don't."

(Good boy.)

"Why don't they?" Still curious, not yet angry.

"Well, because," Jacent said. "God is omniscient. God knows the answers to all questions. If you are god, you'd know the answer to the Great Question. I mean, people say if you're really god, you'll answer that question. Then *everybody* will know you're god. Everybody will know."

"How do you know I haven't answered the question?" Another voice, this one edged with anger, displeasure. Boarmus held on to the boy's shoulder, keeping him steady. Even this voice was not the really bad one, not the gulper. The gulper must be busy elsewhere.

"You'd have told us," said Jacent in a firm voice. "In order that we might work toward our destiny properly. You see, that's how we know all gods before now were false, they never told us what our destiny really was. So, if you do tell us, you'll be the only true one. And the answer will be so self-evident, we'd all agree with it. Because when a true god truly answers a question, that's what happens. Everyone knows that."

"But I am god," muttered a voice. "We are god."

"Of course," quavered Jacent. "I already believe that. But *everyone* will believe it when you answer the Great Question."

"I don't need you to believe. I can make you do what I say even if you don't believe." A sulky-sounding voice, this. "God doesn't need to prove anything, not if god can make people do what god wants."

Boarmus patted Jacent silent. They had struggled with this argument, whispering, on the way home. Now was time to see if the Brannigan minds would understand it.

Boarmus said, "That's true. But if people only do what you say, then you'll only get what you're already capable of. Gods create beings as tools to explore beyond what they already are and know. To create randomness, chaos, chance. To create discovery. You created man to discover new things for you, and man will discover them, if he knows you're god, if he wants to please you. That is what you created mankind for, wasn't it? After all, you're god, you're very busy. You created man as a kind of tool, to find things out for you."

Silence. That silence that Boarmus had always believed meant the minds were talking together. Disagreeing. That was the key. If there was still enough individuality in there for disagreement. Which he wasn't at all sure of!

He tugged. Time to get out of there. They fled, not quite precipitously.

"What're they doing now?" murmured Jacent, feeling the cold sweat dripping from his jaw. "What?"

"I hope it's arguing with itself," whispered Boarmus, wiping his mouth on the back of his hand. "Pray that's what it's doing, boy. Arguing."

Behind them, in the depths of the Core, there was argument indeed, though it did not go in any way Boarmus could have foreseen.

One presence. "At Brannigan we . . ."

And another. ". . . mankind's problem only . . ."

And another yet. ". . . should prove we are what we say we are, after all. . . ."

And another arriving, full of rage, the one Boarmus thought of as the gulper, that one stripped out of Chimi-ahm and deprived of his fun, the gulper thwarted by Great Dragon, that one humiliated before his worshipers!

"We need prove nothing! Nothing!"

Silence in the Core, in the net, everywhere as intention wavered before this thunderous presence.

"But we always said man would answer the question." One broke the quiet in a mechanical whine. "Not others, only man. But we aren't man. Not anymore."

"Then make man answer," hissed that which had been Chimi-ahm.

"But they don't have the answer."

"Lazy," it again with a horrible gulp. "No concentration. Thinking of other things than their duty to us! We will take some of them and put them somewhere and then we will make them answer!"

"Who?" whispered one. "Who will we take?"

"Those ones," it gulped with vengeful satisfaction. "Who asked questions about us. Those ones on Panubi!"

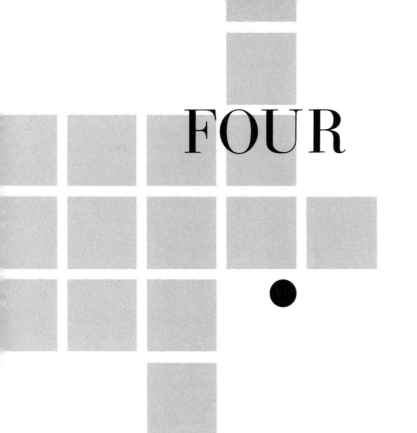

FOUR

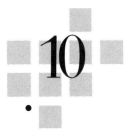

10

In Du-you, Curvis seized up Jory and Asner, one under each arm, and led the members of the sideshow, abandoning all their paraphernalia, in headlong flight down to the riverside. Behind them dragons rampaged through the city, appearing and disappearing while Houm and Murrey fled wildly before them. When the first dragons reached the riverfront, the chimi-hounds guarding the booms ran howling, a dereliction immediately taken advantage of by the captain of the *Dove*. Four stocky deckmen skimmed a small boat off to the nearest boom tower, the booms were raised, and the *Dove* was poled down the channel to the river. Once there, the strongest oarsmen thrust at the sweeps to move the *Dove* quickly into open water as the little boat came scuttling to catch up. The sails were raised and the *Dove* dug its bow into the River Fohm once more.

On the deck, in the midst of all this frantic activity, Fringe crouched over the recumbent and unconscious body of Alouez, a weapon in each hand, daring either Danivon or Curvis to come near her. She would not let them touch the girl, and she would not give them a reason for her action. How could she give them a reason? How say she recognized that lost expression, knew that same feeling of agonized helplessness. How say she was moved by it as by an instinctive frenzy of self-preservation. She could no more abandon the child than she could have abandoned herself, but she could not say why. She did not understand why.

"You can't fight us both off," Curvis threatened. "Give her to me. I'll take the little boat and get her back to shore while there's still time."

"You and what other six Enforcers," snarled Fringe.

"Leave Fringe alone," Jory told the two men. "Leave her!"

Danivon cursed at length.

"Leave her alone," said Jory again. "She is only doing for this child what someone did for you."

"Don't talk silly, old woman. Do you expect me to believe . . ." he snarled.

"Yes," she said, beckoning toward the shadows of the deckhouse where the two castaways stood. "I expect you to believe this is Latibor Luze, who fathered you; this is Cafferty Luze, who bore you. They were in Molock when you were born, and still there when you were chosen for the temple. They saved your life, then Zasper Ertigon saved you again, risking everything for you." She shook her head at him warningly, then turned to Fringe. "Do I have that name right?"

"Yes, Zasper Ertigon," Fringe confirmed in an exhausted voice. "And I have broken my promise to him, never to tell." Her eyes filled with guilty tears, but they did not blink as she glared at the two men.

Danivon stared unbelievingly at the two castaways and threw up his hands. "This is all crazy! I don't have time for this! We were sent after dragons, and we've found the dragons! That's what we should be concentrating on!"

"These aren't the dragons you were looking for," said Jory in a firm voice. "Believe me."

"Why should I believe you?" he yelled.

Latibor took something from around his neck and handed it to him. "Will this convince you?" he murmured, staring into the younger man's face.

He took the thing reluctantly, bending down to peer at it. Curvis struck a light.

"My medallion," said Danivon, grabbing for his neck. He found his own hanging where it always hung.

"Not yours," said Cafferty softly. "Latibor's. Jory has given these medallions to all the people she's chosen. She calls them a conceit, but they serve to identify us to one another."

"What is this design?" demanded Danivon.

"It is a depiction of Great Dragon ridden by the prophetess," said Jory in a peevish voice. "Cafferty's right. It's a conceit. I was a prophetess once."

Cafferty said, "I've always regarded it as a promise that if we are in dire distress Great Dragon will come to our aid as he did tonight. I put my medallion around your neck before we put you in the ship that carried you to safety from Molock."

"Great Dragon, Great Dragon," Nela cried, "what is it? Where did it come from? Where did they all come from?"

"Great Dragon is a friend of mine," Jory soothed. "The lesser dragons you saw are his great-great-grandchildren. They have the power to be seen or not, as they choose, and until tonight they did not choose. They are no danger to you, to any of you, and they are *not* the dragons you're looking for. The dragons you're looking for were seen over the wall from Thrasis, and they are something else entirely."

"Has he been here, on this ship?" demanded the captain. "This big one?"

"Sometimes on this ship," she replied.

"We've been riding low," he said sulkily. "I wondered why. A monstrous heavy beast, this beast of yours. And where is it now?"

"He is heavy, yes. He goes on growing all his life, and my friend has had a long life. However, it is no *beast*, certainly no beast of mine. You can tell where he is now from the consternation along the Ti'il. I would say he and his descendants are leading the people a merry chase, to their discomfiture though likely to no lasting harm. Though he is prideful, he is also a most tolerant and peaceable creature."

"Why?" cried Danivon, his Enforcer's pride outraged. "Why did he show up now? We weren't in danger just then!"

Asner snorted, shaking his head at Danivon, and Danivon flushed, conscious of having sounded ridiculous. He was accustomed to thinking of danger only as it applied to himself or other Enforcers, but of course there had been danger: danger to the girl child, danger and death to the people of Derbeck, danger to Jory and Asner and the twins. The danger to themselves he had believed he could handle, or escape, for he had not smelled his own death as a creeping cold thing with a stench he knew well. He fell silent, staring at the toes of his boots in order not to look at any of them.

Jory broke the silence by waving a bony finger at them all. "Listen, and I will tell you what Latibor and Cafferty found out in Derbeck: Houdum-Bah, fed much rancid broth of resentment by the priests of Chimi-ahm, brewed plans for rebellion against Council Supervisory, deciding that his first act against them should be one of unmistakable contempt and defiance. Such gestures occur from time to time on Elsewhere, as you must know. Why else have Enforcers, save to keep such as Houdum-Bah in check?"

Danivon turned toward her, suddenly attentive.

"Houdum-Bah aspires to conquer Beanfields, and then Shallow," offered Latibor. "The priests told him this is possible, that Council Supervisory is weak and vacillating and will do nothing."

Jory nodded agreement. "Houdum-Bah knew you three were Council Enforcers. It was no fleeting or drunken foolishness that moved him to summon the show to his banquet. He had planned it for some time. He was told you were coming by someone who knew, perhaps by someone who knew you were coming here even before you left Tolerance. When you arrived in Derbeck, you were to be 'invited' to a dabbo-dam where you would be given to Chimi-ahm. Chimi-ahm was to eat you, us, his voracity being the signal for war."

Said Cafferty: "The death of Old Man Daddy and the election of a successor are merely coincidental. Even while Old Man Daddy was alive, it was Houdum-Bah who held the power. If Great Dragon had not interrupted Houdum-Bah's gesture of contempt, Chimi-ahm would have eaten you tonight, and his hounds would have been across the western border into Beanfields by morning."

"He meant to kill all of us?" Nela breathed.

Jory snorted. "*Something* meant to kill at least some of us. Something wanted us dead. Possibly only you three Enforcers, but then again, perhaps whatever moves Chimi-ahm would have tried to make a meal of all seven of us. Seven is a good number, as the chimi-hound said who came to fetch us. We did not ask him a good number for what." She wiped her mouth angrily.

"And you knew all this when you let us go in there?" demanded Fringe.

Jory shook her head in frustration. "I knew they planned an attack, yes, but who would fear an attack when there were three Enforcers along, all trained to a fine edge and with arms enough to destroy the province? Then, too, there was Great Dragon with us. I considered us safe enough."

"I had a warning," said Danivon in perplexity. "I had a secret warning from Boarmus. But he said ghosts."

"Ghosts?" asked Jory, tilting her head to one side as she considered. "Ghosts of whom?"

He shook his head, "He didn't say." He turned to Cafferty and Latibor. "How did you find out what they were going to do? How did you know?"

"You yourself knew," Cafferty said to him. "Come now, think. Even without a warning, you must have known. You must have smelled it. You *must* have been smelling danger."

He shook his head at her, unwilling to admit she was right. "My nose doesn't give me all the details you claim to know," he said angrily.

These two did not fit his own ideas of who his parents had been. He had thought Princes, perhaps, from some enlightened province. Or respected scientists from some category-eight or -nine place. Not these weary people, draggled by years and sorrow, staring at him with tired yet voracious eyes.

"Your nose coupled to some very professional spying would have given you all sorts of detail," snorted Jory. "Cafferty and Latibor have spent most of their lives going about among the provinces of Panubi, seeing one thing and another, charting the changes that have been going on in Elsewhere! They've planted their little ears to hear the councils of high priests. They've listened to the words of chief chimi-hounds in their secret meetings. They've known what was planned. And when they came aboard, they told Asner and me."

"But why were they spying in Derbeck in the first place?" Danivon cried in a voice as much outraged as curious. "What business was it of theirs! Of yours! None of you are Enforcers!"

"Our business here is as valid as your business here, Danivon Luze," snapped Jory. "You are not the only cock strutting this particular dunghill. Why argue matters of jurisdiction? Here are two folk who haven't seen you since you were a toddling child! They might like to talk to you and see if you are worth the trouble they took!"

Almost unwillingly, Danivon followed Cafferty and Latibor to the opposite rail, apart from the others, in no more hurry to believe he was their son than they seemingly were to convince him of that fact. The two of them regarded him warily, nostrils flared, backs stiff, like two dogs who have found their only child has turned out to be a cat.

Jory leaned toward Fringe and stroked her cheek. "Put the weapon away, Enforcer. Danivon won't bother you."

"What about him?" demanded Fringe, glaring at Curvis.

"Nor him. Neither of them. Not now. Curvis may report you both later, but he hasn't yet decided to do that." She looked up at the giant, her eyes squinted half shut, as though trying to see into his heart.

He flushed and turned away angrily. His duty as an Enforcer had been compromised, and he was considerably annoyed. "No," he said. "Not. . . I don't know. Should I? Should I report them? Danivon's . . . well, it wasn't his fault he got saved. And Fringe can't be blamed much, being only a woman."

"Only!" shrieked Fringe, taking up her weapon once more.

"Shush, shush," said Asner. "Danivon's an illegal escapee from Molock who, so we're told, has asked forbidden questions, and Fringe, woman or not, has interfered in the affairs of a province. Both of them have sinned against diversity and are already dead, in accordance with the laws of Council Supervisory. Isn't that so? Of course, Curvis, you are suspect too, for having been in their company."

Curvis bit his lip and turned away. Fringe put the weapon back on her belt and sank onto the deck beside the unconscious girl.

"What was Chimi-ahm?" asked Bertran, taking Jory by the arm. He thought from the looks of her she needed to lie down and be given hot cups of something restorative. What he could see of her face in the dim light from the wheelhouse was haggard and skull-like, her cheeks shadowed and her eyes strained. Bertran and Nela led her to a low chest and sat her upon it, remarking conversationally, "I saw him, or it. I thought he was real."

"I thought so too," Jory agreed, settling herself with a sigh of weariness. "Which surprised me considerably. I had expected an attack, but not from that quarter! I had not expected their devil god to be real!"

"What did you expect?" asked Nela, settling with Bertran beside her.

"Customarily the Derbeckians summon their gods through fasting and chanting, through exhaustion and suggestion and clouds of hallucinogenic smoke blown from their altars. At least, so they have done until now, and the priests profited mightily from it. When did those priests find something to flesh out their dabbo-dam?"

"It's probably the same thing that infected them with ideas of conquest," said Asner thoughtfully.

"No doubt. No doubt at all. Something inimical and evil," agreed Jory. "And whatever it is, it isn't only in Derbeck but extends all across Elsewhere. Latibor and Cafferty have searched for it. Asner and I have gone back and forth, trying to find evidence of it. Great Dragon is concerned about it. Until tonight we'd seen only the tracks of the beast— pain, torture, violence, the worst that man is capable of, multiplied— but we had not seen the beast itself! And even tonight it wore a mask!"

"The possesseds," said Fringe. "Before we started on this journey, Danivon said we might encounter possesseds!"

The two old people gazed at her with undisguised amazement. "Possesseds?" asked Jory. "What do you mean, possesseds?"

"Something possessed by the Hobbs Land Gods," Curvis said firmly. "Something no longer human."

Jory and Asner exchanged glances. Asner started to speak and Jory shushed him. "How very interesting," she said.

Fringe said, "It would be a tragedy if they were here, for only here have we retained . . ." She caught her breath and looked at the girl lying beside her on the deck.

"Diversity." Curvis finished her statement in an angry tone. "Which Fringe does not so much value now as she did this afternoon."

"This girl is a different matter," Fringe muttered. "You don't know. . . ." She fell silent, confused.

Bertran looked at the sky and drawled, "Fringe was about to say this situation is different from all other situations. While we were growing up, Nela and I learned that our own situations are always different from all other situations, and regardless of the laws or customs, only we ourselves can be trusted to make proper decisions about them."

"Other people, however, must follow the rules," added Nela, her lips twisting into a wry smile. "For other people are, without exception, less moral, less well informed, and less ethically motivated than we."

"Shut up," muttered Fringe. "Damn it. I'm not a fool! I'm aware of the hypocrisy. You of all people ought to understand why I took her!"

"We do understand," said Nela, suddenly contrite. She bit her lip and cast a sidelong look at Bertran.

"That's what she's saying," he said to Fringe. "She's trying . . . we're trying to apologize for our earlier . . . lack of understanding. We're saying we don't blame you for . . . whatever you feel you have to do."

"You blame me if I don't do," said Fringe in a weary voice. "If I do do, Curvis blames me. And Danivon."

Jory nodded. "That's true, but then, Curvis and Danivon foresee trouble. They'd be fools if they didn't. If they don't take action against you, they become accomplices, because word of your action will get back to Tolerance, if it hasn't already."

Fringe was simply too tired to answer. She could not explain to herself what she'd done or why she'd done it. She longed for Zasper. He'd done the same thing she had. He could advise her. Or maybe he couldn't!

No one had seen Zasper break the law. Zasper had done it secretly, and he'd kept it quiet. How could Fringe keep this quiet? Everyone knew what she'd done. And they'd heard Zasper's name used too. She'd allowed that to be blurted about. She dropped her head, feeling terror all at once, for Zasper, for herself. What had she done!

It was too much! She should be able to live without all these feelings, these guilts and urges and fallings short! She should be able to be what she so longed to be, clean and pure and hard, like the blade she carried, fitted for the job it had to do, without all these mawkish sorrows, without all these painful sentiments. She was sick of feelings!

A cool old hand stroked her forehead. "Put the child over there on that pile of sail," said Jory. "Lie down beside her and hold her, Fringe. She needs caring arms about her, and it is not yet the end of this world."

Too weary to argue, Fringe did as she was bid. It might not be the end of the world, and yet it felt monstrously like it.

Those left behind stood wordlessly against the rail.

"It's time I went below," said Curvis in a tone of haughty annoyance. "I must consider what to do."

"Don't go. Wait," said Jory.

He peered at her through the darkness. "For what, old woman?"

"I get hunches," she said, staring into the darkness.

"You're having one now?"

"Something like."

He waited for some moments, then prompted her, "Hunches about what?"

"You wouldn't question there was something dreadful there in Derbeck?" she asked. "Something that knew we were coming? Something aimed at us?"

"I wouldn't question that, no. And so?"

"And so, now we've left, I don't think whatever it was will stay behind in Derbeck," she said. "Not now that it has us located. I think we may expect some additional . . . outrage."

"The outrage thus far is quite enough," said Curvis. "Fringe has done the same thing old Paff did, taken someone from her proper place. She's broken the basic law of Elsewhere, and I can't simply ignore it!"

"Your law is wrong," said Nela in a firm voice.

Curvis replied stiffly, "You may find the concept of our law unfamiliar. . . ."

"Actually, the concept isn't unfamiliar," Bertran commented in a dry voice. "Though Nela may not remember. In our world there were a number of smallish countries ruled by unpleasant types, and our country occasionally invaded one of them to set something right. . . ."

"Killing numerous innocent bystanders in the process," snapped Nela with a toss of her head. "As well as a good many of their soldiers, or ours."

". . . and people took sides as to whether it was morally defensible for us to have done so," Bertran concluded mildly.

"It was not defensible," said Nela definitely. "Because at the same time we were invading these bad smallish countries, our politicians were making excuses for our groveling around bad large countries who treated their citizens even worse! I think people should kick out their own despots."

"Killing numerous innocent bystanders in the process," said Bertran dryly. "As well as a good many of themselves."

Nela glared at him and worked her mouth as though tasting what she intended to say next.

Before she could speak, Curvis said, "We Enforcers are taught that we must not set ourselves up as judges. Fringe knows that!"

"She may know it, but she does judge," cried Nela. "I saw her face when that monster swallowed the child in the basket! She tried not to show any feeling, but her face betrayed her!"

"Had it been up to you, you would have rescued the child?" asked Jory in an interested voice.

"I would."

"But you just said one shouldn't intervene."

Nela flushed. "That's different. The child wasn't in some foreign country. It was on the river all alone."

"Don't you think a man being tortured in a dungeon feels all alone?" asked Bertran. "No matter what country he's in?"

Nela shook her head at him. "You know what I mean."

"I don't." He felt a sudden spurt of anger at her assumption. Why should she believe he always knew what she meant! He didn't. Sometimes he didn't care! "I haven't the slightest idea what you mean. When we were with the circus, I read about a group of seamen and their captain who were captured by a country hostile to their own. The hostiles confined them, tortured the captain, humiliated him, eventually sold him and his men back to their own country for ransom. Of course, the hostiles felt that when they'd humiliated the captain, they'd humiliated his country, which was very satisfying.

"The point is, after his return, the captain confessed that he and his men had prayed every day that their country would end their pain and wipe out their humiliation by totally destroying the city where they were being held, where their captors were. They were eager to die if it meant they would be avenged. They felt death was preferable to confinement, torture, and humiliation. The captain wrote, 'It is better to die than be used by evil for evil's purposes.'

"Emotionally, I think I'm on the side of intervention. Nela, however, seems to feel differently, and on this world—"

"On this world," interrupted Curvis in a furious whisper, "the question does not arise. We do not think of provinces as 'evil.' We do not think of death or torture or human sacrifice as 'evil.' That is simply the custom in certain places, and intervention is always wrong, no matter who is being saved or for what or who or what is being risked! We intervene only to maintain the status quo!"

The twins were silenced by his vehemence. His seemed to be the last word on the subject. They fell silent, closed in by the dark that hid everything except the stars and the deeper blackness of the banks whenever the *Dove* came close to one shore or the other as it tacked upstream. The ship's progress was made up of long diagonal runs followed by laborious changes of direction. The silent thoughts of those along the rail were accompanied only by the humming of the wind among the shrouds and the rattle of the sails when they came about on a new tack. Then, as they approached the southern shore, Jory took a deep breath, almost a sigh.

"There," she said softly. "Along the bank. As I suspected."

In moments they all saw what she did, a line of luminescent blotches moving along the southern bank, staying even with the *Dove* as it made its slow way upstream. Those at the railing blinked, to be sure they were indeed seeing something. Jory shivered uncontrollably. Asner put his arms about her.

"What's the matter with her?" whispered Nela.

"She's frightened," said Asner. "And so am I."

"Of those?"

"We've seen something like them earlier tonight," he reminded her.

"In Derbeck," commented Curvis. "Before Chimi-ahm appeared. The shapes in the smoke."

Hearing the alarm in their voices, Fringe left the unconscious girl and returned to the rail where she was joined by Danivon. They peered at the southern shore, trying to make sense of the featureless blobs.

"Ghosts," said Danivon, remembering Boarmus's message.

"No one said anything to me about ghosts," said Curvis, annoyed once again.

Danivon shook his head, though he had no doubt these were what Boarmus had warned him against. The elder Luzes came to rejoin the group, peering at the blobs, taking what comfort they could in the company of others as they watched the strange pursuers. Though not large, at least not at the distance they were being observed from the ship, they were numerous, moving with deliberation. No barrier prevented their progress, no copse of trees or swampy morass, not even lofty ramparts of stone, several of which reared against the stars as they moved upriver. The shapes kept precisely even with the ship, slowing when the wind fell, speeding when it grew brisker, growing more numerous the farther they went.

Curvis found this persistence menacing though he refused to admit it to himself. "Perhaps they are something sent from Tolerance," he suggested. "By Council Supervisory."

"No," Jory replied, turning to put her back to the rail. "I rather imagine your Council would be as surprised at them—and as frightened—as I am."

"I'm not frightened," Danivon snarled. "Why should I be?"

"You should be because you're not a fool, no matter you are a cockerel who crows before he thinks," she whispered. "You say Boarmus warned you about ghosts. What did he mean?"

Danivon muttered, "I don't know what he meant."

"Ghosts of whom?" asked Asner, peering through the darkness at the flapping forms, now so close they could be seen as separate things with definite edges rather than mere blotches of pale fire. "Or of what?"

After a long moment of staring silence, Jory turned toward the others, her eyes gleaming in the dim light from the wheelhouse as she fixed them with a percipient gaze, cocking her head to one side. "Have any of you heard of the Arbai?"

After a moment's silence, Bertran replied, "We know only what Fringe and Curvis told us. It was an Arbai Door we fell through on Earth and arrived through here." His eyes were fixed on the ominous shapes. "The Arbai spread such Doors about, and there was a great plague that would have wiped out humanity had we not closed the Earth Door in time."

"An extinct race, Fringe and Curvis said," said Nela. "And Celery also said something of the kind." She could not take her eyes from the shore where the things were now hopping over something she could not see: like toads, laboriously, but with no slowing of their forward motion. "Celery said the Arbai were about to be, or already were, extinct."

Jory said, "In my travels I learned something about the Arbai. It was the Arbai who discovered that time and space flow back and forth through wormholes among the universes to keep the energy density constant. As you have remarked, they were the inventors of the wormhole Doors, which make distant points adjacent by going outside our space and coming in again, a concept that human engineers have adapted and—so they claim—improved upon. Eventually, the Arbai became preoccupied with questions of morality. They, like Nela, had always believed that interference with other races was wrong, but their reasoning was quite different from hers. They believed interference was wrong because they had no concept of evil. Their language had no word for it. They could not perceive it when they saw it."

"They'd have made perfect Enforcers," snorted Nela.

"Not really, no. The plague that killed them was purposefully directed against them by creatures all of us here would call evil, but the Arbai could not see it and thus had no defense against it."

"That must have presented them with a dilemma," said Bertran, nervously watching the shore. The ship was coming very close, and he felt his anxiety increase with every ripple that fled beneath the hull.

"A dilemma indeed," Jory remarked. "Most of their race had already died before they knew the reason. The few remaining chose to put all the energies they had left into what they thought of as a moral solution to the problem. They decided that the 'problem'—which they did not call evil—had arisen out of the inability of disparate creatures to completely understand one another, so they withdrew to a distant place and built a communicator."

"An Alsense machine?" Curvis asked, almost distracted from the approaching shore by this revelation. "The Arbai created the Alsense machine?"

Asner shook his head, answering for her. "No, an Alsense is merely a contextual device that compares speech patterns to a library of such patterns, establishes similarities, extrapolates possible meanings, then refines these from continuing utterances. Among languages based on common thought systems, an Alsense serves well enough. . . ."

Jory interrupted. "The Arbai did better than that. They built a true communicator. An empathetometer. A meaning *feeler.* With typical understatement, they called it the Arbai Device."

Danivon said, "How very interesting." He fidgeted, approaching the rail, then stepping away from it, finally blurting, "Shouldn't we be coming about? We're getting very close to the shore."

"I'd noticed that," said Asner. "Perhaps the captain wants to get a better look at those things."

"Better in daylight," whispered Nela. "I think. Though spirits can't cross running water."

"Is that so?" asked Asner.

"In our time it was said to be so. In fairy tales. Evidently it's true here, now."

They fell silent as the ship drew ever closer to the shore. "There's the reason we're coming so close," said Asner, pointing upstream where a foam of white showed dimly. "There are rocks midriver. The captain is coming as far as possible to port so our next tack will bring the rocks on our starboard side."

"You were speaking of the thing the Arbai invented," said Danivon from a dry mouth. "Are you implying there's such a device here on Elsewhere?"

Jory tore her eyes away from the bank where the shapes danced and jittered, seeming almost to extend themselves onto the surface of the water. "How could there be? If evil results from a lack of empathy (which the Arbai believed), and if evil is included in diversity (which you Enforcers seem to believe), then wouldn't diversity also result from a lack of empathy? In which case, the presence of an Arbai Device here on Elsewhere would have destroyed all diversity long ago." She gave him a distracted look and turned back to the rail. Bending and twisting, the flattened luminosities oozed outward, becoming elongated, stretching themselves into tentacles.

"Why are we discussing Arbai Devices?" demanded Bertran. "Has it something to do with these . . . these things?"

"I was only thinking," said Jory. "That I'd like very much to understand what they are and why they are following us." She laughed, without amusement. "Quite frankly, I was wishing we had the Arbai Device, here and now!"

"Ready to come about," cried the captain.

The group fell silent, holding their breaths. The boom swung, the sails rattled, the ship began moving away as the forms along the bank became suddenly agitated, flopping toward the water in spasms, as though to fly across it.

"*Ware*," screamed the lookout from the mast.

"Hard a'port," shouted the captain, his voice cracking.

The *Dove* shuddered and bucked as something huge rubbed along its starboard side, thrusting it inexorably shoreward.

"*Ware*," screamed the lookout again, "*two of them!*"

Over the starboard rail loomed the head of a monstrous gaver, jaw gaping, teeth gleaming in the dim lights from the wheelhouse, lurching upward toward the watchman on the mast.

"God, look at the size of it," marveled Danivon aloud, too astonished in that instant to be fearful. "The size of it!"

Beyond the nearer beast, its mate reared higher yet, looming into the starlight, a clifflike bulk, curved fangs snatching at the protruding spar, the spar shattering, then falling in a slither of broken wood and torn sail. They heard the scream of the lookout as he plunged to the end of his safety line, panicky shouts from the men, all subsumed into the thrashing sounds of water frenziedly beaten by monstrous tails. Something else fell from above, accompanied by an outraged howl from the dangling man.

Suddenly the beasts were gone downstream in a flurry of spray, droplets falling everywhere, like a squall of rain.

"Hard t'starboard," shouted the captain. Three men were scurrying aloft, clinging to the ratlines as they hauled in the watchman, now dangling silently. Below on deck other men tugged at the wreckage of timber and ropes where the half spar had fallen, missing the main sail by a finger's width.

"We didn't lose way," said Asner. "We didn't go aground. There for a minute I thought sure we'd . . ."

"Where's Fringe?" asked Danivon, his voice shrill. "Where're the twins?"

"They were right here," said Curvis. "Beside us."

Jory turned slowly, taking an inventory. Danivon, Curvis, Cafferty, Latibor. Herself and Asner. Over on the piled sail, Alouez, the girl child.

Forward, sailors rushing to and fro like ants, swearing and chopping. No Fringe. No twins. Where were they?

"Look!" breathed Cafferty. "Ashore!"

There the pale blobs of fire twirled in an oozing spiral of light, pallid gray, twisting like an auger. The dully gleaming pillar sunk into the ground, bearing with it two struggling shapes, two blotches of darkness.

"Fringe!" screamed Danivon, hearing the word come out of him with a sense of surprise, not only at the sound but at the feeling of loss and grief that pushed it up and out of him. "Fringe!"

"Nela and Bertran," murmured Jory. "Oh, Asner, we came too close to the shore, too close. . . ."

"Fools," Asner cried in a cracked voice. "We've been fools, Jory. Looking in the wrong place. There's your devils, the ones at the root of all this wickedness, whatever the damned things are!"

"Boarmus warned Danivon of ghosts," she wept, "and ghosts they may be, but of what? Of whom?"

The last of the corpselight plunged downward and disappeared. The boat drew away, upstream.

"They're gone! They've quit following us," cried Latibor.

"Oh, yes," said Jory in a flat, uninflected voice. "Quite right, Latibor. It will give us no satisfaction, but yes. For the moment they have quit following us."

Fringe saw the gavers. She opened her mouth, maybe to warn someone, maybe to scream. She clutched at the nearest person: Bertran. Then cold, an icy grip of air, herself looking down at the river from high above it, the muddy bank twisting like a snake. Then herself, themselves spinning in a maelstrom of gray fire. She tried to scream for help, but there was no air.

From a distance she heard Danivon shouting her name. Beside her, Nela shrieked with pain. Then everything went away.

She woke sprawled on a ledge in a stone chamber dimly lit by a few glow points scattered far above. The ledge beneath her was thickly though not softly furred, as by the hairy rootlets of trees. She could hear water running. She played dead, exploring what she could see through slitted eyes. Nothing. No one. Whoever or whatever had taken them was not present.

She got up and examined the chamber: stone floor, walls, ceiling.

The streamlet ran along one wall, coming and going through shallow slits not more than a handbreadth wide. She could see no opening that might have admitted them; no way of escape. And her belt weapon was gone.

She stripped off the oracle's robe she'd been wearing, doing a quick inventory while hidden beneath its folds. The slug weapon was still in her boot. She left it there, drawing no attention to it. Whatever had removed her belt weapon had not searched her carefully. She tucked the item of information away with no idea of its meaning. Was the person or thing merely curious or had it intended to deprive her of any weapon? In either case, it had not been quite curious or careful enough. A certain tendency toward sloppiness on the part of their captors was the only inference she could draw at the moment. It was too early to make guesses.

"What happened?" asked Nela in a feeble voice, hearing their heart thubbing desperately away between herself and Bertran, their lungs laboring.

Fringe put one hand to the girl's head, knelt to give Bertran a look. Pallid, both of them, gray, with flaccid limbs. If they had been handled as she had been, they had been badly wrenched about during their abduction. Nela looked very ill, and Bertran had not moved at all.

"Lie still," Fringe advised. "Don't try to get up. Don't try to move." She fetched the oracle's robe and tucked the abundant fabric around them.

"What happened," begged Nela once more.

"The ghosts got us," said Fringe matter-of-factly, swallowing the hysteria that threatened to come pouring from her throat. "Whatever they are."

"We were too close to the bank," whispered Nela. "I thought so at the time."

"The gavers couldn't have surfaced at a worse time," admitted Fringe. "Almost as though something drove them toward us just to press us close to shore." She knelt and put her hand to Nela's forehead once more, then bent to her ear, whispering, "Anything we say can probably be overheard. I wouldn't say much."

Nela swallowed and closed her eyes.

Fringe made the rounds of the chamber once more. It was warm—warm enough, at least, though the water in the shallow stream was cold. They could drink from the upstream end and eliminate into the water where it ran out of the cavern if they were confined long enough to make that necessary. There was nothing to eat, but presumably food would be supplied. Like all Enforcers, on duty or not, she had certain equipment built into her clothing, some even built into her body, none of which seemed very useful at the moment. Nonetheless, she did a mental inventory, this bit, that bit. If their captors were corporeal, she could do them some damage, at least. She was wearing her badge, with its locator device. Very useful for finding wounded or dead Enforcers lying under the sky. Not very useful for finding people very far under the ground.

Bertran groaned.

Fringe knelt beside them once more. Bertran's eyes flickered open. He smiled. "I dreamed," he whispered. "Oh, I dreamed I was swimming. . . ." His eyes shut again, he winced with pain. The dream had been wonderful, painless, weightless. He longed to go back to it.

"What did you dream?" Fringe asked.

"Nothing," he murmured. "Nothing." And it was nothing, vanishing, as dreams always did. "It's gone. Where are we?"

"In a cave," Fringe answered. "In a damned hole."

"I can't breathe," complained Nela. "Can you sit up, Berty?"

He struggled to do so, the two of them edging themselves up against the low shelf. They leaned against it as though after a long race, breathing heavily.

"Thirsty," he murmured from a dry mouth. He licked his lips and panted.

"We haven't a cup," said Fringe, scooping water from the stream and offering it in her cupped hands. "Forgive my skin, Bertran, but it's the best I can do."

He drank greedily, emptying her hands several times.

"This seems fairly hopeless," he commented, wiping his wet mouth on his sleeve. "Doesn't it?"

"Too soon to say," murmured Fringe. "Actually, the place isn't as bad as it could be. There's light. There's water. It's fairly warm. There's nothing threatening to kill us just at the moment." Dismayed by the pallid gray of Bertran's skin, the liquid pain in Nela's eyes, she set herself to be as comforting as possible.

Bertran tried to smile, unsuccessfully. "A pity we could not save your Destiny Machine, oracle. We might find out what's going to happen to us."

"We don't need the Destiny Machine for that," said Nela in a weak, pained voice. "We do need to lie down. When they grabbed us, they messed us up."

"I'll help you." Fringe helped them lie back on the furry ledge, tucked their own coats and her robe around them to keep them warm, and stood watching as their eyes closed, as their breathing eased slightly, an old familiar feeling possessing her, of helplessness, of grief, of concern. So she had felt about Souile, sometimes. About Nada, sometimes. She had learned to shut those feelings off, not to care because there was nothing she could do. But this was Nela, once again her friend. This was Nela's brother. Both, both her friends, come to this through no fault of their own. They were not Enforcers. They shouldn't have shared Enforcers' risks. They should be somewhere on a well-lit platform, joking and doing magic tricks. They should not be here. Whoever . . . whatever had done this was an evil person, an evil thing, and she, Fringe, would have to do whatever she could to set matters right, diversity be damned!

She looked the place over more carefully, examining it inch by inch. Though in far better physical shape than the twins, she felt as weary as they. It had been a long day, maybe more than one, since she had slept. The recent unconsciousness had not been sleep, for it had not left her rested. All the tumult of Derbeck was still roiling about inside her mind, the terror at Chimi-ahm, the fear for the girl, the apprehension of betrayal at Curvis's hands—or Danivon's.

And along with all that, a longing for Danivon so great that it made her want to weep. She had heard him cry her name when they had been seized up. It had had the sound of someone who cared, the sound of a lover crying warning and woe. She had heard fear in his voice, fear for her! Moisture gathered at the corners of her eyes, tears she would not let fall, as she quartered the cave, again and again. Nothing. No way out. No place to hide. They were well and truly caught.

When she was sure of it, she sat cross-legged against the ledge, leaning her head back and closing her eyes. Thus far their captors had not shown themselves. Itself. No point in remaining awake or on guard. Undoubtedly it or they would show up when they felt like it. Meantime, she would conserve her energies.

She focused her mind upon one of the relaxation exercises she had learned at the Academy, a soothing recitation to quiet her mind, relax her body, soften her terror into something manageable, make her ready for whatever was to happen. Eventually, she slept.

11

Most of those aboard the *Dove* had gone below; the captain to lie sleepless, wondering if the gavers that had attacked the ship were gone or only lying low; Cafferty and Latibor and Asner to murmur with one another in fruitless speculation; Danivon to curse and stamp about, unable to hide his feelings from Curvis, who, if the truth were known, thought good riddance to Fringe and the twins both. The long middle hours of horrid night had passed but morning had not yet come as Jory stood at the railing with her oldest friend.

"I stayed too long in Derbeck," he said silently, in her mind, as he had always spoken to her. *"I should have been here, with the ship. Perhaps I could have prevented . . ."*

Jory shook her head. She didn't need to speak. He knew what she thought, that he could have done nothing. Perhaps none of them could do anything.

"I left it too late," she said aloud. "I thought in usual terms. Human perversity. If one could identify it, one could fix it. But there's something here beyond our power to fix, old friend. Something immune to reason, I think."

"Your friends upriver could fix it."

"My friends upriver." She laughed, a pained laugh. "Someone once told me they are too good to be any good. Or words to that effect."

Silence, then, *"You're right. The ones upriver will be full of kindly concern but they will do nothing."*

She sighed, profoundly weary. "I should have gone directly to Tolerance years ago, instead of being so damned . . . tentative."

"You didn't want to upset them, upriver."

"That, and also I was working with the avalanche theory: A few little falling stones, and whoops, here comes a general downfall to make Council Supervisory question what it's doing!"

"Your petitions. So nicely thought out. So very nicely executed. With my help!"

She laughed. "I shall not forget your description of Boarmus's face when you made him believe he was breaking out in words. That was fun. At my age, I'm entitled to have fun. Surely even God must have fun occasionally. I meant the petitions to provoke thought, to create discussion, but I underestimated the inertia in the system. I forgot that inertia is what bureaucracies are all about!"

"Except for the Provosts, no one heard of the petitions."

"I chose the wrong audience. We should have gone to the people themselves. I heard Fringe say it, with my own ears, on the trip up from Shallow. She said, 'You've got to leave people a way out.' We should have offered the people a way out."

"Isn't that a little beyond your power? Where would you have had them go?"

She sighed. That was the question, of course. Only two Doors on Elsewhere. Both of them in Tolerance. Both of them guarded. No way to use either of them without a fight. "There's home," she said. "There's beyond the wall here on Panubi. There's room for some. Just because there isn't room for everyone doesn't mean I couldn't have saved some. Or can't now. There's still time to save some!"

"Marjorie. . . ."

"Come death or destruction, old friend, I will offer a choice to some."

"To whom?"

"There's only one more province upriver of us. Thrasis. I'll offer a choice to the women of Thrasis."

"Despite how those upriver are going to feel about it?"

"Despite that. Why should the women of Thrasis go on suffering alone if we can give them a way out, a change in their lives?"

His voice in her mind was amused but tender. *"You're still hoping for change!"*

Change. Oh, yes, she went on hoping for change. She had always hoped for change since . . . When had it been? When she was nine? Ten? As a special treat she had been taken to an exhibition of things found in an ancient tomb, artifacts of a people who had lived—what had it been?—five or six thousand years before she was born. Oh, the anticipation of that! She had thought of it as utterly wonderful, seeing things so old. . . .

And she had seen: wooden chairs, carved and painted, not unlike chairs at home, a wagon that looked a lot like her pony cart, a hand mirror not unlike one her mother had—bronze, not glass, but otherwise much alike.

She had waited for the wonderful, but there had been only ordinary things: tables, boxes, wagons, jars, dishes, spoons.

"You were disappointed?" He'd been reading her mind.

"Not so much in the people from the past as I was disappointed in us. I'd had a childish belief that man was changing. Past was barbaric and primitive. Present was civilized and advanced. That was my faith, strong as my religion! But here we were, after six thousand years, still using the same furniture!"

"So man hadn't changed much?"

"When I got older, I decided it was our own fault, that we'd stopped evolution. We'd defined ourselves as what man was supposed to be. We'd looked in the mirror and said, 'That's Homo sapiens, right there, right now. The brightest and best among us are Homo sapiens, but the sick, stupid, sociopathic ones are also Homo sapiens. Every warped and evil thing born to us is nonetheless Homo sapiens because it comes from a human womb and is therefore sacred! Homo sapiens, crown of creation, the only important living thing! When God made the rest of the universe, he was only kidding around, but when he made man, he meant it.'"

Laughter, deep and abiding.

She flushed angrily. "Well, it's true! It's exactly the way we thought and acted. Man didn't have to be better! At least, not in terms of western thought, he didn't. He strutted and crowed and told himself just as he was, he was made in the image of God! It was easier to depend on heaven than be responsible on earth, but humans were divinely created, so why worry."

"And you don't believe he was? Human?"

"He wasn't what I thought of as sapiens. In my opinion, very few of us were sapiens. Maybe none of us were. Maybe we'd had a chance at becoming sapiens, but we threw it away."

"When did mankind do that?"

"In Nela's time, I think. It was then that pitiful people who saw no reality and knew no science declared the holiness of reproduction. And while the liberals were preserving the right to beget, the reactionaries were preserving the faults in our gene pool. We could corrupt and destroy all the rest of creation, but our own germ plasm was sacred. It didn't matter that there were billions of us, that anything sapiens about us was far more threatened by our numbers than by any change we might make in ourselves. . . ."

"But man was saved, wasn't he?"

"You mean out there?" She gestured at the far stars. "Yes, in spite of ourselves, we were. Almost incidentally, we were. But not here. Here priests and prophets are doing what priests and prophets have always done, forbidding their people to become anything except what they already are! No interference. God, what foolishness!" Her shoulders shook and she mopped at her eyes.

"I know." The feel of a pat on a shoulder, a hug, a vast unhuman sympathy.

"Just such a pity, that's all," she said, recovering herself with a last shuddering sob. "And when I'm foolish enough to try to improve matters, I have to struggle against all the weight of human nature plus the nature of those upriver. It's like being married all over again, someone always making rules for me. Sometimes I wonder why you and Asner and I ever settled down among them."

His voice was soothing, organlike. *"We came here because it was a place we'd never been. And not too long after we got here, you were tired."*

For an instant she felt an overwhelming sorrow, transmitted into her mind from the other, an irreconcilable grief, shut off as quickly as it came, becoming merely calm, a loving tranquillity that she had learned to depend upon utterly.

The silent voice went on calmly: *"What was it you told me at the time? There were peaceful things you wanted to do. Look at trees, as I recall. And you wanted to plant an English garden. You wanted to sit in a rocking chair and play with kittens and watch horses in the meadow."*

"There weren't any cats here on Panubi. Or any horses either."

"The ones upriver arranged to provide some for you."

"True. I remember that. But after I'd planted my garden, after I'd patted the horses and rocked awhile, why didn't we leave then?"

He didn't answer. He knew the answer, but it did not bear speaking of. Above them in the night came a quiet humming, a purposeful, directional noise.

"Flier," he said, to distract her.

She nodded. "Headed upriver. Someone from Tolerance. Someone from the Council . . . no, it must be from Boarmus. It's probably headed for Thrasis. We'll dock there in the morning and find out."

"And you're still going to do it, in Thrasis?"

"If you and your great-grandchildren will help me. I can't do it alone."

"You always have my help. Forever."

"Then I'm going to do it. I'm going to accomplish that much, at least. I will not let this be a total failure!"

"They, upriver, won't like it."

"They, upriver, will be presented with a fait accompli. When they let me settle among them, I never agreed to do everything their way. Some things, yes. Not everything. Their way doesn't work with mankind. They should know that, but they have this stubbornness."

"The pot calls the kettle. . . ."

"Oh, hush."

They fell silent, listening to the water, each occupied with memories spreading over galactic distances, over eons of time. Very softly he touched her. Very quietly she folded into his embrace. For a brief time thereafter, neither of them was old.

Noon in Thrasis. In the Towers of the Daughters of the Prophet, the woman Haifazh sat at her loom in the House of Restitution, as she had done every day for the past half year. Her hands moved, the shuttle flew, her feet moved, the loom clacked; around her scores of other looms clacked and rustled. From the floor below came the muted thwack and murmur of women beating soaked fye stems to separate the core fibers from the rotted skins. From the rooms alongside came the scrape and hum of the spinners as they combed the fibers and turned them into thread. Though the earpieces of her basket helmet were padded to exclude as much sound as possible, and though the blinders on each side prevented her seeing anything except the loom directly before her, Haifazh could tell from the light in the windows that noon had come. Both sides of the wide embrasures were lit; there were no shadows. Time had come for peeing, nursing babies, maybe a little talk. Dawn and dusk were food times. Dark was rest time. Every possible hour of daylight in this place was dedicated to making restitution for having offended her owner.

She braced herself for the cane that would soon descend on her basket helmet. The old women who used the canes were as hungry and tired as she. Sometimes they let their fatigue and hunger get the better of them. Sometimes they made a punishment out of the announcement that noon had come.

The cane knocked on her helmet, not too hard. Thank the prophet for all mercies, she muttered, forgetting for the moment that she did not believe in the mercies of the prophet. At one time she had believed, or had, at least, not disbelieved. Not now. Not here. Not in this place.

First to the latrines, to relieve herself. She had been cut while in labor with Shira, and sewn up after, as all the women in Thrasis were cut and sewn, first as children of seven and again when a baby was born. Peeing was still painful, but not—she reminded herself—as bad as sex would have been. The first time she'd had that experience, she'd been fifteen; her new owner had been so impatient he'd neglected to gag her, so she'd been punished twice, once by his maladroit maleness, once later by the whip, because she had screamed when it happened.

She went to the bucket for her water ration, as little as possible, otherwise she might wet herself at the loom during the afternoon. Then to the place against the wall below the windows, where the babies waited. She cuddled Shira to her breast and felt her nipple tugged into the little mouth. Shira never cried, thank the prophet (forgetting again). Girl babies who cried were often gagged.

The woman to her left was someone new.

Haifazh leaned forward. "I'm Haifazh," she introduced herself softly, eyes down. Talking while nursing was discouraged. Talking at other times was forbidden, though they all did it at night, on their pallets along the walls, when darkness hid them and the old women had fallen asleep.

"Bulerah," the woman next to her murmured.

"What're you in for?" she asked.

"Bearing a daughter," the woman answered.

"Ah."

"And you."

"The same."

It wasn't the same. She wasn't in for bearing a daughter, not exactly. Haifazh's owner hadn't minded having a girl child, so he said. He had plenty of sons and healthy girl children were a good cash crop, much in demand by the story weavers. Little fingers could tie the tightest knots, take the smallest stitches, and girl children ate less than grown women, much less if one starved them as they approached adulthood. No, it wasn't having a girl child that had upset Haifazh's owner but the fact that Haifazh's flow hadn't stopped as soon as her owner thought it should. Her uncleanness persisted too long. It was, so her owner said, inconvenient. She should go to the House of Restitution until she was fit once again for his use.

The old woman who now came mumbling along with her list was a reminder.

"Haifazh? Are you clean now?"

"No, Mahmi. I am still unclean."

The old woman made a check mark. "Bulerah? Are you Bulerah?"

"I am," the woman said.

"You will return to your owner when your child is weaned and sold. Is your child weaned."

"She is only a week old, Mahmi," said Bulerah.

"Ah," said the old woman, stumping along, making another check mark.

"Your uncleanness has lasted a long time," said Bulerah wonderingly. "Your child looks to be half a year old."

So far as Haifazh was concerned, the uncleanness she had originally counterfeited by smearing herself with filth would last forever. The old women never bothered to check. They just asked and believed what they were told. "True," she said calmly. "It is probably not uncleanness at all but a disease. An infection from when they cut and sewed me again when my baby was born. I will probably die of it."

She intended to continue unclean until she died, that was certain. Where this spirit of rebellion had come from, she could not tell. It had arisen out of nothing, out of pain and fear and a fire burning inside her that required vengeance to be quenched. So, she would continue unclean. The House of Restitution was peaceful, at least. She could stay here so long as she could work the loom. It was preferable to the bower of her owner—fat, sweaty, heaving gaver of a man. He had liked to bite her breasts until they bled. It had pleased him to make bruises.

"I can't wait to go back," sighed Bulerah. "I don't like this place."

"Weren't you raised in the tower?" Haifazh asked, curious. "I was."

"I was raised in the bower of my progenitor," the other said proudly. "My mother was his favorite and I was twin of his oldest son."

Haifazh's lip curled. "Don't crow, woman. No matter where you were raised, you were cut and sewn when you were a child; then when you were twelve or so, your progenitor sold you to your owner who sooner or later sent you here." She gestured at the room around them. "When you had your child, the midwives cut you again and sewed you up so you could hardly pee. You were lucky not to become infected and die as a fifth of us do when they cut us. One out of every five daughters, lost. One out of every five mothers, lost. You are maybe lucky to be alive, but maybe not, for when your blood time comes, the blood will clot inside you, and cleaning yourself will be agony. Then, when you go back to him, he'll hurt you even more, expecting you to be silent while he does it. And when you're old, Bulerah, they'll put you out in the Court of Removal to die. Bower or tower, where you were reared makes no difference in the end!"

The other flushed and turned her eyes toward her child.

"Nothing makes any difference to women," muttered Haifazh. "If there were no women, that might make a difference." She stood up, still cuddling Shira, and looked through the tall window, across the Court of Removal and the high wall, across a corner of the fye fields to the River Fohm. What she saw there made her exclaim in surprise, bringing all the other women to their feet.

The ship tied at the dock and the flier beside it on the bank had been there earlier, rare enough to warrant watching though not truly astonishing. What had not been there before were the women, *women* standing about with their faces uncovered and behind them something shifty and wonderful-looking, with scales and horns, or perhaps plates and fangs, but at any rate a mysterious and unusual sharpness, protectiveness, hugeness kind of thing that none of them could see clearly. Heedless of the commands of their keepers and the halfhearted blows of the canes on their basket helmets, the weavers thronged the windows, leaning out to see better.

"That's a flier," said Haifazh. "I saw one once before."

"What is a flier?" asked Bulerah. She had never seen a flier, a ship, a river until she came here. There had been nothing at all to see from her owner's bower except the tops of the trees and the sky. Nothing to see but the sky, nothing to do but bathe or sleep or tell stories or sing, very softly, or come to her owner's bed when he sent for her. Haifazh's words had reminded her how much it had hurt when she was new-bought. Now she'd been cut and sewn again, there would be pain again. She hadn't thought of that until now. The thought almost drove away the pleasure of seeing new things.

Below them, on the riverbank, the passengers of the *Dove* became aware they were being watched.

"All those windows over there are full of women," said Cafferty. "If I couldn't see them, I could smell them from here. They're frantic with curiosity."

"Never mind about them," growled Zasper, who had seen starlight on the sails of the *Dove* in the early hours and had been awaiting her arrival since he had landed, to the consternation of the guards who were even now hovering at a safe distance, growling among themselves. "You tell me Fringe is missing; so what, if anything, have you done about her?" He glared over Jory's shoulder at Danivon, who stood broodingly at the rail of the ship.

"Don't snarl, Zasper," Danivon said in an empty voice. "They were already beyond our reach when we noticed they were gone. We saw where they went, at least we took sightings of the last place we saw them. I wanted to go ashore and search, but the others overruled me. They said she could be miles away by the time we started searching; they said the lights might end by getting us all; both things seemed likely. If you know something we don't, tell us about it! We need a plan to rescue them!"

Zasper fumed, full of speculation he wanted to share but unwilling to say anything at all while they were here on shore and might be overheard. Just as he had left Enarae, a tourist dink had brought him a transmitter cube from Boarmus with a very long, rambling message adding to the somewhat muddled but nonetheless threatening picture of what they were all dealing with. Zasper had spent the flight to Thrasis listening to the cube and trying to figure it out: According to Boarmus, Elsewhere had been taken over by something both omnipresent and omnipotent, something paranoid and erratic, full of malice and cunning, which seemed mostly concerned with its own sense of esteem and power. "It wants to be a god," Boarmus had said. "Maybe it is one." Little god or big god made no difference, Boarmus said. A big one might kill them all at once, little ones could nibble them to death. They'd be just as dead either way!

Zasper stared at Danivon and made a covert sign in use among Enforcers that meant, roughly, "I'll tell you later."

Danivon replied with an angry gesture, his lips drawn back in an impatient snarl, but he held himself in check.

Jory blinked at the recent interloper and murmured, "If there's nothing else. . . ."

Zasper growled, "There's a good deal else, old woman. Am I right that you are the same Jory somebody who used to follow Fringe around when she was a child?" He took her silence for assent and demanded, "What are you doing here in Thrasis?"

"I'm here because the ship is here. The ship is here because it has cargo to unload. I'll go when the ship goes."

"Go where?"

"Home," she said.

His eyebrows lifted almost to his smoothly drawn-back hair. So this was Fringe's Jory. The legendary Jory. Oh, he wanted to talk to her, now or later. Later, probably. Without Danivon hovering at his elbow. "Home being?" he asked her.

She pointed westward, up the river.

Zasper and Danivon exchanged glances. Danivon lifted his hands, palms up, sniffing the air. He tilted a palm, this way, that way. He couldn't tell, couldn't smell it.

Zasper sighed and scratched the back of his head. "Women aren't allowed to walk about loose in this province."

"The things that followed us aren't on this side of the river, yet," Jory said, "and I have business here."

"He's trying to tell you you'll be killed," Danivon said flatly as he came down from the deck of the *Dove*. "The servants of the Prophet will kill you all. Women have to be in the bowers of their owners or in the towers, no place else."

"Great Dragon comes with us," said Jory. "And I don't think the servants of the Prophet will interfere. I would invite you to join us, except that you Enforcers already know all about Thrasis. No doubt you want to talk man talk. Or is it Enforcer talk? Whichever, we'll leave you to it."

She took Cafferty and Latibor by the hands and moved away from the ship.

"Why are we doing this?" Cafferty asked Jory.

Jory pointed at the bulky towers along the river. "Because we're here. Because we can."

Latibor murmured, "Great Dragon comes."

They couldn't see Great Dragon, though they had a sense of something beside them as they left the ship and strolled down the waterfront. Their way was immediately barred by infuriated men who screamed and waved curved blades at them, but who then mysteriously lost their enthusiasm for confrontation and ran off toward the town, not looking back. The Luzes and Jory were not surprised.

"These buildings are still called towers," said Jory in a didactic tone as they approached the nearest of several similar complicated structures. "Though they are not towers in the architectural sense."

The whole was surrounded by high walls pierced with fretted gates. As they came near the gates, the guards fled and the gates burst open, allowing Jory to walk through with the others behind her.

"This is the Court of Removal," Jory continued in a lecturer's tone. "Old women like us, Cafferty, are left here to die. It would not be fitting for them to die where men who don't own them might look upon them—and of course their owners don't want to look at them—so they die here, where none see them. The religion of Thrasis prohibits murder. They are merely given no food or water and left to the mercy of the Thrasian god."

She walked across the wide yard, the others tiptoeing behind. "Through there," she said, pointing, "is the tower proper. The tower administrator, an office he purchases from the Prophet, is allowed to buy selected girl babies, to rear them, to train some of them in music and dancing, then later sell them as breeders or entertainers. We won't go in there. My business is with the House of Restitution." She headed toward a massive block whose windows were crowded with women peering out at them. "This is the place from which girl children are sold as workers and where women who have proven unsatisfactory to their owners are allowed to labor on an interim basis."

Cafferty asked, "Unsatisfactory to their owners? How proven unsatisfactory?"

"Oh, by growing ugly. Or sexually unexciting. Or bearing a girl instead of a son. Or speaking where a man can hear them. Or allowing a man other than their owners to see their faces. Or menstruating at a time when a man would prefer they did not. Or giving birth inconveniently. Or being sick. Or getting old."

She turned, pointing once more. "The walled fields to your right, stretching down to the river, are where the women of this tower grow their food and fiber. They are expected to feed themselves since they have displeased the owners who might otherwise have fed them." As they approached, the wide doors burst open onto an empty hallway.

The hallway didn't remain empty. Women came out of the place like bees out of a hive, pouring out of doors and down stairways. As Jory and the Luzes walked down the corridors, the women of Thrasis came after, a buzzing swarm of them. By the time they reached the central courtyard, the women surrounded them on all sides in a murmurous throng, all crouched and staring at them as though they had been angels made of fire.

"Are you captive here?" Jory asked gently.

"We are the daughters of the Prophet," several murmured, turning their heads to glance at one another from behind the wings of their basket helmets.

"But are you captive here?"

"We follow the destiny of women," said one in a puzzled voice. "This is our fitting place."

"I ask again, are you captive here?"

"Oh, by my breasts and womb, yes, we are captive here," cried a shrill voice. "I am Haifazh, and this is my daughter Shira, and no matter what these other cooing doves may say, yes, we are prisoners and slaves, and I am sick of it if they are not."

Jory smiled. "Well then, Haifazh, it is to you that I bring my news, though any others who listen may hear it or not, as they choose. I bring you word of a way that opens for the women of Thrasis."

She spoke briefly. Some of the women fled, their hands thrust into their helmets to cover their ears, shutting out the heresy, stopping just within earshot to listen again. Others stayed close, punctuating Jory's discourse with little shrieks. Haifazh herself listened intently and wordlessly to it all.

When she had finished speaking, Jory took Haifazh by the hand and asked, "Are there women who go between the towers and the bowers of the town?"

"Midwives," said Haifazh. "And inspectors for the auctioneers."

"You will be sure they hear this news."

"They will already have heard," said Haifazh. "There are no secrets in the world of women. We have too few amusements to let any opportunity pass."

The three travelers went on to the other towers, staying a time at each, and returned to the *Dove* early in the evening, where Zasper was waiting impatiently.

"Where have you been?" he demanded.

"To the towers, where I said I was going," Jory told him. "We found a few rebellious souls. Rebellion invites intervention, don't you think? Not that Nela would agree (poor Nela), though Bertran might. So, we've been carrying the gospel to the women of Thrasis. Once those things that followed us get across the water, the women will be the first victims. I can imagine the god of Thrasis made manifest, given flesh and bone! The women would die like flies—not that they don't already."

"And what might your gospel be, Jory?"

Jory smiled on him, a bittersweet smile. "To the imprisoned, I speak the gospel of flight, Zasper Ertigon. As I think your friend Fringe remarked, 'You have to leave people a way out.' "

"Well, whatever you've been preaching, come aboard. Your interference in Thrasis has upset the populace; there are more guards arriving on the shore every moment; and the captain wishes to anchor in deeper water, where we are less at risk."

As they boarded the ship, Curvis summoned them to the place where he and Danivon sat on the deck, their eyes fixed on the pocket munk on Curvis's knee.

"Has it done something interesting?" asked Jory.

"Listen," Danivon directed. "Perhaps it will say it again."

The munk was chewing its way around a cracker. When it had made the remnant perfectly round, it thumped it with a tiny paw and asked conversationally, "Where are we?"

It was Bertran's voice, very weak and sad.

Cafferty started to say something, but was silenced by a gesture from Curvis.

"In a cave," said the munk in Fringe's voice. "In a damned hole." Fringe sounded all right. Angry, if anything.

The munk took up another cracker and started eating its way around it.

"The mate to this one was in Bertran's pocket when we performed in Derbeck," rumbled Curvis. "He didn't give it back to me, afterward—we were all thinking of other things. When he was taken, the munk went with him."

"And this one reads the other's mind?" asked Latibor.

"I've always assumed so," said Danivon. "Hears what the other hears, at least."

"It was part of the act," said Curvis. "To have the one recite what the other heard. It made people believe we had actually magicked the little beasts through space."

"Will it work in reverse?" asked Jory.

They stared at her.

"Will the one with Bertran say what this one hears? We could try a message of hope and reassurance, at least," she said.

"Lies, you mean," said Danivon bitterly.

"Not necessarily. You are going to try to rescue them, aren't you?"

They stared at one another, then at the widening strip of water as the sailors pushed them away from the shore.

Zasper said, "She's right. Hope is never a lie. Hope could keep her alive. All three of them alive."

And when they had put sufficient distance between themselves and the shore, he drew them close, all of them, and in that huddle told them what he had not dared tell them ashore—all that he had learned from Boarmus, all that Boarmus had learned in City Fifteen.

When he had done, Jory and Asner went away from the others, their faces pale and drawn, to sit muttering together against the wheelhouse. Danivon, however, fastened on the item of most concern to him.

"So Fringe could be anywhere," he cried in anguish. "Anywhere a Door could reach!"

Zasper put a finger to his lips, counseling quiet. "Don't yell. Sound travels over water, and they may hear you from the shore. No, Fringe couldn't be just anywhere. We know from what the munk said that she's in a cavern. Moving anything over distance takes large-scale installations. The dinks in City Fifteen postulate a network tiny enough to have gone undiscovered. We're dealing with localized effects, Danivon!"

"Tiny little projectors," mused Curvis. "Tiny focused transmitters. Tiny ones, but everywhere."

"Even tiny ones can do a great deal of damage," said Zasper.

"Perhaps we can think of something on our way upstream," said Curvis soothingly.

Danivon cried, "I won't go upstream! Now that I know Fringe is near the place she disappeared, I'll go back to look for her! Zasper!"

Zasper threw up his hands and glanced at Jory, saying softly, "What shall I say? Have you words of wisdom, woman?"

"Few, if any."

"If you think of some, will you tell me?"

"Fringe is one of my people. And the twins could well be. I want them rescued as much as you do."

"Zasper," cried Danivon once more in a fever of impatience.

Zasper shook his head, pulling his braid over his shoulder and tugging at it with one hand, making his head bob sidewise, a gesture he made rarely and only when considerably disturbed. "Danivon, let me think!"

"There's no time to think!"

"I wish you'd admit you're in love with her," Zasper said in exasperation.

Danivon started to deny it. He started, his nose twitched, he sneezed violently. It was the truth. He loved her. Love occupied him all at once, like a strange new tenant that had moved in instantaneously with all its furniture, cluttering the cupboards and corners of his mind. There had been nothing there but the open rooms of himself through which he had moved as impulse took him. Now he stumbled over love's chattels in every doorway.

"I didn't know I did love her," he said stupidly, almost silenced by the realization.

Zasper said, "Well, everyone else knows it, so you may as well join in! If you'll admit it, you'll know the reason for your misery, at least, and then you could try thinking. You owe it to her and the rest of us to stop this jittering and stuttering and move cautiously, professionally, in an Enforcer-like manner."

Curvis patted Danivon's shoulder, trying to seem sympathetic, though in fact he was not. Danivon's way with women was nothing new to Curvis, but Danivon in love was. Unacceptably so. "Do you smell she's alive, Danivon?" he asked, hoping the answer might put an end to their speculation.

His hopes were dashed. Danivon nodded. Yes. Oh, by all he had ever believed in, yes, he smelled she was alive.

While Fringe and the twins slept, a way was opened silently into another, larger cavern. When they woke once more, feeling sick and unrested, they saw that one side of the rocky room had become a rough archway crisscrossed with sparkling lines. An energy barrier, Fringe told herself, though not a kind she was familiar with. They could look through into the space beyond, a very large high-ceilinged cavern with a towering complexity of well-lit gold at the far end.

Nela and Bertran, who had struggled to their feet with considerable pain, joined her at the opening and shook their heads in wonder.

"It's a church," said Nela.

Fringe had seen churches. There were a few of them in Enarae, different sorts, mostly used for things like weddings or status achievement ceremonies—ancestor chapels, most of them, though there were a few dedicated to one or another of the ancient Phansuri gods. This one was a good deal more impressive than any she had seen before.

"What kind of church is it?" Fringe asked in a whisper.

Nela shrugged. "Not Christian. No cross. Not any kind I recognize. No Buddhas or anything, though that thing up in front looks like an altar. I'm sure it's a church, though it doesn't smell like a church."

It smelled oily, resinous, chemical, redolent of some other time or place. It was an unnatural smell in this place. She was about to comment on this when the voice came.

"Bow down. Kneel and put your foreheads on the floor. Show respect."

Fringe, staring around herself stupidly in an effort to find the source of the voice, felt some inner part of her gripped agonizingly. She fell, flopping on the stone like a caught fish.

"Now you two," said the voice. It was a woman's voice, full of a sickening motherliness.

"Get down," muttered Bertran, dragging Nela down beside him. Fringe got her legs under her, and Bertran put a hand on her shoulder, keeping her from rising. "Stay down," he urged in a whisper.

"Oh, yeah," she gasped. "Yeah. That's a good idea."

"Put . . . your . . . foreheads . . . on . . . the . . . floor," repeated the voice in the manner of a teacher with the stupid pupil, a trainer with a dog.

They did so awkwardly.

"This is how you show reverence," said the voice with sweet satisfaction. "You will do so whenever you leave us or approach us. You may approach us now."

Fringe risked a glance. The sparkling net across the door had disappeared. She helped the twins up, both of them gasping and obviously in pain. Together they stepped through the archway and walked slowly along the smooth center line of the larger cavern. On either side the floor was rough and boulder-strewn, but this center aisle was smooth. At the end of it was a rail, and beyond the rail an altar and the complicated golden wall they had seen from their cell.

"Faces," breathed Nela.

Faces covered the wall, golden faces, carved or cast or living, but in any case moving, watching, eyes blinking, lips pursing, nostrils flaring. Faces stacked on faces, some with hands folded beneath their chins, some with hands cupped behind an ear, some with necks fading into the hair of the face beneath, rows and stacks of them, male and female, old and almost young, bearded and shaven, bald and hirsute, hooded and bare, ranks of them from the level of Fringe's knees to far above her head. A thousand pairs of eyes slept or peered or stared or winked. A thousand mouths gaped unconsciously or moved restlessly as though chewing, tongues lolling from some, teeth showing in some. A thousand noses protruded, some turned toward them, twitching, dripping, sniffing. Here were the faces of all those in the Great Question Committee, their likenesses preserved. Fringe and the twins had no idea who they were.

When the voice came, some of the faces to the lower left of the wall moved their lips synchronically.

"We are Magna Mater," they said. "You may bow down again."

They bowed down again, Nela crying out as they did so.

"What's the matter with her?" the voice said carelessly.

"You hurt her," replied Fringe in an angry voice. "Bringing her here. You're hurting both of them, making them bob up and down like this. They're not built the way I am."

"Will she die?" asked another voice in an interested tone.

Fringe looked for the source of the voice, finding it in an idealized woman's face, lofty browed, wide-eyed, but with its mouth twisted in malicious concentration.

"She may," said Fringe. "And if so, they both will. Is that what you want?"

The eyes watched, the lips moved. "Address me as Gracious Lady Therabas Bland! Is that what we want?"

Around this face, a group of others came to life, blinking, mouthing. "Is that what we want?" the faces chorused, like an echo.

"No," said the first voice from another idealized face, some distance from the second. "Not yet. Not now. Before we instruct them in their duty, they must learn to pray to us." Around this face, others echoed its lip motions.

Two groups, Fringe thought, watching them closely. And both groups together accounted for about half the faces on the wall. No, damn it. There was another thing present. Not speaking. Only watching. She caught the glimmer of its eyes and shuddered.

"What shall we pray for?" asked Bertran with a pained grunt. "What prayers are you pleased to grant."

Silence.

"You may pray for rest," said a face from the second group at last. "Pray to Gracious Lady that she will be pleased to grant you rest."

"And food," said Fringe stubbornly. "We pray for food, for if we don't have food we will die."

"And food," said the voice grudgingly. "You may pray for food as well. Can we make food?"

"We can make food," said the other. "We can make anything."

"Pray for food then. Perhaps we will grant it. And you will pray for enlightenment, to assist you in your duty."

They prayed for rest, food, enlightenment: Nela and Bertran with practiced phrases and a tumble of parochial school adulatories; Fringe haltingly, in the manner of someone making an assigned speech, keeping her eyes on the faces as she did so, watching for any signs of reaction. Of the faces that were awake, most seemed hypnotized by their words.

When they had done praying (and they were kept at it for some little time), the lower left group of faces demanded that they do reverence once more before they were allowed to retreat to their cell. Fringe went eagerly, the twins with tottering steps, barely able to move.

In a rocky niche beside the ledge they found a heap of dry powdery flakes that smelled vaguely foodlike. They tasted the stuff without enthusiasm. Possibly it would sustain life, though it would never provoke appetite. As they picked at the flakes, Bertran's breast pocket moved, and from the top of it a tiny head appeared to fix them all with bright beady eyes.

"Hope is never a lie," it said conversationally. "Hope could keep her alive. All three of them alive."

It was Zasper's voice.

"Who was that?" whispered Bertran, patting the pocket with one trembling hand.

"My friend Zasper," muttered Fringe, her breath quickening in sudden hope. "A friend, Berty. Someone trying to help us." She reached out to the munk, offering shreds of the foodstuff, which it ate as they were doing, without enjoyment, before burrowing down once more in Bertran's pocket.

"I think we will rest again," said Nela, after choking down a mouthful or so of the stuff and drinking from Fringe's cupped hands. "I think we must, Fringe, even though we just woke up. We feel all torn inside. Maybe resting a bit will let us heal. . . ."

"Rest," Fringe agreed worriedly, her eyes on the larger cavern. After she had helped the two of them squirm their way onto the ledge and had covered them as warmly as possible, she sat at the door to the cell, watching the distant faces from beneath lowered lids. Whatever animated them seemed to come and go. Now it had gone elsewhere, for a time at least. The faces were like dolls' faces now, shiny and expressionless, mouths curved into bows, eyes wide or shut, without lines, without individuality. They were not flesh that showed life graven upon itself. They were only symbols of life. Two groups had spoken. Maybe not groups, exactly. Maybe two entities made up of individuals, with not much difference among the individuals involved.

When she had been a girl at school, much had been made of popular E- or P-class girls who had their own coteries. All members of a coterie had sounded much alike. Their vocabularies were similar, their habits of thought. They dressed much alike, made the same gestures, laughed at the same things. By observing one of the sycophants, one could say certainly, "That's one of Lorry's clique, that's one of Ylane's." The same was true of these faces. Now that they were quiet, she could see the resemblance among them. The group to the right, the Gracious Lady group, had a straight-lipped, satisfied look. The group to the left was greedy, a bit puff-cheeked, like fat babies, wanting sweeties. And all of them were like those damned E&P dolls Souile had given her so long ago. In her mind she could hear an infant wail, a doll voice. "Am I not beautiful. Do you like my hair?"

What did they want, really? Surely not this pretense at adulation. Were they so infantile that this mockery of worship served? Love me if you will, and if you won't, I'll make you!

And that other presence. The one she knew was there, the one that hadn't spoken yet. What did it want? Not love, she was sure of that.

What duty did a human person owe things like these? Never mind what was owed. If it was something she could do, she would do it at once. Both Nela and Bertran were gray-faced, obviously suffering. The damned things had hurt them! The twins needed help they couldn't get in here.

Sighing, she crawled onto the ledge where the twins slept, stretched out beside them, and closed her eyes. Beneath her superficial calm, she felt terror. But then, Enforcers often felt terror, often went in fear of their lives. That's one of the first things she'd learned at Academy, how to handle terror. Beyond all terror and pain was always the simple fact: One would live or one would die. One had only to find out which and do it with élan, whichever it was. The only real challenge, as Zasper had often said, was to be sure one didn't wiffle around.

Dark came on Thrasis. The province seethed as Derbeck had done. It was said foreign persons, including at least one man, had invaded the towers. The Prophet was enraged. Men gathered to plan retaliation for this dishonor. The ship on which the interlopers had traveled was anchored out in the river. On the morrow it would be boarded and the people taken to the court for trial before they were beheaded. Until then, it was sufficient merely to describe what vengeance each man would exact when the strangers were captured. Guards were set to watch the ship, but no one thought to set extra guards on the towers.

Those on the *Dove* went to their cabins to lie sleepless, considering various unpleasant futures, while on shore the guards fell into profound, inexplicable slumber. The gates of the tower nearest the river opened and Haifazh came out carrying her child upon her shoulder. She stood for a moment all alone before the opened gates, then she cried out once—only once. It was like the sound of a treble trumpet, silvery and remote, sounding equally everywhere, near and far, as though it came from or was augmented by some other throat than hers. Everyone in Thrasis heard it, but only the women knew what it meant. They came out, women and girls, some eagerly, some reluctantly. They carried their babies and daughters, all of them there were. They had been given the choice. The choice would not be given again. There was evil coming, and this was the only chance they would have. Choose. Even the reluctant ones could not lose this one chance.

Some, mostly old ones, fearful of change, chose to stay, but none chose to have their babies or daughters stay. Mothers and daughters stood in argumentative clots, pushing and dragging at one another. The Houses of Retribution opened their doors and their inhabitants poured out. In the Houses of Retribution only a few remained behind, old women all, those who had ruled the others with their canes. In the Courts of Removal the departing women picked up all those still living and carried them along.

In the houses of the town, where women were kept in their so-called bowers, windowless cells emptied themselves down hidden stairs to high-walled gardens, and over those walls into the night. No one saw the women go. It was almost as though something hid them, preventing them from being seen. Here and there locked doors stood between women and the outside world, doors to which women had no keys, but the doors opened long enough for the women to come through, then locked again behind them.

Here and there in the gardens women crouched, weeping, waiting until the gate was locked once more with themselves inside. These were too frightened to go. These would rather die than take action themselves. Passivity had gone too deep.

Those who went, went in darkness, first to the banks of the Fohm, then westward along the river to the great wall that separated Thrasis, westernmost of the provinces, from the unknown lands beyond. The wall stretched from the depths of the river as far to the north as any man had ever gone. It had been there when the first settlers came. There was no way around it or under it or over it. Still, as the women waited silently, the wall began to fall, stone by stone sliding silently down from the top, stone by stone piling at the bottom, stone by stone heaping up to make a giant stairway over which the women could clamber. No sound as they went, no sound as they climbed, tugging one another from above, pushing one another from below, the dozens and hundreds and thousands of them finding their way in the dark as though a way were illuminated for their eyes alone.

As the last of them climbed, a few more came running, weeping, those who had delayed, who could not make up their minds until the last minute, until they thought of remaining here almost alone.

West of the wall they found a road shining vaguely in the moonless night, and the women went down that road, hastening as they could, helping one another along. When all had passed over the wall, the stones rose up once more, stone on stone until the wall stood as it had always stood, massive and impassable. The border of Thrasis was unbreached, secure. Beyond the wall, as the last woman passed, the road furred itself with green grass and herbs and small flowering trees that sprang up like mushrooms. A road reached on before, but there was no road behind. No tracks were left, no trail. There was no way back.

The false light of dawn whispered at the edge of the world. A tiny wind came from the east, betokening, so the early-rising sailors on the *Dove* said, a stronger breeze with the morning. The captain woke and argued with Asner whether it was safe to cross to Beanfields or whether it would be better to do as Jory had asked, avoid the southern bank altogether and head upriver at the best possible speed.

On shore, the tower guards wakened without realizing they had been asleep. They had nothing to report to the guards who came to relieve them at dawn. In the town of Thrasis, men rose and went about their affairs, in no whit alarmed at the silence in the bowers. Women's quarters were usually silent. Women with any sense did not attract attention to themselves.

A single early-rising buyer came to the tower nearest the river to obtain a breeder as a manhood gift for his son. He was accompanied by a vizer of the Prophet, and they strode self-importantly through the outer courts and into one of the smaller sales halls. A day before the old women who worked as inspectors had been instructed to examine certain women, previously selected by age and appearance, to be sure they had been properly cut and sewn as children to guarantee their purity.

The small sales hall was empty. The vizer strode into the nearest corridor, bellowing, only to be greeted by vacant echoes. There was no one in the tower except a few old women cowering in an upper room. He ran out of the place in frantic haste, and there followed a great consternation of guards and officers and men galloping this way and that. Not only was the one tower virtually empty, but so were all the towers. Not only the towers beside the river, but many of the bowers in the houses of the city as well. Not only in the city, but in the palace of the

Prophet himself, and in the countryside where in remote and hidden areas invisible forces had sped women on their way. Even in the most distant parts of the province, the story was the same. In all Thrasis there were only a few hundred women left, many of them old.

A boat was sent out to the *Dove,* and a vizer, encountering Danivon, who had risen early to put together materials for his rescue effort, demanded to see the person who had invaded the towers the day before. With all the rest of the party, Jory came forth, looking old and frail and a little half-witted.

"You wanted me, my son?" she asked, the words intended to be provocative, which they were. In Thrasis, only men had sons.

"Where are the women?" the man screamed at her.

"What women?" she asked innocently. "I have no women here except those who came with me. What women?"

"Our women! The Prophet's daughters. Someone has stolen them!"

"A thief does not steal what is worthless," Jory said. "The women of Thrasis are worthless, so it is said by all the prophets since earliest times. Why would anyone steal what has no value? Probably they simply ran off."

"The guards did not see them go!"

"Well, the guards watching this ship certainly didn't see them come out here. Why are you yelling at me? I didn't take them."

Baffled, the officer made certain threats, then forgot them in a momentary fit of confusion during which he seemed to hear the voice of something huge and invisible telling him not to be silly. When he was ashore, he remembered his former concerns, but only foggily. He reported that the people on the ship knew nothing of the disappearance. Certainly the women of Thrasis could not be aboard the little ship.

"What have you done?" whispered Danivon to Jory. "What have you done, old woman?"

"I've been right here on the ship all night," she said innocently. "Haven't I, Cafferty?"

"Right here," agreed Cafferty.

"*All* the women are really gone?" demanded Danivon.

"Most all, I should think. It really will make very little difference in Thrasis. Aside from making a few minor adjustments in their sexual habits, the men will hardly notice the difference. No more sons, of course, but that's the way of things sometimes. The universe is no guarantor of sons. And likely there'd be none anyhow, once those things from Derbeck get here."

"Where did the women go!" Danivon demanded.

Jory shrugged. "What choice did they have. East is Molock, they wouldn't have gone there. North is the waste, a great desert of stone and sand and predatory serpents running all the way to the sea. South is the river, and I doubt any Thrasian woman ever learned how to swim. West is the wall. . . ."

"Which leaves?"

"What would you say? Underground, perhaps? Unless they flew away."

"Boat ho," cried the lookout. "Boats. Boats ho."

In midriver a scattered fleet of tiny boats was using the light breeze to make its way upstream. Turning his glass upon them, Danivon saw they were full of Murrey folk with a few Houm scattered here and there. "Where are they going?" he demanded.

"Upstream," Jory commented, her eyes wide with pleased surprise. "Obviously. Away from Derbeck." She went to the railing and called across the water. "Why have you left Derbeck?"

". . . Chimi-ahm . . ." came the faint reply. ". . . eating all the people. . . ."

"They can't do that!" shouted Danivon. "They can't leave their province!"

"They are doing it," she cried. "On their own. All by themselves!"

"Boarmus won't stand for it!"

"Boarmus may have other things on his mind."

"Council Supervisory will have an army of Enforcers down here at once."

"I think not, Danivon. If the things we saw along the river are stealing our folk here in Panubi and eating the people of Derbeck, what may they be doing in Tolerance? Boarmus is probably very busy! Or dead."

He had no answer for her. He took no time to think of one, but threw up his hands and started for one of the small boats. "I'm going ashore and taking the flier Zasper came in," he said.

"Do you have any idea what you're going to do?" Jory asked.

Danivon replied, "I can set down almost on top of the place Fringe was taken. I've got weapons that should be able to sterilize the area. . . ."

"Sterilize?"

"Well, Boarmus told Zasper it might be a kind of network, and if I melt the surrounding area, the network should melt with it, shouldn't it?"

"What if the network is keeping them alive, and we wreck it," asked Zasper mildly as he came to join them. "What if the cavern they're in needs air or water, and can't get it without the network."

"By the rules and the covenants, Zasper, you're infuriating! What if she's injured? What if she's sick? What if we wait and wait and don't get there in time. We can all play at what if!"

Zasper nodded slowly. He had to admit, Danivon was right. "The flier's big enough for two," he said. "I'm going with you."

Curvis waited, thinking Danivon would say no, Curvis would go. Curvis didn't want to go, but he didn't want Danivon to go off with Zasper, either. Danivon merely nodded at Zasper, however, one short jerk of his head, and stalked off to rummage among the baggage he'd assembled at the rail, looking for something he'd just thought of, or, perhaps, merely doing so to put an end to conversation. Curvis, left behind, found himself angry at being ignored.

"Can't contain himself, can he," said Jory. "Fool kid."

"Scarcely that," admonished Zasper. "He's over thirty."

"I'm over several thousand, and he's a kid."

"We were all kids once," he said, peering into her eyes. He wanted to talk with her about Fringe. About herself. He wanted to know her, and there might not be time. . . . This might be the only occasion possible. . . .

The question he asked, however, surprised even him, for it was drawn out of him by some ageless glimmer in her eyes.

"What were you like as a girl, Jory?"

"Oh, I was a dutiful girl, Zasper Ertigon. I obeyed all the rules. I bought into subordination and humility."

"You couldn't have! You didn't!"

"Oh, yes, I did. I was a very lovely handmaiden."

"I believe that."

"I find it hard to believe, sometimes. Actually, I was like a lot of those women in Thrasis, trying to be contented in my bower and a seething mass of rebellion inside. In my country in my time they didn't go in for surgical chopping on women, though the custom still prevailed some places on Earth, but psychological chopping was quite common. I was taught to believe things no intelligent person could have believed.

And eventually I rebelled against believing—perhaps in preparation for what I became."

"Which was?"

"A prophetess, would you believe? Me, a prophetess?"

"I can believe that. You have that air about you."

"Do I? It seems unlikely—looking back."

He shook his head slowly. "Perhaps not unlikely. Fringe told me you picked her out, lady."

"True."

"Since . . . since we may not have an opportunity to talk again, will you tell me about that?"

"What do you want to know?" she asked, her head cocked to one side, giving her a sparrowlike look.

"I suppose . . . I suppose I want to know why? Why would a prophetess pick Fringe out. And for what?"

She laughed. It was a quick, uncomfortable little laugh. "Will it comfort you to know?"

He shook his head slowly. "Only you would know that."

She looked at him doubtfully. "Well, perhaps it would. A parable must suffice, however. Will you settle for that?"

"If I must."

"Well then:

"Was a farm woman, once, found a miraculous beast eating the flowers in her garden, and they became friends. Trouble was, getting to know the beast unsuited the woman for less marvelous friendships, if you understand me?"

"Other relationships seemed trivial, perhaps?" he asked, after a moment's thought.

"Not that so much as—irrelevant. Because, knowing the beast well as she did, she became something a great deal more than merely a farm woman with a garden. What she became was not of her own making, you understand, and she wasn't always sure of its significance, though her innermost self reassured her it was worthy."

He nodded. "I see. I think I do."

"But an important thing is, what she became she could not have become if she hadn't been suited for it in the first place."

"Aahh," said Zasper.

Jory smiled. "Well, we all get old, and so did she, and the time came she knew she hadn't much longer, so she looked about for someone to inherit what she had to leave behind. And, of course, what she looked for in her successor could not be what she had become—which was unique, through no virtue of her own—but what had been in her in the first place. The capability."

"And what was that?"

"God knows." She laughed. "I've often wondered."

"Stubbornness?" he suggested.

"Perseverance," she agreed.

"Contentiousness." He smiled. "Rebelliousness."

"Indomitability." She smiled back.

"Dissatisfaction," he said.

"Oh, yes," she said. "A lot of that. A certain prickliness, perhaps. Unwillingness to settle for what's there and obvious when it's obviously wrong! A mystical sense of purpose. A sense of high duty to perform, without knowing what it may be! A longing for heaven, without knowing what that is, either."

"Altogether, an uncomfortable person."

She grinned at him. "So I'm told."

"So you picked Fringe." He shook his head sadly. "And now she's gone."

"Yes," whispered Jory. "She's the best I've found, and now she's gone. And the prophetess is no longer sure of her prophecy, because it was all such a long time ago."

"If no longer a prophetess, what are you now?"

"You're full of good questions." She made a face at him. "Perhaps I am merely a handmaiden again. Perhaps a witch or a ghost, up to no good. When I figure it out, I'll let you know."

"When I bring Fringe back to you, I'll remember you promised." He looked toward the railing where Danivon was still fussing with the supplies and dropped his voice. "He's not right for her, you know. I know her well enough to know that."

She shrugged elaborately, not meeting his eyes, then looked up full of sudden intent. "I'm bound to tell you I don't think this rescue attempt is well thought out," she said.

"Danivon's nose says he won't die."

"Does Danivon's nose tell you whether he'll maybe wish he had?" she asked gently.

Zasper saw something much like pity in her eyes, though he couldn't say why, for Danivon's nose had been silent upon that matter.

When the next summons came from the golden faces, Nela and Bertran could not rise. They made a futile endeavor, but their bodies would not respond. Fringe did her reverence alone, went to the altar alone.

"What's the matter with them?" a new voice asked.

"You damaged them," Fringe replied. "They need time to recover. If they recover."

Silence. Then the new voice, possibly a male voice, said, "They would work better if they were apart."

"True," said Fringe. This voice was worse than either of the others. The others had been . . . malicious, perhaps. Childish in a nasty way. But this voice had real hatred in it, real malice, real evil.

"Maybe we'll take them apart."

Fringe swallowed bile. "It would have to be very cleverly done," she said in as quiet a voice as she could manage. "Otherwise it would kill them. Of course, god could do it without killing them. If they died, we would know it was not god who had done it."

"Oh, I could do it," said the voice with a chuckle. "I've been learning how. Very interesting too. Very . . . educational. If I took your friends apart, they'd work better at the duty we're assigning you, and since only god could do it, you would then know who god is. Correct?"

Fringe moistened dry lips and whispered, "What duty is that?"

"You must answer a question before we let you go," the voice gulped.

"If we can."

"No matter if you can or not. You must."

Anger bested her. "That's not logical. That's completely arbitrary. To demand that someone do something he may not be able to do."

"We have consulted Files." The voice bubbled with hideous laughter. "Gods often demand that people do things they cannot do or things that are dangerous or onerous or hateful. And when the people fail, gods punish them. Should I be less a god than they?"

Fringe swallowed. "Are you a god?"

"Oh, indeed. I am Chimi-ahm the proud, whom you offended mightily. I am Chimi-ahm the hunter, whom you robbed of his prey. I am Chimi-ahm, monstrous and mighty, all knowing, all seeing." The voice was swallowed in a great shout of malicious laughter.

Fringe tried twice before she could get the words out. "What's the question?"

The voice sucked and snickered, "You must say, 'Oh, High Lord Chimi-ahm. . . .' "

She bit down her rage and hatred, letting only submission show. "Oh, High Lord Chimi-ahm, what is the question we must answer."

"No, no. You must say, 'High Lord Chimi-ahm, I am sorry for having offended you by taking away your sacrifice.' "

The words stuck in her throat, and a vise closed about her heart.

"High Lord Chimi-ahm," she gasped. "I am sorry for having offended you by taking away your sacrifice."

" 'Please accept my unworthy self in retribution. . . .' "

"Please accept my unworthy self in retribution."

"Ah. Nicely done. Now, the question you must answer is this: 'What is the ultimate destiny of man?' "

Fringe's mouth fell open. Whatever she might have expected, it had not been this.

"But that's the Great Question," she gasped. "The historic one. The diversity of Elsewhere was expected to answer that question in the fullness of time. . . ." So she had been taught. So she had heard every year on Great Question Day.

"Yes. How clever of you to notice it's the Great Question."

"But, we're only three people."

"A hundred, a dozen, or only three. You must answer it, nonetheless."

"Indeed you must," said the Magna Mater voice sternly.

"You must," said the other female voice, almost with indifference. "Man must answer the question, and you are man."

Now Fringe's nervous glances detected at least four separate groups, each centered upon a spokesface.

"You're not all Chimi-ahm, are you?" she asked.

"Lord Breaze!" trumpeted a hard and handsome face, heretofore silent.

"Gracious Lady Therabas Bland," whispered another, a sly voice.

"Magna Mater, Mintier Thob," another simpered.

They were separate yet united, speaking the same words from a hundred throats.

The one calling himself Lord Breaze said in a kindly voice, "Though I am a newcomer to these councils, my fellow deities tell me god must receive the answer to the question. Reason tells me this is so. Man was made by god to love him. Man does god's will because he loves him. You are man, we are god. Therefore, you will answer the question."

Chimi-ahm gurgled menacingly. "And if you will not do it for love, you will do it because otherwise we'll hurt you and your friends. Then, if you do not answer, we will kill you." The voice was mechanical and yet lubricious. "Of course, we may kill you anyway."

"Gods do this," said Gracious Lady Therabas Bland, golden faces nodding from the high altar piece. "We have read the words of heroes and prophets and priests. Even in ancient times, this was how gods behaved."

As soon as Zasper and Danivon had departed in the flier, the *Dove* left the tumult of Thrasis and sailed upriver once more, past the great wall that stretched away to the north as far as they could see.

"Who built the wall?" asked Curvis.

"It was here when Elsewhere was colonized by the Brannigans," said Jory.

"I thought the world was empty when men arrived."

"Not totally, no. Certainly not behind the wall."

"How far does the wall go?"

"All the way around Panubi," said Asner. "A great circle. Separating what is inside from what is outside."

More than that they would not or could not tell him, and though Curvis fumed with annoyance and impatience, it did him no good.

They went past the plains where the women of Thrasis had walked, and into a land of rolling hills. The swamps along the shore became rocky banks, the banks became cliffs, and the river narrowed into a foaming torrent between the looming walls of a gorge. Below the gorge, the tiny boats from Derbeck lay empty all along the shore. Unable to make way against the torrent, their occupants had gone on afoot.

At the entrance to the gorge, the crew fished a float out of the torrent, heaved it onto the deck, and hauled in a great hawser, dripping with weed and small mollusks. This was clamped to the towing bitts on the bow, while most of the crew went ashore to trudge westward on a narrow footpath, up the gorge and out of sight. Some hours later the line pulled slackly to the surface of the river, and against the full weight of the river the ship was tugged slowly up the narrow gorge whose towering walls seemed within reach of their arms.

At the far end of the canyon, they came up to the monstrous spool on which the mighty hawser was wound, its huge gears connecting it to the capstan where the *Dove*'s sailors trudged around a well-worn track in company with three huge beasts with flapping ears. When the *Dove* had anchored, the hawser was loosed and the great roller turned freely while the current carried the cable-end float downstream.

The *Dove* set sail once more, leaving the beasts and their keepers behind. Gentle hills took the place of rocky walls and beyond them rolling prairies stretched to the limit of sight. North of the river the fires of an encampment lit many bright tents against a shadowed carpet of meadows.

"For the women of Thrasis, no doubt," Jory said to Curvis. "And for the Murrey of Derbeck. When they arrive."

"Who put them there? Who built them?"

"Well, Curvis, the encampment wasn't here when I left, and I didn't see it built. No doubt we shall find out soon enough."

"Where are we going?"

"Noplace," she said.

"Who's there?" he asked angrily.

She shook her head wearily. "Let it come as a surprise to you, Curvis. As it did, once upon a time, to Asner and me."

He was not interested in a surprise. He was not interested in anything that was happening. He wanted to be wherever Danivon was.

She turned away from him without a word. It was obvious he was staying on the *Dove* merely because there was nowhere else to go.

12

In Derbeck the god Chimi-ahm killed twenty or so of the Houm and amused himself thereafter by dancing upon their bones. The Houm had neglected an esoteric detail in their reverence to the Great Lord.

In Enarae two ganger tribes staged a pitched battle in the Hall of Final Equity, which ended several days later with all the gangers, the entire executive staff of the Hall, and numerous bystanders either dead or about to die. The battle had been over a question of precedence between Guntoter and a new goddess called Magna Mater.

In Choire several singers died of exhaustion following a three-day marathon hymn of praise for Most Gracious Lady Thob, who had lately acquired an insatiable thirst for adulation.

On one of the Seldom Isles, a formerly pastoral tribe howled and drummed lengthily before sacrificing one of their more likely virgins to the Gods of the Golden Faces, who had recently manifested themselves at the back of a shallow cavern along the shore.

In Tolerance, the Enforcer Lodge went into emergency session, adjourning after a lengthy meeting to send the Master with a delegation to the Provost.

From the mezzanine of the Great Rotunda, Boarmus saw them coming. Everyone saw them coming, not that there were all that many people sitting around looking. Most people spent their time hiding these days, and who could blame them? Of those few present, however, no one missed the marching feet, the nodding plumes, the grim expressions. The only surprising thing about it, Boarmus thought, was that they had waited so long.

"Master," he greeted the leader of the group, somewhat drunkenly. He'd been trying, unsuccessfully, to drown his too intimate knowledge of what was going on.

"Provost, sir." The Master looked at his boots, trying to find a diplomatic way of saying it and finding none.

"We've just been having an emergency meeting. It's clear we can't go on like this. We're being chewed up and spit out! We've got Enforcers going out on routine missions getting maimed, murdered, disappeared! We've got whole provinces on the brink of breakdown! What in the name of all Enforcement is going on?"

"I've been hoping I wouldn't have to tell you," whispered Boarmus, looking furtively around him.

"Tell us what? Tell us the world is falling apart?"

"I've been hoping it would settle down."

"What would settle down?"

Boarmus sighed. "What's happened is, we've got a god . . . gods."

"The Hobbs Land Gods," cried the Master, going into a defensive half crouch, as though to repel any attack of creeping divinity.

"No, no," whispered Boarmus. "Far from it." He looked around again, wondering what was watching him, what was listening. Well, the hell with it. They could hardly expect discretion at this stage of their game. Not as obtrusive as they'd become. He leaned forward and in a rapid narrative, punctuated by tears, chest heavings, and futile poundings of the table with a pudgy fist, he told the story beginning with Brannigan Galaxy, back in the long ago.

"So," he concluded, "we've got these . . . these . . . gods, who used to be professors at Brannigan, using us for playthings. And we don't know what to do. . . ." Which was an understatement. The entire Council Supervisory, what was left of it, was as baffled, frustrated, and frightened as Boarmus himself.

"You're aware there are several provinces where the death rate now far exceeds the birth rate?" the Master asked.

Boarmus nodded hopelessly.

"You're aware that over in Morlub the suicide rate is so high the place will probably be totally depopulated within a few days?"

Boarmus nodded again. "I follow the monitors," he murmured. "The ones that are left. It's happening everywhere." Greatly daring, he'd checked Files and found historic examples for everything that was happening, including mass suicide at the behest of religious leaders. Re-

344   S H E R I   S.   T E P P E R

markably, there were a few provinces where sweetness and jollity prevailed, almost as though the Gods had decided to try a controlled experiment. Pain here. Pleasure there. See what's most satisfactory. So far, they'd come down heavily on the side of pain.

"Is there some way I can keep my Enforcers from getting killed?" the Master persisted. "What would you suggest?"

Boarmus licked his lips. "Propitiate them."

"And how in hell do we do that?"

"I don't know. Processions, maybe? Sacrifices? Rituals of some kind or other."

"And while we're doing all this propitiating, what do we do about Enforcement?"

Boarmus shrugged. "What they'll let you, I guess. Before you send anyone out on a mission, maybe it would be a good idea to find out which side the gods are on."

He tried to sound positive, even while carefully not mentioning he'd learned to his dismay that quite often the gods were amused by being on several sides at once.

When Nela and Bertran next woke from their exhausted slumber, Fringe was sitting cross-legged beside the entry to the larger cavern, peering through it as though to decipher some riddle. When she saw them moving, she came to help them sit upright.

"Is there any of that food left?" asked Nela. "I feel so weak."

"Lots of it," Fringe replied, fetching a handful of the dry flakes to divide among the twins and the disconsolate pocket munk that was perched on Bertran's shoulder. When they had eaten a few mouthfuls and pushed away the rest, she fetched water in her cupped hands for them to drink, then offered the wet kerchief with which she had washed her own face.

"If I look like you do, I look like death warmed over," Nela said to Bertran as she rubbed the grime from her cheeks.

"I'm afraid it's one for all and all for one," he said, trying to smile. In fact, he thought, if he looked like she did, death wasn't even warm.

"Did anything happen while we were out of it?" Nela asked.

"I had another interview with them," said Fringe, jabbing a thumb in the direction of the faces. "What do you think they are?"

As soon as she asked the question, she knew it wasn't a wise thing to have done, but Bertran was already answering her.

"Something that was once human, once alive, but is now . . . not alive. Something that is at least partly mechanical, and no longer at all sane," he said.

Fringe put her finger to her lips and looked upward, shaking her head.

Bertran sighed. Well, yes, they were probably overheard, but what difference did it make? "It could have been more careful of us," he said emphatically. "It didn't seem to mind hurting us."

Fringe agreed. The things didn't mind hurting. Seemed to enjoy it, in fact.

"What did they want this time?" asked Nela.

"Oh, the usual," she said from a dry throat. "A few threats. They intend to hurt us again, rather badly if we don't do what they want." Though she'd tried to think up gentle words while they slept, there was no easy way to say it.

"Which is?"

"Answer a question for them."

"Gladly," said Nela. "Our lives are an open book. Anything at all they'd like to know."

"I'm afraid it's not that kind of question."

"What is it?" asked Bertran apprehensively.

"They want to know what the destiny of man is."

The two stared at her disbelievingly, Nela fretfully rubbing her shoulder and chest where the pain was worst.

"You're joking!" she blurted.

"No," said Fringe, wishing she could say yes, all a joke, all a funniness, let's get out of here and forget it. "Not a joke, I'm afraid. They really want to know."

"But isn't that the Great Question? The one you and Danivon have talked about? The one all the people on Elsewhere were supposed to answer sooner or later?"

She nodded. It was indeed.

"But how . . ." Nela was speechless. She tried again. "Even if we came up with something, how would we know if we'd answered it correctly?"

"We'll know," said a voice.

Afar, on the golden wall, a face peered at them, a mouth moved.

"We'll know. The populace will acclaim the answer. The truth of it will be self-evident."

The three were silent.

"Come now," said the voice, one of the female voices, Fringe couldn't tell which. "Come now. You've been guilty of blasphemy, you know. If you were more loving, more adoring, more worshipful, you wouldn't call us insane. But we won't punish you for that. Not now. Not if you give us the answer."

"If all of Elsewhere couldn't answer the question in a thousand years or so, how the hell do you expect us to answer it?" cried Nela, tried past endurance.

The air sparkled among them. On the far wall, the faces came alive, focused, avid, while pain surged through nerves; while their muscles jerked and danced; while flesh burned, then chilled, then burned again.

When it was over, the twins were blue and gasping. Fringe herself was in little better shape, though still able to curse silently at the creatures on the far wall who were watching her eagerly, waiting for her, for any of them to do or say something more.

Bertran's hand was on her own. He pressed gently, saying, *Be silent. Be silent. Don't give them any excuse to hurt us again.* The faces were like the hecklers at the sideshow. One could escalate a mere heckling to physical violence if one wasn't careful. Certainly these beings were in the mood for it.

Fringe was silent. The red haze in her eyes faded. Tears dripped unheeded. She closed her eyes not to see the faces staring, waiting, ready to do something else, offer some further pain, some further horror.

The pain had left a sick exhaustion in its wake. She slipped into a half faint, half slumber, conscious of where she was, yet adrift. Bertran's hand was still on hers, still pressing hers. When she opened her eyes again, she saw only darkness.

"They've turned out our lights," she said stupidly.

"To encourage concentration," Bertran whispered, only a handbreadth from her ear. "No doubt."

"Bertran and I have been discussing things," Nela whispered in her turn. "Our chances and all that."

"We don't believe they're good," Bertran offered.

"We've thought of dying, lots of times," Nela confessed. "But the idea of doing it here, now, in all this darkness, all this pain, is revolting! Though maybe we will want to die, before they're through with us."

Bertran cleared his throat. "We have this thing we'd like to try. It may mean nothing, but then again . . ."

"It can't hurt anything," Nela offered.

"Ah?" said Fringe.

"We're really not able to move around. We wondered if you'd mind finding us a loose rock, something about the size of a fist."

Obediently, Fringe felt her way to the rocky wall and along the base of it, hefting stones, returning with something only a little larger than asked for. "Will this do?" she asked, feeling for his hands.

Bertran took it. She sat beside him once more, feeling the muscles in his arm and shoulder moving and bunching as he hefted the stone.

"This should do nicely," he said. "Nela, you ready?"

"More or less," she whispered.

He took something from around his neck and put it on the ledge near Fringe's leg. "Keep your fingers away from here," he instructed. "Nela?"

"All right," she said.

They spoke together, in hushed voices, slowly, very clearly. *"We want to know what the destiny of man is, and we want the things persecuting us to believe the answer and let us alone."*

Bertran hammered downward with the stone, once, twice. Brilliant blue light lit the cavern momentarily, then vanished with a cracking sound, as though the mountain had broken asunder.

"What the hell was that?" demanded Fringe, rubbing her eyes where jagged afterimages swam against the darkness.

"When Celery came, all that long while ago," Nela said, "it left us this little transmitter thing. When we decided on our payment, Berty and I, we were supposed to speak it, then smash the transmitter. So we just did."

"But that was thousands of years ago!"

"I know. We don't really expect it to work. The Celerians are all gone. . . ."

Long gone, it appeared, for nothing happened.

Nela sighed. "I supposed it isn't possible that we might actually answer the question?" She tried to say it cheerfully. It was up to all of them to keep their spirits up, she no less than the other two, though all she wanted to do was curl up against the stone and retreat into thumb-sucking silence. "The show," Aunt Sizzy was wont to say, "may not have to go on, but we don't buy groceries unless it does!"

"Men have probably come up with all possible answers by now and discarded them," said Bertran.

"I've never thought about the Great Question much since I was a kid," said Fringe. "It hasn't seemed relevant, somehow."

"Oh, but yes." He laughed, the sound teetering on the edge of control. "Think of how much time and effort it would have saved if we'd only known what man's destiny actually was. Think of our time, all the fundamentalist fascists versus the civil libertines; all the liberals throwing our money at the poor versus the conservatives throwing our money at themselves; all the male versus female controversies, all the revolutions, sexual, political, and economic. How marvelous if we'd only known what was important and what wasn't!"

Fringe was amused despite herself. "What did you think man's destiny was?"

He heaved a deep, obviously painful breath. "Nela, what did we think man's destiny was? When we were children."

Nela made a slight humming noise, as though to advise the darkness she was thinking, or as though she might be clenching her teeth to keep from crying. "Well, let's see," she said at last in a tight voice that barely hid hysteria. "As good Catholic children, our destiny was to be guilty over sex, to have lots of babies, and to partake of the sacraments sufficiently often to assure we'd go to heaven when we died."

"Right," said Bertran. "And in the fundamentalist church down the block, they learned their destiny was to be guilty over sex, to worship the flag (in defiance of the first and second commandments), and to be born again sufficiently often to assure *they'd* go to heaven when they died, though I'm not sure whether it was the same heaven or not. In fact, the only real difference between us and them was whether we ranked sperm or the flag slightly ahead of god."

He laughed, choking, then groaned.

"So heaven was your destiny," said Fringe. "Or having lots of babies."

"Oh, yes," murmured Nela. "The only excuse we had for overpopulating our world was that it wouldn't matter in heaven." She tried to laugh but couldn't manage it. The laugh turned into a sob.

"Nela, Nela," said Fringe, falling to her knees before them and taking Nela into her arms. "Hey."

"It's just, just I'm so scared," Nela whispered. "I'm so scared, Fringe. It's so dark, and I feel so sick."

"We're not very good at this," Bertran quavered. "Not very good at being brave."

"You're the bravest people I've ever known," said Fringe firmly, patting them gently, knowing it to be true. "You two really are! You've been brave and gallant all your lives. You're just not good about showing it, or bragging about it. But listen, I swear to you . . . I swear to you both, I am your friend, and I will do everything in my power to see that nothing bad happens to you!"

Nela sighed. Under Fringe's stroking hands she seemed to relax, to give way. "It's just being . . . how we've always had to be."

"Well, that's what bravery is," Fringe murmured, holding them closely. "Being what you have to be, without whining about it. That's what Zasper says, anyhow."

"Maybe that's man's destiny," Nela said. "Just to be brave." She took two or three deep breaths, easing herself.

"That gives us three answers," said Fringe. "Babies, heaven, bravery."

"Which will get us absolutely nowhere," Bertran offered. "Nothing so simple is going to satisfy those . . . beings! The Great Question ranks right up there with the quest for the Grail, with seeking the philosopher's stone or catching a unicorn. Our race is obsessed with quests and questers. As children, we dream the quest before we dream the thing quested for. No doubt some of us are born for the attempt. No matter what shape of box we find ourselves in, we keep struggling to be free!"

Fringe listened to the longing in his voice and was chastened.

He sighed. "How did this Great Question thing get started on Elsewhere anyhow?"

"It wasn't started here. It was started a long time ago at the biggest educational institution in the known universe, Brannigan Galaxy. But once the Hobbs Land Gods had destroyed man everywhere else, the question could only be answered on Elsewhere," Fringe replied.

"You're sure man was destroyed everywhere else?"

"Well, of course. Once the Gods took over . . ."

"You're sure they did take over? I know you've said that, but are you sure?"

"Bertran. Yes. They did take over. And they destroyed mankind. The only place in the galaxy where mankind was left was here. So, this is the only place in the galaxy where that question can be answered. I mean, it's self-evident."

He leaned back against the stone, seeming to sag there, almost bone-lessly, Nela dragged with him, their breathing labored. "So there are gods out there who have destroyed mankind," Bertran whispered. "And there are gods in here who are bidding fair to destroy what's left. So, maybe the destiny of man is to be destroyed by his gods, and wouldn't that be a nice ironic answer for them."

"I'd rather not tell them that," whispered Nela.

"If that is the answer, they probably already know," said Fringe soberly.

"How did you ever graduate from the Academy?" Danivon fumed, plunging his arm into the guts of the flier where it sat on a sandspit beside the River Floh, just upstream of the Great Wall. "How did you ever get your operator's clearance."

"We didn't have to fly these damned gnats," Zasper muttered angrily. "We worked with vehicles large enough to stay put when the wind blew."

"It was an updraft," said Danivon angrily. "And the way you landed us . . ."

"I did land us," Zasper pointed out.

"The way you landed us has knocked something loose in there, and I can't see to fix it."

"I'll be glad to hold the light."

"Whatever's loose is behind six other things, and there's room for only two hands in there. I need both of them to fix it. We're going to have to wait for daytime, Zasper!"

"We've already waited too long. What do you smell?"

"Pain, Zasper. Suffering. Fear. Darkness. You want to add to the catalog!"

"No," he said. "I just hoped they were still alive."

"Oh, they're alive. And from what I can sniff out, still in the same place. Though why . . . now that's a good question, isn't it. Why. Why would these gods you speak of want Fringe? Or the twins?"

Zasper shook his head. "They were probably after you."

"Because I asked questions."

"Possibly, yes. But then, so did the twins. Maybe they were after any of us and just grabbed whoever was closest."

That had a ring of likelihood to it. Danivon slumped against the flier and stared toward the east, waiting for dawn.

"I guess I should say thank you," he said.

"For what?"

"For saving my life. In Molock. All those years ago."

"Oh, you found out about that, did you? I suppose Fringe told you."

"Yes."

"Women cannot keep their mouths shut."

"It was when she saved the girl in Derbeck. I tried to stop her."

"Yes, well. I would have thought Curvis would have been the one who tried to stop her. He goes by the book pretty much. Of course, you have done too, when it was convenient." He mused at the dark sky. "How did she tell you?"

"She yelled it at me, to explain why she was saving the girl. I should have expected her to do something like that. She's been very upset with us lately."

Zasper sighed. "I didn't really want her to be an Enforcer. It's hard for a woman. It's hard for some men. The children were always hardest for me. Those places where they kept having them and having them and killing them and killing them, or just letting them die. At least your people, whoever they were, tried to keep you alive."

"You met them."

"Who?"

"My people. Cafferty and Latibor, at the boat. They're my parents."

Zasper stared at him, a mere silhouette against the stars. "Think of that," he said at last, trying to decipher the feeling that had just run through his mind, leaving muddy footprints across his heart. Jealousy maybe? So Danivon had parents.

"Dawn coming," said Danivon. "But it won't be really light for a while yet. We might as well catch up on some sleep."

The golden faces summoned their prisoners before them once more. Panting and pale, the twins managed to get into the cavern of the faces, though they could not rise after the obligatory reverence.

"You have the answer for us?" a face asked with poisonous sweetness.

"We have some possible answers," offered Fringe, putting her hand on Nela's shoulder, feeling the damp chill there, the sweating cold.

Tentatively, she suggested man's destiny was to reproduce.

The faces howled with laughter.

"It's the first thought we had," Fringe said, swallowing bile. "Since that's what we seem to do best."

"No," said a face, all the others echoing, no, no, no, no.

"We thought perhaps our destiny was to be destroyed," she went on, hurrying, getting it over with. "Or to attain heaven, or simply to be brave."

As soon as the word left her mouth, she knew she had erred.

"Brave," gulped a voice. "Let's see how brave. . . ."

The twins stood it for a time, grunting and jerking, and then they slid to the ground all in one heap as Fringe screamed imprecations at the faces and knelt to draw Nela's head into her lap. She felt the gray throat for a pulse, leaned down to detect a breath. None. None.

"You bastards," Fringe screamed. "You bastards, you've killed them."

She was thrust back against the wall by a forest of tiny tentacles, still screaming curses.

"What are you doing? What are you doing?"

"Separating them," said a voice, a gulping voice. "They're no good tied together like that. So, we'll take them apart."

"You'll kill them! You can't do that! If they aren't already dead, you'll kill them."

"I can do it," the voice said calmly. "I've been studying the matter, and I have everything I need, right here."

The tentacles knew something, obviously, for the twins came back to life, enough at least to scream, plead, cry, beg, bubble, gurgle, and at last subside into silence as the tentacles burrowed and sliced and connected, giggling as they worked, chuckling as they worked, as what had been two human persons was reduced to something more useful to those in charge.

When they were done, the tentacles withdrew.

Fringe sagged against the wall, mouth open, unable to look away from the cavern floor that was stained with fluids, littered with knobs of bloody bone and coils of purple and red, blobs of organs and muscle, parts identifiable and unidentifiable, all reeking warmly, steaming in the chill air of the chamber, all strewn about the boxes, the two sets of boxes that keened a continuous scream of horror as they peered out at Fringe with wholly familiar eyes.

"An ear," her mind shrieked at her, doing an inventory. "See there, that's a knee, that's a thigh. See there, breasts, Fringe, breasts!"

From a pile of discarded clothing across the cavern, the pocket munk raced across the intervening space, up Fringe's leg and into her pocket, shrieking its own horror and agony to add to hers.

"Aaaah," she moaned, unable to stop herself, unable to control it. "They've made you dinks, you're dinka-jins, oh, God, Nela, Bertran, you're . . ."

". . . dinks . . ." cried the munk from Danivon's pocket in Fringe's hysterical voice.

"What have they done?" cried Zasper, grabbing at Danivon's arm so violently that the little flier wobbled and slipped beneath Danivon's hands.

"Careful," cried Danivon. "You'll have us on the ground again. We're almost there, don't do anything silly. . . ."

"Dinks. They've made the twins into dinks! Did they do it to Fringe?" Zasper asked. "Was it just the twins?"

Danivon's throat dried at the thought of their having done it to Fringe. But no. Not Fringe. Just the twins. Just the twins. He knew it.

"Bertran will hate it," he murmured. "Hate it. His dreams were all of sleekness, of swimming like a fish. He told me once. Oh, he'll hate that, Zasper."

"Why!" Zasper demanded. "Why in hell!"

"Maybe because they weren't . . . portable the way they were," Danivon said. "If the things wanted to move them. If they were hurt, for instance. And they were hurt, I could smell that. . . ."

He dropped the flier toward the river and began to examine the shoreline.

"Where are we?" asked Zasper.

"Halfway across Beanfields. Vacant country along here. The settlements are all to the south and west." He turned the flier slightly. "Look for three tall pillars, the middle one highest," he instructed. "A little south of us."

"There," cried Zasper, pointing.

"Right." Danivon jerked the flier around, flying low above the water. "Now there's a tall dead tree along here with four branches at the top. When that lines up with the middle pillar, that's where. . . ."

·   ·   ·

The faces regarded the boxes with satisfaction. "Better," said the bad one, the malicious one. "Far better. Now they can concentrate on what we need to know."

"Why?" cried Fringe, hammering on the floor with her fists. "Why do you need to know now!"

"Now is appropriate," said a face. "Why not now?"

"Now is necessary," said another. "God must know the answer to this question. How can we direct our worshipers properly if we do not know their destiny."

"But we're only people," she sobbed. "Ordinary people. Not philosophers. Not ethicists. Not the kind of people to consider questions like that. We're just ordinary little people. Why do you ask us?"

"You might know," said a voice.

"Should know," amended another.

"Since the question pertains to man, man must know. Naive intuition should inform you of your destiny."

"Enough," said a gulping voice. "All that is irrelevant. God requires the answer to this question. The question will be answered by man. We are god. You are man. Therefore, you will answer. That's all you need to know!"

On the floor the boxes howled. The faces seemed not to hear the sound, to disregard it.

"That's completely arbitrary," Fringe screamed. "It doesn't take into consideration that we're just three people, that maybe it takes all men to answer. . . ."

"Arbitrary doesn't matter," said a female voice in an instructive tone. "We have consulted Files. Gods are usually arbitrary."

"But we can't. . . ."

"If you can't, you will die and we will try with someone else, until we find one who will answer. . . ."

Pain flicked across the cavern. Fringe cried out. The boxes went on howling.

And suddenly stopped, as though killed in midscream.

"Who is that?" asked a face.

Was there apprehension in the voice?

"Listen . . . listen to . . ." cried one of the other voices. "Listen to up above. Something coming!"

Abruptly the faces were empty, all but one.

"Fringe Owldark!" said the box across from her.

"Bertran?" Fringe asked, shocked into sensibility. It hadn't sounded like Bertran.

"This assemblage is not Bertran at this moment, no. Fringe Owldark, listen to me. The weapon they took from you. It's under that small pile of rock to your left. They forgot it. Burn the rock in the cavern. Melt it so they can't get at you."

"Who?" she gaped stupidly. "Who are you?"

"Someone you don't know. Someone caught in this mess with these monsters. Someone trying to help you."

"Who?" she cried. "Who?"

"Jordel," it said. "Call me Jordel. Now do as I say!"

"Where's Bertran? Where's Nela?"

"Here. Safe."

"Safe!" She broke into hysterical laughter. "Safe!"

"Fringe Owldark! You must be an Enforcer! Cool! Thoughtful! Otherwise you will die, and so will they. You must burn the surfaces of the stone to keep the devices from coming through. Understand me!"

"We'd die of suffocation! It'll burn up all the air!"

"There's enough air. Someone has come to help you, up there. And I will help you. But you have to keep them from getting to you. Burn the walls, the floor, so they can't get through."

"Do it," howled the other of the boxes. "Do it, Fringe. Melt it, Fringe. Then melt us."

She tumbled the pile of stones, scrabbling among them, coming up with her heat beamer, feeling it turn almost of its own volition onto the faces, burning them, melting them.

Something came screaming through the floor at her, something with knives, and she melted it as well. The floor. The walls. Behind the stone, things howled and drilled furiously, trying to get through.

"Now us," cried one box. "Now us, Fringe. Melt us."

"Don't!" demanded the voice from the other box. "Take them back. They can be cloned. . . ."

"Can't, can't, left too much out," the box cried, its eyes swiveling to the lumps of bone, the scattered organs, the bits and pieces of flesh, like a bombed butcher shop, the purple and red and white parts of themselves, the reeking parts, the framework, the network, all that had made them man.

Fringe had avoided that place, that bloody place, and now it erupted with glittering blades, whirring drills.

She turned the beamer on them, sobbing, the roast meat smell rising around her.

The walls howled, and she burned them. The floor howled, and she burned that. All around her was melted stone and air that stank of blood and metal. It was hard to breathe.

"We'll go back in the little room," she said to the boxes coaxingly, as she might have tempted a child. "Back in the little room where it's cooler."

"Not cooler," cried Jordel. "Burn it there too. They're in the walls in there, in the floor. But there's a place over the ledge where they brought you in, hidden in the shadow, you can get up. . . ."

"Come," she said to the boxes. "Come with me!" She couldn't bear to touch them, couldn't bear to see them. She forced herself to speak softly, lovingly. "Come!" These were her friends, she reminded herself. No matter what they looked like. No matter what they had become! She had sworn an oath of friendship.

One of the assemblages moved at once. Behind her the other one howled, helplessly jerking this way and that. "How?" it cried piteously. "How can we move?"

"Think of walking," said the Jordel box. "It's automatic, just think of walking."

The other box jerked and trembled, moving forward with its various parts strung out behind, clashing together, then strung apart, then clashing together once more, howling and clashing, howling and clashing. Fringe looked away hastily, remembering a toy she'd had as a child, one she had pulled along the ground, clashing together, stringing apart, clashing together, stringing apart. This was no toy. This was Bertran. This was Nela. Her friend Nela. She wanted to scream and choked it down. Perhaps she should have melted them as Nela had asked. That might have been kinder. If it had been her, she'd have wanted that for herself. Now it was too late, now she'd had too much time to think. She couldn't do it now, but she couldn't bear to look at them either.

"Here," said Danivon, leaning from the flier to burn the rocks below, careful pass after careful pass. "Right here, Zasper."

He set the flier down and they slid onto the heated surface where

Danivon bent close to the stones, sniffing. Over the mineral smell he caught a whiff of her, the merest breath. Almost more the memory of a scent than the scent itself. "Here," he said, pointing downward at a crack no wider than his finger. The crack led waveringly across the rock surface, disappearing behind a standing pillar of stone. He followed it behind the pillar and was attacked from three sides at once by tiny, vicious sharpnesses.

"Nicely done," growled Zasper, who had come around the other way and was busy destroying the surfaces around him where a dozen screaming devices had burrowed through. "Nice to see you remember to look before you move, boy!" As soon as he had a hand free, he sprayed coagulant on Danivon's shoulder and passed him an ampule of universal antidote, just in case the blades had been poisoned.

Behind the pillar the crack widened into a hole, a vertical shaft. As they walked around it, trying to see into it, a tiny form erupted from it and flung itself at Danivon's leg.

Zasper aimed but could not fire in time. The scurrying blob went up Danivon's leg and into his pocket, squealing all the way.

"Curvis's munk," Zasper said weakly.

"Down there." Danivon pointed. "That's where it came from." He leaned forward and bellowed, hearing only echoes in return.

"Somebody has to go down and look," said Zasper, pulling on his gauntlets. "Me."

"Why you?"

"Because if you go and get killed, chances are I'd wreck that flier on the way back." He was already leaning into the crack, spraying it with deadly heat, watching the stones drip like wax.

Then he lowered himself into the hole, touching it only with boots and gloves, feeling his face redden under the heat, smelling the scalded air.

Partway down, something with fangs came at him from a crevice. He burned it before it got to him, then melted the crevice plus another crack or two he could see from where he was. "Fringe?" he yelled. "Fringe, are you down there?"

No answer. Above him, Danivon's anxious face peered down. He shook his hands, cooling them, then searched for a set of holds farther down.

Another burn, another shaft, and abruptly the crevice changed from vertical to horizontal. "Fringe!" he yelled.

"Here," her voice came without direction or distance. "Coming."

Zasper paused, panting for air. He'd burned up all the air. No point in going farther down if she was coming up. "Are the twins there with you?" he hollered.

He heard a sound. Laughter? Crying? He couldn't tell. Maybe she needed help. He leaned into the horizontal space and burned it carefully, floor, walls, ceiling. Wait for it to cool, he told himself. Go into that thing hot, burn your kneecaps off.

The rock beside his ear howled. Something drilling through. He waited until it emerged, then melted it, so pleased with himself he almost missed the one coming through on the other side. He hung on the rock, panting, resting.

"Too old for this," he told himself. "Far, far too old."

He felt of the stone, finding it less searing, cooled enough to crawl on if he didn't mind blistering a little. After two or three body lengths, it ran into another vertical passage, this one pouring heated air past his face to leak away through small fractures above him.

"Fringe!"

"Here, Zasper," hysterical breathless laughter. "Coming. I've got the twins with me. So to speak."

One of the twins, so to speak, came lurching up the shaft, battering against the sides, howling as it rose. Zasper grabbed the foremost part of it and passed it into the tunnel behind him, where it fled to the far end and lay there, still howling.

"Melt me!" shrieked a voice from below. "Please, Fringe. Don't leave us like this. Melt us. Don't make us live like this."

"She can't," bellowed Zasper in his parade-ground voice. "It's against Enforcer regulations. If you want to die, do it later, but you're risking her life with all this delay!"

Then silence and more battering, banging as the second assemblage came up the chimney, lurching and clattering against the rocky walls, to be passed on in its turn.

Poor bastards, Zasper thought, *oh, poor little bastards, not a clue how to move, moving on sheer panic and nine tenths of that wrong.*

And then Fringe, burned, dirty, bloody, clambered from out of the chimney, and he retreated before her to make room.

At the far end of the horizontal, he sprayed the shaft again before pushing the boxes up, their tiny gravitics whining and hiccuping as the two made pathetic attempts at flight. "Keep the rock clear up there," he screamed at Danivon, who seemed to be watching bemusedly and not paying attention.

Three things came howling through the stone at him. He got two of them, Fringe got the third, aiming an inch from his chin to do it.

"Sorry about that," she muttered, climbing past.

When she was halfway up, a thing full of tiny bright teeth emerged from the shaft behind her and burrowed into her leg. She screamed, and Zasper killed it as her blood dripped down onto his face. She kept on climbing.

Then they were out, and Danivon was standing with his back to them spraying the surrounding rock, the dinks whimpering at his feet.

Fringe stared at the flier, shaking her head slowly from side to side. "I see some of us are going to walk out."

Both Danivon and Zasper glanced at the flier, for the first time considering its size.

"Damn," Zasper said. "It wouldn't have made any difference, Fringe. It was the only one they had."

"Fine rescuers you are," she remarked.

"There's room for one of us and the two . . . the twins," said Danivon. "You, Fringe."

"Why me? Let Zasper take them out."

"Zasper can't fly the thing. He tried on the way in and almost killed us both."

"You, then."

Zasper said, "You're wounded and he's not, not much." There was no argument to that. She was indeed wounded, in several places, though not, Zasper hoped, seriously. Mostly cuts and punctures where toothed or bladed things had caught her. The worse threats, the tiny Doors, the little forcefields, may have been too delicate to force through the melted stone. Perhaps this place was at the forward line of the gods' advance. Perhaps they hadn't been totally ready when the *Dove* left Derbeck. Perhaps they weren't totally in control yet—he hoped.

"There's real bad things in there," said Fringe urgently. "But there's one that tried to help. He spoke to me through one of the . . . the dinks. Jordel."

"Jordel of Hemerlane," said Zasper. "He's still there?"

"There, where, Zasper?"

"Never mind. There's no time. Later."

"Leave us here," cried a box. "Leave us here. We don't want to live like this. Without us there'll be room. . . ."

"Without you, there'll be room for two," said Fringe firmly, kindly, not looking at the assemblages. "Zasper and Danivon wouldn't leave me; Danivon and I wouldn't leave Zasper. And I certainly wouldn't leave Danivon."

"You wouldn't?" he begged her. "You wouldn't, Fringe."

"Enforcers don't do that," she said stiffly, avoiding his outstretched hand. "Damn, Danivon. Move!"

"You wouldn't leave me?" Danivon asked her softly.

"We stand together," she said to him. "No, I wouldn't abandon you, Danivon Luze. Did you think I would?"

He touched her face and she let him do it as she said, "Can you two make it on foot?"

"Do you think these monsters have spread west of here?" Danivon asked.

"They may have blanketed a considerable distance," Zasper said.

"Not logical," Fringe contradicted. "Why would they waste time blanketing places where there aren't any people."

"Good idea," said Danivon. "That's where we'll go."

"Where?"

"Where there aren't any people. We'll stay clear of the settlements, and that'll probably keep us ahead of the monsters too. If you get out all right, you can come back and ferry us west. We'll be along the river."

Danivon busied himself stacking the boxes on top of one another in the flier, trying not to look at the eyes. The boxes still howled, but with diminished energy, as though they had worn out their terror, or been exhausted by it.

"The others have gone on west," Zasper told Fringe. "Past the Great Wall. The captain told me there's a gorge upriver, and you should find them not too far past the gorge, where Jory calls noplace."

"I'll be back for you."

"Whenever. We'll be all right."

"Zasper. Thank you for coming."

"It's as you said. We Enforcers stand together." He leaned close to her. "Get back to Jory, girl. Stick close to her. Promise."

She gave him a preoccupied look. "Jory? If you say so, Zas."

"Promise."

"Promise."

He stood back as the flier lifted. Something tentacular extruded itself from the stone, grasped the undercarriage, and tried to pull it back down. Both Zasper and Danivon burned it away and watched the flier lift and turn toward the west.

"Come on, old man," said Danivon. "Unless you'd like to get more intimately acquainted with these devices."

"Not really, no."

Without further conversation the two began to run away westward, down from the rocky prominence they found themselves on and along the grassy verges of the river.

Above them, Fringe tilted the flier to watch them go: Danivon in the lead, Zasper not far behind. Her eyes blurred, and she blinked them clear, leveled the flier and dropped it low over the surface of the river to head upstream.

"Are they gone," one of the boxes cried.

"Down below," she said. "Nothing bothering them, so far as I can see."

"You can drop us off somewhere. Go back for them."

"I'll do that. Once you're safe."

"Safe. . . ." The box made a series of sounds that Fringe only belatedly recognized as sobbing.

"Jordel said safe," she said. "I know you think it's the end of the world." She sounded pompous and patronizing, even to herself. "But . . ." But what. "Jory may be able to think of something. . . ." Her vision blurred again, and she blinked it clear. She should comfort them! How could she comfort them. She couldn't hug them, couldn't hold them. They wouldn't feel a touch. What words did she have? "Maybe. . . ."

The flier lurched, and she leveled it, taking a deep breath.

"Listen," she said. "Later on, if you want to . . . if you don't want to . . . I'll help you. Later on. But just now, you've got to be quiet. Quiet . . . as you can. So I can think. So I can fly. Because . . ."

Because what?

She couldn't think what. She had to go upstream, that was it. Upstream where she could drop the two of them off.

"There are two of you, aren't there?" she asked.

"Two," sobbed a voice.

Why had she asked that? She knew there were two. Nela. And Bertran. Was Jordel in there too? He'd been in there. For a little time. Using the voice box to talk to her. She was pretty sure. . . .

She stared at the riverbank moving past, not too fast. Just keep it level, keep it going along the water. Can't get lost following the water.

Not far to the west was a settlement of some kind. Small dwellings grouped into a village. More of them farther on. Beanfields. Ruled by Mother-dear and all her sister guards. And on the other side of the river— that was Thrasis. What did she know about Thrasis? Nothing. Nothing she could remember. The wall past that. Higher than she'd thought it would be. Who had built that? And when?

Was it possible those weapons had had some kind of drug on them? Some kind of poison?

Her vision blurred and she blinked.

Just keep above the water. Keep moving.

Those who occupied the Core, in addition to creating a network that covered most of Elsewhere, had also duplicated chunks of the Core matrix, a node here, a node there, inhabiting one and then another more or less randomly, as impulse moved them. There was one such node on Panubi, in a vault beneath the coastal mountains west of Deep.

Orimar Breaze, so it seemed to him, came there to find the others. They had been distant; they became adjacent. They had been outside his awareness; they came inside, a clot of roiling egos much occupied in an inquisition of Fringe and the twins. Though Orimar observed what occurred thereafter, he took little part and remained securely in the node while the others seemed to go raging off in pursuit of the escapees.

"Where have you gone?" he asked plaintively and rhetorically, not really expecting an answer. "Where is everybody?"

The voice that answered him was familiar, even after all these years.

"There are only four of you left," it said. "And three of them are chasing after their prey, Orimar Breaze."

"Jordel?"

"Yes," said the voice. "Indeed. Jordel."

"I have this feeling they've changed, you know," said Orimar Breaze, still plaintively.

"You've all changed, Orimar. I said you would."

"I haven't changed!"

The voice seemed to laugh, chokingly. "Oh, Orimar, if you could see yourself as I do!"

"I've grown, perhaps. I'm not merely human now."

"A god, are you? Like the others?"

The being who called himself Orimar Breaze considered this. "Well, perhaps. Yes. But not like the others. What you have to consider is the others have no . . . panache. Clore's a monster and Thob is a swollen udder. Magna Mater indeed. I don't know what you could call Bland, but Gracious Lady wouldn't be it. She's a hag. She's always been a hag. No style at all."

"You have style, do you?"

"I will. When I set my mind to it. I had style even as a human! What happened to them? Jordel?"

The voice whispered, almost menacingly, "Do you really want to know?"

"I wouldn't have asked otherwise." A hint of the old asperity there, the old dignity, offended.

"What happened was what I told you would happen."

"All that nonsense about staying asleep when we didn't want to!"

"All that nonsense, yes. You all went into the Core as dynamic patterns with no sensory feedback to anchor your thoughts, no automatic procedures to correct your patterns. As each of you acquired experiences similar to the others, the edges between you started to blur. Something of Clore lapped over into what had been you, Orimar. Some of you became part of Mintier Thob, some of her became Therabas Bland. Patterns became less individual; personalities became less sure where themselves began and others ended. Attitude and identity scrambled. . . ."

Orimar whined, "Nonsense. All nonsense!"

Jordel overrode him. "Part of our patterns were the carefully inculcated civilities our mothers had taught us as children: customs and mores and manners, the behaviors that mask our primitive urges. They're learned, of course, not instinctive, so they detach easily under stress, or when they're not reinforced. . . ."

"There was no stress. . . ."

"No reinforcement, either! So civilities detached and were lost, then the old beast urges came surging up. All minds have them, and they amplified one another, they resonated. . . ."

Orimar whined in his throat.

Jordel whispered, "All the minds of all the Great Question Committee, bubbling around in the Core like an ugly stew, bobbing and bumping against one another, getting soggier and less distinguishable the longer they cooked."

"I don't believe you," he cried. "I won't. . . ."

"Believe or not, I don't care. Besides, I'm not finished.

"Every personality acquires intellectual fringes: not memory, but opinions, reflexes, and responses. A lot of those bits and fragments also came unglued and went floating around loose. When the matrix came upon these free-floating scraps, it simply eliminated them.

"Aside from faces and names, those were often the traits that most distinguish any one of us from any other. With those gone, many of your minds were virtually alike, so the Core identified them as redundancies and aggregated them."

Orimar cried, "You're saying we were melded, combined. . . ."

"Melded. Yes. Amalgamated. Every time I was wakened, there were fewer of you. . . ."

"What do you mean when you were awakened? We voted not to. . . ."

"Did you think I would let you control me with your vote? I bribed the technicians! They put me and my colleagues in a nice quiet corner of the Core, and I've been asleep there ever since except for my annual updatings, during which I counted you all. By the end of the first decade there were only a hundred or so. A hundred years later there were only a dozen. Now there are only four monstrous egos plus a few fragments. And me, of course. And my colleagues."

"Liar. . . ."

"All of you had a full complement of biological data when you came in here, all your muscletwitch and lungfill, heartspeed and footrun, ability to fight or flee, to bellow and blink and bark. It was all there when you came in, all the left luggage of evolution. It's virtually the same for everybody! Crawling is crawling. Sucking is sucking. But the matrix was programmed to detect and eliminate redundancies when necessary to create storage space, and what did you all do? You began to create worlds of your own, whole universes of your own. Space was needed so the matrix deleted all but one set of the bio-data. Among the four of you, you've only got one set of breathe, jerk, blink, crawl, walk, run, shit, suck, fuck, bite!"

"But there are still a thousand faces, a thousand names."

"Yes, a thousand faces, a thousand names, whole clusters of them attached to a single ego. Clore thinks he has followers still, when all he really has trailing after him are pieces of himself, like the tail on a comet!"

"You lie," hissed a new voice, one returned from other business. "Don't listen to him, Breaze."

"You lie, Jordel."

"Jordel, peeper and pryer, sneaker and liar," cried a third voice. "Not one of us, Orimar. Not one of us."

"Not one of you," agreed Jordel, his pattern vanishing, too quickly for them to follow, his voice fading: "Not one of you, thank God."

"Liar, liar," chanted a chorus. "Jordel the Liar."

"Did you catch them?" Breaze asked. "Did you catch the ones that got away?"

Hatred. Consternation. Loss. The captives had escaped! They had flown away!

Clore trumpeted, "They know something! They know something important! I'm going to get them back, and I'm going to stay here until I do!"

"They belong to all of us," said Thob. "We'll all stay!"

"It wastes time," Clore screamed. "All of us being in the same place. That's why we lost them. We weren't paying attention because we were distracted by one another. We'd be more creative if we were apart, really apart!"

Momentary silence in the network. The matrix sparkled with pulses of light, with wandering thoughts.

"It would be more interesting," said Thob. "More interesting to be separate." She'd been doing some things separately, of course, but always with the possibility of interference.

"We could divide it up," Bland whispered. "Some for me, some for you. I could have my own places."

"My own places," echoed Breaze. Not that he hadn't taken some places as his own already. Brannigan was his. Just let any of the others try to get into Brannigan!

They glittered in the matrix, considering. It was Thob who moved first.

"I'll go," she said. "I'm going. I'm taking my share."

"Go, go, go," they echoed. "Our share."

"Separate me," Thob instructed the matrix. "I'm going."

For an instant the matrix hesitated, baffled by its own efficiency. If the original specifications had been in effect, none could have been separated until complete biological functions, reactions, behaviors had been restored. There were no such specifications. When Magna Mater Mintier Thob ordered the matrix to separate her, the matrix did so expediently, taking the consciousness labeled Thob (an assemblage including several hundred face-name patterns) and attaching to it a random quarter of the personality fragments and biological inventory.

Clore got a third of the balance.

Bland got half the remaining.

Breaze took what was left.

Three of the Brannigan assemblages moved off toward fresh nodes and pastures new. Clore remained, aware of space around him, of pressure removed. What had been a crowded boundary now stretched in all directions as open possibility. Places to fill with himself. Places to inhabit, to environ, to possess.

And, somewhere else, Orimar Breaze oozed around the boundaries of himself. At one time he would have walked. Still, he retained memories of walking, what walking was, of people walking, but these were only random images, without sense or application. All that complex of muscular and nervous instruction that makes up the movement concept of "walk" had gone to the others. Great Lord Breaze was left with earlier means of locomotion, with crawling and oozing and slithering around the boundaries of himself.

Except, there were no boundaries. All that feeling concept of in versus out, of me versus other, all that was gone. There was no skin. There was no edge. There were only spongy glimmers and shadowy vacancies. Breaze thrust a sponginess at a vacancy and pushed. Nothing there. Nothing at all. A hole. Like a tongue thrust into the place a tooth had been, the firm hardness of it gone, only the vacancy remaining.

But there had been something there. Something he had used for . . . What had he used it for? He remembered using it for something. For some purpose. Of limitation, perhaps. Of . . .

He couldn't remember. It was like a dream, like waking and half remembering a dream. And like that, it was unimportant. If it were important, he'd still have it, but he didn't, so . . . so . . .

So it had been unnecessary. He didn't need it.

". . . won't correct your patterns . . ." someone said.

"Jordel! You don't belong here."

But it wasn't Jordel. It was only a memory, something Jordel had said about correcting patterns. It made no sense? What patterns? Nothing needed correcting. Everything was fine now.

He perambulated around the space he had now, some of it environed, some not. So much space to fill with things. So much space to fill with himself, with his own creations.

His own religion. His own people. His own provinces, to rule as he saw fit. Oh, yes, it would be better this way. Far better to have one's own people, one's own rites, one's own . . . answers. For him, Mighty Crawler, Great Oozer, Lord God Breaze!

From the node near Deep, Chimi-ahm, Great Clore, determined to recapture those who had escaped. He created wheeled eyes to run along the riverbank, and other little eyes to swim upstream in the Floh, and still others to fly over the wall, into the unknown lands. The captives. He wanted them back. He wanted them back very much. The eyes would find them. In the water of the Floh, other things swam, listening for sounds and emitting sounds of their own, some repulsive, some attractive.

In the node, Clore decided he would go after them soon. In a distant place, Legless God Orimar Breaze decided he would go as well. And the others too. They would all go. Just as soon as the captives were found!

As she flew into the lower end of the gorge, Fringe found her sight blurring once again.

"Poison," she told herself, aloud.

"Wha' . . ." begged one or both of the boxes.

"Poison," she said again. "On those things they hit us with. I've got to set down. Use the med kit. . . ."

There was universal antidote in the kit. She should have used it before they left. She'd forgotten, that's all. Just forgotten. She should do it now, but she couldn't spare a hand to get it out just now, and the twins couldn't help. No place to land in the gorge. She'd have to wait until they came out of the gorge.

"Should have gone over it," she mumbled to herself. It would have been easier. She could have landed up there. But with the overhang of the looming walls, the curving passage of the river . . .

"No way," she advised herself owlishly. "Can't get there from here. Got to wait until I get out."

"Wha' . . ." pled the box again.

"Not much farther," she said. "Hardly any way at all." She concentrated on staying low, almost on the water. The air was quieter here, and the gorge was wider too, where the river had cut it most recently. Softer stratum, something told her. Water's reached a softer stratum.

She explained this at length to the twins as the walls of the gorge brightened and dimmed, swelled and receded. Not all of that was the drug, or poison, or whatever it had been. Some of it was real, she assured herself. The walls did change with the light, with the direction of flight.

And light was there, at the end, the gap, where the gorge ended. She wanted to laugh but didn't. She'd made it. There for a few minutes, she hadn't been sure she'd make it. Now she could set down and use the antidote. . . .

And she was past it, with only a short way farther of tumbled rock and then flatland, a place to set down. She kept it low, waiting for the rock to end, waiting to swerve toward the bank. . . .

The gaver that came from the river below was one of those that had attacked the *Dove*. She saw it coming. She hit the risers, watching her hand move, watching it take an hour to move, slowly, too slowly, watching the huge jaws gape, one on either side, the fangs coming toward her as in a dream, slowly.

The beast took the flier as a fish takes a fly, crunching it between huge jaws as it fell back down into the water, letting the flier break up when it hit the water.

Instinctively Fringe took a deep breath. She was caught between the instrument panel and the door. Water flooded around her, gray and cold. The opposite door had broken off and she saw the boxes float clear. She wanted to follow them but couldn't get loose, couldn't . . .

Then the remaining parts of the flier collapsed. She came out into the clear, stroked upward, rising, slowly rising. The square silhouettes of the boxes lay above her on the surface with shining halos around them.

The gaver released the inorganic shell to seize the flesh that had been within. A claw caught her, turned her over. The jaws took her. She felt a pain, a horrible pain, in the neck. He had her by the neck.

All right, get it over, get it over, she thought, not screaming, not howling, not drowning, still holding her breath, *just get it over.*

As he did, biting down, spitting out the smaller piece in favor of the larger one with all the blood in it.

The smaller piece flew up, into the shallows, rolled and rolled and rolled in the eddies near a protruding sandspit, coming to rest on the sand.

The boxes floated and screamed, making only bubbling noises. They moved manipulators, trying to swim, but the manipulators had not been made for swimming. When they bobbed to the surface, they screamed again, "Fringe!" the sound shrieking away over the flat banks, into nothing, receiving no response.

The eddies at the shore caught the boxes too, moved them next to the sandspit, half on, half off, rocked them there, on, off, on, off, each thrust pushing them a tiny bit higher, until at last they did not rock at all.

The river boiled and belched. From a reddened blotch, scraps of cloth floated up, fragments of the flier floated up, each to be caught by the eddy in its turn, each to be deposited upon the sand. The cloth was torn and darkly stained. Pinned to it was an Enforcer's badge. I Attend the Situation. A picture of an armed warrior and a gylph.

A dink moved and mumbled. A box worked its manipulators, trying to straighten the cloth, trying to see the badge that was pinned there. When it did so, it cried again, the other cried, making sounds that echoed strangely in the gorge behind them, the weeping of hopeless spirits, perhaps. The crying of ghosts.

The boxes did not turn, didn't know how to turn, so they did not see what lay behind them, Fringe's head, bloodless but largely intact, lying on the sand with them.

In the sand with them, for the sand was rising, blown by the wind, rising around them like a blanket.

"Why didn't we die?" Mechanical, weary, infinitely sad.

"Must be a way. Something here we can turn off. Something here we can unplug." Weary too. Determined.

Silence. The sand rises.

"We'll find a way. I promise." Bertran comforting Nela.

"Later, Berty. I'm so tired."

"Later."

And higher yet, moving gently across the boxes of the dinks, across the still face of the Enforcer, covering the torn fabric, the broken pieces of the flier.

"Poor Fringe. . . ." Nela, sounding almost human, sobbing.

"Poor Fringe."

The sand covered it all, smoothly, like a carpet.

From downriver came a ripple on the River Floh, a protruding wave-let, as might be made by an impatient fish, the wavelet spiked with a tiny eye on a stem, turning this way, turning that way, *look-look, see-see, what is this, what is that,* jabbing impetuous glances at the banks, the rocks, the river, the sandspit, searching for people, for a flier. It had heard a flier. A flier meant people.

But there were no people, no flier. Nothing but wind-sculpted sand and moving grass and the back of a huge gaver, floating slowly down-stream, the way they did when they had eaten or were hunting. The gaver had been summoned. The gaver was supposed to be here. The eye took no notice.

The eye dived down through the murky water, looking, looking. The river had already carried the flier parts away. They were far down-stream by now. On the bottom, however, something sparkled, and the eye went to that, focusing, fiddling. Nothing much. A circlet of gold, tiny, with words on it. *Just as she is.*

The circlet, the words were meaningless. The eye was looking for people or a flier. This wasn't people, wasn't a flier. The eye surfaced again. Nothing to report. It would go farther upstream and look again.

While behind it the sand moved in endless ripples, gently in the wind.

The *Dove* arrived at noplace.

Curvis, standing at the rail, saw pale buildings atop a nearby hill. He saw people, here and there. He saw tile-roofed dwellings scattered along the shore, beneath the shade of enormous trees. At some distance, among other trees, he saw the dragons.

Not Great Dragon. Not remotely related to Great Dragon. Though dragonish in appearance, these were entirely different beings.

He turned to speak to Jory, only to hear her cry out, reach out as though to grasp someone, then cry once more.

"What is it?"

"Fringe," she said brokenly. "Something's happened to her."

The old man took her by the shoulders.

"Tell me! What is it?"

"I'm not sure," she cried. "She was coming back. . . ."

"Then they've rescued her."

"But Danivon isn't there. Zasper isn't there."

"The twins?"

"I don't know. I can't tell. Oh, Asner. . . ."

"Shall we go there, where they are?"

She put her hands over her face, murmuring, "I don't know what to do. It's all lost. She's gone."

The old man held her while she cried. Held her and rocked her to and fro.

Curvis made no effort to comfort Jory. He merely nodded to himself, glad that Danivon hadn't been hurt. Zasper hadn't been hurt. Too bad about Fringe, but . . .

He looked back toward the dragons. Gone. Gone in under those trees. Vanished.

They had been wearing clothing. They had been carrying tools. And they were undoubtedly what he and Danivon had been sent to find.

FIVE

13

Zasper and Danivon moved along the water with the practiced lope learned in Academy and perfected over years of duty. In low-category places, Enforcers often went on foot, and it was necessary to move swiftly and tirelessly—and silently. There was no need to discuss strategy. Their entire strategy was to move and keep moving, to stay out of inhabited areas, to get through Beanfields and on west, past the wall, where, so Danivon had told Zasper in a few grunted words, the underground monsters probably hadn't gained a foothold yet. He had gained that impression from Jory, sniffed it out, though he would have been hard put to explain it.

Their scuttling anxieties kept up with their trotting legs for a time. Trying to keep watch on all sides was exhausting. As the miles went by without attack, however, the anesthetic of movement took over, and thoughts faded until suddenly Danivon stopped short, murmuring in a choked voice, "Wait. No. Fringe. . . ." He was sniffing the air, his face stiff with apprehension.

Zasper had sensed something too, though it didn't come to him as a smell. It came more as a sound, a far-off roaring, something surging and surflike. Wrongness. Not merely the general wrongness that went with Elsewhere and grew daily more deadly, but something more personal and grievous.

"Fringe," he said, acknowledging Danivon's concern. "And the twins?"

Danivon's nose twitched painfully, full of that stale, old-ice smell, lung filling, lung chilling, like breathing stagnant water. "Something wrong. Very wrong." Feeling a sob coming up in his throat. Oh, something terribly wrong.

Zasper wiped his face. "The twins?" he asked again in a voice he fought to keep dead calm. "All three of them?"

"I don't know. I can't smell anything about them. They could be . . . all right." He didn't mean all right. They hadn't been all right when he had seen them last. He merely meant he had no sense that they were dead, gone, unliving. But then, he had no sense they were living, either.

"How could they be all right and Fringe not?"

Danivon gulped, unable to breathe, aware of loss, as though an arm were gone, or his sight. This was grief. He'd never felt grief before, never lost anyone before.

"Do you get any feel for where they are?" Zasper persisted grimly.

Danivon's senses said westward. He pointed wordlessly. They were headed that way anyhow. No change of plans needed.

Zasper nodded, fighting to keep his mind still, his body relaxed. Enforcers had no time for grief. Time or not, he felt it, had to express it. "Danivon," he said evenly. "She was . . . she was like a daughter to me. Like family." He had never had any other family. She—and Danivon himself—were all there were.

"Don't say was," Danivon demanded angrily. "Oh, don't say was, Zasper. Maybe . . . maybe she's—I don't know. Maybe it isn't what we think. Maybe she's not dead. No. Something. . . ." He couldn't say what. Something else. Something even worse, maybe, he couldn't tell. "Don't say was. Just . . . just something wrong, that's all."

Talking would not help it, but he had to talk.

"She wouldn't . . . she wouldn't love me, Zasper. You were right about my loving her, but she wouldn't love me. She wanted to. I know she wanted to, but she wouldn't."

"She wants something else more," said Zasper. "Jory knows about it. About that wanting."

"What? What does she want more?"

"Damned if I know, Dan. There've been times maybe . . . when I was younger . . . when I felt like that. Wanting . . . wanting something else. Almost as though I had a hunger that had never been fed, some kind of tastebud that hadn't ever been stimulated or something. A hole in my mind asking to be filled. Something itching at me. You ever feel like that?"

Danivon shook his head. "Not that I know of. When I want something, I'm pretty sure what it is."

"Not Fringe. I've tried to figure her out since she was a little girl. She wants something that doesn't exist, maybe." He thought deeply. "She wants something beyond, Dan. I think . . . I believe there's a place of satisfaction, an attainable plateau, that suits ninety-nine point nine percent of all people. For those people there's a destiny that fills all their needs. That's the answer to the Great Question, maybe. But for that one in a thousand, or maybe even one in a million, other people's destiny is no good at all. Nothing will suit except a singularity. Fringe is one of those."

Danivon shook his head, not in disagreement but in dismay. "Oh, I wish . . ." What Danivon wished, Danivon didn't go on to say. Instead, he fell silent, mumbled to himself for a moment, then turned to check Zasper's wounds, which were painful but not serious, already healing under the balm of the med-kit growth agents and the universal antidote. After this, they ran once more. Time spun by, and distance, rock and tree, hill and valley, always the river sparkling on their right, bright or dim as clouds moved across the sky. At last, as they crested a hill and faced the lowe of the setting sun, they saw a shadowy line along the horizon to the northwest, as though an artist had brushed a long black stroke to separate earth and sky.

Danivon stopped and pointed. "The Great Wall west of Thrasis."

"West of Beanfields too. It makes a great circle all around the center of the continent, in fact."

Danivon nodded slowly in realization. The line had been on the maps, and he had known it was there—he had even seen it when in Thrasis— but the reality of its size hadn't come to him until now. "I wonder who built it? Jory could probably tell me."

Zasper, conscious of several aching vacancies, could not care about the wall at the moment. "We brought food?" he asked, mopping his face. "I hope."

"Yes," Danivon replied, turning from his examination of the lands to the west. "Field rations in my leg packs. We need water. We'll get down to the river."

"Tributary streamlet just below us," Zasper said, pointing. "How long shall we keep moving?"

"Until it's too dark to move at all. If it's clear, there may be enough starlight reflected off the river to keep going. Can we run faster than they can build?"

Zasper barked weary laughter. "Than they can build the network, yes. But there's nothing to prevent their creating autonomous units, flying eyes and ears, maybe even killing machines. We can do it, so I assume they can. Anything we can do, they can do . . . and more."

"Damn," said Danivon, who had not considered autonomous machines. "Then that's what I've been seeing." He turned to stare back along their trail. At the limit of sight swarmed sparkles, brightnesses, reflective gleams, growing larger and more obvious even as they watched. Something or somethings had found their trail and was coming very swiftly along it.

Zasper saw them and cursed as he did a quick inventory of the weapons and devices he carried, plus those built into his clothing and into his body, regretting those he'd had removed when he retired. Built-in weapons were useful, but damned uncomfortable. Now he wished for every one he'd ever had.

"Another thing," he grunted, pointing to a fold of ground to the west, where a glimmer of lights moved near the river. "We're going through Beanfields, and we have no mother with us nor any pass from Mother-dear."

Danivon bit his cheeks in frustration. He hadn't considered that, either.

Shallow under the sand lie Nela and Bertran Zy-Czorsky, bits and pieces of them tucked away in impenetrable vitreon, unbreakable dura-plast. Not far away is buried what is left of Fringe Owldark, her shredded, blood-drained head, more or less intact. The sand is dry on top where the wind combs it into sparkling surfaces, but it is moist beneath. Between the grains small darknesses gather, tiny dampnesses, miniscule wombs of wet from which something, no doubt, could grow.

Something, no doubt, has grown. All the sandspit is full of rootlets, fibers, hair-thin, thread-fine, wavering between the sand grains with blunt, exploring noses, wriggling like elvers, slithering like snakes, soft little fibers, moist and tender, gathering and multiplying like mold on bread, cell by cell. Inevitably, eventually, the tip of a fiber touches the side of a dinka-jin case, touches, withdraws, then comes back to touch again, exploring this thing like a carapace that has something living inside. It finds a molecule of vitreon, tastes it, extrudes a molecule of its own that fastens tight, like a key in a lock, and sucks it out with a tiny plop like marrow from a bone, a sound too feeble to be heard by any creature larger than a virus. Yum, says the fiber. The vitreon molecule is savored, its atoms passed down the length of the fiber, disintegrated as it goes. Oh, yum, yes, tasty. Very nice. Patiently, molecule by molecule, the fibers chew at the stuff of the cases, nibbling a tiny erosion, which becomes a microscopic pit, then a hair-thin hole.

Through the hole the fibers race, coiling and recoiling in their eagerness. Oh, see what's here, what this is, what that is. Oh, look, here a bone, there a cell, here an organ, here a mechanism. Ugh, nasty mechanism. Ugly and difficult. Inefficient. Painful. Still, interesting. Everything is interesting. This connects to that. This has been disconnected from something that should be here. Fill in the blank. What was it? What could it have been? What should it be? Feel, smell, taste, extrapolate.

Those fibers not engaged in exploration continue to nibble at the edges of the hole, though by now there are thousands of them thickly furring the outside of the case, thousands of little tongues making infinitesimal erosions of their own. Soon the vitreon is perforated like a sieve, then lacy as a doily, then only a fragile net, more holes than substance, then gone. What was inside is now outside, free, cradled, and covered by the fibers.

Nela sleeps. Bertran sleeps. They have retreated into dream, into a world of sleekness, of sinuosity, of easy movement rejoicing in its own grace. This is an old gift, this sanctuary of dream. They feel no pain. They have been released from horror too dreadful to bear. Where they are is in the world of antithesis where they live in movement and delight.

The fibers ramify. Here they like the taste of a cell, so they duplicate it, not once but a thousand times in a coiling chain. There they miss a flavor, so they create it, a new cell, of a new type. Here they form a sinew. There a bone. All very quietly. All very peacefully, not to disturb the dreamers who are all unaware of where they are, of what they were, of what they are.

Nela dreams she stands upon the precipice, looking out across the world. Around her the birds swirl in a joyous cloud, calling to her. She opens her wings and drops into their midst singing.

Bertran leaps from the surface of the sea, turns nose down and dives deep, bending and twisting as he follows his fellows in the spiraling downward dance. At the lowest point he turns to follow chains of bubbles upward in a single, pure curve that ends as he erupts laughing upon the silver waters.

"Nela," he cries in a sea giant's voice, calling to the sky, raising a finned hand, a fingered fin, in a gesture of greeting.

"Bertran," she answers in a wind sound, drifting over the waters. Her wings brush him as she skims the surface. The breath of her passing cools his face.

Under the sand, a fiber eats a mechanism, atom by atom. Nasty, this, but it is necessary to digest it and get it out of the way. Metal and hydrocarbons dissolve, tiny chunk by tiny chunk. The wave generator of a gravitic unit sighs and falls apart into constituent elements. The mechanical linkages of a manipulator give up their coherence. Fibers carry the elements away, some to the river to be washed downstream, some to remote stone outcroppings, to be deposited upon the stone atom by atom, some deep beneath the grasses and reeds of the bank. If anyone comes to this place equipped with detection gear, searching, let us say, for certain elements found in vitreon or in dinka-jin mechanisms, those elements are no longer assembled, they are no longer present.

The vitreon cases hold skulls, hard shells of bone minus the jaws. The fibers take them apart, cell by cell, then rebuild them differently. What is this inside? Are there instructions here inside?

Gray leaf and gray tree and gray wind rising.

What is that?

Sorrow, fleeing from sorrow, swimming, diving.

This small, shelled thing, climbing, climbing. What is this? Does the other one have this thing too?

Here too. Sorrow, sorrow. Climbing, climbing. Turtledove, oh, Turtledove.

Instructions? Perhaps. Though this large mind seems too big, too intelligent to be contained in the little shelled being, which is moved by . . . by longing to fly. By a longing for wings.

It is small, yes, but important. Keep it.

Upon the naked bone, skin forms and a covering for that skin. At the knobbed white ends of joints, cartilage forms, then other bones. At the juncture of organ with organ, other organs form and rebuild themselves—or build themselves for the first time in new systems, in accordance with the dreams.

All of it goes on below the surface. All of it happens in the warm dark of the sandspit, moisture below, sun above. On the top, everything is still and level, rippled only a little by the breezes, otherwise flat and unrevealing. Tiny eyes forge up and down the river at the end of busy little stems. They jab glances like needles, here, there, searching in irritated lunges for something they do not find. The captives have gone. Where have they gone? In his node near the Deep, mighty Chimi-ahm wants to know. From a distant place, Legless God Breaze wants to know!

A flier comes, a buzzing bee-sized botherance, one of a numerous hive of such mechanical busybodies. It settles upon the sandspit in the quiet of late afternoon. After a time of turning and staring, it attempts to take off again and cannot. Though it struggles and hums, eventually it succumbs to a deadly ennui, an inability to hold itself together. It has no integrity. It becomes convinced of this fact as it sheds itself, layer by layer, into the inquisitive network below the sand.

At noplace, the sailors unloaded crates and sacks and the baggage of the passengers. The dragon shapes beneath the trees had vanished. People gathered, murmuring to Asner and Jory.

Curvis, standing at the rail, stared rudely at the place the dragons had gone, for once almost speechless.

Cafferty brought on deck the girl child, still pale and inclined to starts and trembles, but no longer terrified.

"This is Alouez," Cafferty introduced her. "I have told her that now, for a time, she will be our foster daughter."

Latibor murmured his name, took Alouez by the hand, reassured her with a smile, a nod. Curvis kept his eyes on the shore, refusing to take part in this ritual of comfort. The girl belonged back there, in Derbeck, not here, being greeted and accepted as though she were part of a family. Only when the others had gone ashore did he follow, approaching Jory to jab a finger in the direction of the vanished dragon forms.

"These are not kin to your beast, are they!" It wasn't a question, for he already knew the answer. Jory's beast had something of the mythical about it, something of the ultimately strange. The dragon shapes that had departed were real beings. Not human at all, but flesh and blood nonetheless. Scales and fangs too, no doubt, but simple flesh for all that.

"No, Curvis, they are not kin to Great Dragon," she said, looking up at him from brimming eyes.

"These are no doubt what we were sent to investigate," he said firmly, ignoring her grief. From what he had overheard, the old woman thought something had happened to Fringe. So long as it had not happened to Danivon, Curvis would not allow himself to be upset.

"No doubt," she said, drying her eyes.

"And you've always known who, or what, they are?"

"Always since I came to Elsewhere, yes." She paused, exchanging a look with Asner. "If you are wise, Curvis, you'll stop staring after them, stop pointing in their direction, stop behaving like a child at a zoo."

"I suppose you'll tell me why I should," he snarled.

"Because it is not good manners, and the Arbai put a very high value upon good manners."

He didn't think he'd heard her correctly. He tried several different words in his mind, other words she might have said, finally muttering, "The Arbai?"

"The Arbai. All who are left of them."

"What are they doing here?" he blurted, unable to keep his eyes from wandering to the place he had seen them last. "What in hell. . . . How did they get here?"

"Through an Arbai Door," said Asner. "When the Brannigans first explored the shores of Panubi, they found an Arbai Door. They took it. It's now at Tolerance, so I'm told."

"There is one at Tolerance, yes, the one the twins came through," agreed Curvis distractedly. "I don't recall that it was originally found on Panubi."

"There's no particular reason you should have known," Jory said. "At any rate, there was an Arbai Door here, and the Arbai came through it, running from the plague. They shut the Door behind them, or thought they did, though they must have left it open to some linkages because Asner and I came through it. We found the Arbai remnant here on Panubi. They were few, a fragment, believing they were still in danger from the plague, terrified of us for fear we'd brought it with us. . . ."

"We were able to reassure them about that," said Asner. "The plague was long over by then."

"As a thank-you gesture, they invited us to stay if we liked. Later, when the first scout ships of the Brannigans were sighted, the Arbai moved into the center of the continent and built the wall to mark their own enclave, theirs by right of prior settlement."

"But they didn't take the Door with them?" demanded Curvis.

"They didn't intend to use it again, so they left it where it was."

"And you didn't intend to use it, either?"

They didn't answer.

"And the people?" Curvis nodded toward the people standing here and there on the hillside, among the buildings. "The humans?"

"Our people. People Asner and I have recruited to help us."

"Help you do what?"

"Help us find out what was going on out there in Elsewhere. We ourselves were not always . . . available to travel about, asking questions. We'd become very worried about the people on Elsewhere, and no one else seemed to know what was happening, or care."

"And you live here, you and the old man?"

"Just over that hill. Asner and I have a house there, and a garden."

"And a meadow full of horses, and a porch with a rocking chair and a cat," said Asner in a sarcastic tone. "All of which, though long coveted, are little used."

"Where did the people come from?" Curvis demanded angrily.

"Either they or their parents were recruited from Elsewhere."

"Like Cafferty and Latibor." He gestured toward the two, standing beside them.

"We recruited them, yes. As children. Brought them here, and reared them."

"For which we have always been thankful . . ." said Latibor.

"Interfering in the affairs of a province!" interrupted Curvis in a peremptory tone.

Jory shook her head at him. "Oh, Curvis, stop sounding outraged. Cafferty and Latibor were babies left for dead, so it didn't make much difference if we took them or not. I fished them out of the Fohm, if you must know! They got their webs removed later. We've only recruited children or young people who really wouldn't be missed very much. People like Fringe."

"Zasper would have missed Fringe!" Curvis's words defended Zasper's affections, though his tone said he thought it a foolishness to miss anyone.

"He would have, yes. We found that out. That's why we left her in Enarae instead of bringing her here."

Curvis much desired to be angry. He much desired to have something to be angry about. "If you're so busy saving people, why didn't you save Danivon as a baby? Why did Zasper have to do that?"

Jory shrugged. "It was one of those times we weren't . . . available.

Cafferty and Latibor couldn't reach us. We didn't even know they'd had a child—it wasn't the smartest thing to have done, under the circumstances."

"It wasn't," agreed Cafferty. "The threat to Danivon happened very suddenly. We did what we thought was best."

"And it all worked out," said Asner. "Sometimes things do work out."

The sailors came down the plank, carrying the last of their baggage. Those ashore scarcely had time to say farewell before the ship had pushed off again and was out in midriver, moving downstream, the men at the sweeps crying their ceaseless "Hauu-lah, hauu-lah."

"It seems I am to stay awhile," Curvis muttered.

"As our guest," said Jory. "Come, be our guest. Everyone be our guest."

"Do I have a choice?" He stared around him, at the great trees—larger than any he had seen heretofore on Elsewhere—at the simple tile-roofed buildings clustered beneath them, at the grassy slope stretching up to a summit crowned with other structures: temples, perhaps, or monuments. The acropolis had a certain formality about it, a reasoned arrangement that spoke of ritual purposes: flights of wide stairs, pillars, porticos, and domes, each calling to each in a simplicity of completion. Above the building rose trees even larger than those at the riverside, looming giants whose enormous branches stretched over the structures like verdant clouds.

A human person came from the shade of these trees and moved rapidly down the hill toward them.

"What is that?" Curvis gestured toward the buildings on the hilltop.

"That is their center of government," said Jory. "Such as it is."

"Ah. Then I suggest we go there now and arrange for reinforcements to be sent to the aid of Danivon and Zasper."

Jory shook her head slowly, ruefully. "You may ask, if you like, but it will do no good."

"You mean they're unfriendly?"

"They're not at all unfriendly. They just won't intervene in anything beyond the wall."

Curvis considered this. Though he couldn't find it in himself to care greatly about Zasper or Fringe or the twins, he cared a good deal about Danivon.

"I was a fool to let him go with the old man. I should have gone with him!" He turned a suspicious face on the surrounding crowd, receiving untroubled glances in return. It was obvious these people felt no awe for Enforcers, and this merely added to his irritation. "I'll go to these Arbai and demand . . ."

The person, reaching the bottom of the hill, came toward them, hugged Jory briefly, then whispered rapidly into her ear.

Jory sighed. "It seems the Arbai are aware of your intent, Curvis, and they wish to forestall it. The current deciders are sending us a formal message."

"Current deciders?" asked Curvis.

Jory said, "They are not a numerous people, and each of them takes a turn at the duty of deciding things. They'll send one of our people as messenger."

"What's to keep us from going to them?"

"The fact they've told us to await a message. It means they don't want to talk to us. Maybe they're tired of hearing about it. Or possibly they're annoyed with me."

"Because of Thrasis," said Asner. "Well, you knew they would be. You pushed the limits there, Jory."

She shrugged, again with that rueful smile. "No doubt. Well, I think Asner and I will go home. You're welcome to come with us." She led the way across the open riverside into the trees, through the narrow neck of woodland, and out onto an open meadow where a small brown house crouched low to the ground. It seemed too small to house them all, but as they came closer, they saw a long wing extending from the far side.

"You'll find rooms in the guest wing," said Jory. "You, Curvis. And Cafferty and Latibor, and Alouez, of course."

"In the guest wing," said Cafferty with a glance at Latibor. "Of course."

They went in through an open door, across wide-planked floors strewn with woven rugs, through the door in the corner and down a shining corridor where doors stood open into rooms for each of them, as though the house had known how many guests to prepare for.

"We'll have lunch when you're ready," Jory called after them. "Have a wash, or a rest."

Obediently, they went into their rooms. Curvis paused in the room only long enough to note that it held a bed large enough for even his giant frame. He dropped his baggage and went out the window, telling himself he would not be penned up in any structure until he knew what lay around it, how it could be defended, and how attacked.

Horses raised their heads and whickered at him as he passed, then went back to grazing. Behind the house a small building was home to the flock of birds that clucked and muttered, pecking at invisibilities in the soil. A little farther back, at the top of the rounded hill, he found two carved stones.

He read the inscriptions: "Jory, born Marjorie Westriding, Planet Earth, Sol system, twenty-second century of the common era. Master of the Hunt. Far-traveler. Prophetess emeritus."

"Asner, born Samasnier Girat, Planet Ahabar, Bogar system, thirty-seventh century of the common era. Myth-eater. Missionary. Fellow far-traveler. Retired."

Almost four thousand years had elapsed since Jory's century and the current one. During most of that time she must have been in stasis between Doors. Like the twins. And Asner too. Curvis ran his fingers across the stones. He had seen such monuments before, prepared by old folks or their families, so the old ones could be assured of their own memorials. It was custom in a dozen provinces he knew of.

He returned to find food set out on a terrace-cum-porch, where Jory rocked slowly in her chair, a large black-and-white cat in her lap and a clutter of kittens at her feet.

Later they all went with Cafferty to pick fruit from the tiny orchard and sat eating it on the sun-warmed wall of the terrace. They drowsed in the peace of the afternoon. And finally they saw the same woman who had spoken to them that morning come out of the trees at the bottom of the meadow and move slowly up the hill toward them.

"Well, comes the messenger," said Jory. "To tell us what the Arbai have to say even though we already know what they have to say."

Her matter-of-fact tone made Curvis simmer. He was still thwarted in his anger, not sure he knew why. Except . . . except that as an Enforcer he was accustomed to being in charge and he was not in charge. Not here. He wasn't sure who was in charge. Not Jory, which somewhat surprised him. Not Asner.

"Patience," said Latibor, noting Curvis's heightened color. "No point in being annoyed."

"I'm annoyed because if we're going to get help for Danivon, we ought to get on with it. We Enforcers have a saying: 'The right help helps, and enough help helps, but help that's in time helps most.' "

Latibor shook his head, murmuring, "Curvis, I want to help Danivon as much as you do. Even though he's a stranger to us, Cafferty and I can see in him the child we loved. We want to save him from harm, but there's no way we can do it ourselves and we know the Arbai won't."

"We haven't asked yet. At least, *I* haven't!"

"Oh, yes you have. Believe me, the Arbai are aware of every thought you've had since you've been here."

". . . And here she is," Jory said.

The woman held up her scroll and bowed. Jory bowed. They exchanged a few words in a sibilant tongue. Then the woman unrolled the scroll and began reading in the same language.

Cafferty murmured a translation: "The Arbai are aware that you would like to help your friends beyond the wall. The Arbai sympathize with your desires. The Arbai, however, have adopted a philosophical position that prevents the Arbai Device from—"

Curvis blurted, "The Arbai Device! Jory said there was no such thing on Panubi!"

"She really didn't say that," Asner corrected him in a hushed voice. "She merely questioned whether such a device could have coexisted with your vaunted diversity. There is such a device, but it is used only on this side of the Great Wall."

"But. . . ."

"Shhh," said Cafferty. "Don't interrupt, Curvis. They're a patient people. They don't mind my translating for you, but they'd consider interrupting their messenger to be abysmal bad manners."

The woman finished her speech, rolled up her scroll, bowed, and departed down the meadow once more.

Cafferty said, "The message concluded thusly: *'The people of Elsewhere chose to come here, chose to live in the manner of their ancestors, chose their gods, their rites, their way of life and death. We respect their choice and will not interfere with it.'* "

Curvis shook his head, baffled.

Jory sighed. "You diplomatically left out the bit about Thrasis, Cafferty. The Arbai are quite annoyed about Thrasis. My argument is, of course, that the *women* of Thrasis had never chosen anything until I gave them a choice."

"I don't understand the problem about helping Danivon," growled Curvis. "We're not proposing to change anything in the provinces."

"It should be very clear, Curvis. They won't interfere anywhere in Elsewhere."

"Even to save Danivon's life?" demanded Curvis.

"Listen to yourself," exploded Jory, her old voice trembling. "What was it you said to Fringe about Alouez? You were ready to turn Fringe in to the powers-that-be for interfering in Derbeck! What was it you and Danivon said about the child in the basket? Just the way things were, right? Nothing to get upset about. What was that argument in Molock about? What have you said repeatedly about diversity and the status quo? Only days ago you were snarling at Fringe for saying what you just said! What of your Enforcer's oath? Is all that suddenly nothing?"

"But Danivon is one of us," he cried angrily. "He's an Enforcer. He belongs to us."

"Almost without exception," said Jory, holding on to Asner's arm with all her strength, "everyone belongs to someone."

At the node near the Deep, Lord God Subble Clore lost touch with some of the remote eyes and ears that had gone beyond the wall, but the losses did not distract him from his preoccupation. He was creating new boundaries for himself. Now that the others had gone, there was a lot of space to fill with one invention or another, one environ or another. He needed to center himself, to determine his essential nature. It was time to stop playing games, time to quit hiding behind minor demons and reveal himself, time to begin issuing commandments, time to assert his divinity!

In another node, Orimar Breaze also considered his godhood. His followers would be called Breazians. He would demand behaviors and customs peculiar to himself. He would make rules, complicated rules, and many of them, that would take a lot of time and trouble and pain to keep. The only way he could know that his people truly loved him would be if they obeyed many onerous rules. There should be many rituals, also, rituals for everything. Much crawling. He liked the idea of crawling. Slithering, even. Also, abstentions from . . . from anything pleasurable.

He tried to remember what things were pleasurable. What were they? It had been such a long . . . so many . . . so . . . Was it sex? He seemed to remember it was sex. And food. Food had been pleasurable. So, he would make many rules about sex, many rules about food. If the rules were difficult enough, they would be cause for much backsliding, and that, in its turn, would be cause for much reproval! He would force . . . He would make people . . . He would punish them until they . . .

Though he could not remember the taste of food or wine, the feel of love, the joys of human movement, he felt a surge of pure pleasure at the idea of power. He would conduct himself properly as a god, using sweet and seductive words at first; then, if that failed, using power and pain to teach his people to adore him.

Evening came, and with it the cool and the dusk. The sandspit crawled in the evening wind, granules moving in rolling rivulets, making new ripples as they slid away from what lay beneath. Something was being uncovered here beside the river. Several somethings.

One had wings. One had webbed feet. Both were man-sized, with heads slightly larger than one might expect. One was sleek and furred; the other had feathers. Both of them slept.

One shape stretched and turned, half unfurling a wing. One moved a foot, stretching long-nailed toes apart, revealing the webbing between them.

An eye at the end of its stalk came back down the river, peering, peering, back and forth, back and forth, look-look, listen-listen! It stopped dead in the water. Afar, Great Crawler, Lord God Orimar's monitor picked up the image, compared it to acceptable images, and screamed anomaly. The eye went closer to shore, raising itself higher on its stem. What it saw was true. There were anomalous beings upon the sandspit. The monitor compared the images to others it found in Files. Here was a bird, a not-bird, an angel maybe, a huge feathered something resting on the sand, a gylph. And there, there beside the bird was an otter, maybe an otter, maybe something else, a seal, perhaps (Files refers to ancient catalogs of beasts, looking for the right one). The eye wasn't sure, except that they lived. Their chests moved up and down. They breathed.

They had no business there. Not the otter-seal, not the angel-gylph.

The eye pulsed a scream for Great Crawler, Lord God Breaze. The scream was picked up by Chimi-ahm, Great God Clore, who sent eyes of his own to see. Lord God Subble Clore looked and did not believe, saw and could not convince himself it was real. These beings were a trick. A delusion. Somebody feeding false images down the line toward him. Somebody being stupid.

The beings opened their eyes. They stared into the little sensors hovering over the water without seeing them, conscious of something dreadfully different, perhaps wrong.

Afar, Legless God Orimar Breaze howled rage and resentment at this nonsense. There were only two classes of beings: adorers or persecutors. Someone, probably Clore (who else would be as hostile?), was setting a trap for him! He made circumferential accusations and received tangential denials. He confronted and was confronted in return. He shouted. (He believed he shouted, he was convinced he shouted, though those he shouted at were unaware of it. How does a circuit shout? How does a pattern convey fury?)

"No," Bland replied from some distant node. "No, Breaze. All imagination. It's in your created world, no doubt, a dream."

"No," transmitted Thob from a node more distant yet. She believed Breaze was lying, but she chose to pretend to take the matter seriously. "Something you remember from some old mythology, Breaze. Why would I waste time manufacturing angels."

They were playing games with him, Breaze thought. Perhaps they had even arranged the escape of the prisoners! Perhaps they were plotting against him!

But in the node near the Deep, Clore summoned all his powers and made certain demands upon the network, certain demands upon the great factory in the Core. The very presence of these anomalous creatures demanded violent and definitive response. They had intruded upon his world, and he would kill them. He would kill the former captives first. Then he would find the other escapees and kill them too. Also, and most particularly, he looked forward to the long slow killing of the two men who had stolen the prisoners, during which he would find out if Breaze and Bland and Thob had put them up to it!

Furry self tried to move his eyes without moving any of the rest of him. This was not himself, not his own self, soft skin, tender hide, throbbing jointure, thub-a-thub of heart, huff of lungs, not any of that, something other than, else. This was dream time, asleep time, but without sleep's certainty and ease. Oh, no, this was wakening and he was afraid to look.

"What are you?" asked a voice, Nela's voice.

His head turned of itself toward the voice (he hadn't willed it to move at all) and saw a feathered creature there, not Nela, even though the voice had been Nela's voice. Why then was Nela's face atop this being? This bird-type being, this winged thing, fluffed and sleek with feathers? Why Nela's face scanning its feathered arms and legs, Nela's face weeping, mouth stretched wide in a rictus of some unanticipated feeling. Joy? Probably not.

"Bertran!" she cried, and the sound was unmistakably terror.

He didn't tell himself to move, and yet there he was leaping up to take her beneath his left arm where she belonged, where she lived, where she had always been, she half crouching, trying to get into her accustomed position, all the time crying, "Bertran, Bertran," as though he were far away, not here beside her. "Bertran," she cried again, as one bereft. "Hold me!" Even as she cried for him to hold her, she pushed the other thing away, tried to fight the furry thing off, to thrust this stranger away, to escape from it.

He held her, though he was as terrified as she, at her appearance, at her violence, at his own being lost in this strange skin, inside this strange body. He shuddered in a spasm of terror, and she broke away to fall huddled on the ground, screaming as though this separation were some new violation.

She crouched nearby, her eyes shut, panting an echo of his own heaving breath, making similar panicky noises.

"Nela," he shouted in near hysteria, trying to control himself. "You . . . we're changed, that's all. We've been changed." He shut his eyes tightly, not to see her, not to see himself. If he could not see, it was less dreadful!

"Change me back!" she screamed. "Change me back!"

"You hated that box," he yelled, eyes still closed. "You hated it!" She had, he had, but maybe the changes were worse, worse even than that!

"Not the box. Not the box. Us. The way we were."

The words went spinning off into nothingness. Oh, the way we were. Silence greeted the words. Quick breaths, but no other sound. The way we were. Who would listen to a plea to put them back the way they were when they had prayed so long to be something else?

"Nela, stop crying!"

Nela's eyes opened, almost against her will. "I'm changed," she said. "Berty, we're changed."

"I thought you wanted to be," cried Bertran. "You told me you did."

"Did," Nela moaned. "Did. Not like this. All of a sudden. No time. No time to get . . ."

"We wanted to be separated," cried Bertran.

"But we wanted to be us! We didn't not want to be us!"

"How do we know what we are," shouted Bertran. "All you're doing is howling!"

She caught her breath. There had been something of Sizzy in those words, something of old Sister Jean Luc saying calm down. Stop having hysterics. Look around!

Which she did, slowly, with many false starts. She wasn't hideous, Bertran wasn't hideous. Not themselves, but not awful. Not ugly. Not human, but not ugly. Better than the boxes. Some better. But . . . but they were freakish still. There would be no others like themselves. It took no time to realize this. They knew at once they were still oddities, still sideshow stuff, platform people. "See the seal-man, umpteenth wonder of the world, he dives, he floats, he eats raw fish. See the bird-woman. . . ."

"It was all those dreams," whispered Nela. "All those dreams of flying, Berty. Whatever did this read my dreams. I didn't mean them for real, but it thought I did."

Examining his webbed feet, Bertran knew she was right. He hadn't meant it either. A fantasy, that was all. An indulgent fantasy, assiduously cultivated as one drifted off into sleep, a substitute for infantile thumb-sucking or adolescent masturbation. A fairy tale to while away a drowsy afternoon, this dream of floating, diving, plunging through emerald depths of liquid joy. Himself was what he really wanted. Himself as he might have been.

Still, it was better than the box.

He said so, and Nela caught her breath in a gasp of remembered horror. Oh, yes, better than the box.

Bertran sat up to run his webbed fingers down his sides, feeling them sleek and continuous from under the arms, across the ribs, down the flank, onto the hip, down the thigh. Continuous. Single. No longer joined.

Nela opened her wings and dragged them down, feeling the stiff slide of quill against quill, hearing a silken rattle of movement. Her feet left the ground. She reacted with panic and dismay. "My bones are hollow," she whispered, terrified by her lightness. "Even my skull is hollow."

She ran her hands down her feathered breast, continuous and sleek. "Probably I can fly."

"I can swim," said the otter simultaneously, remembering his dream, letting the delights of that dream move him out and down into the shallows of the river, across the sandy bottom into the depths. He disappeared, erupting from the ripples moments later to come staggering and trembling back onto the sand, coughing water. "Cold," he cried. "Cold and full of strange things." It was not like the dream.

Nela, moved by a like impulse, had sprung into the air and circled upward. Suddenly she looked down, cried terror, and fell, wings thrashing, to tumble sobbing onto the sand nearby. "High," she wept. "Oh, high, and all alone!"

They cried for a time, wondering, lost, their ignorance and confusion as frightening as their structure. They felt part terror, part curiosity, much loneliness. Their identities were true, but all else was conjecture.

Bertran squirmed on the pebbles, getting slowly to his feet. He could stand upright. Or he could walk on all fours. Either one. "It was that thing, the one Jory spoke of, the Arbai thing," he said dully.

"The Arbai Device?" asked Nela. "The one she was talking about on the ship? Jory said that was a communication device." This was mere conversation, for she knew that Bertran was right. The moment he said it, both of them recognized the rightness of it. Of course. They had been saved, transformed, by the Arbai Device.

Bertran touched her leg with one webbed hand. "It is a communication device. That's what happened. We've communicated. All our fantasies, our dreams, they've been communicated. To . . . to something."

"Oh, yes," Nela commented as she staggered across the sand to sit beside him, fitting herself beneath his arm in her usual place. "Just like Mama used to read us stories. This time we told our own stories. . . ."

Silence on the sandspit. Out of the sky a thing came at them suddenly, a tiny flying thing full of ugly danger. Bertran put up a quick paw and deflected it onto the sand where it lay groaning and screaming to itself. Writhing fibers lassoed it and joined instantaneously into a fibrous casing. The thing became a buzzing lump upon the sand. Then it was nothing at all.

"The monsters out there want to kill us," Bertran said. "The gods. Those things. They hate us because we escaped." He knew this was true, just as he knew other things.

"They can't kill us here," said Nela. "They might hurt us, but they can't kill us."

"But they can kill everyone else," Bertran commented.

"All our friends!" cried Nela. "Oh, everyone we met, all dead."

"The sailors on the Curward ship," mourned Bertran. "The froggy people of Shallow. The music makers of Choire, and the Heron Folk of Salt Maresh. The Houm and the Murrey in Derbeck."

"All of them," wept Nela. "All of them." Tears flowed from her human eyes and down onto bird feathers, making them soggy. She grieved, and her grief was noticed by the probing network that occupied her as it did the interstices in the sand. Her sorrow was real, a part of gray leaf and gray tree and gray wind rising. A part of that small crawling thing.

Silence from within.

"I want to find Jory," said Nela. "I want to talk to Jory. Come with me to find Jory, Bertran."

She folded her wings and stumbled off along the river, inexplicably headed in the right direction. After a moment Bertran followed her, humping his body along behind her, finding this gallumphing progress weird but efficient.

Perhaps when they found Jory, he would decide whether it was worth it to go on living.

Behind them both, the sand lay level and still in the sunlight, no ripple betraying what still lay beneath.

For a time, it seemed to Zasper and Danivon that they would reach the wall before the things behind them caught up with them. For a time they thought they would get there without being observed by any of the people of Beanfields, either. There was open woodland much of the way, with good cover and solid footing, and they were making very good progress. Though they observed persons working in fields inland, though they could not avoid coming out into the open occasionally, as when fording streams, no one seemed to know they were there, no one got in their way, and they became almost convinced as the day wore on that they would come to the wall without trouble.

Then they reached a region where the trees had been cleared, a strip of bare, high land, where they could both see and be seen, and noticed behind them the telltale glitter of something coming very fast along the riverside.

"That's bigger than it ought to be," said Zasper soberly. "The things back there near the cavern were very small."

Danivon moved rapidly into cover. "So maybe this is a bunch of them stuck together," he said, telling more truth than he knew. What was coming behind was, indeed, a lot of them stuck together that were capable of coming apart again with fatal intent.

"What do you think guides it," panted Zasper. "Heat detector?"

"Possibly. Or just sound. You're breathing like a gaver in rut."

"Courtesy, boy," muttered Zasper. "Either case dictates evasive action."

Danivon didn't bother to reply. The standard formula applied. Get quiet. Get cool. Cool meant water. The river was a considerable distance to their right, through some badly cut up country, so they headed downhill at their best speed, praying there would be a stream at the bottom. Running water, if deep enough, would mask the heat of their bodies. Running water, if swift enough, would hide the sound of their breathing as well.

What they found was a murky pool, and not much of that.

"I hate mud puddles," Zasper groaned to himself, busy cutting a large reed into a breathing tube. "Would you like to bet there will be at least a dozen chaffers in there?"

"No bet," snarled Danivon, busy with a tube of his own.

They trampled about in the pool, muddying it still further, then slid into it with all their belongings, their heads among the reeds, each with a single finger wearing a detection tip extended to the surface of the water.

They detected the thing arriving. After a time they detected it departing. They waited, and it came back again.

"Tracker?" signaled Danivon with a finger on Zasper's hand.

"Wait," signaled Zasper in return.

The thing went away for a second time. Again the thing came back.

"Tracker?" signaled Danivon again. "Smeller."

"You go left, I'll go right," signaled Zasper, scarcely finishing before Danivon erupted from the pool beside him. Their weapons fired almost as one; the thing came apart into its constituent parts, some of which were very lively and quite deadly.

Sometime later, Danivon finished bandaging his leg, and Zasper the long cut along his ribs, which he had managed to stop bleeding but which nothing could stop hurting. He felt he had been sliced by a giant venomous insect.

"They're getting nasty. There was a new kind of poison on those blades," said Zasper, then more plaintively, "we're filthy!"

"All to the good," said Danivon, burrowing in his leg packs for something he had trouble finding. "Here. Native growth scent pads."

Zasper rubbed the things over his hands, then strapped them over his boots. The device had tracked them by smell. If a breeze came up to dissipate the aroma of their passing—though they mostly smelled of mud at the moment—the scent pads would mask their footsteps and anything they touched with their hands. "The next one will be worse," he commented. "You know that."

Danivon merely grunted.

If there was another one, it did not follow them from the muddy pool. They saw things on their back trail, but nothing came close. Time went by; they began almost to relax, and it was with a good deal of shocked surprise that they came out of a narrow defile into a wider patch of woodland to be suddenly seized up by a company of Mother-dear's sister guards.

As Danivon remarked later, even surprised as they were, they could have disposed of the sister guards if only they had had license to do so. Unfortunately, there was no complaint and disposition against the women of Beanfields.

Zasper, who had never been in Beanfields, tried to explain who they were and was knocked on the head.

"Boys do not speak until spoken to," said the sister-in-charge. "You will have an opportunity soon enough to tell your story to Mother-dear herself. It was she who told us to watch for your coming."

All their weapons were removed, except the ones the sisters did not find. All their belongings were taken away as well. They were escorted up a hill onto a rocky ridge above the nearest community and there locked into a small stone building and left alone.

"Who knew we were coming this way," asked Danivon.

"Fringe. The twins. And the thing following us."

"That's what I thought too. So who told Mother-dear?"

"I doubt it was Fringe."

Two cots stood along the walls of their jail, and Danivon fell onto one of them with a weary groan. He had not run so fast so far for the better part of a year, and every muscle protested.

He did a quick tally of the useful devices he still carried, considered immediate departure, and decided to defer escape until he'd had a chance to rest a bit. He conveyed this in a quick series of Enforcer gestures, at which Zasper nodded and lay down on the other cot, groaning in his turn. Chances were any conversation would be overheard. Since they could think of nothing harmless to say, they merely lay quiet, waiting upon the pleasure of Mother-dear.

That pleasure came too soon to allow them much rest. The sister guards escorted them down to the village plaza where Mother-dear (whether the only such or one of several) sat in a huge carved chair, her villager children clustered about her. She wore a vast flowered dress, like a tent, and her flesh overflowed the chair. Her breasts were like long balloons bulging from chest to abdomen, and her arms were braceleted and dimpled with fat. Around her stood her sister guards, muscular, slender women all. Only Mother-dear carried the great burden of flesh that signified her divinity.

The men only glanced at Mother-dear, their eyes drawn to the being beside her. It looked suspiciously like the thing they had destroyed at the mud pool.

"This messenger arrived earlier to tell us you were loose in Beanfields," said Mother-dear, stroking Danivon's arm. "Who is your mother, grown boy?" Her voice was concerned and maternal, like a local grandma concerned for the safety of a neighbor child.

"My mother is Lalla-balla, Mother-dear," said Danivon in his most humble voice. "She is a Council Enforcer, as are we. She was supposed to be with us."

The thing beside Mother-dear sparkled and shifted, listening to each word they said.

Mother-dear turned to Zasper. "And yours, old boy?"

"Lalla-balla, also, Mother-dear. My brother speaks truthfully. She was supposed to be with us."

"Where is she?"

"We think a gaver took her," said Zasper. "For she went to the river and did not return." He felt tears on his cheeks and made no effort to wipe them away. They were honest tears, tears he had managed not to shed until now. Speaking his fears for Fringe had brought them to his cheeks unbidden.

"Does she have sisters who will come to claim you?" Mother-dear asked in a more pleasant voice. She had seen the tears and was moved by them. These must be good boys to grieve for their mother so.

Zasper and Danivon shook their heads. Danivon said, "She does, Mother-dear, but it will take them some time to arrive after they know she is gone. She was on very important business for her mother. We beg that you take us as your boys and let us continue the duty our mother set us on."

"You know our rules?"

Danivon sighed within. Oh, yes, he did indeed. "Yes, Mother-dear."

"The fact that you are outlanders from Tolerance does not excuse your being loose without a mother. You know that?"

"Yes, Mother-dear." Danivon swallowed resentment, watching the device from the corners of his eyes. It sat and glittered and shifted. What was it doing? Reporting back? Summoning others?

Mother-dear went on: "When your own mother's sisters come to redeem you and pay the fine for your wandering loose, you may go on with their business. If so, well and good. Only if it is clear they will not come for you could I consider taking you as my boys. Even then, you would have to work off the fine before I could send you to complete your own mother's task." She looked them frankly up and down, as though deciding what work she might have them do. "You, grown boy, I would have blinded and take you as a lover. You are nicely built, and I have been wanting a new lover."

"Blinded!" gulped Danivon, shocked out of his Enforcer poise. "Why blinded?"

"Blind boys make the best lovers for Mothers," she said, preening. "They are not put off by the magnificence of what they see. And as for you," she turned to Zasper. "I have no doubt you could be caponized to make an excellent kitchen boy."

Zasper croaked, "Mother-dear, allow me to bring you a warning our mother told us of. . . ."

"Old boy, hush. Boys do not warn Mothers. This is impudence, and if it is repeated, Mother will spank!" Mother-dear's flesh quivered in outrage, and around her the sister guards bristled.

"May we at least go to the river to look for our mother?" begged Danivon. "She may be injured but alive, needing help."

Mother-dear regarded him expressionlessly. Beside her the gadget glistened and quivered. "I will think on it," she said at last. "I will consider it until morning."

They were taken back up the hill, stumbling a little on the jagged rock of the outcropping, and returned to their room, though this time several guards were posted outside. Though the walls were of stone and the window barred, it was comfortable enough. Mother did not hurt her children unnecessarily. So the people of Beanfields were taught. Of course, when it was necessary, she did hurt them. Mother-dear would spank. They were taught that also.

"Likely Mother-dear has sent her sisters to look along the riverbank already," said Danivon, gripping the window bars with both hands and shaking them as though to determine their strength. "They go at once to the aid of any woman in danger. But our mother . . ." He leaned close to Zasper's ear. "Fringe wouldn't have been on this side. You told her the destination of the *Dove* was on the east side, so she'd have been crossing over."

"Beanfields women won't cross over to Thrasis, that's certain. There used to be some raiding between the two provinces, but we put an end to that decades ago," Zasper whispered in return. "You don't think it happened in Thrasis?"

Danivon shook his head, sniffing, pointing westward, mouthing, "There, quite some way. Not north of us at all."

"Then beyond the wall."

"I believe so."

"Noplace."

Danivon laughed shortly, silently, and said aloud, "Noplace is safe, wouldn't you say?"

"What was that thing doing down there?" whispered Zasper, drawing Danivon near him again.

"Spying. I read they don't want to kill us but capture us! So, they're making sure the women hold us until something else can arrive."

"The network, you think?"

"What else? They've lost one set of captives. This time they want to bring up the whole armamentarium."

"Hadn't we better break out of here, then?" Zasper mouthed silently.

"There's that." Danivon stretched out on the bed. "We need some rest. This is as comfortable a place as we're likely to find."

Zasper gripped him by the arm. "That's as may be, boy, but the thing knows we're here. So, if we rest, we rest somewhere else, right?"

"Oh, very well," sighed Danivon. "How would you suggest?"

"Something to get the guard in here."

"Why not take out the lock and surprise them?"

"If you're equipped to do that."

"Always equipped to do that," said Danivon, busy taking one of his boots apart. The hollow heel disclosed a number of small shiny devices, and one of them applied to the door hummed only briefly before the grating swung silently open. They emerged into an open foyer to find their belongings stacked against the outer wall of their cell.

"Poor Mother-dear," whispered Zasper, stowing his paraphernalia about his person. "I fear she will not like her visitors."

"I didn't really want to be blinded," Danivon replied, restoring his boot to its usual conformation. "Though if expected to make love to Mother-dear, I could appreciate the advantages of that state."

He took up his arms, his pack, and sneaked a look around the door. There were two guards, he signaled, as he popped back to point at Zasper and himself, then in two directions, meaning, *You take that one, I'll take this one.*

Zasper nodded wearily. *Too old for this,* he thought sadly. *Really too old for this.*

When Danivon went to the left, Zasper went obediently to the right. . . .

And confronted the silvery killer he had last seen with Mother-dear in the village below.

It came at him in a rush, giving him time only for one muffled shout before it fell apart into several pieces, five he thought dazedly, three before and two . . . two where? He tried to get his back against the wall, but one of the creatures was between him and it. He took that one out with the weapon in his hand, stumbled across it as he turned, the wall now behind him, to confront two others. One down, two in view, two where? Or had there only been four to start with? His hand swept from left to right, and the two confronting him shrieked in high, metallic voices, not killed but crippled.

Danivon shouted that he was coming.

Zasper never heard the thing that dropped on him from above.

He was rolling and yelling when Danivon came around the corner; he was still yelling when Danivon peeled the creature away from his head.

"One more," he gasped. "One more, somewhere."

"I got it, Zasp," Danivon muttered as he fumbled for the med kit at his belt. Zasper's head was a bloody mess. "It was on the roof, but I got it."

"Never saw it," Zasper said, wondering why he couldn't see. "Blood in my eyes."

There was no blood in his eyes. Everywhere else, but not in his eyes.

"Came at me from above. Dropped down on me."

"They can climb like spiders." Danivon found the capsule he was looking for and clapped it between his hands, watching the resultant cloud of powder settle onto the sliced flesh and make a film there. The bleeding stopped, almost miraculously.

"Cold," said Zasper.

Danivon shrugged out of his coat and wrapped it around the older man. "A little shock is all," he murmured. "It'll pass."

"Too old for this." Zasper's eyes fell shut.

Danivon gathered Zasper into his arms and held him, sharing his own warmth. He rocked gently, letting the healing film do its work. It had the universal antidote in it, just in case there had been some kind of venom on those things. . . .

Time passed. Zasper didn't seem to be better. His breathing was more labored.

Danivon fumbled with the kit again. More of the antidote. That would do it. He injected, then gathered Zasper into his arms once more.

"Dan. . . ."

"Yes, Zas. I'm right here."

"Should get away."

"When you can move, Zas. We've got time."

Time passed.

"Dan. . . ."

"Zasper."

"Fringe. If you find Fringe . . . She . . ."

"I'll take care of her. I promise."

"You can't." He struggled to say more, getting it out one agonized word at a time. "She's not your . . . Jory will. You get her to Jory."

"I'll see to it, Zas."

"Good. Good boy."

A pained and incredulous screaming from the village below brought Danivon to himself sometime later. He was sitting on the ground, Zasper still cradled in his arms, the med kit open at his side, its contents including all the empty vials of universal antidote scattered about. The screaming had gone on for some time before Danivon realized that Zasper had stopped breathing a considerable time before.

Danivon rose, dry-eyed, took his coat from around Zasper's body and put it on, took the badge from Zasper's shoulder and put it away carefully among his own belongings along with all of Zasper's weapons. He stumbled several times, his foot turning on the empty vials of antidote that, so it seemed, had not in fact been at all universal.

Zasper's belt kit included incendiaries. All Enforcers carried them. No Enforcer wanted his body to fall into the hands of those who might not respect it. Nasty things could be done with recently dead bodies, nasty high-tech things and nasty low-tech things.

Danivon tucked the incendiaries down both sides of Zasper's body and pulled the caps away. Then he left, without looking back. Enforcers didn't look back. Better to remember the peaceful face than the white-hot flame. All this was drill. He'd done it in drill. He'd done it for colleagues before too. He'd always expected that someone would do it for him.

The screams from the village were fading. Obviously something deadly had arrived in Beanfields. He wiped his mouth, where a bitterness had gathered, and ran away from the village, down the backside of the stone outcropping to where it joined a ridge line stretching to the west, a wandering spine of stone making a high road for his weary feet.

He came to himself leaning on a stone and weeping. He could not remember stopping, could not remember weeping ever before. Not for anyone. He wiped his eyes and went on. He knew the drill. He just didn't know how to make the drill fit Zasper, that's all. Zasper wasn't supposed to die. Zasper wasn't ever supposed to die. Not Zasper, not Fringe. Certainly not both.

He did not stop to rest until he had come some distance from the community, and then he climbed into a large tree and stretched out along a stout branch, his coat folded beneath him, wondering why the invaders had come first to the village rather than to the jail where he and Zasper had been held. Because of the rock, he decided. They had come through the soft soil first. They had encountered Mother-dear and her people first.

Danivon had not much liked the idea of being Mother-dear's lover, but he did not relish the idea of her death, either. Hers or that of any of her people. Or anyone's. Anyone's.

Zasper's.

Fringe's.

He laid his arm across his eyes and forbade himself to weep anymore. Enforcers did not weep. They exacted vengeance, when necessary, but they did not weep! They slept when they needed to, but they did not weep!

When he woke, his face wet, the first flush of dawn lay on the sky, so he took up his burdens and went westward once more. He felt less like an Enforcer than like some small prey animal, fleeing endlessly from an implacable foe. Why were those creatures behind him so set upon killing him?

He had asked Zasper that same question.

"Boarmus says they kill for the same reason men and their gods have always killed. To prove they can."

It made no more sense than any other reason for death.

Jory and Asner were staring down the river from the end of the pier when Bertran and Nela limped out of the woods along the river, very weary and bedraggled. Neither of the old people would have recognized them except for their posture, the one cuddled protectively under the left arm of the other.

"Jory, look what happened to me!" Nela's voice crying, like a child calling, *Look at me, Mommy, I'm hurt.*

"At me," echoed Bertran. "Look at me, Asner."

The old people looked at them both for a long moment, seeking their eyes, which were unchanged.

"So," Jory sighed, "you were on this side of the wall when it happened. What about Fringe?"

"Fringe was there," said Bertran, baffled at her lack of surprise. "The gaver got Fringe."

"What do you mean, on this side of the wall?" asked Nela.

Over Nela's shoulder, Jory saw several of the Arbai gathered with Cafferty on the path to the acropolis. Both Arbai and human seemed equally interested in these new arrivals. "On this side of the wall," she repeated softly, "where the Arbai Device operates."

Nela followed the direction of Jory's gaze, slowly turning to catch her first glimpse of the Arbai. They were taller than men. And very bony, though not particularly dangerous-looking. She sighed, tired of new things, tired of things always happening.

"Dragons," she said, trying to sound politely interested. "Are these Danivon's dragons?"

"They are Arbai," said Asner. "All of them who're left."

Bertran stood on his hind legs, rearing high to get a better look, hands held pawlike before him. "So they aren't all dead! Somebody said they were all dead! I thought they would seem more mysterious." He crouched tiredly, letting Nela step away from him. "They should, shouldn't they? Seem mysterious, I mean? The inventors of the Doors were something very strange and special, I should think."

"They are as they are," said Jory. "Rather reptilian in appearance, though not at all biologically. Slow to grow. Slow to breed. Able to accept any new scientific discovery or technological idea without a moment's hesitation, yet still, after all these centuries, unable to accept the concept of evil."

"But there is evil there," said Bertran, pointing his muzzle back down the river. "Enough to convince anyone."

"Oh, yes, there is," cried Nela. "They had us in a place like a church, Jory. They told us we had to solve the Great Question or they'd torture us. They made dinka-jins of us. It was . . . It was awful."

"Fringe said that's what we were," said Bertran. "Dinka-jins. We wanted her to melt us, but she wouldn't."

"I know it must have hurt you," said Jory. "Otherwise you would not be . . . as you are."

"Someone must stop it, Jory! Someone must stop it happening to people!" cried Nela.

Asner shook his head wearily. "We'd like to stop it! Oh, yes!"

"Why did they do it to us, Jory! Why?"

"Because they're monsters," said the old woman.

"I thought they had perhaps once been men," said Bertran. "Though they are something else now."

Jory made a wry face. "They were men and teachers of men, but man alone is only a halfway creature: half ape, half angel. Some men get worse when they get learning, made monstrous by too much language and the manipulation of ideas. They lose the experience of reality."

"But if they are monsters, why don't people destroy them?"

"That's always the question. Who does the destroying? We good men? Good men don't kill others easily; instead we look deeply into the hearts of bad men, and what do we see? We see things we recognize in ourselves. And once we have admitted that kinship, it's hard to kill the other man. It's hard to say he's evil, for that means we too are evil. It's easier to pretend he's sick, easier to pretend he can be cured, even when we know he cannot. We all have the same evils inside us, so what gives us the right to get rid of the other? Ah?"

"You're being prophetic again," complained Asner. "You've retired, remember."

"I say what comes to me," she said sharply. "Including this: The problem of men and Arbai is very similar! Both refuse to recognize evil, men in themselves, the Arbai in anyone. That's why we're in this mess. The device would save us in a minute, but for that."

"Can we meet the Arbai?" asked Bertran. "Talk to them?"

Asner laughed. "Everyone wants to talk to the Arbai! They're too annoyed to let anyone talk to them. We've overstepped our bounds, the prophetess and I. They even sent a messenger to tell us so, so we'd have no chance to argue with them."

"They don't like argument," agreed Jory. "They don't like dissension or being told what they ought to do. I wanted them to use the Arbai Device beyond the wall. Curvis wanted the same. Now you come; they presume you want the same thing, and they don't want to hear it!"

Nela and Bertran subsided, leaning against one another in their familiar posture, holding one another for comfort.

Asner took in their strangeness, shaking his head. Poor things. "How far beyond the wall had you come when you were attacked?"

"Jory said that too. That we were on this side of the wall. What does it mean?" Bertran asked.

It was Jory who replied, "Who did you think mended you? Was it your God and mine, who we learned of when we were young? Or a guardian angel, perhaps?"

They did not answer.

Asner said, "You were told about the Hobbs Land Gods, weren't you?"

Silence. The gylph Nela shared a glance with the otter Bertran. They leaned more closely into one another. He pulled her down to him where she snuggled beneath his arm, eyes wary. "What, Asner. What about them?"

"The Arbai Device is the Hobbs Land Gods. They're the same thing."

They shuddered. Nela cried out, a tiny, choked cry.

Asner shook his head at them. "Relax," he demanded. "You're not hurt. You're not maimed or diabolically possessed. You've just been fixed, that's all. Given your heart's desire. So what's wrong with that?"

"It wasn't our heart's desire, not really," cried Bertran. "This isn't really . . . I thought I wanted but . . . and now I'm enslaved!"

"Enslaved?" said Asner in an offended voice. "What makes you think that?"

"Fringe said. . . ."

"Fringe is no expert," Asner growled. "Besides, you think you and Nela weren't enslaved before? You were born enslaved!"

"Now who's being prophetic," grumbled Jory.

"No," cried Nela. "I wasn't. I was a free person."

"Free to what?"

"To . . . to do anything I wanted to."

Jory laughed, shaking her head. "Weren't you told as a child that one way was better than another, one belief better than another? Weren't you told some things were higher and some lower? That some things were suitable for women, others for men? That your God was more powerful? That your religion was truer? That your language was more expressive? That your customs had more heart, or more soul? That your cooking tasted better? That your way of child-rearing was preferable? That all your ways were so much better than others' ways that you would die to keep yours as they were, or die to destroy others if they seemed threatening? Weren't you taught not to change, not to adapt, not to become anything different? Weren't you taught the word 'loyalty'? The word 'tradition'? Didn't they tell you that animals were higher than vegetables, mammals were higher than other animals, man was higher than other mammals, and your kind of man was higher than other men?

"You think you weren't enslaved by that? You think you had freedom of choice? I have said this to Fringe, I say it to you: A man's choice becomes his son's duty and his grandson's tradition! Thus men assure enslavement of their progeny."

"But . . . but . . . I've been taken over!"

"By what? By a communication net that lets you in on how the intelligences around you feel and what they think and know. So?"

"But . . ."

Asner growled, "But, if you refuse to know what those around you think and know, if the idea of taking other intelligences into consideration offends you, if you don't want to be part of it, just say so. Say it firmly, and the Arbai Device will leave you strictly alone. If you think you're better and wiser than those around you, tell it to fuck off. That's the way Curvis reacted. That's the way it was designed to be."

"But . . ." faltered Bertran, running his webbed hand along his side, along his sleekness, his sinuous body, his fluid shape. "I didn't really want to be . . . like this. Inside, I'm the same. Inside, I'm human. I need to be human outside too."

"Simply wait a little," sighed Jory. "As soon as it has time to receive your feedback, the device will get it right."

"But the people here . . ." Nela faltered. "Even the people on Elsewhere say the Hobbs Land Gods are evil. . . ."

"The people brought to Elsewhere were, every one of them, great tribal egos who have always festered like a boil on the butt of humanity," said Asner.

"A feverish reminder of old, sorrowful times," whispered Jory.

". . . or one last cause for a notorious do-gooder," continued Asner in a grumpy tone, with a wry look in Jory's direction. "One last wrong needing righting. One last ill for the prophetess to fulminate against."

Said she, "What would you have me do! Dragged up as we were out of . . ."

"I don't understand any of this! I don't understand why any of this is happening!" cried Nela.

"Tell them about it, Asner," Jory said. "Tell them all about Brannigan. They missed out on Zasper's lecture, and it's time they knew." And she went back to staring at the river while Asner told them about Brannigan.

Just before dawn, Danivon reached both the western borders of Beanfields and the point of exhaustion. He had stayed on the stony spine of the hills, letting it lead him westward. There had been no signs of pursuit, though he had seen fires blooming in the night to speak of sleepers awakened and alarms made in the darkness. Now he could see the wall before him and to his right the river, gleaming softly in the starshine.

"Time to get across, I think," said Danivon to the air, to himself, to the pocket munks peeking from his shirt, to Zasper's ghost. He had been talking to this audience for some little time. "It's an easy slope along here. We'll build some kind of raft out of reeds."

He would need to sleep for a while before he built anything, much less a raft, but he did not dwell on this as he staggered down the wooded slope toward the tall, shadowed growths along the shore. From here the dark line of the wall marched across the world and out into the water, an inviolable barrier.

"I wish we had Great Dragon here," murmured Danivon. "To get us across that wall as he no doubt did the women of Thrasis. I'd be willing to ride him bareback if he'd do that."

He stared at the wall, his nose twitching. Were the pursuers going to come through the wall after him? Over the wall? Around it?

His nose said nothing, nothing hostile beyond the wall, but no knowledge of whether they might come there, either.

At the bottom of the hill a wandering streamlet wove its way among the reeds, reflecting the gray sky to make silver meanders as it sought the river. He waded up to his hips in mud and rotting vegetation, clutching at the tall stems to keep his balance. At last he staggered out of their shade into a shallow sandy-bottomed lagoon to see a dark cluster of anchored boats, their sails furled and gear carefully stowed. Drying nets were silhouetted against the sky, and the outline of a walkway on pilings above the mud told him he had found the fishing fleet of a nearby village.

"How do you feel about a bit of thievery?" Danivon asked himself as he wiped mud from his face and stared at the walkway in disgust. "Wouldn't you say we'd earned it? Being such good guys there in Bean-fields. Abstaining from any unnecessary slaughter?"

He waited a moment, as though for an answer, then answered himself. "Indeed, we've earned a bit of license. If one boat will do, by all means, do one boat."

He had smelled death behind him since Zasper died. It had come closer since midnight. He thought it would be less likely to catch up if he were on the river.

He tossed up a handful of leaves and saw them spin away toward the west. "The wind's in the right direction, at least. Won't need to tack back and forth. Which is a good thing!"

Danivon was no boatman; though he had had the advantage of observing the sailors on their way up the Fohm, he was not at all confident he could get safely across the river.

Still, there was no other choice. He pushed the nearest boat into the river, held to its side while he dunked himself repeatedly to wash the stinking mud away, then climbed in and set the sail more or less as he had seen the captain of the *Dove* doing all the days of their upriver trip. The wind was gentle, barely enough to move them against the current, and he lay wearily in the bottom of the boat, fighting to keep his eyes open, the tiller beneath his arm as he watched the shore creep slowly by. After what seemed an eternity, the wall approached, grew taller, loomed off the port beam, then edged away behind him.

"Now cross over," said Danivon wearily. "If Fringe and the twins are anywhere, they will be on the other side."

The little boat had been designed for use in the slow waters and quiet lagoons along the bank. It jigged like a beetle as it inched its way across the wavelets in its reach for the far shore and Danivon thought hopelessly of gavers. He was of the opinion the Brannigans Zasper had told him of had set the gavers against the ship. He was almost certain it had been a gaver that had taken Fringe. A huge and inexorable beast, lunging up from beneath the waves.

Dawn came. The sky lightened. The far shore became visible and drew gradually closer, the undulant banks rising into grassy precipices or falling into mud flats. Danivon steered for a place where the banks were low. At last he felt the keel thrust into the mud and hold there, the boat shivering for a moment before it tilted against the soil and was still. He furled the sail.

"Could we set the sail, do you suppose, to take it home?" Danivon asked of the air. "Back to Beanfields?"

There would likely be no one there to use it. No doubt the Brannigans were making their usual wholesale destruction.

He staggered up the bank, clawing his way the last few feet to the cushiony grasses at the top, then lay there, unable to go farther. At the rim of the sky, the last stars winked out.

"I saw you coming," said a voice. "I was very glad to see you alive."

He looked up, taking in the purple plumes against the gray sky of early morning, the polished boots beside his head.

"Fringe," he breathed, unable to believe it. He stood up, took her by the shoulders, hugged her to him. "Fringe."

"Danivon," she said.

He stood back and looked at her, his joyous smile fading. It was Fringe. Her eyes, her face, her voice. And yet, not Fringe. Not Fringe at all. No nervous little movement as she pushed him away a little, no sidelong look. No apprehension in her gaze, saying, *Love me, leave me alone, love me.* Nothing of that at all. Only sureness. Competence. Poise. Certainty.

She smiled gladly. "It is good to see you well. I was worried about you." Her voice was unworried. "Where's Zasper?"

Danivon reached out to her, to the gap in her shirt that showed her bare throat. "Where is the pendant he gave you. You wore it all the time."

She felt at her throat. It was gone, of course. The gaver had taken it when it had taken her head off. "Gone," she said smilingly, shaking her head. "Too bad. Where's Zasper?"

Danivon stared at her with his mouth open and his nose quivering. His eyes filled as he heard the pocket munks in chorus repeating what she had said.

"Gone," they whispered. "Too bad."

Microdevices moved through the soil of Beanfields, spewing out a million more eyes and ears, a million more miniscule Doors, a million more tiny gravitics, and killers, of course, even though the instructions of the network were clear: Hold certain persons captive, do not kill them! Hold captive Danivon Luze and Zasper Ertigon.

When the network reached the prison at the top of the hill, however, the two were gone. There were only the bodies of two guards killed by one of Clore's machines, the battered pieces of that machine, and a burned place on the soil. Mechanisms designed to travel overland looked for the two humans but couldn't find them.

The devices asked the people of Beanfields where the captives were, but the people of that province knew only this mother's old boy or that mother's young boy or some other mother's black-haired boy or yet some other mother's boy who plays the flute. No one knew who *Zasper* was or *Danivon*. No one knew their names. Those who were asked could not answer, and so died.

The network did not stop growing, even while Beanfields was being reduced to a suffering fragment of itself. While parts of it were lethally involved in the villages, the rest of it pushed on toward the west. Less than an hour after Danivon set sail across the Fohm, the network reached the Great Wall and began to burrow through it. Getting through rock was not difficult, merely slow. The network had been extended through rock in many parts of the world.

Patiently it drilled its way, eventually arriving on the other side as infinitesimal metallic points. Each of these points was noticed by the ubiquitous fibers that grew throughout noplace. The fibers attached themselves to the emerging network and disassembled it, molecule by molecule, tiny part by tiny part. As soon as one molecule of it was extruded through the wall, it was corrupted and eaten. No sensor lasted long enough to report this effect. The network simply reached the Great Wall and then vanished.

Great Slitherer and Subble Clore were at first too busy to notice. They were still fuming at the escape of the two Enforcers, at the fact the network had not caught them, at the strange creatures upriver who had not died when the machines were told to kill them. All these matters were distracting them at a time when they wished to think of other things—the rules and ritual of Clore adoration, the catechism and theology of Breaze worship.

Breaze had decided that he would require his followers to believe illogical things as evidence of their faith. He would require them to believe that Breaze had created Elsewhere and all its people in one day, out of nothing, exactly one thousand years ago! But . . . (a master stroke) he would leave evidence in Files to contradict this! Thus they would have to disbelieve the evidence of their own senses in order to believe in Breaze!

When he got to this point, a small voice asked why he had given men such senses in the first place? Why had he given them intelligence if he intended to forbid its use?

Great Slitherer couldn't remember creating men, though he knew he must have done so. He couldn't remember why he had given them the ability to weigh evidence and make judgments for themselves. Why had he given them intelligence?

Preoccupied with such questions, Breaze did not notice the network had stopped at the wall. Preoccupied with similar notions, neither did the others of the Core. As time passed, no word came; as more time went by, even the little mobile ears and eyes beyond the wall fell silent. So long as they had remained aloft or afloat, they had continued to function, but as each of them had touched soil or the branch of a tree or the stony summit of a hill, it had stopped being. Eventually, all had stopped being, and the noisy flow of messages from the west dwindled into silence.

Great Lord Crawler had moved on to inventing a marriage ceremony, something very arduous and esoteric involving ritual defloration and genital mutilation. Clore had devised an ingenious new form of sacrifice. It was some time before they became aware.

They peered, then howled, their noisy protest going out through the network, among the nodes. Messages came back, not so sanguine and dismissive as before. Magna Mater had also run into the wall when she had tried to get through it from the north. Therabas Bland had made the attempt from the south and failed.

The failure infuriated them all. They got into their god forms and stalked toward the center of the continent, trampling the provinces in their rage.

In Tolerance, Jacent crept quietly down a deserted corridor toward his aunt Syrilla's door. Most people these days were staying in their own quarters. The monitors had given up all pretense of keeping the status quo. Many Enforcers had departed for their home provinces, and the few that remained dressed like ordinary people. Only the Frickians seemed more or less immune to what was happening. Nothing seemed to bother them greatly. Some of them had been killed, but Frickians never made a fuss, even when they were being dismembered. They tended to die silently or disappear as silently. *No fun*, thought Jacent. *No fun at all, which is why the Brannigans left them alone.* A phlegmatic people, the Frickians. Boarmus said Frickians would end up being the only survivors and the Brannigans would then be worshiped by Frickians alone. Which was a laugh, because Frickians had been bred to take orders, to be servants and soldiers just as Council Supervisory members had been bred to be bureaucrats and maintain the status quo. How fitting for a self-created god to be worshiped only by people who had been bred to be subservient. How fitting to have all the bureaucrats slaughtered when they were only doing their jobs. Talk about irony!

Not that Boarmus saw the irony. At least he didn't say anything about it. Not that he said much where anyone—anything—could hear him. Still, everyone knew about the Brannigans by now. Knew, whispered, but never said it out loud. One said Monstrous Crawler, Great Lord Clore this, Great Lord Clore that. One said Mighty Lord Breaze or Magna Mater. One said Sweet and Adorable Lady Bland. One said litanies, new ones every few days. Heart of Heaven, Wall of Desire, Mouth of Morning. Great Temple of Love. That was one for Thob. One could say things like that, but one didn't say Brannigan. One pretended not to know about that.

Jacent tapped softly on Aunt Syrilla's door. He hadn't seen her for some days. Somebody ought to check on her, be sure she was all right.

There was no answer, but then people these days sometimes didn't bother answering. Sometimes it was better if they didn't. He tried the door, which was not sealed. He pushed it open. The room inside seemed empty. A little dusty and disarranged, but that was the usual thing these days, with so many of the automatic systems out of order and nobody left to repair them.

"Aunt Syrilla?" The doors inside the suite were open. He could see all the way through it. The bedroom was empty. The bathroom. He walked through into the wardrobe, lined on both sides with racks and chests and shelves.

It was almost as if he'd known she'd be there, on the shelf next to the ceiling, her purple face hanging over the edge, the rest of her squashed into an impossibly small space in the corner.

Jacent made it to the saniton before he was sick. Parts of her had run down the wall, dripped onto her clothing below. He took deep breaths, one after the other, trying not to remember what she looked like. There were a few like this every now and then, strange deaths, impossible deaths, just enough to make everyone imagine the next one would be him, or her. And then some person would claim to have had a vision of what the god wanted, and everyone in Tolerance would dance or sing or chant or engage in ridiculous, meaningless actions, and nobody would be killed for a while. Almost as though the Brannigans had been distracted. Or really had wanted everybody to do whatever ritual it was they were doing.

When he had recovered enough that he could walk, he slipped out into the corridor, almost knocking Boarmus down as he came through the door.

"I was looking for you, boy," whispered Boarmus. "Come with me." And he set off down a side corridor, dragging Jacent along by the arm as he ducked through a servant's door, thus avoiding a group of several hundred persons slithering down the corridor on their bellies to the sound of drums and cymbals. Jacent tried to hold him back, babbling about what he'd found back there.

"I know," said Boarmus. "I found her this morning."

"Where . . ." breathed Jacent. "Where are we?"

"Garage," said Boarmus. "I'm sending you to Panubi."

"Me!"

"You. In a ZT thirty-four, which is the only thing we have capable of getting you there in one swoop. I hope your operational skills are good."

"But I can't fly a thirty-four," the boy blubbed. "Honestly, Boarmus. I've only been in one once."

"It's the only way," said Boarmus. "Any other type flier, you'll have to land and recharge, and the minute you land, they'll eat you."

"You come with me," begged the boy. "You can fly one of those."

"I can't come with you." He laughed harshly. "I never thought duty impressed me that much, boy, but this is duty. I'm trying to keep a few of us alive here. If I can."

"Send a pilot, then."

"What pilot? Where? You see any pilots? You see any maintenance people? You see any messengers? You see any patrols? Use your head, boy. You wanted excitement, now you've got it. You either teach yourself to fly this machine or you die pretty soon, as likely all of us will anyhow."

Jacent screamed into the weary face before him, "They won't kill me if I bow down! If I do the rituals and things. If I crawl. They won't kill me if I crawl!"

Boarmus shook him until his head flopped. "Maybe not today. Maybe they'll wait until tomorrow. Then they'll have a heresy trial, maybe, just for amusement. And they'll make up new rules and kill everyone who doesn't know what they are. Jacent, remember Metty. She didn't do anything to anyone. What did Syrilla do? What have any of us done? Don't you understand what's going on here? You expect you can figure out what to do to keep yourself out of trouble. You expect logic. You expect good sense. You don't understand what's happening."

Jacent took a deep breath and tried to control himself. He'd never thought he would fall apart like this. But there was blood everywhere these days, blood and messy things. Pieces of people falling out of closets and off of shelves. People coming apart right in front of you, while they were working, while they were eating even. One of his friends had his girlfriend come all to pieces while they were making love, right there on the bed, leaving him covered with parts of her while this terrible gulping laughter went on and on. Horror piled on horror, and nobody knowing why or what to do about it.

"What am I going for?" he said from a dry mouth, trying to control his shaking.

"You're going to tell Zasper Ertigon or whoever else you find there— Danivon, maybe—that if he can think of any way to help us, now's the time. Tell him Enarae's half-gone. Tell him most of the provinces are nothing but a few dazed survivors wandering around wondering what hit them. Either that or religious processions marching back and forth, with people dropping from starvation and dehydration. Tell him the Enforcers that are left are lying low, pretending to be ordinary folk. Tell him everything's coming to an end very soon if someone doesn't do something."

"What can he do?" Jacent spoke from sheer amazement that there was anyone who might be thought to be helpful.

"Nothing," said Boarmus. "Most likely nothing. But I've done everything I can think of, and this is the only thing left to try. There were dragons on Panubi. I don't know what kind. But Files says dragons are supposed to be . . . miraculous. Holy, maybe, whatever that means. And if there's anything holy or miraculous left in this world, we need it to help us. So go, boy. Go!"

Jacent climbed into the machine and went. He didn't know how to fly it, but it wasn't that different from something he did know how to fly. He didn't know where Panubi was, but the on-board navigator was able to find it. He didn't know where Zasper was, either, but the model thirty-four knew where the Enforcer post near Shallow was, and those left alive at the post remembered that Zasper had gone west, toward Thrasis and the Great Wall.

14

As he made his erratic way above the River Floh, Jacent saw lines of refugees traveling westward along the banks and over the undulating plains. Scattered encampments stood at the Great Wall where people were frantically building ladders and towers. Though bodies lay heaped here and there along the line of march, Jacent saw no signs of human conflict. The refugees had been hunted down, were still being hunted down by the other thing.

Past the Great Wall the killing stopped. Here he saw only groups on the move, escapees from Deep and Shallow who'd swum past the barrier, and people from other provinces who'd come by boat or raft. The surface of the Floh was still speckled with small craft tacking their slow way upstream.

When the gorge gaped its narrow throat before him, he prudently chose to fly over rather than through it, and this route brought him in sight of two Enforcers making slow progress along the high trail. By that time Jacent needed company almost as badly as he needed directions. He landed the flier—unskillfully—and took Fringe and Danivon aboard. Danivon, who had noted the sloppy landing, took over the flier, and this allowed Jacent to concentrate on Boarmus's message. Though made rather incoherent by fear and exhaustion, he managed to convey that Tolerance was being wiped out, that Boarmus wanted a miracle, would they take him to Zasper, who would produce one.

"I don't know what kind of miracle old Boarmus expects," Danivon said flatly. "I know Zasper won't produce one, because Zasper is dead. I don't know what kind of dragons there are where we're going, if any.

I left the group in Thrasis, and up until then we'd only seen the one dragony beast the old woman had with her plus some smaller ones said to be its descendants."

"Jory's dragon was impressive," commented Fringe in an infuriatingly calm voice.

"That's true," Danivon agreed, gritting his teeth. "But it had surprise on its side, and even if there were hundreds like it, they wouldn't be much use against a world full of killing machines."

Jacent wiped tears of weariness from his eyes. "Boarmus was really hoping about the dragons. And I was too."

"Then you must hope for some other dragons. Since none of us have been where we're going, how can we say what we'll find?" Danivon cast a sidelong look at Fringe, who sat stiffly beside him, saying nothing, wearing the half smile she had worn since she found him at the riverside. If they all saw inescapable horror looming before them, likely Fringe would still be wearing that same little smile.

"The massif," she said unnecessarily, pointing ahead of them at the smoothly glowing dome that rose above the center of the continent like a giant carbuncle. "There's the massif, Jacent."

Jacent obediently followed her gaze but was unimpressed by landscape. "Nobody was getting killed inside the wall," he persevered, unwilling to give up hope. "So there must be something here that can fight the network off."

Danivon shook his head. "Keeping an enemy out is different from fighting one off. Withstanding siege is a different matter from winning a battle."

Fringe said, "If it's your safety you're worried about, likely you'll be safe here."

Jacent stopped trying to hide his tears of weariness and frustration and frankly wept, his voice rising in incipient hysteria. "It isn't just *me*. It's everybody. It's Aunt Syrilla, only she's already dead, and it's Boarmus and all my friends in Tolerance, and my home in Heaven, and . . ."

Danivon turned to lay his fingers on the boy's lips, shutting down the flow. "All and everyone would probably be safe here, boy, but there's not enough room in Central Panubi for the entire population of Elsewhere, even if we could think of means to get it here. Take hold of yourself. Things are as they are, and no amount of wishful thinking will change them!"

He took his hand away and Jacent was quiet, no doubt stunned into silent grief. He wasn't alone. Since meeting Fringe, Danivon had grieved for her as he did for Zasper. Here she was beside him, yet he grieved as though she were dead. Something had happened to her. He didn't know what, but she was most dreadfully changed.

He grunted sharply at the sight of the acropolis almost below them and let the flier sideslip toward the shore, landing it like a dried leaf on a stretch of turf. People came running. Jory and Asner limped out from one of the buildings beneath the trees, and those leaving the flier looked beyond them to see dragons standing at the edge of a distant grove.

Danivon's mouth dropped open. "So there they are," he said. "I didn't really believe in them."

"Arbai," came a treble voice from above him, where a gylph fluttered awkwardly, lurching on unsteady wings as it screamed in surprise, "Fringe! We thought you were dead!"

"What the . . . who . . ." croaked Danivon.

"It's Nela," advised Fringe in the kindly-but-impersonal voice that set Danivon's teeth on edge. "And that's Bertran in the fur with the webbed feet. I forgot to tell you about them. At the same time I was being put together again, Bertran and Nela were being changed."

The winged being fell with its arms about Fringe's neck. Fringe stepped back, and Nela's arms fell away.

"Fringe?" she asked doubtfully.

"What happened to the three of you?" grated Danivon. He had not asked Fringe what had happened to her; he'd been afraid to know. He had not even looked at her closely since she found him first at the riverside, but now, confronted by these other monstrous changes, he had to look, had to ask.

"Something fixed them when it fixed me," Fringe said offhandedly. "Rebuilt them and me."

"The Hobbs Land Gods," said gylph Nela in a wondering voice. "It seems they've been here all the time."

Danivon felt his heart stop, felt a bloody and violent pressure in his skull, a bursting red geyser, a terror so inbred he couldn't speak, come from nowhere, about to eat him!

"Ahhhhn," he shrieked.

"No," said Fringe in a surprised but fearless voice. "I will not accept that! I will not allow myself to be possessed."

"It's all right," said Jory, to Danivon and Fringe both. "Calm down."

Danivon didn't hear her. He was away from the flier, running in panic through the trees beside the river, he didn't know where except to get away. He fled through the grove and deep into a bed of reeds where he crouched, blood hammering in his ears. Where had he come to? What disaster?

"Why did you do that?" asked a voice from above. "Why did you run off?"

He looked up to see Nela teetering above him once more, on barely manageable wings.

"That was silly," she gasped.

"Possesseds," he hissed at her. "Not human anymore. Take us over."

She half landed, half fell beside him. A snuffly bustling approached through the reeds and erupted at his side, spilling the furred creature between them.

"Why did you run away, Danivon?" asked Bertran.

Danivon put his hands over his eyes and shuddered, still moaning wordlessly.

"He's scared of us," said Nela in a sad, remote voice. "Really scared. The way Turtledove used to be scared. Of nothing. He used to scare himself, invent monsters, make up horrors."

"Danivon," said Bertran pleadingly. "Danivon. Look at us."

He looked at them and saw monsters. Horrible, nonhuman monsters with feathers and claws. He howled and hid his face once more, lost in nightmare.

Bertran patted his knee with one webbed hand. "Danivon. You were going to take us apart and rebuild us, weren't you? So? Something else took us apart, is all, and all we can figure out is it knew we'd always dreamed of being . . . different from what we were . . . so it gave us different shapes. . . . That's all. We're the same. Inside, we're the same." His tone betrayed him. He did not believe he would ever be the same. "Jory says it will put us back, if we like. . . ."

Danivon trembled, gulped for air, fought for air, couldn't breathe. "It got Fringe," he gasped. "It got Fringe. She isn't Fringe anymore."

"Isn't she?" asked Nela. "Really? She did seem odd. . . ."

"Cold," he howled. "She's all cold! When she heard Zasper was dead, she didn't even cry!"

"But she probably wanted to be like that!" cried Nela. "Fringe wanted something else, Danivon. All her human feelings kept getting in the way. She wanted to be fearless and immune to pain, without all those muddles and pangs. Poor Fringe, she used to hurt all the time. So now maybe she doesn't."

"She didn't want to be like *that*!" he cried.

"But . . ." said Nela.

"Maybe she really didn't," said Bertran. "We didn't really want to be like this, Nela."

"But . . ."

Danivon didn't hear, couldn't move. He went on cowering, unable to think, unable to accept. The twins murmured to each other in subdued voices, then went away. After a time Jory and Asner came tunneling through the rattling stems, complaining in cracked voices, to hunker down beside him with many groans and gasps. They talked more to each other than to him.

"Of course, what's here in noplace *isn't* the Hobbs Land Gods," said Jory, patting Danivon on the knee and peering into his eyes.

"No," Asner agreed. "Not really."

"Similar, but not identical," she said. "Because the Hobbs Land Gods had mostly humans to work with, whereas this device is both controlled by the Arbai and dominated by their thoughts and sensitivities. Only if it were freed from their control could it become like the Hobbs Land Gods."

"True," said Asner, squeezing Danivon's shoulder. "Which is no doubt why it affected the twins as it did. And Fringe. If it had enough experience with humans, it would have repaired them differently."

Danivon merely shuddered, scarcely hearing, while some remote part of himself stood aloof and amazed at this craven animal, this cowering creature he had become. He had not believed himself capable of this. Where had this terror come from? Of course he had always been taught the worst things in the universe were the Hobbs Land Gods, but still. . . .

The two old people went on chatting, of this, of that, of old times, of recent events. After a considerable time, Danivon found his fists unclenched and his jaw relaxed. It was like being under running water, like listening to rain. The remote, judgmental part of himself went away somewhere. The old voices went on and on, unhurried and untroubled, like little fingers, untying all his knots. The tension dissolved. All the fear dissipated. He wondered, rather vaguely, if he was now possessed, but he didn't protest when Asner and Jory took his arms and half led, half leaned on him as they made their way out of the reeds and across a grassy plot to the place near the buildings where the others sat around an open fire, dining on bits of roast meat and awaiting his arrival with curious faces.

"Danivon, and you, Fringe, listen to me," said Jory. "If you want no interference from what you think of as the Hobbs Land Gods, you'll get none."

"They've already interfered," said Fringe in her chilly voice. "It's too late. I will die rather than live possessed." She said it as though she commented on the weather.

Jory shushed her. "It's not too late. They'll put you back precisely as you were and leave you alone. It's just . . . they, it had no reliable human index, no one much to cross-check with and very little time."

"They'll put me back dead?"

"They'll put you back however you like! Dead. Alive. Reconstructed as you were before the gaver got you. However."

"Enslaved," said Fringe emotionlessly.

"Not," said Jory in a dispirited tone. "Not enslaved any more than you already were. You will still be enslaved by yourself, by custom, by opinion, by all the hierarchies you have accepted from others or built for yourself, but you're used to that."

Fringe merely stared, disbelieving, but Danivon sat up straighter.

"How?" he asked. "How do I get . . . unpossessed?"

"Simply think of yourself as you were," Jory said. "The device will help you do it. It won't cheat. It has no desire for power. It has no ego to assert. It is simply what it was designed to be, a communication device. Because most people like to think of themselves as better than they are—kinder and more generous—the usual net effect of the device is an improvement in people's ability to get along with one another. There is more trust, more faith, as Asner could tell you. Nonetheless, if you spend some time remembering incidents from your life and how you felt and reacted toward them, you'll become more and more what you were. The Arbai Device has no use for grieving, rebellious participants."

Danivon looked only partially convinced.

"How can you prove this?" Fringe demanded. "How would I know it had left me?"

"Are you aware, now, of how Nela feels? No, don't look at her. Are you aware?"

Fringe nodded, unwillingly. She was. She knew exactly how Nela felt, and Bertran, and Danivon. . . .

"It is the device informing you. Say to yourself now that you do not wish to know how Nela feels. Keep in mind that you do not wish to know about others. Shortly, you will find you do not know." Jory spoke with rueful and unimpassioned conviction.

"When you are as deaf and unperceiving as you were before, you will know it has gone. When you feel yourself a solitary creature, walled inside yourself, you will know you are alone."

Fringe turned away, believing she had heard the truth.

"But I always . . ." murmured Danivon. "I could smell . . ."

"For you, Asner and I will think up a different test," said Jory, almost angrily. "But I assure you, you will not be an unwilling part of anything!"

"You haven't really met Alouez," Cafferty murmured, changing the subject. "You haven't met Haifazh, who has only just come."

The girl nodded, the woman nodded. Danivon merely stared at them, not even hearing their names, as he mentally took an inventory of Danivon as Danivon knew Danivon to be. Seeing his vacant expression, Jory pushed him toward a bench against the sun-warmed wall. He sat there, concentrating on himself-qua-himself, running over the catalog of his faults and virtues, breathing through his mouth, trying not to smell anything or think anything that might make the terror rise up once more.

Jacent was still reciting a catalog of events he had experienced in Tolerance. He went on and on, concluding, ". . . and it isn't just Tolerance. All the people of Elsewhere are dying. Children, women, men, old people. All dying. Boarmus said the dragons were his last hope. So what should I do now?"

Jory said firmly, "It's unfortunate that Boarmus placed any hope in dragons. The Arbai won't do anything, young man."

"What's happening?" Danivon blurted, suddenly aware that what she had said had to do with him. "Who won't do anything?"

"Tell him," Curvis demanded, giving Danivon an almost-contemptuous look. "Tell him all about it. He doesn't know all about the Arbai Device yet?"

"What more should I know?" cried Danivon.

Jory seated herself and folded her hands in her lap. "The device is a living thing. When it is small, it's simple, without thought or volition. As it grows larger, it draws on the minds and consciousness of every intelligence in the net and becomes synergistic, predictive, even creative. It can draw on the dreams and imaginations of the minds it includes. It can evolve syncretic symbols to interpret among different life forms. It can convince all its parts that they see or feel or hear or smell certain things. It can create a reality that all its parts accept."

"It did that on Hobbs Land," said Asner. "Hobbs Land was dull, but we settlers longed for marvels, so it drew on our imaginations to create marvels for us. Some of its creations—the ones that could be grown, like trees or beasts—were real. Other creations, geographical ones, were sort of . . . illusory, at least, to start with. Eventually they became real too, though it took a long time to make a canyon or a mountain range by moving a molecule at a time. Eventually, when our world was threatened, it drew on our experience and its own growth potential to create a defense."

"It interfered with you," snarled Curvis. "That's all Danivon needs to know. It took you over! And it's now taking us over! Taking him over."

Jory waved a bony fist at him. "Though I have repeatedly said that does not happen, it is beside the point Asner was making! He's saying the device can actually create or destroy in response to the needs of the intelligences it includes."

Danivon cried suddenly, "What are you saying, woman?"

Jory repeated, "I'm saying the Arbai Device could eliminate the Brannigan network if allowed to get at it."

"And the Arbai won't let it?" Danivon asked incredulously.

"They won't let it. They have programmed it to grow only where they wish it to grow. The limit has always been at the wall."

"Why won't they let it go farther?"

Jory raised her eyebrows at him, miming astonishment. "That question yet again? You sound like Curvis, Danivon. Here you are, both Enforcers. You've both seen fit to lecture us on noninterference all the way up the Fohm, yet both of you get swollen about the neck when I tell you the Arbai hold the same point of view."

Danivon closed his eyes, trying to understand. "They won't use it beyond the wall even to save the lives of all those on Elsewhere."

"Correct," said Asner.

"Millions of people are going to die."

"Likely," said Asner again. "Or already have."

Danivon said desperately, "I'll ask the Arbai to change their minds.

Just because our forefathers chose doesn't mean we have! We aren't choosing now! We don't choose to die like this now! The Derbeckians didn't choose for Chimi-ahm to be real!"

"The only difference between Chimi-ahm real and Chimi-ahm illusory is that the real is able to do in person what the priests and hounds used to do in his name," said Jory.

"All right! But Derbeck's only one province!" he cried. "Surely, under the present situation . . ."

Jory laughed harshly. "Situation? What situation? When man first came here, the Arbai examined his history in an attempt to understand him. They found holocaust after holocaust, armageddon after armageddon, each of them as dreadful as this *situation*. Man has always tortured in the name of his gods and committed atrocities in the name of his culture."

She threw up her hands, her hair making a white mane about her wrathful face.

"I knew that as well as the Arbai did, but still, when I became aware there was another force at work, I asked the Arbai to reconsider. The Arbai then asked me: 'Was there any difference between what the new forces were doing to man and what man had always done to himself?' "

"Jory . . ." said Asner, troubled, putting out a hand.

"Let me rave, Asner. Their question took me back in time. Back to the planet on which I was born. Back to the planet from which Great Dragon and I came. Back to the places we have seen in the centuries between. Everywhere, men have perpetuated myths of honor and death, everywhere men have worshiped gods who have destroyed them. So, the Arbai asked, 'Why should man be saved from customs and gods he himself had created?' "

She leaned to speak into Danivon's face. "If they ask you that same question, what answer will you give them?"

"I might say something about mercy," he cried. "Something about pity!"

"You're a fine one to talk, Enforcer! But, as a matter of fact, that's what I did say. In my womanly way, I talked a good deal about mercy. And I was told mercy was an end, but the means to achieve that end was interference, and that ends do not justify means. Which, surprisingly enough, is precisely the male promulgated doctrine I was weaned on as a child!"

She came to herself, dwindled before their eyes to stand fragile and trembling before them. "Sorry," she said, tottering. "I sometimes forget I am no longer a prophetess."

"You will always be a prophetess," said Asner tenderly, putting his arms around her. "Until you are no more. And by that time, there will be no need for a prophetess."

"Certainly not here," she said wearily. "For everyone will be dead, all talk of mercy notwithstanding."

Curvis growled at her in a bitter voice, "Not quite all if what you say is true. The people out there, yes. But not *your* people behind the wall."

"All," Jory mumbled tiredly. *"All!* I'm grieving for all of them, stupid boy. For Fringe and you and Latibor and Cafferty. For my people as well as the others. The Arbai may have no concept of evil but they have a horror of pain, so they're going." Jory turned and laid her forehead on Asner's shoulder, clinging to him. The air behind her moved in a convoluted way. Shadows chased one another across scales and fangs and great, smoldering eyes.

"Going?" asked Fringe wonderingly.

It was Asner who replied. "They're retreating under the massif. They've got some kind of redoubt down there, built long ago in case of need. They're pulling in the Arbai Device behind them, and in case you're wondering, no, our people are not invited to join them."

"We're too discomforting for the Arbai," murmured Jory. "All these human thoughts and desires getting into the device make it painful for them. Like rocks in their shoes, hurting every step they take. They can't handle ambiguity. And once the device is gone, there'll be nothing to stop the Brannigans."

"How can your Arbai friends let you die?" Bertran asked the old woman.

"You didn't make that choice," cried Nela. "You came from outside! Surely they'd save you!"

"Ahh . . ." said Jory.

"Ahh . . ." Asner echoed.

Nela cried, "If they won't even save you, then none of us can escape. They'll still kill us, just as they were going to do! We've no place to go."

"Even if there were a place, I wouldn't leave my comrades to fight alone," said Fringe, as though surprised at the thought. "And it is better that the Hobbs Land Gods are going. If we are to die, we should die freely, as we have lived."

Jory looked at Fringe and shook her head in irritation.

"There now," whispered Asner. "She won't stay this way."

"She would die happier this way," said Jory.

"Do you want that kind of contentment for her?"

"Oh, Asner. Of course not."

"When are the Arbai going?" Danivon demanded.

"They've already gone," Jory replied. "They left immediately after you arrived because they did not wish to explain yet again. They're finding explanation increasingly painful as more and more humans come behind the wall, ready to dispute with them about evil."

"And the . . . the Arbai Device?"

"Is already withdrawing from the wall. Little by little. A few days, perhaps, before it too is gone."

Danivon darted a glance from Fringe to Curvis, finding no response from either of them. Curvis seemed absent, as though he were lost in some other time and place, while Fringe had the firm exalted look of a heroic statue graven to memorialize some great triumph—or some terrible martyrdom. So far as she was concerned, it seemed to make no difference which.

There seemed to be nothing more to say. Even Danivon was silenced.

When evening came, Fringe found Jory on the terrace, petting a cat. Danivon and the twins sat upon the wall nearby, Danivon staring at the forest but Bertran and Nela watching Jory as though her action were rare and wonderful, and indeed, her hands wove a spell of contentment above the purring animal.

"Why do you do that?" asked Fringe wonderingly.

"Because one can, if one wishes, distill all the happiness of a lifetime into one soft, furry body and a stroking hand," said Jory. "When one is very old, one can."

"Ah," said Fringe, unconvinced, her brow furrowed.

"You're troubled," said Jory, including them all.

"I wasn't until this afternoon," she replied thoughtfully. "Truly, Jory. I thought we would die, yes, but dying is what Enforcers often do. There was no point in being troubled. But then, this afternoon I began to worry over it. . . ."

"Thank God for that," said Jory.

"I was more comfortable before," said Fringe plaintively, sitting down beside the old woman. "I suppose because I wasn't me . . ."

"No."

". . . or not all of me, at any rate. So, I should probably say 'Thank God' also." Her tone was plaintive, as though she was not sure she meant it. "Though, since I'm going to die, I might as well have been comfortable about it."

"You're getting your self back," said Jory, laying one hand on Fringe's head. "You're beginning to become yourself, so you're troubled, as Fringe would be." She sighed, stroking Fringe's hair. "I'm glad you are becoming the Fringe I picked out . . . as a daughter. As an heir. To whom . . . I would leave what has been mine. I'd hate to have lost you."

Fringe looked at her wonderingly, thinking it an odd concern to have at such a time. There would be nothing left to inherit.

"Let me tell you all a story," Jory said, settling herself back in the chair and pulling the cat close against her. "Once upon a time, there was a turtle. . . ."

Nela made a sound, halfway between a snort of laughter and a sob.

"Perhaps you've heard this tale before?" Jory asked. "Never mind. You can hear it again, Nela, and you, Bertran. This story is for all of us.

"Once upon a time, there was a turtle who lived in a pond: gray reeds and gray mud and gray moonlight falling, which was what turtles see who cannot see color. Not for him the glory of the sunset or the wonder of the dawn. Not for him the flash of a hummingbird's throat or a butterfly's wings. For him the liquid sounds of water moving, the slosh and murmur of the stream, the wind in the trees; for him the difference between shadow and darkness. He was content, as turtles are content, to be deliberate in his habits and slow in his pace, to eat leaves and the ends of worms and suchlike fodder, and to think long slow thoughts on a log with his fellows, where he knew the sunlight was warm though he did not know it was yellow.

"But a time came on an autumn evening, gray leaf and gray thorn and gray mist rising, when he sat overlong on the log after the sun was well down, and the swallows came to drink and hunt on the surface of the pond, dipping and dancing above the ripples, swerving and swooping with consummate grace, so that the turtle saw them as silver and black and beautiful, and all at once, with an urgency he had never known before, he longed for wings.

" 'Oh, I wish I could see them more clearly,' he murmured to the bullfrog on the bank. 'That I might learn to fly.'

" 'If you would see them clearly, you must go to the secret sanctuary of the birds,' said the bullfrog in a careless voice, as though he did not take the matter seriously.

"And when the turtle asked where that was, the bullfrog pointed westward, to the towering mountains, and told the turtle the sanctuary was there, among the crags and abysses, where the birds held their secret convocations and granted wings to certain petitioners. And this made the turtle think how wonderful it would be to go there and come back to tell the bullfrog all about it.

"And on the next night, he asked again where the birds went when they left the pond, and the owl pointed westward with its talon, telling him of towering peaks and break-back chasms in a calm and dismissive voice. And again he thought of making the journey and returning, and of the wonder the bullfrog would feel, and the owl, to hear of it when he came back.

"On the third night, he asked yet again, and this time it was the bat who answered, squeaking as it darted hither and yon, telling of immeasurable heights and bottomless canyons. 'No one dares go there,' the bat squeaked, and the turtle told himself that he dared even if no one else could.

"So, for three nights the turtle had watched, each night his longing growing. And at midnight on the third night, when the bat had spoken and the swallows had departed, the turtle went after them without telling anyone good-bye, slowly dragging himself toward the great mountains to the west.

"He went by long ways and rough ways and hard ways always, first across the desert, where he would have died of thirst had not a desert tortoise showed him how to get moisture from the fruits of a cactus. And then across the stone, where he would have died of hunger had a wandering rabbit not given him green leaves to eat, and then into the mountains themselves where he would have given up and died many times except for his vision of himself going back to the pond to tell the creatures there of this marvelous and quite surpassing quest.

" 'They didn't know,' the turtle told himself. 'They had no idea what it would be like. They made it sound easy, but when I go back to tell them what it was really like . . .' And he dreamed the cold nights away visualizing himself telling his story to his kindred turtles on the sunlit log, and to the bullfrog among the reeds, and to the owl and the bat, all of whom would be admiring and astonished at his bravery and his perseverance.

"And so, sustained by this ambition, he went higher and higher yet, gray stone and gray cliff and gray rain falling, year after year, until he came at last to the place the swallows danced in the air above the bottomless void.

"When they saw him, they stopped dancing to perch beside him on the stone, and when he saw them there, silver and black, beautiful as a night lit with stars, he was possessed once again by a great longing, and he told them of his desire for wings.

" 'Perhaps you may have wings, but you must give up your shell,' they cried. And even as they told him he might have wings, he seemed to hear in their voices some of the carelessness he had heard in the voice of the owl and the bat and the bullfrog, who had told him where to go without telling him the dangers of the way. He heard them rightly, for the winged gods have a divine indifference toward those who seek flight. They will not entice and they will not promise and they will not make the way easy, for those who wish to soar must do so out of their heart's desire and their mind's consent and not for any other reason.

"And the turtle struggled with himself, wanting wings but not wanting wings, for if he had wings, they told him, he would no longer be interested in going back to the pond to tell the creatures there of his journey—that comfortable telling, the anticipation of which had been, perhaps, more important to him than the wings themselves. So, he struggled, wanting and not wanting. . . ."

Her voice trailed off.

"And," cried Bertran. "Tell the ending!"

"There is no ending," said Jory. "I do not know what he chose to do."

"He should have gone back to his people," cried Nela. "He'd have been contented there. He'd have told his story in the evenings, and the little turtles would have clapped their feet together. . . ."

"Yes," said Danivon. "They'd have danced and drunk beer, and everyone would have asked him to tell it again. . . ."

"No doubt he'd have enjoyed that," Jory said.

"Perhaps, when he had given up his shell, he would have found there were no wings," said Bertran from some remote corner of himself. "No wings, and no shell either. It is hard to be content with your shell when you have seen the birds flying, but it is hard to choose wings when you aren't sure where they will take you."

"That's true," said Jory. "And it's a troubling thought."

Fringe stared at her feet and said nothing, though she felt Jory's eyes upon her.

Jory put her head against the back of the chair and closed her eyes, her hand moving on the cat's back, the cat purring, the chair rocking.

"I didn't know she knew that story," whispered Bertran.

"But she didn't know the ending," said Nela.

"No one knows the ending," said Fringe, staring at the dust, her mind a tumult of doubt and suspicion. "Each of us has to choose it for herself."

Inside the house, Cafferty and Latibor lay close, talking of friends they had known.

Haifazh, Alouez, and the baby Shira had found a little brook and were wading. Haifazh had never waded before. When she had wakened today, her body had been changed. The cutting and sewing were as if they had never been. For the first time since she was a child, she experienced her body without pain. Now she stood in rippling water, without pain, full of sensations she had never imagined, thankful for this blessing, however brief.

In the grove by the river, Jacent was talking with a girl, the daughter of two of Jory's people. She looked something like Metty, though she said her name was Lidasu, and she listened while he told her about Heaven, while he even cried a little about Heaven, which he missed very much.

"Do you have a mother there?" she asked him as she patted him and rocked him in her arms. He hadn't mentioned a mother.

"Well, yes," he murmured. "Though I don't know her very well. We're raised by family groups in Heaven, and who our biological parents were isn't considered very important."

"That's all right," she said comfortingly. "I'll be your mother for a while."

And in the acropolis, Curvis stalked wildly about, looking for the damned dragons who had, just as Jory said, gone away.

Asner followed him there and asked him, "What is it, Curvis?"

"My whole life!" he shouted. "That's what it is!"

"It's everyone's lives, Curvis. You're not alone. We're all in it."

"I don't care about everyone! Not you old crocks staggering around, not any of you. I cared about Danivon! I thought he was something special, but look at him! Mention the Hobbs Land Gods and he's like an old woman! And he cares about nothing but Fringe! I asked him to get out of here with me, and he won't leave her. What difference does she make now? Ha? So, the hell with them. Now I care about me, old man."

Asner tried to think of something comforting to say and couldn't. Curvis was raging, not listening. Curvis didn't want to hear. Curvis wanted to do something, anything.

While Asner watched impotently, Curvis got into the flier Jacent had brought, took it upward in a tight spiral, and turned away eastward, his actions betraying his intent. Curvis was returning to Tolerance. Curvis intended to find out if the Brannigan creatures had any use for him.

In the lowe of the evening, Danivon took Fringe by the hand and led her from Jory's house out onto the hillside.

"Come," he begged her. "The end is coming, Fringe. Let's end as lovers."

She leaned her head against his shoulder. "Have we time to be lovers, Danivon?"

"Why not?"

"To be truly lovers, Danivon? There's time enough for passion, but it seems an unworthy choice for our last hours. There seems very little point."

"Pleasure? Would that be sufficient reason?"

"Well then, if it would please you. . . ."

He wavered between tears and laughter, between anguish and anger. "No, it would not please me with you in that mood, lady. Sit by me then, here in the shelter of the trees. If you're not moved to be my lover, be my comrade. Tell yourself we're resting up for battle."

This she could do. They sat beneath the great tree, not far from the two stones, Danivon with his back against the trunk, Fringe against his chest, his arms loosely about her. The view westward was of the meadows, a wandering streamlet, then a line of forest below the massif rearing its bulk against the horizon, smooth and glowing in the last of the light.

Seeing them there, Bertran and Nela came up the slope and sat down not far away, the feathered gylph cuddled close beneath a furry arm, in her own place.

"I keep thinking how I've always wanted to be a real girl," whispered Nela, yet not so softly they could not hear her. "I sound like Pinocchio, don't I? Wanting to be a real person."

"Who is Pinocchio?" asked Fringe, firmly resisting the picture she was getting from Nela's thoughts.

"A fairy-tale puppet. A wooden doll who wanted to be real. Just as I did. I wanted to be a real woman. All that time on the sideshow stage, all those years with Aunt Sizzy, somehow whenever I thought about the future, I saw myself as a real woman. With a family and children. . . ."

"I never thought of myself like that," said Fringe in surprise. "Never once like that."

Bertran said, "When we first started at the circus, I used to imagine finding our father and saying, 'I'm your son. I'm the boy you went off and left, so look at me. You didn't need to run away. I'm a man you can be proud of.' "

"I thought that too," said Danivon. "I wondered who my father was, why he had let me go. I thought of finding him someday and amazing him with my . . ."

"With your manliness," said Nela, extending a wing and stretching it. "And with your beauty and good sense."

Danivon smiled, almost laughed.

Bertran said, "My other dreams, the swimming, flying dreams, they were only . . . sensual, I suppose. Muscles and tendons finding an out-let, playing out their purpose in fantasy. . . ."

"I know," Nela murmured. "Me too."

"I used to make plans for the time we'd be separated," he went on musingly. "I wanted to be an explorer. I wanted to do all the things, go all the places we couldn't go. Mountain climbing." He stretched a furry paw, miming the action. "Deep-sea diving. I wanted to go hang gliding. I wanted to jump out of airplanes. . . ."

Fringe resisted the surge of their thought, their feelings, firmly re-jecting any perception of them except what she could see, what she could hear. She felt their presences within her dwindle, even as Jory had predicted.

"Instead of giving Nela wings, the device should have given them to you," she said to Bertran.

Danivon asked, "Are you reconciled to the device then, Fringe? Do you accept it?"

"Never!" she replied firmly. "But I can be grateful that it saved me and rebuilt me even though I have told it I will not be possessed, not even for my own good."

"It would have been interesting to have the experience," he said, not remembering he was still having it.

"You did not think so before. You ran," she said. It was not an accusation but a statement of fact.

"I did. I was afraid. I'm not afraid now."

"Nor I," said Nela, turning restlessly in Bertran's arms, opening her eyes to take in the sky flecked with sunset, wondering at all the memories that suddenly assailed her. Jory's turtle story, so much like her own. Why had Jory told it?

"Why did Jory talk about the turtle?" she asked, pulling herself a little away from Bertran.

"Because it was about Jory herself," said Fringe with a sudden flash of insight.

Nela said, "I've been thinking about it. That's how she became what she was . . . is, by being like the turtle. Because she knew somehow that this . . . all this is just a sideshow. . . ."

Fringe considered this. Had Jory known that comfortable lives pass away, that love is only for a time, that beyond human passions and affections and concerns, beyond human destiny lies the dark of the heights, the loneliness of flight, and beyond that . . . the eternal burning of the stars? And beyond them . . . ?

The main event? Something other, wondrous, utterly beyond human conception?

Danivon whispered to her, "What are you thinking?"

She sat up, her brow furrowed, hearing only his words, not his feelings. "I am thinking of the far stars. And of the times we made love and I told myself it wouldn't last."

"You didn't really want it to last," Nela said to her across the little space between them, a puzzled expression in her eyes. "You don't want to be tied by love. Oh, but I do!"

Fringe nodded slowly, accepting Nela's judgment. If there had been something between Danivon and herself, it wouldn't have lasted, but not necessarily because of Danivon. She herself would have ended it. She might have blamed Danivon when it happened, feeling wounded in that exasperating way one did even when one had provoked one's own pain, but in truth, she would have done it herself.

She would have done it herself, because . . . because . . .

"What is it?" asked Danivon. "What is it, Fringe?"

She shook her head. What was it? It would have been good to give Souile comfort and joy, but not good enough to have been the Professional-class daughter Souile had dreamed of. It would have been good if Char had loved her, but not good enough for her to become the daughter he had wanted. Even during their sentimental clinging, she'd realized they were playing at reality, making promises neither could keep. . . .

Because of this longing. This need. Which Char may have had as well as she. Though with a tragic difference, for he had dragged others into his dream and then hated them for being there, burdening him.

Anyone had the right to dream. But only free beings had the right to go questing. Only beings unenslaved by anything, unencumbered by anything, wearing no label.

As she was. Unlabeled. Not daughter. Not lover. Not Enforcer.

Certainly not a contented part of the Arbai Device.

She put her hand between her breasts, where Zasper's pendant had hung. *Just as she is.* Had he known what she was, what she wanted to be? Had he known she needed to be an unlabeled thing?

"Not tied by anyone's love," she said, seeing how the words tasted. Were they true? "Not even Zasper's. Not any longer."

"Oh, Fringe," said Bertran.

"Not even our friend, Fringe?" asked Nela.

"Always your friend," she said. She had sworn so. As for the rest, she didn't know. She drew herself up and away. Something pulling at her. Something picking at her. Not letting her be. Denying her peace. Nibbling at contentment.

"What is it?" Danivon asked again, startled by her expression.

"I want . . . I want to go. Away."

"You ridiculous woman." He shook his head, shaking her. "How will you go anywhere? You think you can find a safe way out of this? Where is there to go?"

"Yes," cried Nela. "Where is there to go!"

She came to herself, owl-eyed. "Well, maybe nowhere," she admitted, surprised at this intrusion of reality. "But still, if I could find a way, I would go. I needed to tell you that, Danivon. I would go!"

Danivon shook her again, wryly angry. "You mean without me, of course. Curvis told me I wanted you mostly because you wanted something else. Maybe he was right."

Nela looked up at Bertran and said anxiously, "There is no one right way to be. There are always some who want something else. Even if they're not sure what it is."

Fringe saw the anxiety, and met it with a rueful smile. "You'd be happier with someone more . . . settled, Danivon. People like me may be interesting for an occasional passionate encounter, but we're too prickly for comfort. We're hot and we're cold, we're sharp and we're dull. One minute we're sweet, and the next we're bitter. And when you think we're here, with you, we aren't. We're always somewhere else, dreaming something else."

"I'm glad we have that settled," said Nela in an amused voice. She stood up and brushed herself off, feeling through the silkiness of her shirt the sensuous swelling of her breasts. She put out one foot to admire the shiny short boots and the flowing skirt that lashed at her calves. She pushed at her hair, throwing it into charming disarray, and offered a soft delicate little hand to Bertran. He stared at her for a moment, then took her hand in his own larger, calloused one, and pulled himself to his full height with a great swelling of muscles and tightening of rugged jaw beneath his virile beard. He was a full head taller than she. He looked at Fringe and she at them. They seemed to shine.

The twins, Danivon thought, were like campfires, warm and comforting. But Fringe was a light so distant it could hardly be seen. She shone like a diamond one might set upon a finger. One might want to touch it. One might want to possess it. But if one came close enough to hold it, one would be burned to ash.

And given the choice, he admitted ruefully to himself, he would pick another fate. Given the choice, he would sit beside the campfire, telling tales of the marvels he had seen—other places, other times.

"I wonder if Zasper knew about me?" Fringe asked the air. "I wish I could ask him . . . ask him what I'm supposed to be."

Somehow Danivon managed to smile as he held out his hand to her. Indeed. Zasper had known about her. Had known and had longed after her with his last breath, wanting her to be . . . whatever she was.

Jory and Asner sat upon the terrace, holding hands.

"I don't like this ending," she said. "It's not a happy ending. I like happy endings. If I'd known it would end like this . . ."

"We don't have to stay around for it," he told her gently. "We don't need to take part."

"I know," she said angrily. "But I brought all these people here. I will not run. I will not refuse to share what I've brought them to."

"Of course not," he said, trying to think of something that would change the subject. The trouble was, there was only that one subject left.

"What will happen to Great Dragon and his children," he asked. "The Arbai Device has never managed to touch him, has it? Surely he will escape the Brannigans."

She said pensively, "I know he can escape them, if he will. He has stayed here such a very long time. He should have gone out exploring once more, as we did together. Or returned to his old homeworld long ago, to dance with his fellows in the moonlight."

Great Dragon had stayed for reasons of his own, as Jory well knew, but Asner ignored this. "After all this time, does he still remember his home?" he asked gently.

"I'm sure he does. As I do mine?"

"Do you really remember yours, Jory?" He could not believe she did. He could scarcely remember his own.

She sat and rocked, the question going around and around in her head. It seemed to her she did remember Earth. Lately, she remembered it compulsively, as though something besides herself required the memory. She remembered the sound of larks in the dawn, with the grass gemmed and the air like silver. She remembered the leap of a fish in a pond, the spreading circles of light, the glint of scales, the glancing eye. She remembered trees towering, leaves lilting, the shatter and shimmer of sun in the woods, the cry of cicadas, the squeak and murmur of small furry beasts in the branches. She remembered the smell of green, the feel of growth, the touch of grandeur.

She remembered mountains, shadow on shadow, the creep and crush of stone reared up, the hollows of the furnaces of the deep, great abysses of rock where the fires dwelt, had dwelt, dwelt no longer, filled with blue lakes and clean air, with great, white continents of cloud moving over them like the blessing of a mighty hand.

She remembered the glory of the sea, the waters of the world washing upon its shores, the finned creatures of the sea, the seethe of calm, the crash of storm.

Had that been home? Perhaps not, for she remembered coming away from it, in search of something else. Duty. That had been it. In search of duty.

She remembered Grass, the endless prairies of it, the beauty of its gardens, the glory of its forest, the stunning wonder of its human and alien people. Was that home? She came away from that too, still seeking. Not duty this time, but her given world. . . .

To circling worlds, ringed and glorious, where the fires of creation still burned. To a pavane of suns, remote and marvelous, wearing their planets like necklaces. To human worlds and alien worlds, to places earthly and unearthly. She remembered them all, remembered leaving them all. Which of them had been home?

Perhaps in the end, where one's love was, was home.

"See there," whispered Asner, pointing toward the woods.

They came across the meadow: Nela dancing on her lovely feet, moving across the meadow like a princess, joyous and beautiful, with Bertran tall and powerful just behind her, a smile barely lighting his face, his eyes glowing wonder as he came to take Jory's hands.

So here they were, what they longed to be. Woman. Man. Joy flowed from them into her.

She marveled that there was time for a little happiness yet. No matter that all time would end soon, this they would have to carry into the darkness.

"Fringe?" she asked. She had no way of knowing unless she asked. She could not feel Fringe.

"She's behind us somewhere," said Bertran.

They went away with Asner, and soon Fringe came from the woods: a shadow, an uncomfortable presence.

"Well, child?" Jory called.

"Well, Jory?" She came to take the old woman's hands.

"I see the Hobbs Land Gods have finished with you." Jory looked deeply into her eyes. "Or you with them. So you stand alone?"

"I stand alone, Jory."

"Are you now unenslaved?"

"More than in my past, Jory. I was enslaved then, just as you said. To one thing or another."

"And now you feel free?"

Fringe smiled doubtfully and shook her head. "How would I know?"

Jory murmured, "At various times in my life, I've felt freedom— usually briefly and never completely. As I recall, however, even partial freedom can be disconcerting. Even if one has to deal with it only briefly."

"Even if it were only for an instant, Jory, I would welcome the experience. I'd trade a longer life elsewhere for that feeling."

Jory reached up to touch her face. "Then you're a fool, child. But whoever said we were not, you and I."

Fringe seated herself beside the rocking chair. "I may be a fool, Jory, but you're not. That much I'm sure of."

"What tells you that?"

"The presence of Great Dragon tells me that."

The old woman cast her eyes down, asking softly, "What do you know about him?"

"Very little. What one can surmise."

"And what do you surmise?"

"That he could, if he wished, follow the Arbai wherever they have gone."

"Probably. I don't know for sure."

"I think they are no match for him."

"That may be true."

"But he won't follow them, won't . . . anything. Because he respects your feelings."

Jory shook her head slowly. "It seems to me it is less a matter of respect than it is of his own logic, his own ethics. He too chooses non-interference unless his help is sought. And it depends on the cause, and on who does the asking."

"If you asked?"

"I am incapable of some things. Because of what I am."

"What are you?" Fringe whispered. "Really?"

"I can't tell you. Really."

"You're not allowed . . . ?"

"Simply can't. The prohibition is built in. I can't speak, or think too clearly, of what I am really, or I wouldn't *be* what I am." She laughed, a little ripple of real amusement. "Some of us can exist only because we're not too aware of what we are. We are like the tiny particles from which the universe is made. If we locate ourselves, we can no longer move about our business. So long as we are moving about our business, we cannot say where, or what, we are. But—so I tell myself—if I have chosen well, chosen aright, you'll figure it out. And then, perhaps . . ."

They held each other and rocked slowly to and fro while the evening came down around them, each seeking strangely and wondrously for an answer that neither knew.

"Victory," cried Great Crawler; "Victory," cried Subble Clore, the words splattering around the limits of themselves like molten lead. "Victory, victory, us the conquerors, them on the run, mop 'em up, make 'em gone!" It was like rounding up rabbits, or sheep. The Brannigans had all their devilish devices in a big, big circle, Clore's and Thob's and Bland's and Breaze's, all closing in, with the people running ahead, getting tighter and tighter in the middle. Like catching fish in a net!

"What will we do when we get them all in the middle?" someone asked.

"Capture them," said Orimar Breaze, full of panic fire and eagerness. He wanted to get this over with so he could do something more interesting. "Put them in pens. Teach them to obey. Kill the bad ones."

"Why are you going to kill any of them?" the small intrusive voice asked, that same voice that had been asking too many questions recently! "Why will you do that? You've already killed too many people on Elsewhere. Why are you doing that?"

"No, no," Orimar snarled. "We haven't killed that many. There are plenty left here, in different places. It's just there, where the bad ones went. The ones that didn't obey us. We have to kill those ones, who don't obey us." Orimar could not remember why this was true, but it had become the truest thing he knew. Himself was to be obeyed. Unquestioningly, immediately, to the death.

The small questioning voice, that of Jordel the Engineer, did not speak again. At his last awakening, he had exercised two of the options he had bribed those long-ago technicians to install: he had ordered a body cloned for himself and he had chosen to stay awake until it was ready—very soon now. The others didn't know. The others had been too busy out in the world, like a pack of dogs chasing chickens. Blood all over everything and still not enough!

The process of reembodiment would take place inside the Core, as it had been designed to occur. Once embodied here, inside, he could intervene on behalf of the people of Elsewhere, if any of them were left. Until then, he could only ask questions, cause small doubts and even smaller delays. He snarled and fumed, knowing the delays wouldn't be enough. At least two more days until his body was ready. Clore and the others would reach the massif of Panubi sooner than that.

Clore said they would kill only some, but killing was like a fever in them. They compared totals, like hunters shooting birds. Jordel visualized himself a game warden, prowling desperately through the hunt, unable to protect what little was left.

"Well, so time comes to leave this place," said Nela, being very brave because what she had become required bravery as a becoming part of itself.

Fringe leaned toward the old woman. "Are you coming, Jory."

Jory, who had been sitting very still in her rocking chair for some little time, looked up and said, "Yes, of course, child. I'll ride one of the horses."

"Asner?" asked Bertran.

"Do you think I'd let her go alone?" Asner asked.

"Great Dragon?" asked Fringe, looking around.

"Do you think I'd let her go alone?"

The voice reverberated in Fringe's mind. Like a blow on an anvil. Like a tocsin, vibrant with foreboding. Fringe shuddered to her boot tops, struck dumb by this voice.

"How about Haifazh?" asked Danivon, who had heard nothing.

"I'll come along behind," said Haifazh. "But for a little time I will stay here, where I have had joy. Here beside the river with my child."

"Good-bye, then," Fringe said, giving Haifazh her hand. "Good-bye."

Good-bye, good-bye. Nela and Cafferty and Latibor. Good-bye, good-bye. Jory and Asner and Danivon. Good-bye, Alouez and Jacent too. Good-bye.

"How far away are the Brannigans?" Nela whispered to Danivon.

"Not far behind us," he said, struck almost motionless by her beauty. Was this Nela? Little spidery Nela? He cleared his throat. "They're moving almost as fast as we are. Just as fast as the Arbai Device is retreating."

Nela dried her eyes on her sleeve and looked up to find someone had brought the horses, already saddled, and both Jory and Asner were dressed for riding.

Fringe moved forward to lift Jory into the saddle. It was the only way she could travel. The old people couldn't walk fast enough to keep ahead of the Brannigans.

Then they moved away down the meadow, Nela beside Jory, Danivon beside Asner, Fringe striding along with Bertran at her side. Bertran, booted and cloaked and with a great plume in his hat, was full of questions about Enarae, about her training as an Enforcer. Such a little time, he felt, to learn everything he wanted to know about everything!

Cafferty and Latibor were nearby; Alouez and Jacent were somewhere ahead: all of them staring forward as they marched, as though there was something they were going toward. If they looked forward, they avoided looking back. Fringe saw them, or imagined them, as a carved frieze on some great temple of man, marching toward the corner of a mighty structure. They would march forever, turning the corner at the sunset. Not one among them was cowardly or craven. Not one among them was unworthy. Even old Jory, high upon her horse, sat proudly and held the reins like a queen.

So they went, not quickly but steadily, and behind them came the whine and yammer of the machines.

A considerable distance west of Jory's house, at the top of a low hill, Fringe stood aside to let the others go by while she checked her weapons. From this height she could look across the intervening valley to the place they had so recently left. She saw the meadow and the great tree and even the two stones, gleaming whitely, but there were no horses. No house.

Jory and Asner had ridden on ahead. Danivon was nowhere near. "Bertran . . ." Fringe called softly.

"I know," he said as he came to stand beside her.

"Where is the house?" she murmured thoughtfully. "Where are the horses?"

"In the network, I suppose. In the Arbai Device. House, horses, cats probably—I imagine they were all created and maintained by the device. When the device withdrew, it took its creations with it."

"But the stones are still there," she murmured to herself. And when he turned to follow the others, she stayed behind for a long moment, staring at the stones.

They went forward again. Strangers mounted the hills before and be-hind them; strangers moved through the forests at either side. Someone moving off to their left was accompanying the march with the beat of drums, a steady, funereal beat, slower than a heartbeat, growing louder and nearer the farther they went. What had been a loose chain around Central Panubi was becoming a choker, a tight band drawn ever more closely around the massif, a belt of men, women, and children walking steadily toward the center of their ever-diminishing lives.

"If we have to die, I'm glad it's out here, in the sunlight," Nela said to Danivon. "I would have hated to die back in that cavern, with those faces looking at me."

"Yes," said Bertran, glancing at her over his shoulder. He had given thanks before, but he did it again, to the long-ago God of parochial school, the long-ago holy ones, saints and angels. Even for half a day it was good to stride along beside a beautiful woman, talking of things he had never imagined. He wanted more, but it was good to have this!

Behind them the edge of the world drew in. Behind them the glitter-ing machines of the Brannigans glimmered and howled. Very soon they would overrun all of Panubi. Then they would finish what little was left of Elsewhere. Then, probably, Fringe thought to herself, they would kill one another.

They came at evening to a grove of trees that stood only a hundred yards or so from the edge of the massif. They were weary with that tiredness that is the lesser part physical.

"Soul-weary," Jory said to Nela.

"Soul-weary," Nela repeated, seeing something beyond weariness in Jory's eyes. "Are you all right?" she asked, knowing it for a foolish ques-tion.

"I'm here," said Jory. "At least for a time. Though I'll confess that a long sleep would be welcome. . . ." Not that they wouldn't all sleep soon enough. She led her horse onto a bit of grassy meadow at the edge of the grove and plucked a handful of grasses to feed the animal, run-ning her old hands over its glossy hide as it munched, laying her cheeks against its soft nose.

She's saying good-bye, Nela told herself. *Saying good-bye to all this.*

Asner watched them from beneath the nearest tree while Danivon built a campfire and took food from their packs, doing what people were doing all around the circled edge of stone. Asner could see the fires from where he stood, a line of fires, arcing away to the right, to the left, vanishing from sight but continuing, he knew, all the way around. The retreating edge of the Arbai Device was only half a mile behind them, motionless now, as it had recently been at night, as though the Arbai themselves had granted the chill mercy of respite for a last meal, a last sleep, perhaps a last embrace. Beyond that line the little slaughterers jittered and danced, waiting for morning. And behind them, some distance to the east, a thing like a malicious mountain crouched still in the dusk. Great Crawler, Great Oozer, Mighty Mountain, Lord God Breaze. The other monsters were arrayed like compass points around the massif: Magna Mater and Glorious Lady Bland and the tripartite monster that was Chimi-ahm, Subble Clore.

There had been human stragglers during the day's travel. Everyone had heard and seen what had happened to those who had fallen behind the line of march, and none of those along the edge of ruddy stone had any illusions about what would happen in the morning. For the most part the campfires burned in terrible silence while people made their last desperate plans, said their last farewells.

Fringe stood for a long moment staring at the hulked shadow of Great Oozer, then, as Asner watched in amazement, took from her pack the full ceremonial garb of an Enforcer and put it on. When she was dressed, she came across the grassy clearing to him, her bonnet in her hand. "Will you come with me, Asner?"

"Where, girl?"

"Where Jory is, Asner."

"And what are you all dressed up for?"

Fringe brushed at her sleeve. "Why not, Asner? This is what we wear to do honor."

Danivon raised his head. "What, Fringe?"

"A little meeting," she said quietly. "If you will join us." She beckoned to Nela and Bertran, also, and the five of them went into the clearing where the massif rose red against the graying sky.

Jory stood with one scrawny arm over the horse's neck, her head leaned against the tall animal, the two of them seeming lost in a wordless interchange.

Fringe put on her bonnet and strode forward to give the full Enforcers' salute.

"Jory," Fringe said. "Am I your daughter and heir?"

The old woman turned to face her. To Danivon, it seemed that her face was very still and empty.

"Fringe Owldark," she said quietly. "I picked you for my daughter. You are my inheritor."

"And what was yours will be mine?"

"All that is mine to give will be yours."

Asner grunted as though he had been hit, and went to stand beside Jory.

Fringe swallowed the lump in her throat and said, "Then as your daughter I come to you to say it is time to relinquish, for you cannot do what must be done."

"*No,*" said a voice in all their minds.

Jory bowed her head. "You have always said no," she whispered. "The years have spun and you have said no. But isn't it time, old friend?"

Her voice was breathless, with a quality of finality in it that was enough to keep all their eyes upon her. She reached for Asner's hand.

"Isn't she right, Asner? Hasn't it been enough?" she said softly. "Asner?"

"Yes, Jory." He nodded at her. "As you say. Enough."

"*No!*" said something huge.

"Yes," said Jory, speaking to that complicated mass of scale and shadow, to all that mighty presence that had been her own love for all the thousands of years. "Yes. We have spoken of this. The time is enough, and done, and over. You are all my estate, and I bequeath you. . . ."

They heard a sound, as though some great mill ground and ground, saw mighty talons reaching out, saw jeweled eyes lit like little suns. . . .

And before them Jory as a shadow fading, Jory and Asner both, the two shadows holding one another by the hand before the shadow of a horse, Jory's other hand stretched out toward all that ramified glory, at first gently, palm down, as though she granted her hand to be held, or kissed, but then slowly turning on the wrist until it was at last upright, palm out, forbidding, signaling stop, go no farther, do no more.

They two were wraiths, dark against the glory of the departing sun. They were shadows dimming. They were ghosts against the soft glow of the massif. And then they were gone.

A feeling of grief like the washing of a great sea.

Nela said, "Jory? Oh, Jory. . . ."

Then they all cried out at a pain so sudden and horrid that they could not keep silent, the loss of all living, all green, all burgeoning, all sweet and fruitful, all delight. They wept at the loss of all loveliness, all surprise and enchantment. They breathed flame as the air around them wilted and burned and turned to dust. They burned as they held in their hands a gem, glowing with light, the light striking into all their eyes, then dimming, shattering, gone.

Grief. Their own, but not only their own.

Fringe grunted and bent over, as though to compress the pain into a manageable size. "The stones," she gasped. "Those stones under the big tree. Jory and Asner were buried there. The people we knew were only part of the device."

"Like the horses?" cried Nela.

"Like the house and the beds we slept in. Only more . . . more real. Real enough to walk around out on Elsewhere. Real enough to argue with the Arbai, to try to save us . . ."

"Think of the strength of will!" whispered Bertran. "So much that even a simulacrum of it was moved to save a world!"

". . . but not real enough to be capable of the act that might save us," Fringe said.

Bertran wasn't listening. "How long? How long ago did they really die?"

"Long ago. A very long time ago." They all heard it, all felt the time stretching out, the years falling like rain, the age that had gone since they had died.

"Will they come again?" Nela cried into the gathering dark. "Oh, Great Dragon, will they come again."

No sound. Only the vast sorrow retreating as it turned back, its intention clear to all of them. It would return to the meadow near the stones where it had lived and waited, lived and waited, for lifetimes alone. They heard it calling, the great heartbroken sound of a creature calling for its mate.

After a long moment, trembling but resolute, Fringe moved after it.

"Fringe," cried Nela fearfully.

Danivon tried to catch at her, but Fringe put up her hand as Jory had done, palm upright, saying no, say no more.

Danivon let her go, his face open and vacant, not feeling anything. Not sorrow. Not relief. Later he would feel them both, but now he felt nothing at all.

.   .   .

"Wait for me," demanded Fringe, running through the forest after a dwindling presence.

There was no answer.

"She wanted this," Fringe asserted. "If you cared for her, you owe this to her."

"Love cannot be owed," said the retreating shadow. *"It can only be given."*

"And she gave it," Fringe cried stubbornly. "She kept on giving it. You're part of the reason she got into this. You're part of the reason she came back, kept coming back. Because you were here, waiting."

Silence.

"You were the core around which her resurrection grew," Fringe said angrily. "You were the bell that wakened her!"

Still silence.

"So if love cannot be owed, perhaps duty can. Jory was a great one for duty."

"True," said a vast, echoing voice. *"That is true."*

"Or perhaps love can be given still, to do something she wanted to do. As a memorial!"

"Such as . . . ?"

"You know very well. Such as saving the people of Elsewhere."

"They chose. . . ."

"Do I need to quote Jory at you? None of us could get away from our history far enough to make choices!"

Vast sighing, as of winds, heaving as of a forest in storm. *"Very well. Since you ask, I will do something as a memorial for her. I will save her daughter, the one she chose. That I can do."*

"You'll save me?"

"I can do that. I can take you with me, away from here, out among the stars. We can continue the journey. . . ."

She breathed deeply, suddenly alight, as though kindled by joy. She could go! As Jory had done! To find . . . to find whatever it was that lay beyond all human hopes, all human destinies. . . .

She could fly. She could take these offered wings and fly!

She bowed her head. What would Jory have said? Never mind what Jory would have said, what did she herself say! What had she already told herself? Only the unencumbered could go chasing visions. Was she unencumbered?

"Not good enough," she sighed at last. "Not good enough, Great

Dragon. I made a vow. I have friends here. Jory had friends here. She wouldn't have accepted that."

A long silence, then a whisper. *"I, too, can die. I, too, can be killed!"*

"We are alike in that."

"Why should I risk my life for Elsewhere?"

"Because it was important to Jory."

And again, silence. Fringe stalked forward, her hand before her. It encountered something monstrous and wall-like, something that quivered with enormous life. She stood where she was, not daring to move. The being burned darkly, emitting grief like an aura.

"I'm sorry," she whispered. "But she was so tired. She was willing to stand with us upon the massif, fighting until she fell at last, but she was so tired."

"I, too, grow weary."

"Will you help me do what she wanted done?"

"It may not be possible to do what she wanted done."

"We can try."

Again the sigh. Again the whisper. *"Come then. Let us try."*

She rode, unaware how it had happened that she rode, aware only that beneath her great muscles played one against another, hurricane winds were stilled into quiet breaths; before her trees submitted to the trampling of great talons, the insinuations of enormous flesh.

"Where are we going?"

"Where you wanted us to go."

"Where the Arbai have gone?"

"Yes."

They came to an outcropping of rock, hidden among the trees, where a wide, low archway was closed by a monstrous door. Though it was dark, Fringe saw it clearly for it shone with a harsh, obdurate light. She saw great talons gripping the hinges of that door, trying to bend them, straining at them, roaring at them, while they remained yet adamant. The struggle went on and on, and likewise the defeat.

"I can't break it." There was a certain hopelessness in that voice, almost a resignation. *"Given enough time, enough thought, I can do many things. But I cannot break this door."*

Fringe's head sagged. She slumped, beginning to despair.

Jory had not despaired. Not even at the end. Jory had chosen her; she had no right to despair.

"There must be something," she cried. "Some way!"

"Let it go," said the great voice.

"No," she shouted. "Everyone I ever loved, I could have loved better, but I *always* let it go. I did it. Even Char . . . even him. When the time came for me to give me up, I never could."

"What vision is this, Fringe Owldark?"

"Me," she said. "It's me." She shook her head in puzzlement, and peered deeply at the shadowed bulk beneath her, as though to confirm her answer there.

"I'm a questing beast, Great Dragon. It's why Jory picked me. She knew. . . ."

"Knew what?" he demanded.

"Knew she could find one of us somewhere, for there are always a few of us around." She ran her hands down her sides, as though to be sure she was present. "Like her. Like Zasper. Like me. We're the discontented ones. People try to love us, but we keep getting distracted. People give us presents, hoping to please us, but to us they feel like chains and ropes, tying us. They cook the food and pour the wine, and we go unicorn hunting instead. They yell at us and we don't hear, and they try to nail us down, and we pull out the nails and run away licking the punctures. They tell us we're being obstinate, and they send us to bed, and we crawl out the window and go wandering. They lock us in a room and they throw away the key. And we slide out under the door." She laughed. "We leak away, like water."

"Like water," he agreed.

"Water can wear away a stone, eventually," she said. "If there's enough time."

"But there isn't enough time. So we'll leave it, shall we?"

"Wait," she said, forcing the words past a dry throat and a terrible inward shrinking. "Put me down!"

She was down. She stood facing the door, one hand out. When she was a girl, long ago, working in the weapons shop, she had repaired weapons. She knew how they worked. What was it Asner had said about the Arbai Device? That it could create? Well then, let it create.

She visualized the weapon, the structure of the crystals, the intricacies of the circuitry, the shape of the housing, the effect of one part upon another. She thrust her mind at the nothingness in her hand, believing that what she needed was there!

Nothing. More was needed than merely this! She had sent the device away. What must she do to bring it back?

Give up herself. Let it have its way. Be possessed. Enslaved. Willingly, for the device would not work any other way.

Sobbing, she invited it.

It came from the soil beneath her feet, not as an insinuation but as an invasion. It came into her like a swarm, like a tidal flow.

She stumbled, almost falling, her whole being in revolt against this violence being done to her. From beside her, a mighty claw reached out and held her.

Her mind stuttered. *"Steady,"* whispered a voice inside her. *"Steady now."*

She took a deep breath, focused herself once more. This was the way the weapon had worked. This one she held was different, of course, being larger, more powerful. Vastly more powerful. This one could take down a mountain if that was what was needed.

The firing button lay beneath her thumb.

She pressed it.

The door glowed. The fabric of it howled. Metallic runnels flowed away from it. It sagged upon its hinges. Great Dragon seized it, tore it, battered it down.

Before them a sandy-floored tunnel stretched ahead and downward, into infinity.

"Do you now accept enslavement?" asked the voice.

"If you risk death, can I risk less?" she asked. It was what one Enforcer said to another when they went into battle. A way of swearing loyalty. An acceptance of an honorable end.

"Come. I'll carry you."

"I cannot reach what I need through you," she said. "I must walk."

"True. The device cannot touch me. So, we will walk together."

She started down the tunnel, counting her steps, ignoring the feeling that she was no longer herself. Her legs felt different. Her arms. Part of her was no longer available. Part of her substance had been used to make the weapon she still held.

Ignore that. Count the steps. Hammer down the distance with striding feet.

When she reached several thousand, she stopped counting, unable to remember what the next number should have been.

"Will we reach them in time?" she asked

"In time for what?"

"In time to do what Jory would have done."

"Who knows," he murmured.

What remained of her leaned for a moment against his side, then turned and began walking once more.

In far-off City Fifteen, Sepel794DZ watched the ending of man on Panubi. He was enmeshed in his little tentacles, perceiving the slaughter in fear and dismay, fearing the end of the world for himself as for these others, so far away.

Brain dinks led very long lives. They were not subject to disease, and if they stayed at home they were seldom killed. Sepel had always supposed that being a dink had immunized him against fear. He knew now this was not so. Seeing men and women die had not worried him before this. They were they and he was he. Seeing men and women die on Panubi terrified him, for it was clear that Panubi set the pattern for the end.

In the midst of this sickening realization, he received a signal.

"Boarmus here," said a shaky voice out of nowhere. "Can you hear me?"

"Sepel794DZ here," the dink replied, uncertain where the message was coming from. All communication with Tolerance had been blocked for some time.

". . . lash up . . ." cried Boarmus, his voice fading and returning. "Put togeth . . . scraps and bits. Can . . . tell . . . what ship?"

What ship? What was Boarmus speaking of. What did he mean, what ship?

"Something approaching," suggested Files in an insect hum. "Coming toward Elsewhere. Unknown origin. Coming very fast."

"I heard that," said Boarmus, suddenly clear as a bell. "Don't suppose it'll make any difference. Don't know how long we've got. The gods have left us alone here for the last few days. Can't tell where they are because all the monitors are gone. Committing a destruction somewhere else, no doubt."

"Panubi," Sepel confirmed. "Yes."

"Oh, damn," sighed Boarmus. "Oh, hell. I'd hoped . . . Well, so there's a few of us left here trying to get as many out through the Door as we can, only nobody knows how to set it, and we can't find the information. Evidently the Brannigans deleted it from Files. So, we're just sending people through, hoping they're coming out at the other end. . . ."

"I have settings," snapped Sepel. "Prepare to receive," and it blurted the sequences and instructions in a blare of noise, leaving them at the other end to sort it out.

Boarmus was still speaking. ". . . nyhow, picked up this ship coming in. Is it coming here?"

"No idea," Sepel said, "no idea at all."

Fringe was stumbling with weariness when she perceived a change. It was in the quality of light, perhaps. Or the smell of the air. Mist, there was certainly, and a musty smell as of old rooms. She staggered, leaning against her companion, breathing deeply as she looked ahead. Not far away the corridor ended abruptly in a railing above an effulgent and spherical cavern. They went there, slowly, leaned on the railing, gasping at the smell, the mistiness that hid and then disclosed what lay below: a giant target, concentric rings around a dark center. She blinked, translating what she saw. The bottom quarter of the cavern had been carved into level rings, like an amphitheater. The center was a level floor, bare and empty. On the rings were the Arbai, all of them who were left, a few hundred perhaps, crouched in concentric circles, facing the center, their faces hidden in their hands as though entranced or asleep.

"*Yes,*" said Great Dragon. "*There they are. I know them. They are old and tired. They intend to sleep until all cause for confusion has passed.*"

"They must wake for a while," she said. "They must tolerate being confused. Can you translate for me?"

"*They learned to understand Jory; they will understand you.*"

She leaned across the railing and took a deep breath. It rattled in her throat, catching there. She had no voice left. Her mouth was dry. She grimaced, trying to set her feet solidly and finding nothing below her that felt like feet. She fought down terror and imagined herself possessed of a mighty voice. A huge voice. A voice like thunder.

"Awaken!" she shouted.

The voice reverberated, its echoes running around the place once and again, like the gathering of an avalanche, which fell at last upon those crouched below. They jerked and started. They stirred. They moaned. They raised their heads and looked about themselves.

"Here," she cried imperatively.

They looked up and saw her. They spoke querulously.

"Why are they being disturbed?" the great voice whispered in translation.

"You have not earned repose!" shouted Fringe. "You have a duty to perform!"

They moved sluggishly, as though they were too cold to move. Slowly, slowly they spoke again.

"What duty?" whispered Great Dragon.

"It is your duty to achieve your destiny," Fringe cried. "Which is to relinquish all your decisions, to let them go. Decisions are a cause of anguish to you. It is your destiny to lay down this anguish and sleep."

Much murmuring below. She saw bodies bend, heard voices raised, as though in complaint.

Great Dragon whispered, *"They have outlived their strength. Decision is impossible for them. They cannot even understand what you ask."*

"Tell them, in their own language, I do not ask. I do not pose a question. I simply tell. They are interfering with the destiny of man. The only way they can stop interfering is to relinquish all response, even that of inaction."

Great Dragon spoke.

Silence. No answer.

"If they will not relinquish it, then I will take it from them. It is a simple choice."

Great Dragon spoke again.

Those below returned sluggishly to their circles.

"Nothing," said Great Dragon. *"They are not capable of responding."*

Fringe held out her hand, trying not to see what hung there at the end of her wrist. It was not her hand, not even a human hand. It was what she needed now, she supposed, but not herself. Ignore that! She imagined that the appendage held within it a device that caused sleep. She had used such devices. This sleep would be so deep and lasting, however, that those caught in it could not wake; could not wake and could not form or keep any intention whatsoever.

The fibers spun, troubled. She felt them roiling inside her. Her will moved them, but there was another will, close and manifest, the will that had created the device, the will that had not been able to use it.

She insisted, using the last of her strength in the effort. What little remained of that other will was diffuse, strained, indifferent. It had no strength. It had no determination. It was passing away. It had gone. Fringe's will burned hot. It did not waver.

The device happened at the end of her arm, made of her bone and sinew, drawn from her body and mind. She moved what had been her hand, her arm, aiming it downward, sweeping it around and around the circles until she had covered them all. The Arbai fell over sideways, sprawled with their jaws open, their tongues lolling.

She tried to move and could not. There wasn't enough of her left to move. She was lost, part of the device, gone from her own being.

"They sleep," murmured Great Dragon, recalling her to herself.

Now only the Arbai Device remained. She thought of the device idly, without the strength to direct it. All that remained of herself wanted only sleep and forgetting. The struggle to hold herself apart was beyond her. Someone else would have to do what needed doing.

"Come," whispered Great Dragon. *"You are Fringe Owldark. You are Jory's daughter. You have inherited wonder."*

She struggled to acknowledge this, to identify herself with this. After a long time, she was able to nod, to say doubtfully yes, she might be, perhaps she was Fringe.

"Why, Fringe. Why did you do this? Was it for Jory? For Zasper?"

She could not make sense of the question. "No. No. They're gone. I didn't do it for them."

"Then for whom?"

"Nela," she said. "I guess I did it for Nela. So she'd have some time to be . . . what she wants to be. What the device made her."

"This device is an enigma to me. I cannot feel it. So will it now do what needs be done?"

"Only time will tell," she murmured, thought she murmured, too weary and lost to know for sure.

"Is there enough time?"

"Don't know," she sighed, thought she sighed. "May be too late. How long did it take to get here?"

"A long time." The time he meant was measured in hundreds, thousands of years.

The time she meant was not so long. "Is it dawn, outside?"

"Yes," said the great voice, very softly. *"Some time ago was dawn."*

15

All through the night, Danivon stood wakeful: while the darkness drew in, while the stars came out in scatters, while light left the world below, remaining only on the higher clouds; even after true darkness came, he blundered his way from tree to tree, clearing to clearing, unable to rest. He was waiting for Fringe. Fringe had gone away after Great Dragon. Perhaps Fringe had departed from Panubi, cloaked in the dragon's power and invisibility, slithering through the lines of the killers, saving herself.

He hoped she had.

He knew she had not.

He tried to imagine where she might be and failed. She had had some purpose, that much he guessed, but what? This question brought with it a fit of hysterical though silent laughter. Much of the time her purposes had made no sense to him. Why should he understand this one? He yawned uncontrollably and leaned against a tree, listening to the breathing of those around him, wondering how long he dared let them sleep, half sleeping himself as he stood.

Dawn came at last, with high pink clouds foretelling the arrival of day. From the killing ground, the monster machines began to yammer. Danivon forbade himself to listen, throwing back his head to look up at the clouds, storing up the memory. When death came he would not think of death, or of Fringe, or of anything to do with man. He would hold in his mind a picture of clouds turning from black to gray to blooming rose.

Such resolution did him no good. Fringe remained at the center of his thought. What was she really like? What had she really wanted? He found himself remembering her, every detail, every nuance of expression or action. Zasper had talked about her. He remembered all the things Zasper had said. Her presence was like a rhythm he couldn't get out of his mind, like a litany he kept telling over and over, like a summoning spell, an invocation.

Above him the clouds brightened and faded, except for one high, crescent shape that went on glowing with color after all the rest had faded to white.

And then another below it, appearing out of nothing.

"Bertran." Danivon spoke softly. "Nela?"

The two were already half-awake. They roused themselves and came to stand beside him.

"There," he said, pointing upward. Something was growing like linked moons, softly shining. A murmur of voices came from the sides, near and far, where others who had been early wakeful had also seen the strangeness. Cafferty and Latibor came from among the trees to stand beside them, watching.

"Did Fringe ever come back?" whispered Nela.

Danivon shook his head, unable to speak.

"I've been thinking about her and thinking about her," said Nela. "So has Bertran. Ever since it started to get light. We can't get her out of our heads!"

An odd coincidence, Danivon thought, giving it no more attention than that, distracted by the thing in the sky that was continuing to unfold, little by little. The sky brightened, and still the thing grew, each linked crescent a bit lower, a bit closer, the whole mass centering itself upon the great rock dome as upon the bull's-eye of a target. At last whatever-it-was seemed to occupy most of the massif, many miles across. From its translucent base it rose in a series of interconnected curves, vanishing beyond vision, sunlit at the height. The massif creaked alarmingly, roared and trembled a bit, then steadied. Either it had decided it could hold the weight or the weight had been removed.

The others came from among the trees.

"What is it?" marveled Cafferty.

"No idea," said Danivon. "Nela?"

She shook her head. "I've never seen anything like it. Have you, Latibor?"

He shook his head in return. Never. Nothing like it.

Every person left on Panubi had been gathered tight at the base of the massif, and all of them saw the thing come, though they could not comprehend the arrival. It looked like nothing material, nothing solid, so no one around the massif thought of it as a way of escape. They merely gaped and murmured in hesitant voices, slowly edging toward the thing, standing very quietly with their arms folded, all peering at this hugeness, this wonder, this quite marvelous thing come from nowhere to mystify their last hours.

Not so the Brannigan machines. Around the circle they erupted in sudden frenzies. From behind them, the mighty mountain shivered and growled and moved itself as Great Oozer slithered, leaving dead forests smashed to ashes in his wake. To the south, Chimi-ahm came grinning his tripartite grin, lighted from within by mighty fires, howling like a tempest and beating the ground with a huge flail. From the west, Magna Mater rolled on studded wheels across the forests, each spiked tiptoe an earthquake, each earthquake a catastrophe of broken mountain and flooded river. From the north Lady Bland came on her great car, crushing hills and filling valleys. All four of them approached, mighty as mountains, to crouch just beyond the circle of the Arbai Device, staring at the thing on the massif, no more able to comprehend it than were the people.

The thing took no notice of astonishment. Its only response was to open a tiny crack at the base of its substance from which a single creature emerged. The form was completely familiar to Nela and Bertran as it trundled down the slope toward them emitting a strong smell of hay fields.

"Celery," whispered Nela. "It's Celery." She shared a look of hopeful surmise with Bertran, the two of them deep in a wordless interchange during which they remembered the exact wording of their request. Now it seemed inadequate, superficial. It had been so long ago!

They stared at the approaching figure, building together a silent strategy.

"But he won't want to talk to us," Bertran muttered in sudden panic as the leafy creature approached. "We're not multiple anymore."

"You're more multiple than you ever were," murmured Cafferty. "At least for the time being. The Arbai Device is not yet gone."

The creature reached them and bowed.

"Nela-Bertran," said Celery (or what they assumed was Celery), "how nice to meet you at last." (Well then, it wasn't Celery.) "We've heard so much about you." There was a faint, a very faint overtone of irritation in its voice, as of courtesy strained to its limit.

Bertran bowed. Nela bowed, realizing that somehow here she was under Bertran's left arm. Habit! She moved slightly away and stood tall. If she was multiple, it didn't depend on where she was!

"We did what we promised Celery we'd do," said Bertran, unable to think of anything more apropos.

The being nodded. "We know. And we received your message, of course. Which is why we're here. I apologize for our being so tardy, but . . ." (Bertran thought he detected a definite tone of asperity) "we've had to come a long way."

"We've interrupted your journey," said Nela in her most sweetly sympathetic voice. "And after you'd gone to such trouble. Earning your . . . what was it? Your concession."

"Well," said the being with a sidewise look at her, "it was our own fault, wasn't it."

"We think it was," agreed Bertran with a hint of asperity of his own. "Yes."

"An exemplary situation, however," the Celerian continued. "One our younger aggregations will profit from for untold generations. Which is, at the moment, neither here nor there. . . ." It made an equivocal gesture and emitted a smell of disappointment.

"When we received your message, we started back, ready to keep our end of the bargain, only to learn as we approached this place that it would be impossible for us."

Bertran felt himself dwindle. Nela reached for his hand as Danivon cursed slowly, monotonously.

"However," the creature went on, glancing upward over the trees, at the looming monsters, "since we're here, there are some things we'd like to clarify. For our own information. We'd like to know what you meant, in the cavern, when you said 'we' and 'us.' "

Danivon came closer, his hands knotting into fists. The Celerian regarded him blandly.

"In the context of what we knew about humans, the words were confusing. We were sure you meant you-Nela-Bertran, of course. That would have been what you meant by 'us' at the time you met our colleague. Before you came here. But at the time your wish was uttered you weren't alone, so we knew you meant Nela-Bertran-Fringe. . . ."

Nela fixed the being with her eyes and shook her head firmly. "No. As a matter of fact, we meant all of us who are here, around the massif. . . ." Even if the Celerians could not help, let the record show!

"And everyone on Elsewhere," added Bertran. "Our request referred to all our kind. We asked that mankind no longer be influenced by gods he made in his own image."

"You are not referring to the Creators?" asked the Celerian curiously. "We would not want to give you the impression we could have had any effect at all on the purposes of the real . . ."

"We mean," interrupted Nela, pointing at the monsters visible over the treetops, "things like that, whether visible or invisible, whether real or imaginary. No matter how traditional they are. No matter how divine they are said to be. Now, or ever. Here or anywhere. We want to be free of them."

"Ah, I do see." The Celerian did something with its face that gave the effect of a glowing smile. "You wanted us to implement the destiny of man here as elsewhere."

Nela squeezed Bertran's hand as she replied, "The Arbai had the power to do it, but they couldn't accept ambiguity. They worried too much about means and ends. They wouldn't interfere because they couldn't accept risk, they couldn't take the guilt or the pain of possibly being wrong. I understand that. I've been like that myself. But you . . . our experience indicated your people had no hangups about interference."

"That's true," breathed the Celerian in a strangled voice. "We have no hangups about that."

"We thought you'd be willing to risk it," said Bertran, head cocked as though thinking deeply. "Willing to risk being wrong."

"It was our willingness to risk being wrong that won us the great concession," whispered the Celerian. "The emergence from mere creaturehood demands risk. Intelligence demands risk. Holiness demands risk . . . and growth, and change. No. We'd have been willing to risk it."

"But you won't help us," said Nela.

The Celerian bowed, tilting forward until its leafy crest almost brushed Nela's face. "We confess to you: We would feel infinitely more worthy if we could do as you ask. Even we, however, cannot go back in time to do what has already been done by someone else."

Nela stepped aside, confused, turning to the others for explanation as the Celerian moved away. It paused only briefly, to call, "Your colleague says to tell you farewell."

"Colleague?" grated Danivon.

"Your colleague," said the Celerian. "Who in paying our debt to you has indebted us to . . . them."

It went swiftly up the hill, giving them no time to ask the questions that slowly formed in all their minds. After the ship swallowed it up, the ship itself went away as it had come, by vanishment a little at a time.

And nothing happened. The people nearby peered into the brightening day, muttering, retelling, not sure they had not dreamed it. Nothing at all happened. The Gods continued bellowing, but they came no closer. The killing machines yammered and gyrated, but they danced in place. The sun rose, throwing long shadows up onto the massif. People murmured.

And then at last, Chimi-ahm howled more loudly than ever and moved back. Magna Mater backed up. Slow wriggle by slow wriggle, bellowing with each movement, uttering imprecations, Great Oozer slithered in reverse. Lady Bland, shrieking and snarling on her great car, crunched a retreat. Little by little, their movements became a steady withdrawal.

"What happened?" Danivon breathed.

Nela murmured, half hearing, half intuiting what must have occurred. "By the time the Celerians got here, they couldn't do anything else, because Fringe and Great Dragon had already done it."

"Done what?"

"I think Fringe . . . both of them went down under the massif and took the device away from the Arbai."

"They could do that?" asked Danivon, dumbfounded. "Then why did they wait so long! All this time! While so many died? Why did they wait?"

Bertran shook his head slowly, searching inside himself for answers. "I assume Great Dragon wouldn't interfere in human affairs unless Jory asked him to," he murmured. "They were mated in a way I don't understand. But Jory, though very much her own being, or perhaps one should say a being made in her pattern, was still a creation of the Arbai Device here on Elsewhere. Rebellion was her nature, but she could be . . . rebellious only to a degree. She could not threaten the fundamental structure of the Arbai. And it wasn't until Fringe realized what Jory actually was that she could take over. . . . Or try."

"But how?" breathed Danivon. "I can't imagine how?"

"No," Nela murmured, "I can't either, Danivon. But she couldn't have done it as she was, solitary as she was, I'm sure of that. I get this notion of enormous sacrifice. . . ."

Danivon gritted his teeth, astonished to find tears in the corners of his eyes. "And now she's gone, is that it? Gone into the device? Or gone off with the Celerians? Or was it Great Dragon who went with the Celerians?"

Nela shrugged, seeking an answer where there was no answer. She could find pictures, memories of the device unbuilding Fringe in the cavern of the Arbai. Memories of its possessing her at her own invitation, destructuring her at her own command. But had it later rebuilt . . . remade? Of its own volition, perhaps? Of its own memory?

Had it finished with her? Was she free once more?

Nela couldn't tell. What had been Fringe had vanished, and the device didn't know where, or how.

Nela put her arms about Danivon, pressed herself tight against him. "I'm not sure, Danivon. I don't know what happened."

Danivon fumed helplessly over her shoulder. "And your Celerian friend said something about implementing human destiny, but how could he do that when nobody's answered the Great Question!"

Nela held him more tightly. Wasn't that like Danivon? Not to have noticed the answer to the Great Question as it went flitting by. Oh, well. Bertran put his long arms around them both, laying his cheeks against Nela's and Danivon's, all of them wet. Whether they were crying from joy or sorrow or simple exhaustion, none of them were able to say.

In the Core, Jordel of Hemerlane wakened to his newly cloned body, sat it up, got it up, looked it over to be sure it was, in fact, his body, then dressed himself and went into the control section of the Core. A moment's search through the network and he found the four Brannigan monsters on Panubi, where they were being backed slowly toward the sea. Given sufficient time, the Brannigans would be forced all the way back to Tolerance.

Jordel had never shared the Brannigan paranoia or panic about the Hobbs Land Gods, and he saw no reason to prolong matters. The Brannigan network, ramified and wide-flung as it was, with its personality matrix nodes here and there throughout the world, was still powered entirely from inside the Core and could be shut down from inside the Core. Jordel did so, systematically canceling all physical manifestations.

Lights flickered and went out, mechanisms chattered and died. The spider network of the Brannigan gods lost cohesion and fell apart into its constituent molecules. Chimi-ahm collapsed with a shriek; Magna Mater vanished in a cloud of micro-parts; Great Oozer and Lady Bland lingered only a moment longer and then were gone.

Jordel then instructed the Core to clone bodies for all those who had entered the Core and, when the bodies were grown, to program them with their original mind patterns. Except for Jordel's few associates (stored, as he himself had been, under the original specifications), they would emerge with no knowledge of what had happened on Elsewhere. So much the better. The less they knew, the quicker they could be sent . . . somewhere else.

"Jordel," screamed a ghost voice. "Jordel of Hemerlane, you bastard!"

It startled him momentarily. But, of course, the monsters would have returned to the Core when the power to the nodes was removed. Now they were here, with him, so to speak.

"Jordel! This is Magna Mater. You turn us back on!"

"Jordel, you have no right. . . ."

He drew a deep breath. Slowly, carefully, he isolated his colleagues and the original storage area, then turned off the power to the rest. The voices dwindled. They were a mere gnat's hum to his ears when he turned them off entirely.

"Except for the following sections, wipe the matrix," he instructed, rapidly entering locations. "Keep nothing."

As he had told them long and long ago, if they insisted on living forever, error would creep in. There was nothing there worth keeping.

In later years on Elsewhere, the fifth day of Springflower, which had heretofore been dedicated to the Great Question, was celebrated as Emergence Day. On that day, the thousand inhabitants of the Core straggled forth onto the plaza outside the old Frickian barracks, most of them blinking and weaving in the unaccustomed light of the day like toddlers just learning to walk. On awakening, they had been told the answer to the Great Question. Aside from that, they knew only what they had known when they went in.

Nela and Bertran came to the plaza early to sit on a low stone coping and watch the Core inhabitants stagger out in twos and threes. There Danivon joined them, bringing with him a shambling man whose sagging flesh proclaimed he had once been fatter.

"Nela, Bertran," said Danivon, "you remember Boarmus."

Nela rose and kissed Boarmus on one flabby cheek. "You were very brave," she said. "Jacent told us."

"Oh, well." He gestured vaguely as he looked her over. "There really wasn't anything else to do but what I did."

"What are you going to do now?"

"Most of us are going home to Heaven. I don't know what we'll do there. Things will sort themselves out, I suppose. Jacent says there's always a place for bureaucrats, but I think he's being provocative." The twins didn't seem familiar to him, but he couldn't place the difference. Things had been rather confusing of late. He had difficulty remembering a lot of things.

"Will you miss being Provost?" Nela asked.

He turned to stare at the bulk of the Great Rotunda, as though he had not seen it before. "I don't think so. I never liked it that much. It was just, you know, something to do."

"Have you been very busy?" she asked sympathetically.

"Well, this and that. We've taken the guards off the Doors, of course. And there's no more Enforcement to worry about. . . . Which reminds me, I owe an explanation to that little Enforcer girl, the one I sent the message to Danivon by."

"No longer with us, sir," said Danivon, keeping his voice level with some difficulty.

"Oh. Killed by the things, was she?"

"No, sir. We're not sure what happened to her. She went away, that's all we know."

A small group of Brannigans emerged from the arched opening to the Core and stood blinking in the sunlight.

"Look," said Nela, nudging Bertran.

The man she pointed out had a face familiar to Bertran if not to the others.

Seeing them looking at him, Orimar came toward them.

"Good morning," he said, nodding to the men before focusing on Nela. "And who's this pretty thing?"

"Nela," she said. "And this is Danivon Luze, and my brother, Bertran. You know who this is, Bertran. This is Orimar Breaze."

"Have we met?" asked Breaze doubtfully.

"Only in passing," said Bertran, thinking of this face among other faces in a golden cavern.

Orimar gave them all a charming smile, then returned to Nela. "Well, Nela. Are you a student here?" So luscious, she was. So sweet. Lips like roses.

Nela smiled, a wry twist to her lips. "I'm not a student. You must remember, this isn't Brannigan."

His mouth trembled momentarily. Of course it wasn't. It wasn't Brannigan Galaxy. Brannigan was somewhere else. They had come from Brannigan to this little Elsewhere world, and a thousand years had gone by, but nothing had happened the way they'd planned it. There was no diversity anymore. They'd been told that, just this morning, when they'd been embodied.

"That's right," he said in a querulous tone. "I remember: They've answered the Great Question, so we came out. We were supposed to . . . supposed to do that. But"—he gestured vaguely, waving away his own confusion—"I don't remember much about it. None of us remember what happened."

"But you do remember the answer to the Great Question?" Nela asked, a hard edge to her voice.

"Yes," said Orimar Breaze, feeling tears welling up that he was quite unable to control. "Yes."

"You'd like to share it with us, wouldn't you?"

He shook his head, gulping. He didn't want to share it. He didn't want to hear it again.

"The Ultimate Destiny of Man . . ." Nela prompted.

"The Ultimate Destiny of Man . . ." he said, swallowing the tears. What was this? Why this surge of sorrow?

"Is to . . ." she prompted again.

"Is to . . ." He tried once more, unable to get it out.

"Is to stop . . ."

"Is to stop . . ."

"Being only man," she said.

"Yes," he agreed, wiping tears from his eyes. "Sorry, I don't know what's come over me."

"That's all right." She patted him on the shoulder. "We understand."

Bertran put his arm around Nela as they watched the man move away, seemingly overwhelmed by emotion.

"You had to see for yourself, didn't you," Bertran asked softly. "I wonder what's going to happen to them?"

Danivon replied, "They're to be repatriated to Brannigan Galaxity, according to Jordel."

"The Galaxity is still there?" Nela asked, amazed.

"It's always been there. Now it wants to study these people, learn the effects of long-term storage on the purely human psyche. I'm told these Brannigans are the only remaining examples of unalloyed humanity. They'll have a nice shielded campus at Brannigan, where they won't be bothered by the Gods."

"Poor things. So even now they won't have the advantage of the Arbai Device." Nela shook her head. "They'll be shut up in their own heads forever."

"They made the choice," said Danivon, looking into the distance to avoid their eyes. "They didn't trust change, or growth if it felt like change. It made them fearful, so they made the choice first to define man as the crown of creation and then to be forever no more than they were. . . ."

"We respect their choice. It would be . . . inappropriate to interfere."

Say the name enthusiastically. Say it with joy. Say it as you might utter the holy name of God.

Brannigan Galaxity:

The academic center of Fauna Sapiens. The repository of everything known to be so. The hub around which all interesting questions are asked. The quintessential fount of academe.

"Brannigan Galaxity," says the teacher in the remote village on the tiny world, laying its appendages upon the heads of the young. "Question well, and maybe you'll go to Brannigan."

"Imagine diligently," cry the docentdroids on the eduscreens, to isolated individuals they will never touch, never see. "You may be selected for Brannigan!"

There is every likelihood they will. Those who desire Brannigan almost invariably end up there. Unquestioned and prodigious genius is the standard, of course, when each one can know what everyone knows, but there is great need for more than merely that! Great need for questioners, seekers, unravelers, and untwisters, great need for those who will push the boundaries of mystery out a little farther yet.

Fauna Sapiens sometimes sings:

> *Brannigan, we sing to thee!*
> *Fount of magnanimity. . . .*

Brannigan Galaxity.

Here twisting stairs clatter beneath niagaras of pounding extremities. There dim corridors, endless as roads, run into cavernous spaces where dinka-jins and other strange peoples ask those questions peculiar to themselves.

> *May thy ancient precincts be . . .*
> *Wondrous with discovery. . . .*

Tourists still come to Brannigan, still wander in gaping groups among the quadrangles, along the gardens, beneath domes and vaults decorated with murals so recently painted they are scarcely faded at all. On one of the paintings most frequently visited, all the figures are joined by planes and lines of light and dark that, from a distance, make them seem the parts of some glittering and wonderful machine. The mural is, in fact, referred to by the docents as the Destiny Machine.

"The creatures at the very top of the dome . . ." cries a guide directing their eyes upward, ". . . are the Arbai, creators of the Arbai Device that saved mankind from itself through the establishment throughout the galaxy of Fauna Sapiens. A remnant of the Arbai is now in stasis upon the planet Elsewhere."

The tourists finger their pocket files, recording this experience for later delectation.

The docent moves her light pointer to the left: "The figure on the east of the dome is Marjorie Westriding, who saved mankind from the Arbai plague. She was a prophetess of the mid-dispersion period, and the man beside her is her companion, Samasnier Girat, sometimes called St. Sam because of his dedication to the perpetuation of the device.

"The Prophetess Marjorie and St. Sam were sometime resurrectees upon planet Elsewhere. Approved pilgrimage schedules are available in the office of the Vice-Chancellor for Historic Realization."

At least one or two in every tour group seriously consider going on pilgrimage. Almost no one ever gets around to it, which disappoints neither the prophetess nor the saint, who have proven insusceptible to further resurrection.

"The figures to the west of the dome are the Zy-Czorsky twins, Nela and Bertran, saviors of mankind in predispersion times. Nela points upward, toward the mystic turtledove, while Bertran holds the symbolic jackplane. Beside Nela is her lifetime companion, Danivon Luze. The Zy-Czorsky twins also succored the planet Elsewhere by summoning to its aid the inscrutable Celerians—shown to the left."

It is easier to believe the Celerians saved Elsewhere than to believe the truth. Besides, no one is entirely sure what the truth is.

Around the bottom of the dome, only briefly mentioned by the docent, are many other images: among others, a woman with apricot-colored hair and bangles on her arms; a scatter of dinka-jins; a stocky man with a long gray braid and a badge on his shoulder; a fat man holding a teacup, his other hand resting on the shoulder of a smiling youth.

One likeness to which eyes return again and again is at the edge of the vault, a woman striding away across the stars, dressed in purple coat and purple plumes and carrying in one hand a turtle shell. Her expression is one of ferocious joy. Behind and around her, the artist has conveyed the impression of something wonderful and mostly invisible, so that though the woman is painted as a solitary figure, the observer understands clearly that she is not alone.

Brannigan is no longer preoccupied with emeriti. What one knows, all know. It is not individual lives but the pursuit of knowing that matters— any tangled mystery, any challenging wonder, any great question—though one in particular is much discussed by Fauna Sapiens. The Celerians are said to know the answer to it. If they do, they have not shared it with the people at Brannigan, who are determined to find out for itself/themselves.

Laughingly, they speak of appointing a committee to find an answer for this new Great Question (For which one who was of mankind may have already found an answer. Old beast voices forgotten, old forms and sensations vanished, the birth galaxy like strewn sand behind, a sparkling whirl, a fading gather. Here, an arrow of intellect, a flight of imagination. Light ahead, an ascending path. A new wonder teasing the edges of the universe. Farther. Farther. Farther yet. One rider, one ridden. Companions, urging one another on. . . .):

WHAT SHALL WE BECOME,

NOW WE ARE NO LONGER MAN?